An Unusual Angle

"Egan gets at the old familiar material, schooldays in the suburbs, and provokes his readers to redefine it. This redefinition, moreover, is not in terms of traditional metaphysics . . . In other words, he is pushing back the limits of literary pasturage."

—Veronica Brady, *Xeno Fiction*

Quarantine

"*Quarantine* explores quite convincingly what it may mean to be human a hundred years from now. Egan's future fascinates, and the interiority of the narrative as well as the anonymous, powerful meta-organizations in which no one really seems to know the whole story evoke the edgy, European feel of Kafka or Lem . . . He adroitly finesses quantum theory to the nth degree, making the consequences utterly real—and at the same time, utterly unreal—to his characters."

—Kathleen Ann Goonan, *Science Fiction Eye*

"*Quarantine* becomes both philosophical treatise and procedural whodunnit, a hard feat to pull off, but the two threads do eventually converge in a stunning ending."

—Colin Harvey, *Strange Horizons*

Permutation City

"Wonderful mind-expanding stuff, and well-written too."

—*The Guardian*

"Immensely exhilarating. Sweeps the reader along like a cork on a tidal wave."

—*Sydney Morning Herald*

Distress

"A dizzying intellectual adventure."

—*The New York Times*

"The plot offers both adventure and depth, with themes of information, science and human relationships interwoven in complex and often profound ways. Egan is a major voice in SF, and this impressive work should help win him the wide readership he deserves."

—*Publishers Weekly*

Diaspora

"A conceptual tour de force . . . This is science fiction with an emphasis on science."

—Gerald Jones, *The New York Times*

"Vast in scope, episodic, complex, and utterly compelling: a hard science-fiction yarn that's worth every erg of the considerable effort necessary to follow."

—*Kirkus Reviews*

"Egan's remarkable gift for infusing theoretical physics with vibrant immediacy, creating sympathetic characters that stretch the definition of humanity, results in an exhilarating galactic adventure that echoes the best efforts of Greg Bear, Larry Niven, and other masters of hard sf. A top-notch purchase for any library."

—*Library Journal*

Teranesia

"Egan knows his material, has a keen talent for extrapolation, a vivid imagination and a passion for intellectual banter."

—*San Francisco Examiner*

"Egan is perhaps SF's most committed rationalist in the mould of Richard Dawkins. If it cannot be measured, weighed and analyzed, for Egan it does not exist . . . *Teranesia* show why the genre needs him."

—Colin Harvey, *Strange Horizons*

"One of the very best."

—*Locus*

Schild's Ladder

"Egan focuses on the wonders of quantum physics, bringing a complex topic to life in a story of risk and dedication at the far end of time and space."

—*Library Journal*

"[Egan is able to] dramatize the interplay between intellect and emotion in the advance of science. He finds unexpected poignancy in a confrontation between those scientists who are impatient to destroy the new universe before it destroys us and those who want to find a way to coexist with it—and with any life-forms that it might have engendered. Even 20,000 years in the future, such issues can still provoke recognizable human passions."

—Gerald Jones, *The New York Times*

Incandescence

"Greg Egan has no equal in the field of hard SF novels. His themes are cosmic with galactic civilizations and plots spanning millennia. Compelling throughout, [*Incandescence*] contrasts some fascinating moral quandaries of knowing decadence with the mind-expanding discoveries of isolated peasants and eventually blends its narrative threads in a surprising twist."

—Tony Lee, *Starburst*

"Audacious as ever, Egan makes you believe it is possible . . . breathtaking."

—*New Scientist*

"The driving forces of this novel are a pure scientific puzzle and the intellectual joy of finding answers . . . Those who like their science hard will appreciate his thorough research and intricate speculations."

—Krista Hutley, *Booklist*

Zendegi

"Both beautifully written and relentlessly intelligent, *Zendegi* is like a marvelous, precision-engineered watch. It never sacrifices its thematic content to its science, or its richly drawn characters to either, but enmeshes them fully, treating them as the deeply interconnected pieces of the human experience that they are."

—io9.com

"A thought-provoking, intensely personal story about conflicting instincts and desires as technology recapitulates humanity."

—*Publishers Weekly* (starred review)

"It might look, at first glance, like a plot we've already seen hashed out ad nauseam, but have faith in Egan's ability to create stunning, complex futures, with grand themes given a human dimension: he delivers something extraordinary, with no easy answers. Despite its tragedies, the story is remarkably hopeful and certainly one of the best of its kind."

—Regina Schroeder, *Booklist* (starred review)

The Clockwork Rocket (Orthogonal Book One)
"The perfect SF novel. A pitch-perfect example of how to imagine aliens. Captivating from the first page to the superb last paragraph."

—Liviu Suciu, *Fantasy Book Critic*

"Greg Egan is a master of 'what if' science fiction. Other physics? Different biology? Egan's characters work out the implications and outcomes as they struggle to survive and prevail. The most original alien race since Vernor Vinge's Tines."

—David Brin, Hugo and Nebula Award-winning author
of *Earth* and *Existence*

The Eternal Flame (Orthogonal Book Two)
"More than any Egan story to date, the books of the Orthogonal trilogy place science in a broader social context."

—Karen Burnham, *Strange Horizons*

The Arrows of Time (Orthogonal Book Three)
"An intellectual quest which involves us, the readers . . . It is as valid an apotheosis as anything which involves the physical or the spiritual, made rarer because it celebrates curiosity, knowledge, and understanding."

—Andy Sawyer, *Strange Horizons*

THE BEST OF
GREG EGAN

THE BEST OF GREG EGAN

20 Stories of Hard Science Fiction

GREG EGAN

Night Shade Books
NEW YORK

CONTENTS

LEARNING TO BE ME

I WAS SIX YEARS OLD when my parents told me that there was a small, dark jewel inside my skull, learning to be me.

Microscopic spiders had woven a fine golden web through my brain, so that the jewel's teacher could listen to the whisper of my thoughts. The jewel itself eavesdropped on my senses, and read the chemical messages carried in my bloodstream; it saw, heard, smelled, tasted and felt the world exactly as I did, while the teacher monitored its thoughts and compared them with my own. Whenever the jewel's thoughts were *wrong*, the teacher—faster than thought—rebuilt the jewel slightly, altering it this way and that, seeking out the changes that would make its thoughts correct.

Why? So that when I could no longer be me, the jewel could do it for me.

I thought: if hearing that makes *me* feel strange and giddy, how must it make *the jewel* feel? Exactly the same, I reasoned; it doesn't know it's the jewel, and it too wonders how the jewel must feel, it too reasons: "Exactly the same; it doesn't know it's the jewel, and it too wonders how the jewel must feel . . ."

And it too wonders—

(I knew, because *I* wondered)

—it too wonders whether it's the real me, or whether in fact it's only the jewel that's learning to be me.

As a scornful twelve-year-old, I would have mocked such childish concerns. Everybody had the jewel, save the members of obscure religious sects, and dwelling upon the strangeness of it struck me as unbearably pretentious. The jewel was the jewel, a mundane fact of life, as ordinary as excrement. My friends and I told bad jokes about it, the same way we told bad jokes about sex, to prove to each other how blasé we were about the whole idea.

Yet we weren't quite as jaded and imperturbable as we pretended to be. One day when we were all loitering in the park, up to nothing in particular, one of the gang—whose name I've forgotten, but who has stuck in my mind as always being far too clever for his own good—asked each of us in turn: "Who *are* you? The jewel, or the real human?" We all replied—unthinkingly, indignantly—"The real human!" When the last of us had answered, he cackled and said, "Well, I'm not. *I'm* the jewel. So you can eat my shit, you losers, because *you'll* all get flushed down the cosmic toilet—but me, I'm gonna live forever."

We beat him until he bled.

By the time I was fourteen, despite—or perhaps because of—the fact that the jewel was scarcely mentioned in my teaching machine's dull curriculum, I'd given the question a great deal more thought. The pedantically correct answer when asked "Are you the jewel or the human?" had to be "The human"—because only the human brain was physically able to reply. The jewel received input from the senses, but had no control over the body, and its intended reply coincided with what was actually said only because the device was a perfect imitation of the brain. To tell the outside world "I am the jewel"—with speech, with writing, or with any other method involving the body—was patently false (although to *think it* to oneself was not ruled out by this line of reasoning).

However, in a broader sense, I decided that the question was simply misguided. So long as the jewel and the human brain shared the same sensory input, and so long as the teacher kept their thoughts in perfect step, there was only *one* person, *one* identity, *one* consciousness. This one person merely happened to have the (highly desirable) property that if *either* the jewel *or* the human brain were to be destroyed, he or she would survive unimpaired. People had always had two lungs and two kidneys, and for almost a century, many had lived with two hearts. This was the same: a matter of redundancy, a matter of robustness, nothing more.

That was the year that my parents decided I was mature enough to be told that they had both undergone the switch—three years before. I pretended to take the news calmly, but I hated them passionately for not having told me at the time. They had disguised their stay in hospital with lies about a business trip overseas. For three years I had been living with jewel-heads, and they hadn't even told me. It was *exactly* what I would have expected of them.

"We didn't seem any different to you, did we?" asked my mother.

"No," I said—truthfully, but burning with resentment nonetheless.

"That's why we didn't tell you," said my father. "If you'd known we'd switched, at the time, you might have *imagined* that we'd changed in some way. By waiting until now to tell you, we've made it easier for you to convince yourself that we're still the same people we've always been." He put an arm around me and squeezed me. I almost screamed out, "Don't *touch* me!", but I remembered in time that I'd convinced myself that the jewel was No Big Deal.

I should have guessed that they'd done it, long before they confessed; after all, I'd known for years that most people underwent the switch in their early thirties. By then, it's downhill for the organic brain, and it would be foolish to have the jewel mimic this decline. So, the nervous system is rewired; the reins of the body are handed over to the jewel, and the teacher is deactivated. For a week, the outward-bound impulses from the brain are compared with those from the jewel, but by this time the jewel is a perfect copy, and no differences are ever detected.

The brain is removed, discarded, and replaced with a spongy tissue-cultured object, brain-shaped down to the level of the finest capillaries, but no more capable of thought than a lung or a kidney. This mock-brain removes exactly as much oxygen and glucose from the blood as the real thing, and faithfully performs a number of crude, essential biochemical functions. In time, like all flesh, it will perish and need to be replaced.

The jewel, however, is immortal. Short of being dropped into a nuclear fireball, it will endure for a billion years.

My parents were machines. My parents were gods. It was nothing special. I hated them.

WHEN I WAS SIXTEEN, I fell in love, and became a child again.

Spending warm nights on the beach with Eva, I couldn't believe that a mere machine could ever feel the way I did. I knew full well that if my jewel had been given control of my body, it would have spoken the very same words as I had, and executed with equal tenderness and clumsiness my every awkward caress—but I couldn't accept that its inner life was as rich, as miraculous, as joyful as mine. Sex, however pleasant, I could accept as a purely mechanical function, but there was something between us (or so I believed) that had nothing to do with lust, nothing to do with words, nothing to do with *any* tangible action of our bodies that some spy in the sand dunes with parabolic microphone and infrared binoculars might have discerned. After we made love, we'd gaze up in silence at the handful of visible stars, our souls conjoined in a secret place that no crystalline computer could hope to reach in a billion years of striving. (If I'd said *that* to my sensible, smutty, twelve-year-old self, he would have laughed until he hemorrhaged.)

I knew by then that the jewel's "teacher" didn't monitor every single neuron in the brain. That would have been impractical, both in terms of handling the data, and because of the sheer physical intrusion into the tissue. Someone-or-other's theorem said that sampling certain critical neurons was almost as good as sampling the lot, and—given some very reasonable assumptions that nobody could disprove—bounds on the errors involved could be established with mathematical rigor.

At first, I declared that *within these errors*, however small, lay the difference between brain and jewel, between human and machine, between love and its imitation. Eva, however, soon pointed out that it was absurd to make a radical, qualitative distinction on the basis of the sampling density; if the next model teacher sampled more neurons and halved the error rate, would *its* jewel then be "half-way" between "human" and "machine"? In theory—and eventually, in practice—the error rate could be made smaller than any number I cared to name. Did I really believe that a discrepancy of one in a billion made any difference at all—when every human being was permanently losing thousands of neurons every day, by natural attrition?

She was right, of course, but I soon found another, more plausible, defense for my position. Living neurons, I argued, had far more internal structure than the crude optical switches that served the same function in the jewel's so-called "neural net." That neurons fired or did not fire reflected only one level of their behavior; who knew what the subtleties of biochemistry—the quantum mechanics of the specific organic molecules involved—contributed to the nature of human consciousness? Copying the abstract neural topology wasn't enough. Sure, the jewel could pass the fatuous Turing test—no outside observer could tell it from a human—but that didn't prove that *being* a jewel felt the same as *being* human.

Eva asked, "Does that mean you'll never switch? You'll have your jewel removed? You'll let yourself *die* when your brain starts to rot?"

"Maybe," I said. "Better to die at ninety or a hundred than kill myself at thirty, and have some machine marching around, taking my place, pretending to be me."

"How do you know *I* haven't switched?" she asked, provocatively. "How do you know that I'm not just 'pretending to be me'?"

"I know you haven't switched," I said, smugly. "I just *know*."

"How? I'd look the same. I'd talk the same. I'd act the same in every way. People are switching younger, these days. *So how do you know I haven't?*"

I turned onto my side toward her, and gazed into her eyes. "Telepathy. Magic. The communion of souls."

My twelve-year-old self started snickering, but by then I knew exactly how to drive him away.

AT NINETEEN, ALTHOUGH I was studying finance, I took an undergraduate philosophy unit. The Philosophy Department, however, apparently had nothing to say about the Ndoli Device, more commonly known as "the jewel." (Ndoli had in fact called it "the *dual*", but the accidental, homophonic nick-name had stuck.) They talked about Plato and Descartes and Marx, they talked about St. Augustine and—when feeling particularly modern and adventurous—Sartre, but if they'd heard of Gödel, Turing, Hamsun or Kim, they refused to admit it. Out of sheer frustration, in an essay on Descartes I suggested that the notion of human consciousness as "software" that could be "implemented" equally well on an organic brain or an optical crystal was in fact a throwback to Cartesian dualism: for "software" read "soul." My tutor superimposed a neat, diagonal, luminous red line over each paragraph that dealt with this idea, and wrote in the margin (in vertical, bold-face, 20-point Times, with a contemptuous 2 Hertz flash): IRRELEVANT!

I quit philosophy and enrolled in a unit of optical crystal engineering for non-specialists. I learned a lot of solid-state quantum mechanics. I learned a lot of fascinating mathematics. I learned that a neural net is a device used only for solving problems that are far too hard to be *understood*. A sufficiently flexible neural net can be configured by feedback to mimic almost any system—to produce the same patterns of output from the same patterns of input—but achieving this sheds no light whatsoever on the nature of the system being emulated.

"Understanding," the lecturer told us, "is an overrated concept. Nobody really *understands* how a fertilized egg turns into a human. What should we do? Stop having children until ontogenesis can be described by a set of differential equations?"

I had to concede that she had a point there.

It was clear to me by then that nobody had the answers I craved—and I was hardly likely to come up with them myself; my intellectual skills were, at best, mediocre. It came down to a simple choice: I could waste time fretting about the mysteries of consciousness, or, like everybody else, I could stop worrying and get on with my life.

WHEN I MARRIED DAPHNE, at twenty-three, Eva was a distant memory, and so was any thought of the communion of souls. Daphne was thirty-one, an executive in the merchant bank that had hired me during my PhD, and everyone agreed that the marriage would benefit my career. What she got out of it, I was never quite sure. Maybe she actually liked me. We had an agreeable sex life, and we comforted each other when we were down, the way any kind-hearted person would comfort an animal in distress.

Daphne hadn't switched. She put it off, month after month, inventing ever more ludicrous excuses, and I teased her as if I'd never had reservations of my own.

"I'm afraid," she confessed one night. "What if *I* die when it happens—what if all that's left is a robot, a puppet, a *thing*? I don't want to *die*."

Talk like that made me squirm, but I hid my feelings. "Suppose you had a stroke," I said glibly, "which destroyed a small part of your brain. Suppose the doctors implanted a machine to take over the functions which that damaged region had performed. Would you still be 'yourself'?"

"Of course."

"Then if they did it twice, or ten times, or a thousand times—"

"That doesn't necessarily follow."

"Oh? At what magic percentage, then, would you stop being 'you'?"

She glared at me. "All the old clichéd arguments—"

"Fault them, then, if they're so old and clichéd."

She started to cry. "I don't have to. Fuck you! I'm scared to death, and you don't give a shit!"

I took her in my arms. "Shh. I'm sorry. But *everyone* does it sooner or later. You mustn't be afraid. I'm here. I love you." The words might have been a recording, triggered automatically by the sight of her tears.

"Will you do it? With me?"

I went cold. "What?"

"Have the operation, on the same day? Switch when I switch?"

Lots of couples did that. Like my parents. Sometimes, no doubt, it was a matter of love, commitment, sharing. Other times, I'm sure, it was more a matter of neither partner wishing to be an unswitched person living with a jewel-head.

I was silent for a while, then I said, "Sure."

In the months that followed, all of Daphne's fears—which I'd mocked as "childish" and "superstitious"—rapidly began to make perfect sense, and my own "rational" arguments came to sound abstract and hollow. I backed out at the last minute; I refused the anesthetic, and fled the hospital.

Daphne went ahead, not knowing I had abandoned her.

I never saw her again. I couldn't face her; I quit my job and left town for a year, sickened by my cowardice and betrayal—but at the same time euphoric that I had *escaped*.

She brought a suit against me, but then dropped it a few days later, and agreed, through her lawyers, to an uncomplicated divorce. Before the divorce came through, she sent me a brief letter:

> *There was nothing to fear, after all. I'm exactly the person I've always been. Putting it off was insane; now that I've taken the leap of faith, I couldn't be more at ease.*
>
> *Your loving robot wife,*
> *Daphne*

By the time I was twenty-eight, almost everyone I knew had switched. All my friends from university had done it. Colleagues at my new job, as young as twenty-one, had done it. Eva, I heard through a friend of a friend, had done it six years before.

The longer I delayed, the harder the decision became. I could talk to a thousand people who had switched, I could grill my closest friends for hours about their childhood memories and their most private thoughts, but however compelling their words, I knew that the Ndoli Device had spent decades buried in their heads, learning to fake exactly this kind of behavior.

Of course, I always acknowledged that it was equally impossible to be *certain* that even another *unswitched* person had an inner life in any way the same as my own—but it didn't seem unreasonable to be more inclined to give the benefit of the doubt to people whose skulls hadn't yet been scraped out with a curette.

I drifted apart from my friends, I stopped searching for a lover. I took to working at home (I put in longer hours and my productivity rose, so the company didn't mind at all). I couldn't bear to be with people whose humanity I doubted.

I wasn't by any means unique. Once I started looking, I found dozens of organizations exclusively for people who hadn't switched, ranging from a social club that might as easily have been for divorcees, to a paranoid, paramilitary "resistance front", who thought they were living out *Invasion of the Body Snatchers*. Even the members of the social club, though, struck me as extremely maladjusted; many of them shared my concerns, almost precisely, but my own ideas from other lips sounded obsessive and ill-conceived. I was briefly involved with an unswitched woman in her early forties, but all we ever talked about was our fear of switching. It was masochistic, it was suffocating, it was insane.

I decided to seek psychiatric help, but I couldn't bring myself to see a therapist who had switched. When I finally found one who hadn't, she tried to talk me into helping her blow up a power station, to let THEM know who was boss.

I'd lie awake for hours every night, trying to convince myself, one way or the other, but the longer I dwelt upon the issues, the more tenuous and elusive they became. Who was "I", anyway? What did it mean that "I" was "still alive", when my personality was utterly different from that of two decades before? My earlier selves were as good as dead—I remembered them no more clearly than I remembered contemporary acquaintances—yet this loss caused me only the slightest discomfort. Maybe the destruction of my organic brain would be the merest hiccup, compared to all the changes that I'd been through in my life so far.

Or maybe not. Maybe it would be exactly like dying.

Sometimes I'd end up weeping and trembling, terrified and desperately lonely, unable to comprehend—and yet unable to cease contemplating—the dizzying prospect of my own nonexistence. At other times, I'd simply grow "healthily" sick of the whole tedious subject. Sometimes I felt certain that the nature of the jewel's inner life was the most important question humanity could ever confront. At other times, my qualms seemed fey and laughable. Every day, hundreds of thousands of people switched, and the world apparently went on as always; surely that fact carried more weight than any abstruse philosophical argument?

Finally, I made an appointment for the operation. I thought, what is there to lose? Sixty more years of uncertainty and paranoia? If the human race *was* replacing itself with clockwork automata, I was better off dead; I lacked the blind conviction to join the psychotic underground—who, in any case, were tolerated by the authorities only so long as they remained ineffectual. On the other hand, if all my fears were unfounded—if my sense of identity could survive the switch as easily as it had already survived such traumas as sleeping and waking, the constant death of brain cells, growth, experience, learning and forgetting—then I would gain not only eternal life, but an end to my doubts and my alienation.

I WAS SHOPPING FOR food one Sunday morning, two months before the operation was scheduled to take place, flicking through the images of an on-line grocery catalog, when a mouth-watering shot of the latest variety of apple caught my fancy. I decided to order half a dozen. I didn't, though. Instead, I hit the key which displayed the next item. My mistake, I knew, was easily remedied; a single key-stroke could take me back to the apples. The screen showed pears, oranges, grapefruit. I tried to look down to see what my clumsy fingers were up to, but my eyes remained fixed on the screen.

I panicked. I wanted to leap to my feet, but my legs would not obey me. I tried to cry out, but I couldn't make a sound. I didn't feel injured, I didn't feel weak. Was I paralyzed? Brain-damaged? I could still *feel* my fingers on the keypad, the soles of my feet on the carpet, my back against the chair.

I watched myself order pineapples. I felt myself rise, stretch, and walk calmly from the room. In the kitchen, I drank a glass of water. I should have been trembling, choking, breathless; the cool liquid flowed smoothly down my throat, and I didn't spill a drop.

I could only think of one explanation: *I had switched.* Spontaneously. The jewel had taken over, while my brain was still alive; all my wildest paranoid fears had come true.

While my body went ahead with an ordinary Sunday morning, I was lost in a claustrophobic delirium of helplessness. The fact that everything I did was exactly what I had planned to do gave me no comfort. I caught a train to the beach, I swam for half an hour; I might as well have been running amok with an ax, or crawling naked down the street, painted with my own excrement and howling like a wolf. *I'd lost control.* My body had turned into a living strait-jacket, and I couldn't struggle, I couldn't scream, I couldn't even close my eyes. I saw my reflection, faintly, in a window on the train, and I couldn't begin to guess what the mind that ruled that bland, tranquil face was thinking.

Swimming was like some sense-enhanced, holographic night-mare; I was a volitionless object, and the perfect familiarity of the signals from my body only made the experience more horribly *wrong.* My arms had no right to the lazy rhythm of their strokes; I wanted to thrash about like a drowning man, I wanted to show the world my distress.

It was only when I lay down on the beach and closed my eyes that I began to think rationally about my situation.

The switch *couldn't* happen "spontaneously." The idea was absurd. Millions of nerve fibers had to be severed and spliced, by an army of tiny surgical robots which weren't even present in my brain—which weren't due to be injected for another two months. Without deliberate intervention, the Ndoli Device was utterly passive, unable to do anything but *eavesdrop.* No failure of the jewel or the teacher could possibly take control of my body away from my organic brain.

Clearly, there had been a malfunction—but my first guess had been wrong, absolutely wrong.

I wish I could have done *something*, when the understanding hit me. I should have curled up, moaning and screaming, ripping the hair from my scalp, raking my flesh with my fingernails. Instead, I lay flat on my back in the dazzling sunshine. There was an itch behind my right knee, but I was, apparently, far too lazy to scratch it.

Oh, I ought to have managed, at the very least, a good, solid bout of hysterical laughter, when I realized that *I* was the jewel.

The teacher had malfunctioned; it was no longer keeping me aligned with the organic brain. I hadn't suddenly become powerless; I had *always been* powerless. My will to act upon "my" body, upon the world, had *always* gone straight into a vacuum, and it was only because I had been ceaselessly manipulated, "corrected" by the teacher, that my desires had ever coincided with the actions that seemed to be mine.

There are a million questions I could ponder, a million ironies I could savor, but I *mustn't*. I need to focus all my energy in one direction. My time is running out.

When I enter hospital and the switch takes place, if the nerve impulses I transmit to the body are not exactly in agreement with those from the organic brain, the flaw in the teacher will be discovered. *And rectified.* The organic brain has nothing to fear; *his* continuity will be safeguarded, treated as precious, sacrosanct. There will be no question as to which of us will be allowed to prevail. *I* will be made to conform, once again. *I* will be "corrected." *I* will be murdered.

Perhaps it is absurd to be afraid. Looked at one way, I've been murdered every microsecond for the last twenty-eight years. Looked at another way, I've only existed for the seven weeks that have now passed since the teacher failed, and the notion of my separate identity came to mean anything at all—and in one more week this aberration, this nightmare, will be over. Two months of misery; why should I begrudge losing that, when I'm on the verge of inheriting eternity? Except that it won't be *I* who inherits it, since that two months of misery is all that defines me.

The permutations of intellectual interpretation are endless, but ultimately, I can only act upon my desperate will to survive. I don't *feel like* an aberration, a disposable glitch. How can I possibly hope to survive? I must conform—of my own free will. I must choose to make myself *appear* identical to that which they would force me to become.

After twenty-eight years, surely I am still close enough to him to carry off the deception. If I study every clue that reaches me through our shared senses, surely I can put myself in his place, forget, temporarily, the revelation of my separateness, and force myself back into synch.

It won't be easy. He met a woman on the beach, the day I came into being. Her name is Cathy. They've slept together three times, and he thinks he loves her. Or at least, he's said it to her face, he's whispered it to her while she's slept, he's written it, true or false, into his diary.

I feel nothing for her. She's a nice enough person, I'm sure, but I hardly know her. Preoccupied with my plight, I've paid scant attention to her conversation, and the act of sex was, for me, little more than a distasteful piece of involuntary voyeurism. Since I realized what was at stake, I've *tried* to succumb to the same emotions as my alter ego, but how can I love her when communication between us is impossible, when she doesn't even know *I* exist?

If she rules his thoughts night and day, but is nothing but a dangerous obstacle to me, how can I hope to achieve the flawless imitation that will enable me to escape death?

He's sleeping now, so I must sleep. I listen to his heartbeat, his slow breathing, and try to achieve a tranquility consonant with these rhythms. For a moment, I am discouraged. Even my *dreams* will be different; our divergence is ineradicable, my goal is laughable, ludicrous, pathetic. Every nerve impulse, for a week? My fear of detection and my attempts to conceal it will, unavoidably, distort my responses; this knot of lies and panic will be impossible to hide.

Yet as I drift toward sleep, I find myself believing that I *will* succeed. I *must*. I dream for a while—a confusion of images, both strange and mundane, ending with a grain of salt passing through the eye of a needle—then I tumble, without fear, into dreamless oblivion.

I STARE UP AT the white ceiling, giddy and confused, trying to rid myself of the nagging conviction that there's something I *must not* think about.

Then I clench my fist gingerly, rejoice at this miracle, and remember.

Up until the last minute, I thought he was going to back out again—but he didn't. Cathy talked him through his fears. Cathy, after all, has switched, and he loves her more than he's ever loved anyone before.

So, our roles are reversed now. This body is *his* strait-jacket, now . . .

I am drenched in sweat. *This is hopeless, impossible.* I can't read his mind, I can't guess what he's trying to do. Should I move, lie still, call out, keep silent? Even if the computer monitoring us is programmed to ignore a few trivial discrepancies, as soon as *he* notices that his body won't carry out his will, he'll panic just as I did, and I'll have no chance at all of making the right guesses. Would *he* be sweating, now? Would *his* breathing be constricted, like this? *No.* I've been awake for just thirty seconds, and already I have betrayed myself. An optical-fiber cable trails from under my right ear to a panel on the wall. Somewhere, alarm bells must be sounding.

If I made a run for it, what would they do? Use force? I'm a citizen, aren't I? Jewel-heads have had full legal rights for decades; the surgeons and engineers can't do anything to me without my consent. I try to recall the clauses on the waiver he signed, but he hardly gave it a second glance. I tug at the cable that holds me prisoner, but it's firmly anchored, at both ends.

When the door swings open, for a moment I think I'm going to fall to pieces, but from somewhere I find the strength to compose myself. It's my neurologist, Dr Prem. He smiles and says, "How are you feeling? Not too bad?"

I nod dumbly.

"The biggest shock, for most people, is that they don't feel different at all! For a while you'll think, 'It can't be this simple! It can't be this easy! It can't be this *normal!*' But you'll soon come to accept that *it is.* And life will go on, unchanged." He beams, taps my shoulder paternally, then turns and departs.

Hours pass. *What are they waiting for?* The evidence must be conclusive by now. Perhaps there are procedures to go through, legal and technical experts to be consulted, ethics committees to be assembled to deliberate on my fate. I'm soaked in perspiration, trembling uncontrollably. I grab the cable several times and yank with all my strength, but it seems fixed in concrete at one end, and bolted to my skull at the other.

An orderly brings me a meal. "Cheer up," he says. "Visiting time soon."

Afterward, he brings me a bedpan, but I'm too nervous even to piss.

Cathy frowns when she sees me. "What's wrong?"

I shrug and smile, shivering, wondering why I'm even trying to go through with the charade. "Nothing. I just . . . feel a bit sick, that's all."

She takes my hand, then bends and kisses me on the lips. In spite of everything, I find myself instantly aroused. Still leaning over me, she smiles and says, "It's over now, okay? There's nothing left to be afraid of. You're a little shook up, but you know in your heart you're still who you've always been. And I love you."

I nod. We make small talk. She leaves. I whisper to myself, hysterically, "I'm still who I've always been. I'm still who I've always been."

YESTERDAY, THEY SCRAPED MY skull clean, and inserted my new, non-sentient, space-filling mock-brain.

I feel calmer now than I have for a long time, and I think at last I've pieced together an explanation for my survival.

Why do they deactivate the teacher, for the week between the switch and the destruction of the brain? Well, they can hardly keep it running while the brain is being trashed—but why an entire week? To reassure people that the jewel, unsupervised, can still stay in synch; to persuade them that the life the jewel is going to live will be exactly the life that the organic brain "would have lived"—whatever that could mean.

Why, then, only for a week? Why not a month, or a year? Because the jewel *cannot* stay in synch for that long—not because of any flaw, but for precisely the reason that makes it worth using in the first place. The jewel is immortal. The brain is decaying. The jewel's imitation of the brain leaves out—deliberately—the fact that *real* neurons *die*. Without the teacher working to contrive, in effect, an identical deterioration of the jewel, small discrepancies must eventually arise. A fraction of a second's difference in responding to a stimulus is enough to arouse suspicion, and—as I know too well—from that moment on, the process of divergence is irreversible.

No doubt, a team of pioneering neurologists sat huddled around a computer screen, fifty years ago, and contemplated a graph of the probability of this radical divergence, versus time. How would they have chosen *one week?* What probability would have been acceptable? A tenth of a percent? A hundredth? A thousandth? However safe they decided to be, it's hard to imagine them choosing a value low enough to make the phenomenon rare on a global scale, once a quarter of a million people were being switched every day.

In any given hospital, it might happen only once a decade, or once a century, but every institution would still need to have a policy for dealing with the eventuality.

What would their choices be?

They could honor their contractual obligations and turn the teacher on again, erasing their satisfied customer, and giving the traumatized organic brain the chance to rant about its ordeal to the media and the legal profession.

Or, they could quietly erase the computer records of the discrepancy, and calmly remove the only witness.

So, THIS IS IT. Eternity.

I'll need transplants in fifty or sixty years' time, and eventually a whole new body, but that prospect shouldn't worry me—*I* can't die on the operating table. In a thousand years or so, I'll need extra hardware tacked on to cope with my memory storage requirements, but I'm sure the process will be uneventful. On a time scale of millions of years, the structure of the jewel is subject to cosmic-ray damage, but error-free transcription to a fresh crystal at regular intervals will circumvent that problem.

In theory, at least, I'm now guaranteed either a seat at the Big Crunch, or participation in the heat death of the universe.

I ditched Cathy, of course. I might have learned to like her, but she made me nervous, and I was thoroughly sick of feeling that I had to play a role.

As for the man who claimed that he loved her—the man who spent the last week of his life helpless, terrified, suffocated by the knowledge of his impending death—I can't yet decide how I feel. I ought to be able to empathize—considering that I once expected to suffer the very same fate myself—yet somehow he simply isn't *real* to me. I know my brain was modeled on his—giving him a kind of causal primacy—but in spite of that, I think of him now as a pale, insubstantial shadow.

After all, I have no way of knowing if his sense of himself, his deepest inner life, his experience of *being*, was in any way comparable to my own.

AXIOMATIC

❚❚ . . . LIKE YOUR BRAIN has been frozen in liquid nitrogen, and then smashed into a thousand shards!"

I squeezed my way past the teenagers who lounged outside the entrance to The Implant Store, no doubt fervently hoping for a holovision news team to roll up and ask them why they weren't in school. They mimed throwing up as I passed, as if the state of not being pubescent and dressed like a member of Binary Search was so disgusting to contemplate that it made them physically ill.

Well, maybe it did.

Inside, the place was almost deserted. The interior reminded me of a video ROM shop; the display racks were virtually identical, and many of the distributors' logos were the same. Each rack was labeled: PSYCHEDELIA. MEDITATION AND HEALING. MOTIVATION AND SUCCESS. LANGUAGES AND TECHNICAL SKILLS. Each implant, although itself less than half a millimeter across, came in a package the size of an old-style book, bearing gaudy illustrations and a few lines of stale hyperbole from a marketing thesaurus or some rent-an-endorsement celebrity. "*Become* God! *Become* the Universe!" "The Ultimate Insight! The Ultimate Knowledge! The Ultimate Trip!" Even the perennial, "This implant changed my life!"

I picked up the carton of *You Are Great!*—its transparent protective wrapper glistening with sweaty fingerprints—and thought numbly: If I bought this thing and used it, I would actually believe that. No amount of evidence to the contrary would be *physically able* to change my mind. I put it back on the shelf, next to *Love Yourself A Billion* and *Instant Willpower, Instant Wealth*.

I knew exactly what I'd come for, and I knew that it wouldn't be on display, but I browsed a while longer, partly out of genuine curiosity, partly just to give myself time. Time to think through the implications once again. Time to come to my senses and flee.

The cover of *Synesthesia* showed a blissed-out man with a rainbow striking his tongue and musical staves piercing his eyeballs. Beside it, *Alien Mind-Fuck* boasted "a mental state so bizarre that even as you experience it, you won't know what it's like!" Implant technology was originally developed to provide instant language skills for business people and tourists, but after disappointing sales and a takeover by an entertainment conglomerate, the first mass-market implants appeared: a cross between video games and hallucinogenic drugs. Over the years, the range of confusion and dysfunction on offer grew wider, but there's only so far you can take that trend; beyond a certain point, scrambling the neural connections doesn't leave anyone *there* to be entertained by the strangeness, and the user, once restored to normalcy, remembers almost nothing.

The first of the next generation of implants—the so-called axiomatics—were all sexual in nature; apparently that was the technically simplest place to start. I walked over to the Erotica section, to see what was available—or at least, what could legally be displayed. Homosexuality, heterosexuality, autoeroticism. An assortment of harmless fetishes. Eroticization of various unlikely parts of the body. Why, I wondered, would anyone choose to have their brain rewired to make them crave a sexual practice they otherwise would have found abhorrent, or ludicrous, or just plain boring? To comply with a partner's demands? Maybe, although such extreme submissiveness was hard to imagine, and could scarcely be sufficiently widespread to explain the size of the market. To enable a part of their own sexual identity, which, unaided, would have merely nagged and festered, to triumph over their inhibitions, their ambivalence, their revulsion? Everyone has conflicting desires, and people can grow tired of both wanting and not wanting the very same thing. I understood *that*, perfectly.

The next rack contained a selection of religions, everything from Amish to Zen. (Gaining the Amish disapproval of technology this way apparently posed no problem; virtually every religious implant enabled the user to embrace far stranger contradictions.) There was even an implant called *Secular Humanist* ("You WILL hold these truths to be self-evident!"). No *Vacillating Agnostic*, though; apparently there was no market for doubt.

For a minute or two, I lingered. For a mere fifty dollars, I could have bought back my childhood Catholicism, even if the Church would not have approved. (At least, not officially; it would have been interesting to know exactly who was subsidizing the product.) In the end, though, I had to admit that I wasn't really tempted. Perhaps it would have solved my problem, but not in the way that I wanted it solved—and after all, getting my own way was the whole point of coming here. Using an implant wouldn't rob me of my free will; on the contrary, it was going to help me to assert it.

Finally, I steeled myself and approached the sales counter.

"How can I help you, sir?" The young man smiled at me brightly, radiating sincerity, as if he really enjoyed his work. I mean, really, *really*.

"I've come to pick up a special order."

"Your name, please, sir?"

"Carver. Mark."

He reached under the counter and emerged with a parcel, mercifully already wrapped in anonymous brown. I paid in cash, I'd brought the exact change: $399.95. It was all over in twenty seconds.

I left the store, sick with relief, triumphant, exhausted. At least I'd finally bought the fucking thing; it was in my hands now, no one else was involved, and all I had to do was decide whether or not to use it.

After walking a few blocks toward the train station, I tossed the parcel into a bin, but I turned back almost at once and retrieved it. I passed a pair of armored cops, and I pictured their eyes boring into me from behind their mirrored faceplates, but what I was carrying was perfectly legal. How could the government ban a device which did no more than engender, in those who *freely chose* to use it, a particular set of beliefs—without also arresting everyone who shared those beliefs naturally? Very easily, actually, since the law didn't have to be consistent, but the implant manufacturers had succeeded in convincing the public that restricting their products would be paving the way for the Thought Police.

By the time I got home, I was shaking uncontrollably. I put the parcel on the kitchen table, and started pacing.

This wasn't for Amy. I had to admit that. Just because I still loved her, and still mourned her, didn't mean I was doing this for *her*. I wouldn't soil her memory with that lie.

In fact, I was doing it to free myself from her. After five years, I wanted my pointless love, my useless grief, to finally stop ruling my life. Nobody could blame me for that.

SHE HAD DIED IN an armed hold-up, in a bank. The security cameras had been disabled, and everyone apart from the robbers had spent most of the time face-down on the floor, so I never found out the whole story. She must have moved, fidgeted, looked up, she must have done *something*; even at the peaks of my hatred, I couldn't believe that she'd been killed on a whim, for no comprehensible reason at all.

I knew who had squeezed the trigger, though. It hadn't come out at the trial; a clerk in the Police Department had sold me the information. The killer's name was Patrick Anderson, and by turning prosecution witness, he'd put his accomplices away for life, and reduced his own sentence to seven years.

I went to the media. A loathsome crime-show personality had taken the story and ranted about it on the airwaves for a week, diluting the facts with self-serving rhetoric, then grown bored and moved on to something else.

Five years later, Anderson had been out on parole for nine months.

Okay. *So what?* It happens all the time. If someone had come to me with such a story, I would have been sympathetic, but firm.

"Forget her, she's dead. Forget him, he's garbage. Get on with your life."

I didn't forget her, and I didn't forget her killer. I had loved her, whatever that meant, and while the rational part of me had swallowed the fact of her death, the rest kept twitching like a decapitated snake. Someone else in the same state might have turned the house into a shrine, covered every wall and mantelpiece with photographs and memorabilia, put fresh flowers on her grave every day, and spent every night getting drunk watching old home movies. I didn't do that, I couldn't. It would have been grotesque and utterly false; sentimentality had always made both of us violently ill. I kept a single photo. We hadn't made home movies. I visited her grave once a year.

Yet for all of this outward restraint, inside my head my obsession with Amy's death simply kept on growing. I didn't *want* it, I didn't *choose* it, I didn't feed it or encourage it in any way. I kept no electronic scrapbook of the trial. If people raised the subject, I walked away. I buried myself in my work; in my spare time I read, or went to the movies, alone. I thought about searching for someone new, but I never did anything about it, always putting it off until that time in the indefinite future when I would be human again.

Every night, the details of the incident circled in my brain. I thought of a thousand things I "might have done" to have prevented her death, from not marrying her in the first place (we'd moved to Sydney because of my job), to magically arriving at the bank as her killer took aim, tackling him to the ground and beating him senseless, or worse. I knew these fantasies were futile and self-indulgent, but that knowledge was no cure. If I took sleeping pills, the whole thing simply shifted to the daylight hours, and I was literally unable to work. (The computers that help us are slightly less appalling every year, but air traffic controllers *can't* daydream.)

I had to do something.

Revenge? Revenge was for the morally retarded. Me, I'd signed petitions to the U.N., calling for the world-wide, unconditional abolition of capital punishment. I'd meant it then, and I still meant it. Taking human life was *wrong;* I'd believed that, passionately, since childhood. Maybe it started out as religious dogma, but when I grew up and shed all the ludicrous claptrap, the sanctity of life was one of the few beliefs I judged to be worth keeping. Aside from any pragmatic reasons, human consciousness had always seemed to me the most astonishing, miraculous, *sacred* thing in the universe. Blame my upbringing, blame my genes; I could no more devalue it than believe that one plus one equaled zero.

Tell some people you're a pacifist, and in ten seconds flat they'll invent a situation in which millions of people will die in unspeakable agony, and all your loved ones will be raped and tortured, if you don't blow someone's brains out. (There's always a contrived reason why you can't merely *wound* the omnipotent, genocidal madman.) The amusing thing is, they seem to hold you in even greater contempt when you admit that, yes, you'd do it, you'd kill under those conditions.

Anderson, however, clearly was not an omnipotent, genocidal madman. I had no idea whether or not he was likely to kill again. As for his capacity for reform, his abused childhood, or the caring and compassionate alter ego that may have been hiding behind the facade of his brutal exterior, I really didn't give a shit, but nonetheless I was convinced that it would be wrong for me to kill him.

I bought the gun first. That was easy, and perfectly legal; perhaps the computers simply failed to correlate my permit application with the release of my wife's killer, or perhaps the link was detected, but judged irrelevant.

I joined a "sports" club full of people who spent three hours a week doing nothing but shooting at moving, human-shaped targets. A recreational activity, harmless as fencing; I practiced saying that with a straight face.

Buying the anonymous ammunition from a fellow club member *was* illegal; bullets that vaporized on impact, leaving no ballistics evidence linking them to a specific weapon. I scanned the court records; the average sentence for possessing such things was a five-hundred dollar fine. The silencer was illegal, too; the penalties for ownership were similar.

Every night, I thought it through. Every night, I came to the same conclusion: despite my elaborate preparations, I wasn't going to kill anyone. Part of me wanted to, part of me didn't, but I knew perfectly well which was strongest. I'd spend the rest of my life dreaming about it, safe in the knowledge that no amount of hatred or grief or desperation would ever be enough to make me act against my nature.

I UNWRAPPED THE PARCEL. I was expecting a garish cover—sneering body builder toting sub-machine gun—but the packaging was unadorned, plain gray with no markings except for the product code, and the name of the distributor, Clockwork Orchard.

I'd ordered the thing through an on-line catalog, accessed via a coin-driven public terminal, and I'd specified collection by "Mark Carver" at a branch of The Implant Store in Chatswood, far from my home. All of which was paranoid nonsense, since the implant was legal—and all of which was perfectly reasonable, because I felt far more nervous and guilty about buying it than I did about buying the gun and ammunition.

The description in the catalog had begun with the statement *Life is cheap!* then had waffled on for several lines in the same vein: *People are meat. They're nothing, they're worthless.* The exact words weren't important, though; they weren't a part of the implant itself. It wouldn't be a matter of a voice in my head, reciting some badly written spiel which I could choose to ridicule or ignore; nor would it be a kind of mental legislative decree, which I could evade by means of semantic quibbling. Axiomatic implants were derived from analysis of actual neural structures in real people's brains, they weren't based on the expression of the axioms in language. The spirit, not the letter, of the law would prevail.

I opened up the carton. There was an instruction leaflet, in seventeen languages. A programmer. An applicator. A pair of tweezers. Sealed in a plastic bubble labeled STERILE IF UNBROKEN, the implant itself. It looked like a tiny piece of gravel.

I had never used one before, but I'd seen it done a thousand times on holovision. You placed the thing in the programmer, "woke it up", and told it how long you wanted it to be active. The applicator was strictly for tyros; the jaded cognoscenti balanced the implant on the tip of their little finger, and daintily poked it up the nostril of their choice.

The implant burrowed into the brain, sent out a swarm of nano-machines to explore, and forge links with, the relevant neural systems, and then went into active mode for the predetermined time—anything from an hour to infinity—doing whatever it was designed to do. Enabling multiple orgasms of the left kneecap. Making the color blue taste like the long-lost memory of mother's milk. Or, hard-wiring a premise: *I will succeed. I am happy in my job. There is life after death. Nobody died in Belsen. Four legs good, two legs bad...*

I packed everything back into the carton, put it in a drawer, took three sleeping pills, and went to bed.

PERHAPS IT WAS A matter of laziness. I've always been biased toward those options which spare me from facing the very same set of choices again in the future; it seems so *inefficient* to go through the same agonies of conscience more than once. To *not* use the implant would have meant having to reaffirm that decision, day after day, for the rest of my life.

Or perhaps I never really believed that the preposterous toy would work. Perhaps I hoped to prove that my convictions—unlike other people's—were engraved on some metaphysical tablet that hovered in a spiritual dimension unreachable by any mere machine.

Or perhaps I just wanted a moral alibi—a way to kill Anderson while still believing it was something that the *real* me could never have done.

At least I'm sure of one thing. I didn't do it for Amy.

I WOKE AROUND DAWN the next day, although I didn't need to get up at all; I was on annual leave for a month. I dressed, ate breakfast, then unpacked the implant again and carefully read the instructions.

With no great sense of occasion, I broke open the sterile bubble and, with the tweezers, dropped the speck into its cavity in the programmer.

The programmer said, "Do you speak English?" The voice reminded me of one of the control towers at work; deep but somehow genderless, businesslike without being crudely robotic—and yet, unmistakably inhuman.

"Yes."

"Do you want to program this implant?"

"Yes."

"Please specify the active period."

"Three days." Three days would be enough, surely; if not, I'd call the whole thing off.

"This implant is to remain active for three days after insertion. Is that correct?"

"Yes."

"This implant is ready for use. The time is seven forty-three a.m. Please insert the implant before eight forty-three a.m., or it will deactivate itself and reprogramming will be required. Please enjoy this product and dispose of the packaging thoughtfully."

I placed the implant in the applicator, then hesitated, but not for long. This wasn't the time to agonize; I'd agonized for months, and I was sick of it. Any more indecisiveness and I'd need to buy a second implant to convince me to use the first. I wasn't committing a crime; I wasn't even coming close to guaranteeing that I would commit one. Millions of people held the belief that human life was nothing special, but how many of them were murderers? The next three days would simply reveal how *I* reacted to that belief, and although the attitude would be hard-wired, the consequences were far from certain.

I put the applicator in my left nostril, and pushed the release button. There was a brief stinging sensation, nothing more.

I thought, *Amy would have despised me for this.* That shook me, but only for a moment. Amy was dead, which made her hypothetical feelings irrelevant. Nothing I did could hurt her now, and thinking any other way was crazy.

I tried to monitor the progress of the change, but that was a joke; you can't check your moral precepts by introspection every thirty seconds. After all, my assessment of myself as being unable to kill had been based on decades of observation (much of it probably out of date). What's more, that assessment, that self-image, had come to be as much a *cause* of my actions and attitudes as a reflection of them—and apart from the direct changes the implant was making to my brain, it was breaking that feedback loop by providing a rationalization for me to act in a way that I'd convinced myself was impossible.

After a while, I decided to get drunk, to distract myself from the vision of microscopic robots crawling around in my skull. It was a big mistake; alcohol makes me paranoid. I don't recall much of what followed, except for catching sight of myself in the bathroom mirror, screaming, "HAL's breaking First Law! HAL's breaking First Law!" before vomiting copiously.

I woke just after midnight, on the bathroom floor. I took an anti-hangover pill, and in five minutes my headache and nausea were gone. I showered and put on fresh clothes. I'd bought a jacket especially for the occasion, with an inside pocket for the gun.

It was still impossible to tell if the thing had done anything to me that went beyond the placebo effect; I asked myself, out loud, "Is human life sacred? Is it wrong to kill?" but I couldn't concentrate on the question, and I found it hard to believe that I ever had in the past; the whole idea seemed obscure and difficult, like some esoteric mathematical theorem. The prospect of going ahead with my plans made my stomach churn, but that was simple fear, not moral outrage; the implant wasn't meant to make me brave, or calm, or resolute. I could have bought those qualities too, but that would have been cheating.

I'd had Anderson checked out by a private investigator. He worked every night but Sunday, as a bouncer in a Surry Hills nightclub; he lived nearby, and usually arrived home, on foot, at around four in the morning. I'd driven past his terrace house several times, I'd have no trouble finding it. He lived alone; he had a lover, but they always met at her place, in the afternoon or early evening.

I loaded the gun and put it in my jacket, then spent half an hour staring in the mirror, trying to decide if the bulge was visible. I wanted a drink, but I restrained myself. I switched on the radio and wandered through the house, trying to become less agitated. Perhaps taking a life was now no big deal to me, but I could still end up dead, or in prison, and the implant apparently hadn't rendered me uninterested in my own fate.

I left too early, and had to drive by a circuitous route to kill time; even then, it was only a quarter past three when I parked, a kilometer from Anderson's house. A few cars and taxis passed me as I walked the rest of the way, and I'm sure I was trying so hard to look at ease that my body language radiated guilt and paranoia—but no ordinary driver would have noticed or cared, and I didn't see a single patrol car.

When I reached the place, there was nowhere to hide—no gardens, no trees, no fences—but I'd known that in advance. I chose a house across the street, not quite opposite Anderson's, and sat on the front step. If the occupant appeared, I'd feign drunkenness and stagger away.

I sat and waited. It was a warm, still, ordinary night; the sky was clear, but gray and starless thanks to the lights of the city. I kept reminding myself: *You don't have to do this, you don't have to go through with it.* So why did I stay? The hope of being liberated from my sleepless nights? The idea was laughable; I had no doubt that if I killed Anderson, it would torture me as much as my helplessness over Amy's death.

Why did I stay? It was nothing to do with the implant; at most, that was neutralizing my qualms; it wasn't forcing me to *do* anything.

Why, then? In the end, I think I saw it as a matter of honesty. I had to accept the unpleasant fact that I honestly wanted to kill Anderson, and however much I had also been repelled by the notion, to be true to myself I had to do it—anything less would have been hypocrisy and self-deception.

At five to four, I heard footsteps echoing down the street. As I turned, I hoped it would be someone else, or that he would be with a friend, but it was him, and he was alone. I waited until he was as far from his front door as I was, then I started walking. He glanced my way briefly, then ignored me. I felt a shock of pure fear—I hadn't seen him in the flesh since the trial, and I'd forgotten how physically imposing he was.

I had to force myself to slow down, and even then I passed him sooner than I'd meant to. I was wearing light, rubber-soled shoes, he was in heavy boots, but when I crossed the street and did a U-turn toward him, I couldn't believe he couldn't hear my heartbeat, or smell the stench of my sweat. Meters from the door, just as I finished pulling out the gun, he looked over his shoulder with an expression of bland curiosity, as if he might have been expecting a dog or a piece of windblown litter. He turned around to face me, frowning. I just stood there, pointing the gun at him, unable to speak. Eventually he said, "What the fuck do you want? I've got two hundred dollars in my wallet. Back pocket."

I shook my head. "Unlock the front door, then put your hands on your head and kick it open. Don't try closing it on me."

He hesitated, then complied.

"Now walk in. Keep your hands on your head. Five steps, that's all. Count them out loud. I'll be right behind you."

I reached the light switch for the hall as he counted four, then I slammed the door behind me, and flinched at the sound. Anderson was right in front of me, and I suddenly felt trapped. The man was a vicious killer; *I* hadn't even thrown a punch since I was eight years old. Did I really believe the gun would protect me? With his hands on his head, the muscles of his arms and shoulders bulged against his shirt. I should have shot him right then, in the back of the head. This was an execution, not a duel; if I'd wanted some quaint idea of honor, I would have come without a gun and let him take me to pieces.

I said, "Turn left." Left was the living room. I followed him in, switched on the light. "Sit." I stood in the doorway, he sat in the room's only chair. For a moment, I felt dizzy and my vision seemed to tilt, but I don't think I moved, I don't think I sagged or swayed; if I had, he probably would have rushed me.

"What do you want?" he asked.

I had to give that a lot of thought. I'd fantasized this situation a thousand times, but I could no longer remember the details—although I did recall that I'd usually assumed that Anderson would recognize me, and start volunteering excuses and explanations straight away.

Finally, I said, "I want you to tell me why you killed my wife."

"I didn't kill your wife. Miller killed your wife."

I shook my head. "That's not true. I *know*. The cops told me. Don't bother lying, because I *know*."

He stared at me blandly. I wanted to lose my temper and scream, but I had a feeling that, in spite of the gun, that would have been more comical than intimidating. I could have pistol-whipped him, but the truth is I was afraid to go near him.

So I shot him in the foot. He yelped and swore, then leaned over to inspect the damage. "Fuck you!" he hissed. "Fuck you!" He rocked back and forth, holding his foot. "I'll break your fucking neck! I'll fucking kill you!" The wound bled a little through the hole in his boot, but it was nothing compared to the movies. I'd heard that the vaporizing ammunition had a cauterizing effect.

I said, "Tell me why you killed my wife."

He looked far more angry and disgusted than afraid, but he dropped his pretense of innocence. "It just happened," he said. "It was just one of those things that happens."

I shook my head, annoyed. "No. *Why?* Why did it happen?"

He moved as if to take off his boot, then thought better of it. "Things were going wrong. There was a time lock, there was hardly any cash, everything was just a big fuck-up. I didn't mean to do it. It just happened."

I shook my head again, unable to decide if he was a moron, or if he was stalling. "Don't tell me 'it just happened.' *Why* did it happen? Why did you do it?"

The frustration was mutual; he ran a hand through his hair and scowled at me. He was sweating now, but I couldn't tell if it was from pain or from fear. "What do you want me to say? I lost my temper, all right? Things were going badly, and I lost my fucking temper, and there she was, all right?"

The dizziness struck me again, but this time it didn't subside. I understood now; he wasn't being obtuse, he was telling the entire truth. I'd smashed the occasional coffee cup during a tense situation at work. I'd even, to my shame, kicked our dog once, after a fight with Amy. Why? *I'd lost my fucking temper, and there she was.*

I stared at Anderson, and felt myself grinning stupidly. It was all so clear now. I understood. I understood the absurdity of every-thing I'd ever felt for Amy—my "love", my "grief." It had all been a joke. She was meat, she was nothing. All the pain of the past five years evaporated; I was drunk with relief. I raised my arms and spun around slowly. Anderson leaped up and sprung toward me; I shot him in the chest until I ran out of bullets, then I knelt down beside him. He was dead.

I put the gun in my jacket. The barrel was warm. I remembered to use my handkerchief to open the front door. I half-expected to find a crowd outside, but of course the shots had been inaudible, and Anderson's threats and curses were not likely to have attracted attention.

A block from the house, a patrol car appeared around a corner. It slowed almost to a halt as it approached me. I kept my eyes straight ahead as it passed. I heard the engine idle. Then stop. I kept walking, waiting for a shouted command, thinking: if they search me and find the gun, I'll confess; there's no point in prolonging the agony.

The engine spluttered, revved noisily, and the car roared away.

Perhaps I'm *not* the number one most obvious suspect. I don't know what Anderson was involved in since he got out; maybe there are hundreds of other people who had far better reasons for want-ing him dead, and perhaps when the cops have finished with them, they'll get around to asking me what I was doing that night. A month seems an awfully long time, though. Anyone would think they didn't care.

The same teenagers as before are gathered around the entrance, and again the mere sight of me seems to disgust them. I wonder if the taste in fashion and music tattooed on their brains is set to fade in a year or two, or if they have sworn lifelong allegiance. It doesn't bear contemplating.

This time, I don't browse. I approach the sales counter without hesitation.

This time, I know exactly what I want.

What I want is what I felt that night: the unshakeable conviction that Amy's death—let alone Anderson's—simply didn't matter, any more than the death of a fly or an amoeba, any more than breaking a coffee cup or kicking a dog.

My one mistake was thinking that the insight I gained would simply vanish when the implant cut out. It hasn't. It's been clouded with doubts and reservations, it's been undermined, to some degree, by my whole ridiculous panoply of beliefs and superstitions, but I can still recall the peace it gave me, I can still recall that flood of joy and relief, and *I want it back*. Not for three days; for the rest of my life.

Killing Anderson *wasn't* honest, it wasn't "being true to myself." Being true to myself would have meant living with all my contradictory urges, suffering the multitude of voices in my head, accepting confusion and doubt. It's too late for that now; having tasted the freedom of certainty, I find I can't live without it.

"How can I help you, sir?" The salesman smiles from the bottom of his heart.

Part of me, of course, still finds the prospect of what I am about to do totally repugnant.

No matter. That won't last.

APPROPRIATE LOVE

"**Y**OUR HUSBAND IS GOING to survive. There's no question about it."

I closed my eyes for a moment and almost screamed with relief. At some point during the last thirty-nine sleepless hours, the uncertainty had become far worse than the fear, and I'd almost succeeded in convincing myself that when the surgeons had said it was touch-and-go, they'd meant there was no hope at all.

"However, he *is* going to need a new body. I don't expect you want to hear another detailed account of his injuries, but there are too many organs damaged, too severely, for individual transplants or repairs to be a viable solution."

I nodded. I was beginning to like this Mr Allenby, despite the resentment I'd felt when he'd introduced himself; at least he looked me squarely in the eye and made clear, direct statements. Everyone else who'd spoken to me since I'd stepped inside the hospital had hedged their bets; one specialist had handed me a Trauma Analysis Expert System's printout, with one-hundred-and-thirty-two "prognostic scenarios" and their respective probabilities.

A new body. That didn't frighten me at all. It sounded so clean, so simple. Individual transplants would have meant cutting Chris open, again and again—each time risking complications, each time subjecting him to a form of assault, however beneficial the intent. For the first few hours, a part of me had clung to the absurd hope that the whole thing had been a mistake; that Chris had walked away from the train wreck, unscratched; that it was someone else in the operating theater—some thief who had stolen his wallet. After forcing myself to abandon this ludicrous fantasy and accept the truth—that he had been injured, mutilated, almost to the point of death—the prospect of a new body, pristine and whole, seemed an almost equally miraculous reprieve.

Allenby went on. "Your policy covers that side of things completely; the technicians, the surrogate, the handlers."

I nodded again, hoping that he wouldn't insist on going into all the details. I *knew* all the details. They'd grow a clone of Chris, intervening *in utero* to prevent its brain from developing the capacity to do anything more than sustain life. Once born, the clone would be forced to a premature, but healthy, maturity, by means of a sequence of elaborate biochemical lies, simulating the effects of normal aging and exercise at a sub-cellular level. Yes, I still had misgivings—about hiring a woman's body, about creating a brain-damaged "child"—but we'd agonized about these issues when we'd decided to include the expensive technique in our insurance policies. Now was *not* the time to have second thoughts.

"The new body won't be ready for almost two years. In the mean time, the crucial thing, obviously, is to keep your husband's brain alive. Now, there's no prospect of him regaining consciousness in his present situation, so there's no compelling reason to try to maintain his other organs."

That jolted me at first—but then I thought: *Why not?* Why not cut Chris free from the wreck of his body, the way he'd been cut free from the wreck of the train? I'd seen the aftermath of the crash replayed on the waiting room TV: rescue workers slicing away at the metal with their clean blue lasers, surgical and precise. Why not complete the act of liberation? *He* was his brain—not his crushed limbs, his shattered bones, his bruised and bleeding organs. What better way could there be for him to await the restoration of health, than in a perfect, dreamless sleep, with no risk of pain, unencumbered by the remnants of a body that would ultimately be discarded?

"I should remind you that your policy specifies that the least costly medically sanctioned option will be used for life support while the new body is being grown."

I almost started to contradict him, but then I remembered: it was the only way that we'd been able to shoe-horn the premiums into our budget; the base rate for body replacements was so high that we'd had to compromise on the frills. At the time, Chris had joked, "I just hope they don't get cryonic storage working in our lifetimes. I don't much fancy you grinning up at me from the freezer, every day for two years."

"You're saying you want me to keep nothing but his brain alive— *because that's the cheapest method?*"

Allenby frowned sympathetically. "I know, it's unpleasant having to think about costs, at a time like this. But I stress that the clause refers to *medically sanctioned* procedures. We certainly wouldn't insist that you do anything unsafe."

I nearly said, angrily: you won't *insist* that I do *anything*. I didn't, though; I didn't have the energy to make a scene—and it would have been a hollow boast. In theory, the decision would be mine alone. In practice, Global Assurance were paying the bills. They couldn't dictate treatment, directly—but if I couldn't raise the money to bridge the gap, I knew I had no choice but to go along with whatever arrangements they were willing to fund.

I said, "You'll have to give me some time, to talk to the doctors, to think things over."

"Yes, of course. Absolutely. I should explain, though, that of all the various options—"

I put up a hand to silence him. "*Please.* Do we have to go into this right now? I told you, I need to talk to the doctors. I *need* to get some sleep. I know: eventually, I'm going to have to come to terms with all the details . . . the different life support companies, the different services they offer, the different kinds of machines . . . whatever. But it can wait for twelve hours, can't it? *Please.*"

It wasn't just that I was desperately tired, probably still in shock—and beginning to suspect that I was being railroaded into some off-the-shelf "package solution" that Allenby had already costed down to the last cent. There was a woman in a white coat standing nearby, glancing our way surreptitiously every few seconds, as if waiting for the conversation to end. I hadn't seen her before, but that didn't prove that she wasn't part of the team looking after Chris; they'd sent me six different doctors already. If she had news, I wanted to hear it.

Allenby said, "I'm sorry, but if you could just bear with me for a few more minutes, I really *do* need to explain something."

His tone was apologetic, but tenacious. I didn't feel tenacious at all; I felt like I'd been struck all over with a rubber mallet. I didn't trust myself to keep arguing without losing control—and anyway, it seemed like letting him say his piece would be the fastest way to get rid of him. If he snowed me under with details that I wasn't ready to take in, then I'd just switch off, and make him repeat it all later.

I said, "Go on."

"Of all the various options, the least costly doesn't involve a life support *machine* at all. There's a technique called biological life support that's recently been perfected in Europe. Over a two-year period, it's more economical than other methods by a factor of about twenty. What's more, the risk profile is extremely favorable."

"Biological life support? I've never even heard of it."

"Well, yes, it is quite new, but I assure you, it's down to a fine art."

"Yes, but *what is it?* What does it actually entail?"

"The brain is kept alive by sharing a second party's blood supply."

I stared at him. "*What?* You mean . . . create some two-headed . . . ?"

After so long without sleep, my sense of reality was already thinly stretched. For a moment, I literally believed that I was dreaming—that I'd fallen asleep on the waiting room couch and dreamed of good news, and now my wish-fulfilling fantasy was decaying into a mocking black farce, to punish me for my ludicrous optimism.

But Allenby didn't whip out a glossy brochure, showing satisfied customers beaming cheek-to-cheek with their hosts. He said, "No, no, no. Of course not. The brain is removed from the skull completely, and encased in protective membranes, in a fluid-filled sac. And it's sited internally."

"Internally? *Where*, internally?"

He hesitated, and stole a glance at the white-coated woman, who was still hovering impatiently nearby. She seemed to take this as some kind of signal, and began to approach us. Allenby, I realized, hadn't meant her to do so, and for a moment he was flustered—but he soon regained his composure, and made the best of the intrusion.

He said, "Ms Perrini, this is Dr Gail Sumner. Without a doubt, one of this hospital's brightest young gynecologists."

Dr Sumner flashed him a gleaming that-will-be-all-thanks smile, then put one hand on my shoulder and started to steer me away.

I WENT—ELECTRONICALLY—TO EVERY BANK on the planet, but they all seemed to feed my financial parameters into the same equations, and even at the most punitive interest rates, no one was willing to loan me a tenth of the amount I needed to make up the difference. Biological life support was just *so much* cheaper than traditional methods.

My younger sister, Debra, said, "Why not have a total hysterectomy? Slash and burn, yeah! That'd teach the bastards to try colonizing your womb!"

Everyone around me was going mad. "And then what? Chris ends up dead, and I end up mutilated. That's not my idea of victory."

"You would have made a point."

"I don't *want* to make a point."

"But you don't want to be forced to carry him, do you? Listen: if you hired the right PR people—on a contingency basis—and made the right gestures, you could get seventy, eighty per cent of the public behind you. Organize a boycott. Give this insurance company enough bad publicity, and enough financial pain, and they'll end up paying for whatever you want."

"No."

"You can't just think of yourself, Carla. You have to think of all the other women who'll be treated the same way, if you don't put up a fight."

Maybe she was right—but I knew I couldn't go through with it. I couldn't turn myself into a *cause célèbre* and battle it out in the media; I just didn't have that kind of strength, that kind of stamina. And I thought: why should I *have to?* Why should I have to mount some kind of national PR campaign, just to get a simple contract honored fairly?

I sought legal advice.

"Of course they can't *force* you to do it. There are laws against slavery."

"Yes—but in practice, what's the alternative? What else can I actually *do?*"

"Let your husband die. Have them switch off the life support machine he's on at present. That's not illegal. The hospital can, and will, do just that, with or without your consent, the moment they're no longer being paid."

I'd already been told this half a dozen times, but I still couldn't quite believe it. "How can it be legal to murder him? It's not even euthanasia—he has every chance of recovering, every chance of leading a perfectly normal life."

The solicitor shook her head. "The technology exists to give just about anyone—however sick, however old, however badly injured—a *perfectly normal life.* But it all costs money. Resources are limited. Even if doctors and medical technicians were compelled to provide their services, free of charge, to whoever demanded them . . . and like I said, there are laws against slavery . . . well, someone, somehow, would still have to miss out. The present government sees the market as the best way of determining who that is."

"Well, I have no intention of letting him die. All I want to do is keep him on a life support *machine*, for two years—"

"You may want it, but I'm afraid you simply can't afford it. Have you thought of hiring someone else to carry him? You're using a surrogate for his new body, why not use one for his brain? It would be expensive—but not as expensive as mechanical means. You might be able to scrape up the difference."

"There shouldn't *be* any fucking difference! Surrogates get paid a fortune! What gives Global Assurance the right to use *my* body for free?"

"Ah. There's a clause in your policy . . ." She tapped a few keys on her workstation, and read from the screen: " . . . *while in no way devaluing the contribution of the co-signatory as carer, he or she hereby expressly waives all entitlement to remuneration for any such services rendered; furthermore, in all calculations pursuant to paragraph 97 (b) . . .*"

"I thought *that* meant that neither of us could expect to get paid for nursing duties if the other spent a day in bed with the flu."

"I'm afraid the scope is much broader than that. I repeat, they *do not* have the right to compel you to do anything—but nor do they have any obligation to pay for a surrogate. When they compute the costs for the cheapest way of keeping your husband alive, this provision entitles them to do so on the basis that you *could* choose to provide him with life support."

"So ultimately, it's all a matter of . . . *accounting?*"

"Exactly."

For a moment, I could think of nothing more to say. I *knew* I was being screwed, but I seemed to have run out of ways to articulate the fact.

Then it finally occurred to me to ask the most obvious question of all.

"Suppose it had been the other way around. Suppose I'd been on that train, instead of Chris. Would they have paid for a surrogate then—or would they have expected *him* to carry *my* brain inside him for two years?"

The solicitor said, poker-faced, "I really wouldn't like to hazard a guess on that one."

CHRIS WAS BANDAGED IN places, but most of his body was covered by a myriad of small machines, clinging to his skin like beneficial parasites; feeding him, oxygenating and purifying his blood, dispensing drugs, perhaps even carrying out repairs on broken bones and damaged tissue, if only for the sake of staving off further deterioration. I could see part of his face, including one eye socket—sewn shut—and patches of bruised skin here and there. His right hand was entirely bare; they'd taken off his wedding ring. Both legs had been amputated just below the thighs.

I couldn't get too close; he was enclosed in a sterile plastic tent, about five meters square, a kind of room within a room. A three-clawed nurse stood in one corner, motionless but vigilant—although I couldn't imagine the circumstances where its intervention would have been of more use than that of the smaller robots already in place.

Visiting him was absurd, of course. He was deep in a coma, not even dreaming; I could give him no comfort. I sat there for hours, though, as if I needed to be constantly reminded that his body *was* injured beyond repair; that he really did need my help, *or he would not survive.*

Sometimes my hesitancy struck me as so abhorrent that I couldn't believe that I'd not yet signed the forms and begun the preparatory treatment. *His life was at stake! How could I think twice? How could I be that selfish?* And yet, this guilt itself made me almost as angry and resentful as everything else: the coercion that wasn't quite coercion, the sexual politics that I couldn't quite bring myself to confront.

To refuse, to let him die, was unthinkable. And yet . . . would I have carried the brain of a total stranger? No. Letting a stranger die wasn't unthinkable at all. Would I have done it for a casual acquaintance? No. A close friend? For some, perhaps—but not for others.

So, just how much did I love him? Enough?

Of course!

Why "of course"?

It was a matter of . . . *loyalty?* That wasn't the word; it smacked too much of some kind of unwritten contractual obligation, some notion of "duty," as pernicious and idiotic as patriotism. Well, "duty" could go fuck itself; that wasn't it at all.

Why, then? Why was he special? What made him different from the closest friend?

I had no answer, no right words—just a rush of emotion-charged images of Chris. So I told myself: *now* is not the time to analyze it, to dissect it. I don't need an answer; I *know* what I feel.

I lurched between despising myself, for entertaining—however theoretically—the possibility of letting him die, and despising the fact that I was being bullied into doing something with my body that I did *not* want to do. The solution, of course, would have been to do neither—but what did I expect? Some rich benefactor to step out from behind a curtain and make the dilemma vanish?

I'd seen a documentary, a week before the crash, showing some of the hundreds of thousands of men and women in central Africa, who spent their whole lives nursing dying relatives, simply because they couldn't afford the AIDS drugs that had virtually wiped out the disease in wealthier countries, twenty years before. If *they* could have saved the lives of their loved ones by the minuscule "sacrifice" of carrying an extra kilogram and a half for two years . . .

In the end, I gave up trying to reconcile all the contradictions. I had a right to feel angry and cheated and resentful—but the fact remained that *I wanted Chris to live.* If I wasn't going to be manipulated, it had to work both ways; reacting blindly against the way I'd been treated would have been no less stupid and dishonest than the most supine cooperation.

It occurred to me—belatedly—that Global Assurance might not have been entirely artless in the way they'd antagonized me. After all, if I let Chris die, they'd be spared not just the meager cost of biological life support, with the womb thrown in rent-free, but the whole expensive business of the replacement body as well. A little calculated crassness, a little reverse psychology . . .

The only way to keep my sanity was to transcend all this bullshit; to declare Global Assurance and their machinations irrelevant; to carry his brain—not because I'd been coerced; not because I felt guilty, or obliged; not to prove that I couldn't be manipulated—but for the simple reason that I loved him enough to want to save his life.

THEY INJECTED ME WITH a gene-tailored blastocyst, a cluster of cells which implanted in the uterine wall and fooled my body into thinking that I was pregnant.

Fooled? My periods ceased. I suffered morning sickness, anemia, immune suppression, hunger pangs. The pseudo-embryo grew at a literally dizzying rate, much faster than any child, rapidly forming the protective membranes and amniotic sac, and creating a placental blood supply that would eventually have the capacity to sustain an oxygen-hungry brain.

I'd planned to work on as if nothing special was happening, but I soon discovered that I couldn't; I was just too sick, and too exhausted, to function normally. In five weeks, the thing inside me would grow to the size that a fetus would have taken *five months* to reach. I swallowed a fistful of dietary supplement capsules with every meal, but I was still too lethargic to do much more than sit around the flat, making desultory attempts to stave off boredom with books and junk TV. I vomited once or twice a day, urinated three or four times a night. All of which was bad enough—but I'm sure I felt far more miserable than these symptoms alone could have made me.

Perhaps half the problem was the lack of any simple way of *thinking about* what was happening to me. Apart from the actual structure of the "embryo," I *was* pregnant—in every biochemical and physiological sense of the word—but I could hardly let myself go along with the deception. Even half-pretending that the mass of amorphous tissue in my womb was *a child* would have been setting myself up for a complete emotional meltdown. But—what was it, then? *A tumor?* That was closer to the truth, but it wasn't exactly the kind of substitute image I needed.

Of course, intellectually, I knew precisely what was inside me, and precisely what would become of it. I was *not* pregnant with a child who was destined to be ripped out of my womb to make way for my husband's brain. I did *not* have a vampiric tumor that would keep on growing until it drained so much blood from me that I'd be too weak to move. I was carrying a benign growth, a tool designed for a specific task—a task that I'd decided to accept.

So why did I feel perpetually confused, and depressed—and at times, so desperate that I fantasized about suicide and miscarriage, about slashing myself open, or throwing myself down the stairs? I was tired, I was nauseous, I didn't expect to be dancing for joy—but why was I so fucking unhappy that I couldn't stop thinking of death?

I could have recited some kind of explanatory mantra: *I'm doing this for Chris. I'm doing this for Chris.*

I didn't, though. I already resented him enough; I didn't want to end up hating him.

EARLY IN THE SIXTH week, an ultrasound scan showed that the amniotic sac had reached the necessary size, and Doppler analysis of the blood flow confirmed that it, too, was on target. I went into hospital for the substitution.

I could have paid Chris one final visit, but I stayed away. I didn't want to dwell upon the mechanics of what lay ahead.

Dr Sumner said, "There's nothing to worry about. Fetal surgery far more complex than this is routine."

I said, through gritted teeth, "This *isn't* fetal surgery."

She said, "Well . . . no." As if the news were a revelation.

When I woke after the operation, I felt sicker than ever. I rested one hand on my belly; the wound was clean and numb, the stitches hidden. I'd been told that there wouldn't even be a scar.

I thought: *He's inside me. They can't hurt him now. I've won that much.*

I closed my eyes. I had no trouble imagining Chris, the way he'd been—*the way he would be, again.* I drifted half-way back to sleep, shamelessly dredging up images of all the happiest times we'd had. I'd never indulged in sentimental reveries before—it wasn't my style, I hated living in the past—but any trick that sustained me was welcome now. I let myself hear his voice, see his face, feel his touch—

His body, of course, was dead now. Irreversibly dead. I opened my eyes and looked down at the bulge in my abdomen, and pictured what it contained: a lump of meat from his corpse. A lump of gray meat, torn from the skull of his corpse.

I'd fasted for surgery, my stomach was empty, I had nothing to throw up. I lay there for hours, wiping sweat off my face with a corner of the sheet, trying to stop shaking.

IN TERMS OF BULK, I was five months pregnant.

In terms of weight, seven months.

For two years.

If Kafka had been a woman . . .

I didn't grow used to it, but I did learn to cope. There were ways to sleep, ways to sit, ways to move that were easier than others. I was tired all day long, but there were times when I had enough energy to feel almost normal again, and I made good use of them. I worked hard, and I didn't fall behind. The Department was launching a new blitz on corporate tax evasion; I threw myself into it with more zeal than I'd ever felt before. My enthusiasm was artificial, but that wasn't the point; I needed the momentum to carry me through.

On good days, I felt optimistic: weary, as always, but triumphantly persistent. On bad days, I thought: You bastards, you think this will make me hate him? It's *you* I'll resent, *you* I'll despise. On bad days, I made plans for Global Assurance. I hadn't been ready to fight them before, but when Chris was safe, and my strength had returned, I'd find a way to hurt them.

The reactions of my colleagues were mixed. Some were admiring. Some thought I'd let myself be exploited. Some were simply revolted by the thought of *a human brain* floating in my womb—and to challenge my own squeamishness, I confronted these people as often as I could.

"Go on, touch it," I said. "It won't bite. It won't even kick."

There was a brain in my womb, pale and convoluted. *So what?* I had an equally unappealing object in my own skull. In fact, my whole body was full of repulsive-looking offal—a fact which had never bothered me before.

So I conquered my visceral reactions to the organ *per se*—but thinking about Chris himself remained a difficult balancing act.

I resisted the insidious temptation to delude myself that I might be "in touch" with him—by "telepathy," through the bloodstream, by any means at all. Maybe pregnant mothers had some genuine empathy with their unborn children; I'd never been pregnant, it wasn't for me to judge. Certainly, a child in the womb could hear its mother's voice—but a comatose brain, devoid of sense organs, was a different matter entirely. At best—or worst—perhaps certain hormones in my blood crossed the placenta and had some limited effect on his condition.

On his mood?

He was in a coma, he had no *mood*.

In fact, it was easiest, and safest, not to think of him as even being *located* inside me, let alone experiencing anything there. I was carrying a part of him; the surrogate mother of his clone was carrying another. Only when the two were united would he truly exist again; for now, he was in limbo, neither dead nor alive.

This pragmatic approach worked, most of the time. Of course, there were moments when I suffered a kind of panic at the renewed realization of the bizarre nature of what I'd done. Sometimes I'd wake from nightmares, believing—for a second or two—that Chris was dead and his spirit had possessed me; or that his brain had sent forth nerves into my body and taken control of my limbs; or that he was fully conscious, and going insane from loneliness and sensory deprivation. But I wasn't possessed, my limbs still obeyed me, and every month a PET scan and a "uterine EEG" proved that he was still comatose—undamaged, but mentally inert.

In fact, the dreams I hated the most were those in which I was carrying a child. I'd wake from *these* with one hand on my belly, rapturously contemplating the miracle of the new life growing inside me—until I came to my senses and dragged myself angrily out of bed. I'd start the morning in the foulest of moods, grinding my teeth as I pissed, banging plates at the breakfast table, screaming insults at no one in particular while I dressed. Lucky I was living alone.

I couldn't really blame my poor besieged body for trying, though. My over-sized, marathon pregnancy dragged on and on; no wonder it tried to compensate me for the inconvenience with some stiff medicinal doses of maternal love. How ungrateful my rejection must have seemed; how baffling to find its images and sentiments rejected as *inappropriate*.

So . . . I trampled on Death, and I trampled on Motherhood. Well, *hallelujah*. If sacrifices had to be made, what better victims could there have been than those two emotional slave-drivers? And it was easy, really; logic was on my side, with a vengeance. Chris was *not* dead; I had no reason to mourn him, whatever had become of the body I'd known. And the thing in my womb was *not* a child;

permitting a disembodied brain to be the object of motherly love would have been simply farcical.

We think of our lives as circumscribed by cultural and biological taboos, but if people really want to break them, they always seem to find a way. Human beings are capable of anything: torture, genocide, cannibalism, rape. After which—or so I'd heard—most can still be kind to children and animals, be moved to tears by music, and generally behave as if all their emotional faculties are intact.

So, what reason did I have to fear that my own minor—and utterly selfless—transgressions could do me any harm at all?

I NEVER MET THE new body's surrogate mother, I never saw the clone as a child. I did wonder, though—once I knew that the thing had been born—whether or not she'd found her "normal" pregnancy as distressing as I'd found mine. Which is easiest, I wondered: carrying a brain-damaged child-shaped object, with no potential for human thought, grown from a stranger's DNA—or carrying the sleeping brain of your lover? Which is the hardest to keep from loving in inappropriate ways?

At the start, I'd hoped to be able to blur all the details in my mind—I'd wanted to be able to wake one morning and pretend that Chris had merely been *sick*, and was now *recovered*. Over the months, though, I'd come to realize that it was never going to work that way.

When they took out the brain, I should have felt—at the very least—relieved, but I just felt numb, and vaguely disbelieving. The ordeal had gone on for so long; it *couldn't* be over with so little fuss: no trauma, no ceremony. I'd had surreal dreams of laboriously, but triumphantly, giving birth to a healthy pink brain—but even if I'd wanted that (and no doubt the process could have been induced), the organ was too delicate to pass safely through the vagina. This "Caesarean" removal was just one more blow to my biological expectations; a good thing, of course, in the long run, since my biological expectations could never be fulfilled . . . but I still couldn't help feeling slightly cheated.

So I waited, in a daze, for the proof that it had all been worthwhile.

The brain couldn't simply be transplanted into the clone, like a heart or a kidney. The peripheral nervous system of the new body wasn't identical to that of the old one; identical genes weren't sufficient to ensure that. Also—despite drugs to limit the effect—parts of Chris's brain had atrophied slightly from disuse. So, rather than splicing nerves directly between the imperfectly matched brain and body—which probably would have left him paralyzed, deaf, dumb and blind—the impulses would be routed through a computerized "interface," which would try to sort out the discrepancies. Chris would still have to be rehabilitated, but the computer would speed up the process enormously, constantly striving to bridge the gap between thought and action, between reality and perception.

The first time they let me see him, I didn't recognize him at all. His face was slack, his eyes unfocused; he looked like a large, neurologically impaired child—which, of course, he was. I felt a mild twinge of revulsion. The man I'd seen after the train wreck, swarming with medical robots, had looked far more human, far more whole.

I said, "Hello. It's me."

He stared into space.

The technician said, "It's early days."

She was right. In the weeks that followed, his progress (or the computer's) was astounding. His posture and expression soon lost their disconcerting neutrality, and the first helpless twitches rapidly gave way to coordinated movement; weak and clumsy, but encouraging. He couldn't talk, but he could meet my eyes, he could squeeze my hand.

He was *in there*, he was *back*, there was no doubt about that.

I worried about his silence—but I discovered later that he'd deliberately spared me his early, faltering attempts at speech.

One evening in the fifth week of his new life, when I came into the room and sat down beside the bed, he turned to me and said clearly, "They told me what you did. Oh God, Carla, I love you!"

His eyes filled with tears. I bent over and embraced him; it seemed like the right thing to do. And I cried, too—but I even as I did so, I couldn't help thinking: None of this can really touch me. It's just one more trick of the body, and I'm immune to all that now.

WE MADE LOVE ON the third night he spent at home. I'd expected it to be difficult, a massive psychological hurdle for both of us, but that wasn't the case at all. And after everything we'd come through, why should it have been? I don't know what I'd feared; some poor misguided avatar of the Incest Taboo, crashing through the bedroom window at the critical moment, spurred on by the ghost of a discredited nineteenth-century misogynist?

I suffered no delusion at any level—from the merely subconscious, right down to the endocrine—that Chris was *my son*. Whatever effects two years of placental hormones might have had on me, whatever behavioral programs they "ought" to have triggered, I'd apparently gained the strength and the insight to undermine completely.

True, his skin was soft and unweathered, and devoid of the scars of a decade of hacking off facial hair. He might have passed for a sixteen-year-old, but I felt no qualms about *that*—any middle-aged man who was rich enough and vain enough could have looked the same.

And when he put his tongue to my breasts, I did not lactate.

We soon started visiting friends; they were tactful, and Chris was glad of that—although personally, I'd have happily discussed any aspect of the procedure. Six months later, he was working again; his old job had been taken, but a new firm was recruiting (and they wanted a youthful image).

Piece by piece, our lives were reassembled.

Nobody, looking at us now, would think that anything had changed.

But they'd be wrong.

To love a *brain* as if it were a *child* would be ludicrous. Geese might be stupid enough to treat the first animal they see upon hatching as their mother, but there are limits to what a sane human being will swallow. So, reason triumphed over instinct, and I conquered my inappropriate love; under the circumstances, there was never really any contest.

Having deconstructed one form of enslavement, though, I find it all too easy to repeat the process, to recognize the very same chains in another guise.

Everything special I once felt for Chris is transparent to me now. I still feel genuine friendship for him, I still feel desire, but there used to be something more. If there hadn't been, I doubt he'd be alive today.

Oh, the signals keep coming through; some part of my brain still pumps out cues for *appropriate* feelings of tenderness, but these messages are as laughable, and as ineffectual, now, as the contrivances of some tenth rate tear-jerking movie. I just can't suspend my disbelief anymore.

I have no trouble going through the motions; inertia makes it easy. And as long as things are working—as long as his company is pleasant and the sex is good—I see no reason to rock the boat. We may stay together for years, or I may walk out tomorrow. I really don't know.

Of course I'm still glad that he survived—and to some degree, I can even admire the courage and selflessness of the woman who saved him. I know that I could never do the same.

Sometimes when we're together, and I see in his eyes the very same helpless passion that I've lost, I'm tempted to pity myself. I think: I was *brutalized*, no wonder I'm a cripple, no wonder I'm so fucked-up.

And in a sense, that's a perfectly valid point of view—but I never seem to be able to subscribe to it for long. The new truth has its own cool passion, its own powers of manipulation; it assails me with words like "freedom" and "insight," and speaks of the end of all deception. It grows inside me, day by day, and it's far too strong to let me have regrets.

INTO DARKNESS

THE TONE FROM THE buzzer rises in both pitch and loudness the longer it's on, so I leap out of bed knowing that it's taken me less than a second to wake. I swear I was dreaming it first, though, dreaming the sound long before it was real. That's happened a few times. Maybe it's just a trick of the mind; maybe some dreams take shape only in the act of remembering them. Or maybe I dream it every night, every sleeping moment, just in case.

The light above the buzzer is red. Not a rehearsal.

I dress on my way across the room to thump the acknowledgment switch; as soon as the buzzer shuts off, I can hear the approaching siren. It takes me as long to lace my shoes as everything else combined. I grab my backpack from beside the bed and flick on the power. It starts flashing LEDs as it goes through its self-checking routines.

By the time I'm at the curb, the patrol car is braking noisily, rear passenger door swinging open. I know the driver, Angelo, but I haven't seen the other cop before. As we accelerate, a satellite view of The Intake in false-color infrared—a pitch black circle in a landscape of polychromatic blotches—appears on the car's terminal. A moment later, this is replaced by a street map of the region—one of the newer far northern suburbs, all cul-de-sacs and crescents—with The Intake's perimeter and center marked, and a dashed line showing where The Core should be. The optimal routes are omitted;

too much clutter and the mind balks. I stare at the map, trying to commit it to memory. It's not that I won't have access to it, inside, but it's always faster to just *know*. When I close my eyes to see how I'm going, the pattern in my head looks like nothing so much as a puzzle-book maze.

We hit the freeway, and Angelo lets loose. He's a good driver, but I sometimes wonder if this is the riskiest part of the whole business. The cop I don't know doesn't think so; he turns to me and says, "I gotta tell you one thing; I respect what you do, but you must be fucking crazy. I wouldn't go inside that thing for a million dollars." Angelo grins—I catch it in the rear-view mirror—and says, "Hey, how much is the Nobel prize, anyway? More than a million?"

I snort. "I doubt it. And I don't think they give the Nobel prize for the eight hundred meter steeplechase." The media seem to have decided to portray me as some kind of expert; I don't know why—unless it's because I once used the phrase "radially anisotropic" in an interview. It's true that I carried one of the first scientific "payloads," but any other Runner could have done that, and these days it's routine. The fact is, by international agreement, no one with even a microscopic chance of contributing to the theory of The Intake is allowed to risk their life by going inside. If I'm atypical in any way, it's through a *lack* of relevant qualifications; most of the other volunteers have a background in the conventional rescue services.

I switch my watch into chronograph mode, and synch it to the count that the terminal's now showing, then do the same to my backpack's timer. Six minutes and twelve seconds. The Intake's manifestations obey exactly the same statistics as a radioactive nucleus with a half-life of eighteen minutes; seventy-nine per cent last six minutes or more—but multiply anything by 0.962 every minute, and you wouldn't believe how fast it can fall. I've memorized the probabilities right out to an hour (ten per cent), which may or may not have been a wise thing to do. Counter to intuition, The Intake does *not* become more dangerous as time passes, any more than a single radioactive nucleus becomes "more unstable." At any given moment—assuming that it hasn't yet vanished—it's just as likely as ever to stick around for another eighteen minutes. A mere ten per cent of manifestations last for an hour or more—but *of that ten per cent,* half will still be there eighteen minutes later. The danger has not increased.

For a Runner, inside, to ask what the odds are *now,* he or she must be alive to pose the question, and so the probability curve must start afresh from that moment. History can't harm you; the "chance" of *having survived* the last x minutes is one hundred per cent, once you've done it. As the unknowable future becomes the unchangeable past, risk must collapse into certainty, one way or another.

Whether or not any of us really think this way is another question. You can't help having a gut feeling that time is running out, that the odds are being whittled away. Everyone keeps track of the time since The Intake materialized, however theoretically irrelevant that is. The truth is, these abstractions make no difference in the end. You do what you can, as fast as you can, regardless.

It's two in the morning, the freeway is empty, but it still takes me by surprise when we screech onto the exit ramp so soon. My stomach is painfully tight. I wish I felt *ready,* but I never do. After ten real calls, after nearly two hundred rehearsals, I never do. I always wish I had more time to compose myself, although I have no idea what state of mind I'd aim for, let alone how I'd achieve it. Some lunatic part of me is always hoping for a *delay.* If what I'm really hoping is that The Intake will have vanished before I can reach it, I shouldn't be here at all.

The coordinators tell us, over and over: "You can back out any time you want to. Nobody would think any less of you." It's true, of course (up to the point where backing out becomes physically impossible), but it's a freedom I could do without. Retiring would be one thing, but once I've accepted a call I don't want to have to waste my energy on second thoughts, I don't want to have to endlessly reaffirm my choice. I've psyched myself into half believing that *I* couldn't live with myself, however understanding other people might be, and that helps a little. The only trouble is, this lie might be self-fulfilling, and I really don't want to become that kind of person.

I close my eyes, and the map appears before me. I'm a mess, there's no denying it, but I can still do the job, I can still get results. That's what counts.

I can tell when we're getting close, without even searching the skyline; there are lights on in all of the houses, and families standing in their front yards. Many people wave and cheer as we pass, a sight that always depresses me. When a group of teenagers, standing on a street corner drinking beer, scream abuse and gesture obscenely, I can't help feeling perversely encouraged.

"Dickheads," mutters the cop I don't know. I keep my mouth shut.

We take a corner, and I spot a trio of helicopters, high on my right, ascending with a huge projection screen in tow. Suddenly, a corner of the screen is obscured, and my eye extends the curve of the eclipsing object from this one tiny arc to giddy completion.

From the outside, by day, The Intake makes an impressive sight: a giant black dome, completely non-reflective, blotting out a great bite of the sky. It's impossible not to believe that you're confronting a massive, solid object. By night, though, it's different. The shape is still unmistakable, cut in a velvet black that makes the darkest night seem gray, but there's no illusion of solidity; just an awareness of a different kind of void.

The Intake has been appearing for almost ten years now. It's always a perfect sphere, a little more than a kilometer in radius, and usually centered close to ground level. On rare occasions, it's been known to appear out at sea, and, slightly more often, on uninhabited land, but the vast majority of its incarnations take place in populated regions.

The currently favored hypothesis is that a future civilization tried to construct a wormhole that would let them sample the distant past, bringing specimens of ancient life into their own time to be studied. They screwed up. Both ends of the wormhole came unstuck. The thing has shrunk and deformed, from—presumably—some kind of grand temporal highway, bridging geological epochs, to a gateway that now spans less time than it would take to cross an atomic nucleus at the speed of light. One end—The Intake—is a kilometer in radius; the other is about a fifth as big, spatially concentric with the first, but displaced an almost immeasurably small time into the future. We call the inner sphere—the wormhole's destination, which seems to be inside it, but isn't—The Core.

Why this shriveled-up piece of failed temporal engineering has ended up in the present era is anyone's guess; maybe we just happened to be half-way between the original endpoints, and the thing collapsed symmetrically. Pure bad luck. The trouble is, it hasn't quite come to rest. It materializes somewhere on the planet, remains fixed for several minutes, then loses its grip and vanishes, only to appear at a new location a fraction of a second later. Ten years of analyzing the data has yielded no method for predicting successive locations, but there must be some remnant of a navigation system in action; why else would the wormhole cling to the Earth's surface (with a marked preference for inhabited, dry land) instead of wandering off on a random course into interplanetary space? It's as if some faithful, demented computer keeps valiantly trying to anchor The Intake to a region which might be of interest to its scholarly masters; no Paleozoic life can be found, but twenty-first century cities will do, since there's nothing much else around. And every time it fails to make a permanent connection and slips off into hyperspace, with infinite dedication, and unbounded stupidity, it tries again.

Being of interest is bad news. Inside the wormhole, time is mixed with one spatial dimension, and—whether by design or physical necessity—any movement which equates to traveling from the future into the past is forbidden. Translated into the wormhole's present geometry, this means that when The Intake materializes around you, motion away from the center is impossible. You have an unknown time—maybe eighteen minutes, maybe more, maybe less—to navigate your way to the safety of The Core, under these bizarre conditions. What's more, light is subject to the same effect; it only propagates inward. Everything closer to the center than you lies in the invisible future. You're running into darkness.

I have heard people scoff at the notion that any of this could be difficult. I'm not quite enough of a sadist to hope that they learn the truth, first hand.

Actually, outward motion isn't quite literally impossible. If it were, everyone caught in The Intake would die at once. The heart has to circulate blood, the lungs have to inhale and exhale, nerve impulses have to travel in all directions. Every single living cell relies on shuffling chemicals back and forth, and I can't even guess what the effect would be on the molecular level, if electron clouds could fluctuate in one direction but not the reverse.

There is some leeway. Because the wormhole's entire eight hundred meters spans such a minute time interval, the distance scale of the human body corresponds to an even shorter period—short enough for quantum effects to come into play. Quantum uncertainty in the space-time metric permits small, localized violations of the classical law's absolute restriction.

So, instead of everyone dying on the spot, blood pressure goes up, the heart is stressed, breathing becomes laborious, and the brain may function erratically. Enzymes, hormones, and other biological molecules are all slightly deformed, causing them to bind less efficiently to their targets, interfering to some degree with every biochemical process; hemoglobin, for example, loses its grip on oxygen more easily. Water diffuses out of the body—because random thermal motion is suddenly not so random—leading to gradual dehydration.

People already in very poor health can die from these effects. Others are just made nauseous, weak and confused—on top of the inevitable shock and panic. They make bad decisions. They get trapped.

One way or another, a few hundred lives are lost, every time The Intake materializes. Intake Runners may save ten or twenty people, which I'll admit is not much of a success rate, but until some genius works out how to rid us of the wormhole for good, it's better than nothing.

The screen is in place high above us, when we reach the "South Operations Center"—a couple of vans, stuffed with electronics, parked on someone's front lawn. The now-familiar section of street map appears, the image rock steady and in perfect focus, in spite of the fact that it's being projected from a fourth helicopter, and all four are jittering in the powerful inward wind. People inside can see out, of course; this map—and the others, at the other compass points—will save dozens of lives. In theory, once outdoors, it should be simple enough to head straight for The Core; after all, there's no easier direction to find, no easier path to follow. The trouble is, a straight line inward is likely to lead you into obstacles, and when you can't retrace your steps, the most mundane of these can kill you.

So, the map is covered with arrows, marking the optimal routes to The Core, given the constraint of staying safely on the roads. Two more helicopters, hovering above The Intake, are doing one better: with high-velocity paint guns under computer control, and laser-ring inertial guidance systems constantly telling the shuddering computers their precise location and orientation, they're drawing the same arrows in fluorescent/reflective paint on the invisible streets below. You can't see the arrows ahead of you, but you can look back at the ones you've passed. It helps.

There's a small crowd of coordinators, and one or two Runners, around the vans. This scene always looks forlorn to me, like some small-time rained-out amateur athletics event, air traffic notwithstanding. Angelo calls out, "Break a leg!" as I run from the car. I raise a hand and wave without turning. Loudspeakers are blasting the standard advice inward, cycling through a dozen languages. In the corner of my eye I can see a TV crew arriving. I glance at my watch. Nine minutes. I can't help thinking, *seventy-one per cent*, although The Intake is, clearly, one hundred per cent still there. Someone taps me on the shoulder. Elaine. She smiles and says, "John, see you in The Core," then sprints into the wall of darkness before I can reply.

Dolores is handing out assignments on RAM. She wrote most of the software used by Intake Runners around the world, but then, she makes her living writing computer games. She's even written a game which models The Intake itself, but sales have been less than spectacular; the reviewers decided it was in bad taste. "What's next? Let's play Airline Disaster?" Maybe they think flight simulators should be programmed for endless calm weather. Meanwhile, televangelists sell prayers to keep the wormhole away; you just slip that credit card into the home-shopping slot for instant protection.

"What have you got for me?"

"Three infants."

"Is that *all?*"

"You come late, you get the crumbs."

I plug the cartridge into my backpack. A sector of the street map appears on the display panel, marked with three bright red dots. I strap on the pack, and then adjust the display on its movable arm so I can catch it with a sideways glance, if I have to. Electronics can be made to function reliably inside the wormhole, but everything has to be specially designed.

It's not ten minutes, not quite. I grab a cup of water from a table beside one of the vans. A solution of mixed carbohydrates, supposedly optimized for our metabolic needs, is also on offer, but the one time I tried it I was sorry; my gut isn't interested in absorbing anything at this stage, optimized or not. There's coffee too, but the very last thing I need right now is a stimulant. Gulping down the water, I hear my name, and I can't help tuning in to the TV reporter's spiel.

" . . . John Nately, high school science teacher and unlikely hero, embarking on this, his *eleventh* call as a volunteer Intake Runner. If he survives tonight, he'll have set a new national record—but of course, the odds of making it through grow slimmer with every call, and by now . . ."

The moron is spouting crap—the odds *do not* grow slimmer, a veteran faces no extra risk—but this isn't the time to set him straight. I swing my arms for a few seconds in a half-hearted warm-up, but there's not much point; every muscle in my body is tense, and will be for the next eight hundred meters, whatever I do. I try to blank my mind and just concentrate on the run-up—the faster you hit The Intake, the less of a shock it is—and before I can ask myself, for the first time tonight, what the fuck I'm really doing here, I've left the isotropic universe behind, and the question is academic.

The darkness doesn't swallow you. Perhaps that's the strangest part of all. You've seen it swallow other Runners; why doesn't it swallow *you?* Instead, it recedes from your every step. The borderline isn't absolute; quantum fuzziness produces a gradual fade-out, stretching visibility about as far as each extended foot. By day, this is completely surreal, and people have been known to suffer fits and psychotic episodes at the sight of the void's apparent retreat. By night, it seems merely implausible, like chasing an intelligent fog.

At the start, it's almost too easy; memories of pain and fatigue seem ludicrous. Thanks to frequent rehearsals in a compression harness, the pattern of resistance as I breath is almost familiar. Runners once took drugs to lower their blood pressure, but with sufficient training, the body's own vasoregulatory system can be made flexible enough to cope with the stress, unaided. The odd tugging sensation on each leg as I bring it forward would probably drive me mad, if I didn't (crudely) understand the reason for it: inward motion is resisted, when pulling, rather than pushing, is involved, because *information* travels outward. If I trailed a ten-meter rope behind me, I wouldn't be able to take a single step; pulling on the rope would pass information about my motion from where I am to a point further out. That's forbidden, and it's only the quantum leeway that lets me drag each foot forward at all.

The street curves gently to the right, gradually losing its radial orientation, but there's no convenient turn-off yet. I stay in the middle of the road, straddling the double white line, as the border between past and future swings to the left. The road surface seems always to slope toward the darkness, but that's just another wormhole effect; the bias in thermal molecular motion—cause of the inward wind, and slow dehydration—produces a force, or pseudo-force, on solid objects, too, tilting the apparent vertical.

"—me! *Please!*"

A man's voice, desperate and bewildered—and almost indignant, as if he can't help believing that I must have heard him all along, that I must have been feigning deafness out of malice or indifference. I turn, without slowing; I've learned to do it in a way that makes me only slightly dizzy. Everything appears almost normal, looking outward—apart from the fact that the streetlights are out, and so most illumination is from helicopter floodlights and the giant street map in the sky. The cry came from a bus shelter, all vandal-proof plastic and reinforced glass, at least five meters behind me, now; it might as well be on Mars. Wire mesh covers the glass; I can just make out the figure behind it, a faint silhouette.

"Help me!"

Mercifully—for me—I've vanished into this man's darkness; I don't have to think of a gesture to make, an expression to put on my face, appropriate to the situation. I turn away, and pick up speed. I'm not inured to the death of strangers, but I am inured to my helplessness.

After ten years of The Intake, there are international standards for painted markings on the ground around every potential hazard in public open space. Like all the other measures, it helps, slightly. There are standards, too, for eventually eliminating the hazards— designing out the corners where people can be trapped—but that's going to cost billions, and take decades, and won't even touch the real problem: interiors. I've seen demonstration trap-free houses and office blocks, with doors, or curtained doorways, in *every* corner of *every* room, but the style hasn't exactly caught on. My own house is far from ideal; after getting quotes for alterations, I decided that the cheapest solution was to keep a sledgehammer beside every wall.

I turn left, just in time to see a trail of glowing arrows hiss into place on the road behind me.

I'm almost at my first assignment. I tap a button on my back-pack and peer sideways at the display, as it switches to a plan of the target house. As soon as The Intake's position is known, Dolores's software starts hunting through databases, assembling a list of loca-tions where there's a reasonable chance that we can do some good. Our information is never complete, and sometimes just plain wrong; Census data is often out of date, building plans can be inaccurate, misfiled, or simply missing—but it beats walking blind into houses chosen at random.

I slow almost to a walk, two houses before the target, to give myself time to grow used to the effects. Running inward lessens the outward components—relative to the wormhole—of the body's cyclic motions; slowing down always feels like precisely the wrong thing to do. I often dream of running through a narrow canyon, no wider than my shoulders, whose walls will stay apart only so long as I move fast enough; that's what my body thinks of *slowing down*.

The street here lies about thirty degrees off radial. I cross the front lawn of the neighboring house, then step over a knee-high brick wall. At this angle, there are few surprises; most of what's hidden is so easy to extrapolate that it almost seems visible in the mind's eye. A corner of the target house emerges from the darkness on my left; I get my bearings from it and head straight for a side window. Entry by the front door would cost me access to almost half of the house, including the bedroom which Dolores's highly erratic Room Use Predictor nominates as the one most likely to be the child's. People can file room use information with us directly, but few bother.

I smash the glass with a crowbar, open the window, and clamber through. I leave a small electric lamp on the windowsill—carrying it with me would render it useless—and move slowly into the room. I'm already starting to feel dizzy and nauseous, but I force myself to concentrate. One step too many, and the rescue becomes ten times more difficult. Two steps, and it's impossible.

It's clear that I have the right room when a dresser is revealed, piled with plastic toys, talcum powder, baby shampoo, and other paraphernalia spilling onto the floor. Then a corner of the crib appears on my left, pointed at an unexpected angle; the thing was probably neatly parallel to the wall to start with, but slid unevenly under the inward force. I sidle up to it, then inch forward, until a lump beneath the blanket comes into view. I hate this moment, but the longer I wait, the harder it gets. I reach sideways and lift the child, bringing the blanket with it. I kick the crib aside, then walk forward, slowly bending my arms, until I can slip the child into the harness on my chest. An adult is strong enough to drag a small baby a short distance outward. It's usually fatal.

The kid hasn't stirred; he or she is unconscious, but breathing. I shudder briefly, a kind of shorthand emotional catharsis, then I start moving. I glance at the display to recheck the way out, and finally let myself notice the time. Thirteen minutes. Sixty-one per cent. More to the point, The Core is just two or three minutes away, downhill, non-stop. One successful assignment means ditching the rest. There's no alternative; you can't lug a child with you, in and out of buildings; you can't even put it down somewhere and come back for it later.

As I step through the front door, the sense of relief leaves me giddy. Either that, or renewed cerebral blood flow. I pick up speed as I cross the lawn—and catch a glimpse of a woman, shouting, "Wait! Stop!"

I slow down; she catches up with me. I put a hand on her shoulder and propel her slightly ahead of me, then say, "Keep moving, as fast as you can. When you want to speak, fall behind me. I'll do the same. Okay?"

I move ahead of her. She says, "That's my daughter you've got. Is she all right? Oh, please . . . Is she alive?"

"She's fine. Stay calm. We just have to get her to The Core now. Okay?"

"I want to hold her. I want to take her."

"Wait until we're safe."

"I want to take her there myself."

Shit. I glance at her sideways. Her face is glistening with sweat and tears. One of her arms is bruised and blotchy, the usual symptom of trying to reach out to something unreachable.

"I really think it would be better to wait."

"What right have you got? She's *my* daughter! Give her to me!" The woman is indignant, but remarkably lucid, considering what she's been through. I can't imagine what it must have felt like, to stand by that house, hoping insanely for some kind of miracle, while everyone in the neighborhood fled past her, and the side-effects made her sicker and sicker. However pointless, however idiotic her courage, I can't help admiring it.

I'm lucky. My ex-wife, and our son and daughter, live half-way across town from me. I have no friends who live nearby. My emotional geography is very carefully arranged; I don't give a shit about anyone who I could end up unable to save.

So what do I do—sprint away from her, leave her running after me, screaming? Maybe I should. *If I gave her the child, though, I could check out one more house.*

"Do you know how to handle her? Never try to move her backward, away from the darkness. *Never.*"

"I know that. I've read all the articles. I *know* what you're meant to do."

"Okay." I must be crazy. We slow down to a walk, and I pass the child to her, lowering it into her arms from beside her. I realize, almost too late, that we're at the turn-off for the second house. As the woman vanishes into the darkness, I yell after her, "*Run!* Follow the arrows, and *run!*"

I check the time. Fifteen minutes already, with all that stuffing around. I'm still alive, though—so the odds now are, as always, fifty-fifty that the wormhole will last another eighteen minutes. Of course I could die at any second—but that was equally true when I first stepped inside. I'm no greater fool now than I was then. For what that's worth.

The second house is empty, and it's easy to see why. The computer's guess for the nursery is in fact a study, and the parents' bedroom is outward of the child's. Windows are open, clearly showing the path they must have taken.

A strange mood overtakes me, as I leave the house behind. The inward wind seems stronger than ever, the road turns straight into the darkness, and I feel an inexplicable tranquility wash over me. I'm moving as fast as I can, but the edge of latent panic, of sudden death, is gone. My lungs, my muscles, are battling all the same restraints, but I feel curiously detached from them; aware of the pain and effort, yet somehow uninvolved.

The truth is, I know exactly why I'm here. I can never quite admit it, outside—it seems too whimsical, too bizarre. Of course I'm glad to save lives, and maybe that's grown to be part of it. No doubt I also crave to be thought of as a hero. The real reason, though, is too strange to be judged either selfless or vain:

The wormhole makes tangible the most basic truths of existence. You cannot see the future. You cannot change the past. All of life consists of running into darkness. This is why I'm here.

My body grows, not numb, but separate, a puppet dancing and twitching on a treadmill. I snap out of this and check the map, not a moment too soon. I have to turn right, sharply, which puts an end to any risk of somnambulism. Looking up at the bisected world makes my head pound, so I stare at my feet, and try to recall if the pooling of blood in my left hemisphere ought to make me more rational, or less.

The third house is in a borderline situation. The parents' bedroom is slightly outward from the child's, but the doorway gives access to only half the room. I enter through a window that the parents could not have used.

The child is dead. I see the blood before anything else. I feel, suddenly, very tired. A slit of the doorway is visible, and I know what must have happened. The mother or father edged their way in, and found they could just reach the child—could take hold of one hand, but no more. Pulling inward is resisted, but people find that confusing; they don't expect it, and when it happens, they fight it. When you want to snatch someone you love out of the jaws of danger, you pull with all your strength.

The door is an easy exit for me, but less so for anyone who came in that way—especially someone in the throes of grief. I stare into the darkness of the room's inward corner, and yell, "Crouch down, as low as you can," then mime doing so. I pluck the demolition gun from my backpack, and aim high. The recoil, in normal space, would send me sprawling; here it's a mere thump.

I step forward, giving up my own chance to use the door. There's no immediate sign that I've just blasted a meter-wide hole in the wall; virtually all of the dust and debris is on the inward side. I finally reach a man kneeling in the corner, his hands on his head; for a brief moment I think he's alive, that he took this position to shield himself from the blast. No pulse, no respiration. A dozen broken ribs, probably; I'm not inclined to check. Some people can last for an hour, pinned between walls of brick and an invisible, third wall that follows them ruthlessly into the corner, every time they slip, every time they give ground. Some people, though, do exactly the worst thing; they squeeze themselves into the inward-most part of their prison, obeying some instinct which, I'm sure, makes sense at the time.

Or maybe he wasn't confused at all. Maybe he just wanted it to be over.

I hoist myself through the hole in the wall. I stagger through the kitchen. The fucking plan is wrong wrong wrong, a door I'm expecting doesn't exist. I smash the kitchen window, then cut my hand on the way out.

I refuse to glance at the map. I don't want to know the time. Now that I'm alone, with no purpose left but saving myself, everything is jinxed. I stare at the ground, at the fleeting magic golden arrows, trying not to count them.

One glimpse of a festering hamburger discarded on the road, and I find myself throwing up. Common sense tells me to turn and face backward, but I'm not quite that stupid. The acid in my throat and nose brings tears to my eyes. As I shake them away, something impossible happens.

A brilliant blue light appears, high up in the darkness ahead, dazzling my dark adapted eyes. I shield my face, then peer between my fingers. As I grow used to the glare, I start to make out details.

A cluster of long, thin, luminous cylinders is hanging in the sky, like some mad upside-down pipe organ built of glass, bathed in glowing plasma. The light it casts does nothing to reveal the houses and streets below. I must be hallucinating; I've seen shapes in the darkness before, although never anything so spectacular, so persistent. I run faster, in the hope of clearing my head. The apparition doesn't vanish, or waver; it merely grows closer.

I halt, shaking uncontrollably. I stare into the impossible light. What if it's not in my head? There's only one possible explanation. Some component of the wormhole's hidden machinery has revealed itself. The idiot navigator is showing me its worthless soul.

With one voice in my skull screaming, *No!* and another calmly asserting that I have no choice, that this chance might never come again, I draw the demolition gun, take aim, and fire. As if some puny weapon in the hands of an amoeba could scratch the shimmering artifact of a civilization whose failures leave us cowering in awe.

The structure shatters and implodes in silence. The light contracts to a blinding pinprick, burning itself into my vision. Only when I turn my head am I certain that the real light is gone.

I start running again. Terrified, elated. I have no idea what I've done, but the wormhole is, so far, unchanged. The afterimage lingers in the darkness, with nothing to wipe it from my sight. Can hallucinations leave an afterimage? *Did the navigator choose to expose itself, choose to let me destroy it?*

I trip on something and stagger, but catch myself from falling. I turn and see a man crawling down the road, and I bring myself to a rapid halt, astonished by such a mundane sight after my transcendental encounter. The man's legs have been amputated at the thighs; he's dragging himself along with his arms alone. That would be hard enough in normal space, but here, the effort must almost be killing him.

There are special wheelchairs which can function in the wormhole (wheels bigger than a certain size buckle and deform if the chair stalls) and if we know we'll need one, we bring one in, but they're too heavy for every Runner to carry one just in case.

The man lifts his head and yells, "Keep going! Stupid fucker!" without the least sign of doubt that he's not just shouting at empty space. I stare at him and wonder why I don't take the advice. He's huge: big-boned and heavily muscled, with plenty of fat on top of that. I doubt that I could lift him—and I'm certain that if I could, I'd stagger along more slowly than he's crawling.

Inspiration strikes. I'm in luck, too; a sideways glance reveals a house, with the front door invisible but clearly only a meter or two inward of where I am now. I smash the hinges with a hammer and chisel, then maneuver the door out of the frame and back to the road. The man has already caught up with me. I bend down and tap him on the shoulder. "Want to try sledding?"

I step inward in time to hear part of a string of obscenities, and to catch an unwelcome close-up of his bloody forearms. I throw the door down onto the road ahead of him. He keeps moving; I wait until he can hear me again.

"Yes or no?"

"Yes," he mutters.

It's awkward, but it works. He sits on the door, leaning back on his arms. I run behind, bent over, my hands on his shoulders, pushing. Pushing is the one action the wormhole doesn't fight, and the inward force makes it downhill all the way. Sometimes the door slides so fast that I have to let go for a second or two, to keep from overbalancing.

I don't need to look at the map. I *know* the map, I know precisely where we are; The Core is less than a hundred meters away. In my head I recite an incantation: *The danger does not increase. The danger does not increase.* And in my heart I know that the whole conceit of "probability" is meaningless; the wormhole is reading my mind, waiting for the first sign of hope, and whether that comes fifty meters, or ten meters, or two meters from safety, that's when it will take me.

Some part of me calmly judges the distance we cover, and counts: *Ninety-three, ninety-two, ninety-one* . . . I mumble random numbers to myself, and when that fails, I reset the count arbitrarily: *Eighty-one, eighty-seven, eighty-six, eighty-five, eighty-nine* . . .

A new universe, of light, stale air, noise—and people, *countless people*—explodes into being around me. I keep pushing the man on the door, until someone runs toward me and gently prizes me away. Elaine. She guides me over to the front steps of a house, while another Runner with a first-aid kit approaches my bloodied passenger. Groups of people stand or sit around electric lanterns, filling the streets and front yards as far as I can see. I point them out to Elaine. "Look. Aren't they beautiful?"

"John? You okay? Get your breath. It's over."

"Oh, fuck." I glance at my watch. "Twenty-one minutes. Forty-five per cent." I laugh, hysterically. "I was afraid of *forty-five per cent?*"

My heart is working twice as hard as it needs to. I pace for a while, until the dizziness begins to subside. Then I flop down on the steps beside Elaine.

A while later, I ask, "Any others still out there?"

"No."

"Great." I'm starting to feel almost lucid. "So . . . how did you go?"

She shrugs. "Okay. A sweet little girl. She's with her parents somewhere round here. No complications; favorable geometry." She shrugs again. Elaine is like that; favorable geometry or not, it's never a big deal.

I recount my own experience, leaving out the apparition. I should talk to the medical people first, straighten out what kind of hallucination is or isn't possible, before I start spreading the word that I took a pot shot at a glowing blue pipe organ from the future.

Anyway, if I did any good, I'll know soon enough. If The Intake *does* start drifting away from the planet, that shouldn't take long to make news; I have no idea at what rate the parting would take place, but surely the very next manifestation would be highly unlikely to be on the Earth's surface. Deep in the crust, or half-way into space—

I shake my head. There's no use building up my hopes, prematurely, when I'm still not sure that any of it was real.

Elaine says, "What?"

"Nothing."

I check the time again. Twenty-nine minutes. Thirty-three per cent. I glance down the street impatiently. We can see out into the wormhole, of course, but the border is clearly delineated by the sudden drop in illumination, once outward-bound light can no longer penetrate. When The Intake moves on, though, it won't be a matter of looking for subtle shifts in the lighting. While the wormhole is in place, its effects violate the Second Law of Thermodynamics (biased thermal motion, for a start, clearly decreases entropy). In parting, it more than makes amends; it *radially homogenizes* the space it occupied, down to a length scale of about a micron. To the rock two hundred meters beneath us, and the atmosphere above—both already highly uniform—this will make little difference, but every house, every garden, every blade of grass—every structure visible to the naked eye—will vanish. Nothing will remain but radial streaks of fine dust, swirling out as the high-pressure air in The Core is finally free to escape.

Thirty-five minutes. Twenty-six per cent. I look around at the weary survivors; even for those who left no family or friends behind, the sense of relief and thankfulness at having reached safety has no doubt faded. They—we—just want the waiting to be over. Everything about the passage of time, everything about the wormhole's uncertain duration, has reversed its significance. Yes, the thing might set us free at any moment—but so long as it hasn't, we're as likely as not to be stuck here for eighteen more minutes.

Forty minutes. Twenty-one per cent.

"Ears are really going to pop tonight," I say. Or worse; on rare occasions, the pressure in The Core can grow so high that the subsequent decompression gives rise to the bends. That's at least another hour away, though—and if it started to become a real possibility, they'd do an air drop of a drug that would cushion us from the effect.

Fifty minutes. Fifteen per cent.

Everyone is silent now; even the children have stopped crying.

"What's your record?" I ask Elaine.

She rolls her eyes. "Fifty-six minutes. You were there. Four years ago."

"Yeah. I remember."

"Just relax. Be patient."

"Don't you feel a little silly? I mean, if I'd known, I would have taken my time."

One hour. Ten per cent. Elaine has dozed off, her head against my shoulder. I'm starting to feel drowsy myself, but a nagging thought keeps me awake.

I've always assumed that the wormhole moves because its efforts to stay put eventually fail—but what if the truth is precisely the opposite? What if it moves because its efforts to move have always, eventually, succeeded? What if the navigator breaks away to try again, as quickly as it can—but its crippled machinery can do no better than a fifty-fifty chance of success, for every eighteen minutes of striving?

Maybe I've put an end to that striving. Maybe I've brought The Intake, finally, to rest.

Eventually, the pressure itself can grow high enough to be fatal. It takes almost five hours, it's a one-in-one-hundred-thousand case, but it has happened once already, there's no reason at all it couldn't happen again. That's what bothers me most: I'd never know. Even if I saw people dying around me, the moment would never arrive when I knew, for certain, that this was the final price.

Elaine stirs without opening her eyes. "*Still?*"

"Yeah." I put an arm around her; she doesn't seem to mind.

"Well. Don't forget to wake me when it's over."

UNSTABLE ORBITS IN THE
SPACE OF LIES

ALWAYS FEEL SAFEST SLEEPING on the freeway—or at least, those
stretches of it that happen to lie in regions of approximate equilibrium between the surrounding attractors. With our sleeping bags laid
out carefully along the fading white lines between the northbound
lanes (perhaps because of a faint hint of geomancy reaching up from
Chinatown—not quite drowned out by the influence of scientific
humanism from the east, liberal Judaism from the west, and some
vehement anti-spiritual, anti-intellectual hedonism from the north),
I can close my eyes safe in the knowledge that Maria and I are not
going to wake up believing, wholeheartedly and irrevocably, in Papal
infallibility, the sentience of Gaia, the delusions of insight induced
by meditation, or the miraculous healing powers of tax reform.

So when I wake to find the sun already clear of the horizon—
and Maria gone—I don't panic. No faith, no world view, no belief
system, no culture, could have reached out in the night and claimed
her. The borders of the basins of attraction *do* fluctuate, advancing
and retreating by tens of meters daily—but it's highly unlikely that
any of them could have penetrated this far into our precious wasteland of anomie and doubt. I can't think why she would have walked
off and left me, without a word—but Maria does things, now and

then, that I find wholly inexplicable. And vice versa. Even after a year together, we still have that.

I don't panic—but I don't linger, either. I don't want to get too far behind. I rise to my feet, stretching, and try to decide which way she would have headed; unless the local conditions have changed since she departed, that should be much the same as asking where I want to go, myself.

The attractors can't be fought, they can't be resisted—but it's possible to steer a course between them, to navigate the contradictions. The easiest way to start out is to make use of a strong, but moderately distant attractor to build up momentum—while taking care to arrange to be deflected at the last minute by a countervailing influence.

Choosing the first attractor—the belief to which surrender must be feigned—is always a strange business. Sometimes it feels, almost literally, like *sniffing the wind*, like following an external trail; sometimes it seems like pure introspection, like trying to determine "my own" true beliefs . . . and sometimes the whole idea of making a distinction between these apparent opposites seems misguided. Yeah, very fucking Zen—and that's how it strikes me now . . . which in itself just about answers the question. The balance here is delicate, but one influence *is* marginally stronger: Eastern philosophies are definitely more compelling than the alternatives, from where I stand—and knowing the purely geographical reasons for this doesn't really make it any less true. I piss on the chain-link fence between the freeway and the railway line, to hasten its decay, then I roll up my sleeping bag, take a swig of water from my canteen, hoist my pack, and start walking.

A bakery's robot delivery van speeds past me, and I curse my solitude; without elaborate preparations, it takes at least two agile people to make use of them: one to block the vehicle's path, the other to steal the food. Losses through theft are small enough that the people of the attractors seem to tolerate them; presumably, greater security measures just aren't worth the cost—although no doubt the inhabitants of each ethical monoculture have their own unique "reasons" for not starving us amoral tramps into submission. I take out a sickly carrot which I dug from one of my vegetable gardens when I passed by last night; it makes a pathetic breakfast, but as I chew on it, I think about the bread rolls that I'll steal when I'm back with Maria again, and my anticipation almost overshadows the bland, woody taste of the present.

The freeway curves gently south-east. I reach a section flanked by deserted factories and abandoned houses, and against this background of relative silence, the tug of Chinatown, straight ahead now, grows stronger and clearer. That glib label—"Chinatown"— was always an oversimplification, of course; before Meltdown, the area contained at least a dozen distinct cultures besides Hong Kong and Malaysian Chinese, from Korean to Cambodian, from Thai to Timorese—and several varieties of every religion from Buddhism to Islam. All of that diversity has vanished now, and the homogeneous amalgam that finally stabilized would probably seem utterly bizarre to any individual pre-Meltdown inhabitant of the district. To the present day citizens, of course, the strange hybrid feels exactly right; that's the definition of *stability*, the whole reason the attractors exist. If I marched right into Chinatown, not only would I find myself sharing the local values and beliefs, I'd be perfectly happy to stay that way for the rest of my life.

I don't expect that I'll march right in, though—any more than I expect the Earth to dive straight into the Sun. It's been almost four years since Meltdown, and no attractor has captured me yet.

I'VE HEARD DOZENS OF "explanations" for the events of that day, but I find most of them equally dubious—rooted as they are in the world views of particular attractors. One way in which I sometimes think of it, on January 12th, 2018, the human race must have crossed some kind of unforeseen threshold—of global population, perhaps—and suffered a sudden, irreversible change of psychic state.

Telepathy is not the right word for it; after all, nobody found themselves drowning in an ocean of babbling voices; nobody suffered the torment of empathic overload. The mundane chatter of consciousness stayed locked inside our heads; our quotidian mental privacy remained unbreached. (Or perhaps, as some have suggested, everyone's mental privacy was *so thoroughly breached* that the sum of our transient thoughts forms a blanket of featureless white noise covering the planet, which the brain filters out effortlessly.)

In any case, for whatever reason, the second-by-second soap operas of other people's inner lives remained, mercifully, as inaccessible as ever . . . but our skulls became completely permeable to each other's values and beliefs, each other's deepest convictions.

At first, this meant pure chaos. My memories of the time are confused and nightmarish; I wandered the city for a day and a night (I think), finding God (or some equivalent) anew every six seconds—seeing no visions, hearing no voices, but wrenched from faith to faith by invisible forces of dream logic. People moved in a daze, cowed and staggering—while ideas moved between us like lightning. Revelation followed contradictory revelation. I wanted it to stop, badly—I would have prayed for it to stop, if God had stayed the same long enough to be prayed to. I've heard other tramps compare these early mystical convulsions to drug rushes, to orgasms, to being picked up and dumped by ten meter waves, ceaselessly, hour after hour—but looking back, I find myself reminded most of a bout of gastroenteritis I once suffered: a long, feverish night of interminable vomiting and diarrhea. Every muscle, every joint in my body ached, my skin burned; I felt like I was dying. And every time I thought I lacked the strength to expel anything more from my body, another spasm took hold of me. By four in the morning, my helplessness seemed positively transcendental: the peristaltic reflex possessed me like some harsh—but ultimately benevolent—deity. At the time, it was the most religious experience I'd ever been through.

All across the city, competing belief systems fought for allegiance, mutating and hybridizing along the way . . . like those random populations of computer viruses they used to unleash against each other in experiments to demonstrate subtle points of evolutionary theory. Or perhaps like the historical clashes of the very same beliefs—with the length and time scales drastically shortened by the new mode of interaction—and a lot less bloodshed, now that the ideas themselves could do battle in a purely mental arena, rather than employing sword-wielding Crusaders or extermination camps. Or, like a swarm of demons set loose upon the Earth to possess all but the righteous . . .

The chaos didn't last long. In some places seeded by pre-Meltdown clustering of cultures and religions—and in other places, by pure chance—certain belief systems gained enough of an edge, enough of a foothold, to start spreading out from a core of believers into the surrounding random detritus, capturing adjacent, disordered populations where no dominant belief had yet emerged. The more territory these snowballing attractors conquered, the faster they grew. Fortunately—in this city, at least—no single attractor was able to expand unchecked; they all ended up hemmed in, sooner or later, by equally powerful neighbors—or confined by sheer lack of population at the city's outskirts, and near voids of non-residential land.

Within a week of Meltdown, the anarchy had crystallized into more-or-less the present configuration, with ninety-nine percent of the population having moved—or changed—until they were content to be exactly where—and who—they were.

I happened to end up between attractors—affected by many, but captured by none—and I've managed to stay in orbit ever since. Whatever the knack is, I seem to have it; over the years, the ranks of the tramps have thinned, but a core of us remain free.

In the early years, the people of the attractors used to send up robot helicopters to scatter pamphlets over the city, putting the case for their respective metaphors for what had happened—as if a well-chosen analogy for the disaster might be enough to win them converts; it took a while for some of them to understand that the written word had been rendered obsolete as a vector for indoctrination. Ditto for audiovisual techniques—and that still hasn't sunk in everywhere. Not long ago, on a battery-powered TV set in an abandoned house, Maria and I picked up a broadcast from a network of rationalist enclaves, showing an alleged "simulation" of Meltdown as a color-coded dance of mutually carnivorous pixels, obeying a few simple mathematical rules. The commentator spouted jargon about self-organizing systems—and lo, with the magic of hindsight, the flickers of color rapidly evolved into the familiar pattern of hexagonal cells, isolated by moats of darkness (unpopulated except for the barely visible presence of a few unimportant specks; we wondered which ones were meant to be *us*).

I don't know how things would have turned out if there hadn't been the pre-existing infrastructure of robots and telecommunications to allow people to live and work without traveling outside their own basins—the regions guaranteed to lead back to the central attractor—most of which are only a kilometer or two wide. (In fact, there must be many places where that infrastructure wasn't present, but I haven't been exactly plugged into the global village these last few years, so I don't know how they've fared.) Living on the margins of this society makes me even more dependent on its wealth than those who inhabit its multiple centers, so I suppose I should be glad that most people are content with the status quo—and I'm certainly delighted that they can co-exist in peace, that they can trade and prosper.

I'd rather die than join them, that's all.

(Or at least, that's true right here, right now.)

THE TRICK IS TO keep moving, to maintain momentum. There are no regions of perfect neutrality—or if there are, they're too small to find, probably too small to inhabit, and they'd almost certainly drift as the conditions within the basins varied. *Near enough* is fine for a night, but if I tried to live in one place, day after day, week after week, then whichever attractor held even the slightest advantage would, eventually, begin to sway me.

Momentum, and confusion. Whether or not it's true that we're spared each other's inner voices because so much uncorrelated babbling simply cancels itself out, my aim is to do just that with the more enduring, more coherent, more pernicious parts of the signal. At the very center of the Earth, no doubt, the sum of all human beliefs adds up to pure, harmless noise; here on the surface, though, where it's physically impossible to be equidistant from everyone, I'm forced to keep moving to average out the effects as best I can.

Sometimes I daydream about heading out into the countryside, and living in glorious clear-headed solitude beside a robot-tended farm, stealing the equipment and supplies I need to grow all my own food. *With Maria?* If she'll come; sometimes she says yes, sometimes she says no. Half a dozen times, we've told ourselves that we're setting out on such a journey . . . but we've yet to discover a trajectory out of the city, a route that would take us safely past all the intervening attractors, without being gradually deflected back toward the urban center. There must be a way out, it's simply a matter of finding it—and if all the rumors from other tramps have turned out to be dead ends, that's hardly surprising: the only people who could know for certain how to leave the city are those who've stumbled on the right path and actually departed, leaving no hints or rumors behind.

Sometimes, though, I stop dead in the middle of the road, and ask myself what I "really want":

To escape to the country, and lose myself in the silence of my own mute soul?

To give up this pointless wandering and rejoin *civilization?* For the sake of prosperity, stability, certainty: to swallow, and be swallowed by, one elaborate set of self-affirming lies?

Or, to keep orbiting this way until I die?

The answer, of course, depends on where I'm standing.

MORE ROBOT TRUCKS PASS me, but I no longer give them a second glance. I picture my hunger as an object—another weight to carry, not much heavier than my pack—and it gradually recedes from my attention. I let my mind grow blank, and I think of nothing but the early morning sunshine on my face, and the pleasure of walking.

After a while, a startling clarity begins to wash over me; a deep tranquility, together with a powerful sense of understanding. The odd part is, I have no idea what it is that I think I *understand*; I'm experiencing the pleasure of insight without any apparent cause, without the faintest hope of replying to the question: *insight into what?* The feeling persists, regardless.

I think: I've traveled in circles, all these years, and where has it brought me?

To this moment. To this chance to take my first real steps along the path to enlightenment.

And all I have to do is keep walking, straight ahead.

For four years, I've been following a false *tao*—pursuing an illusion of freedom, striving for no reason but the sake of striving—but now I see the way to transform that journey into—

Into what? A short-cut to damnation?

"Damnation"? There's no such thing. Only *samsara*, the treadmill of desires. Only the futility of striving. My understanding is clouded, now—but I know that if I traveled a few steps further, the truth would soon become clear to me.

For several seconds, I'm paralyzed by indecision—shot through with pure dread—but then, drawn by the possibility of redemption, I leave the freeway, clamber over the fence, and head due south.

These side streets are familiar. I pass a car yard full of sun-bleached wrecks melting in slow motion, their plastic chassis triggered by disuse into auto-degradation; a video porn and sex-aids shop, facade intact, dark within, stinking of rotting carpet and mouse shit; an outboard motor showroom, the latest—four-year-old—fuel cell models proudly on display already looking like bizarre relics from another century.

Then the sight of the cathedral spire rising above all this squalor hits me with a giddy mixture of nostalgia and *déjà vu*. In spite of everything, part of me still feels like a true Prodigal Son, coming home for the first time—not passing through for the fiftieth. I mumble prayers and phrases of dogma, strangely comforting formulae reawakened from memories of my last perihelion.

Soon, only one thing puzzles me: how could I have known God's perfect love—and then walked away? It's unthinkable. *How could I have turned my back on Him?*

I come to a row of pristine houses; I know they're uninhabited, but here in the border zone the diocesan robots keep the lawns trimmed, the leaves swept, the walls painted. A few blocks further, south-west, and I'll never turn my back on the truth again. I head that way, gladly.

Almost gladly.

The only trouble is . . . with each step south it grows harder to ignore the fact that the scriptures—let alone Catholic dogma—are full of the most grotesque errors of fact and logic. Why should a revelation from a perfect, loving God be such a dog's breakfast of threats and contradictions? Why should it offer such a flawed and confused view of humanity's place in the universe?

Errors of fact? The metaphors had to be chosen to suit the world view of the day; should God have mystified the author of Genesis with details of the Big Bang, and primordial nucleosynthesis? *Contradictions?* Tests of faith—and humility. How can I be so arrogant as to set my wretched powers of reasoning against the Word of the Almighty? God transcends everything, logic included.

Logic especially.

It's no good. Virgin births? Miracles with loaves and fishes? Resurrection? Poetic fables only, not to be taken literally? If that's the case, though, what's left but a few well-intentioned homilies, and a lot of pompous theatrics? If God *did in fact* become man, suffer, die, and rise again to save me, then I owe Him everything . . . but if it's just a beautiful story, then I can love my neighbor with or without regular doses of bread and wine.

I veer south-east.

The truth about the universe (here) is infinitely stranger, and infinitely more grand: it lies in the Laws of Physics that have come to Know Themselves through humanity. Our destiny and purpose are encoded in the fine structure constant, and the value of the density omega. The human race—in whatever form, robot or organic—will keep on advancing for the next ten billion years, until we can give rise to the hyperintelligence which will *cause* the finely tuned Big Bang required to bring us into existence.

If we don't die out in the next few millennia.

In which case, other intelligent creatures will perform the task. It doesn't matter who carries the torch.

Exactly. None of it matters. Why should I care what a civilization of post-humans, robots, or aliens, might or might not do ten billion years from now? What does any of this grandiose shit have to do with me?

I finally catch sight of Maria, a few blocks ahead of me—and right on cue, the existentialist attractor to the west firmly steers me away from the suburbs of cosmic baroque. I increase my pace, but only slightly—it's too hot to run, but more to the point, sudden acceleration can have some peculiar side-effects, bringing on unexpected philosophical swerves.

As I narrow the gap, she turns at the sound of my footsteps.

I say, "Hi."

"Hi." She doesn't seem exactly thrilled to see me—but then, this isn't exactly the place for it.

I fall into step beside her. "You left without me."

She shrugs. "I wanted to be on my own for a while. I wanted to think things over."

I laugh. "If you wanted to *think*, you should have stayed on the freeway."

"There's another spot ahead. In the park. It's just as good."

She's right—although now I'm here to spoil it for her. I ask myself for the thousandth time: *Why do I want us to stay together?* Because of what we have in common? But we owe most of that to the very fact that we *are* together—traveling the same paths, corrupting each other with our proximity. Because of our differences, then? For the sake of occasional moments of mutual incomprehensibility? But the longer we're together, the more that vestige of mystery will be eroded; orbiting each other can only lead to a spiraling together, an end to all distinctions.

Why, then?

The honest answer (here and now) is: food and sex—although tomorrow, elsewhere, no doubt I'll look back and brand that conclusion a cynical lie.

I fall silent as we drift toward the equilibrium zone. The last few minutes' confusion still rings in my head, satisfyingly jumbled, the giddy succession of truncated epiphanies effectively canceling each other out, leaving nothing behind but an amorphous sense of distrust. I remember a school of thought from pre-Meltdown days which proclaimed, with bovine good intentions—confusing laudable tolerance with sheer credulity—that there was something of value in *every human philosophy* . . . and what's more, when you got right down to it, they all really spoke the same "universal truths", and were all, ultimately, *reconcilable.* Apparently, none of these supine ecumenicists have survived to witness the palpable disproof of their hypothesis; I expect they all converted, three seconds after Meltdown, to the faith of whoever was standing closest to them at the time.

Maria mutters angrily, "Wonderful!" I look up at her, then follow her gaze. The park has come into view, and if it's time to herself she wanted, she has more than me to contend with. At least two dozen other tramps are gathered in the shade. That's rare, but it does happen; equilibrium zones are the slowest parts of everybody's orbits, so I suppose it's not surprising that occasionally a group of us end up becalmed together.

As we come closer, I notice something stranger: everybody reclining on the grass is facing the same way. Watching something— or someone—hidden from view by the trees.

Someone. A woman's voice reaches us, the words indistinct at this distance, but the tone mellifluous. Confident. Gentle but persuasive.

Maria says nervously, "Maybe we should stay back. Maybe the equilibrium's shifted."

"Maybe." I'm as worried as she is—but intrigued as well. I don't feel much of a tug from any of the familiar local attractors—but then, I can't be sure that my curiosity itself isn't a new hook for an old idea.

I say, "Let's just . . . skirt around the rim of the park. We can't ignore this; we have to find out what's going on." If a nearby basin has expanded and captured the park, then keeping our distance from the speaker is no guarantee of freedom; it's not her words, or her lone presence, that could harm us—but Maria (knowing all this, I'm sure) accepts my "strategy" for warding off the danger, and nods assent.

We position ourselves in the middle of the road at the eastern edge of the park, without noticeable effect. The speaker, middle-aged I'd guess, looks every inch a tramp, from the dirt-stiff clothes to the crudely-cut hair to the weathered skin and lean build of a half-starved perennial walker. Only the voice is wrong. She's set up a frame, like an easel, on which she's stretched a large map of the city; the roughly hexagonal cells of the basins are neatly marked in a variety of colors. People used to swap maps like this all the time, in the early years; maybe she's just showing off her prize possession, hoping to trade it for something worthwhile. I don't think much of her chances; by now, I'm sure, every tramp relies on his or her own mental picture of the ideological terrain.

Then she lifts a pointer and traces part of a feature I'd missed: a delicate web of blue lines, weaving through the gaps between the hexagons.

The woman says, "But of course it's no accident. We haven't stayed out of the basins all these years by sheer good luck—or even skill." She looks out across the crowd, notices us, pauses a moment, then says calmly, "*We've been captured by our own attractor.* It's nothing like the others—it's not a fixed set of beliefs, in a fixed location—but it's still an attractor, it's still drawn us to it from whatever unstable orbits we might have been on. I've mapped it—or part of it—and I've sketched it as well as I can. The true detail may be infinitely fine—but even from this crude representation, you should recognize paths that you've walked yourselves."

I stare at the map. From this distance, the blue strands are impossible to follow individually; I can see that they cover the route that Maria and I have taken over the last few days, but—

An old man calls out, "You've scrawled a lot of lines between the basins. What does that prove?"

"Not between *all* the basins." She touches a point on the map. "Has anyone ever been here? Or here? Or here? No? Here? Or here? *Why not?* They're all wide corridors between attractors—they look as safe as any of the others. So why have we never been to these places? For the same reason nobody living in the fixed attractors has: they're not part of our territory; they're not part of *our own* attractor."

I know she's talking nonsense, but the phrase alone is enough to make me feel panicky, claustrophobic. *Our own attractor.* We've been captured by *our own attractor.* I scan the rim of the city on the map;

the blue line never comes close to it. In fact, the line gets about as far from the center as I've ever traveled, myself . . .

Proving what? Only that this woman has had no better luck than I have. If she'd escaped the city, she wouldn't be here to claim that escape was impossible.

A woman in the crowd—visibly pregnant—says, "You've drawn your own paths, that's all. You've stayed out of danger—I've stayed out of danger—we all know what places to avoid. That's all you're telling us. That's all we have in common."

"No!" The speaker traces a stretch of the blue line again. "This is *who we are*. We're not aimless wanderers; we're the people of this strange attractor. We have an identity—a unity—after all."

There's laughter, and a few desultory insults from the crowd. I whisper to Maria, "Do you know her? Have you seen her before?"

"I'm not sure. I don't think so."

"You wouldn't have. Isn't it obvious? She's some kind of robot evangelist—"

"She doesn't talk much like one."

"*Rationalist*—not Christian or Mormon."

"Rationalists don't send evangelists."

"No? *Mapping strange attractors*; if that's not rationalist jargon, what is it?"

Maria shrugs. "Basins, attractors—they're all rationalist words, but everybody uses them. You know what they say: the Devil has the best tunes, but the rationalists have the best jargon. Words have to come from somewhere."

The woman says, "I'll build my church on sand. And I'll ask no one to follow me—and yet, you will. You all will."

I say, "Let's go." I take Maria's arm, but she pulls free angrily.

"Why are you so against her? Maybe she's right."

"Are you crazy?"

"Everyone else has an attractor—why can't we have one of our own? Stranger than all the rest. Look at it: it's the most beautiful thing on the map."

I shake my head, horrified. "How can you say that? We've stayed *free*. We've struggled so hard to stay free."

She shrugs. "Maybe. Or maybe we've been captured by what you call freedom. Maybe we don't need to struggle anymore. Is that so bad? If we're doing what we want, either way, why should we care?"

Without any fuss, the woman starts packing up her easel, and the crowd of tramps begins to disperse. Nobody seems to have been much affected by the brief sermon; everyone heads off calmly on their own chosen orbits.

I say, "The people in the basins are *doing what they want.* I don't want to be like them."

Maria laughs. "Believe me, you're not."

"No, you're right, I'm not: they're rich, fat and complacent; I'm starving, tired, and confused. And for what? Why am I living this way? That robot's trying to take away the one thing that makes it all worthwhile."

"Yeah? Well, I'm tired and hungry, too. And maybe an attractor of my own will *make it all worthwhile.*"

"*How?*" I laugh derisively. "Will you worship it? Will you pray to it?"

"No. But I won't have to be afraid anymore. If we really have been captured—if the way we live is stable, after all—then putting one foot wrong won't matter: we'll be drawn back to our own attractor. We won't have to worry that the smallest mistake will send us sliding into one of the basins. If that's true, aren't you glad?"

I shake my head angrily. "That's bullshit—dangerous bullshit. Staying out of the basins is a skill, it's a gift. You know that. We navigate the channels, carefully, balancing the opposing forces—"

"Do we? I'm sick of feeling like a tight-rope walker."

"Being *sick of it* doesn't mean it isn't true! Don't you see? She *wants* us to be complacent! The more of us who start to think orbiting is easy, the more of us will end up captured by the basins—"

I'm distracted by the sight of the prophet hefting her possessions and setting off. I say, "Look at her: she may be a perfect imitation—but she's a robot, she's a fake. They've finally understood that their pamphlets and their preaching machines won't work, so they've sent a machine to lie to us about our freedom."

Maria says, "Prove it."

"What?"

"You've got a knife. If she's a robot, go after her, stop her, cut her open. Prove it."

The woman, the robot, crosses the park, heading north-west, away from us. I say, "You know me; I could never do that."

"If she's a robot, she won't feel a thing."

"But she looks human. I couldn't do it. I couldn't stick a knife into a perfect imitation of human flesh."

"Because you know she's not a robot. You know she's telling the truth."

Part of me is simply glad to be arguing with Maria, for the sake of proving our separateness—but part of me finds everything she's saying too painful to leave unchallenged.

I hesitate a moment, then I put down my pack and sprint across the park toward the prophet.

She turns when she hears me, and stops walking. There's no one else nearby. I halt a few meters away from her, and catch my breath. She regards me with patient curiosity. I stare at her, feeling increasingly foolish. I can't pull a knife on her: she might not be a robot, after all—she might just be a tramp with strange ideas.

She says, "Did you want to ask me something?"

Almost without thinking, I blurt out, "How do you know nobody's ever left the city? How can you be so sure it's never happened?"

She shakes her head. "I didn't say that. The attractor looks like a closed loop to me. Anyone who's been captured by it could never leave. But other people may have escaped."

"What *other people?*"

"People who weren't in the attractor's basin."

I scowl, confused. "What basin? I'm not talking about the people of the basins, I'm talking about us."

She laughs. "I'm sorry. I don't mean the basins that lead to the fixed attractors. Our strange attractor has a basin, too: all the points that lead to *it*. I don't know what this basin's shape is: like the attractor itself, the detail could be infinitely fine. Not every point in the gaps between the hexagons would be part of it: some points must lead to the fixed attractors—that's why some tramps have been captured by them. Other points would belong to the strange attractor's basin. But others—"

"What?"

"Other points might lead to infinity. To escape."

"Which points?"

She shrugs. "Who knows? There could be two points, side by side, one leading into the strange attractor, one leading—eventually—out of the city. The only way to find out which is which would be to start at each point, and see what happens."

"But you said we'd all been captured, already—"

She nods. "After so many orbits, the basins must have emptied into their respective attractors. The attractors are the stable part: the basins lead into the attractors, but the attractors lead into themselves. Anyone who was destined for a fixed attractor must be in it by now—and anyone who was destined to leave the city has already gone. Those of us who are still in orbit will stay that way. We have to understand that, accept that, learn to live with it . . . and if that means inventing our own faith, our own religion—"

I grab her arm, draw my knife, and quickly scrape the point across her forearm. She yelps and pulls free, then clasps her hand to the wound. A moment later, she takes it away to inspect the damage, and I see the thin red line on her arm, and a rough wet copy on her palm.

"You lunatic!" she yells, backing away.

Maria approaches us. The probably-flesh-and-blood prophet addresses her: "He's mad! Get him off me!" Maria takes hold of my arm, then, inexplicably, leans toward me and puts her tongue in my ear. I burst out laughing. The woman steps back uncertainly, then turns and hurries away.

Maria says, "Not much of a dissection—but as far as it went, it was in my favor. I win."

I hesitate, then feign surrender.

"You win."

By NIGHTFALL, WE END up on the freeway again; this time, to the east of the city center. We gaze at the sky above the black silhouettes of abandoned office towers, our brains mildly scrambled by the residual effects of a nearby cluster of astrologers, as we eat the day's prize catch: a giant vegetarian pizza.

Finally, Maria says, "Venus has set. I think I ought to sleep now." I nod. "I'll wait up for Mars."

Traces of the day's barrage drift through my mind, more or less at random—but I can still recall most of what the woman in the park told me.

After so many orbits, the basins must have emptied . . .

So by now, we've all ended up *captured*. But how could she know that? How could she be sure?

And what if she's wrong? What if we haven't all, yet, arrived in our final resting place?

The astrologers say: None of her filthy, materialist, reductionist lies can be true. Except the ones about destiny. We like destiny. Destiny is fine.

I get up and walk a dozen meters south, neutralizing their contribution. Then I turn and watch Maria sleeping.

There could be two points, side by side, one leading into the strange attractor, one leading—eventually—out of the city. The only way to find out which is which would be to start at each point, and see what happens.

Right now, everything she said sounds to me like some heavily distorted and badly misunderstood rationalist model. And here I am, grasping at hope by seizing on half of her version, and throwing out the rest. *Metaphors mutating and hybridizing, all over again . . .*

I walk over to Maria, crouch down and bend to kiss her, gently, upside-down on the forehead. She doesn't even stir.

Then I lift my pack and set off down the freeway, believing for a moment that I can feel the emptiness beyond the city reach through, reach over, all the obstacles ahead, and claim me.

CLOSER

NOBODY WANTS TO SPEND eternity alone.

("Intimacy," I once told Sian, after we'd made love, "is the only cure for solipsism."

She laughed and said, "Don't get too ambitious, Michael. So far, it hasn't even cured me of masturbation.")

True solipsism, though, was never my problem. From the very first time I considered the question, I accepted that there could be no way of proving the reality of an external world, let alone the existence of other minds—but I also accepted that taking both on faith was the only practical way of dealing with everyday life.

The question which obsessed me was this: Assuming that other people existed, how did they apprehend that existence? How did they experience *being?* Could I ever truly understand what consciousness was like for another person—any more than I could for an ape, or a cat, or an insect?

If not, I was alone.

I desperately wanted to believe that other people were somehow *knowable*, but it wasn't something I could bring myself to take for granted. I knew there could be no absolute proof, but I wanted to be persuaded, I needed to be compelled.

No LITERATURE, NO POETRY, no drama, however personally resonant I found it, could ever quite convince me that I'd glimpsed the author's soul. Language had evolved to facilitate cooperation in the conquest of the physical world, not to describe subjective reality. Love, anger, jealousy, resentment, grief—all were defined, ultimately, in terms of external circumstances and observable actions. When an image or metaphor rang true for me, it proved only that I shared with the author a set of definitions, a culturally sanctioned list of word associations. After all, many publishers used computer programs—highly specialized, but unsophisticated algorithms, without the remotest possibility of self-awareness—to routinely produce both literature, and literary criticism, indistinguishable from the human product. Not just formularized garbage, either; on several occasions, I'd been deeply affected by works which I'd later discovered had been cranked out by unthinking software. This didn't prove that human literature communicated nothing of the author's inner life, but it certainly made clear how much room there was for doubt.

UNLIKE MANY OF MY friends, I had no qualms whatsoever when, at the age of eighteen, the time came for me to "switch." My organic brain was removed and discarded, and control of my body handed over to my "jewel"—the Ndoli Device, a neural-net computer implanted shortly after birth, which had since learned to imitate my brain, down to the level of individual neurons. I had no qualms, not because I was at all convinced that the jewel and the brain experienced consciousness identically, but because, from an early age, I'd identified myself solely with the jewel. My brain was a kind of bootstrap device, nothing more, and to mourn its loss would have been as absurd as mourning my emergence from some primitive stage of embryological neural development. Switching was simply what humans *did* now, an established part of the life cycle, even if it was mediated by our culture, and not by our genes.

Seeing each other die, and observing the gradual failure of their own bodies, may have helped convince pre-Ndoli humans of their common humanity; certainly, there were countless references in their literature to the equalizing power of death. Perhaps concluding that the universe would go on without them produced a shared sense of hopelessness, or insignificance, which they viewed as their defining attribute.

Now that it's become an article of faith that, sometime in the next few billion years, physicists will find a way for *us* to go on without *the universe*, rather than vice versa, that route to spiritual equality has lost whatever dubious logic it might ever have possessed.

SIAN WAS A COMMUNICATIONS engineer. I was a holovision news editor. We met during a live broadcast of the seeding of Venus with terraforming nanomachines—a matter of great public interest, since most of the planet's as-yet-uninhabitable surface had already been sold. There were several technical glitches with the broadcast which might have been disastrous, but together we managed to work around them, and even to hide the seams. It was nothing special, we were simply doing our jobs, but afterward I was elated out of all proportion. It took me twenty-four hours to realize (or decide) that I'd fallen in love.

However, when I approached her the next day, she made it clear that she felt nothing for me; the chemistry I'd imagined "between us" had all been in my head. I was dismayed, but not surprised. Work didn't bring us together again, but I called her occasionally, and six weeks later my persistence was rewarded. I took her to a performance of "Waiting for Godot" by augmented parrots, and *I* enjoyed myself immensely, but I didn't see her again for more than a month.

I'd almost given up hope, when she appeared at my door without warning one night and dragged me along to a "concert" of interactive computerized improvisation. The "audience" was assembled in what looked like a mock-up of a Berlin nightclub of the 2050s. A computer program, originally designed for creating movie scores, was fed with the image from a hover-camera which wandered about the set. People danced and sang, screamed and brawled, and engaged in all kinds of histrionics in the hope of attracting the camera and shaping the music. At first, I felt cowed and inhibited, but Sian gave me no choice but to join in.

It was chaotic, insane, at times even terrifying. One woman stabbed another to "death" at the table beside us, which struck me as a sickening (and expensive) indulgence, but when a riot broke out at the end, and people started smashing the deliberately flimsy furniture, I followed Sian into the melee, cheering.

The music—the excuse for the whole event—was garbage, but I didn't really care. When we limped out into the night, bruised and aching and laughing, I knew that at least we'd shared something that had made us feel closer. She took me home and we went to bed together, too sore and tired to do more than sleep, but when we made love in the morning, I already felt so at ease with her that I could hardly believe it was our first time.

Soon we were inseparable. My tastes in entertainment were very different from hers, but I survived most of her favorite "artforms," more or less intact. She moved into my apartment, at my suggestion, and casually destroyed the orderly rhythms of my carefully arranged domestic life.

I had to piece together details of her past from throwaway lines; she found it far too boring to sit down and give me a coherent account. Her life had been as unremarkable as mine: she'd grown up in a suburban, middle-class family, studied her profession, found a job. Like almost everyone, she'd switched at eighteen. She had no strong political convictions. She was good at her work, but put ten times more energy into her social life. She was intelligent, but hated anything overtly intellectual. She was impatient, aggressive, roughly affectionate.

And I could not, for one second, imagine what it was like inside her head.

For a start, I rarely had any idea what she was thinking—in the sense of knowing how she would have replied if asked, out of the blue, to describe her thoughts at the moment before they were interrupted by the question. On a longer time scale, I had no feeling for her motivation, her image of herself, her concept of who she was and what she did and why. Even in the laughably crude sense that a novelist pretends to "explain" a character, I could not have explained Sian.

And if she'd provided me with a running commentary on her mental state, and a weekly assessment of the reasons for her actions in the latest psychodynamic jargon, it would all have come to nothing but a heap of useless words. If I could have pictured myself in her circumstances, imagined myself with her beliefs and obsessions, empathized until I could anticipate her every word, her every decision, then I still would not have understood so much as a single moment when she closed her eyes, forgot her past, wanted nothing, and simply *was*.

OF COURSE, MOST OF the time, nothing could have mattered less. We were happy enough together, whether or not we were strangers—and whether or not my "happiness" and Sian's "happiness" were in any real sense the same.

Over the years, she became less self-contained, more open. She had no great dark secrets to share, no traumatic childhood ordeals to recount, but she let me in on her petty fears and her mundane neuroses. I did the same, and even, clumsily, explained my peculiar obsession. She wasn't at all offended. Just puzzled.

"What could it actually mean, though? To know what it's like to be someone else? You'd have to have their memories, their personality, their body—everything. And then you'd just *be* them, not yourself, and *you* wouldn't know anything. It's nonsense."

I shrugged. "Not necessarily. Of course, perfect knowledge would be impossible, but you can always get *closer*. Don't you think that the more things we do together, the more experiences we share, the closer we become?"

She scowled. "Yes, but that's not what you were talking about five seconds ago. Two years, or two thousand years, of 'shared experiences' *seen through different eyes* means nothing. However much time two people spent together, how could you know that there was even the briefest instant when they both experienced what they were going through 'together' in the same way?"

"I know, but . . ."

"If you admit that what you want is impossible, maybe you'll stop fretting about it."

I laughed. "Whatever makes you think I'm as rational as that?"

WHEN THE TECHNOLOGY BECAME available, it was Sian's idea, not mine, for us to try out all the fashionable somatic permutations. Sian was always impatient to experience something new. "If we really are going to live forever," she said, "we'd better stay curious if we want to stay sane."

I was reluctant, but any resistance I put up seemed hypocritical. Clearly, this game wouldn't lead to the perfect knowledge I longed for (and knew I would never achieve), but I couldn't deny the possibility that it might be one crude step in the right direction.

First, we exchanged bodies. I discovered what it was like to have breasts and a vagina—what it was like for me, that is, not what it had been like for Sian. True, we stayed swapped long enough for the shock, and even the novelty, to wear off, but I never felt that I'd gained much insight into *her* experience of the body she'd been born with. My jewel was modified only as much as was necessary to allow me to control this unfamiliar machine, which was scarcely more than would have been required to work another male body. The menstrual cycle had been abandoned decades before, and although I could have taken the necessary hormones to allow myself to have periods, and even to become pregnant (although the financial disincentives for reproduction had been drastically increased in recent years), that would have told me absolutely nothing about Sian, who had done neither.

As for sex, the pleasure of intercourse still felt very much the same—which was hardly surprising, since nerves from the vagina and clitoris were simply wired into my jewel as if they'd come from my penis. Even being penetrated made less difference than I'd expected; unless I made a special effort to remain aware of our respective geometries, I found it hard to care who was doing what to whom. Orgasms were better, though, I had to admit.

At work, no one raised an eyebrow when I turned up as Sian, since many of my colleagues had already been through exactly the same thing. The legal definition of identity had recently been shifted from the DNA fingerprint of the body, according to a standard set of markers, to the serial number of the jewel. When even *the law* can keep up with you, you know you can't be doing anything very radical or profound.

After three months, Sian had had enough. "I never realized how clumsy you were," she said. "Or that ejaculation was so *dull*."

Next, she had a clone of herself made, so we could both be women. Brain-damaged replacement bodies—Extras—had once been incredibly expensive, when they'd needed to be grown at virtually the normal rate, and kept constantly active so they'd be healthy enough to use. However, the physiological effects of the passage of time, and of exercise, don't happen by magic; at a deep enough level, there's always a biochemical signal produced, which can ultimately be faked. Mature Extras, with sturdy bones and perfect muscle tone, could now be produced from scratch in a year—four months' gestation and eight months' coma—which also allowed them to be more thoroughly brain-dead than before, soothing the ethical qualms of those who'd always wondered just how much was going on inside the heads of the old, active versions.

In our first experiment, the hardest part for me had always been, not looking in the mirror and seeing Sian, but looking at Sian and seeing myself. I'd missed her, far more than I'd missed being myself. Now, I was almost happy for my body to be absent (in storage, kept alive by a jewel based on the minimal brain of an Extra). The symmetry of being her twin appealed to me; surely now we were closer than ever. Before, we'd merely swapped our physical differences. Now, we'd abolished them.

The symmetry was an illusion. I'd changed gender, and she hadn't. I was with the woman I loved; she lived with a walking parody of herself.

One morning she woke me, pummeling my breasts so hard that she left bruises. When I opened my eyes and shielded myself, she peered at me suspiciously. "Are you in there? Michael? I'm going crazy. *I want you back.*"

For the sake of getting the whole bizarre episode over and done with for good—and perhaps also to discover for myself what Sian had just been through—I agreed to the third permutation. There was no need to wait a year; my Extra had been grown at the same time as hers.

Somehow, it was far more disorienting to be confronted by "myself" without the camouflage of Sian's body. I found my own face unreadable; when we'd both been in disguise, that hadn't bothered me, but now it made me feel edgy, and at times almost paranoid, for no rational reason at all.

Sex took some getting used to. Eventually, I found it pleasurable, in a confusing and vaguely narcissistic way. The compelling sense of equality I'd felt, when we'd made love as women, never quite returned to me as we sucked each other's cocks—but then, when we'd both been women, Sian had never claimed to feel any such thing. It had all been my own invention.

The day after we returned to the way we'd begun (well, almost—in fact, we put our decrepit, twenty-six-year-old bodies in storage, and took up residence in our healthier Extras), I saw a story from Europe on an option we hadn't yet tried, tipped to become all the rage: hermaphroditic identical twins. Our new bodies could be our biological children (give or take the genetic tinkering required to ensure hermaphroditism), with an equal share of characteristics from both of us. We would *both* have changed gender, *both* have lost partners. We'd be equal in every way.

I took a copy of the file home to Sian. She watched it thoughtfully, then said, "Slugs are hermaphrodites, aren't they? They hang in mid-air together on a thread of slime. I'm sure there's even something in Shakespeare, remarking on the glorious spectacle of copulating slugs. Imagine it: you and me, making slug love."

I fell on the floor, laughing.

I stopped, suddenly. "*Where*, in Shakespeare? I didn't think you'd even *read* Shakespeare."

EVENTUALLY, I CAME TO believe that with each passing year, I knew Sian a little better—in the traditional sense, the sense that most couples seemed to find sufficient. I knew what she expected from me, I knew how not to hurt her. We had arguments, we had fights, but there must have been some kind of underlying stability, because in the end we always chose to stay together. Her happiness mattered to me, very much, and at times I could hardly believe that I'd ever thought it possible that all of her subjective experience might be fundamentally *alien* to me. It was true that every brain, and hence every jewel, was unique—but there was something extravagant in supposing that the nature of consciousness could be radically different between individuals, when the same basic hardware, and the same basic principles of neural topology, were involved.

Still. Sometimes, if I woke in the night, I'd turn to her and whisper, inaudibly, compulsively, "I don't know you. I have no idea who, or what, you are." I'd lie there, and think about packing and leaving. I was *alone*, and it was farcical to go through the charade of pretending otherwise.

Then again, sometimes I woke in the night, absolutely convinced that I was *dying*, or something else equally absurd. In the sway of some half-forgotten dream, all manner of confusion is possible. It never meant a thing, and by morning, I was always myself again.

WHEN I SAW THE story on Craig Bentley's service—he called it "research," but his "volunteers" paid for the privilege of taking part in his experiments—I almost couldn't bring myself to include it in the bulletin, although all my professional judgment told me it was everything our viewers wanted in a thirty second techno-shock piece: bizarre, even mildly disconcerting, but not too hard to grasp.

Bentley was a cyberneurologist; he studied the Ndoli Device, in the way that neurologists had once studied the brain. Mimicking the brain with a neural-net computer had not required a profound understanding of its higher-level structures; research into these structures continued, in their new incarnation. The jewel, compared to the brain, was of course both easier to observe, and easier to manipulate.

In his latest project, Bentley was offering couples something slightly more up-market than an insight into the sex lives of slugs. He was offering them eight hours with identical minds.

I made a copy of the original, ten-minute piece that had come through on the fiber, then let my editing console select the most titillating thirty seconds possible, for broadcast. It did a good job; it had learned from me.

I couldn't lie to Sian. I couldn't hide the story, I couldn't pretend I wasn't interested. The only honest thing to do was to show her the file, tell her exactly how I felt, and ask her what *she* wanted.

I did just that. When the HV image faded out, she turned to me, shrugged, and said mildly, "Okay. It sounds like fun. Let's try it."

BENTLEY WORE A T-SHIRT with nine computer-drawn portraits on it, in a three-by-three grid. Top left was Elvis Presley. Bottom right was Marilyn Monroe. The rest were various stages in between.

"This is how it will work. The transition will take twenty minutes, during which time you'll be disembodied. Over the first ten minutes, you'll gain equal access to each other's memories. Over the second ten minutes, you'll both be moved, gradually, toward the compromise personality.

"Once that's done, your Ndoli Devices will be identical—in the sense that both will have all the same neural connections with all the same weighting factors—but they'll almost certainly be in different states. I'll have to black you out, to correct that. Then you'll wake—"

Who'll wake?

"—in identical electromechanical bodies. Clones can't be made sufficiently alike.

"You'll spend the eight hours alone, in perfectly matched rooms. Rather like hotel suites, really. You'll have HV to keep you amused if you need it—*without* the videophone module, of course. You might think you'd both get an engaged signal, if you tried to call the same number simultaneously—but in fact, in such cases the switching equipment arbitrarily lets one call through, which would make your environments different."

Sian asked, "Why can't we phone each other? Or better still, meet each other? If we're exactly the same, we'd say the same things, do the same things—we'd be one more identical part of each other's environment."

Bentley pursed his lips and shook his head. "Perhaps I'll allow something of the kind in a future experiment, but for now I believe it would be too . . . potentially traumatic."

Sian gave me a sideways glance, which meant: *This man is a killjoy.*

"The end will be like the beginning, in reverse. First, your personalities will be restored. Then, you'll lose access to each other's memories. Of course, your memories of *the experience itself* will be left untouched. Untouched by me, that is; I can't predict how your separate personalities, once restored, will act—filtering, suppressing, reinterpreting those memories. Within minutes, you may end up with very different ideas about what you've been through. All I can guarantee is this: for the eight hours in question, the two of you *will* be identical."

WE TALKED IT OVER. Sian was enthusiastic, as always. She didn't much care what it would be *like*; all that really mattered to her was collecting one more novel experience.

"Whatever happens, we'll be ourselves again at the end of it," she said. "What's there to be afraid of? You know the old Ndoli joke."

"What old Ndoli joke?"

"Anything's bearable—so long as it's finite."

I couldn't decide how I felt. The sharing of memories notwithstanding, we'd both end up *knowing*, not each other, but merely a transient, artificial third person. Still, for the first time in our lives, we would have been through exactly the same experience, from exactly the same point of view—even if the experience was only spending eight hours locked in separate rooms, and the point of view was that of a genderless robot with an identity crisis.

It was a compromise—but I could think of no realistic way in which it could have been improved.

I called Bentley, and made a reservation.

IN PERFECT SENSORY DEPRIVATION, my thoughts seemed to dissipate into the blackness around me before they were even half-formed. This isolation didn't last long, though; as our short-term memories merged, we achieved a kind of telepathy: one of us would think a message, and the other would "remember" thinking it, and reply in the same way.

—I really can't wait to uncover all your grubby little secrets.

—I think you're going to be disappointed. Anything I haven't already told you, I've probably repressed.

—Ah, but *repressed* is not *erased*. Who knows what will turn up?

—*We'll* know, soon enough.

I tried to think of all the minor sins I must have committed over the years, all the shameful, selfish, unworthy thoughts, but nothing came into my head but a vague white noise of guilt. I tried again, and achieved, of all things, an image of Sian as a child. A young boy slipping his hand between her legs, then squealing with fright and pulling away. But she'd described that incident to me, long ago. Was it her memory, or my reconstruction?

—My memory. I think. Or perhaps *my* reconstruction. You know, half the time when I've told you something that happened before we met, the memory of the telling has become far clearer to me than the memory itself. Almost replacing it.

—It's the same for me.

—Then in a way, our memories have already been moving toward a kind of symmetry, for years. We both remember what was *said*, as if we'd both heard it from someone else.

Agreement. Silence. A moment of confusion. Then:

—This neat division of "memory" and "personality" Bentley uses; is it really so clear? Jewels are neural-net computers, you can't talk about "data" and "program" in any absolute sense.

—Not in general, no. His classification must be arbitrary, to some extent. But who cares?

—It matters. If he restores "personality," but allows "memories" to persist, a misclassification could leave us . . .

—What?

—It depends, doesn't it? At one extreme, so thoroughly "restored," so completely unaffected, that the whole experience might as well not have happened. And at the other extreme . . .

—Permanently . . .

— . . . closer.

—Isn't that the point?

—I don't know anymore.

Silence. Hesitation.

Then I realized that I had no idea whether or not it was my turn to reply.

I WOKE, LYING ON a bed, mildly bemused, as if waiting for a mental hiatus to pass. My body felt slightly awkward, but less so than when I'd woken in someone else's Extra. I glanced down at the pale, smooth plastic of my torso and legs, then waved a hand in front of my face. I looked like a unisex shop-window dummy—but Bentley had shown us the bodies beforehand, it was no great shock. I sat up slowly, then stood and took a few steps. I felt a little numb and hollow, but my kinesthetic sense, my proprioception, was fine; I felt *located* between my eyes, and I felt that this body was *mine*. As with any modern transplant, my jewel had been manipulated directly to accommodate the change, avoiding the need for months of physiotherapy.

I glanced around the room. It was sparsely furnished: one bed, one table, one chair, one clock, one HV set. On the wall, a framed reproduction of an Escher lithograph: "Bond of Union," a portrait of the artist and, presumably, his wife, faces peeled like lemons into helices of rind, joined into a single, linked band. I traced the outer surface from start to finish, and was disappointed to find that it lacked the Möbius twist I was expecting.

No windows, one door without a handle. Set into the wall beside the bed, a full-length mirror. I stood a while and stared at my ridiculous form. It suddenly occurred to me that, if Bentley had a real love of symmetry games, he might have built one room as the mirror image of the other, modified the HV set accordingly, and altered one jewel, one copy of me, to exchange right for left. What looked like a mirror could then be nothing but a window between the rooms. I grinned awkwardly with my plastic face; my reflection looked appropriately embarrassed by the sight. The idea appealed to me, however unlikely it was. Nothing short of an experiment in nuclear physics could reveal the difference. No, not true; a pendulum free to precess, like Foucault's, would twist the same way in both rooms, giving the game away. I walked up to the mirror and thumped it. It didn't seem to yield at all, but then, either a brick wall, or an equal and opposite thump from behind, could have been the explanation.

I shrugged and turned away. Bentley *might* have done anything—for all I knew, the whole set-up could have been a computer simulation. My body was irrelevant. The room was irrelevant. The point was . . .

I sat on the bed. I recalled someone—Michael, probably—wondering if I'd panic when I dwelt upon my nature, but I found no reason to do so. If I'd woken in this room with no recent memories, and tried to sort out who I was from my past(s), I'd no doubt have gone mad, but I knew *exactly* who I was, I had two long trails of anticipation leading to my present state. The prospect of being changed back into Sian or Michael didn't bother me at all; the wishes of both to regain their separate identities endured in me, strongly, and the desire for personal integrity manifested itself as relief at the thought of their reemergence, not as fear of my own demise. In any case, my memories would not be expunged, and I had no sense of having goals which one or the other of them would not pursue. I felt more like their lowest common denominator than any kind of synergistic hypermind; I was less, not more, than the sum of my parts. My purpose was strictly limited: I was here to enjoy the strangeness for Sian, and to answer a question for Michael, and when the time came I'd be happy to bifurcate, and resume the two lives I remembered and valued.

So, how did I experience consciousness? The same way as Michael? The same way as Sian? So far as I could tell, I'd undergone no fundamental change—but even as I reached that conclusion, I began to wonder if I was in any position to judge. Did *memories* of being Michael, and *memories* of being Sian, contain so much more than the two of them could have put into words and exchanged verbally? Did I really *know* anything about the nature of their existence, or was my head just full of second-hand description—intimate, and detailed, but ultimately as opaque as language? If my mind *were* radically different, would that difference be something I could even perceive—or would all my memories, in the act of remembering, simply be recast into terms that seemed familiar?

The past, after all, was no more knowable than the external world. Its very existence also had to be taken on faith—and, granted existence, it too could be misleading.

I buried my head in my hands, dejected. *I* was the closest they could get, and what had come of me? Michael's hope remained precisely as reasonable—and as unproven—as ever.

AFTER A WHILE, MY mood began to lighten. At least Michael's search was over, even if it had ended in failure. Now he'd have no choice but to accept that, and move on.

I paced around the room for a while, flicking the HV on and off. I was actually starting to get *bored*, but I wasn't going to waste eight hours and several thousand dollars by sitting down and watching soap operas.

I mused about possible ways of undermining the synchronization of my two copies. It was inconceivable that Bentley could have matched the rooms and bodies to such a fine tolerance that an engineer worthy of the name couldn't find some way of breaking the symmetry. Even a coin toss might have done it, but I didn't have a coin. Throwing a paper plane? That sounded promising—highly sensitive to air currents—but the only paper in the room was the Escher, and I couldn't bring myself to vandalize it. I might have smashed the mirror, and observed the shapes and sizes of the fragments, which would have had the added bonus of proving or disproving my earlier speculations, but as I raised the chair over my head, I suddenly changed my mind. Two conflicting sets of short-term memories had been confusing enough during a few minutes of sensory deprivation; for several hours interacting with a physical environment, it could be completely disabling. Better to hold off until I was desperate for amusement.

So I lay down on the bed and did what most of Bentley's clients probably ended up doing.

As they coalesced, Sian and Michael had both had fears for their privacy—and both had issued compensatory, not to say defensive, mental declarations of frankness, not wanting the other to think that they had something to hide. Their curiosity, too, had been ambivalent; they'd wanted to *understand* each other, but, of course, not to *pry*.

All of these contradictions continued in me, but—staring at the ceiling, trying not to look at the clock again for at least another thirty seconds—I didn't really have to make a decision. It was the most natural thing in the world to let my mind wander back over the course of their relationship, from both points of view.

It was a very peculiar reminiscence. Almost everything seemed at once vaguely surprising and utterly familiar—like an extended attack of *deja vu*. It's not that they'd often set out deliberately to deceive each other about anything substantial, but all the tiny white lies, all the concealed trivial resentments, all the necessary, laudable, essential, loving deceptions, that had kept them together in spite of their differences, filled my head with a strange haze of confusion and disillusionment.

It wasn't in any sense a conversation; I was no multiple personality. Sian and Michael simply weren't there—to justify, to explain, to deceive each other all over again, with the best intentions. Perhaps I should have attempted to do all this on their behalf, but I was constantly unsure of my role, unable to decide on a position. So I lay there, paralyzed by symmetry, and let their memories flow.

After that, the time passed so quickly that I never had a chance to break the mirror.

WE TRIED TO STAY together.

We lasted a week.

Bentley had made—as the law required—snapshots of our jewels prior to the experiment. We could have gone back to them—and then had him explain to us *why*—but self-deception is only an easy choice if you make it in time.

We couldn't forgive each other, because there was nothing to forgive. Neither of us had done a single thing that the other could fail to understand, and sympathize with, completely.

We knew each other too well, that's all. Detail after tiny fucking microscopic detail. It wasn't that the truth hurt; it didn't, any longer. It numbed us. It smothered us. We didn't know each other as we knew ourselves; it was worse than that. In the self, the details blur in the very processes of thought; mental self-dissection is possible, but it takes great effort to sustain. Our mutual dissection took no effort at all; it was the natural state into which we fell in each other's presence. Our surfaces *had* been stripped away, but not to reveal a glimpse of the soul. All we could see beneath the skin were the cogs, spinning.

And I knew, now, that what Sian had always wanted most in a lover was the alien, the unknowable, the mysterious, the opaque. The whole point, for her, of being with someone else was the sense of confronting *otherness*. Without it, she believed, you might as well be talking to yourself.

I found that I now shared this view (a change whose precise origins I didn't much want to think about . . . but then, I'd always known she had the stronger personality, I should have guessed that *something* would rub off).

Together, we might as well have been alone, so we had no choice but to part.

Nobody wants to spend eternity alone.

CHAFF

E L NIDO DE LADRONES—THE Nest of Thieves—occupies a roughly elliptical region, fifty thousand square kilometers in the western Amazon Lowlands, straddling the border between Colombia and Peru. It's difficult to say exactly where the natural rain forest ends and the engineered species of El Nido take over, but the total biomass of the system must be close to a trillion tonnes. A trillion tonnes of structural material, osmotic pumps, solar energy collectors, cellular chemical factories, and biological computing and communications resources. All under the control of its designers.

The old maps and databases are obsolete; by manipulating the hydrology and soil chemistry, and influencing patterns of rainfall and erosion, the vegetation has reshaped the terrain completely: shifting the course of the Putumayo River, drowning old roads in swampland, raising secret causeways through the jungle. This biogenic geography remains in a state of flux, so that even the eye-witness accounts of the rare defectors from El Nido soon lose their currency. Satellite images are meaningless; at every frequency, the forest canopy conceals, or deliberately falsifies, the spectral signature of whatever lies beneath.

Chemical toxins and defoliants are useless; the plants and their symbiotic bacteria can analyze most poisons, and reprogram their metabolisms to render them harmless—or transform them into food—faster than our agricultural warfare expert systems can invent new molecules. Biological weapons are seduced, subverted, domesticated; most of the genes from the last lethal plant virus we introduced were found three months later, incorporated into a benign vector for El Nido's elaborate communications network. The assassin had turned into a messenger boy. Any attempt to burn the vegetation is rapidly smothered by carbon dioxide—or more sophisticated fire retardants, if a self-oxidizing fuel is employed. Once we even pumped in a few tonnes of nutrient laced with powerful radioisotopes—locked up in compounds chemically indistinguishable from their natural counterparts. We tracked the results with gamma-ray imaging: El Nido separated out the isotope-laden molecules—probably on the basis of their diffusion rates across organic membranes—sequestered and diluted them, and then pumped them right back out again.

So when I heard that a Peruvian-born biochemist named Guillermo Largo had departed from Bethesda, Maryland, with some highly classified genetic tools—the fruits of his own research, but very much the property of his employers—and vanished into El Nido, I thought: At last, an excuse for the Big One. The Company had been advocating thermonuclear rehabilitation of El Nido for almost a decade. The Security Council would have rubber-stamped it. The governments with nominal authority over the region would have been delighted. Hundreds of El Nido's inhabitants were suspected of violating US law—and President Golino was aching for a chance to prove that she could play hard ball south of the border, whatever language she spoke in the privacy of her own home. She could have gone on prime time afterward and told the nation that they should be proud of Operation Back to Nature, and that the thirty thousand displaced farmers who'd taken refuge in El Nido from Colombia's undeclared civil war—and who had now been liberated forever from the oppression of Marxist terrorists and drug barons—would have saluted her courage and resolve.

I never discovered why that wasn't to be. Technical problems in ensuring that no embarrassing side-effects would show up downriver in the sacred Amazon itself, wiping out some telegenic endangered species before the end of the present administration? Concern that some Middle Eastern warlord might somehow construe the act as license to use his own feeble, long-hoarded fission weapons on a troublesome minority, destabilizing the region in an undesirable manner? Fear of Japanese trade sanctions, now that the rabidly anti-nuclear Eco-Marketeers were back in power?

I wasn't shown the verdicts of the geopolitical computer models; I simply received my orders—coded into the flicker of my local K-Mart's fluorescent tubes, slipped in between the updates to the shelf price tags. Deciphered by an extra neural layer in my left retina, the words appeared blood red against the bland cheery colors of the supermarket aisle.

I was to enter El Nido and retrieve Guillermo Largo.

Alive.

DRESSED LIKE A LOCAL real estate agent—right down to the gold-plated bracelet-phone, and the worst of all possible three-hundred-dollar haircuts—I visited Largo's abandoned home in Bethesda: a northern suburb of Washington, just over the border into Maryland. The apartment was modern and spacious, neatly furnished but not opulent—about what any good marketing software might have tried to sell him, on the basis of salary less alimony.

Largo had always been classified as *brilliant but unsound*—a potential security risk, but far too talented and productive to be wasted. He'd been under routine surveillance ever since the gloriously euphemistic Department of Energy had employed him, straight out of Harvard, back in 2005—clearly, too routine by far . . . but then, I could understand how thirty years with an unblemished record must have given rise to a degree of complacency. Largo had never attempted to disguise his politics—apart from exercising the kind of discretion that was more a matter of etiquette than subterfuge; no Che Guevara T-shirts when visiting Los Alamos—but he'd never really acted on his beliefs, either.

A mural had been jet-sprayed onto his living room wall in shades of near infrared (visible to most hip fourteen-year-old Washingtonians, if not to their parents). It was a copy of the infamous Lee Hing-cheung's *A Tiling of the Plane with Heroes of the New World Order*, a digital image that had spread across computer networks at the turn of the century. Early nineties political leaders, naked and interlocked—Escher meets the Kama Sutra—deposited steaming turds into each other's open and otherwise empty brain cases—an effect borrowed from the works of the German satirist George Grosz. The Iraqi dictator was shown admiring his reflection in a hand mirror—the image an exact reproduction of a contemporary magazine cover in which the mustache had been retouched to render it suitably Hitleresque. The US President carried—horizontally, but poised ready to be tilted—an egg-timer full of the gaunt hostages whose release he'd delayed to clinch his predecessor's election victory. Everyone was shoe-horned in, somewhere—right down to the Australian Prime Minister, portrayed as a pubic louse, struggling (and failing) to fit its tiny jaws around the mighty presidential cock. I could imagine a few of the neo-McCarthyist troglodytes in the Senate going apoplectic, if anything so tedious as an inquiry into Largo's defection ever took place—but what should we have done? Refused to hire him if he owned so much as a *Guernica* tea-towel?

Largo had blanked every computer in the apartment before leaving, including the entertainment system—but I already knew his taste in music, having listened to a few hours of audio surveillance samples full of bad Korean Ska. No laudable revolutionary ethno-solidarity, no haunting Andean pipe music; a shame—I would have much preferred that. His bookshelves held several battered college-level biochemistry texts, presumably retained for sentimental reasons, and a few dozen musty literary classics and volumes of poetry, in English, Spanish, and German. Hesse, Rilke, Vallejo, Conrad, Nietzsche. Nothing modern—and nothing printed after 2010. With a few words to the household manager, Largo had erased every digital work he'd ever owned, sweeping away the last quarter of a century of his personal archaeology.

I flipped through the surviving books, for what it was worth. There was a pencilled-in correction to the structure of guanine in one of the texts . . . and a section had been underlined in "Heart of Darkness." The narrator, Marlow, was pondering the mysterious fact that the servants on the steamboat—members of a cannibal tribe, whose provisions of rotting hippo meat had been tossed overboard—hadn't yet rebelled and eaten him. After all:

> *No fear can stand up to hunger, no patience can wear it out, disgust simply does not exist where hunger is; and as to superstition, beliefs, and what you may call principles, they are less than chaff in a breeze.*

I couldn't argue with that—but I wondered why Largo had found the passage noteworthy. Perhaps it had struck a chord, back in the days when he'd been trying to rationalize taking his first research grants from the Pentagon? The ink was faded—and the volume itself had been printed in 2003. I would rather have had copies of his diary entries for the fortnight leading up to his disappearance—but his household computers hadn't been systematically tapped for almost twenty years.

I sat at the desk in his study, and stared at the blank screen of his work station. Largo had been born into a middle-class, nominally Catholic, very mildly leftist family in Lima, in 1980. His father, a journalist with *El Comercio*, had died from a cerebral blood clot in 2029. His seventy-eight-year-old mother still worked as an attorney for an international mining company—going through the motions of *habeas corpus* for the families of disappeared radicals in her spare time, a hobby her employers tolerated for the sake of cheap PR brownie points in the shareholder democracies. Guillermo had one elder brother, a retired surgeon, and one younger sister, a primary school teacher, neither of them politically active.

Most of his education had taken place in Switzerland and the States; after his PhD, he'd held a succession of research posts in government institutes, the biotechnology industry, and academia—all with more or less the same real sponsors. Fifty-five, now, thrice divorced but still childless, he'd only ever returned to Lima for brief family visits.

After *three decades* working on the military applications of molecular genetics—unwittingly at first, but not for long—what could have triggered his sudden defection to El Nido? If he'd managed the cynical doublethink of reconciling defense research and pious liberal sentiments for so long, he must have got it down to a fine art. His latest psychological profile suggested as much: fierce pride in his scientific achievements balanced the self-loathing he felt when contemplating their ultimate purpose—with the conflict showing signs of decaying into comfortable indifference. A well-documented dynamic in the industry.

And he seemed to have acknowledged—deep in his heart, thirty years ago—that his "principles" were *less than chaff in a breeze*.

Perhaps he'd decided, belatedly, that if he was going to be a whore he might as well do it properly, and sell his skills to the highest bidder—even if that meant smuggling genetic weapons to a drugs cartel. I'd read his financial records, though: no tax fraud, no gambling debts, no evidence that he'd ever lived beyond his means. Betraying his employers, just as he'd betrayed his own youthful ideals to join them, might have seemed like an appropriately nihilistic gesture . . . but on a more pragmatic level, it was hard to imagine him finding the money, and the consequences, all that tempting. What could El Nido have offered him? A numbered satellite account, and a new identity in Paraguay? All the squalid pleasures of life on the fringes of the Third World plutocracy? He would have had everything to gain by living out his retirement in his adopted country, salving his conscience with one or two vitriolic essays on foreign policy in some unread left-wing netzine—and then finally convincing himself that any nation that granted him such unencumbered rights of free speech probably deserved everything he'd done to defend it.

Exactly what he *had* done to defend it, though—what tools he'd perfected, and stolen—I was not permitted to know.

As DUSK FELL, I locked the apartment and headed south down Wisconsin Avenue. Washington was coming alive, the streets already teeming with people looking for distraction from the heat. Nights in the cities were becoming hallucinatory. Teenagers sported bioluminescent symbionts, the veins in their temples, necks, and pumped-up forearm muscles glowing electric blue, walking circulation diagrams who cultivated hypertension to improve the effect. Others used retinal symbionts to translate IR into visible light, their eyes flashing vampire red in the shadows.

And others, less visibly, had a skull full of White Knights.

Stem cells in the bone marrow infected with Mother—an engineered retrovirus—gave rise to something half-way between an embryonic neuron and a white blood cell. White Knights secreted the cytokines necessary to unlock the blood-brain barrier—and once through, cellular adhesion molecules guided them to their targets, where they could flood the site with a chosen neurotransmitter—or even form temporary quasi-synapses with genuine neurons. Users often had half a dozen or more sub-types in their bloodstream simultaneously, each one activated by a specific dietary additive: some cheap, harmless, and perfectly legitimate chemical not naturally present in the body. By ingesting the right mixture of innocuous artificial colorings, flavors and preservatives, they could modulate their neurochemistry in almost any fashion—until the White Knights died, as they were programmed to do, and a new dose of Mother was required.

Mother could be snorted, or taken intravenously . . . but the most efficient way to use it was to puncture a bone and inject it straight into the marrow—an excruciating, messy, dangerous business, even if the virus itself was uncontaminated and authentic. The good stuff came from El Nido. The bad stuff came from basement labs in California and Texas, where gene hackers tried to force cell cultures infected with Mother to reproduce a virus expressly designed to resist their efforts—and churned out batches of mutant strains ideal for inducing leukemia, astrocytomas, Parkinson's disease, and assorted novel psychoses.

Crossing the sweltering dark city, watching the heedlessly joyful crowds, I felt a penetrating, dream-like clarity come over me. Part of me was numb, leaden, blank—but part of me was electrified, all-seeing. I seemed to be able to stare into the hidden landscapes of the people around me, to see deeper than the luminous rivers of blood; to pierce them with my vision right to the bone.

Right to the marrow.

I drove to the edge of a park I'd visited once before, and waited. I was already dressed for the part. Young people strode by, grinning, some glancing at the silver 2025 Ford Narcissus and whistling appreciatively. A teenaged boy danced on the grass, alone, tirelessly—blissed out on Coca-Cola, and not even getting paid to fake it.

Before too long, a girl approached the car, blue veins flashing on her bare arms. She leaned down to the window and looked in, inquiringly.

"What you got?" She was sixteen or seventeen, slender, dark-eyed, coffee-colored, with a faint Latino accent. She could have been my sister.

"Southern Rainbow." All twelve major genotypes of Mother, straight from El Nido, cut with nothing but glucose. Southern Rainbow—and a little fast food—could take you anywhere.

The girl eyed me skeptically, and stretched out her right hand, palm down. She wore a ring with a large multifaceted jewel, with a pit in the center. I took a sachet from the glove compartment, shook it, tore it open, and tipped a few specks of powder into the pit. Then I leaned over and moistened the sample with saliva, holding her cool fingers to steady her hand. Twelve faces of the "stone" began to glow immediately, each one in a different color. The immunoelectric sensors in the pit, tiny capacitors coated with antibodies, were designed to recognize several sites on the protein coats of the different strains of Mother—particularly the ones the bootleggers had the most trouble getting right.

With good enough technology, though, those proteins didn't have to bear the slightest relationship to the RNA inside.

The girl seemed to be impressed; her face lit up with anticipation. We negotiated a price. Too low by far; she should have been suspicious.

I looked her in the eye before handing over the sachet.

I said, "What do you need this shit for? The world is the world. You have to take it as it is. Accept it as it is: savage and terrible. Be strong. Never lie to yourself. That's the only way to survive."

She smirked at my apparent hypocrisy, but she was too pleased with her luck to turn nasty. "I hear what you're saying. It's a bad planet out there." She forced the money into my hand, adding, with wide-eyed mock-sincerity, "And this is the last time I do Mother, I promise."

I gave her the lethal virus, and watched her walk away across the grass and vanish into the shadows.

THE COLOMBIAN AIR FORCE pilot who flew me down from Bogotá didn't seem too thrilled to be risking his life for a DEA bureaucrat. It was seven hundred kilometers to the border, and five different guerrilla organizations held territory along the way: not a lot of towns, but several hundred possible sites for rocket launchers.

"My great-grandfather," he said sourly, "died in fucking Korea fighting for General Douglas fucking MacArthur." I wasn't sure if that was meant to be a declaration of pride, or an intimation of an outstanding debt. Both, probably.

The helicopter was eerily silent, fitted out with phased sound absorbers, which looked like giant loudspeakers but swallowed most of the noise of the blades. The carbon-fiber fuselage was coated with an expensive network of chameleon polymers—although it might have been just as effective to paint the whole thing sky blue. An endothermic chemical mixture accumulated waste heat from the motor, and then discharged it through a parabolic radiator as a tightly focused skywards burst, every hour or so. The guerrillas had no access to satellite images, and no radar they dared use; I decided that we had less chance of dying than the average Bogotá commuter. Back in the capital, buses had been exploding without warning, two or three times a week.

Colombia was tearing itself apart; *La Violencia* of the 1950s, all over again. Although all of the spectacular terrorist sabotage was being carried out by organized guerrilla groups, most of the deaths so far had been caused by factions within the two mainstream political parties butchering each other's supporters, avenging a litany of past atrocities which stretched back for generations. The group who'd actually started the current wave of bloodshed had negligible support; *Ejército de Simon Bolívar* were lunatic right-wing extremists who wanted to "reunite" with Panama, Venezuela, and Ecuador—after two centuries of separation—and drag in Peru and Bolivia, to realize Bolívar's dream of *Gran Colombia*. By assassinating President Marín, though, they'd triggered a cascade of events that had nothing to do with their ludicrous cause. Strikes and protests, street battles, curfews, martial law. The repatriation of foreign capital by nervous investors, followed by hyperinflation, and the collapse of the local financial system. Then a spiral of opportunistic violence. Everyone, from the paramilitary death squads to the Maoist splinter groups, seemed to believe that their hour had finally come.

I hadn't seen so much as a bullet fired—but from the moment I'd entered the country, there'd been acid churning in my guts, and a heady, ceaseless adrenaline rush coursing through my veins. I felt wired, feverish . . . alive. Hypersensitive as a pregnant woman: I could smell blood, everywhere. When the hidden struggle for power which rules all human affairs finally breaks through to the surface, finally ruptures the skin, it's like witnessing some giant primordial creature rise up out of the ocean. Mesmerizing, and appalling. Nauseating—and exhilarating.

Coming face to face with the truth is always exhilarating.

FROM THE AIR, THERE was no obvious sign that we'd arrived; for the last two hundred kilometers, we'd been passing over rain forest—cleared in patches for plantations and mines, ranches and timber mills, shot through with rivers like metallic threads—but most of it resembling nothing so much as an endless expanse of broccoli. El Nido permitted natural vegetation to flourish all around it—and then imitated it . . . which made sampling at the edges an inefficient way to gather the true genetic stock for analysis. Deep penetration was difficult, though, even with purpose-built robots—dozens of which had been lost—so edge samples had to suffice, at least until a few more members of Congress could be photographed committing statutory rape and persuaded to vote for better funding. Most of the engineered plant tissues self-destructed in the absence of regular chemical and viral messages drifting out from the core, reassuring them that they were still *in situ*—so the main DEA research facility was on the outskirts of El Nido itself, a collection of pressurized buildings and experimental plots in a clearing blasted out of the jungle on the Colombian side of the border. The electrified fences weren't topped with razor wire; they turned ninety degrees into an electrified roof, completing a chain-link cage. The heliport was in the center of the compound, where a cage within the cage could, temporarily, open itself to the sky.

Madeleine Smith, the research director, showed me around. In the open, we both wore hermetic biohazard suits—although if the modifications I'd received in Washington were working as promised, mine was redundant. El Nido's short-lived defensive viruses occasionally percolated out this far; they were never fatal, but they could be severely disabling to anyone who hadn't been inoculated. The forest's designers had walked a fine line between biological "self-defense" and unambiguously military applications. Guerrillas had always hidden in the engineered jungle—and raised funds by collaborating in the export of Mother—but El Nido's technology had never been explicitly directed toward the creation of lethal pathogens.

So far.

"Here, we're raising seedlings of what we hope will be a stable El Nido phenotype, something we call beta seventeen." They were unremarkable bushes with deep green foliage and dark red berries; Smith pointed to an array of camera-like instruments beside them. "Real-time infrared microspectroscopy. It can resolve a medium-sized RNA transcript, if there's a sharp surge in production in a sufficient number of cells, simultaneously. We match up the data from these with our gas chromatography records, which show the range of molecules drifting out from the core. If we can catch these plants in the act of sensing a cue from El Nido—and if their response involves switching on a gene and synthesizing a protein—we may be able to elucidate the mechanism, and eventually short-circuit it."

"You can't just . . . sequence all the DNA, and work it out from first principles?" I was meant to be passing as a newly-appointed administrator, dropping in at short notice to check for gold-plated paper clips—but it was hard to decide exactly how naïve to sound.

Smith smiled politely. "El Nido DNA is guarded by enzymes which tear it apart at the slightest hint of cellular disruption. Right now, we'd have about as much of a chance of *sequencing it* as I'd have of . . . reading your mind by autopsy. And we still don't know how those enzymes work; we have a lot of catching up to do. When the drug cartels started investing in biotechnology, forty years ago, *copy protection* was their first priority. And they lured the best people away from legitimate labs around the world—not just by paying more, but by offering more creative freedom, and more challenging goals. El Nido probably contains as many patentable inventions as the entire agrotechnology industry produced in the same period. And all of them a lot more exciting."

Was that what had brought Largo here? *More challenging goals?* But El Nido was complete, the challenge was over; any further work was mere refinement. And at fifty-five, surely he knew that his most creative years were long gone.

I said, "I imagine the cartels got more than they bargained for; the technology transformed their business beyond recognition. All the old addictive substances became too easy to synthesize biologically—too cheap, too pure, and too readily available to be profitable. And addiction itself became bad business. The only thing that really sells now is novelty."

Smith motioned with bulky arms toward the towering forest outside the cage—turning to face south-east, although it all looked the same. "*El Nido* was more than they bargained for. All they really wanted was coca plants that did better at lower altitudes, and some gene-tailored vegetation to make it easier to camouflage their labs and plantations. They ended up with a small *de facto* nation full of gene hackers, anarchists, and refugees. The cartels are only in control of certain regions; half the original geneticists have split off and founded their own little jungle utopias. There are at least a dozen people who know how to program the plants—how to switch on new patterns of gene expression, how to tap into the communications networks—and with that, you can stake out your own territory."

"Like having some secret, shamanistic power to command the spirits of the forest?"

"Exactly. Except for the fact that it actually works."

I laughed. "Do you know what cheers me up the most? Whatever else happens . . . the *real* Amazon, the *real* jungle, will swallow them all in the end. It's lasted—what? Two million years? *Their own little utopias!* In fifty years' time, or a hundred, it will be as if El Nido had never existed."

Less than chaff in a breeze.

Smith didn't reply. In the silence, I could hear the monotonous click of beetles, from all directions. Bogotá, high on a plateau, had been almost chilly. Here, it was as sweltering as Washington itself.

I glanced at Smith; she said, "You're right, of course." But she didn't sound convinced at all.

IN THE MORNING, OVER breakfast, I reassured Smith that I'd found everything to be in order. She smiled warily. I think she suspected that I wasn't what I claimed to be, but that didn't really matter. I'd listened carefully to the gossip of the scientists, technicians and soldiers; the name *Guillermo Largo* hadn't been mentioned once. If they didn't even know about Largo, they could hardly have guessed my real purpose.

It was just after nine when I departed. On the ground, sheets of light, delicate as auroral displays, sliced through the trees around the compound. When we emerged above the canopy, it was like stepping from a mist-shrouded dawn into the brilliance of noon.

The pilot, begrudgingly, took a detour over the center of El Nido. "We're in Peruvian air space, now," he boasted. "You want to spark a diplomatic incident?" He seemed to find the possibility attractive.

"No. But fly lower."

"There's nothing to see. You can't even see the river."

"Lower." The broccoli grew larger, then suddenly snapped into focus; all that undifferentiated *green* turned into individual branches, solid and specific. It was curiously shocking, like looking at some dull familiar object through a microscope, and seeing its strange particularity revealed.

I reached over and broke the pilot's neck. He hissed through his teeth, surprised. A shudder passed through me, a mixture of fear and a twinge of remorse. The autopilot kicked in and kept us hovering; it took me two minutes to unstrap the man's body, drag him into the cargo hold, and take his seat.

I unscrewed the instrument panel and patched in a new chip. The digital log being beamed via satellite to an air force base to the north would show that we'd descended rapidly, out of control.

The truth wasn't much different. At a hundred meters, I hit a branch and snapped a blade on the front rotor; the computers compensated valiantly, modeling and remodeling the situation, trimming the active surfaces of the surviving blades—and no doubt doing fine for each five-second interval between bone-shaking impacts and further damage. The sound absorbers went berserk, slipping in and out of phase with the motors, blasting the jungle with pulses of intensified noise.

Fifty meters up, I went into a slow spin, weirdly smooth, showing me the thickening canopy as if in a leisurely cinematic pan. At twenty meters, free fall. Air bags inflated around me, blocking off the view. I closed my eyes, redundantly, and gritted my teeth. Fragments of prayers spun in my head—the detritus of childhood, afterimages burned into my brain, meaningless but unerasable. I thought: *If I die, the jungle will claim me. I am flesh, I am chaff. Nothing will remain to be judged.* By the time I recalled that this wasn't true jungle at all, I was no longer falling.

The air bags promptly deflated. I opened my eyes. There was water all around, flooded forest. A panel of the roof between the rotors blew off gently with a hiss like the dying pilot's last breath, and then drifted down like a slowly crashing kite, turning muddy silver, green, and brown as it snatched at the colors around it.

The life raft had oars, provisions, flares—and a radio beacon. I cut the beacon loose and left it in the wreckage. I moved the pilot back into his seat, just as the water started flooding in to bury him.

Then I set off down the river.

EL NIDO HAD DIVIDED a once-navigable stretch of the Rio Putumayo into a bewildering maze. Sluggish channels of brown water snaked between freshly raised islands of soil, covered in palms and rubber plants, and the inundated banks where the oldest trees—choco-late-colored hardwood species (predating the geneticists, but not nec-essarily unmodified)—soared above the undergrowth and out of sight.

The lymph nodes in my neck and groin pulsed with heat, savage but reassuring; my modified immune system was dealing with El Nido's viral onslaught by generating thousands of new killer T-cell clones *en masse*, rather than waiting for a cautious antigen-mediated response. A few weeks in this state, and the chances were that a self-directed clone would slip through the elimination process and burn me up with a novel autoimmune disease—but I didn't plan on staying that long.

Fish disturbed the murky water, rising up to snatch sur-face-dwelling insects or floating seed pods. In the distance, the thick coils of an anaconda slid from an overhanging branch and slipped languidly into the water. Between the rubber plants, hummingbirds hovered in the maws of violet orchids. So far as I knew, none of these creatures had been tampered with; they had gone on inhabiting the prosthetic forest as if nothing had changed.

I took a stick of chewing gum from my pocket, rich in cyclamates, and slowly roused one of my own sets of White Knights. The stink of heat and decaying vegetation seemed to fade, as certain olfactory pathways in my brain were numbed, and others sensitized—a kind of inner filter coming into play, enabling any signal from the newly acquired receptors in my nasal membranes to rise above all the other, distracting odors of the jungle.

Suddenly, I could smell the dead pilot on my hands and clothes, the lingering taint of his sweat and feces—and the pheromones of spider monkeys in the branches around me, pungent and distinc-tive as urine. As a rehearsal, I followed the trail for fifteen minutes, paddling the raft in the direction of the freshest scent, until I was finally rewarded with chirps of alarm and a glimpse of two skinny gray-brown shapes vanishing into the foliage ahead.

My own scent was camouflaged; symbionts in my sweat glands were digesting all the characteristic molecules. There were long-term side-effects from the bacteria, though, and the most recent intelligence suggested that El Nido's inhabitants didn't bother with them. There was a chance, of course, that Largo had been paranoid enough to bring his own.

I stared after the retreating monkeys, and wondered when I'd catch my first whiff of another living human. Even an illiterate peasant who'd fled the violence to the north would have valuable knowledge of the state of play between the factions in here, and some kind of crude mental map of the landscape.

The raft began to whistle gently, air escaping from one sealed compartment. I rolled into the water and submerged completely. A meter down, I couldn't see my own hands. I waited and listened, but all I could hear was the soft *plop* of fish breaking the surface. No rock could have holed the plastic of the raft; it had to have been a bullet.

I floated in the cool milky silence. The water would conceal my body heat, and I'd have no need to exhale for ten minutes. The question was whether to risk raising a wake by swimming away from the raft, or to wait it out.

Something brushed my cheek, sharp and thin. I ignored it. It happened again. It didn't feel like a fish, or anything living. A third time, and I seized the object as it fluttered past. It was a piece of plastic a few centimeters wide. I felt around the rim; the edge was sharp in places, soft and yielding in others. Then the fragment broke in two in my hand.

I swam a few meters away, then surfaced cautiously. The life raft was decaying, the plastic peeling away into the water like skin in acid. The polymer was meant to be cross-linked beyond any chance of biodegradation—but obviously some strain of El Nido bacteria had found a way.

I floated on my back, breathing deeply to purge myself of carbon dioxide, contemplating the prospect of completing the mission on foot. The canopy above seemed to waver, as if in a heat haze, which made no sense. My limbs grew curiously warm and heavy. It occurred to me to wonder exactly what I might be smelling, if I hadn't shut down ninety per cent of my olfactory range. I thought: *If I'd bred bacteria able to digest a substance foreign to El Nido, what else would I want them to do when they chanced upon such a meal? Incapacitate whoever had brought it in? Broadcast news of the event with a biochemical signal?*

I could smell the sharp odors of half a dozen sweat-drenched people when they arrived, but all I could do was lie in the water and let them fish me out.

AFTER WE LEFT THE river, I was carried on a stretcher, blindfolded and bound. No one talked within earshot. I might have judged the pace we set by the rhythm of my bearers' footsteps, or guessed the direction in which we traveled by hints of sunlight on the side of my face . . . but in the waking dream induced by the bacterial toxins, the harder I struggled to interpret those cues, the more lost and confused I became.

At one point, when the party rested, someone squatted beside me—and waved a scanning device over my body? That guess was confirmed by the pinpricks of heat where the polymer transponders had been implanted. Passive devices—but their resonant echo in a satellite microwave burst would have been distinctive. The scanner found, and fried, them all.

Late in the afternoon, they removed the blindfold. Certain that I was totally disoriented? Certain that I'd never escape? Or maybe just to flaunt El Nido's triumphant architecture.

The approach was a hidden path through swampland; I kept looking down to see my captors' boots not quite vanishing into the mud, while a dry, apparently secure stretch of high ground nearby was avoided.

Closer in, the dense thorned bushes blocking the way seemed to yield for us; the chewing gum had worn off enough for me to tell that we moved in a cloud of a sweet, ester-like compound. I couldn't see whether it was being sprayed into the air from a cylinder—or emitted bodily by a member of the party with symbionts in his skin, or lungs, or intestines.

The village emerged almost imperceptibly out of the impostor jungle. The ground—I could feel it—became, step by step, unnaturally firm and level. The arrangement of trees grew subtly ordered—defining no linear avenues, but increasingly *wrong* nonetheless. Then I started glimpsing "fortuitous" clearings to the left and right, containing "natural" wooden buildings, or shiny biopolymer sheds.

I was lowered to the ground outside one of the sheds. A man I hadn't seen before leaned over me, wiry and unshaven, holding up a gleaming hunting knife. He looked to me like the archetype of human as animal, human as predator, human as unselfconscious killer.

He said, "Friend, this is where we drain out all of your blood." He grinned and squatted down. I almost passed out from the stench of my own fear, as the glut overwhelmed the symbionts. He cut my hands free, adding, "And then put it all back in again." He slid one arm under me, around my ribs, raised me up from the stretcher, and carried me into the building.

GUILLERMO LARGO SAID, "FORGIVE me if I don't shake your hand. I think we've almost cleaned you out, but I don't want to risk physical contact in case there's enough of a residue of the virus to make your own hyped-up immune system turn on you."

He was an unprepossessing, sad-eyed man; thin, short, slightly balding. I stepped up to the wooden bars between us and stretched my hand out toward him. "Make contact any time you like. I never carried a virus. Do you think I believe your *propaganda?*"

He shrugged, unconcerned. "It would have killed you, not me— although I'm sure it was meant for both of us. It may have been keyed to my genotype, but you carried far too much of it not to have been caught up in the response to my presence. That's history, though, not worth arguing about."

I didn't actually believe that he was lying; a virus to dispose of both of us made perfect sense. I even felt a begrudging respect for the Company, for the way I'd been used—there was a savage, unsentimental honesty to it—but it didn't seem politic to reveal that to Largo.

I said, "If you believe that I pose no risk to you now, though, why don't you come back with me? You're still considered valuable. One moment of weakness, one bad decision, doesn't have to mean the end of your career. Your employers are very pragmatic people; they won't want to punish you. They'll just need to watch you a little more closely in future. Their problem, not yours; you won't even notice the difference."

Largo didn't seem to be listening, but then he looked straight at me and smiled. "Do you know what Victor Hugo said about Colombia's first constitution? He said it was written for a country of angels. It only lasted twenty-three years—and on the next attempt, the politicians lowered their sights. Considerably." He turned away, and started pacing back and forth in front of the bars. Two Mestizo peasants with automatic weapons stood by the door, looking on impassively. Both incessantly chewed what looked to me like ordinary coca leaves; there was something almost reassuring about their loyalty to tradition.

My cell was clean and well furnished, right down to the kind of bioreactor toilet that was all the rage in Beverly Hills. My captors had treated me impeccably, so far, but I had a feeling that Largo was planning something unpleasant. Handing me over to the Mother barons? I still didn't know what deal he'd done, what he'd sold them in exchange for a piece of El Nido and a few dozen bodyguards. Let alone why he thought this was better than an apartment in Bethesda and a hundred grand a year.

I said, "What do you think you're going to do, if you stay here? Build your own *country for angels*? Grow your own bioengineered utopia?"

"Utopia?" Largo stopped pacing, and flashed his crooked smile again. "No. How can there ever be a *utopia*? There is no *right way to live*, which we've simply failed to stumble upon. There is no set of rules, there is no system, there is no formula. Why should there be? Short of the existence of a creator—and a perverse one, at that— why should there be some blueprint for perfection, just waiting to be discovered?"

I said, "You're right. In the end, all we can do is be true to our nature. See through the veneer of civilization and hypocritical morality, and accept the real forces that shape us."

Largo burst out laughing. I actually felt my face burn at his response—if only because I'd misread him, and failed to get him on side; not because he was laughing at the one thing I believed in.

He said, "Do you know what I was working on, back in the States?"

"No. Does it matter?" The less I knew, the better my chances of living.

Largo told me anyway. "I was looking for a way to render mature neurons *embryonic*. To switch them back into a less differentiated state, enabling them to behave the way they do in the fetal brain: migrating from site to site, forming new connections. Supposedly as a treatment for dementia and stroke . . . although the work was being funded by people who saw it as the first step toward viral weapons able to rewire parts of the brain. I doubt that the results could ever have been very sophisticated—no viruses for imposing political ideologies—but all kinds of disabling or docile behavior might have been coded into a relatively small package."

"And you sold that to the cartels? So they can hold whole cities to ransom with it, next time one of their leaders is arrested? To save them the trouble of assassinating judges and politicians?"

Largo said mildly, "I sold it to the cartels, but not as a weapon. No infectious military version exists. Even the prototypes—which merely regress selected neurons, but make no programmed changes— are far too cumbersome and fragile to survive at large. And there are other technical problems. There's not much reproductive advantage for a virus in carrying out elaborate, highly specific modifications to its host's brain; unleashed on a real human population, mutants that simply ditched all of that irrelevant shit would soon predominate."

"Then . . . ?"

"I sold it to the cartels as *a product*. Or rather, I combined it with their own biggest seller, and handed over the finished hybrid. A new kind of Mother."

"Which does what?" He had me hooked, even if I was digging my own grave.

"Which turns a subset of the neurons in the brain into something like White Knights. Just as mobile, just as flexible. Far better at establishing tight new synapses, though, rather than just flooding the interneural space with a chosen substance. And not controlled by dietary additives; controlled by molecules they secrete themselves. Controlled by each other."

That made no sense to me. "*Existing neurons* become mobile? Existing brain structures . . . melt? You've made a version of Mother that turns people's brains to mush—and you expect them to pay for that?"

"Not mush. Everything's part of a tight feedback loop: the firing of these altered neurons influences the range of molecules they secrete—which in turn controls the rewiring of nearby synapses. Vital regulatory centers and motor neurons are left untouched, of course. And it takes a strong signal to shift the Gray Knights; they don't respond to every random whim. You need at least an hour or two without distractions before you can have a significant effect on any brain structure.

"It's not altogether different from the way ordinary neurons end up encoding learned behavior and memories—only faster, more flexible . . . and much more widespread. There are parts of the brain that haven't changed in a hundred thousand years, which can be remodeled completely in half a day."

He paused, and regarded me amiably. The sweat on the back of my neck went cold.

"You've used the virus—?"

"Of course. That's why I created it. For myself. That's why I came here in the first place."

"For do-it-yourself neurosurgery? Why not just slip a screwdriver under one eyeball and poke it around until the urge went away?" I felt physically sick. "At least . . . cocaine and heroine—and even White Knights—exploited *natural* receptors, *natural* pathways. You've taken a structure that evolution has honed over millions of years, and—"

Largo was greatly amused, but this time he refrained from laughing in my face. He said gently, "For most people, navigating their own psyche is like wandering in circles through a maze. That's what *evolution* has bequeathed us: a miserable, confusing prison. And the only thing crude drugs like cocaine or heroine or alcohol ever did was build short cuts to a few dead ends—or, like LSD, coat the walls of the maze with mirrors. And all that White Knights ever did was package the same effects differently.

"*Gray Knights* allow you to reshape the entire maze, at will. They don't confine you to some shrunken emotional repertoire; they empower you completely. They let you control *exactly who you are.*"

I had to struggle to put aside the overwhelming sense of revulsion I felt. Largo had decided to fuck himself in the head; that was his problem. A few users of Mother would do the same—but one more batch of poisonous shit to compete with all the garbage from the basement labs wasn't exactly a national tragedy.

Largo said affably, "I spent thirty years as someone I despised. I was too weak to change—but I never quite lost sight of what I wanted to become. I used to wonder if it would have been less contemptible, less hypocritical, to resign myself to the fact of my weakness, the fact of my corruption. But I never did."

"And you think you've erased your old personality, as easily as you erased your computer files? What are you now, then? A saint? *An angel?*"

"No. But I'm exactly what I want to be. With Gray Knights, you can't really be anything else."

I felt giddy for a moment, light-headed with rage; I steadied myself against the bars of my cage.

I said, "So you've scrambled your brain, and you feel better. And you're going to live in this fake jungle for the rest of your life, collaborating with drug pushers, kidding yourself that you've achieved redemption?"

"The rest of my life? Perhaps. But I'll be watching the world. And hoping."

I almost choked. "Hoping for *what?* You think your habit will ever spread beyond a few brain-damaged junkies? You think Gray Knights are going to sweep across the planet and transform it beyond recognition? Or were you lying—is the virus really infectious, after all?"

"No. But it gives people what they want. They'll seek it out, once they understand that."

I gazed at him, pityingly. "What people *want* is food, sex, and power. That will never change. Remember the passage you marked in 'Heart of Darkness'? What do you think that *meant?* Deep down, we're just animals with a few simple drives. Everything else is *less than chaff in a breeze.*"

Largo frowned, as if trying to recall the quote, then nodded slowly. He said, "Do you know how many different ways an ordinary human brain can be wired? Not an arbitrary neural network of the same size—but an actual, working *Homo sapiens* brain, shaped by real embryology and real experience? There are about ten-to-the-power-of-ten-million possibilities. A huge number: a lot of room for variation in personality and talents, a lot of space to encode the traces of different lives.

"But do you know what Gray Knights do to that number? They multiply it by the same again. They grant the part of us that was fixed, that was tied to 'human nature', the chance to be as different from person to person as a lifetime's worth of memories.

"Of course Conrad was right. Every word of that passage was true—when it was written. But now it doesn't go far enough. Because now, all of human nature is *less than chaff in a breeze.* 'The horror', the heart of darkness, is *less than chaff in a breeze.* All the 'eternal verities'—all the sad and beautiful insights of all the great writers from Sophocles to Shakespeare—are *less than chaff in a breeze.*"

I LAY AWAKE ON my bunk, listening to the cicadas and frogs, wondering what Largo would do with me. If he didn't see himself as capable of murder, he wouldn't kill me—if only to reinforce his delusions of self-mastery. Perhaps he'd just dump me outside the research station—where I could explain to Madeleine Smith how the Colombian air force pilot had come down with an El Nido virus in midair, and I'd valiantly tried to take control.

I thought back over the incident, trying to get my story straight. The pilot's body would never be recovered; the forensic details didn't have to add up.

I closed my eyes and saw myself breaking his neck. The same twinge of remorse passed over me. I brushed it aside irritably. So I'd killed him—and the girl, a few days earlier—and a dozen others before that. The Company had very nearly disposed of me. Because it was expedient—and because it was possible. That was the way of the world: power would always be used, nation would subjugate nation, the weak would always be slaughtered. Everything else was pious self-delusion. A hundred kilometers away, Colombia's warring factions were proving the truth of that, one more time.

But if Largo had infected me with his own special brand of Mother? And if everything he'd told me about it was true?

Gray Knights only moved if you willed them to move. All I had to do in order to remain unscathed was to choose that fate. To wish only to be exactly who I was: a killer who'd always understood that he was facing the deepest of truths. Embracing savagery and corruption because, in the end, there was no other way.

I kept seeing them before me: the pilot, the girl.

I had to feel nothing—and wish to feel nothing—and keep on making that choice, again and again.

Or everything I was would disintegrate like a house of sand, and blow away.

One of the guards belched in the darkness, then spat.

The night stretched out ahead of me, like a river that had lost its way.

LUMINOUS

I WOKE, DISORIENTATED, UNSURE WHY. I knew I was lying on the narrow, lumpy single bed in Room 22 of the Hotel Fleapit; after almost a month in Shanghai, the topography of the mattress was depressingly familiar. But there was something wrong with the way I was lying; every muscle in my neck and shoulders was protesting that nobody could end up in this position from natural causes, however badly they'd slept.

And I could smell blood.

I opened my eyes. A woman I'd never seen before was kneeling over me, slicing into my left triceps with a disposable scalpel. I was lying on my side, facing the wall, one hand and one ankle cuffed to the head and foot of the bed.

Something cut short the surge of visceral panic before I could start stupidly thrashing about, instinctively trying to break free. Maybe an even more ancient response—catatonia in the face of danger—took on the adrenaline and won. Or maybe I just decided that I had no right to panic when I'd been expecting something like this for weeks.

I spoke softly, in English. "What you're in the process of hacking out of me is a necrotrap. One heartbeat without oxygenated blood, and the cargo gets fried."

My amateur surgeon was compact, muscular, with short black hair. Not Chinese; Indonesian, maybe. If she was surprised that I'd woken prematurely, she didn't show it. The gene-tailored hepatocytes I'd acquired in Hanoi could degrade almost anything from morphine to curare; it was a good thing the local anesthetic was beyond their reach.

Without taking her eyes off her work, she said, "Look on the table next to the bed."

I twisted my head around. She'd set up a loop of plastic tubing full of blood—mine, presumably—circulated and aerated by a small pump. The stem of a large funnel fed into the loop, the intersection controlled by a valve of some kind. Wires trailed from the pump to a sensor taped to the inside of my elbow, synchronizing the artificial pulse with the real. I had no doubt that she could tear the trap from my vein and insert it into this substitute without missing a beat.

I cleared my throat and swallowed. "Not good enough. The trap knows my blood pressure profile exactly. A generic heartbeat won't fool it."

"You're bluffing." But she hesitated, scalpel raised. The hand-held MRI scanner she'd used to find the trap would have revealed its basic configuration, but few fine details of the engineering—and nothing at all about the software.

"I'm telling you the truth." I looked her squarely in the eye, which wasn't easy given our awkward geometry. "It's new, it's Swedish. You anchor it in a vein forty-eight hours in advance, put yourself through a range of typical activities so it can memorize the rhythms . . . then you inject the cargo into the trap. Simple, foolproof, effective." Blood trickled down across my chest onto the sheet. I was suddenly very glad that I hadn't buried the thing deeper, after all.

"So how do you retrieve the cargo, yourself?"

"That would be telling."

"Then tell me now, and save yourself some trouble." She rotated the scalpel between thumb and forefinger impatiently. My skin did a cold burn all over, nerve ends jangling, capillaries closing down as blood dived for cover.

I said, "*Trouble* gives me hypertension."

She smiled down at me thinly, conceding the stalemate—then peeled off one stained surgical glove, took out her notepad, and made a call to a medical equipment supplier. She listed some devices which would get around the problem—a blood pressure probe, a more sophisticated pump, a suitable computerized interface—arguing heatedly in fluent Mandarin to extract a promise of a speedy delivery. Then she put down the notepad and placed her ungloved hand on my shoulder.

"You can relax now. We won't have long to wait."

I squirmed, as if angrily shrugging off her hand—and succeeded in getting some blood on her skin. She didn't say a word, but she must have realized at once how careless she'd been; she climbed off the bed and headed for the washbasin, and I heard the water running.

Then she started retching.

I called out cheerfully, "Let me know when you're ready for the antidote."

I heard her approach, and I turned to face her. She was ashen, her face contorted with nausea, eyes and nose streaming mucus and tears.

"Tell me where it is!"

"Uncuff me, and I'll get it for you."

"No! No deals!"

"Fine. Then you'd better start looking, yourself."

She picked up the scalpel and brandished it in my face. "Screw the cargo. *I'll do it!*" She was shivering like a feverish child, uselessly trying to stem the flood from her nostrils with the back of her hand.

I said coldly, "If you cut me again, you'll lose more than the cargo."

She turned away and vomited; it was thin and gray, blood-streaked. The toxin was persuading cells in her stomach lining to commit suicide *en masse*.

"Uncuff me. It'll kill you. It doesn't take long."

She wiped her mouth, steeled herself, made as if to speak—then started puking again. I knew, first-hand, exactly how bad she was feeling. Keeping it down was like trying to swallow a mixture of shit and sulphuric acid. Bringing it up was like evisceration.

I said, "In thirty seconds, you'll be too weak to help yourself—even if I told you where to look. So if I'm not free . . ."

She produced a gun and a set of keys, uncuffed me, then stood by the foot of the bed, shaking badly but keeping me targeted. I dressed quickly, ignoring her threats, bandaging my arm with a miraculously spare clean sock before putting on a T-shirt and a jacket. She sagged to her knees, still aiming the gun more or less in my direction—but her eyes were swollen half-shut, and brimming with yellow fluid. I thought about trying to disarm her, but it didn't seem worth the risk.

I packed my remaining clothes, then glanced around the room as if I might have left something behind. But everything that really mattered was in my veins; Alison had taught me that that was the only way to travel.

I turned to the burglar. "There is no antidote. But the toxin won't kill you. You'll just wish it would, for the next twelve hours. Goodbye."

As I headed for the door, hairs rose suddenly on the back of my neck. It occurred to me that she might not take me at my word—and might fire a parting shot, believing she had nothing to lose.

Turning the handle, without looking back, I said, "But if you come after me—next time, I'll kill you."

That was a lie, but it seemed to do the trick. As I pulled the door shut behind me, I heard her drop the gun and start vomiting again.

Halfway down the stairs, the euphoria of escape began to give way to a bleaker perspective. If one careless bounty hunter could find me, her more methodical colleagues couldn't be far behind. Industrial Algebra were closing in on us. If Alison didn't gain access to Luminous soon, we'd have no choice but to destroy the map. And even that would only be buying time.

I paid the desk clerk for the room until the next morning, stressing that my companion should not be disturbed, and added a suitable tip to compensate for the mess the cleaners would find. The toxin denatured in air; the bloodstains would be harmless in a matter of hours. The clerk eyed me suspiciously, but said nothing.

Outside, it was a mild, cloudless summer morning. It was barely six o'clock, but Kongjiang Lu was already crowded with pedestrians, cyclists, buses—and a few ostentatious chauffeured limousines, plowing through the traffic at about ten kph. It looked like the night shift had just emerged from the Intel factory down the road; most of the passing cyclists were wearing the orange, logo-emblazoned overalls.

Two blocks from the hotel I stopped dead, my legs almost giving way beneath me. It wasn't just shock—a delayed reaction, a belated acceptance of how close I'd come to being slaughtered. The burglar's clinical violence was chilling enough—but what it implied was infinitely more disturbing.

Industrial Algebra were paying big money, violating international law, taking serious risks with their corporate and personal futures. The arcane abstraction of the defect was being dragged into the world of blood and dust, boardrooms and assassins, power and pragmatism.

And the closest thing to certainty humanity had ever known was in danger of dissolving into quicksand.

It HAD ALL STARTED out as a joke. Argument for argument's sake. Alison and her infuriating heresies.

"A mathematical theorem," she'd proclaimed, "only becomes true when a physical system tests it out: when the system's behavior depends in some way on the theorem being *true* or *false*."

It was June, 1994. We were sitting in a small paved courtyard, having just emerged yawning and blinking into the winter sunlight from the final lecture in a one-semester course on the philosophy of mathematics—a bit of light relief from the hard grind of the real stuff. We had fifteen minutes to kill before meeting some friends for lunch. It was a social conversation—verging on mild flirtation—nothing more. Maybe there were demented academics lurking in dark crypts somewhere, who held views on the nature of mathematical truth which they were willing to die for. But we were twenty years old, and we *knew* it was all angels on the head of a pin.

I said, "Physical systems don't create mathematics. Nothing *creates* mathematics—it's timeless. All of number theory would still be exactly the same, even if the universe contained nothing but a single electron."

Alison snorted. "Yes, because even *one electron*, plus a space-time to put it in, needs all of quantum mechanics and all of general relativity—and all the mathematical infrastructure they entail. One particle floating in a quantum vacuum needs half the major results of group theory, functional analysis, differential geometry—"

"Okay, okay! I get the point. But if that's the case . . . the events in the first picosecond after the Big Bang would have 'constructed' every last mathematical truth required by *any* physical system, all the way to the Big Crunch. Once you've got the mathematics which underpins the Theory of Everything . . . that's it, that's all you ever need. End of story."

"But it's not. To *apply* the Theory of Everything to a particular system, you still need all the mathematics for dealing with *that system*—which could include results far beyond the mathematics which the TOE itself requires. I mean, fifteen billion years after the Big Bang, someone can still come along and prove, say . . . Fermat's Last Theorem." Andrew Wiles at Princeton had recently announced a proof of the famous conjecture, although his work was still being scrutinized by his colleagues, and the final verdict wasn't yet in. "Physics never needed *that* before."

I protested, "What do you mean, 'before'? Fermat's Last Theorem never has—and never will—have anything to do with any branch of physics."

Alison smiled sneakily. "No *branch*—no. But only because the class of physical systems whose behavior depends on it is so ludicrously specific: the brains of mathematicians who are trying to validate the Wiles proof.

"Think about it. Once you start trying to prove a theorem, then even if the mathematics is so 'pure' that it has no relevance to any other object in the universe . . . you've just made it relevant to *yourself*. You have to choose *some* physical process to test the theorem—whether you use a computer, or a pen and paper . . . or just close your eyes and shuffle *neurotransmitters*. There's no such thing as a proof which doesn't rely on physical events—and whether they're inside or outside your skull doesn't make them any less real."

"Fair enough," I conceded warily. "But that doesn't mean—"

"And maybe Andrew Wiles's brain—and body, and notepaper—comprised the first physical system whose behavior depended on the theorem being true or false. But I don't think human actions have any special role . . . and if some swarm of quarks had done the same thing blindly, fifteen billion years before—executed some purely random interaction which just happened to test the conjecture in some way—then *those quarks* would have constructed FLT long before Wiles. We'll never know."

I opened my mouth to complain that no swarm of quarks could have tested the infinite number of cases encompassed by the theorem, but I caught myself just in time. That was true, but it hadn't stopped Wiles. A finite sequence of logical steps linked the axioms of number theory—which included some simple generalities about *all* numbers—to Fermat's own sweeping assertion. And if a mathematician could test those logical steps by manipulating a finite number of physical objects for a finite amount of time—whether they were pencil marks on paper, or neurotransmitters in his or her brain—then all kinds of physical systems could, in theory, mimic the structure of the proof . . . with or without any awareness of what it was they were "proving."

I leaned back on the bench and mimed tearing out hair. "If I wasn't a die-hard Platonist before, you're forcing me into it! Fermat's Last Theorem didn't *need* to be proved by anyone—or stumbled on by any random swarm of quarks. If it's true, it was always true. Everything implied by a given set of axioms is logically connected to them, timelessly, eternally . . . even if the links couldn't be traced by people—or quarks—in the lifetime of the universe."

Alison was having none of this; every mention of *timeless and eternal truths* brought a faint smile to the corners of her mouth, as if I was affirming my belief in Santa Claus. She said, "So who, or what, pushed the consequences of 'There exists an entity called zero' and 'Every X has a successor', *et cetera*, all the way to FLT and beyond, before the universe had a chance to test out any of it?"

I stood my ground. "What's joined by logic is just . . . *joined*. Nothing has to happen—consequences don't have to be 'pushed' into existence by anyone, or anything. Or do you imagine that the first events after the Big Bang, the first wild jitters of the quark-gluon plasma, stopped to fill in all the logical gaps? You think the quarks reasoned: well, so far we've done A and B and C—but now we mustn't do D, because D would be logically inconsistent with the other mathematics we've 'invented' so far . . . even if it would take a five-hundred-thousand-page proof to spell out the inconsistency?"

Alison thought it over. "No. But what if event D took place, regardless? What if the mathematics it implied *was* logically inconsistent with the rest—but it went ahead and happened anyway . . . because the universe was too young to have computed the fact that there was any discrepancy?"

I must have sat and stared at her, open-mouthed, for about ten seconds. Given the orthodoxies we'd spent the last two-and-a-half years absorbing, this was a seriously outrageous statement.

"You're claiming that . . . *mathematics* might be strewn with primordial defects in consistency? Like space might be strewn with cosmic strings?"

"Exactly." She stared back at me, feigning nonchalance. "If space-time doesn't join up with itself smoothly, everywhere . . . why should mathematical logic?"

I almost choked. "Where do I begin? What happens—now—when some physical system tries to link theorems across the defect? If theorem D has been rendered 'true' by some over-eager quarks, what happens when we program a computer to disprove it? When the software goes through all the logical steps which link A, B and C—which the quarks have also made true—to the contradiction, the dreaded not-D . . . does it succeed, or doesn't it?"

Alison side-stepped the question. "Suppose they're both true: D and not-D. Sounds like the end of mathematics, doesn't it? The whole system falls apart, instantly. From D and not-D together you can prove anything you like: one equals zero, day equals night. But that's just the boring-old-fart Platonist view—where logic travels faster than light, and computation takes no time at all. People live with omega-inconsistent theories, don't they?"

Omega-inconsistent number theories were non-standard versions of arithmetic, based on axioms which "almost" contradicted each other—their saving grace being that the contradictions could only show up in "infinitely long proofs" (which were formally disallowed, quite apart from being physically impossible). That was perfectly respectable modern mathematics—but Alison seemed prepared to replace "infinitely long" with just plain "long"—as if the difference hardly mattered, in practice.

I said, "Let me get this straight. What you're talking about is taking ordinary arithmetic—no weird counter-intuitive axioms, just the stuff every ten-year-old *knows* is true—and proving that it's inconsistent, in a finite number of steps?"

She nodded blithely. "Finite, but large. So the contradiction would rarely have any physical manifestation—it would be 'computationally distant' from everyday calculations, and everyday physical events. I mean . . . one cosmic string, somewhere out there, doesn't destroy the universe, does it? It does no harm to anyone."

I laughed dryly. "So long as you don't get too close. So long as you don't tow it back to the solar system and let it twitch around slicing up planets."

"Exactly."

I glanced at my watch. "Time to come down to Earth, I think. You know we're meeting Julia and Ramesh—?"

Alison sighed theatrically. "I know, I know. And this would bore them witless, poor things—so the subject's closed, I promise." She added wickedly, "Humanities students are so *myopic*."

We set off across the tranquil leafy campus. Alison kept her word, and we walked in silence; carrying on the argument up to the last minute would have made it even harder to avoid the topic once we were in polite company.

Half-way to the cafeteria, though, I couldn't help myself.

"If someone ever *did* program a computer to follow a chain of inferences across the defect . . . what do you claim would actually happen? When the end result of all those simple, trustworthy logical steps finally popped up on the screen—which group of primordial quarks would win the battle? And please don't tell me that the whole computer just conveniently vanishes."

Alison smiled, tongue-in-cheek at last. "Get real, Bruno. How can you expect me to answer that, when the mathematics needed to predict the result doesn't even *exist* yet? Nothing I could say would be true or false—until someone's gone ahead and done the experiment."

I SPENT MOST OF the day trying to convince myself that I wasn't being followed by some accomplice (or rival) of the surgeon, who might have been lurking outside the hotel. There was something disturbingly Kafkaesque about trying to lose a tail who might or might not have been real: no particular face I could search for in the crowd, just the abstract idea of a pursuer. It was too late to think about plastic surgery to make me look Han Chinese—Alison had raised this as a serious suggestion, back in Vietnam—but Shanghai had over a million foreign residents, so with care even an Anglophone of Italian descent should have been able to vanish.

Whether or not I was up to the task was another matter.

I tried joining the ant-trails of the tourists, following the path of least resistance from the insane crush of the Yuyuan Bazaar (where racks bursting with ten-cent watch-PCs, mood-sensitive contact lenses, and the latest karaoke vocal implants, sat beside bamboo cages of live ducks and pigeons) to the one-time residence of Sun Yatsen (whose personality cult was currently undergoing a mini-series-led revival on Phoenix TV, advertised on ten thousand buses and ten times as many T-shirts). From the tomb of the writer Lu Xun ("Always think and study . . . visit the generals then visit the victims, see the realities of your time with open eyes"—no prime time for *him*) to the Hongkou McDonalds (where they were giving away small plastic Andy Warhol figurines, for reasons I couldn't fathom).

I mimed leisurely window-shopping between the shrines, but kept my body language sufficiently unfriendly to deter even the loneliest Westerner from attempting to strike up a conversation. If foreigners were unremarkable in most of the city, they were positively eye-glazing here—even to each other—and I did my best to offer no one the slightest reason to remember me.

Along the way I checked for messages from Alison, but there were none. I left five of my own, tiny abstract chalk marks on bus shelters and park benches—all slightly different, but all saying the same thing: CLOSE BRUSH, BUT SAFE NOW. MOVING ON.

By early evening, I'd done all I could to throw off my hypothetical shadow, so I headed for the next hotel on our agreed but unwritten list. The last time we'd met face-to-face, in Hanoi, I'd mocked all of Alison's elaborate preparations. Now I was beginning to wish that I'd begged her to extend our secret language to cover more extreme contingencies. FATALLY WOUNDED. BETRAYED YOU UNDER TORTURE. REALITY DECAYING. OTHERWISE FINE.

The hotel on Huaihai Zhonglu was a step up from the last one, but not quite classy enough to refuse payment in cash. The desk clerk made polite small-talk, and I lied as smoothly as I could about my plans to spend a week sight-seeing before heading for Beijing. The bellperson smirked when I tipped him too much—and I sat on my bed for five minutes afterward, wondering what significance to read into *that*.

I struggled to regain a sense of proportion. Industrial Algebra *could* have bribed every single hotel employee in Shanghai to be on the lookout for us—but that was a bit like saying that, in theory, they could have duplicated our entire twelve-year search for defects, and not bothered to pursue us at all. There was no question that they wanted what we had, badly—but what could they actually do about it? Go to a merchant bank (or the Mafia, or a Triad) for finance? That might have worked if the cargo had been a stray kilogram of plutonium, or a valuable gene sequence—but only a few hundred thousand people on the planet would be capable of understanding what the defect *was*, even in theory. Only a fraction of that number would believe that such a thing could really exist . . . and even fewer would be both wealthy and immoral enough to invest in the business of exploiting it.

The stakes appeared to be infinitely high—but that didn't make the players omnipotent.

Not yet.

I changed the dressing on my arm, from sock to handkerchief, but the incision was deeper than I'd realized, and it was still bleeding thinly. I left the hotel—and found exactly what I needed in a twenty-four-hour emporium just ten minutes away. Surgical grade tissue repair cream: a mixture of collagen-based adhesive, antiseptic, and growth factors. The emporium wasn't even a pharmaceuticals outlet—it just had aisle after aisle packed with all kinds of unrelated odds and ends, laid out beneath the unblinking blue-white ceiling panels. Canned food, PVC plumbing fixtures, traditional medicines, rat contraceptives, video ROMS. It was a random cornucopia, an almost organic diversity—as if the products had all just grown on the shelves from whatever spores the wind had happened to blow in.

I headed back to the hotel, pushing my way through the relentless crowds, half seduced and half sickened by the odors of cooking, dazed by the endless vista of holograms and neon in a language I barely understood. Fifteen minutes later, reeling from the noise and humidity, I realized that I was lost.

I stopped on a street corner and tried to get my bearings. Shanghai stretched out around me, dense and lavish, sensual and ruthless—a Darwinian economic simulation self-organized to the brink of catastrophe. The Amazon of commerce: this city of sixteen million had more industry of every kind, more exporters and importers, more wholesalers and retailers, traders and resellers and recyclers and scavengers, more billionaires and more beggars, than most nations on the planet.

Not to mention more computing power.

China itself was reaching the cusp of its decades-long transition from brutal totalitarian communism to brutal totalitarian capitalism: a slow seamless morph from Mao to Pinochet set to the enthusiastic applause of its trading partners and the international financial agencies. There'd been no need for a counter-revolution—just layer after layer of carefully reasoned Newspeak to pave the way from previous doctrine to the stunningly obvious conclusion that private property, a thriving middle class, and a few trillion dollars worth of foreign investment were exactly what the Party had been aiming for all along.

The apparatus of the police state remained as essential as ever. Trade unionists with decadent bourgeois ideas about uncompetitive wages, journalists with counter-revolutionary notions of exposing corruption and nepotism, and any number of subversive political activists spreading destabilizing propaganda about the fantasy of free elections, all needed to be kept in check.

In a way, Luminous was a product of this strange transition from communism to not-communism in a thousand tiny steps. No one else, not even the US defense research establishment, possessed a single machine with so much power. The rest of the world had succumbed long ago to networking, giving up their imposing super-computers with their difficult architecture and customized chips for a few hundred of the latest mass-produced work stations. In fact, the biggest computing feats of the twenty-first century had all been farmed out over the Internet to thousands of volunteers, to run on their machines whenever the processors would otherwise be idle. That was how Alison and I had mapped the defect in the first place: seven thousand amateur mathematicians had shared the joke, for twelve years.

But now the net was the very opposite of what we needed—and only Luminous could take its place. And though only the People's Republic could have paid for it, and only the People's Institute for Advanced Optical Engineering could have built it . . . only Shanghai's QIPS Corporation could have sold time on it to the world—while it was still being used to model hydrogen bomb shock waves, pilotless fighter jets, and exotic anti-satellite weapons.

I finally decoded the street signs, and realized what I'd done: I'd turned the wrong way coming out of the emporium, it was as simple as that.

I retraced my steps, and I was soon back on familiar territory.

WHEN I OPENED THE door of my room, Alison was sitting on the bed.

I said, "What is it with locks in this city?"

We embraced, briefly. We'd been lovers, once—but that was long over. And we'd been friends for years afterward—but I wasn't sure if that was still the right word. Our whole relationship now was too functional, too spartan. Everything revolved around the defect, now.

She said, "I got your message. What happened?"

I described the morning's events.

"You know what you should have done?"

That stung. "I'm still here, aren't I? The cargo's still safe."

"You should have killed her, Bruno."

I laughed. Alison gazed back at me placidly, and I looked away. I didn't know if she was serious—and I didn't much want to find out.

She helped me apply the repair cream. My toxin was no threat to her—we'd both installed exactly the same symbionts, the same genotype from the same unique batch in Hanoi. But it was strange to feel her bare fingers on my broken skin, knowing that no one else on the planet could touch me like this, with impunity.

Ditto for sex, but I didn't want to dwell on that.

As I slipped on my jacket, she said, "So guess what we're doing at five a.m. tomorrow?"

"Don't tell me: I fly to Helsinki, and you fly to Cape Town. Just to throw them off the scent."

That got a faint smile. "Wrong. We're meeting Yuen at the Institute—and spending half an hour on Luminous."

"*You* are brilliant." I bent over and kissed her on the forehead. "But I always knew you'd pull it off."

And I should have been delirious—but the truth was, my guts were churning; I felt almost as trapped as I had upon waking cuffed to the bed. If Luminous had remained beyond our reach (as it should have, since we couldn't afford to hire it for a microsecond at the going rate) we would have had no choice but to destroy all the data, and hope for the best. Industrial Algebra had no doubt dredged up a few thousand fragments of the original Internet calculations—but it was clear that, although they knew exactly what we'd found, they still had no idea where we'd found it. If they'd been forced to start their own random search—constrained by the need for secrecy to their own private hardware—it might have taken them centuries.

There was no question now, though, of backing away and leaving everything to chance. We were going to have to confront the defect in person.

"How much did you have to tell him?"

"Everything." She walked over to the washbasin, removed her shirt, and began wiping the sweat from her neck and torso with a flannel. "Short of handing over the map. I showed him the search algorithms and their results, and all the programs we'll need to run on Luminous—all stripped of specific parameter values, but enough for him to validate the techniques. He wanted to see direct evidence of the defect, of course, but I held out on that."

"And how much did he believe?"

"He's reserved judgment. The deal is, we get half an hour's unimpeded access—but he gets to observe everything we do."

I nodded, as if my opinion made any difference, as if we had any choice. Yuen Ting-fu had been Alison's supervisor for her PhD on advanced applications of ring theory, when she'd studied at Fu-tan University in the late nineties. Now he was one of the world's leading cryptographers, working as a consultant to the military, the security services, and a dozen international corporations. Alison had once told me that she'd heard he'd found a polynomial-time algorithm for factoring the product of two primes; that had never been officially confirmed . . . but such was the power of his reputation that almost everyone on the planet had stopped using the old RSA encryption method as the rumor had spread. No doubt time on Luminous was his for the asking—but that didn't mean he couldn't still be imprisoned for twenty years for giving it away to the wrong people, for the wrong reasons.

I said, "And you trust him? He may not believe in the defect now, but once he's convinced—"

"He'll want exactly what *we* want. I'm sure of that."

"Okay. But are you sure IA won't be watching, too? If they've worked out why we're here, and they've bribed someone—"

Alison cut me off impatiently. "There are still a few things you can't buy in this city. Spying on a military machine like Luminous would be suicidal. No one would risk it."

"What about spying on unauthorized projects being run on a military machine? Maybe the crimes cancel out, and you end up a hero."

She approached me, half naked, drying her face on my towel. "We'd better hope not."

I laughed suddenly. "You know what I like most about Luminous? They're not really letting Exxon and McDonnell-Douglas use the same machine as the People's Liberation Army. Because the whole computer vanishes every time they pull the plug. There's no paradox at all, if you look at it that way."

ALISON INSISTED THAT WE stand guard in shifts. Twenty-four hours earlier, I might have made a joke of it; now I reluctantly accepted the revolver she offered me, and sat watching the door in the neon-tinged darkness while she went out like a light.

The hotel had been quiet for most of the evening—but now it came to life. There were footsteps in the corridor every five minutes—and rats in the walls, foraging and screwing and probably giving birth. Police sirens wailed in the distance; a couple screamed at each other in the street below. I'd read somewhere that Shanghai was now the murder capital of the world—but was that *per capita*, or in absolute numbers?

After an hour, I was so jumpy that it was a miracle I hadn't blown my foot off. I unloaded the gun, then sat playing Russian roulette with the empty barrel. In spite of everything, I still wasn't ready to put a bullet in anyone's brain for the sake of defending the axioms of number theory.

INDUSTRIAL ALGEBRA HAD APPROACHED us in a perfectly civilized fashion, at first. They were a small but aggressive UK-based company, designing specialized high-performance computing hardware for industrial and military applications. That they'd heard about the search was no great surprise—it had been openly discussed on the Internet for years, and even joked about in serious mathematical

journals—but it seemed an odd coincidence when they made contact with us just days after Alison had sent me a private message
from Zürich mentioning the latest "promising" result. After half
a dozen false alarms—all due to bugs and glitches—we'd stopped
broadcasting the news of every unconfirmed find to the people who
were donating runtime to the project, let alone any wider circle. We
were afraid that if we cried wolf one more time, half our collaborators would get so annoyed that they'd withdraw their support.

IA had offered us a generous slab of computing power on the
company's private network—several orders of magnitude more than
we received from any other donor. *Why?* The answer kept changing. Their deep respect for pure mathematics . . . their wide-eyed
fun-loving attitude to life . . . their desire to be seen to be sponsoring
a project so wild and hip and unlikely to succeed that it made SETI
look like a staid blue-chip investment. It was—they'd finally "conceded"—a desperate bid to soften their corporate image, after years
of bad press for what certain unsavory governments did with their
really rather nice smart bombs.

We'd politely declined. They'd offered us highly paid consulting jobs. Bemused, we'd suspended all net-based calculations—and
started encrypting our mail with a simple but highly effective algorithm Alison had picked up from Yuen.

Alison had been collating the results of the search on her own
work station at her current home in Zürich, while I'd helped coordinate things from Sydney. No doubt IA had been eavesdropping on
the incoming data, but they'd clearly started too late to gather the
information needed to create their own map; each fragment of the
calculations meant little in isolation. But when the work station was
stolen (all the files were encrypted, it would have told them nothing)
we'd finally been forced to ask ourselves: *If the defect turns out to be
genuine, if the joke is no joke . . . then exactly what's at stake? How much
money? How much power?*

On June 7, 2006, we met in a sweltering, crowded square in
Hanoi. Alison wasted no time. She was carrying a backup of the
data from the stolen work station in her notepad—and she solemnly
proclaimed that, this time, the defect was real.

The notepad's tiny processor would have taken centuries to repeat the long random trawling of the space of arithmetic statements which had been carried out on the net—but, led straight to the relevant computations, it could confirm the existence of the defect in a matter of minutes.

The process began with Statement S. Statement S was an assertion about some ludicrously huge numbers—but it wasn't mathematically sophisticated or contentious in any way. There were no claims here about infinite sets, no propositions concerning "every integer." It merely stated that a certain (elaborate) calculation performed on certain (very large) whole numbers led to a certain result—in essence, it was no different from something like "5+3 = 4×2." It might have taken me ten years to check it with a pen and paper—but I could have carried out the task with nothing but primary school mathematics and a great deal of patience. A statement like this could not be undecidable; it had to be either true or false.

The notepad decided it was true.

Then the notepad took statement S . . . and in four hundred and twenty-three simple, impeccably logical steps, used it to prove not-S.

I repeated the calculations on my own notepad—using a different software package. The result was exactly the same. I gazed at the screen, trying to concoct a plausible reason why two different machines running two different programs could have failed in identical ways. There'd certainly been cases in the past of a single misprinted algorithm in a computing textbook spawning a thousand dud programs. But the operations here were too simple, too basic.

Which left only two possibilities. Either conventional arithmetic was intrinsically flawed, and the whole Platonic ideal of the natural numbers was ultimately self-contradictory . . . or Alison was right, and an alternative arithmetic had come to hold sway in a "computationally remote" region, billions of years ago.

I was badly shaken—but my first reaction was to try to play down the significance of the result. "The numbers being manipulated here are greater than the volume of the observable universe, measured in cubic Planck lengths. If IA were hoping to use this on their foreign exchange transactions, I think they've made a slight error of scale." Even as I spoke, though, I knew it wasn't that simple. The raw numbers might have been trans-astronomical—but it was the mere 1024 bits of the notepad's binary representations which had actually, physically misbehaved. Every truth in mathematics was encoded, reflected, in countless other forms. If a paradox like this—which at first glance sounded like a dispute about numbers too large to apply even to the most grandiose cosmological discussions—could affect the behavior of a five-gram silicon chip, then there could easily be a billion other systems on the planet at risk of being touched by the very same flaw.

But there was worse to come.

The theory was, we'd located part of the boundary between two incompatible systems of mathematics—both of which were *physically true*, in their respective domains. Any sequence of deductions which stayed entirely on one side of the defect—whether it was the "near side", where conventional arithmetic applied, or the "far side", where the alternative took over—would be free from contradictions. But any sequence which crossed the border would give rise to absurdities—hence S could lead to not-S.

So, by examining a large number of chains of inference, some of which turned out to be self-contradictory and some not, it should have been possible to map the area around the defect precisely—to assign every statement to one system or the other.

Alison displayed the first map she'd made. It portrayed an elaborately crenelated fractal border, rather like the boundary between two microscopic ice crystals—as if the two systems had been diffusing out at random from different starting points, and then collided, blocking each other's way. By now, I was almost prepared to believe that I really was staring at a snapshot of the creation of mathematics—a fossil of primordial attempts to define the difference between truth and falsehood.

Then she produced a second map of the same set of statements, and overlaid the two. The defect, the border, had shifted—advancing in some places, retreating in others.

My blood went cold. "*That* has got to be a bug in the software."

"It's not."

I inhaled deeply, looking around the square—as if the heedless crowd of tourists and hawkers, shoppers and executives, might offer some simple "human" truth more resilient than mere arithmetic. But all I could think of was *1984*: Winston Smith, finally beaten into submission, abandoning every touchstone of reason by conceding that *two and two make five*.

I said, "Okay. Go on."

"In the early universe, some physical system must have tested out mathematics which was isolated, cut off from all the established results—leaving it free to decide the outcome at random. That's how the defect arose. But by now, *all* the mathematics in this region has been tested, all the gaps have been filled in. When a physical system tests a theorem on the near side, not only has it been tested a billion times before—but all the *logically adjacent* statements around it have been decided, and they imply the correct result in a single step."

"You mean . . . peer pressure from the neighbors? No inconsistencies allowed, you have to conform? If x−1 = y−1, and x+1 = y+1, then x is left with no choice but to equal y . . . because there's nothing 'nearby' to support the alternative?"

"Exactly. Truth is determined locally. And it's the same, deep into the far side. The alternative mathematics has dominated there, and every test takes place surrounded by established theorems which reinforce each other, and the 'correct'—non-standard—result."

"At the border, though—"

"At the border, every theorem you test is getting contradictory advice. From one neighbor, x−1 = y−1 . . . but from another, x+1 = y+2. And the topology of the border is so complex that a near-side theorem can have more far-side neighbors than near-side ones—and vice versa.

"So the truth at the border isn't fixed, even now. Both regions can still advance or retreat—*it all depends on the order in which the theorems are tested*. If a solidly near-side theorem is tested first, and it lends support to a more vulnerable neighbor, that can guarantee that they both stay near-side." She ran a brief animation which demonstrated the effect. "But if the order is reversed, the weaker one *will* fall."

I watched, light-headed. Obscure—but supposedly eternal—truths were tumbling like chess pieces. "And . . . you think that physical processes going on *right now*—chance molecular events which keep inadvertently testing and retesting different theories along the border—cause each side to gain and lose territory?"

"Yes."

"So there's been a kind of . . . random tide washing back and forth between the two kinds of mathematics, for the past few billion years?" I laughed uneasily, and did some rough calculations in my head. "The expectation value for a random walk is the square root of N. I don't think we have anything to worry about. The tide isn't going to wash over any useful arithmetic in the lifetime of the universe."

Alison smiled humorlessly, and held up the notepad again. "The tide? No. But it's the easiest thing in the world to dig a channel. To bias the random flow." She ran an animation of a sequence of tests which forced the far-side system to retreat across a small front—exploiting a "beach-head" formed by chance, and then pushing on to undermine a succession of theorems. "Industrial Algebra, though—I imagine—would be more interested in the reverse. Establishing a whole network of narrow channels of non-standard mathematics running deep into the realm of conventional arithmetic—which they could then deploy against theorems with practical consequences."

I fell silent, trying to imagine tendrils of contradictory arithmetic reaching down into the everyday world. No doubt IA would aim for surgical precision—hoping to earn themselves a few billion dollars by corrupting the specific mathematics underlying certain financial transactions. But the ramifications would be impossible to predict—or control. There'd be no way to limit the effect, spatially—they could target certain mathematical truths, but they couldn't confine the change to any one location. *A few billion dollars, a few billion neurons, a few billion stars . . . a few billion people.* Once the basic rules of counting were undermined, the most solid and distinct objects could be rendered as uncertain as swirls of fog. This was not a power I would have entrusted to a cross between Mother Theresa and Carl Friedrich Gauss.

"So what do we do? Erase the map—and just hope that IA never find the defect for themselves?"

"No." Alison seemed remarkably calm—but then, her own long-cherished philosophy had just been confirmed, not razed to the ground—and she'd had time on the flight from Zürich to think through all the *Realmathematik*. "There's only one way to be sure that they can never use this. We have to strike first. We have to get hold of enough computing power to map the entire defect. And then we either iron the border flat, so it *can't* move—if you amputate all the pincers, there can be no pincer movements. Or—better yet, if we can get the resources—we push the border in, from all directions, and shrink the far-side system down to nothing."

I hesitated. "All we've mapped so far is a tiny fragment of the defect. We don't know how large the far side could be. Except that it can't be small—or the random fluctuations would have swallowed it long ago. And it *could* go on forever; it could be infinite, for all we know."

Alison gave me a strange look. "You still don't get it, do you, Bruno? You're still thinking like a Platonist. The universe has only been around for fifteen billion years. It hasn't had time to create infinities. The far side *can't* go on forever—because somewhere beyond the defect, there are theorems which don't belong to *any* system. Theorems which have never been touched, never been tested, never been rendered true or false.

"And if we have to reach beyond the existing mathematics of the universe in order to surround the far side . . . then that's what we'll do. There's no reason why it shouldn't be possible—just so long as we get there first."

WHEN ALISON TOOK MY place, at one in the morning, I was certain I wouldn't get any sleep. When she shook me awake three hours later, I still felt like I hadn't.

I used my notepad to send a priming code to the data caches buried in our veins, and then we stood together side-by-side, left-shoulder-to-right-shoulder. The two chips recognized each other's magnetic and electrical signatures, interrogated each other to be sure—and then began radiating low power microwaves. Alison's note-pad picked up the transmission, and merged the two complementary data streams. The result was still heavily encrypted—but after all the precautions we'd taken so far, shifting the map into a hand-held computer felt about as secure as tattooing it onto our foreheads.

A taxi was waiting for us downstairs. The People's Institute for Advanced Optical Engineering was in Minhang, a sprawling technology park some thirty kilometers south of the city center. We rode in silence through the gray predawn light, past the giant ugly tower blocks thrown up by the landlords of the new millennium, riding out the fever as the necrotraps and their cargo dissolved into our blood.

As the taxi turned into an avenue lined with biotech and aerospace companies, Alison said, "If anyone asks, we're PhD students of Yuen's, testing a conjecture in algebraic topology."

"Now you tell me. I don't suppose you have any specific conjecture in mind? What if they ask us to elaborate?"

"On *algebraic topology*? At five o'clock in the morning?"

The Institute building was unimposing—sprawling black ceramic, three stories high—but there was a five-meter electrified fence, and the entrance was guarded by two armed soldiers. We paid the taxi driver and approached on foot. Yuen had supplied us with visitor's passes—complete with photographs and fingerprints. The names were our own; there was no point indulging in unnecessary deception. If we were caught out, pseudonyms would only make things worse.

The soldiers checked the passes, then led us through an MRI scanner. I forced myself to breathe calmly as we waited for the results; in theory, the scanner could have picked up our symbionts' foreign proteins, lingering breakdown products from the necrotraps, and a dozen other suspicious trace chemicals. But it all came down to a question of what they were looking for; magnetic resonance spectra for billions of molecules had been cataloged—but no machine could hunt for all of them at once.

One of the soldiers took me aside and asked me to remove my jacket. I fought down a wave of panic—and then struggled not to overcompensate: if I'd had nothing to hide, I would still have been nervous. He prodded the bandage on my upper arm; the surrounding skin was still red and inflamed.

"What's this?"

"I had a cyst there. My doctor cut it out, this morning."

He eyed me suspiciously, and peeled back the adhesive bandage—with ungloved hands. I couldn't bring myself to look; the repair cream should have sealed the wound completely—at worst there should have been old, dried blood—but I could *feel* a faint liquid warmth along the line of the incision.

The soldier laughed at my gritted teeth, and waved me away with an expression of distaste. I had no idea what he thought I might have been hiding—but I saw fresh red droplets beading the skin before I closed the bandage.

Yuen Ting-fu was waiting for us in the lobby. He was a slender, fit-looking man in his late sixties, casually dressed in denim. I let Alison do all the talking: apologizing for our lack of punctuality (although we weren't actually late), and thanking him effusively for granting us this precious opportunity to pursue our unworthy research. I stood back and tried to appear suitably deferential. Four soldiers looked on impassively; they didn't seem to find all this groveling excessive. And no doubt I would have been giddy with awe, if I really had been a student granted time here for some run-of-the-mill thesis.

We followed Yuen as he strode briskly through a second checkpoint and scanner (this time, no one stopped us) then down a long corridor with a soft gray vinyl floor. We passed a couple of white-coated technicians, but they barely gave us a second glance. I'd had visions of a pair of obvious foreigners attracting as much attention here as we would have wandering through a military base—but that was absurd. Half the runtime on Luminous was sold to foreign corporations—and because the machine was most definitely *not* linked to any communications network, commercial users had to come here in person. Just how often Yuen wangled free time for his students—whatever their nationality—was another question, but if he believed it was the best cover for us, I was in no position to argue. I only hoped he'd planted a seamless trail of reassuring lies in the university records and beyond, in case the Institute administration decided to check up on us in any detail.

We stopped in at the operations room, and Yuen chatted with the technicians. Banks of flatscreens covered one wall, displaying status histograms and engineering schematics. It looked like the control center for a small particle accelerator—which wasn't far from the truth.

Luminous was, literally, a computer made of light. It came into existence when a vacuum chamber, a cube five meters wide, was filled with an elaborate standing wave created by three vast arrays of high-powered lasers. A coherent electron beam was fed into the chamber—and just as a finely machined grating built of solid matter could diffract a beam of light, a sufficiently ordered (and sufficiently intense) configuration of light could diffract a beam of matter.

The electrons were redirected from layer to layer of the light cube, recombining and interfering at each stage, every change in their phase and intensity performing an appropriate computation— and the whole system could be reconfigured, nanosecond by nanosecond, into complex new "hardware" optimized for the calculations at hand. The auxiliary supercomputers controlling the laser arrays could design, and then instantly build, the perfect machine of light to carry out each particular stage of any program.

It was, of course, fiendishly difficult technology, incredibly expensive and temperamental. The chance of ever putting it on the desktops of Tetris-playing accountants was zero, so nobody in the West had bothered to pursue it.

And this cumbersome, unwieldy, impractical machine ran faster than all the pieces of silicon hanging off the Internet, combined.

We continued on to the programming room. At first glance, it might have been the computing center in a small primary school, with half a dozen perfectly ordinary work stations sitting on white formica tables. They just happened to be the only six in the world which were hooked up to Luminous.

We were alone with Yuen now—and Alison cut the protocol and just glanced briefly in his direction for approval, before hurriedly linking her notepad to one of the work stations and uploading the encrypted map. As she typed in the instructions to decode the file, all the images running through my head of what would have happened if I'd poisoned the soldier at the gate receded into insignificance. We now had half an hour to banish the defect—and we still had no idea how far it extended.

Yuen turned to me; the tension on his face betrayed his own anxieties, but he mused philosophically, "If our arithmetic seems to fail for these large numbers—does it mean the mathematics, the ideal, is really flawed and mutable—or only that the behavior of matter always falls short of the ideal?"

I replied, "If every class of physical objects 'falls short' in exactly the same way—whether it's boulders or electrons or abacus beads . . . what is it that their common behavior is obeying—or defining—if not the mathematics?"

He smiled, puzzled. "Alison seemed to think you were a Platonist."

"Lapsed. Or . . . defeated. I don't see what it can *mean* to talk about standard number theory still being true for these statements—in some vague Platonic sense—if no real objects can ever reflect that truth."

"We can still imagine it. We can still contemplate the abstraction. It's only the physical act of validation that must fall through. Think of transfinite arithmetic: no one can physically test the properties of Cantor's infinities, can they? We can only reason about them from afar."

I didn't reply. Since the revelations in Hanoi, I'd pretty much lost faith in my power to "reason from afar" about anything I couldn't personally describe with Arabic numerals on a single sheet of paper. Maybe Alison's idea of "local truth" was the most we could hope for; anything more ambitious was beginning to seem like the comic-book "physics" of swinging a rigid beam ten billion kilometers long around your head, and predicting that the far end would exceed the speed of light.

An image blossomed on the work station screen: it began as the familiar map of the defect—but Luminous was already extending it at a mind-boggling rate. Billions of inferential loops were being spun around the margins: some confirming their own premises, and thus delineating regions where a single, consistent mathematics held sway . . . others skewing into self-contradiction, betraying a border crossing. I tried to imagine what it would have been like to follow one of those Möbius-strips of deductive logic in my head; there were no difficult concepts involved, it was only the sheer size of the statements which made that impossible. But would the contradictions have driven me into gibbering insanity—or would I have found every step perfectly reasonable, and the conclusion simply unavoidable? Would I have ended up calmly, happily conceding: *Two and two make five?*

As the map grew—smoothly rescaled to keep it fitting on the screen, giving the unsettling impression that we were retreating from the alien mathematics as fast as we could and only just avoiding being swallowed—Alison sat hunched forward, waiting for the big picture to be revealed. The map portrayed the network of statements as an intricate lattice in three dimensions (a crude representational convention, but it was as good as any other). So far, the border between the regions showed no sign of overall curvature—just variously sized random incursions in both directions. For all we knew, it was possible that the far-side mathematics enclosed the near side completely—that the arithmetic we'd once believed stretched out to infinity was really no more than a tiny island in an ocean of contradictory truths.

I glanced at Yuen; he was watching the screen with undisguised pain. He said, "I read your software, and I thought: sure, this looks fine—but some glitch on your machines is the real explanation. Luminous will soon put you right."

Alison broke in jubilantly, "Look, it's turning!"

She was right. As the scale continued to shrink, the random fractal meanderings of the border were finally being subsumed by an overall convexity—a convexity of the far side. It was as if the viewpoint was backing away from a giant spiked sea-urchin. Within minutes, the map showed a crude hemisphere, decorated with elaborate crystalline extrusions at every scale. The sense of observing some palaeomathematical remnant was stronger than ever, now: this bizarre cluster of theorems really did look as if it had exploded out from some central premise into the vacuum of unclaimed truths, perhaps a billionth of a second after the Big Bang—only to be checked by an encounter with our own mathematics.

The hemisphere slowly extended into a three-quarters sphere . . . and then a spiked whole. The far side was bounded, finite. It was the island, not us.

Alison laughed uneasily. "Was that true before we started—or did we just make it true?" *Had the near side enclosed the far side for billions of years—or had Luminous broken new ground, actively extending the near side into mathematical territory which had never been tested by any physical system before?*

We'd never know. We'd designed the software to advance the mapping along a front in such a way that any unclaimed statements would be instantly recruited into the near side. If we'd reached out blindly, far into the void, we might have tested an isolated statement—and inadvertently spawned a whole new alternative mathematics to deal with.

Alison said, "Okay—now we have to decide. Do we try to seal the border—or do we take on the whole structure?" The software, I knew, was busy assessing the relative difficulty of the tasks.

Yuen replied at once, "Seal the border, nothing more. You mustn't destroy this." He turned to me, imploringly. "Would you smash up a fossil of *Australopithecus*? Would you wipe the cosmic background radiation out of the sky? This may shake the foundations of all my beliefs—but it encodes the truth about our history. We have no right to obliterate it, like vandals."

Alison eyed me nervously. *What was this—majority rule?* Yuen was the only one with any power here; he could pull the plug in an instant. And yet it was clear from his demeanor that he wanted a consensus—he wanted our moral support for any decision.

I said cautiously, "If we smooth the border, that'll make it literally impossible for IA to exploit the defect, won't it?"

Alison shook her head. "We don't know that. There may be a quantum-like component of spontaneous defections, even for statements which appear to be in perfect equilibrium."

Yuen countered, "Then there could be spontaneous defections *anywhere*—even far from any border. Erasing the whole structure will guarantee nothing."

"It will guarantee that IA won't find it! Maybe pin-point defections *do* occur, all the time—but the next time they're tested, they'll always revert. They're surrounded by explicit contradictions, they have no chance of getting a foothold. You can't compare a few transient glitches with this . . . *armory* of counter-mathematics!"

The defect bristled on the screen like a giant caltrop. Alison and Yuen both turned to me expectantly. As I opened my mouth, the work station chimed. The software had examined the alternatives in detail: destroying the entire far side would take Luminous twenty-three minutes and seventeen seconds—about a minute less than the time we had left. Sealing the border would take more than an hour.

I said, "That can't be right."

Alison groaned. "But it is! There's random interference going on at the border from other systems all the time—and doing anything finicky there means coping with that noise, fighting it. Charging ahead and pushing the border inward is different: you can exploit the noise to speed the advance. It's not a question of *dealing with a mere surface* versus *dealing with a whole volume.* It's more like . . . trying to carve an island into an absolutely perfect circle, while waves are constantly crashing on the beach—versus bulldozing the whole thing into the ocean."

We had thirty seconds to decide—or we'd be doing neither today. And maybe Yuen had the resources to keep the map safe from IA, while we waited a month or more for another session on Luminous—but I wasn't prepared to live with that kind of uncertainty.

"I say we get rid of the whole thing. Anything less is too dangerous. Future mathematicians will still be able to study the map—and if no one believes that the defect itself ever really existed, that's just too bad. IA are too close. We can't risk it."

Alison had one hand poised above the keyboard. I turned to Yuen; he was staring at the floor with an anguished expression. He'd let us state our views—but in the end, it was his decision.

He looked up, and spoke sadly but decisively.

"Okay. Do it."

Alison hit the key—with about three seconds to spare. I sagged into my chair, light-headed with relief.

WE WATCHED THE FAR side shrinking. The process didn't look quite as crass as *bulldozing an island*—more like dissolving some quirkily beautiful crystal in acid. Now that the danger was receding before our eyes, though, I was beginning to suffer faint pangs of regret. Our mathematics had coexisted with this strange anomaly for fifteen billion years, and it shamed me to think that within months of its discovery, we'd backed ourselves into a corner where we'd had no choice but to destroy it.

Yuen seemed transfixed by the process. "So are we breaking the laws of physics—or enforcing them?"

Alison said, "Neither. We're merely changing what the laws imply."

He laughed softly. "'Merely.' For some esoteric set of complex systems, we're rewriting the high-level rules of their behavior. Not including the human brain, I hope."

My skin crawled. "Don't you think that's . . . unlikely?"

"I was joking." He hesitated, then added soberly, "Unlikely for humans—but *someone* could be relying on this, somewhere. We might be destroying the whole basis of their existence: certainties as fundamental to them as a child's multiplication tables are to us."

Alison could barely conceal her scorn. "This is junk mathematics—a relic of a pointless accident. Any kind of life which evolved from simple to complex forms would have no use for it. Our mathematics works for . . . rocks, seeds, animals in the herd, members of the tribe. *This* only kicks in beyond the number of particles in the universe—"

"Or smaller systems which represent those numbers," I reminded her.

"And you think life somewhere might have a burning need to do *non-standard trans-astronomical arithmetic*, in order to survive? I doubt that very much."

We fell silent. Guilt and relief could fight it out later, but no one suggested halting the program. In the end, maybe nothing could outweigh the havoc the defect would have caused if it had ever been harnessed as a weapon—and I was looking forward to composing a long message to Industrial Algebra, informing them of precisely what we'd done to the object of their ambitions.

Alison pointed to a corner of the screen. "What's that?" A narrow dark spike protruded from the shrinking cluster of statements. For a moment I thought it was merely avoiding the near side's assault— but it wasn't. It was slowly, steadily growing longer.

"Could be a bug in the mapping algorithm." I reached for the keyboard and zoomed in on the structure. In close-up, it was several thousand statements wide. At its border, Alison's program could be seen in action, testing statements in an order designed to force tendrils of the near side ever deeper into the interior. This slender extrusion, ringed by contradictory mathematics, should have been corroded out of existence in a fraction of a second. Something was actively countering the assault, though—repairing every trace of damage before it could spread.

"If IA have a bug here—" I turned to Yuen. "They couldn't take on Luminous directly, so they couldn't stop the whole far side shrinking—but a tiny structure like this . . . what do you think? Could they stabilize it?"

"Perhaps," he conceded. "Four or five hundred top-speed work stations could do it."

Alison was typing frantically on her notepad. She said, "I'm writing a patch to identify any systematic interference—and divert all our resources against it." She brushed her hair out of her eyes. "Look over my shoulder will you, Bruno? Check me as I go."

"Okay." I read through what she'd written so far. "You're doing fine. Stay calm." Her hands were trembling.

The spike continued to grow steadily. By the time the patch was ready, the map was rescaling constantly to fit it on the screen.

Alison triggered the patch. An overlay of electric blue appeared along the spike, flagging the concentration of computing power— and the spike abruptly froze.

I held my breath, waiting for IA to notice what we'd done— and switch their resources elsewhere? If they did, no second spike would appear—they'd never get that far—but the blue marker on the screen would shift to the site where they'd regrouped and tried to make it happen.

But the blue glow didn't move from the existing spike. And the spike didn't vanish under the weight of Luminous's undivided efforts.

Instead, it began to grow again, slowly.

Yuen looked ill. "This is *not* Industrial Algebra. There's no computer on the planet—"

Alison laughed derisively. "What are you saying now? Aliens who need the far side are defending it? Aliens *where?* Nothing we've done has had time to reach even . . . Jupiter." There was an edge of hysteria in her voice.

"Have you measured how fast the changes propagate? Do you know, for certain, that they can't travel faster than light—with the far-side mathematics undermining the logic of relativity?"

I said, "Whoever it is, they're not defending all their borders. They're putting everything they've got into the spike."

"They're aiming at something. A specific target." Yuen reached over Alison's shoulder for the keyboard. "We're shutting this down. Right now."

She turned on him, blocking his way. "Are you crazy? We're almost holding them off! I'll rewrite the program, fine-tune it, get an edge in efficiency—"

"No! We stop threatening them, then see how they react. We don't know what harm we're doing—"

He reached for the keyboard again.

Alison jabbed him in the throat with her elbow, hard. He staggered backward, gasping for breath, then crashed to the floor, bringing a chair down on top of him. She hissed at me, "Quick—shut him up!"

I hesitated, loyalties fracturing; his idea had sounded perfectly sane to me. But if he started yelling for security—

I crouched down over him, pushed the chair aside, then clasped my hand over his mouth, forcing his head back with pressure on the lower jaw. We'd have to tie him up—and then try brazenly marching out of the building without him. But he'd be found in a matter of minutes. Even if we made it past the gate, we were screwed.

Yuen caught his breath and started struggling; I clumsily pinned his arms with my knees. I could hear Alison typing, a ragged staccato; I tried to get a glimpse of the work station screen, but I couldn't turn that far without taking my weight off Yuen.

I said, "Maybe he's right—maybe we should pull back, and see what happens." *If the alterations could propagate faster than light . . . how many distant civilizations might have felt the effects of what we'd done?* Our first contact with extraterrestrial life could turn out to be an attempt to obliterate mathematics which they viewed as . . . what? A precious resource? A sacred relic? An essential component of their entire world view?

The sound of typing stopped abruptly. "Bruno? Do you feel—?"

"What?"

Silence.

"*What?*"

Yuen seemed to have given up the fight. I risked turning around.

Alison was hunched forward, her face in her hands. On the screen, the spike had ceased its relentless linear growth—but now an elaborate dendritic structure had blossomed at its tip. I glanced down at Yuen; he seemed dazed, oblivious to my presence. I took my hand from his mouth, warily. He lay there placidly, smiling faintly, eyes scanning something I couldn't see.

I climbed to my feet. I took Alison by the shoulders and shook her gently; her only response was to press her face harder into her hands. The spike's strange flower was still growing—but it wasn't spreading out into new territory; it was sending narrow shoots back in on itself, crisscrossing the same region again and again with ever finer structures.

Weaving a net? Searching for something?

It hit me with a jolt of clarity more intense than anything I'd felt since childhood. It was like reliving the moment when the whole concept of *numbers* had finally snapped into place—but with an adult's understanding of everything it opened up, everything it implied. It was a lightning-bolt revelation—but there was no taint of mystical confusion: no opiate haze of euphoria, no pseudo-sexual rush. In the clean-lined logic of the simplest concepts, I saw and understood exactly how the world worked—

—except that it was all wrong, it was all false, it was all impossible. *Quicksand.*

Assailed by vertigo, I swept my gaze around the room—counting frantically: *Six work stations. Two people. Six chairs.* I grouped the work stations: three sets of two, two sets of three. One and five, two and four; four and two, five and one.

I weaved a dozen cross-checks for consistency—*for sanity* . . . but everything added up.

They hadn't stolen the old arithmetic; they'd merely blasted the new one into my head, on top of it.

Whoever had resisted our assault with Luminous had reached down with the spike and rewritten our neural metamathematics— the arithmetic which underlay our own reasoning *about* arithmetic—enough to let us glimpse what we'd been trying to destroy.

Alison was still uncommunicative, but she was breathing slowly and steadily. Yuen seemed fine, lost in a happy reverie. I relaxed slightly, and began trying to make sense of the flood of far-side arithmetic surging through my brain.

On their own terms, the axioms were . . . trivial, obvious. I could see that they corresponded to elaborate statements about trans-astronomical integers, but performing an exact translation was far beyond me—and thinking about the entities they described in terms of the huge integers they represented was a bit like thinking about *pi* or *the square root of two* in terms of the first ten thousand digits of their decimal expansion: it would be missing the point entirely. These alien "numbers"—the basic objects of the alternative arithmetic—had found a way to embed themselves in the integers, and to relate to each other in a simple, elegant way—and if the messy corollaries they implied upon translation contradicted the rules integers were supposed to obey . . . well, only a small, remote patch of obscure truths had been subverted.

Someone touched me on the shoulder. I started—but Yuen was beaming amiably, all arguments and violence forgotten.

He said, "Lightspeed is *not* violated. All the logic which requires that remains intact." I could only take him at his word; the result would have taken me hours to prove. Maybe the aliens had done a better job on him—or maybe he was just a superior mathematician in either system.

"Then . . . where are they?" At lightspeed, our attack on the far side could not have been felt any further away than Mars—and the strategy used to block the corrosion of the spike would have been impossible with even a few seconds' time lag.

"The atmosphere?"

"You mean—*Earth's?*"

"Where else? Or maybe the oceans."

I sat down heavily. Maybe it was no stranger than any conceivable alternative, but I still balked at the implications.

Yuen said, "To us, their structure wouldn't look like 'structure' at all. The simplest unit might involve a group of thousands of atoms—representing a trans-astronomical number—not necessarily even *bonded together* in any conventional way, but breaking the normal consequences of the laws of physics, obeying a different set of high-level rules which arise from the alternative mathematics. People have often mused about the chances of intelligence being coded into long-lived vortices on distant gas giants . . . but *these* creatures won't be in hurricanes or tornadoes. They'll be drifting in the most innocuous puffs of air—invisible as neutrinos."

"Unstable—"

"Only according to our mathematics. Which does not apply."

Alison broke in suddenly, angrily. "Even if all of this is true—where does it get us? Whether the defect supports a whole invisible ecosystem or not—IA will still find it, and use it, in exactly the same way."

For a moment I was dumbstruck. *We were facing the prospect of sharing the planet with an undiscovered civilization—and all she could think about was IA's grubby machinations?*

She was absolutely right, though. Long before any of these extravagant fantasies could be proved or disproved, IA could still do untold harm.

I said, "Leave the mapping software running—but shut down the shrinker."

She glanced at the screen. "No need. They've overpowered it—or undermined its mathematics." The far side was back to its original size.

"Then there's nothing to lose. Shut it down."

She did. No longer under attack, the spike began to reverse its growth. I felt a pang of loss as my limited grasp of the far-side mathematics suddenly evaporated; I tried to hold on, but it was like clutching at air.

When the spike had retracted completely, I said, "Now we try doing an Industrial Algebra. We try bringing the defect closer."

We were almost out of time, but it was easy enough—in thirty seconds, we rewrote the shrinking algorithm to function in reverse.

Alison programmed a function key with the commands to revert to the original version—so that if the experiment backfired, one keystroke would throw the full weight of Luminous behind a defense of the near side again.

Yuen and I exchanged nervous glances. I said, "Maybe this wasn't such a good idea."

Alison disagreed. "We need to know how they'll react to this. Better we find out now than leave it to IA."

She started the program running.

The sea-urchin began to swell, slowly. I broke out in a sweat. The far-siders hadn't harmed us, so far—but this felt like tugging hard at a door which you really, badly, didn't want to see thrown open.

A technician poked her head into the room and announced cheerfully, "Down for maintenance in two minutes!"

Yuen said, "I'm sorry, there's nothing—"

The whole far side turned electric blue. Alison's original patch had detected a systematic intervention.

We zoomed in. Luminous was picking off vulnerable statements of the near side—but something else was repairing the damage.

I let out a strangled noise that might have been a cheer. Alison smiled serenely. She said, "I'm satisfied. IA don't stand a chance."

Yuen mused, "Maybe they have a reason to defend the status quo—maybe they rely on the border itself, as much as the far side."

Alison shut down our reversed shrinker. The blue glow vanished; both sides were leaving the defect alone. And there were a thousand questions we all wanted answered—but the technicians had thrown the master switch, and Luminous itself had ceased to exist.

THE SUN WAS BREAKING through the skyline as we rode back into the city. As we pulled up outside the hotel, Alison started shaking and sobbing. I sat beside her, squeezing her hand. I knew she'd felt the weight of what might have happened, all along, far more than I had.

I paid the driver, and then we stood on the street for a while, silently watching the cyclists go by, trying to imagine how the world would change as it endeavored to embrace this new contradiction between the exotic and the mundane, the pragmatic and the Platonic, the visible and the invisible.

SILVER FIRE

I WAS IN MY OFFICE at home, grading papers for Epidemiology 410, when the call came through from John Brecht in Maryland. Real-time, not a polite message to be dealt with whenever I chose. I'd grown into the habit of thinking of Colonel Brecht as "my old boss." Apparently that had been premature.

He said, "We've found a little Silver Fire anomaly which I think might interest you, Claire. A little blip on the autocorrelation transform which just won't go away. And seeing as you're on vacation—"

"*My students* are on vacation. I still have work to do."

"Oh, I think Columbia can find someone to take over those menial tasks for a week or two."

I regarded him in silence for a moment, trying to decide whether or not to tell him to find someone else to take over his own *menial tasks*.

I said, "What exactly are we talking about?"

Brecht smiled. "A faint trail. Hovering on the verge of signifi-cance. Your specialty." A map appeared on the screen; his face shrank to an inset. "It seems to start in North Carolina, around Greensboro, heading west." The map was peppered with dots marking the loca-tions of recent Silver Fire cases—color-coded by the time elapsed since a notional "day of infection", the dots themselves positioned wherever the patient had been at the time. Having been told exactly what to look for, I could just make out a vague spectral progression cutting through the scattered blossoms of localized outbreaks: a kind of smudged rainbow trail from red to violet, dissolving into uncertainty just west of Knoxville, Tennessee. Then again . . . if I squinted, I could discern another structure, about as convincing, sweeping down in an amazingly perfect arc from Kentucky. A few more minutes, and I'd see the hidden face of Groucho Marx. The human brain is far too good at finding patterns; without rigorous statistical tools we're helpless, animists grasping at meaning in every random puff of air.

I said, "So how do the numbers look?"

"The P value's borderline," Brecht conceded. "But I still think it's worth checking out."

The visible part of this hypothetical trail spanned at least ten days. *Three days* after exposure to the virus, the average person was either dead or in intensive care—not driving blithely across the countryside. Maps tracing the precise routes of infection generally looked like random walks with mean free paths five or ten kilometers long; even air travel, at worst, tended to spawn a multitude of scattered small outbreaks. If we'd stumbled on someone who was infectious but asymptomatic, then that was definitely *worth checking out*.

Brecht said, "As of now, you have full access to the notifications database. I'd offer you our provisional analysis—but I'm sure you can do better with the raw data, yourself."

"No doubt."

"Good. Then you can leave tomorrow."

I WOKE BEFORE DAWN and packed in ten minutes, while Alex lay cursing me in his sleep. Then I realized I had three hours to kill, and absolutely nothing left to do, so I crawled back into bed. When I woke for the second time, Alex and Laura were both up, and eating breakfast.

As I sat down opposite Laura, though, I wondered if I was dreaming: one of those insidiously reassuring no-need-to-wake-because-you-already-have dreams. My fourteen-year-old daughter's face and arms were covered in alchemical and zodiacal symbols in iridescent reds, greens and blues. She looked like a character in some dire VR-as-psychedelia movie who'd been mauled by the special effects software.

She stared back at me defiantly, as if I'd somehow expressed disapproval. In fact, I hadn't yet worked my way around to such a mundane emotion—and by the time I did, I kept my mouth firmly shut. Knowing Laura, these were definitely not fakes which would wash off—but transdermal enzyme patches could still erase them as bloodlessly as the dye-bearing ones which had implanted them. So I was good, I didn't say a word: no cheap reverse-psychology ("Oh, aren't they *sweet?*"), no (honest) complaints about the harassment I'd get from her principal if they weren't gone by the start of term.

Laura said, "Did you know that Isaac Newton spent more time on alchemy than he did on the theory of gravity?"

"Yes. Did you know he also died a virgin? Role models are great, aren't they?"

Alex gave me a sideways warning look, but didn't buy in. Laura continued, "There's a whole secret history of science that's been censored from the official accounts. Hidden knowledge that's only coming to light now that everyone has access to the original sources."

It was hard to know how to respond honestly to this without groaning aloud. I said evenly, "I think you'll find that most of it has actually 'come to light' before. It's just turned out to be of limited interest. But sure, it's fascinating to see some of the blind alleys people have explored."

Laura smiled at me pityingly. "*Blind alleys!*" She finished picking the toast crumbs off her plate, then she rose and left the room with a spring in her step, as if she'd won some kind of battle.

I said plaintively, "What did I miss? When did all this start?"

Alex was unfazed. "I think it's mostly just the music. Or rather, three seventeen-year-old boys with supernaturally perfect skin and big brown contact lenses, called The Alchemists—"

"Yes, I *know* the band—but New Hermetics is more than the bubblegum music, it's a major cult—"

He laughed. "Oh, come on! Wasn't your sister deeply in lust with the lead singer of some quasi-Satanic heavy metal group? I don't recall her ending up nailing black cats to upside-down crucifixes."

"That was never *lust*. She just wanted to discover his hair-care secrets."

Alex said firmly, "Laura is fine. Just . . . relax and sit it out. Unless you want to buy her a copy of *Foucault's Pendulum*?"

"She'd probably miss the irony."

He prodded me on the arm; mock-violence, but genuine anger. "*That's* unfair. She'll chew up New Hermetics and spit it out in . . . six months, at the most. How long did Scientology last? A week?"

I said, "*Scientology* is crass, transparent gibberish. New Hermetics has five thousand years of cultural adornment to draw on. It's every bit as insidious as Buddhism or Catholicism: there's a tradition, there's a whole esthetic—"

Alex cut in, "Yes—and in six months' time, she'll understand: the esthetic can be appreciated without swallowing any of the bullshit. Just because alchemy was a blind alley, that doesn't mean it isn't still elegant and fascinating . . . but *being* elegant and fascinating doesn't render a word of it true."

I reflected on that for a while, then I leaned over and kissed him. "I hate it when you're right: you always make it sound so obvious. I'm too damn protective, aren't I? She'll work it all out for herself."

"You know she will."

I glanced at my watch. "*Shit*. Can you drive me to La Guardia? I'm never going to get a cab, now."

EARLY IN THE PANDEMIC, I'd pulled a few strings and arranged for a group of my students to observe a Silver Fire patient close up. It had seemed wrong to bury ourselves in the abstractions of maps and graphs, numerical models and extrapolations—however vital they were to the battle—without witnessing the real physical condition of an individual human being.

We didn't have to don biohazard suits; the young man lay in a glass-walled, hermetically sealed room. Tubes brought him oxygen, water, electrolytes and nutrients—along with antibiotics, antipyretics, immunosuppressants, and pain killers. No bed, no mattress; the patient was embedded in a transparent polymer gel: a kind of buoyant semi-solid which limited pressure sores and drew away the blood and lymphatic fluid weeping out through what used to be his skin.

I surprised myself by crying, silently and briefly, hot tears of anger. Rage dissipating into a vacuum; I knew there was no one to blame. Half the students had medical degrees—but if anything, they seemed more shaken than the green statisticians who'd never set foot in a trauma ward or an operating theater—probably because they could better imagine what the man would have been feeling without a skull full of opiates.

The official label for the condition was Systemic Fibrotic Viral Scleroderma—but SFVS was unpronounceable, and apparently people's eyes glazed over if news readers spelled out four whole letters. I used the new name like everyone else—but I never stopped loathing it. It was too fucking poetic by far.

When the Silver Fire virus infected fibroblasts in the subcutaneous connective tissue, it caused them to go into overdrive, manufacturing vast quantities of collagen—in a variant form transcribed from the normal gene but imperfectly assembled. This denatured protein formed solid plaques in the extracellular space, disrupting the nutrient flow to the dermis above—and eventually becoming so bulky as to shear it off completely. Silver Fire flayed you from within. A good strategy for releasing large amounts of virus, maybe—though when it had stumbled on the trick, no one knew. The presumed animal host in which the parent strain lived, benignly or otherwise, was yet to be found.

If the lymph-glistening sickly white of naked collagen plaques was "silver", the fever, the autoimmune response, and the sensation of being burned alive was "fire." Mercifully, the pain couldn't last long, either way. The standard First World palliative treatment included constant deep anesthesia—and if you didn't get that level of high-tech intervention, you went into shock, fast, and died.

Two years after the first outbreaks, the origin of the virus remained unknown, a vaccine was still a remote prospect—and though patients could be kept alive almost indefinitely, all attempts to effect a cure by purging the body of the virus and grafting cultured skin had failed.

Four hundred thousand people had been infected, worldwide; nine out of ten were dead. Ironically, rapid onset due to malnutrition had all but eliminated Silver Fire in the poorest nations; most outbreaks in Africa had burned themselves out on the spot. The US not only had more hospitalized victims on life support, per capita, than any other nation; it was heading for the top of the list in the rate of new cases.

A handshake or even a ride in a packed bus could transmit the virus—with a low probability for each contact event, but it added up. The only thing that helped in the medium term was isolating potential carriers—and to date it had seemed that no one could remain infectious and healthy for long. If the "trail" Brecht's computers had found was more than a statistical mirage, cutting it short might save dozens of lives—and understanding it might save thousands.

IT WAS ALMOST NOON when the plane touched down at the Triad airport on the outskirts of Greensboro. There was a hire car waiting for me; I waved my notepad at the dashboard to transmit my profile, then waited as the seating and controls rearranged themselves slightly, piezoelectric actuators humming. As I started to reverse out of the parking bay, the stereo began a soothing improvisation, flashing up a deadpan title: *Music for Leaving Airports on June 11, 2008.*

I got a shock driving into town: there were dozens of large plots of tobacco visible from the road. The born-again weed was encroaching everywhere, and not even the suburbs were safe. The irony had become clichéd, but it was still something to witness the reality firsthand: even as nicotine was finally going the way of absinthe, more tobacco was being cultivated than ever before—because tobacco mosaic virus had turned out to be an extremely convenient and efficient vector for introducing new genes. The leaves of these plants would be loaded with pharmaceuticals or vaccine antigens—and worth twenty times as much as their unmodified ancestors at the height of demand.

My first appointment was still almost an hour away, so I drove around town in search of lunch. I'd been so wound up since Brecht's call, I was surprised at just how good I felt to have arrived. Maybe it was no more than traveling south, with the sudden slight shift in the angle of the light—a kind of beneficent latitudinal equivalent of jet lag. Certainly, everything in downtown Greensboro appeared positively luminous after NYC, with modern buildings in pastel shades looking curiously harmonious beside the gleamingly preserved historic ones.

I ended up eating sandwiches in a small diner—and going through my notes again, obsessively. It was seven years since I'd done anything like this for real, and I'd had little time to make the mental transition from theoretician back to practitioner.

There'd been four new cases of Silver Fire in Greensboro in the preceding fortnight. Health authorities everywhere had long ago given up trying to establish the path of infection for every last case; given the ease of transmission, and the inability to question the patients themselves, it was a massively labor-intensive process which yielded few tangible benefits. The most useful strategy wasn't backtracking, but rather quarantining the family, workmates and other known contacts of each new case, for about a week. Carriers were infectious for two or three days at the most before becoming—very obviously—sick themselves; you didn't need to go looking for them. Brecht's rainbow trail either meant an exception to this rule . . . or a ripple of new cases propagating from town to town without any single carrier.

Greensboro's population was about a quarter of a million— though it depended on exactly where you drew the boundaries. North Carolina had never gone in much for implosive urbanization; growth in rural areas had actually outstripped growth in the major cities in recent years, and the microvillage movement had taken off here in a big way—at least as much as on the west coast.

I displayed a contoured population density map of the region on my notepad; even Raleigh, Charlotte and Greensboro were only modest elevations against the gently undulating background of the countryside—and only the Appalachians themselves cut a deep trench through this inverted topography. Hundreds of small new communities dotted the map, between the already numerous established towns. The microvillages weren't literally self-sustaining, but they were definitely high-tech Green, with photovoltaics, small-scale local water treatment, and satellite links in lieu of connections to any centralized utilities. Most of their income came from cottage service industries: software, design, music, animation.

I switched on an overlay showing the estimated magnitude of population flows, on the timescale relevant to Silver Fire. The major roads and highways glowed white hot, and the small towns were linked into the skein by their own slender capillaries . . . but the microvillages all but vanished from the scene: everyone worked from home. So it wasn't all that unlikely for a random Silver Fire outbreak to have spread straight down the interstate, rather than diffusing in a classic drunkard's walk across this relatively populous landscape.

Still . . . the whole point of being here was to find out the one thing that none of the computer models could tell me: whether or not the assumptions they were based on were dangerously flawed.

I LEFT THE DINER and set to work. The four cases came from four separate families; I was in for a long day.

All the people I interviewed were out of quarantine, but still suffering various degrees of shock. Silver Fire hit like an express train: there was no time to grasp what was happening before a perfectly healthy child or parent, spouse or lover, all but died in front of your eyes. The last thing you needed was a two-hour interrogation by a total stranger.

It was dusk by the time I reached the last family—and any joy I'd felt at being back in the field had long since worn off. I sat in the car for a minute, staring at the immaculate garden and lace curtains, listening to the crickets, wishing I didn't have to go in and face these people.

Diane Clayton taught high school mathematics; her husband, Ed, was an engineer, working night shifts for the local power company. They had a thirteen-year-old daughter, Cheryl. Mike, eighteen, was in the hospital.

I sat with the three of them, but it was Ms Clayton who did most of the talking. She was scrupulously patient and courteous with me—but after a while, it became clear that she was still in a kind of daze. She answered every question slowly and thoughtfully—but I had no idea if she really knew what she was saying, or whether she was just going through the motions on autopilot.

Mike's father wasn't much help, since the shift work had kept him out of synch with the rest of the family. I tried increasing eye contact with Cheryl, encouraging her to speak. It was absurd, but I felt guilty even as I did it—as if I'd come here to sell the family some junk product, and now I was trying to bypass parental resistance.

"So . . . Tuesday night he definitely stayed home?" I was filling in a chart of Mike Clayton's movements for the week before symptoms appeared—hour-by-hour. It was a fastidious, nit-picking Gestapo routine that made the old days of merely asking for a list of sexual partners and fluids exchanged seem positively idyllic.

"Yes, that's right." Diane Clayton screwed her eyes shut and ran through her memories of the night again. "I watched some television with Cheryl, then went to bed around . . . eleven. Mike must have been in his room all the time." He'd been on vacation from UNC Greensboro, with no reason to spend his evenings studying—but he might have been socializing electronically, or watching a movie.

Cheryl glanced at me uncertainly, then said shyly, "I think he went out."

Her mother turned to her, frowning. "Tuesday night? No!"

I asked Cheryl, "Do you have any idea where?"

"Some nightclub, I think."

"He said that?"

She shrugged. "He was dressed for it."

"But he didn't say where?"

"No."

"Could it have been somewhere else? A friend's place? A party?" My information was that no nightclubs in Greensboro were open on Tuesdays.

Cheryl thought it over. "He said he was going dancing. That's all he said."

I turned back to Diane Clayton; she was clearly upset at being cut out of the discussion. "Do you know who he might have gone with?"

If Mike was in a steady relationship he hadn't mentioned the fact, but she gave me the names of three old school friends. She kept apologizing to me for her "negligence."

I said, "It's all right. Really. No one can remember every last detail."

She was still distraught when I left, an hour later. Her son leaving the house without telling her—or the fact that he'd told her, and it had slipped her mind—was now (somehow) the reason for the whole tragedy.

I felt partly to blame for her distress, myself—though I didn't see how I could have handled things any differently. The hospital would have offered her expert counseling—that wasn't my job at all. And there was sure to be more of the same ahead; if I started taking it personally, I'd be a wreck in a matter of days.

I managed to track down all three friends before eleven—about the latest I dared call anyone—but none of them had been with Mike on Tuesday night, or had any idea where he'd been. They helped me cross-check some other details, though. I ended up sitting in the car making calls for almost two hours.

Maybe there'd been a party, maybe there hadn't. Maybe it had been a pretext for something else; the possibilities were endless. Blank spots on the charts were a matter of course; I could have spent a month in Greensboro trying to fill them all in, without success. If the hypothetical carrier *had* been at this hypothetical party (and the other three members of the Greensboro Four definitely hadn't— they were all accounted for on the night) I'd just have to pick up the trail further on.

I checked into a motel and lay awake for a while, listening to the traffic on the interstate. Thinking of Alex and Laura—and trying to imagine the unimaginable.

But it couldn't happen to them. They were mine. I'd protect them.

How? By moving to Antarctica?

Silver Fire was rarer than cancer, rarer than heart disease, rarer than death by automobile. Rarer than gunshot wounds, in some cities. But there was no strategy for avoiding it—short of complete physical isolation.

And Diane Clayton was now torturing herself for failing to keep her eighteen-year-old son locked up for the summer vacation. Asking herself, over and over: *What did I do wrong? Why did this happen? What am I being punished for?*

I should have taken her aside, looked her squarely in the eye, and reminded her: "This is not your fault! There's nothing you could have done to prevent it!"

I should have said: *It just happened. People suffer like this for no reason. There is no sense to be made of your son's ruined life. There is no meaning to be found here. Just a random dance of molecules.*

I WOKE EARLY AND skipped breakfast; I was on the I-40, heading west, by seven thirty. I drove straight past Winston-Salem; a couple of people had been infected there recently—but not recently enough to be part of the trail.

Sleep had taken the edge off my pessimism. The morning was cool and clear, and the countryside was stunning—or at least, it was where it hadn't been turned over to monotonous biotech crops, or worse: golf courses.

Still, some things had definitely changed for the better. It was on the I-40—more than twenty years before—that I'd first heard a radio evangelist preaching the eighties' gospel of hate: AIDS as God's instrument, HIV as the righteous virus sent down from Heaven to smite adulterers, junkies and faggots. (I'd been young and hot-headed, then; I'd pulled off at the next exit, phoned the radio station, and heaped abuse on some poor receptionist.) But proponents of this subtle theology had fallen curiously silent ever since an immortalized cell line derived from the bone marrow of a Kenyan prostitute had proved more than a match for the omnipotent deity's secret weapon. And if Christian fundamentalism wasn't exactly dead and buried, its power base had certainly gone into decline; the kind of ignorance and insularity it relied upon seemed to be becoming almost impossible to sustain against the tide of information.

Local audio had long since shifted to the net, of course, evangelists and all; the old frequencies had fallen silent. And I was out of range of cellular contact with the beast with 20,000 channels . . . but the car did have a satellite link. I switched on my notepad, hoping for some light relief.

I'd programmed Ariadne, my knowledge miner, to scan all available media outlets for references to Silver Fire. Maybe it was sheer masochism, but there was something perversely fascinating about the distorted shadow the real pandemic cast in the shallows of media space: rumors and misinformation, hysteria, exploitation.

The tabloid angles, as always, were predictably inane: Silver Fire was a disease from space / the inevitable result of fluoridation / the reason half a dozen celebrities had disappeared from the public gaze. Three false modes of transmission were on offer: today it was tampons, Mexican orange juice, and mosquitoes (again). Several young victims with attractive "before" shots and family members willing to break down on camera had been duly rounded up. New century, same old fox shit.

The most bizarre item in Ariadne's latest sweep wasn't classic tabloid at all, though. It was an interview on a program called *The Terminal Chat Show* (23:00 GMT, Thursdays, on Britain's Channel 4) with a Canadian academic, James Springer, who was touring the UK (in the flesh) to promote his new hypertext, *The Cyber Sutras*.

Springer was a balding, middle-aged, avuncular man. He was introduced as Associate Professor of Theory at McGill University; apparently only the hopelessly reductionist asked: "Theory of *what?*" His area of expertise was described as "computers and spirituality"— but for reasons I couldn't quite fathom, his opinion was sought on Silver Fire.

"The crucial thing," he insisted smoothly, "is that Silver Fire is the very first plague of the Information Age. AIDS was certainly post-industrial and post-modernist, but its onset predated the emergence of true Information Age cultural sensibilities. AIDS, for me, embodied the whole negative zeitgeist of Western materialism confronting its inevitable *fin de siècle* crisis of confidence—but with Silver Fire, I think we're free to embrace far more positive metaphors for this so-called 'disease.'"

The interviewer inquired warily, "So . . . you're hopeful that Silver Fire victims will be spared the stigmatization and hysteria that accompanied AIDS?"

Springer nodded cheerfully. "Of course! We've made enormous strides forward in cultural analysis since those days! I mean, if Burroughs' *Cities of the Red Night* had only penetrated the collective subconscious more fully when it appeared, the whole course of the AIDS plague might have been radically different—and that's a hot topic in Uchronic Studies which one of my doctoral students is currently pursuing. But there's no doubt that Information Age cultural forms have fully prepared us for Silver Fire. When I look at global techno-anarchist raves, trading-card tattoo body comics, and affordable desktop implementations of the Dalai Lama . . . it's clear to me that Silver Fire is a sequence of RNA whose time has come. If it didn't exist, we'd have to synthesize it!"

MY NEXT STOP WAS a town called Statesville. A brother and sister in their late teens, Ben and Lisa Walker, and the sister's boyfriend, Paul Scott, were in hospital in Winston-Salem. The families had only just returned home.

Lisa and Ben had been living with their widower father and a nine-year-old brother. Lisa had worked in a local store, alongside the owner—who'd remained symptom-free. Ben had worked in a vaccine-extraction plant, and Paul Scott had been unemployed, living with his mother. Lisa seemed the most likely of the three to have become infected first; in theory, all it took was an accidental brush of skin against skin as a credit card changed hands—albeit with only a 1-in-100 chance of transmission. In the larger cities, some people who dealt with the public in the flesh had taken to wearing gloves—and some (arguably paranoid) subway commuters covered every square centimeter of skin below the neck, even in midsummer—but the absolute risk was so small that few strategies like this had become widespread.

I grilled Mr Walker as gently as I could. His children's movements for most of the week were like clockwork; the only time during the window of infection when they'd been anywhere but work or home was Thursday night. Both had been out until the early hours, Lisa visiting Paul, Ben visiting his girlfriend, Martha Amos. Whether the couples had gone anywhere, or stayed in, he wasn't certain—but there wasn't much happening locally on a week night, and they hadn't mentioned driving out of town.

I phoned Martha Amos; she told me that she and Ben had been at her house, alone, until about two. Since she hadn't been infected, presumably Ben had picked up the virus from his sister sometime later—and Lisa had either been infected by Paul that night, or vice versa.

According to Paul's mother, he'd barely left the house all week, which made him an unlikely entry point. Statesville seemed to be making perfect sense: customer to Lisa in the store (Thursday afternoon), Lisa to Paul (Thursday night), Lisa to Ben (Friday morning). Next stop, I'd ask the store owner what she remembered about their out-of-town customers that day.

But then Ms Scott said, "Thursday night, Paul was over at the Walkers until late. That's the only time he went out, that I can think of."

"He went to see Lisa? She didn't come here?"

"No. He left for the Walkers, about half past eight."

"And they were just going to hang around the house? They had nothing special planned?"

"Paul doesn't have a lot of money, you know. They can't afford to go out much—it's not easy for them." She spoke in a relaxed, confiding tone—as if the relationship, with all its minor tribulations, had merely been put on hold. I hoped someone would be around to support her when the truth struck home in a couple of days.

I called at Martha Amos's house. I hadn't paid close enough attention to her when I'd phoned; I could see now that she was not in good shape.

I asked her, "Did Ben happen to tell you where his sister went with Paul Scott on Thursday night?"

She stared at me expressionlessly.

"I'm sorry, I know this is intrusive—but no one else seems to know. If you can remember anything he said, it could be very helpful."

Martha said, "He told me to say he was with me. I always covered for him. His father wouldn't have . . . *approved*."

"Hang on. Ben wasn't with you on Thursday night?"

"I went with him a couple of times. But it's not my kind of thing. The people are all right. The music's shit, though."

"Where? Are you talking about some bar?"

"No! *The villages*. Ben and Paul and Lisa went out to the villages, Thursday night." She suddenly focused on me properly, for the first time since I'd arrived; I think she'd finally realized that she hadn't been making a lot of sense. "They hold 'Events.' Which are just dance parties, really. It's no big deal. Only—Ben's father would assume it's all about *drugs*. Which it's not." She put her face in her hands. "But that's where they caught Silver Fire, isn't it?"

"I don't know."

She was shaking; I reached across and touched her arm. She looked up at me and said wearily, "You know what hurts the most?"

"What?"

"I didn't go with them. I keep thinking: *If I'd gone, it would have been all right*. They wouldn't have caught it then. I would have kept them safe."

She searched my face—as if for some hint as to what she might have done. *I was hunting down Silver Fire, wasn't I?* I ought to have been able to tell her, precisely, how she could have warded off the curse: what magic she hadn't performed, what sacrifice she hadn't made.

And I'd seen this a thousand times before—but I still didn't know what to say. All it took was the shock of grief to peel away the veneer of understanding: *Life is not a morality play. Disease is just disease; it carries no hidden meaning. There are no gods we failed to appease, no elemental spirits we failed to bargain with.* Every sane adult knew this—but the knowledge was still only skin deep. At some level, we still hadn't swallowed the hardest-won truth of all: *The universe is indifferent.*

Martha hugged herself, rocking gently. "I know it's crazy, thinking like that. But it still hurts."

I SPENT THE REST of the day trying to find someone who could tell me more about Thursday night's "Event" (such as where, exactly, it had taken place—there were at least four possibilities within a twenty kilometer radius). I had no luck, though; it seemed micro-village culture was very much a minority taste, and Statesville's only three enthusiasts were now *incommunicado*. Drugs weren't the issue with most of the people I talked to; they just seemed to think the villagers were boring tech-heads with appalling taste in music.

Another night, another motel. It was beginning to feel like old times.

Mike Clayton had gone dancing, somewhere, on the Tuesday night. *Out in the villages?* Presumably he hadn't traveled quite this far, but an unknown person—a tourist, maybe—might easily have been at both Events: Tuesday night near Greensboro, Thursday night near Statesville. If this was true, it would narrow down the possibilities considerably—at least compared with the number of people who'd simply passed through the towns themselves.

I pored over road maps for a while, trying to decide which village would be easiest to add to the next day's itinerary. I'd searched the directories for some kind of "microvillage night life" web site—in vain, but that didn't mean anything. The address had no doubt made its way, by electronic diffusion, to everyone who was genuinely interested—and whichever village I went to, half a dozen people were sure to know all about the Events.

I climbed into bed around midnight—but then reached for my notepad again, to check with Ariadne. Silver Fire had made the big time: video fiction. There was a reference in the latest episode of NBC's "hit sci-fi drama", *Mutilated Mystic Empaths in N-Space*.

I'd heard of the series, but never watched it before, so I quickly scanned the pilot. "Don't you know the first law of astronavigation!

Ask a *computer* to solve equations in *17-dimensional hypergeometry* . . . and its rigid, deterministic, linear mind would shatter like a diamond dropped into a black hole! Only *twin telepathic Buddhist nuns*, with seventh-dan black belts in karate, and enough self-discipline to *hack their own legs from their bodies*, could ever hope to master the *intuitive skills* required to navigate the treacherous quantum fluctuations of N-space and rescue that stranded fleet!"

"My God, Captain, you're right—but where will we find . . . ?"

MME was set in the 22nd century—but the Silver Fire reference was no clumsy anachronism. Our heroines miscalculate a difficult trans-galactic jump (breathing the wrong way during the recitation of a crucial mantra), and end up in Present Day San Francisco. There, a small boy and his dog, on the run from mafia hit men, help them repair a vital component in their Tantric Energy Source. After humiliating the assassins with a perfectly choreographed display of legless martial arts amid the scaffolding of a high-rise construction site, they track down the boy's mother to a hospital, where she turns out to be infected with Silver Fire.

The camera angles here grow coy. The few glimpses of actual flesh are sanitized fantasies: glowing ivory, smooth and dry.

The boy (whose recently slaughtered accountant-for-the-mob father concealed the truth from him), bursts into tears when he sees her. But the MMEs are philosophical:

"These well-meaning doctors and nurses will tell you that your Mom has suffered a terrible fate—but in time, the truth will be understood by all. Silver Fire is the closest we can come, in this world, to the Ecstasy of Unbeing. You observe only the frozen shell of her body . . . but inside, in the realm of *shunyata*, a great and wonderful transformation is at work."

"Really?"

"Really."

Boy dries tears, theme music soars, dog jumps up and licks everyone's faces. Cathartic laughter all round.

(Except, of course, from the mother.)

THE NEXT DAY, I had appointments in two small towns further along the highway. The first patient was a divorced forty-five-year-old man, a technician at a textile factory. Neither his brother nor his colleagues could offer me much help; for all they knew, he could have driven to a different town (or village) every single night during the period in question.

In the next town, a couple in their mid-thirties and their eight-year-old daughter had died. The symptoms must have hit all three more-or-less simultaneously—and escalated more rapidly than usual—because no one had managed to call for help.

The woman's sister told me without hesitation, "Friday night, they would have gone out to the villages. That's what they usually did."

"And they would have taken their daughter?"

She opened her mouth to reply—but then froze and just stared at me, mortified—as if I was blaming her sister for recklessly exposing the child to some unspeakable danger. There were photographs of all three on the mantelpiece behind her. This woman had discovered their disintegrating bodies.

I said gently, "No place is safer than any other. It only looks that way in hindsight. They could have caught Silver Fire anywhere at all—and I'm just trying to trace the path of the infection, after the event."

She nodded slowly. "They always took Phoebe. She loved the villages; she had friends in most of them."

"Do you know which village they went to, that night?"

"I think it was Herodotus."

Out in the car, I found it on the map. It wasn't much further from the highway than the one I'd chosen purely for convenience; I could probably drive out there and still make it to the next motel by a civilized hour.

I clicked on the tiny dot; the information window told me: *Herodotus, Catawba County. Population 106, established 2004.*

I said, "More."

The map said, "That's all."

SOLAR PANELS, TWIN SATELLITE dishes, vegetable gardens, water tanks, boxy prefabricated buildings . . . there was no single component of the village which couldn't have been found on almost any large rural property. It was only seeing all of them thrown together in the middle of the countryside that was startling. Herodotus resembled nothing so much as a 20th century artist's impression of a pioneering settlement on some Earth-like—but definitely alien—planet.

A major exception was the car park, discreetly hidden behind the huge banks of photovoltaic cells. With only a bus and two other cars, there was room for maybe a hundred more vehicles. Visitors were clearly welcome in Herodotus; there wasn't even a meter to feed.

Despite the prefabs, there was no army-camp feel to the layout; the buildings obeyed some symmetry I couldn't quite parse, clustered around a central square—but they certainly weren't lined up in rows like quonset huts. As I entered the square, I could see a basketball game in progress in a court off to one side; teenagers playing, and younger children watching. It was the only obvious sign of life. I approached—feeling a bit like a trespasser, even if this was as much a public space as the main street of any ordinary town.

I stood by the other spectators and watched the game for a while. None of the children spoke to me, but it didn't feel like I was being actively snubbed. The teams were mixed-sex, and play was intense but good-natured. The kids were Anglo-, African-, Chinese-American. I'd heard rumors that certain villages were "effectively segregated"—whatever that meant—but it might well have been nothing but propaganda.

The microvillage movement had stirred some controversy when it started, but the lifestyle wasn't exactly radical. A hundred or so people—who would have worked from their homes in towns or cities anyway—pooled their resources and bought some cheap land out in the country, making up for the lack of amenities with a few state-of-the-art technological fixes. Residents were just as likely to be stockbrokers as artists or musicians—and though any characterization was bound to be unfair, most villages were definitely closer to yuppie sanctuaries than anarchist communes.

I couldn't have faced the physical isolation, myself—and no amount of bandwidth would have compensated—but if the people here were happy, all power to them. I was ready to concede that in fifty years' time, living in Queens would be looked on as infinitely more perverse and inexplicable than living in a place like Herodotus.

A young girl, six or seven years old, tapped my arm. I smiled down at her. "Hello."

She said, "Are you on the trail of happiness?"

Before I could ask her what she meant, someone called out, "Hello there!"

I turned; it was a woman—in her mid-twenties, I guessed—shielding her eyes from the sun. She approached, smiling, and offered me her hand.

"I'm Sally Grant."

"Claire Booth."

"You're a bit early for the Event. It doesn't start until nine thirty."

"I—"

"So if you want a meal at my place, you'd be welcome."

I hesitated. "That's very kind of you."

"Ten dollars sound fair? That's what I'd charge if I opened the cafeteria—only there were no bookings tonight, so I won't be."

I nodded.

"Well, drop in around seven. I'm number twenty-three."

"Thank you. Thank you very much."

I sat on a bench in the village square, shaded from the sunset by the hall in front of me, listening to the cries from the basketball court. I knew I should have told Ms Grant straight away what I was doing here; shown her my ID, asked the questions I was permitted to ask, and left. *But mightn't I learn more by staying to watch the Event? Informally?* Even a few crude firsthand observations of the demographics of this unmodeled contact between the villagers and the other local populations might be useful—and though the carrier was obviously long gone, this was still a chance to get a very rough profile of the kind of person I was looking for.

Uneasily, I came to a decision. There was no reason not to stay for the party—and no need to make the villagers anxious and defensive by telling them why I was here.

From the inside, the Grants' house looked more like a spacious, modern apartment than a factory-built box which had been delivered on the back of a truck to the middle of nowhere. I'd been unconsciously expecting the clutter of a mobile home, with too many mod-cons per cubic meter to leave room to breathe, but I'd misjudged the scale completely.

Sally's husband, Oliver, was an architect. She edited travel guides by day; the cafeteria was a sideline. They were founding residents, originally from Raleigh; there were still only a handful of later arrivals. Herodotus, they explained, was self-sufficient in (vegetarian) staple foods, but there were regular deliveries of all the imports any small town relied on. They both made occasional trips to Greensboro, or interstate, but their routine work was pure telecommuting.

"And when you're not on holidays, Claire?"

"I'm an administrator at Columbia."

"That must be fascinating." It certainly turned out to be a good choice; my hosts changed the subject back to themselves immediately.

I asked Sally, "So what clinched the move for you? Raleigh's not exactly the crime capital of the nation." I found it hard to believe that the real estate prices could have driven them out, either.

She replied without hesitation, "Spiritual criteria, Claire."

I blinked.

Oliver laughed pleasantly. "It's all right, you haven't come to the wrong place!" He turned to his wife. "Did you see her face? You'd think she'd stumbled onto some enclave of *Mormons* or *Baptists!*"

Sally explained, apologetically, "I meant the word in its broadest sense, of course: an understanding that we need to *resensitize ourselves* to the *moral dimensions* of the world around us."

That left me none the wiser, but she was clearly expecting a sympathetic response. I said tentatively, "And you think . . . living in a small community like this makes your civic responsibilities clearer, more readily apparent?"

Now Sally was bemused. "Well . . . yes, I suppose it does. But that's just politics, really, isn't it? Not *spirituality*. I meant—" She raised her hands, and beamed at me. "I just *meant*, the reason you're here, yourself! We came to Herodotus to find—for a lifetime—what you've come here to find for a few hours, yourself!"

I HEARD THE OTHER cars begin to arrive while I sat drinking coffee with Sally in the living room. Oliver had excused himself for an urgent meeting with a construction manager in Tokyo. I passed the time with small-talk about Alex and Laura, and my Worst Ever New York Experience horror stories—some of which were true. It wasn't a lack of curiosity that kept me from probing Sally about the Event—I was just afraid of alerting her to the fact that I had no idea what I'd let myself in for. When she left me for a minute, I scanned the room—without rising from my chair—for any sign of what she might have *come here to find for a lifetime*. All I had time to take in were a few CD covers, the half-dozen visible ones on a large rotating rack. Most looked like modern music/video, from bands I'd never heard of. There was one familiar title, though: James Springer's *The Cyber Sutras*.

By the time the three of us crossed the square and approached the village hall—a barn-like structure, resembling a very large cargo container—I was quite tense. There were thirty or forty people in the square, most but not all in their late teens or early twenties, dressed in the kind of diverse mock-casual clothing that might have been seen outside any nightclub in the country. *So what was I afraid was going to happen?* Just because Ben Walker couldn't tell his father about it, and Mike Clayton couldn't tell his mother, didn't mean I'd wandered into some southern remake of *Twin Peaks*. Maybe bored kids just snuck out to the villages to pop hallucinogens at dance parties—my own youth resurrected before my eyes, with safer drugs and better light shows.

As we approached the hall, a small group of people filed in through the self-opening doors, giving me a brief glimpse of bodies silhouetted against swirling lights, and a blast of music. My anxiety began to seem absurd. Sally and Oliver were into psychedelics, that was all—and Herodotus's founders had apparently decided to create a congenial environment in which to use them. I paid the sixty-dollar entry fee, smiling with relief.

Inside, the walls and ceiling were ablaze with convoluted patterns: soft-edged multi-hued fractals pulsing with the music, like vast color-coded simulations of turbulent fluids cascading down giant fret-boards at Mach 5. The dancers cast no shadows; these were high-power wall-screens, not projections. Stunning resolution—and astronomically expensive.

Sally pressed a fluorescent-pink capsule into my hand. Harmony or Halcyon, maybe; I no longer knew what was fashionable. I tried to thank her, and offer some excuse about "saving it for later"—but she didn't hear a word, so we just smiled at each other meaninglessly. The hall's sound insulation was extraordinary (which was lucky for the other villagers); I would never have guessed from outside that my brain was going to be puréed.

Sally and Oliver vanished into the crowd. I decided to hang around for half an hour or so, then slip out and drive on to the motel. I stood and watched the people dancing, trying to keep my head clear despite the stupefying backdrops . . . though I doubted that I could learn much about the carrier that I didn't already know. *Probably under 25. Probably not towing small children.* Sally had given me all the details I needed to obtain information on Events from here to Memphis—past and future. The search was still going to be difficult, but at least I was making progress.

A sudden loud cheer from the crowd broke through the music—*and the room was transformed before my eyes.* For a moment I was utterly disorientated—and even when the world began to make visual sense again, it took me a while to get the details straight.

The wall-screens now showed dancers in identical rooms to the one I was standing in; only the ceiling continued to play the abstract animation. These identical rooms all had wall-screens themselves, which also showed identical rooms full of dancers . . . much like the infinite regress between a pair of mirrors.

And at first, I thought the "other rooms" were merely realtime images of the Herodotus dance hall itself. But . . . the swirling vortex pattern on the ceiling joined seamlessly with the animation on the ceilings of "adjacent" rooms, combining to form a single complex image; there was no repetition, reflected or otherwise. And the crowds of dancers were *not* identical—though they all looked sufficiently alike to make it hard to be sure, from a distance. Belatedly, I turned around and examined the closest wall, just four or five meters away. A young man "behind" the screen raised a hand in greeting, and I returned the gesture automatically. We couldn't quite make convincing eye contact—and wherever the cameras were placed, that would have been a lot to ask for—but it was, still, almost possible to believe that nothing really separated us but a thin wall of glass.

The man smiled dreamily and walked away.

I had goose bumps. This was nothing new in principle, but the technology here had been pushed to its limits. The sense of being in an infinite dance hall was utterly compelling; I could see no "furthest hall" in any direction (and when they ran out of real ones, they could have easily recycled them). The flatness of the images, the incorrect scaling as you moved, the lack of parallax (worst of all when I tried to peer into the "corner rooms" between the main four . . . which "should" have been possible, but wasn't) served more to make the space beyond the walls appear exotically distorted than to puncture the effect. The brain actually struggled to compensate, to cover up the flaws—and if I'd swallowed Sally's capsule, I doubt I would have been nit-picking. As it was, I was grinning like a child on a fairground ride.

I saw people dancing facing the walls, loosely forming couples or groups across the link. I was mesmerized; I forgot all thoughts of leaving. After a while, I bumped into Oliver, who was swaying happily by himself. I screamed into his ear, "These are all other villages?" He nodded, and shouted back, "East is east and west is west!" Meaning . . . the virtual layout followed real geography—it just abolished the intervening distances? I recalled something James Springer had said in his *Terminal Chat Show* interview: *We must invent a new cartography, to rechart the planet in its newborn, Protean state. There is no separation, now. There are no borders.*

Yeah . . . and the world was just one giant party. Still, at least they weren't splicing in live connections to war zones. I'd seen enough we-dance/you-dodge-shells "solidarity" in the nineties to last a lifetime.

It suddenly occurred to me: *If the carrier really was traveling from Event to Event . . . then he or she was "here" with me. right now. My quarry had to be one of the dancers in this giant, imaginary hall.*

And this fact implied no opportunity—let alone any kind of danger. It wasn't as if Silver Fire carriers conveniently fluoresced in the dark. But it still felt like the strangest moment of a long, strange night: to understand that the two of us were finally "connected", to understand that I'd "found" the object of my search.

Even if it did me no good at all.

JUST AFTER MIDNIGHT—AS THE novelty was wearing off, and I was finally making up my mind to leave—some of the dancers began cheering loudly again. This time it took me even longer to see why. People started turning to face the east, and excitedly pointing something out to each other.

Weaving through one of the distant crowds of dancers—in a village three screens removed—were a number of human figures. They might have been naked, some male some female, but it was hard to be sure: they could only be seen in glimpses . . . and they were shining so brightly that most details were swamped in their sheer luminosity.

They glowed an intense silver-white. The light transformed their immediate surroundings—though the effect was more like a halo of luminous gas, diffusing through the air, than a spotlight cast on the crowd. The dancers around them seemed oblivious to their presence—as did those in the intervening halls; only the people in Herodotus paid them the kind of attention their spectacular appearance deserved. I couldn't yet tell whether they were pure animation, with plausible paths computed through gaps in the crowd, or unremarkable (but real) actors, enhanced by software.

My mouth was dry. I couldn't believe that the presence of these silver figures could be pure coincidence—but what were they meant to signify? Did the people of Herodotus know about the string of local outbreaks? That wasn't impossible; an independent analysis might have been circulated on the net. Maybe this was meant as some kind of bizarre "tribute" to the victims.

I found Oliver again. The music had softened, as if in deference to the vision, and he seemed to have come down a little; we managed to have something approaching a conversation.

I pointed to the figures—who were now marching smoothly straight through the image of the image of a wall-screen, proving themselves entirely virtual.

He shouted, "They're walking the trail of happiness!"

I mimed incomprehension.

"Healing the land for us! Making amends! Undoing the trail of tears!"

The trail of tears? I was lost for a while, then a memory from high school surfaced abruptly. The "Trail of Tears" was the brutal forced march of the Cherokee from what was now part of Georgia, all the way to Oklahoma, in the 1830s. Thousands had died along the way; some had escaped, and hidden in the Appalachians. Herodotus, I was fairly sure, was hundreds of kilometers from the historical route of the march—but that didn't seem to be the point. As the silver figures moved across the dance floor twice-removed, I could see them spreading their arms wide, as if performing some kind of benediction.

I shouted, "But what does *Silver Fire* have to do with—?"

"Their bodies are frozen—so their spirits are free to walk the Trail of Happiness through cyberspace for us! Didn't you know? That's what Silver Fire is *for!* To renew everything! To bring happiness to the land! *To make amends!*" Oliver beamed at me with absolute sincerity, radiating pure good will.

I stared at him in disbelief. This man, clearly, hated no one . . . but what he'd just spewed out was nothing but a New Age remix of the rantings of that radio evangelist, twenty years before, who'd seized upon AIDS as the incontrovertible proof of his own *spiritual beliefs*.

I shouted angrily, "Silver Fire is a merciless, agonizing—"

Oliver tipped his head back and laughed, uproariously, without a trace of malice—as if I was the one telling ghost stories.

I turned and walked away.

The trail-walkers split into two streams as they crossed the hall immediately to the east of us. Half went north, half went south, as they "detoured around" Herodotus. They couldn't move among us— but this way, the illusion remained almost seamless.

And if I'd been drugged out of my skull? If I'd embraced the whole mythology of the Trail of Happiness—and come here hoping to see it confirmed? In the morning, would I have half-believed that the roaming spirits of Silver Fire patients had marched right past me?

Bestowing their luminous blessing on the crowd.

Near enough to touch.

I THREADED MY WAY toward the camouflaged exit. Outside, the cool air and the silence were surreal; I felt more disembodied and dream-like than ever. I staggered toward the car park, and waved my note-pad to make the hire car flash its lights.

My head cleared as I approached the highway. I decided to drive on through the night; I was so agitated that I didn't think I had much chance of sleeping. I could find a motel in the morning, shower, and catch a nap before my next appointment.

I still didn't know what to make of the Event—what solid link there could be between the carrier and the villagers' mad syncretic cyberbabble. If it was nothing but coincidence, the irony was grotesque—but what was the alternative? *Some "pilgrim" on the Trail of Happiness, deliberately spreading the virus?* The idea was ludicrous— and not just because it was unthinkably obscene. A carrier could only *know* that he or she had been infected if distinctive symptoms had appeared . . . but *distinctive symptoms* only marked the brutal end stage of the disease; a prolonged mild infection—if such a thing existed—would be indistinguishable from influenza. Once Silver Fire progressed far enough to affect the visible layers of the skin, the only options for cross-country travel all involved flashing lights and sirens.

At about half past three in the morning, I switched on my note-pad. I wasn't exactly drowsy, but I wanted something to keep me alert.

Ariadne had plenty.

First, a heated debate on *The Reality Studio*—a program on the Intercampus Ideas Network. A freelance zoologist from Seattle named Andrew Feld spoke first—putting the case that Silver Fire "proved beyond doubt" his "controversial and paradigm-subverting" S-force theory of life, which "combined the transgressive genius of Einstein and Sheldrake with the insights of the Maya and the latest developments in superstrings, to create a new, life-affirming biology to take the place of soulless, mechanistic Western science."

In reply, virologist Margaret Ortega from UCLA explained in detail why Feld's ideas were superfluous, failed to account for—or clashed directly with—numerous observed biological phenomena . . . and were neither more nor less "mechanistic" than any other theory which didn't leave everything in the universe to the whim of God. She also ventured the opinion that most people were capable of *affirming life* without casually discarding all of human knowledge in the process.

Feld was a clueless idiot on a wish-fulfillment trip. Ortega wiped the floor with him.

But when the nationwide audience of students voted, he was declared winner by a majority of two to one.

Next item: Protesters were blockading the Medical Research Laboratories of the Max Planck Institute in Hamburg, calling for an end to Silver Fire research. Safety was not the issue. Protest organizer and "acclaimed cultural agitator" Kid Ransom had held an impromptu press conference:

"We must reclaim Silver Fire from the gray, small-minded scientists, and learn to tap its wellspring of mythical power for the benefit of all humanity! These technocrats who seek to *explain* everything are like vandals rampaging through a gallery, scrawling equations on all the beautiful works of art!"

"But how will humanity ever find a cure for this disease, without research?"

"There is no such thing as disease! There is only transformation!"

There were four more news stories, all concerning (mutually exclusive) proclamations about the "secret truth" (or secret ineffability) behind Silver Fire—and maybe each one, alone, would have seemed no more than a sad, sick joke. But as the countryside materialized around me—the purple-gray ridge of the Black Mountains to the north starkly beautiful in the dawn—I was slowly beginning to understand. *This was not my world anymore.* Not in Herodotus, not in Seattle, not in Hamburg or Montreal or London. Not even in New York.

In my world, there were no nymphs in trees and streams. No gods, no ghosts, no ancestral spirits. *Nothing*—outside our own cultures, our own laws, our own passions—existed in order to punish us or comfort us, to affirm any act of hatred or love.

My own parents had understood this, perfectly—but theirs had been the first generation, ever, to be so free of the shackles of superstition. And after the briefest flowering of understanding, my own generation had grown complacent. At some level, we must have started taking it for granted that *the way the universe worked* was now obvious to any child . . . even though it went against everything innate to the species: the wild, undisciplined love of patterns, the craving to extract meaning and comfort from everything in sight.

We thought we were passing on everything that mattered to our children: science, history, literature, art. Vast libraries of information lay at their fingertips. But we hadn't fought hard enough to pass on the hardest-won truth of all: *Morality comes only from within. Meaning comes only from within. Outside our own skulls, the universe is indifferent.*

Maybe, in the West, we'd delivered the death blows to the old doctrinal religions, the old monoliths of delusion . . . but that victory meant nothing at all.

Because taking their place now, everywhere, was the saccharine poison of *spirituality.*

I checked into a motel in Asheville. The parking lot was full of campervans, people heading for the national parks; I was lucky, I got the last room.

My notepad chimed while I was in the shower. An analysis of the latest data reported to the Centers for Disease Control showed the "anomaly" extending almost two hundred kilometers further west along the I-40—about half-way to Nashville. *Five more people on the Trail of Happiness.* I sat and stared at the map for a while—then I dressed, packed my bag again, and checked out.

I made ten calls as I was driving up into the mountains, canceling all my appointments with relatives from Asheville to Jefferson City, Tennessee. The time had passed for being cautious and methodical, for gathering every last scrap of data along the way. I *knew* the transmission had to be taking place at the Events—the only question was whether it was accidental or deliberate.

Deliberate how? With a vial full of fibroblasts, teeming with Silver Fire? It had taken researchers at the NIH over a year to learn how to culture the virus—and they'd only succeeded in March. I couldn't believe that their work had been replicated by amateurs in less than three months.

The highway plunged between the lavish wooded slopes of the Great Smoky Mountains, following the Pigeon River most of the way. I programmed a predictive model—by voice—as I drove. I had a calendar for the Events, now, and I had five approximate dates of infection. Case notifications would always be too late; the only way to catch up was to extrapolate. And I could only assume that the carrier would continue moving steadily westwards, never lingering, always traveling on to the next Event.

I reached Knoxville around midday, stopped for lunch, then drove straight on.

The model said: *Pliny, Saturday Jan 14, 9.30 pm.* My first chance to search the infinite dance hall for the carrier, without an impassable wall between us.

My first chance to be in the presence of Silver Fire.

I ARRIVED EARLY—BUT NOT so early as to attract the attention of Pliny's equivalents of Sally and Oliver. I stayed in the car for an hour, improvising ways to look busy, recording the license numbers of arriving vehicles. There were a lot of four-wheel drives and utilities, and a few campervans. Many villagers favored bicycles—but the carrier would have to have been a real fanatic—and extremely fit—to have cycled all the way from Greensboro.

The Event followed much the same pattern as the one in Herodotus the night before—though Herodotus itself wasn't taking part. The crowd was similar, too: mostly young, but with enough exceptions to keep me from looking completely out of place. I wandered around, trying to commit every face to memory without attracting too much attention. *Had all these people swallowed the Silver Fire myth, as I'd heard it from Oliver?* The possibility was almost too bleak to contemplate. The only thing that gave me any hope was that when I'd compared the number of villages listed on the Event calendar with the number in the region, it was less than one in twenty. The microvillage movement itself had nothing to do with this insanity.

Someone offered me a pink capsule—not for free, this time. I gave her twenty dollars, and pocketed the drug for analysis. There was a slender chance that someone was passing out doctored capsules—although stomach acid tended to make short work of the virus.

A handsome blond kid—barely in his twenties—hovered around me for a while as the trail-walkers appeared. When they'd vanished into the west, he approached me, took my elbow, and made an offer I couldn't quite hear over the music—though I thought I got the gist of it. I was too distracted to feel amazed or flattered—let alone tempted—and I got rid of him in five seconds flat. He walked away looking wounded—but not long afterward, I saw him leaving with a woman half my age.

I stayed to the very end—and on Saturday nights, that meant five in the morning. I staggered out into the light, discouraged, although I didn't know what I'd seriously hoped to see. *Someone walking around with an aerosol spray, administering doses of Silver Fire?* When I reached the car park I realized that many of the cars had arrived after I'd gone in—and some might have come and gone unseen. I recorded the license plates I'd missed, trying to be discreet, but almost past caring; I hadn't slept for thirty-six hours.

THE NEAREST EVENT WEST of Pliny, on Sunday night, was past the Mississippi and half-way across Arkansas; I made a calculated guess that the carrier would take this as an opportunity for a night off.

Monday evening, I drove into Eudoxus—population 165, established 2002, about an hour from Nashville—ready to spend all night in the car park if I had to. I needed to record every license plate, or there wasn't much point being here.

I hadn't told Brecht what I was doing; I still had no solid evidence, and I was afraid of sounding paranoid. I'd called Alex before leaving Nashville, but I hadn't told him much, either. Laura had declined to speak to me when he'd called out and told her I was on the line, but that was nothing new. I missed them both already, more than I'd anticipated—but I wasn't sure how I'd manage when I finally made it home, to a daughter who was turning away from reason, and a husband who took it for granted that any bright adolescent would recapitulate five thousand years of intellectual progress in six months.

Thirty-five vehicles arrived between ten and eleven—none I'd seen before—and then the flow tapered off abruptly. I scanned the entertainment channels on my notepad, satisfied by anything with color and movement; I'd had enough of Ariadne's bad news.

Just before midnight, a blue Ford campervan rolled up and parked in the corner opposite me. A young man and a young woman got out; they seemed excited, but a little wary—as if they couldn't quite believe that their parents weren't watching from the shadows.

As they crossed the car park, I realized that the guy was the blond kid who'd spoken to me in Pliny.

I waited five minutes, then went and checked their license plate; it was a Massachusetts registration. I hadn't recorded it on Saturday night, so I would have missed the fact that they were following the Trail, if one of them hadn't—

Hadn't what?

I stood there frozen behind the van, trying to stay calm, replaying the incident in my mind. I knew I hadn't let him paw me for long—*but how long would it have taken?*

I glanced up at the disinterested stars, trying to savor the irony because it tasted much better than the fear. I'd always known there'd be a risk—and the odds were still heavily in my favor. I could put myself into quarantine in Nashville in the morning; nothing I did right now would make the slightest difference—

But I wasn't thinking straight. If they'd *traveled together* all the way from Massachusetts—or even from Greensboro—one should have infected the other long ago. The probability of the two of them sharing the same freakish resistance to the virus was negligible, even if they were brother and sister.

They couldn't both be unwitting, asymptomatic carriers. So either they had nothing to do with the outbreaks—

—or they were transporting the virus outside their bodies, and handling it with great care.

A bumper sticker boasted: STATE-OF-THE-ART SECURITY! I placed a hand against the rear door experimentally; the van didn't emit so much as a warning beep. I tried shaking the handle aggressively; still nothing. If the system was calling a security firm in Nashville for an armed response, I had all the time I needed. If it was trying to call its owners, it wouldn't have much luck getting a signal through the aluminum frame of the village hall.

There was no one in sight. I went back to my car, and fetched the toolkit.

I knew I had no legal right. There were emergency powers I could have invoked—but I had no intention of calling Maryland and spending half the night fighting my way through the correct procedures. And I knew I was putting the prosecution case at risk, by tainting everything with illegal search and seizure.

I didn't care. They weren't going to have the chance to send one more person down the Trail of Happiness, even if I had to burn the van to the ground.

I levered a small, tinted fixed window out of its rubber frame in the door. Still no wailing siren. I reached in, groped around, and unlocked the door.

I'd thought they must have been half-educated biochemists, who'd learned enough cytology to duplicate the published fibroblast culturing techniques.

I was wrong. They were medical students, and they'd half-learned other skills entirely.

They had their friend cushioned in polymer gel, contained in something like a huge tropical fish tank. They had oxygen set up, a urethral catheter, and half a dozen drips. I played my torch beam over the inverted bottles, checking the various drugs and their concentrations. I went through them all twice, hoping I'd missed one—but I hadn't.

I shone the beam down onto the girl's skinless white face, peering through the delicate streamers of red rising up through the gel. She was in an opiate haze deep enough to keep her motionless and silent—but she was still conscious. Her mouth was frozen in a rictus of pain.

And she'd been like this for sixteen days.

I staggered back out of the van, my heart pounding, my vision going black. I collided with the blond kid; the girl was with him, and they had another couple in tow.

I turned on him and started punching him, screaming incoherently; I don't remember what I said. He put up his hands to shield his face, and the others came to his aid: pinning me gently against the van, holding me still without striking a single blow.

I was crying now. The campervan girl said, "Shh. It's all right. No one's going to hurt you."

I pleaded with her. "Don't you understand? She's in pain! *All this time, she's been in pain!* What did you think she was doing? *Smiling?*"

"Of course she's smiling. This is what she always wanted. She made us promise that if she ever caught Silver Fire, she'd walk the Trail."

I rested my head against the cool metal, closed my eyes for a moment, and tried to think of a way to get through to them.

But I didn't know how.

When I opened my eyes, the boy was standing in front of me. He had the most gentle, compassionate face imaginable. He wasn't a torturer, or a bigot, or even a fool. He'd just swallowed some beautiful lies.

He said, "Don't you understand? All *you* see in there is a woman dying in pain—*but we all have to learn to see more.* The time has come to regain the lost skills of our ancestors: the power to see visions, demons and angels. The power to see the spirits of the wind and the rain. The power to walk the Trail of Happiness."

REASONS TO BE CHEERFUL

1

IN SEPTEMBER 2004, NOT long after my twelfth birthday, I entered a state of almost constant happiness. It never occurred to me to ask why. Though school included the usual quota of tedious lessons, I was doing well enough academically to be able to escape into daydreams whenever it suited me. At home, I was free to read books and web pages about molecular biology and particle physics, quaternions and galactic evolution, and to write my own Byzantine computer games and convoluted abstract animations. And though I was a skinny, uncoordinated child, and every elaborate, pointless organized sport left me comatose with boredom, I was comfortable enough with my body on my own terms. Whenever I ran—and I ran everywhere—it felt good.

I had food, shelter, safety, loving parents, encouragement, stimulation. Why shouldn't I have been happy? And though I can't have entirely forgotten how oppressive and monotonous classwork and schoolyard politics could be, or how easily my usual bouts of enthusiasm were derailed by the most trivial problems, when things were actually going well for me I wasn't in the habit of counting down the days until it all turned sour. Happiness always brought with it the belief that it would last, and though I must have seen this optimistic forecast disproved a thousand times before, I wasn't old and cynical enough to be surprised when it finally showed signs of coming true.

When I started vomiting repeatedly, Dr Ash, our GP, gave me a course of antibiotics and a week off school. I doubt it was a great shock to my parents when this unscheduled holiday seemed to cheer me up rather more than any mere bacterium could bring me down, and if they were puzzled that I didn't even bother feigning misery, it would have been redundant for me to moan constantly about my aching stomach when I was throwing up authentically three or four times a day.

The antibiotics made no difference. I began losing my balance, stumbling when I walked. Back in Dr Ash's surgery, I squinted at the eye chart. She sent me to a neurologist at Westmead Hospital, who ordered an immediate MRI scan. Later the same day, I was admitted as an in-patient. My parents learned the diagnosis straight away, but it took me three more days to make them spit out the whole truth.

I had a tumor, a medulloblastoma, blocking one of the fluid-filled ventricles in my brain, raising the pressure in my skull. Medulloblastomas were potentially fatal, though with surgery followed by aggressive radiation treatment and chemotherapy, two out of three patients diagnosed at this stage lived five more years.

I pictured myself on a railway bridge riddled with rotten sleepers, with no choice but to keep moving, trusting my weight to each suspect plank in turn. I understood the danger ahead, very clearly . . . and yet I felt no real panic, no real fear. The closest thing to terror I could summon up was an almost exhilarating rush of vertigo, as if I was facing nothing more than an audaciously harrowing fairground ride.

There was a reason for this.

The pressure in my skull explained most of my symptoms, but tests on my cerebrospinal fluid had also revealed a greatly elevated level of a substance called Leu-enkephalin—an endorphin, a neuropeptide which bound to some of the same receptors as opiates like morphine and heroin. Somewhere along the road to malignancy, the same mutant transcription factor that had switched on the genes enabling the tumor cells to divide unchecked had apparently also switched on the genes needed to produce Leu-enkephalin.

This was a freakish accident, not a routine side-effect. I didn't know much about endorphins then, but my parents repeated what the neurologist had told them, and later I looked it all up. Leu-enkephalin wasn't an analgesic, to be secreted in emergencies when pain threatened survival, and it had no stupefying narcotic effects to immobilize a creature while injuries healed. Rather, it was the primary means of signaling happiness, released whenever behavior or circumstances warranted pleasure. Countless other brain activities modulated that simple message, creating an almost limitless palette of positive emotions, and the binding of Leu-enkephalin to its target neurons was just the first link in a long chain of events mediated by other neurotransmitters. But for all these subtleties, I could attest to one simple, unambiguous fact: Leu-enkephalin made you feel *good*.

My parents broke down as they told me the news, and I was the one who comforted them, beaming placidly like a beatific little child martyr from some tear-jerking oncological mini-series. It wasn't a matter of hidden reserves of strength or maturity; I was physically incapable of feeling bad about my fate. And because the effects of the Leu-enkephalin were so specific, I could gaze unflinchingly at the truth in a way that would not have been possible if I'd been doped up to the eyeballs with crude pharmaceutical opiates. I was clear-headed but emotionally indomitable, positively radiant with courage.

I HAD A VENTRICULAR shunt installed, a slender tube inserted deep into my skull to relieve the pressure, pending the more invasive and risky procedure of removing the primary tumor; that operation was scheduled for the end of the week. Dr Maitland, the oncologist, had explained in detail how my treatment would proceed, and warned me of the danger and discomfort I faced in the months ahead. Now I was strapped in for the ride and ready to go.

Once the shock wore off, though, my un-blissed-out parents decided that they had no intention of sitting back and accepting mere two-to-one odds that I'd make it to adulthood. They phoned around Sydney, then further afield, hunting for second opinions.

My mother found a private hospital on the Gold Coast—the only Australian franchise of the Nevada-based "Health Palace" chain—where the oncology unit was offering a new treatment for medulloblastomas. A genetically engineered herpes virus introduced into the cerebrospinal fluid would infect only the replicating tumor cells, and then a powerful cytotoxic drug, activated only by the virus, would kill the infected cells. The treatment had an 80 percent five-year survival rate, without the risks of surgery. I looked up the cost myself, in the hospital's web brochure. They were offering a package deal: three months' meals and accommodation, all pathology and radiology services, and all pharmaceuticals, for sixty thousand dollars.

My father was an electrician, working on building sites. My mother was a sales assistant in a department store. I was their only child, so we were far from poverty-stricken, but they must have taken out a second mortgage to raise the fee, saddling themselves with a further fifteen or twenty years' debt. The two survival rates were not that different, and I heard Dr Maitland warn them that the figures couldn't really be compared, because the viral treatment was so new. They would have been perfectly justified in taking her advice and sticking to the traditional regime.

Maybe my enkephalin sainthood spurred them on somehow. Maybe they wouldn't have made such a great sacrifice if I'd been my usual sullen and difficult self, or even if I'd been nakedly terrified rather than preternaturally brave. I'll never know for sure—and either way, it wouldn't make me think any less of them. But just because the molecule wasn't saturating their skulls, that's no reason to expect them to have been immune to its influence.

On the flight north, I held my father's hand all the way. We'd always been a little distant, a little mutually disappointed in each other. I knew he would have preferred a tougher, more athletic, more extroverted son, while to me he'd always seemed lazily conformist, with a world view built on unexamined platitudes and slogans. But on that trip, with barely a word exchanged, I could feel his disappointment being transmuted into a kind of fierce, protective, defiant love, and I grew ashamed of my own lack of respect for him. I let the Leu-enkephalin convince me that, once this was over, everything between us would change for the better.

FROM THE STREET, THE Gold Coast Health Palace could have passed for one more high-rise beach front hotel—and even from the inside, it wasn't much different from the hotels I'd seen in video fiction. I had a room to myself, with a television wider than the bed, complete with network computer and cable modem. If the aim was to distract me, it worked. After a week of tests, they hooked a drip into my ventricular shunt and infused first the virus, and then three days later, the drug.

The tumor began shrinking almost immediately; they showed me the scans. My parents seemed happy but dazed, as if they'd never quite trusted a place where millionaire property developers came for scrotal tucks to do much more than relieve them of their money and offer first-class double-talk while I continued to decline. But the tumor kept on shrinking, and when it hesitated for two days in a row the oncologist swiftly repeated the whole procedure, and then the tendrils and blobs on the MRI screen grew skinnier and fainter even more rapidly than before.

I had every reason to feel unconditional joy now, but when I suffered a growing sense of unease instead I assumed it was just Leu-enkephalin withdrawal. It was even possible that the tumor had been releasing such a high dose of the stuff that literally nothing could have made me *feel better*—if I'd been lofted to the pinnacle of happiness, there'd be nowhere left to go but down. But in that case, any chink of darkness in my sunny disposition could only confirm the good news of the scans.

One morning I woke from a nightmare—my first in months—with visions of the tumor as a clawed parasite thrashing around inside my skull. I could still hear the click of carapace on bone, like the rattle of a scorpion trapped in a jam jar. I was terrified, drenched in sweat . . . *liberated*. My fear soon gave way to a white-hot rage: the thing had drugged me into compliance, but now I was free to stand up to it, to bellow obscenities inside my head, to exorcize the demon with self-righteous anger.

I did feel slightly cheated by the sense of anticlimax that came from chasing my already-fleeing nemesis downhill, and I couldn't entirely ignore the fact that imagining my anger to be driving out the cancer was a complete reversal of true cause and effect—a bit like watching a forklift shift a boulder from my chest, then pretending to have moved it myself by a mighty act of inhalation. But I made what sense I could of my belated emotions, and left it at that.

Six weeks after I was admitted, all my scans were clear, and my blood, CSF and lymphatic fluid were free of the signature proteins of metastasizing cells. But there was still a risk that a few resistant tumor cells remained, so they gave me a short, sharp course of entirely different drugs, no longer linked to the herpes infection. I had a testicular biopsy first—under local anesthetic, more embarrassing than painful—and a sample of bone marrow taken from my hip, so my potential for sperm production and my supply of new blood cells could both be restored if the drugs wiped them out at the source. I lost hair and stomach lining, temporarily, and I vomited more often, and far more wretchedly, than when I'd first been diagnosed. But when I started to emit self-pitying noises, one of the nurses steelily explained that children half my age put up with the same treatment for months.

These conventional drugs alone could never have cured me, but as a mopping-up operation they greatly diminished the chance of a relapse. I discovered a beautiful word: *apoptosis*—cellular suicide, programmed death—and repeated it to myself, over and over. I ended up almost relishing the nausea and fatigue; the more miserable I felt, the easier it was to imagine the fate of the tumor cells, membranes popping and shriveling like balloons as the drugs commanded them to take their own lives. *Die in pain, zombie scum!* Maybe I'd write a game about it, or even a whole series, culminating in the spectacular *Chemotherapy III: Battle for the Brain.* I'd be rich and famous, I could pay back my parents, and life would be as perfect in reality as the tumor had merely made it seem to be.

I WAS DISCHARGED EARLY in December, free of any trace of disease. My parents were wary and jubilant in turn, as if slowly casting off the fear that any premature optimism would be punished. The side-effects of the chemotherapy were gone; my hair was growing back, except for a tiny bald patch where the shunt had been, and I had no trouble keeping down food. There was no point returning to school now, two weeks before the year's end, so my summer holidays began immediately. The whole class sent me a tacky, insincere, teacher-or-chestrated get-well email, but my friends visited me at home, only slightly embarrassed and intimidated, to welcome me back from the brink of death.

So why did I feel so bad? Why did the sight of the clear blue sky through the window when I opened my eyes every morning—with the freedom to sleep-in as long as I chose, with my father or mother home all day treating me like royalty, but keeping their distance and letting me sit unnagged at the computer screen for sixteen hours if I wanted—why did that first glimpse of daylight make me want to bury my face in the pillow, clench my teeth and whisper: *"I should have died. I should have died."*?

Nothing gave me the slightest pleasure. Nothing—not my favorite netzines or web sites, not the *njari* music I'd once reveled in, not the richest, the sweetest, the saltiest junk food that was mine now for the asking. I couldn't bring myself to read a whole page of any book, I couldn't write ten lines of code. I couldn't look my real-world friends in the eye, or face the thought of going online.

Everything I did, everything I imagined, was tainted with an overwhelming sense of dread and shame. The only image I could summon up for comparison was from a documentary about Auschwitz that I'd seen at school. It had opened with a long tracking shot, a newsreel camera advancing relentlessly toward the gates of the camp, and I'd watched that scene with my spirits sinking, already knowing full well what had happened inside. I wasn't delusional; I didn't believe for a moment that there was some source of unspeakable evil lurking behind every bright surface around me. But when I woke and saw the sky, I felt the kind of sick foreboding that would only have made sense if I'd been staring at the gates of Auschwitz.

Maybe I was afraid that the tumor would grow back, but not *that* afraid. The swift victory of the virus in the first round should have counted for much more, and on one level I did think of myself as lucky, and suitably grateful. But I could no more rejoice in my escape, now, than I could have felt suicidally bad at the height of my enkephalin bliss.

My parents began to worry, and dragged me along to a psychologist for "recovery counseling." The whole idea seemed as tainted as everything else, but I lacked the energy for resistance. Dr Bright and I "explored the possibility" that I was subconsciously choosing to feel miserable because I'd learned to associate happiness with the risk of death, and I secretly feared that recreating the tumor's main symptom could resurrect the thing itself. Part of me scorned this facile explanation, but part of me seized on it, hoping that if I owned up to such subterranean mental gymnastics it would drag the whole process into the light of day, where its flawed logic would become untenable. But the sadness and disgust that everything induced in me—birdsong, the pattern of our bathroom tiles, the smell of toast, the shape of my own hands—only increased.

I wondered if the high levels of Leu-enkephalin from the tumor might have caused my neurons to reduce their population of the corresponding receptors, or if I'd become "Leu-enkephalin-tolerant" the way a heroin addict became opiate-tolerant, through the production of a natural regulatory molecule that blocked the receptors. When I mentioned these ideas to my father, he insisted that I discuss them with Dr Bright, who feigned intense interest but did nothing to show that he'd taken me seriously. He kept telling my parents that everything I was feeling was a perfectly normal reaction to the trauma I'd been through, and that all I really needed was time, and patience, and understanding.

I WAS BUNDLED OFF to high school at the start of the new year, but when I did nothing but sit and stare at my desk for a week, arrangements were made for me to study online. At home, I did manage to work my way slowly through the curriculum, in the stretches of zombie-like numbness that came between the bouts of sheer, paralyzing unhappiness. In the same periods of relative clarity, I kept thinking about the possible causes of my affliction. I searched the biomedical literature and found a study of the effects of high doses of Leu-enkephalin in cats, but it seemed to show that any tolerance would be short-lived.

Then, one afternoon in March—staring at an electron micrograph of a tumor cell infected with herpes virus, when I should have been studying dead explorers—I finally came up with a theory that made sense. The virus needed special proteins to let it dock with the cells it infected, enabling it to stick to them long enough to use other tools to penetrate the cell membrane. But if it had acquired a copy of the Leu-enkephalin gene from the tumor's own copious RNA transcripts, it might have gained the ability to cling, not just to replicating tumor cells, but to every neuron in my brain with a Leu-enkephalin receptor.

And then the cytotoxic drug, activated only in infected cells, would have come along and killed them all.

Deprived of any input, the pathways those dead neurons normally stimulated were withering away. Every part of my brain able to feel pleasure was dying. And though at times I could, still, simply feel nothing, mood was a shifting balance of forces. With nothing to counteract it, the slightest flicker of depression could now win every tug-of-war, unopposed.

I didn't say a word to my parents; I couldn't bear to tell them that the battle they'd fought to give me the best possible chance of survival might now be crippling me. I tried to contact the oncologist who'd treated me on the Gold Coast, but my phone calls floundered in a Muzak-filled moat of automated screening, and my email was ignored. I managed to see Dr Ash alone, and she listened politely to my theory, but she declined to refer me to a neurologist when my only symptoms were psychological: blood and urine tests showed none of the standard markers for clinical depression.

The windows of clarity grew shorter. I found myself spending more and more of each day in bed, staring out across the darkened room. My despair was so monotonous, and so utterly disconnected from anything real, that to some degree it was blunted by its own absurdity: no one I loved had just been slaughtered, the cancer had almost certainly been defeated, and I could still grasp the difference between what I was feeling and the unarguable logic of real grief, or real fear.

But I had no way of casting off the gloom and feeling what I wanted to feel. My only freedom came down to a choice between hunting for reasons to justify my sadness—deluding myself that it was my own, perfectly natural response to some contrived litany of misfortunes—or disowning it as something alien, imposed from without, trapping me inside an emotional shell as useless and unresponsive as a paralyzed body.

My father never accused me of weakness and ingratitude; he just silently withdrew from my life. My mother kept trying to get through to me, to comfort or provoke me, but it reached the point where I could barely squeeze her hand in reply. I wasn't literally paralyzed or blind, speechless or feeble-minded. But all the brightly lit worlds I'd once inhabited—physical and virtual, real and imaginary, intellectual and emotional—had become invisible, and impenetrable. Buried in fog. Buried in shit. Buried in ashes.

By the time I was admitted to a neurological ward, the dead regions of my brain were clearly visible on an MRI scan. But it was unlikely that anything could have halted the process even if it had been diagnosed sooner.

And it was certain that no one had the power to reach into my skull and restore the machinery of happiness.

2

THE ALARM WOKE ME at ten, but it took me another three hours to summon up the energy to move. I threw off the sheet and sat on the side of the bed, muttering half-hearted obscenities, trying to get past the inescapable conclusion that I shouldn't have bothered. Whatever pinnacles of achievement I scaled today (managing not only to go shopping, but to buy something other than a frozen meal) and whatever monumental good fortune befell me (the insurance company depositing my allowance before the rent was due) I'd wake up tomorrow feeling exactly the same.

Nothing helps, nothing changes. Four words said it all. But I'd accepted that long ago; there was nothing left to be disappointed about. And I had no reason to sit here lamenting the bleeding obvious for the thousandth time.

Right?

Fuck it. Just keep moving.

I swallowed my "morning" medication, the six capsules I'd put out on the bedside table the night before, then went into the bathroom and urinated a bright yellow stream consisting mainly of the last dose's metabolites. No antidepressant in the world could send me to Prozac Heaven, but this shit kept my dopamine and serotonin levels high enough to rescue me from total catatonia—from liquid food, bedpans and sponge baths.

I splashed water on my face, trying to think of an excuse to leave the flat when the freezer was still half full. Staying in all day, unwashed and unshaven, did make me feel worse: slimy and lethargic, like some pale parasitic leech. But it could still take a week or more for the pressure of disgust to grow strong enough to move me.

I stared into the mirror. Lack of appetite more than made up for lack of exercise—I was as immune to carbohydrate comfort as I was to runner's high—and I could count my ribs beneath the loose skin of my chest. I was 30 years old, and I looked like a wasted old man. I pressed my forehead against the cool glass, obeying some vestigial instinct which suggested that there might be a scrap of pleasure to be extracted from the sensation. There wasn't.

In the kitchen, I saw the light on the phone: there was a message waiting. I walked back into the bathroom and sat on the floor, trying to convince myself that it didn't have to be bad news. No one had to be dead. And my parents couldn't break up twice.

I approached the phone and waved the display on. There was a thumbnail image of a severe-looking middle-aged woman, no one I recognized. The sender's name was Dr Z. Durrani, Department of Biomedical Engineering, University of Cape Town. The subject line read: "New Techniques in Prosthetic Reconstructive Neuroplasty." That made a change; most people skimmed the reports on my clinical condition so carelessly that they assumed I was mildly retarded. I felt a refreshing absence of disgust, the closest I could come to respect, for Dr Durrani. But no amount of diligence on her part could save the cure itself from being a mirage.

Health Palace's no-fault settlement provided me with a living allowance equal to the minimum wage, plus reimbursement of approved medical costs; I had no astronomical lump sum to spend as I saw fit. However, any treatment likely to render me financially self-sufficient could be paid for in full, at the discretion of the insurance company. The value of such a cure to Global Assurance—the total remaining cost of supporting me until death—was constantly falling, but then so was medical research funding, worldwide. Word of my case had got around.

Most of the treatments I'd been offered so far had involved novel pharmaceuticals. Drugs *had* freed me from institutional care, but expecting them to turn me into a happy little wage-earner was like hoping for an ointment that made amputated limbs grow back. From Global Assurance's perspective, though, shelling out for anything more sophisticated meant gambling with a much greater sum—a prospect that no doubt sent my case manager scrambling for his actuarial database. There was no point indulging in rash expenditure decisions when there was still a good chance that I'd suicide in my forties. Cheap fixes were always worth a try, even if they were long shots, but any proposal radical enough to stand a real chance of working was guaranteed to fail the risk/cost analysis.

I knelt by the screen with my head in my hands. I could erase the message unseen, sparing myself the frustration of knowing exactly what I'd be missing out on . . . but then, not knowing would be just as bad. I tapped the PLAY button and looked away; meeting the gaze of even a recorded face gave me a feeling of intense shame. I understood why: the neural circuitry needed to register positive non-verbal messages was long gone, but the pathways that warned of responses like rejection and hostility had not merely remained intact, they'd grown skewed and hypersensitive enough to fill the void with a strong negative signal, whatever the reality.

I listened as carefully as I could while Dr Durrani explained her work with stroke patients. Tissue-cultured neural grafts were the current standard treatment, but she'd been injecting an elaborately tailored polymer foam into the damaged region instead. The foam released growth factors that attracted axons and dendrites from surrounding neurons, and the polymer itself was designed to function as a network of electrochemical switches. Via microprocessors scattered throughout the foam, the initially amorphous network was programmed first to reproduce generically the actions of the lost neurons, then fine-tuned for compatibility with the individual recipient.

Dr Durrani listed her triumphs: sight restored, speech restored, movement, continence, musical ability. My own deficit—measured in neurons lost, or synapses, or raw cubic centimeters—lay beyond the range of all the chasms she'd bridged to date. But that only made it more of a challenge.

I waited almost stoically for the one small catch, in six or seven figures. The voice from the screen said, "If you can meet your own travel expenses and the cost of a three-week hospital stay, my research grant will cover the treatment itself."

I replayed these words a dozen times, trying to find a less favorable interpretation—one task I was usually good at. When I failed, I steeled myself and emailed Durrani's assistant in Cape Town, asking for clarification.

There was no misunderstanding. For the cost of a year's supply of the drugs that barely kept me conscious, I was being offered a chance to be whole again for the rest of my life.

ORGANIZING A TRIP TO South Africa was completely beyond me, but once Global Assurance recognized the opportunity it was facing, machinery on two continents swung into action on my behalf. All I had to do was fight down the urge to call everything off. The thought of being hospitalized, of being powerless again, was disturbing enough, but contemplating the potential of the neural prosthesis itself was like staring down the calendar at a secular Judgment Day. On 7 March 2023, I'd either be admitted into an infinitely larger, infinitely richer, infinitely better world . . . or I'd prove to be damaged beyond repair. And in a way, even the final death of hope was a far less terrifying prospect than the alternative; it was so much closer to where I was already, so much easier to imagine. The only vision of *happiness* I could summon up was myself as a child, running joyfully, dissolving into sunlight—which was all very sweet and evocative, but a little short on practical details. If I'd wanted to be a sunbeam, I could have cut my wrists anytime. I wanted a job, I wanted a family, I wanted ordinary love and modest ambitions—because I knew these were the things I'd been denied. But I could no more imagine what it would be like, finally, to attain them, than I could picture daily life in 26-dimensional space.

I didn't sleep at all before the dawn flight out of Sydney. I was escorted to the airport by a psychiatric nurse, but spared the indignity of a minder sitting beside me all the way to Cape Town. I spent my waking moments on the flight fighting paranoia, resisting the temptation to invent reasons for all the sadness and anxiety coursing through my skull. *No one on the plane was staring at me disdainfully. The Durrani technique was not going to turn out to be a hoax.* I succeeded in crushing these "explanatory" delusions . . . but as ever, it remained beyond my power to alter my feelings, or even to draw a clear line between my purely pathological unhappiness, and the perfectly reasonable anxiety that anyone would feel on the verge of radical brain surgery.

Wouldn't it be bliss, not to have to fight to tell the difference all the time? Forget happiness; even a future full of abject misery would be a triumph, so long as I knew that it was always for a reason.

LUKE DE VRIES, ONE of Durrani's postdoctoral students, met me at the airport. He looked about 25, and radiated the kind of self-assurance I had to struggle not to misread as contempt. I felt trapped and helpless immediately; he'd arranged everything, it was like stepping on to a conveyor belt. But I knew that if I'd been left to do anything for myself the whole process would have ground to a halt.

It was after midnight when we reached the hospital in the suburbs of Cape Town. Crossing the car park, the insect sounds were wrong, the air smelled indefinably alien, the constellations looked like clever forgeries. I sagged to my knees as we approached the entrance.

"Hey!" De Vries stopped and helped me up. I was shaking with fear, and then shame too, at the spectacle I was making of myself.

"This violates my Avoidance Therapy."

"Avoidance Therapy?"

"Avoid hospitals at all costs."

De Vries laughed, though if he wasn't merely humoring me I had no way of telling. Recognizing the fact that you'd elicited genuine laughter was a pleasure, so those pathways were all dead.

He said, "We had to carry the last subject in on a stretcher. She left about as steady on her feet as you are."

"That bad?"

"Her artificial hip was playing up. Not our fault."

We walked up the steps and into the brightly lit foyer.

THE NEXT MORNING—MONDAY, 6 March, the day before the operation—I met most of the surgical team who'd perform the first, purely mechanical, part of the procedure: scraping clean the useless cavities left behind by dead neurons, prizing open with tiny balloons any voids that had been squeezed shut, and then pumping the whole oddly-shaped totality full of Durrani's foam. Apart from the existing hole in my skull from the shunt 18 years before, they'd probably have to drill two more.

A nurse shaved my head and glued five reference markers to the exposed skin, then I spent the afternoon being scanned. The final, three-dimensional image of all the dead space in my brain looked like a spelunker's map, a sequence of linked caves complete with rock falls and collapsed tunnels.

Durrani herself came to see me that evening. "While you're still under anesthetic," she explained, "the foam will harden, and the first connections will be made with the surrounding tissue. Then the microprocessors will instruct the polymer to form the network we've chosen to serve as a starting point."

I had to force myself to speak; every question I asked—however politely phrased, however lucid and relevant—felt as painful and degrading as if I was standing before her naked asking her to wipe shit out of my hair. "How did you find a network to use? Did you scan a volunteer?" Was I going to start my new life as a clone of Luke De Vries—inheriting his tastes, his ambitions, his emotions?

"No, no. There's an international database of healthy neural structures—20,000 cadavers who died without brain injury. More detailed than tomography; they froze the brains in liquid nitrogen, sliced them up with a diamond-tipped microtome, then stained and electron-micrographed the slices."

My mind balked at the number of exabytes she was casually invoking; I'd lost touch with computing completely. "So you'll use some kind of composite from the database? You'll give me a selection of typical structures, taken from different people?"

Durrani seemed about to let that pass as near enough, but she was clearly a stickler for detail, and she hadn't insulted my intelligence yet. "Not quite. It will be more like a multiple exposure than a composite. We've used about 4,000 records from the database—all the males in their twenties or thirties—and wherever someone has neuron A wired to neuron B, and someone else has neuron A wired to neuron C . . . you'll have connections to both B *and* C. So you'll start out with a network that in theory could be pared down to any one of the 4,000 individual versions used to construct it—but in fact, you'll pare it down to your own unique version instead."

That sounded better than being an emotional clone or a Frankenstein collage; I'd be a roughly hewn sculpture, with features yet to be refined. But—

"Pare it down how? How will I go from being potentially anyone, to being . . . ?" *What?* My 12-year-old self, resurrected? Or the 30-year-old I should have been, conjured into existence as a remix of these 4,000 dead strangers? I trailed off; I'd lost what little faith I'd had that I was talking sense.

Durrani seemed to grow slightly uneasy, herself—whatever my judgment was worth on that. She said, "There should be parts of your brain, still intact, which bear some record of what's been lost. Memories of formative experiences, memories of the things that used to give you pleasure, fragments of innate structures that survived the virus. The prosthesis will be driven automatically toward a state that's compatible with everything else in your brain—it will find itself interacting with all these other systems, and the connections that work best in that context will be reinforced." She thought for a moment. "Imagine a kind of artificial limb, imperfectly formed to start with, that adjusts itself as you use it: stretching when it fails to grasp what you reach for, shrinking when it bumps something unexpectedly . . . until it takes on precisely the size and shape of the phantom limb implied by your movements. Which itself is nothing but an image of the lost flesh and blood."

That was an appealing metaphor, though it was hard to believe that my faded memories contained enough information to reconstruct their phantom author in every detail—that the whole jigsaw of who I'd been, and might have become, could be filled in from a few hints along the edges and the jumbled-up pieces of 4,000 other portraits of happiness. But the subject was making at least one of us uncomfortable, so I didn't press the point.

I managed to ask a final question. "What will it be like, before any of this happens? When I wake up from the anesthetic and all the connections are still intact?"

Durrani confessed, "That's one thing I'll have no way of knowing, until you tell me yourself."

SOMEONE REPEATED MY NAME, reassuringly but insistently. I woke a little more. My neck, my legs, my back were all aching, and my stomach was tense with nausea.

But the bed was warm, and the sheets were soft. It was good just to be lying there.

"It's Wednesday afternoon. The operation went well."

I opened my eyes. Durrani and four of her students were gathered at the foot of the bed. I stared at her, astonished: the face I'd once thought of as "severe" and "forbidding" was . . . riveting, magnetic. I could have watched her for hours. But then I glanced at Luke De Vries, who was standing beside her. He was just as extraordinary. I turned one by one to the other three students. Everyone was equally mesmerizing; I didn't know where to look.

"How are you feeling?"

I was lost for words. These people's faces were loaded with so much significance, so many sources of fascination, that I had no way of singling out any one factor: they all appeared wise, ecstatic, beautiful, reflective, attentive, compassionate, tranquil, vibrant . . . a white noise of qualities, all positive, but ultimately incoherent.

But as I shifted my gaze compulsively from face to face, struggling to make sense of them, their meanings finally began to crystallize—like words coming into focus, though my sight had never been blurred.

I asked Durrani, "Are you smiling?"

"Slightly." She hesitated. "There are standard tests, standard images for this, but . . . please, describe my expression. Tell me what I'm thinking."

I answered unselfconsciously, as if she'd asked me to read an eye chart. "You're . . . curious? You're listening carefully. You're interested, and you're . . . hoping that something good will happen. And you're smiling because you think it will. Or because you can't quite believe that it already has."

She nodded, smiling more decisively. "Good."

I didn't add that I now found her stunningly, almost painfully, beautiful. But it was the same for everyone in the room, male and female: the haze of contradictory moods that I'd read into their faces had cleared, but it had left behind a heart-stopping radiance. I found this slightly alarming—it was too indiscriminate, too intense—though in a way it seemed almost as natural a response as the dazzling of a dark-adapted eye. And after 18 years of seeing nothing but ugliness in every human face, I wasn't ready to complain about the presence of five people who looked like angels.

Durrani asked, "Are you hungry?"

I had to think about that. "Yes."

One of the students fetched a prepared meal, much the same as the lunch I'd eaten on Monday: salad, a bread roll, cheese. I picked up the roll and took a bite. The texture was perfectly familiar, the flavor unchanged. Two days before, I'd chewed and swallowed the same thing with the usual mild disgust that all food induced in me.

Hot tears rolled down my cheeks. I wasn't in ecstasy; the experience was as strange and painful as drinking from a fountain with lips so parched that the skin had turned to salt and dried blood.

As painful, and as compelling. When I'd emptied the plate, I asked for another. *Eating was good, eating was right, eating was necessary.* After the third plate, Durrani said firmly, "That's enough." I was shaking with the need for more; she was still supernaturally beautiful, but I screamed at her, outraged.

She took my arms, held me still. "This is going to be hard for you. There'll be surges like this, swings in all directions, until the network settles down. You have to try to stay calm, try to stay reflective. The prosthesis makes more things possible than you're used to . . . but you're still in control."

I gritted my teeth and looked away. At her touch I'd suffered an immediate, agonizing erection.

I said, "That's right. I'm in control."

IN THE DAYS THAT followed, my experiences with the prosthesis became much less raw, much less violent. I could almost picture the sharpest, most ill-fitting edges of the network being—metaphorically—worn smooth by use. To eat, to sleep, to be with people remained intensely pleasurable, but it was more like an impossibly rosy-hued dream of childhood than the result of someone poking my brain with a high voltage wire.

Of course, the prosthesis wasn't sending signals into my brain in order to make my brain feel pleasure. *The prosthesis itself* was the part of me that was feeling all the pleasure—however seamlessly that process was integrated with everything else: perception, language, cognition . . . the rest of me. Dwelling on this was unsettling at first, but on reflection no more so than the thought experiment of staining blue all the corresponding organic regions in a healthy brain, and declaring, "*They* feel all the pleasure, not you!"

I was put through a battery of psychological tests—most of which I'd sat through many times before, as part of my annual insurance assessments—as Durrani's team attempted to quantify their success. Maybe a stroke patient's fine control of a formerly paralyzed hand was easier to measure objectively, but I must have leaped from bottom to top of every numerical scale for positive affect. And far from being a source of irritation, these tests gave me my first opportunity to use the prosthesis in new arenas—to be happy in ways I could barely remember experiencing before. As well as being required to interpret mundanely rendered scenes of domestic situations—what has just happened between this child, this woman, and this man; who is feeling good and who is feeling bad?—I was shown breathtaking images of great works of art, from complex allegorical and narrative paintings to elegant minimalist essays in geometry. As well as listening to snatches of everyday speech, and even unadorned cries of joy and pain, I was played samples of music and song from every tradition, every epoch, every style.

That was when I finally realized that something was wrong.

Jacob Tsela was playing the audio files and noting my responses. He'd been deadpan for most of the session, carefully avoiding any risk of corrupting the data by betraying his own opinions. But after he'd played a heavenly fragment of European classical music, and I'd rated it 20 out of 20, I caught a flicker of dismay on his face.

"What? You didn't like it?"

Tsela smiled opaquely. "It doesn't matter what I like. That's not what we're measuring."

"I've rated it already, you can't influence my score." I regarded him imploringly; I was desperate for communication of any kind. "I've been dead to the world for 18 years. I don't even know who the composer was."

He hesitated. "J.S. Bach. And I agree with you: it's sublime." He reached for the touchscreen and continued the experiment.

So what had he been dismayed about? I knew the answer immediately; I'd been an idiot not to notice before, but I'd been too absorbed in the music itself.

I hadn't scored any piece lower than 18. And it had been the same with the visual arts. From my 4,000 virtual donors I'd inherited, not the lowest common denominator, but the widest possible taste—and in ten days, I still hadn't imposed any constraints, any preferences, of my own.

All art was sublime to me, and all music. Every kind of food was delicious. Everyone I laid eyes on was a vision of perfection.

Maybe I was just soaking up pleasure wherever I could get it, after my long drought, but it was only a matter of time before I grew sated, and became as discriminating, as focused, as *particular*, as everyone else.

"Should I still be like this? *Omnivorous?*" I blurted out the question, starting with a tone of mild curiosity, ending with an edge of panic.

Tsela halted the sample he'd been playing—a chant that might have been Albanian, Moroccan, or Mongolian for all I knew, but which made hair rise on the back of my neck, and sent my spirits soaring. Just like everything else had.

He was silent for a while, weighing up competing obligations. Then he sighed and said, "You'd better talk to Durrani."

DURRANI SHOWED ME A bar graph on the wallscreen in her office: the number of artificial synapses that had changed state within the prosthesis—new connections formed, existing ones broken, weakened or strengthened—for each of the past ten days. The embedded microprocessors kept track of such things, and an antenna waved over my skull each morning collected the data.

Day one had been dramatic, as the prosthesis adapted to its environment; the 4,000 contributing networks might all have been perfectly stable in their owners' skulls, but the Everyman version I'd been given had never been wired up to anyone's brain before.

Day two had seen about half as much activity, day three about a tenth.

From day four on, though, there'd been nothing but background noise. My episodic memories, however pleasurable, were apparently being stored elsewhere—since I certainly wasn't suffering from amnesia—but after the initial burst of activity, the circuitry for defining what pleasure *was* had undergone no change, no refinement at all.

"If any trends emerge in the next few days, we should be able to amplify them, push them forward—like toppling an unstable building, once it's showing signs of falling in a certain direction." Durrani didn't sound hopeful. Too much time had passed already, and the network wasn't even teetering.

I said, "What about genetic factors? Can't you read my genome, and narrow things down from that?"

She shook her head. "At least 2,000 genes play a role in neural development. It's not like matching a blood group or a tissue type; everyone in the database would have more or less the same small proportion of those genes in common with you. Of course, some people must have been closer to you in temperament than others—but we have no way of identifying them genetically."

"I see."

Durrani said carefully, "We could shut the prosthesis down completely, if that's what you want. There'd be no need for surgery—we'd just turn it off, and you'd be back where you started."

I stared at her luminous face. *How could I go back?* Whatever the tests and the bar graphs said . . . *how could this be failure?* However much useless beauty I was drowning in, I wasn't as screwed-up as I'd been with a head full of Leu-enkephalin. I was still capable of fear, anxiety, sorrow; the tests had revealed universal shadows, common to all the donors. Hating Bach or Chuck Berry, Chagall or Paul Klee was beyond me, but I'd reacted as sanely as anyone to images of disease, starvation, death.

And I was not oblivious to my own fate, the way I'd been oblivious to the cancer.

But what was my fate, if I kept using the prosthesis? Universal happiness, universal shadows . . . half the human race dictating my emotions? In all the years I'd spent in darkness, if I'd held fast to anything, hadn't it been the possibility that I carried a kind of seed within me: a version of myself that might grow into a living person again, given the chance? *And hadn't that hope now proved false?* I'd been offered the stuff of which selves were made—and though I'd tested it all, and admired it all, I'd claimed none of it as my own. All the joy I'd felt in the last ten days had been meaningless. I was just a dead husk, blowing around in other peoples' sunlight.

I said, "I think you should do that. Switch it off."

Durrani held up her hand. "Wait. If you're willing, there is one other thing we could try. I've been discussing it with our ethics committee, and Luke has begun preliminary work on the software . . . but in the end, it will be your decision."

"To do what?"

"The network can be pushed in any direction. We know how to intervene to do that—to break the symmetry, to make some things a greater source of pleasure than others. Just because it hasn't happened spontaneously, that doesn't mean it can't be achieved by other means."

I laughed, suddenly light-headed. "So if I say the word . . . *your ethics committee* will choose the music I like, and my favorite foods, and my new vocation? They'll decide who I become?" Would that be so bad? Having died, myself, long ago, to grant life now to a whole new person? To donate, not just a lung or a kidney, but my entire body, irrelevant memories and all, to an arbitrarily constructed—but fully functioning—*de novo* human being?

Durrani was scandalized. "No! We'd never dream of doing that! But we could program the microprocessors to let *you* control the network's refinement. We could give you the power to choose for yourself, consciously and deliberately, the things that make you happy."

DE VRIES SAID, "TRY to picture the control."

I closed my eyes. He said, "Bad idea. If you get into the habit, it will limit your access."

"Right." I stared into space. Something glorious by Beethoven was playing on the lab's sound system; it was difficult to concentrate. I struggled to visualize the stylized, cherry-red, horizontal slider control that De Vries had constructed, line by line, inside my head five minutes before. Suddenly it was more than a vague memory: it was superimposed over the room again, as clear as any real object, at the bottom of my visual field.

"I've got it." The button was hovering around 19.

De Vries glanced at a display, hidden from me. "Good. Now try to lower the rating."

I laughed weakly. *Roll over Beethoven.* "How? How can you try to like something less?"

"You don't. Just try to move the button to the left. Visualize the movement. The software's monitoring your visual cortex, tracking any fleeting imaginary perceptions. Fool yourself into seeing the button moving—and the image will oblige."

It did. I kept losing control briefly, as if the thing was sticking, but I managed to maneuver it down to 10 before stopping to assess the effect.

"Fuck."

"I take it it's working?"

I nodded stupidly. The music was still . . . *pleasant* . . . but the spell was broken completely. It was like listening to an electrifying piece of rhetoric, then realizing half-way through that the speaker didn't believe a word of it—leaving the original poetry and eloquence untouched, but robbing it of all its real force.

I felt sweat break out on my forehead. When Durrani had explained it, the whole scheme had sounded too bizarre to be real. And since I'd already failed to assert myself over the prosthesis—despite billions of direct neural connections, and countless opportunities for the remnants of my identity to interact with the thing and shape it in my own image—I'd feared that when the time came to make a choice, I'd be paralyzed by indecision.

But I knew, beyond doubt, that I should *not* have been in a state of rapture over a piece of classical music that I'd either never heard before, or—since apparently it was famous, and ubiquitous—sat through once or twice by accident, entirely unmoved.

And now, in a matter of seconds, I'd hacked that false response away.

There was still hope. I still had a chance to resurrect myself. I'd just have to do it consciously, every step of the way.

De Vries, tinkering with his keyboard, said cheerfully, "I'll color-code virtual gadgets for all the major systems in the prosthesis. With a few days' practice it'll all be second nature. Just remember that some experiences will engage two or three systems at once . . . so if you're making love to music that you'd prefer not to find so distracting, make sure you turn down the red control, not the blue." He looked up and saw my face. "Hey, don't worry. You can always turn it up again later if you make a mistake. Or if you change your mind."

3

IT WAS NINE P.M. in Sydney when the plane touched down. Nine o'clock on a Saturday night. I took a train into the city center, intending to catch the connecting one home, but when I saw the crowds alighting at Town Hall station I put my suitcase in a locker and followed them up on to the street.

I'd been in the city a few times since the virus, but never at night. I felt as if I'd come home after half a lifetime in another country, after solitary confinement in a foreign gaol. Everything was disorienting, one way or another. I felt a kind of giddy *déjà vu* at the sight of buildings that seemed to have been faithfully preserved, but still weren't quite as I remembered them, and a sense of hollowness each time I turned a corner to find that some private landmark, some shop or sign I remembered from childhood, had vanished.

I stood outside a pub, close enough to feel my eardrums throb to the beat of the music. I could see people inside, laughing and dancing, sloshing armfuls of drinks around, faces glowing with alcohol and companionship. Some alive with the possibility of violence, others with the promise of sex.

I could step right into this picture myself, now. The ash that had buried the world was gone; I was free to walk wherever I pleased. And I could almost feel the dead cousins of these revelers—reborn now as harmonics of the network, resonating to the music and the sight of their soul-mates—clamoring in my skull, begging me to carry them all the way to the land of the living.

I took a few steps forward, then something in the corner of my vision distracted me. In the alley beside the pub, a boy of 10 or 12 sat crouched against the wall, lowering his face into a plastic bag. After a few inhalations he looked up, dead eyes shining, smiling as blissfully as any orchestra conductor.

I backed away.

Someone touched my shoulder. I spun around and saw a man beaming at me. "Jesus loves you, brother! Your search is over!" He thrust a pamphlet into my hand. I gazed into his face, and his condition was transparent to me: he'd stumbled on a way to produce Leu-enkephalin at will—but he didn't know it, so he'd reasoned that some divine wellspring of happiness was responsible. I felt my chest tighten with horror and pity. At least I'd known about my tumor. And even the fucked-up kid in the alley understood that he was just sniffing glue.

And the people in the pub? Did they know what they were doing? Music, companionship, alcohol, sex . . . where did the border lie? When did justifiable happiness turn into something as empty, as pathological, as it was for this man?

I stumbled away, and headed back toward the station. All around me, people were laughing and shouting, holding hands, kissing . . . and I watched them as if they were flayed anatomical figures, revealing a thousand interlocking muscles working together with effortless precision. Buried inside me, the machinery of happiness recognized itself, again and again.

I had no doubt, now, that Durrani really had packed every last shred of the human capacity for joy into my skull. But to claim any part of it, I'd have to swallow the fact—more deeply than the tumor had ever forced me to swallow it—that happiness itself meant nothing. Life without it was unbearable, but as an end in itself, it was not enough. I was free to choose its causes—and to be happy with my choices—but whatever I felt once I'd bootstrapped my new self into existence, the possibility would remain that all my choices had been wrong.

GLOBAL ASSURANCE HAD GIVEN me until the end of the year to get my act together. If my annual psychological assessment showed that Durrani's treatment had been successful—whether or not I actually had a job—I'd be thrown to the even less tender mercies of the privatized remnants of social security. So I stumbled around in the light, trying to find my bearings.

On my first day back I woke at dawn. I sat down at the phone and started digging. My old net workspace had been archived; at current rates it was only costing about ten cents a year in storage fees, and I still had $36.20 credit in my account. The whole bizarre informational fossil had passed intact from company to company through four takeovers and mergers. Working through an assortment of tools to decode the obsolete data formats, I dragged fragments of my past life into the present and examined them, until it became too painful to go on.

The next day I spent twelve hours cleaning the flat, scrubbing every corner—listening to my old *njari* downloads, stopping only to eat, ravenously. And though I could have refined my taste in food back to that of a 12-year-old salt-junky, I made the choice—thoroughly un-masochistic, and more pragmatic than virtuous—to crave nothing more toxic than fruit.

In the following weeks I put on weight with gratifying speed, though when I stared at myself in the mirror, or used morphing software running on the phone, I realized that I could be happy with almost any kind of body. The database must have included people with a vast range of ideal self-images, or who'd died perfectly content with their actual appearances.

Again, I chose pragmatism. I had a lot of catching up to do, and I didn't want to die at 55 from a heart attack if I could avoid it. There was no point fixating on the unattainable or the absurd, though, so after morphing myself to obesity, and rating it zero, I did the same for the Schwarzenegger look. I chose a lean, wiry body—well within the realms of possibility, according to the software—and assigned it 16 out of 20. Then I started running.

I took it slowly at first, and though I clung to the image of myself as a child, darting effortlessly from street to street, I was careful never to crank up the joy of motion high enough to mask injuries. When I limped into a chemist looking for liniment, I found they were selling something called prostaglandin modulators, anti-inflammatory compounds that allegedly minimized damage without shutting down any vital repair processes. I was skeptical, but the stuff did seem to help; the first month was still painful, but I was neither crippled by natural swelling, nor rendered so oblivious to danger signs that I tore a muscle.

And once my heart and lungs and calves were dragged screaming out of their atrophied state, *it was good*. I ran for an hour every morning, weaving around the local back streets, and on Sunday afternoons I circumnavigated the city itself. I didn't push myself to attain ever faster times; I had no athletic ambitions whatsoever. I just wanted to exercise my freedom.

Soon the act of running melted into a kind of seamless whole. I could revel in the thudding of my heart and the feeling of my limbs in motion, or I could let those details recede into a buzz of satisfaction and just watch the scenery, as if from a train. And having reclaimed my body, I began to reclaim the suburbs, one by one. From the slivers of forest clinging to the Lane Cove river to the eternal ugliness of Parramatta Road, I crisscrossed Sydney like a mad surveyor, wrapping the landscape with invisible geodesics then drawing it into my skull. I pounded across the bridges at Gladesville and Iron Cove, Pyrmont, Meadowbank, and the Harbor itself, daring the planks to give way beneath my feet.

I suffered moments of doubt. I wasn't drunk on endorphins—I wasn't pushing myself that hard—but it still felt too good to be true. *Was this glue-sniffing?* Maybe ten thousand generations of my ancestors had been rewarded with the same kind of pleasure for pursuing game, fleeing danger, and mapping their territory for the sake of survival, but to me it was all just a glorious pastime.

Still, I wasn't deceiving myself, and I wasn't hurting anyone. I plucked those two rules from the core of the dead child inside me, and kept on running.

Thirty was an interesting age to go through puberty. The virus hadn't literally castrated me, but having eliminated pleasure from sexual imagery, genital stimulation, and orgasm—and having partly wrecked the hormonal regulatory pathways reaching down from the hypothalamus—it had left me with nothing worth describing as sexual function. My body disposed of semen in sporadic joyless spasms—and without the normal lubricants secreted by the prostate during arousal, every unwanted ejaculation tore at the urethral lining.

When all of this changed, it hit hard—even in my state of relative sexual decrepitude. Compared to wet dreams of broken glass, masturbation was wonderful beyond belief, and I found myself unwilling to intervene with the controls to tone it down. But I needn't have worried that it would rob me of interest in the real thing; I kept finding myself staring openly at people on the street, in shops and on trains, until by a combination of willpower, sheer terror, and prosthetic adjustment I managed to kick the habit.

The network had rendered me bisexual, and though I quickly ramped my level of desire down considerably from that of the database's most priapic contributors, when it came to choosing to be straight or gay, everything turned to quicksand. The network was not some kind of population-weighted average; if it had been, Durrani's original hope that my own surviving neural architecture could hold sway would have been dashed whenever the vote was stacked against it. So I was not just 10 or 15 per cent gay; the two possibilities were present with equal force, and the thought of eliminating *either* felt as alarming, as disfiguring, as if I'd lived with both for decades.

But was that just the prosthesis defending itself, or was it partly my own response? I had no idea. I'd been a thoroughly asexual 12-year-old, even before the virus; I'd always assumed that I was straight, and I'd certainly found some girls attractive, but there'd been no moonstruck stares or furtive groping to back up that purely esthetic opinion. I looked up the latest research, but all the genetic claims I recalled from various headlines had since been discredited—so even if my sexuality had been determined from birth, there was no blood test that could tell me, now, what it would have become. I even tracked down my pre-treatment MRI scans, but they lacked the resolution to provide a direct, neuroanatomical answer.

I didn't want to be bisexual. I was too old to experiment like a teenager; I wanted certainty, I wanted solid foundations. I wanted to be monogamous—and even if monogamy was rarely an effortless state for anyone, that was no reason to lumber myself with unnecessary obstacles. *So who should I slaughter?* I knew which choice would make things easier . . . but if everything came down to a question of which of the 4,000 donors could carry me along the path of least resistance, whose life would I be living?

Maybe it was all a moot point. I was a 30-year-old virgin with a history of mental illness, no money, no prospects, no social skills—and I could always crank up the satisfaction level of my only current option, and let everything else recede into fantasy. I wasn't deceiving myself, I wasn't hurting anyone. It was within my power to want nothing more.

I'D NOTICED THE BOOKSHOP, tucked away in a back street in Leichhardt, many times before. But one Sunday in June, when I jogged past and saw a copy of *The Man Without Qualities* by Robert Musil in the front window, I had to stop and laugh.

I was drenched in sweat from the winter humidity, so I didn't go in and buy the book. But I peered in through the display toward the counter, and spotted a HELP WANTED sign.

Looking for unskilled work had seemed futile; the total unemployment rate was 15 per cent, the youth rate three times higher, so I'd assumed there'd always be a thousand other applicants for every job: younger, cheaper, stronger, and certifiably sane. But though I'd resumed my on-line education, I was getting not so much nowhere, fast as everywhere, slowly. All the fields of knowledge that had gripped me as a child had expanded a hundredfold, and while the prosthesis granted me limitless energy and enthusiasm, there was still too much ground for anyone to cover in a lifetime. I knew I'd have to sacrifice 90 per cent of my interests if I was ever going to choose a career, but I still hadn't been able to wield the knife.

I returned to the bookshop on Monday, walking up from Petersham station. I'd fine-tuned my confidence for the occasion, but it rose spontaneously when I heard that there'd been no other applicants. The owner was in his 60s, and he'd just done his back in; he wanted someone to lug boxes around, and take the counter when he was otherwise occupied. I told him the truth: I'd been neurologically damaged by a childhood illness, and I'd only recently recovered.

He hired me on the spot, for a month's trial. The starting wage was exactly what Global Assurance were paying me, but if I was taken on permanently I'd get slightly more.

The work wasn't hard, and the owner didn't mind me reading in the back room when I had nothing to do. In a way, I was in heaven—ten thousand books, and no access fees—but sometimes I felt the terror of dissolution returning. I read voraciously, and on one level I could make clear judgments: I could pick the clumsy writers from the skilled, the honest from the fakers, the platitudinous from the inspired. But the prosthesis still wanted me to enjoy everything, to embrace everything, to diffuse out across the dusty shelves until I was no one at all, a ghost in the Library of Babel.

She walked into the bookshop two minutes after opening time, on the first day of spring. Watching her browse, I tried to think clearly through the consequences of what I was about to do. For weeks I'd been on the counter five hours a day, and with all that human contact I'd been hoping for . . . *something*. Not wild, reciprocated love at first sight, just the tiniest flicker of mutual interest, the slightest piece of evidence that I could actually desire one human being more than all the rest.

It hadn't happened. Some customers had flirted mildly, but I could see that it was nothing special, just their own kind of politeness—and I'd felt nothing more in response than if they'd been unusually, formally, courteous. And though I might have agreed with any bystander as to who was conventionally good-looking, who was animated or mysterious, witty or charming, who glowed with youth or radiated worldliness . . . I just didn't care. The 4,000 had all loved very different people, and the envelope that stretched between their far-flung characteristics encompassed the entire species. That was never going to change, until I did something to break the symmetry myself.

So for the past week, I'd dragged all the relevant systems in the prosthesis down to 3 or 4. People had become scarcely more interesting to watch than pieces of wood. Now, alone in the shop with this randomly chosen stranger, I slowly turned the controls up. I had to fight against positive feedback; the higher the settings, the more I wanted to increase them, but I'd set limits in advance, and I stuck to them.

By the time she'd chosen two books and approached the counter, I was feeling half defiantly triumphant, half sick with shame. I'd struck a pure note with the network at last; what I felt at the sight of this woman rang true. And if everything I'd done to achieve it was calculated, artificial, bizarre and abhorrent . . . I'd had no other way.

I was smiling as she bought the books, and she smiled back warmly. No wedding or engagement ring—but I'd promised myself that I wouldn't try anything, no matter what. This was just the first step: to notice someone, to make someone stand out from the crowd. I could ask out the tenth, the hundredth woman who bore some passing resemblance to her.

I said, "Would you like to meet for a coffee sometime?"

She looked surprised, but not affronted. Indecisive, but at least slightly pleased to have been asked. And I thought I was prepared for this slip of the tongue to lead nowhere, but then something in the ruins of me sent a shaft of pain through my chest as I watched her make up her mind. If a fraction of that had shown on my face, she probably would have rushed me to the nearest vet to be put down.

She said, "That would be nice. I'm Julia, by the way."

"I'm Mark." We shook hands.

"When do you finish work?"

"Tonight? Nine o'clock."

"Ah."

I said, "How about lunch? When do you have lunch?"

"One." She hesitated. "There's that place just down the road . . . next to the hardware store?"

"That would be great."

Julia smiled. "Then I'll meet you there. About ten past. Okay?"

I nodded. She turned and walked out. I stared after her, dazed, terrified, elated. I thought: This is simple. Anyone in the world can do it. It's like breathing.

I started hyperventilating. I was an emotionally retarded teen-ager, and she'd discover that in five minutes flat. Or, worse, discover the 4,000 grown men in my head offering advice.

I went into the toilet to throw up.

JULIA TOLD ME THAT she managed a dress shop a few blocks away. "You're new at the bookshop, aren't you?"

"Yes."

"So what were you doing before that?"

"I was unemployed. For a long time."

"How long?"

"Since I was a student."

She grimaced. "It's criminal, isn't it? Well, I'm doing my bit. I'm job-sharing, half-time only."

"Really? How are you finding it?"

"It's wonderful. I mean, I'm lucky, the position's well enough paid that I can get by on half a salary." She laughed. "Most people assume I must be raising a family. As if that's the only possible reason."

"You just like to have the time?"

"Yes. Time's important. I hate being rushed."

We had lunch again two days later, and then twice again the next week. She talked about the shop, a trip she'd made to South America, a sister recovering from breast cancer. I almost mentioned my own long-vanquished tumor, but apart from fears about where that might lead, it would have sounded too much like a plea for sympathy. At home, I sat riveted to the phone—not waiting for a call, but watching news broadcasts, to be sure I'd have something to talk about besides myself. *Who's your favorite singer/author/artist/actor? I have no idea.*

Visions of Julia filled my head. I wanted to know what she was doing every second of the day; I wanted her to be happy, I wanted her to be safe. *Why?* Because I'd chosen her. But . . . why had I felt compelled to choose anyone? Because in the end, the one thing that most of the donors must have had in common was the fact that they'd desired, and cared about, one person above all others. *Why?* That came down to evolution. You could no more help and protect everyone in sight than you could fuck them, and a judicious combination of the two had obviously proved effective at passing down genes. So my emotions had the same ancestry as everyone else's; what more could I ask?

But how could I pretend that I felt anything real for Julia, when I could shift a few buttons in my head, anytime, and make those feelings vanish? Even if what I felt was strong enough to keep me from wanting to touch that dial . . .

Some days I thought: it must be like this for everyone. People make a decision, half-shaped by chance, to get to know someone; everything starts from there. Some nights I sat awake for hours, wondering if I was turning myself into a pathetic slave, or a dangerous obsessive. Could anything I discovered about Julia drive me away, now that I'd chosen her? Or even trigger the slightest disapproval? And if, when, she decided to break things off, how would I take it?

We went out to dinner, then shared a taxi home. I kissed her goodnight on her doorstep. Back in my flat, I flipped through sex manuals on the net, wondering how I could ever hope to conceal my complete lack of experience. Everything looked anatomically impossible; I'd need six years of gymnastics training just to achieve the missionary position. I'd refused to masturbate since I'd met her; to fantasize about her, to *imagine her* without consent, seemed outrageous, unforgivable. After I gave in, I lay awake until dawn trying to comprehend the trap I'd dug for myself, and trying to understand why I didn't want to be free.

JULIA BENT DOWN AND kissed me, sweatily. "That was a nice idea." She climbed off me and flopped onto the bed.

I'd spent the last ten minutes riding the blue control, trying to keep myself from coming without losing my erection. I'd heard of computer games involving exactly the same thing. Now I turned up the indigo for a stronger glow of intimacy—and when I looked into her eyes, I knew that she could see the effect on me. She brushed my cheek with her hand. "You're a sweet man. Did you know that?"

I said, "I have to tell you something." *Sweet? I'm a puppet, I'm a robot, I'm a freak.*

"What?"

I couldn't speak. She seemed amused, then she kissed me. "I know you're gay. That's all right; I don't mind."

"I'm not gay." *Anymore?* "Though I might have been."

Julia frowned. "Gay, bisexual . . . I don't care. Honestly."

I wouldn't have to manipulate my responses much longer; the prosthesis was being shaped by all of this, and in a few weeks I'd be able to leave it to its own devices. Then I'd feel, as naturally as anyone, all the things I was now having to choose.

I said, "When I was twelve, I had cancer."

I told her everything. I watched her face, and saw horror, then growing doubt. "You don't believe me?"

She replied haltingly, "You sound so matter-of-fact. *Eighteen years?* How can you just say, 'I lost eighteen years'?"

"How do you want me to say it? I'm not trying to make you pity me. I just want you to understand."

When I came to the day I met her, my stomach tightened with fear, but I kept on talking. After a few seconds I saw tears in her eyes, and I felt like I'd been knifed.

"I'm sorry. I didn't mean to hurt you." I didn't know whether to try to hold her, or to leave right then. I kept my eyes fixed on her, but the room swam.

She smiled. "What are you sorry about? You chose me. I chose you. It could have been different for both of us. But it wasn't." She reached down under the sheet and took my hand. "It wasn't."

JULIA HAD SATURDAYS OFF, but I had to start work at eight. She kissed me goodbye sleepily when I left at six; I walked all the way home, weightless.

I must have grinned inanely at everyone who came into the shop, but I hardly saw them. I was picturing the future. I hadn't spoken to either of my parents for nine years, they didn't even know about the Durrani treatment. But now it seemed possible to repair anything. I could go to them now and say: *This is your son, back from the dead. You did save my life, all those years ago.*

There was a message on the phone from Julia when I arrived home. I resisted viewing it until I'd started things cooking on the stove; there was something perversely pleasurable about forcing myself to wait, imagining her face and her voice in anticipation.

I hit the PLAY button. Her face wasn't quite as I'd pictured it.

I kept missing things and stopping to rewind. Isolated phrases stuck in my mind. *Too strange. Too sick. No one's fault.* My explanation hadn't really sunk in the night before. But now she'd had time to think about it, and she wasn't prepared to carry on a relationship with 4,000 dead men.

I sat on the floor, trying to decide what to feel: the wave of pain crashing over me, or something better, by choice. I knew I could summon up the controls of the prosthesis and make myself happy—happy because I was "free" again, happy because I was better off without her . . . happy because Julia was better off without me. Or even just happy because happiness meant nothing, and all I had to do to attain it was flood my brain with Leu-enkephalin.

I sat there wiping tears and mucus off my face while the vegetables burned. The smell made me think of cauterization, sealing off a wound.

I let things run their course, I didn't touch the controls—but just knowing that I could have changed everything. And I realized then that, even if I went to Luke De Vries and said: I'm cured now, take the software away, I don't want the power to choose anymore . . . I'd never be able to forget where everything I felt had come from.

MY FATHER CAME TO the flat yesterday. We didn't talk much, but he hasn't remarried yet, and he made a joke about us going night-club-hopping together.

At least I hope it was a joke.

Watching him, I thought: he's there inside my head, and my mother too, and ten million ancestors, human, proto-human, remote beyond imagining. What difference did 4,000 more make? Everyone had to carve a life out of the same legacy: half universal, half particular; half sharpened by relentless natural selection, half softened by the freedom of chance. I'd just had to face the details a little more starkly.

And I could go on doing it, walking the convoluted border between meaningless happiness and meaningless despair. Maybe I was lucky; maybe the best way to cling to that narrow zone was to see clearly what lay on either side.

When my father was leaving, he looked out from the balcony across the crowded suburb, down toward the Parramatta river, where a storm drain was discharging a visible plume of oil, street litter, and garden run-off into the water.

He asked dubiously, "You happy with this area?"

I said, "I like it here."

OCEANIC

1

THE SWELL WAS GENTLY lifting and lowering the boat. My breathing grew slower, falling into step with the creaking of the hull, until I could no longer tell the difference between the faint rhythmic motion of the cabin and the sensation of filling and emptying my lungs. It was like floating in darkness: every inhalation buoyed me up, slightly; every exhalation made me sink back down again.

In the bunk above me, my brother Daniel said distinctly, "Do you believe in God?"

My head was cleared of sleep in an instant, but I didn't reply straight away. I'd never closed my eyes, but the darkness of the unlit cabin seemed to shift in front of me, grains of phantom light moving like a cloud of disturbed insects.

"Martin?"

"I'm awake."

"Do you believe in God?"

"Of course." Everyone I knew believed in God. Everyone talked about Her, everyone prayed to Her. Daniel most of all. Since he'd joined the Deep Church the previous summer, he prayed every morning for a kilotau before dawn. I'd often wake to find myself aware of him kneeling by the far wall of the cabin, muttering and pounding his chest, before I drifted gratefully back to sleep.

Our family had always been Transitional, but Daniel was fifteen, old enough to choose for himself. My mother accepted this with diplomatic silence, but my father seemed positively proud of Daniel's independence and strength of conviction. My own feelings were mixed. I'd grown used to swimming in my older brother's wake, but I'd never resented it, because he'd always let me in on the view ahead: reading me passages from the books he read himself, teaching me words and phrases from the languages he studied, sketching some of the mathematics I was yet to encounter first-hand. We used to lie awake half the night, talking about the cores of stars or the hierarchy of transfinite numbers. But Daniel had told me nothing about the reasons for his conversion, and his ever-increasing piety. I didn't know whether to feel hurt by this exclusion, or simply grateful; I could see that being Transitional was like a pale imitation of being Deep Church, but I wasn't sure that this was such a bad thing if the wages of mediocrity included sleeping until sunrise.

Daniel said, "Why?"

I stared up at the underside of his bunk, unsure whether I was really seeing it or just imagining its solidity against the cabin's ordinary darkness. "Someone must have guided the Angels here from Earth. If Earth's too far away to see from Covenant . . . how could anyone find Covenant from Earth, without God's help?"

I heard Daniel shift slightly. "Maybe the Angels had better telescopes than us. Or maybe they spread out from Earth in all directions, launching thousands of expeditions without even knowing what they'd find."

I laughed. "But they had to come *here*, to be made flesh again!" Even a less-than-devout ten-year-old knew that much. God prepared Covenant as the place for the Angels to repent their theft of immortality. The Transitionals believed that in a million years we could earn the right to be Angels again; the Deep Church believed that we'd remain flesh until the stars fell from the sky.

Daniel said, "What makes you so sure that there were ever really Angels? Or that God really sent them Her daughter, Beatrice, to lead them back into the flesh?"

I pondered this for a while. The only answers I could think of came straight out of the Scriptures, and Daniel had taught me years ago that appeals to authority counted for nothing. Finally, I had to confess: "I don't know." I felt foolish, but I was grateful that he was willing to discuss these difficult questions with me. I wanted to believe in God for the right reasons, not just because everyone around me did.

He said, "Archaeologists have shown that we must have arrived about twenty thousand years ago. Before that, there's no evidence of humans, or any co-ecological plants and animals. That makes the Crossing older than the Scriptures say, but there are some dates that are open to interpretation, and with a bit of poetic license every-thing can be made to add up. And most biologists think the native microfauna could have formed by itself over millions of years, start-ing from simple chemicals, but that doesn't mean God didn't guide the whole process. Everything's compatible, really. Science and the Scriptures can both be true."

I thought I knew where he was headed, now. "So you've worked out a way to use science to prove that God exists?" I felt a surge of pride; my brother was a genius!

"No." Daniel was silent for a moment. "The thing is, it works both ways. Whatever's written in the Scriptures, people can always come up with different explanations for the facts. The ships might have left Earth for some other reason. The Angels might have made bodies for themselves for some other reason. There's no way to con-vince a non-believer that the Scriptures are the word of God. It's all a matter of faith."

"Oh."

"Faith's the most important thing," Daniel insisted. "If you don't have faith, you can be tempted into believing anything at all."

I made a noise of assent, trying not to sound too disappointed. I'd expected more from Daniel than the kind of bland assertions that sent me dozing off during sermons at the Transitional church.

"Do you know what you have to do to get faith?"

"No."

"Ask for it. That's all. Ask Beatrice to come into your heart and grant you the gift of faith."

I protested, "We do that every time we go to church!" I couldn't believe he'd forgotten the Transitional service already. After the priest placed a drop of seawater on our tongues, to symbolize the blood of Beatrice, we asked for the gifts of faith, hope and love.

"But have you received it?"

I'd never thought about that. "I'm not sure." I believed in God, didn't I? "I might have."

Daniel was amused. "If you had the gift of faith, you'd *know*."

I gazed up into the darkness, troubled. "Do you have to go to the Deep Church, to ask for it properly?"

"No. Even in the Deep Church, not everyone has invited Beatrice into their hearts. You have to do it the way it says in the Scriptures: 'like an unborn child again, naked and helpless.'"

"I was Immersed, wasn't I?"

"In a metal bowl, when you were thirty days old. Infant Immersion is a gesture by the parents, an affirmation of their own good intentions. But it's not enough to save the child."

I was feeling very disoriented now. My father, at least, approved of Daniel's conversion . . . but now Daniel was trying to tell me that our family's transactions with God had all been grossly deficient, if not actually counterfeit.

Daniel said, "Remember what Beatrice told Her followers, the last time She appeared? 'Unless you are willing to drown in My blood, you will never look upon the face of My Mother.' So they bound each other hand and foot, and weighted themselves down with rocks."

My chest tightened. "And you've done that?"

"Yes."

"*When?*"

"Almost a year ago."

I was more confused than ever. "Did Ma and Fa go?"

Daniel laughed. "No! It's not a public ceremony. Some friends of mine from the Prayer Group helped; someone has to be on deck to haul you up, because it would be arrogant to expect Beatrice to break your bonds and raise you to the surface, like She did with Her followers. But in the water, you're alone with God."

He climbed down from his bunk and crouched by the side of my bed. "Are you ready to give your life to Beatrice, Martin?" His voice sent gray sparks flowing through the darkness.

I hesitated. "What if I just dive in? And stay under for a while?" I'd been swimming off the boat at night plenty of times, there was nothing to fear from that.

"No. You have to be weighted down." His tone made it clear that there could be no compromise on this. "How long can you hold your breath?"

"Two hundred tau." That was an exaggeration; two hundred was what I was aiming for.

"That's long enough."

I didn't reply. Daniel said, "I'll pray with you."

I climbed out of bed, and we knelt together. Daniel murmured, "Please, Holy Beatrice, grant my brother Martin the courage to accept the precious gift of Your blood." Then he started praying in what I took to be a foreign language, uttering a rapid stream of harsh syllables unlike anything I'd heard before. I listened apprehensively; I wasn't sure that I wanted Beatrice to change my mind, and I was afraid that this display of fervor might actually persuade Her.

I said, "What if I don't do it?"

"Then you'll never see the face of God."

I knew what that meant: I'd wander alone in the belly of Death, in darkness, for eternity. And even if the Scriptures weren't meant to be taken literally on this, the reality behind the metaphor could only be worse. Indescribably worse.

"But . . . what about Ma and Fa?" I was more worried about them, because I knew they'd never climb weighted off the side of the boat at Daniel's behest.

"That will take time," he said softly.

My mind reeled. He was absolutely serious.

I heard him stand and walk over to the ladder. He climbed a few rungs and opened the hatch. Enough starlight came in to give shape to his arms and shoulders, but as he turned to me I still couldn't make out his face. "Come on, Martin!" he whispered. "The longer you put it off, the harder it gets." The hushed urgency of his voice was familiar: generous and conspiratorial, nothing like an adult's impatience. He might almost have been daring me to join him in a midnight raid on the pantry—not because he really needed a collaborator, but because he honestly didn't want me to miss out on the excitement, or the spoils.

I suppose I was more afraid of damnation than drowning, and I'd always trusted Daniel to warn me of the dangers ahead. But this time I wasn't entirely convinced that he was right, so I must have been driven by something more than fear, and blind trust.

Maybe it came down to the fact that he was offering to make me his equal in this. I was ten years old, and I ached to become something more than I was; to reach, not my parents' burdensome adulthood, but the halfway point, full of freedom and secrets, that Daniel had reached. I wanted to be as strong, as fast, as quick-witted and widely-read as he was. Becoming as certain of God would not have been my first choice, but there wasn't much point hoping for divine intervention to grant me anything else.

I followed him up onto the deck.

He took cord, and a knife, and four spare weights of the kind we used on our nets from the toolbox. He threaded the weights onto the cord, then I took off my shorts and sat naked on the deck while he knotted a figure-eight around my ankles. I raised my feet experimentally; the weights didn't seem all that heavy. But in the water, I knew, they'd be more than enough to counteract my body's slight buoyancy.

"Martin? Hold out your hands."

Suddenly I was crying. With my arms free, at least I could swim against the tug of the weights. But if my hands were tied, I'd be helpless.

Daniel crouched down and met my eyes. "Ssh. It's all right."

I hated myself. I could feel my face contorted into the mask of a blubbering infant.

"Are you afraid?"

I nodded.

Daniel smiled reassuringly. "You know why? You know who's doing that? Death doesn't want Beatrice to have you. He wants you for himself. So he's here on this boat, putting fear into your heart, because he *knows* he's almost lost you."

I saw something move in the shadows behind the toolbox, something slithering into the darkness. If we went back down to the cabin now, would Death follow us? To wait for Daniel to fall asleep? If I'd turned my back on Beatrice, who could I ask to send Death away?

I stared at the deck, tears of shame dripping from my cheeks. I held out my arms, wrists together.

When my hands were tied—not palm-to-palm as I'd expected, but in separate loops joined by a short bridge—Daniel unwound a long stretch of rope from the winch at the rear of the boat, and coiled it on the deck. I didn't want to think about how long it was, but I knew I'd never dived to that depth. He took the blunt hook at the end of the rope, slipped it over my arms, then screwed it closed to form an unbroken ring. Then he checked again that the cord around my wrists was neither so tight as to burn me, nor so loose as to let me slip. As he did this, I saw something creep over his face: some kind of doubt or fear of his own. He said, "Hang onto the hook. Just in case. Don't let go, no matter what. Okay?" He whispered something to Beatrice, then looked up at me, confident again.

He helped me to stand and shuffle over to the guard rail, just to one side of the winch. Then he picked me up under the arms and lifted me over, resting my feet on the outer hull. The deck was inert, a mineralized endoshell, but behind the guard rails the hull was palpably alive: slick with protective secretions, glowing softly. My toes curled uselessly against the lubricated skin; I had no purchase at all. The hull was supporting some of my weight, but Daniel's arms would tire eventually. If I wanted to back out, I'd have to do it quickly.

A warm breeze was blowing. I looked around, at the flat horizon, at the blaze of stars, at the faint silver light off the water. Daniel recited: "Holy Beatrice, I am ready to die to this world. Let me drown in Your blood, that I might be redeemed, and look upon the face of Your Mother."

I repeated the words, trying hard to mean them.

"Holy Beatrice, I offer You my life. All I do now, I do for You. Come into my heart, and grant me the gift of faith. Come into my heart, and grant me the gift of hope. Come into my heart, and grant me the gift of love."

"And grant me the gift of love."

Daniel released me. At first, my feet seemed to adhere magically to the hull, and I pivoted backward without actually falling. I clung tightly to the hook, pressing the cold metal against my belly, and willed the rope of the winch to snap taut, leaving me dangling in midair. I even braced myself for the shock. Some part of me really did believe that I could change my mind, even now.

Then my feet slipped and I plunged into the ocean and sank straight down.

It was not like a dive—not even a dive from an untried height, when it took so long for the water to bring you to a halt that it began to grow frightening. I was falling through the water ever faster, as if it was air. The vision I'd had of the rope keeping me above the water now swung to the opposite extreme: my acceleration seemed to prove that the coil on the deck was attached to nothing, that its frayed end was already beneath the surface. *That's what the followers had done, wasn't it? They'd let themselves be thrown in without a lifeline.* So Daniel had cut the rope, and I was on my way to the bottom of the ocean.

Then the hook jerked my hands up over my head, jarring my wrists and shoulders, and I was motionless.

I turned my face toward the surface, but neither starlight nor the hull's faint phosphorescence reached this deep. I let a stream of bubbles escape from my mouth; I felt them slide over my upper lip, but no trace of them registered in the darkness.

I shifted my hands warily over the hook. I could still feel the cord fast around my wrists, but Daniel had warned me not to trust it. I brought my knees up to my chest, gauging the effect of the weights. If the cord broke, at least my hands would be free, but even so I wasn't sure I'd be able to ascend. The thought of trying to unpick the knots around my ankles as I tumbled deeper filled me with horror.

My shoulders ached, but I wasn't injured. It didn't take much effort to pull myself up until my chin was level with the bottom of the hook. Going further was awkward—with my hands so close together I couldn't brace myself properly—but on the third attempt I managed to get my arms locked, pointing straight down.

I'd done this without any real plan, but then it struck me that even with my hands and feet tied, I could try shinning up the rope. It was just a matter of getting started. I'd have to turn upside-down, grab the rope between my knees, then curl up—dragging the hook—and get a grip with my hands at a higher point.

And if I couldn't reach up far enough to right myself?

I'd ascend feet-first.

I couldn't even manage the first step. I thought it would be as simple as keeping my arms rigid and letting myself topple backward, but in the water even two-thirds of my body wasn't sufficient to counterbalance the weights.

I tried a different approach: I dropped down to hang at arm's length, raised my legs as high as I could, then proceeded to pull myself up again. But my grip wasn't tight enough to resist the turning force of the weights; I just pivoted around my center of gravity—which was somewhere near my knees—and ended up, still bent double, but almost horizontal.

I eased myself down again, and tried threading my feet through the circle of my arms. I didn't succeed on the first attempt, and then on reflection it seemed like a bad move anyway. Even if I managed to grip the rope between my bound feet—rather than just tumbling over backward, out of control, and dislocating my shoulders—climbing the rope *upside-down with my hands behind my back* would either be impossible, or so awkward and strenuous that I'd run out of oxygen before I got a tenth of the way.

I let some more air escape from my lungs. I could feel the muscles in my diaphragm reproaching me for keeping them from doing what they wanted to do; not urgently yet, but the knowledge that I had no control over when I'd be able to draw breath again made it harder to stay calm. I knew I could rely on Daniel to bring me to the surface on the count of two hundred. But I'd only ever stayed down for a hundred and sixty. Forty more tau would be an eternity.

I'd almost forgotten what the whole ordeal was meant to be about, but now I started praying. *Please Holy Beatrice, don't let me die. I know You drowned like this to save me, but if I die it won't help anyone. Daniel would end up in the deepest shit . . . but that's not a threat, it's just an observation.* I felt a stab of anxiety; on top of everything else, had I just offended the Daughter of God? I struggled on, my confidence waning. *I don't want to die. But You already know that. So I don't know what You want me to say.*

I released some more stale air, wishing I'd counted the time I'd been under; you weren't supposed to empty your lungs too quickly—when they were deflated it was even harder not to take a breath—but holding all the carbon dioxide in too long wasn't good either.

Praying only seemed to make me more desperate, so I tried to think other kinds of holy thoughts. I couldn't remember anything from the Scriptures word for word, but the gist of the most important part started running through my mind.

After living in Her body for thirty years, and persuading all the Angels to become mortal again, Beatrice had gone back up to their deserted spaceship and flown it straight into the ocean. When Death saw Her coming, he took the form of a giant serpent, coiled in the water, waiting. And even though She was the Daughter of God, with the power to do anything, She let Death swallow Her.

That's how much She loved us.

Death thought he'd won everything. Beatrice was trapped inside him, in the darkness, alone. The Angels were flesh again, so he wouldn't even have to wait for the stars to fall before he claimed them.

But Beatrice was part of God. Death had swallowed part of God. This was a mistake. After three days, his jaws burst open and Beatrice came flying out, wreathed in fire. Death was broken, shriveled, diminished.

My limbs were numb but my chest was burning. Death was still strong enough to hold down the damned. I started thrashing about blindly, wasting whatever oxygen was left in my blood, but desperate to distract myself from the urge to inhale.

Please Holy Beatrice—

Please Daniel—

Luminous bruises blossomed behind my eyes and drifted out into the water. I watched them curling into a kind of vortex, as if something was drawing them in.

It was the mouth of the serpent, swallowing my soul. I opened my own mouth and made a wretched noise, and Death swam forward to kiss me, to breathe cold water into my lungs.

Suddenly, everything was seared with light. The serpent turned and fled, like a pale timid worm. A wave of contentment washed over me, as if I was an infant again and my mother had wrapped her arms around me tightly. It was like basking in sunlight, listening to laughter, dreaming of music too beautiful to be real. Every muscle in my body was still trying to prize my lungs open to the water, but now I found myself fighting this almost absentmindedly while I marveled at my strange euphoria.

Cold air swept over my hands and down my arms. I raised myself up to take a mouthful, then slumped down again, giddy and spluttering, grateful for every breath but still elated by something else entirely. The light that had filled my eyes was gone, but it left a violet afterimage everywhere I looked. Daniel kept winding until my head was level with the guard rail, then he clamped the winch, bent down, and threw me over his shoulder.

I'd been warm enough in the water, but now my teeth were chattering. Daniel wrapped a towel around me, then set to work cutting the cord. I beamed at him. "I'm so happy!" He gestured to me to be quieter, but then he whispered joyfully, "That's the love of Beatrice. She'll always be with you now, Martin."

I blinked with surprise, then laughed softly at my own stupidity. Until that moment, I hadn't connected what had happened with Beatrice at all. But of course it was Her. I'd asked Her to come into my heart, and She had.

And I could see it in Daniel's face: a year after his own Drowning, he still felt Her presence.

He said, "Everything you do now is for Beatrice. When you look through your telescope, you'll do it to honor Her creation. When you eat, or drink, or swim, you'll do it to give thanks for Her gifts." I nodded enthusiastically.

Daniel tidied everything away, even soaking up the puddles of water I'd left on the deck. Back in the cabin, he recited from the Scriptures, passages that I'd never really understood before, but which now all seemed to be about the Drowning, and the way I was feeling. It was as if I'd opened the book and found myself mentioned by name on every page.

When Daniel fell asleep before me, for the first time in my life I didn't feel the slightest pang of loneliness. The Daughter of God was with me: I could feel Her presence, like a flame inside my skull, radiating warmth through the darkness behind my eyes.

Giving me comfort, giving me strength.

Giving me faith.

2

THE MONASTERY WAS ALMOST four milliradians northeast of our home grounds. Daniel and I took the launch to a rendezvous point, and met up with three other small vessels before continuing. It had been the same routine every tenth night for almost a year—and Daniel had been going to the Prayer Group himself for a year before that—so the launch didn't need much supervision. Feeding on nutrients in the ocean, propelling itself by pumping water through fine channels in its skin, guided by both sunlight and Covenant's magnetic field, it was a perfect example of the kind of legacy of the Angels that technology would never be able to match.

Bartholomew, Rachel and Agnes were in one launch, and they traveled beside us while the others skimmed ahead. Bartholomew and Rachel were married, though they were only seventeen, scarcely older than Daniel. Agnes, Rachel's sister, was sixteen. Because I was the youngest member of the Prayer Group, Agnes had fussed over me from the day I'd joined. She said, "It's your big night tonight, Martin, isn't it?" I nodded, but declined to pursue the conversation, leaving her free to talk to Daniel.

It was dusk by the time the monastery came into sight, a conical tower built from at least ten thousand hulls, rising up from the water in the stylized form of Beatrice's spaceship. Aimed at the sky, not down into the depths. Though some commentators on the Scriptures insisted that the spaceship itself had sunk forever, and Beatrice had risen from the water unaided, it was still the definitive symbol of Her victory over Death. For the three days of Her separation from

God, all such buildings stood in darkness, but that was half a year away, and now the monastery shone from every porthole.

There was a narrow tunnel leading into the base of the tower; the launches detected its scent in the water and filed in one by one. I knew they didn't have souls, but I wondered what it would have been like for them if they'd been aware of their actions. Normally they rested in the dock of a single hull, a pouch of boatskin that secured them but still left them largely exposed. Maybe being drawn instinctively into this vast structure would have felt even safer, even more comforting, than docking with their home boat. When I said something to this effect, Rachel, in the launch behind me, sniggered. Agnes said, "Don't be horrible."

The walls of the tunnel phosphoresced pale green, but the opening ahead was filled with white lamplight, dazzlingly richer and brighter. We emerged into a canal circling a vast atrium, and continued around it until the launches found empty docks.

As we disembarked, every footstep, every splash echoed back at us. I looked up at the ceiling, a dome spliced together from hundreds of curved triangular hull sections, tattooed with scenes from the Scriptures. The original illustrations were more than a thousand years old, but the living boatskin degraded the pigments on a time scale of decades, so the monks had to constantly renew them.

"Beatrice Joining the Angels" was my favorite. Because the Angels weren't flesh, they didn't grow inside their mothers; they just appeared from nowhere in the streets of the Immaterial Cities. In the picture on the ceiling, Beatrice's immaterial body was half-formed, with cherubs still working to clothe the immaterial bones of Her legs and arms in immaterial muscles, veins and skin. A few Angels in luminous robes were glancing sideways at Her, but you could tell they weren't particularly impressed. They'd had no way of knowing, then, who She was.

A corridor with its own smaller illustrations led from the atrium to the meeting room. There were about fifty people in the Prayer Group—including several priests and monks, though they acted just like everyone else. In church you followed the liturgy; the priest slotted-in his or her sermon, but there was no room for the worshippers to do much more than pray or sing in unison and offer rote responses.

Here it was much less formal. There were two or three different speakers every night—sometimes guests who were visiting the monastery, sometimes members of the group—and after that anyone could ask the group to pray with them, about whatever they liked.

I'd fallen behind the others, but they'd saved me an aisle seat. Agnes was to my left, then Daniel, Bartholomew and Rachel. Agnes said, "Are you nervous?"

"No."

Daniel laughed, as if this claim was ridiculous.

I said, "I'm not." I'd meant to sound loftily unperturbed, but the words came out sullen and childish.

The first two speakers were both lay theologians, Firmlanders who were visiting the monastery. One gave a talk about people who belonged to false religions, and how they were all—in effect—worshipping Beatrice, but just didn't know it. He said they wouldn't be damned, because they'd had no choice about the cultures they were born into. Beatrice would know they'd meant well, and forgive them.

I wanted this to be true, but it made no sense to me. Either Beatrice *was* the Daughter of God, and everyone who thought otherwise had turned away from Her into the darkness, or . . . there was no "or." I only had to close my eyes and feel Her presence to know that. Still, everyone applauded when the man finished, and all the questions people asked seemed sympathetic to his views, so perhaps his arguments had simply been too subtle for me to follow.

The second speaker referred to Beatrice as "the Holy Jester", and rebuked us severely for not paying enough attention to Her sense of humor. She cited events in the Scriptures which she said were practical jokes, and then went on at some length about "the healing power of laughter." It was all about as gripping as a lecture on nutrition and hygiene; I struggled to keep my eyes open. At the end, no one could think of any questions.

Then Carol, who was running the meeting, said, "Now Martin is going to give witness to the power of Beatrice in his life."

Everyone applauded encouragingly. As I rose to my feet and stepped into the aisle, Daniel leaned toward Agnes and whispered sarcastically, "This should be good."

I stood at the lectern and gave the talk I'd been rehearsing for days. Beatrice, I said, was beside me now whatever I did: whether I studied or worked, ate or swam, or just sat and watched the stars. When I woke in the morning and looked into my heart, She was there without fail, offering me strength and guidance. When I lay in bed at night, I feared nothing, because I knew She was watching over me. Before my Drowning, I'd been unsure of my faith, but now I'd never again be able to doubt that the Daughter of God had become flesh, and died, and conquered Death, because of Her great love for us.

It was all true, but even as I said these things I couldn't get Daniel's sarcastic words out of my mind. I glanced over at the row where I'd been sitting, at the people I'd traveled with. What did I have in common with them, really? Rachel and Bartholomew were married. Bartholomew and Daniel had studied together, and still played in the same dive-ball team. Daniel and Agnes were probably in love. And Daniel was my brother . . . but the only difference that seemed to make was the fact that he could belittle me far more efficiently than any stranger.

In the open prayer that followed, I paid no attention to the problems and blessings people were sharing with the group. I tried silently calling on Beatrice to dissolve the knot of anger in my heart. But I couldn't do it; I'd turned too far away from Her.

When the meeting was over, and people started moving into the adjoining room to talk for a while, I hung back. When the others were out of sight I ducked into the corridor, and headed straight for the launch.

Daniel could get a ride home with his friends; it wasn't far out of their way. I'd wait a short distance from the boat until he caught up; if my parents saw me arrive on my own I'd be in trouble. Daniel would be angry, of course, but he wouldn't betray me.

Once I'd freed the launch from its dock, it knew exactly where to go: around the canal, back to the tunnel, out into the open sea. As I sped across the calm, dark water, I felt the presence of Beatrice returning, which seemed like a sign that She understood that I'd had to get away.

I leaned over and dipped my hand in the water, feeling the current the launch was generating by shuffling ions in and out of the cells of its skin. The outer hull glowed a phosphorescent blue, more to warn other vessels than to light the way. In the time of Beatrice, one of her followers had sat in the Immaterial City and designed this creature from scratch. It gave me a kind of vertigo, just imagining the things the Angels had known. I wasn't sure why so much of it had been lost, but I wanted to rediscover it all. Even the Deep Church taught that there was nothing wrong with that, so long as we didn't use it to try to become immortal again.

The monastery shrank to a blur of light on the horizon, and there was no other beacon visible on the water, but I could read the stars, and sense the field lines, so I knew the launch was heading in the right direction.

When I noticed a blue speck in the distance, it was clear that it wasn't Daniel and the others chasing after me; it was coming from the wrong direction. As I watched the launch drawing nearer I grew anxious; if this was someone I knew, and I couldn't come up with a good reason to be traveling alone, word would get back to my parents.

Before I could make out anyone on board, a voice shouted, "Can you help me? I'm lost!"

I thought for a while before replying. The voice sounded almost matter-of-fact, making light of this blunt admission of helplessness, but it was no joke. If you were sick, your diurnal sense and your field sense could both become scrambled, making the stars much harder to read. It had happened to me a couple of times, and it had been a horrible experience—even standing safely on the deck of our boat. This late at night, a launch with only its field sense to guide it could lose track of its position, especially if you were trying to take it somewhere it hadn't been before.

I shouted back our coordinates, and the time. I was fairly confident that I had them down to the nearest hundred microradians, and few hundred tau.

"That can't be right! Can I approach? Let our launches talk?"

I hesitated. It had been drummed into me for as long as I could remember that if I ever found myself alone on the water, I should give other vessels a wide berth unless I knew the people on board. But Beatrice was with me, and if someone needed help it was wrong to refuse them.

"All right!" I stopped dead, and waited for the stranger to close the gap. As the launch drew up beside me, I was surprised to see that the passenger was a young man. He looked about Bartholomew's age, but he'd sounded much older.

We didn't need to tell the launches what to do; proximity was enough to trigger a chemical exchange of information. The man said, "Out on your own?"

"I'm traveling with my brother and his friends. I just went ahead a bit."

That made him smile. "Sent you on your way, did they? What do you think they're getting up to, back there?" I didn't reply; that was no way to talk about people you didn't even know. The man scanned the horizon, then spread his arms in a gesture of sympathy. "You must be feeling left out."

I shook my head. There was a pair of binoculars on the floor behind him; even before he'd called out for help, he could have seen that I was alone.

He jumped deftly between the launches, landing on the stern bench. I said, "There's nothing to steal." My skin was crawling, more with disbelief than fear. He was standing on the bench in the starlight, pulling a knife from his belt. The details—the pattern carved into the handle, the serrated edge of the blade—only made it seem more like a dream.

He coughed, suddenly nervous. "Just do what I tell you, and you won't get hurt."

I filled my lungs and shouted for help with all the strength I had; I knew there was no one in earshot, but I thought it might still frighten him off. He looked around, more startled than angry, as if he couldn't quite believe I'd waste so much effort. I jumped backward, into the water. A moment later I heard him follow me.

I found the blue glow of the launches above me, then swam hard, down and away from them, without wasting time searching for his shadow. Blood was pounding in my ears, but I knew I was moving almost silently; however fast he was, in the darkness he could swim right past me without knowing it. If he didn't catch me soon he'd probably return to the launch and wait to spot me when I came up for air. I had to surface far enough away to be invisible—even with the binoculars.

I was terrified that I'd feel a hand close around my ankle at any moment, but Beatrice was with me. As I swam, I thought back to my Drowning, and Her presence grew stronger than ever. When my lungs were almost bursting, She helped me to keep going, my limbs moving mechanically, blotches of light floating in front of my eyes. When I finally knew I had to surface, I turned face-up and ascended slowly, then lay on my back with only my mouth and nose above the water, refusing the temptation to stick my head up and look around.

I filled and emptied my lungs a few times, then dived again.

The fifth time I surfaced, I dared to look back. I couldn't see either launch. I raised myself higher, then turned a full circle in case I'd grown disoriented, but nothing came into sight.

I checked the stars, and my field sense. The launches should *not* have been over the horizon. I trod water, riding the swell, and tried not to think about how tired I was. It was at least two milliradians to the nearest boat. Good swimmers—some younger than I was— competed in marathons over distances like that, but I'd never even aspired to such feats of endurance. Unprepared, in the middle of the night, I knew I wouldn't make it.

If the man had given up on me, would he have taken our launch? When they cost so little, and the markings were so hard to change? That would be nothing but an admission of guilt. *So why couldn't I see it?* Either he'd sent it on its way, or it had decided to return home itself.

I knew the path it would have taken; I would have seen it go by, if I'd been looking for it when I'd surfaced before. But I had no hope of catching it now.

I began to pray. I knew I'd been wrong to leave the others, but I asked for forgiveness, and felt it being granted. I watched the horizon almost calmly—smiling at the blue flashes of meteors burning up high above the ocean—certain that Beatrice would not abandon me.

I was still praying—treading water, shivering from the cool of the air—when a blue light appeared in the distance. It disappeared as the swell took me down again, but there was no mistaking it for a shooting star. *Was this Daniel and the others—or the stranger?* I didn't have long to decide; if I wanted to get within earshot as they passed, I'd have to swim hard.

I closed my eyes and prayed for guidance. *Please Holy Beatrice, let me know.* Joy flooded through my mind, instantly: it was them, I was certain of it. I set off as fast as I could.

I started yelling before I could see how many passengers there were, but I knew Beatrice would never allow me to be mistaken. A flare shot up from the launch, revealing four figures standing side by side, scanning the water. I shouted with jubilation, and waved my arms. Someone finally spotted me, and they brought the launch around toward me. By the time I was on board I was so charged up on adrenaline and relief that I almost believed I could have dived back into the water and raced them home.

I thought Daniel would be angry, but when I described what had happened all he said was, "We'd better get moving."

Agnes embraced me. Bartholomew gave me an almost respectful look, but Rachel muttered sourly, "You're an idiot, Martin. You don't know how lucky you are."

I said, "I know."

Our parents were standing on deck. The empty launch had arrived some time ago; they'd been about to set out to look for us. When the others had departed I began recounting everything again, this time trying to play down any element of danger.

Before I'd finished, my mother grabbed Daniel by the front of his shirt and started slapping him. "I trusted you with him! *You maniac!* I trusted you!" Daniel half raised his arm to block her, but then let it drop and just turned his face to the deck.

I burst into tears. "It was my fault!" Our parents never struck us; I couldn't believe what I was seeing.

My father said soothingly, "Look . . . he's home now. He's safe. No one touched him." He put an arm around my shoulders and asked warily, "That's right, Martin, isn't it?"

I nodded tearfully. This was worse than anything that had happened on the launch, or in the water; I felt a thousand times more helpless, a thousand times more like a child.

I said, "Beatrice was watching over me."

My mother rolled her eyes and laughed wildly, letting go of Daniel's shirt. "Beatrice? *Beatrice?* Don't you know what could have happened to you? You're too young to have given him what he wanted. He would have had to use the knife."

The chill of my wet clothes seemed to penetrate deeper. I swayed unsteadily, but fought to stay upright. Then I whispered stubbornly, "Beatrice was there."

My father said, "Go and get changed, or you're going to freeze to death."

I lay in bed listening to them shout at Daniel. When he finally came down the ladder I was so sick with shame that I wished I'd drowned.

He said, "Are you all right?"

There was nothing I could say. I couldn't ask him to forgive me.

"Martin?" Daniel turned on the lamp. His face was streaked with tears; he laughed softly, wiping them away. "Fuck, you had me worried. Don't ever do anything like that again."

"I won't."

"Okay." That was it; no shouting, no recriminations. "Do you want to pray with me?"

We knelt side by side, praying for our parents to be at peace, praying for the man who'd tried to hurt me. I started trembling; everything was catching up with me. Suddenly, words began gushing from my mouth—words I neither recognized nor understood, though I knew I was praying for everything to be all right with Daniel, praying that our parents would stop blaming him for my stupidity.

The strange words kept flowing out of me, an incomprehensible torrent somehow imbued with everything I was feeling. I knew what was happening: *Beatrice had given me the Angels' tongue.* We'd had to surrender all knowledge of it when we became flesh, but sometimes She granted people the ability to pray this way, because the language of the Angels could express things we could no longer put into words. Daniel had been able to do it ever since his Drowning, but it wasn't something you could teach, or even something you could ask for.

When I finally stopped, my mind was racing. "Maybe Beatrice planned everything that happened tonight? Maybe She arranged it all, to lead up to this moment!"

Daniel shook his head, wincing slightly. "Don't get carried away. You have the gift; just accept it." He nudged me with his shoulder. "Now get into bed, before we're both in more trouble."

I lay awake almost until dawn, overwhelmed with happiness. Daniel had forgiven me. Beatrice had protected and blessed me. I felt no more shame, just humility and amazement. I knew I'd done nothing to deserve it, but my life was wrapped in the love of God.

3

ACCORDING TO THE SCRIPTURES, the oceans of Earth were storm-tossed, and filled with dangerous creatures. But on Covenant, the oceans were calm, and the Angels created nothing in the ecopoiesis that would harm their own mortal incarnations. The four continents and the four oceans were rendered equally hospitable, and just as women and men were made indistinguishable in the sight of God, so were Freelanders and Firmlanders. (Some commentators insisted that this was literally true: God chose to blind Herself to where we lived, and whether or not we'd been born with a penis. I thought that was a beautiful idea, even if I couldn't quite grasp the logistics of it.)

I'd heard that certain obscure sects taught that half the Angels had actually become embodied as a separate people who could live in the water and breathe beneath the surface, but then God destroyed them because they were a mockery of Beatrice's death. No legitimate church took this notion seriously, though, and archaeologists had found no trace of these mythical doomed cousins. Humans were humans, there was only one kind. Freelanders and Firmlanders could even intermarry—if they could agree where to live.

When I was fifteen, Daniel became engaged to Agnes from the Prayer Group. That made sense: they'd be spared the explanations and arguments about the Drowning that they might have faced with partners who weren't so blessed. Agnes was a Freelander, of course, but a large branch of her family, and a smaller branch of ours, were Firmlanders, so after long negotiations it was decided that the wedding would be held in Ferez, a coastal town.

I went with my father to pick a hull to be fitted out as Daniel and Agnes's boat. The breeder, Diana, had a string of six mature hulls in tow, and my father insisted on walking out onto their backs and personally examining each one for imperfections.

By the time we reached the fourth I was losing patience. I muttered, "It's the skin underneath that matters." In fact, you could tell a lot about a hull's general condition from up here, but there wasn't much point worrying about a few tiny flaws high above the waterline.

My father nodded thoughtfully. "That's true. You'd better get in the water and check their undersides."

"I'm not doing that." We couldn't simply trust this woman to sell us a healthy hull for a decent price; that wouldn't have been sufficiently embarrassing.

"Martin! This is for the safety of your brother and sister-in-law."

I glanced at Diana to show her where my sympathies lay, then slipped off my shirt and dived in. I swam down to the last hull in the row, then ducked beneath it. I began the job with perverse thoroughness, running my fingers over every square nanoradian of skin. I was determined to annoy my father by taking even longer than he wanted—and determined to impress Diana by examining all six hulls without coming up for air.

An unfitted hull rode higher in the water than a boat full of furniture and junk, but I was surprised to discover that even in the creature's shadow there was enough light for me to see the skin clearly. After a while I realized that, paradoxically, this was because the water was slightly cloudier than usual, and whatever the fine particles were, they were scattering sunlight into the shadows.

Moving through the warm, bright water, feeling the love of Beatrice more strongly than I had for a long time, it was impossible to remain angry with my father. He wanted the best hull for Daniel and Agnes, and so did I. As for impressing Diana . . . who was I kidding? She was a grown woman, at least as old as Agnes, and highly unlikely to view me as anything more than a child. By the time I'd finished with the third hull I was feeling short of breath, so I surfaced and reported cheerfully, "No blemishes so far!"

Diana smiled down at me. "You've got strong lungs."

All six hulls were in perfect condition. We ended up taking the one at the end of the row, because it was easiest to detach.

FEREZ WAS BUILT ON the mouth of a river, but the docks were some distance upstream. That helped to prepare us; the gradual deadening of the waves was less of a shock than an instant transition from sea to land would have been. When I jumped from the deck to the pier, though, it was like colliding with something massive and unyielding, the rock of the planet itself. I'd been on land twice before, for less than a day on both occasions. The wedding celebrations would last ten days, but at least we'd still be able to sleep on the boat.

As the four of us walked along the crowded streets, heading for the ceremonial hall where everything but the wedding sacrament itself would take place, I stared uncouthly at everyone in sight. Almost no one was barefoot like us, and after a few hundred tau on the paving stones—much rougher than any deck—I could understand why. Our clothes were different, our skin was darker, our accent was unmistakably foreign . . . but no one stared back. Freelanders were hardly a novelty here. That made me even more selfconscious; the curiosity I felt wasn't mutual.

In the hall, I joined in with the preparations, mainly just lugging furniture around under the directions of one of Agnes's tyrannical uncles. It was a new kind of shock to see so many Freelanders together in this alien environment, and stranger still when I realized that I couldn't necessarily spot the Firmlanders among us; there was no sharp dividing line in physical appearance, or even clothing. I began to feel slightly guilty; if God couldn't tell the difference, what was I doing hunting for the signs?

At noon we all ate outside, in a garden behind the hall. The grass was soft, but it made my feet itch. Daniel had gone off to be fitted for wedding clothes, and my parents were performing some vital task of their own; I only recognized a handful of the people around me. I sat in the shade of a tree, pretending to be oblivious to the plant's enormous size and bizarre anatomy. I wondered if we'd take a siesta; I couldn't imagine falling asleep on the grass.

Someone sat down beside me, and I turned.

"I'm Lena. Agnes's second cousin."

"I'm Daniel's brother, Martin." I hesitated, then offered her my hand; she took it, smiling slightly. I'd awkwardly kissed a dozen strangers that morning, all distant prospective relatives, but this time I didn't dare.

"Brother of the groom, doing grunt work with the rest of us." She shook her head in mocking admiration.

I desperately wanted to say something witty in reply, but an attempt that failed would be even worse than merely being dull. "Do you live in Ferez?"

"No, Mitar. Inland from here. We're staying with my uncle." She pulled a face. "Along with ten other people. No privacy. It's awful."

I said, "It was easy for us. We just brought our home with us." *You idiot. As if she didn't know that.*

Lena smiled. "I haven't been on a boat in years. You'll have to give me a tour sometime."

"Of course. I'd be happy to." I knew she was only making small talk; she'd never take me up on the offer.

She said, "Is it just you and Daniel?"

"Yes."

"You must be close."

I shrugged. "What about you?"

"Two brothers. Both younger. Eight and nine. They're all right, I suppose." She rested her chin on one hand and gazed at me coolly.

I looked away, disconcerted by more than my wishful thinking about what lay behind that gaze. Unless her parents had been awfully young when she was born, it didn't seem likely that more children were planned. So did an odd number in the family mean that one had died, or that the custom of equal numbers carried by each parent wasn't followed where she lived? I'd studied the region less than a year ago, but I had a terrible memory for things like that.

Lena said, "You looked so lonely, off here on your own."

I turned back to her, surprised. "I'm never lonely."

"No?"

She seemed genuinely curious. I opened my mouth to tell her about Beatrice, but then changed my mind. The few times I'd said anything to friends—ordinary friends, not Drowned ones—I'd regretted it. Not everyone had laughed, but they'd all been acutely embarrassed by the revelation.

I said, "Mitar has a million people, doesn't it?"

"Yes."

"An area of ocean the same size would have a population of ten."

Lena frowned. "That's a bit too deep for me, I'm afraid." She rose to her feet. "But maybe you'll think of a way of putting it that even a Firmlander can understand." She raised a hand goodbye and started walking away.

I said, "Maybe I will."

THE WEDDING TOOK PLACE in Ferez's Deep Church, a spaceship built of stone, glass, and wood. It looked almost like a parody of the churches I was used to, though it probably bore a closer resemblance to the Angels' real ship than anything made of living hulls.

Daniel and Agnes stood before the priest, beneath the apex of the building. Their closest relatives stood behind them in two angled lines on either side. My father—Daniel's mother—was first in our line, followed by my own mother, then me. That put me level with Rachel, who kept shooting disdainful glances my way. After my misadventure, Daniel and I had eventually been allowed to travel to the Prayer Group meetings again, but less than a year later I'd lost interest, and soon after I'd also stopped going to church. Beatrice was with me, constantly, and no gatherings or ceremonies could bring me any closer to Her. I knew Daniel disapproved of this attitude, but he didn't lecture me about it, and my parents had accepted my decision without any fuss. If Rachel thought I was some kind of apostate, that was her problem.

The priest said, "Which of you brings a bridge to this marriage?"

Daniel said, "I do." In the Transitional ceremony they no longer asked this; it was really no one else's business—and in a way the question was almost sacrilegious. Still, Deep Church theologians had explained away greater doctrinal inconsistencies than this, so who was I to argue?

"Do you, Daniel and Agnes, solemnly declare that this bridge will be the bond of your union until death, to be shared with no other person?"

They replied together, "We solemnly declare."

"Do you solemnly declare that as you share this bridge, so shall you share every joy and every burden of marriage—equally?"

"We solemnly declare."

My mind wandered; I thought of Lena's parents. Maybe one of the family's children was adopted. Lena and I had managed to sneak away to the boat three times so far, early in the evenings while my parents were still out. We'd done things I'd never done with anyone else, but I still hadn't had the courage to ask her anything so personal.

Suddenly the priest was saying, "In the eyes of God, you are one now." My father started weeping softly. As Daniel and Agnes kissed, I felt a surge of contradictory emotions. I'd miss Daniel, but I was glad that I'd finally have a chance to live apart from him. And I wanted him to be happy—I was jealous of his happiness already—but at the same time, the thought of marrying someone like Agnes filled me with claustrophobia. She was kind, devout, and generous. She and Daniel would treat each other, and their children, well. But neither of them would present the slightest challenge to the other's most cherished beliefs.

This recipe for harmony terrified me. Not least because I was afraid that Beatrice approved, and wanted me to follow it myself.

LENA PUT HER HAND over mine and pushed my fingers deeper into her, gasping. We were sitting on my bunk, face to face, my legs stretched out flat, hers arching over them.

She slid the palm of her other hand over my penis. I bent forward and kissed her, moving my thumb over the place she'd shown me, and her shudder ran through both of us.

"Martin?"

"What?"

She stroked me with one fingertip; somehow it was far better than having her whole hand wrapped around me.

"Do you want to come inside me?"

I shook my head.

"Why not?"

She kept moving her finger, tracing the same line; I could barely think. *Why not?* "You might get pregnant."

She laughed. "Don't be stupid. I can control that. You'll learn, too. It's just a matter of experience."

I said, "I'll use my tongue. You liked that."

"I did. But I want something more now. And you do, too. I can tell." She smiled imploringly. "It'll be nice for both of us, I promise. Nicer than anything you've done in your life."

"Don't bet on it."

Lena made a sound of disbelief, and ran her thumb around the base of my penis. "I can tell you haven't put this inside anyone before. But that's nothing to be ashamed of."

"Who said I was ashamed?"

She nodded gravely. "All right. Frightened."

I pulled my hand free, and banged my head on the bunk above us. Daniel's old bunk.

Lena reached up and put her hand on my cheek.

I said, "I can't. We're not married."

She frowned. "I heard you'd given up on all that."

"All what?"

"Religion."

"Then you were misinformed."

Lena said, "This is what the Angels made our bodies to do. How can there be anything sinful in that?" She ran her hand down my neck, over my chest.

"But the bridge is meant to . . ." *What?* All the Scriptures said was that it was meant to unite men and women, equally. And the Scriptures said God couldn't tell women and men apart, but in the

Deep Church, in the sight of God, the priest had just made Daniel claim priority. So why should I care what any priest thought?

I said, "All right."

"Are you sure?"

"Yes." I took her face in my hands and started kissing her. After a while, she reached down and guided me in. The shock of pleasure almost made me come, but I stopped myself somehow. When the risk of that had lessened, we wrapped our arms around each other and rocked slowly back and forth.

It wasn't better than my Drowning, but it was so much like it that it had to be blessed by Beatrice. And as we moved in each other's arms, I grew determined to ask Lena to marry me. She was intelligent and strong. She questioned everything. It didn't matter that she was a Firmlander; we could meet halfway, we could live in Ferez.

I felt myself ejaculate. "I'm sorry."

Lena whispered, "That's all right, that's all right. Just keep moving."

I was still hard; that had never happened before. I could feel her muscles clenching and releasing rhythmically, in time with our motion, and her slow exhalations. Then she cried out, and dug her fingers into my back. I tried to slide partly out of her again, but it was impossible, she was holding me too tightly. This was it. There was no going back.

Now I was afraid. "I've never—" Tears were welling up in my eyes; I tried to shake them away.

"I know. And I know it's frightening." She embraced me more tightly. "Just feel it, though. Isn't it wonderful?"

I was hardly aware of my motionless penis anymore, but there was liquid fire flowing through my groin, waves of pleasure spreading deeper. I said, "Yes. Is it like that for you?"

"It's different. But it's just as good. You'll find out for yourself, soon enough."

"I hadn't been thinking that far ahead," I confessed.

Lena giggled. "You've got a whole new life in front of you, Martin. You don't know what you've been missing."

She kissed me, then started pulling away. I cried out in pain, and she stopped. "I'm sorry. I'll take it slowly." I reached down to touch the place where we were joined; there was a trickle of blood escaping from the base of my penis.

Lena said, "You're not going to faint on me, are you?"

"Don't be stupid." I did feel queasy, though. "What if I'm not ready? What if I can't do it?"

"Then I'll lose my hold in a few hundred tau. The Angels weren't completely stupid."

I ignored this blasphemy, though it wasn't just any Angel who'd designed our bodies—it was Beatrice Herself. I said, "Just promise you won't use a knife."

"That's not funny. That really happens to people."

"I know." I kissed her shoulder. "I think—"

Lena straightened her legs slightly, and I felt the core break free inside me. Blood flowed warmly from my groin, but the pain had changed from a threat of damage to mere tenderness; my nervous system no longer spanned the lesion. I asked Lena, "Do you feel it? Is it part of you?"

"Not yet. It takes a while for the connections to form." She ran her fingers over my lips. "Can I stay inside you, until they have?"

I nodded happily. I hardly cared about the sensations anymore; it was just contemplating the miracle of being able to give a part of my body to Lena that was wonderful. I'd studied the physiological details long ago, everything from the exchange of nutrients to the organ's independent immune system—and I knew that Beatrice had used many of the same techniques for the bridge as She'd used with gestating embryos—but to witness Her ingenuity so dramatically at work in my own flesh was both shocking and intensely moving. Only giving birth could bring me closer to Her than this.

When we finally separated, though, I wasn't entirely prepared for the sight of what emerged. "Oh, that is disgusting!"

Lena shook her head, laughing. "New ones always look a bit . . . encrusted. Most of that stuff will wash away, and the rest will fall off in a few kilotau."

I bunched up the sheet to find a clean spot, then dabbed at my—her—penis. My newly formed vagina had stopped bleeding, but it was finally dawning on me just how much mess we'd made. "I'm going to have to wash this before my parents get back. I can put it out to dry in the morning, after they're gone, but if I don't wash it now they'll smell it."

We cleaned ourselves enough to put on shorts, then Lena helped me carry the sheet up onto the deck and drape it in the water from the laundry hooks. The fibers in the sheet would use nutrients in the water to power the self-cleaning process.

The docks appeared deserted; most of the boats nearby belonged to people who'd come for the wedding. I'd told my parents I was too tired to stay on at the celebrations; tonight they'd continue until dawn, though Daniel and Agnes would probably leave by midnight. To do what Lena and I had just done.

"Martin? Are you shivering?"

There was nothing to be gained by putting it off. Before whatever courage I had could desert me, I said, "Will you marry me?"

"Very funny. Oh—" Lena took my hand. "I'm sorry, I never know when you're joking."

I said, "We've exchanged the bridge. It doesn't matter that we weren't married first, but it would make things easier if we went along with convention."

"Martin—"

"Or we could just live together, if that's what you want. I don't care. We're already married in the eyes of Beatrice."

Lena bit her lip. "I don't want to live with you."

"I could move to Mitar. I could get a job."

Lena shook her head, still holding my hand. She said firmly, "*No.* You knew, before we did anything, what it would and wouldn't mean. You don't want to marry me, and I don't want to marry you. So snap out of it."

I pulled my hand free, and sat down on the deck. *What had I done?* I'd thought I'd had Beatrice's blessing, I'd thought this was all in Her plan . . . but I'd just been fooling myself.

Lena sat beside me. "What are you worried about? Your parents finding out?"

"Yes." That was the least of it, but it seemed pointless trying to explain the truth. I turned to her. "When could we—?"

"Not for about ten days. And sometimes it's longer after the first time."

I'd known as much, but I'd hoped her experience might contradict my theoretical knowledge. *Ten days.* We'd both be gone by then.

Lena said, "What do you think, you can never get married now? How many marriages do you imagine involve the bridge one of the partners was born with?"

"Nine out of ten. Unless they're both women."

Lena gave me a look that hovered between tenderness and incredulity. "My estimate is about one in five."

I shook my head. "I don't care. We've exchanged the bridge, we have to be together." Lena's expression hardened, then so did my resolve. "Or I have to get it back."

"Martin, that's ridiculous. You'll find another lover soon enough, and then you won't even know what you were worried about. Or maybe you'll fall in love with a nice Deep Church boy, and then you'll both be glad you've been spared the trouble of getting rid of the extra bridge."

"Yeah? Or maybe he'll just be disgusted that I couldn't wait until I really *was* doing it for him!"

Lena groaned, and stared up at the sky. "Did I say something before about the Angels getting things right? Ten thousand years without bodies, and they thought they were qualified—"

I cut her off angrily. "Don't be so fucking blasphemous! Beatrice knew exactly what She was doing. If we mess it up, that's our fault!"

Lena said, matter-of-factly, "In ten years' time, there'll be a pill you'll be able to take to keep the bridge from being passed, and another pill to make it pass when it otherwise wouldn't. We'll win control of our bodies back from the Angels, and start doing exactly what we like with them."

"That's sick. That really is sick."

I stared at the deck, suffocating in misery. *This was what I'd wanted, wasn't it? A lover who was the very opposite of Daniel's sweet, pious Agnes?*

Except that in my fantasies, we'd always had a lifetime to debate our philosophical differences. Not one night to be torn apart by them.

I had nothing to lose, now. I told Lena about my Drowning. She didn't laugh; she listened in silence.

I said, "Do you believe me?"

"Of course." She hesitated. "But have you ever wondered if there might be another explanation for the way you felt, in the water that night? You were starved of oxygen—"

"People are starved of oxygen all the time. Freelander kids spend half their lives trying to stay underwater longer than the last time."

Lena nodded. "Sure. But that's not quite the same, is it? You were pushed beyond the time you could have stayed under by sheer willpower. And . . . you were cued, you were told what to expect."

"That's not true. Daniel never told me what it would be like. I was *surprised* when it happened." I gazed back at her calmly, ready to counter any ingenious hypothesis she came up with. I felt chastened, but almost at peace now. This was what Beatrice had expected of me, before we'd exchanged the bridge: not a dead ceremony in a dead building, but the honesty to tell Lena exactly who she'd be making love with.

We argued almost until sunrise; neither of us convinced the other of anything. Lena helped me drag the clean sheet out of the water and hide it below deck. Before she left, she wrote down the address of a friend's house in Mitar, and a place and time we could meet.

Keeping that appointment was the hardest thing I'd ever done in my life. I spent three solid days ingratiating myself with my Mitar-based cousins, to the point where they would have had to be openly hostile to get out of inviting me to stay with them after the wedding. Once I was there, I had to scheme and lie relentlessly to ensure that I was free of them on the predetermined day.

In a stranger's house, in the middle of the afternoon, Lena and I joylessly reversed everything that had happened between us. I'd been afraid that the act itself might rekindle all my stupid illusions, but when we parted on the street outside, I felt as if I hardly knew her.

I ached even more than I had on the boat, and my groin was palpably swollen, but in a couple of days, I knew, nothing less than a lover's touch or a medical examination would reveal what I'd done.

In the train back to the coast, I replayed the entire sequence of events in my mind, again and again. *How could I have been so wrong?* People always talked about the power of sex to confuse and deceive you, but I'd always believed that was just cheap cynicism. Besides, I hadn't blindly surrendered to sex; I'd thought I'd been guided by Beatrice.

If I could be wrong about that—

I'd have to be more careful. Beatrice always spoke clearly, but I'd have to listen to Her with much more patience and humility.

That was it. That was what She'd wanted me to learn. I finally relaxed and looked out the window, at the blur of forest passing by, another triumph of the ecopoiesis. If I needed proof that there was always another chance, it was all around me now. The Angels had traveled as far from God as anyone could travel, and yet God had turned around and given them Covenant.

4

I WAS NINETEEN WHEN I returned to Mitar, to study at the city's university. Originally, I'd planned to specialize in the ecopoiesis—and to study much closer to home—but in the end I'd had to accept the nearest thing on offer, geographically and intellectually: working with Barat, a Firmlander biologist whose real interest was native microfauna. "Angelic technology is a fascinating subject in its own right," he told me. "But we can't hope to work backward and decipher terrestrial evolution from anything the Angels created. The best we can do is try to understand what Covenant's own biosphere was like, before we arrived and disrupted it."

I managed to persuade him to accept a compromise: my thesis would involve the impact of the ecopoiesis on the native microfauna. That would give me an excuse to study the Angels' inventions, alongside the drab unicellular creatures that had inhabited Covenant for the last billion years.

"The impact of the ecopoiesis" was far too broad a subject, of course; with Barat's help, I narrowed it down to one particular unresolved question. There had long been geological evidence that the surface waters of the ocean had become both more alkaline, and less oxygenated, as new species shifted the balance of dissolved gases. Some native species must have retreated from the wave of change, and perhaps some had been wiped out completely, but there was a thriving population of zooytes in the upper layers at present. So had they been there all along, adapting *in situ*? Or had they migrated from somewhere else?

Mitar's distance from the coast was no real handicap in studying the ocean; the university mounted regular expeditions, and I had plenty of library and lab work to do before embarking on anything so obvious as gathering living samples in their natural habitat. What's more, river water, and even rainwater, was teeming with closely related species, and since it was possible that these were the reservoirs from which the "ravaged" ocean had been re-colonized, I had plenty of subjects worth studying close at hand.

Barat set high standards, but he was no tyrant, and his other students made me feel welcome. I was homesick, but not morbidly so, and I took a kind of giddy pleasure from the vivid dreams and underlying sense of disorientation that living on land induced in me. I wasn't exactly fulfilling my childhood ambition to uncover the secrets of the Angels—and I had fewer opportunities than I'd hoped to get side-tracked on the ecopoiesis itself—but once I started delving into the minutiae of Covenant's original, wholly undesigned biochemistry, it turned out to be complex and elegant enough to hold my attention.

I was only miserable when I let myself think about sex. I didn't want to end up like Daniel, so seeking out another Drowned person to marry was the last thing on my mind. But I couldn't face the prospect of repeating my mistake with Lena; I had no intention of becoming physically intimate with anyone unless we were already close enough for me to tell them about the most important thing in my life. But that wasn't the order in which things happened, here. After a few humiliating attempts to swim against the current, I gave up on the whole idea, and threw myself into my work instead.

Of course, it *was* possible to socialize at Mitar University without actually exchanging bridges with anyone. I joined an informal discussion group on Angelic culture, which met in a small room in the students' building every tenth night—just like the old Prayer Group, though I was under no illusion that this one would be stacked with believers. It hardly needed to be. The Angels' legacy could be analyzed perfectly well without reference to Beatrice's divinity. The Scriptures were written long after the Crossing by people of a simpler age; there was no reason to treat them as infallible. If non-believers could shed some light on any aspect of the past, I had no grounds for rejecting their insights.

"It's obvious that only one faction came to Covenant!" That was Céline, an anthropologist, a woman so much like Lena that I had to make a conscious effort to remind myself, every time I set eyes on her, that nothing could ever happen between us. "*We're* not so homogeneous that we'd all choose to travel to another planet and assume a new physical form, whatever cultural forces might drive one small group to do that. So why should the Angels have been unanimous? The other factions must still be living in the Immaterial Cities, on Earth, and on other planets."

"Then why haven't they contacted us? In twenty thousand years, you'd think they'd drop in and say hello once or twice." David was a mathematician, a Freelander from the southern ocean.

Céline replied, "The attitude of the Angels who came here wouldn't have encouraged visitors. If all we have is a story of the Crossing in which Beatrice persuades every last Angel in existence to give up immortality—a version that simply erases everyone else from history—that doesn't suggest much of a desire to remain in touch."

A woman I didn't know interjected, "It might not have been so clear-cut from the start, though. There's evidence of settler-level technology being deployed for more than three thousand years after the Crossing, long after it was needed for the ecopoiesis. New species continued to be created, engineering projects continued to use advanced materials and energy sources. But then in less than a century, it all stopped. The Scriptures merge three separate decisions into one: renouncing immortality, migrating to Covenant, and abandoning the technology that might have provided an escape route if anyone changed their mind. But we *know* it didn't happen like that.

Three thousand years after the Crossing, something changed. The whole experiment suddenly became irreversible."

These speculations would have outraged the average pious Freelander, let alone the average Drowned one, but I listened calmly, even entertaining the possibility that some of them could be true. The love of Beatrice was the only fixed point in my cosmology; everything else was open to debate.

Still, sometimes the debate was hard to take. One night, David joined us straight from a seminar of physicists. What he'd heard from the speaker was unsettling enough, but he'd already moved beyond it to an even less palatable conclusion.

"Why did the Angels choose mortality? After ten thousand years without death, why did they throw away all the glorious possibilities ahead of them, to come and die like animals on this ball of mud?" I had to bite my tongue to keep from replying to his rhetorical question: because God is the only source of eternal life, and Beatrice showed them that all they really had was a cheap parody of that divine gift.

David paused, then offered his own answer—which was itself a kind of awful parody of Beatrice's truth. "Because they discovered that they weren't immortal, after all. They discovered that *no one can be*. We've always known, as they must have, that the universe is finite in space and time. It's destined to collapse eventually: 'the stars will fall from the sky.' But it's easy to *imagine* ways around that." He laughed. "We don't know enough physics yet, ourselves, to rule out anything. I've just heard an extraordinary woman from Tia talk about coding our minds into waves that would orbit the shrinking universe so rapidly that we could think *an infinite number of thoughts* before everything was crushed!" David grinned joyfully at the sheer audacity of this notion. I thought primly: what blasphemous nonsense.

Then he spread his arms and said, "Don't you see, though? If the Angels *had* pinned their hopes on something like that—some ingenious trick that would keep them from sharing the fate of the universe—*but then they finally gained enough knowledge to rule out every last escape route*, it would have had a profound effect on them. Some small faction could then have decided that since they were mortal after all, they might as well embrace the inevitable, and come to terms with it in the way their ancestors had. In the flesh."

Céline said thoughtfully, "And the Beatrice myth puts a religious gloss on the whole thing, but that might be nothing but a *post hoc* reinterpretation of a purely secular revelation."

This was too much; I couldn't remain silent. I said, "If Covenant really was founded by a pack of terminally depressed atheists, what could have changed their minds? Where did the desire to impose a '*post hoc* reinterpretation' *come from?* If the revelation that brought the Angels here was 'secular', why isn't the whole planet still secular today?"

Someone said snidely, "Civilization collapsed. What do you expect?"

I opened my mouth to respond angrily, but Céline got in first. "No, Martin has a point. If David's right, the rise of religion needs to be explained more urgently than ever. And I don't think anyone's in a position to do that yet."

Afterward, I lay awake thinking about all the other things I should have said, all the other objections I should have raised. (And thinking about Céline.) Theology aside, the whole dynamics of the group was starting to get under my skin; maybe I'd be better off spending my time in the lab, impressing Barat with my dedication to his pointless fucking microbes.

Or maybe I'd be better off at home. I could help out on the boat; my parents weren't young anymore, and Daniel had his own family to look after.

I climbed out of bed and started packing, but halfway through I changed my mind. I didn't really want to abandon my studies. And I'd known all along what the antidote was for all the confusion and resentment I was feeling.

I put my rucksack away, switched off the lamp, lay down, closed my eyes, and asked Beatrice to grant me peace.

I WAS WOKEN BY someone banging on the door of my room. It was a fellow boarder, a young man I barely knew. He looked extremely tired and irritable, but something was overriding his irritation.

"There's a message for you."

My mother was sick, with an unidentified virus. The hospital was even further away than our home grounds; the trip would take almost three days.

I spent most of the journey praying, but the longer I prayed, the harder it became. I *knew* that it was possible to save my mother's life with one word in the Angels' tongue to Beatrice, but the number of ways in which I could fail, corrupting the purity of the request with my own doubts, my own selfishness, my own complacency, just kept multiplying.

The Angels created nothing in the ecopoiesis that would harm their own mortal incarnations. The native life showed no interest in parasitizing us. But over the millennia, our own DNA had shed viruses. And since Beatrice Herself chose every last base pair, that must have been what She intended. Aging was not enough. Mortal injury was not enough. Death had to come without warning, silent and invisible.

That's what the Scriptures said.

The hospital was a maze of linked hulls. When I finally found the right passageway, the first person I recognized in the distance was Daniel. He was holding his daughter Sophie high in his outstretched arms, smiling up at her. The image dispelled all my fears in an instant; I almost fell to my knees to give thanks.

Then I saw my father. He was seated outside the room, his head in his hands. I couldn't see his face, but I didn't need to. He wasn't anxious, or exhausted. He was crushed.

I approached in a haze of last-minute prayers, though I knew I was asking for the past to be rewritten. Daniel started to greet me as if nothing was wrong, asking about the trip—probably trying to soften the blow—then he registered my expression and put a hand on my shoulder.

He said, "She's with God now."

I brushed past him and walked into the room. My mother's body was lying on the bed, already neatly arranged: arms straightened, eyes closed. Tears ran down my cheeks, angering me. Where had my love been when it might have prevented this? When Beatrice might have heeded it?

Daniel followed me into the room, alone. I glanced back through the doorway and saw Agnes holding Sophie.

"She's with God, Martin." He was beaming at me as if something wonderful had happened.

I said numbly, "She wasn't Drowned." I was almost certain that she hadn't been a believer at all. She'd remained in the Transitional church all her life—but that had long been the way to stay in touch with your friends when you worked on a boat nine days out of ten.

"I prayed with her, before she lost consciousness. She accepted Beatrice into her heart."

I stared at him. Nine years ago he'd been certain: you were Drowned, or you were damned. It was as simple as that. My own conviction had softened long ago; I couldn't believe that Beatrice really was so arbitrary and cruel. But I knew my mother would not only have refused the full-blown ritual; the whole philosophy would have been as nonsensical to her as the mechanics.

"Did she say that? Did she tell you that?"

Daniel shook his head. "But it was clear." Filled with the love of Beatrice, he couldn't stop smiling.

A wave of revulsion passed through me; I wanted to grind his face into the deck. *He didn't care what my mother had believed.* Whatever eased his own pain, whatever put his own doubts to rest, had to be the case. To accept that she was damned—or even just dead, gone, erased—was unbearable; everything else flowed from that. *There was no truth in anything he said, anything he believed. It was all just an expression of his own needs.*

I walked back into the corridor and crouched beside my father. Without looking at me, he put an arm around me and pressed me against his side. I could feel the blackness washing over him, the helplessness, the loss. When I tried to embrace him he just clutched me more tightly, forcing me to be still. I shuddered a few times, then stopped weeping. I closed my eyes and let him hold me.

I was determined to stay there beside him, facing everything he was facing. But after a while, unbidden, the old flame began to glow in the back of my skull: the old warmth, the old peace, the old certainty. Daniel was right, my mother was with God. *How could I have doubted that?* There was no point asking how it had come about; Beatrice's ways were beyond my comprehension. But the one thing I knew firsthand was the strength of Her love.

I didn't move, I didn't free myself from my father's desolate embrace. But I was an impostor now, merely praying for his comfort, interceding from my state of grace. Beatrice had raised me out of the darkness, and I could no longer share his pain.

5

AFTER MY MOTHER'S DEATH, my faith kept ceding ground, without ever really wavering. Most of the doctrinal content fell away, leaving behind a core of belief that was a great deal easier to defend. It didn't matter if the Scriptures were superstitious nonsense or the Church was full of fools and hypocrites; Beatrice was still Beatrice, the way the sky was still blue. Whenever I heard debates between atheists and believers, I found myself increasingly on the atheists' side— not because I accepted their conclusion for a moment, but because they were so much more honest than their opponents. Maybe the priests and theologians arguing against them had the same kind of direct, personal experience of God as I did—or maybe not, maybe they just desperately needed to believe. But they never disclosed the true source of their conviction; instead, they just made laughable attempts to "prove" God's existence from the historical record, or from biology, astronomy, or mathematics. Daniel had been right at the age of fifteen—you couldn't prove any such thing—and listening to these people twist logic as they tried made me squirm.

I felt guilty about leaving my father working with a hired hand, and even guiltier when he moved onto Daniel's boat a year later, but I knew how angry it would have made him if he thought I'd abandoned my career for his sake. At times that was the only thing that kept me in Mitar: even when I honestly wanted nothing more than to throw it all in and go back to hauling nets, I was afraid my decision would be misinterpreted.

It took me three years to complete my thesis on the migration of aquatic zooytes in the wake of the ecopoiesis. My original hypothesis, that freshwater species had replenished the upper ocean, turned out to be false. Zooytes had no genes as such, just families of enzymes that re-synthesized each other after cell division, but comparisons of these heritable molecules showed that, rather than rain bringing new life from above, an ocean-dwelling species from a much greater depth had moved steadily closer to the surface, as the Angels' creations drained oxygen from the water. That wouldn't have been much of a surprise, if the same techniques hadn't also shown that several species found in river water were even closer relatives of the surface-dwellers. But those freshwater species weren't anyone's ancestors; they were the newest migrants. Zooytes that had spent a billion years confined to the depths had suddenly been able to survive (and reproduce, and mutate) closer to the surface than ever before, and when they'd stumbled on a mutation that let them thrive in the presence of oxygen, they'd finally been in a position to make use of it. The ecopoiesis might have driven other native organisms into extinction, but the invasion from Earth had enabled this ancient benthic species to mount a long overdue invasion of its own. Unwittingly or not, the Angels had set in motion the sequence of events that had released it from the ocean to colonize the planet.

So I proved myself wrong, earned my degree, and became famous amongst a circle of peers so small that we were all famous to each other anyway. Vast new territories did not open up before me. Anything to do with native biology was rapidly becoming an academic cul-de-sac; I'd always suspected that was how it would be, but I hadn't fought hard enough to end up anywhere else.

For the next three years, I clung to the path of least resistance: assisting Barat with his own research, taking the teaching jobs no one else wanted. Most of Barat's other students moved on to better things, and I found myself increasingly alone in Mitar. But that didn't matter; I had Beatrice.

At the age of twenty-five, I could see my future clearly. While other people deciphered—and built upon—the Angels' legacy, I'd watch from a distance, still messing about with samples of seawater from which all Angelic contaminants had been scrupulously removed.

Finally, when it was almost too late, I made up my mind to jump ship. Barat had been good to me, but he'd never expected loyalty verging on martyrdom. At the end of the year a bi-ecological (native and Angelic) microbiology conference was being held in Tia, possibly the last event of its kind. I had no new results to present, but it wouldn't be hard to find a plausible excuse to attend, and it would be the ideal place to lobby for a new position. My great zooyte discovery hadn't been entirely lost on the wider community of biologists; I could try to rekindle the memory of it. I doubted there'd be much point offering to sleep with anyone; ethical qualms aside, my bridge had probably rusted into place.

Then again, maybe I'd get lucky. Maybe I'd stumble on a fellow Drowned Freelander who'd ended up in a position of power, and all I'd have to do was promise that my work would be for the greater glory of Beatrice.

Tia was a city of ten million people on the east coast. New towers stood side-by-side with empty structures from the time of the Angels, giant gutted machines that might have played a role in the ecopoiesis. I was too old and proud to gawk like a child, but for all my provincial sophistication I wanted to. These domes and cylinders were twenty times older than the illustrations tattooed into the ceiling of the monastery back home. They bore no images of Beatrice; nothing of the Angels did. But why would they? They predated Her death.

The university, on the outskirts of Tia, was a third the size of Mitar itself. An underground train ringed the campus; the students I rode with eyed my unstylish clothes with disbelief. I left my luggage in the dormitory and headed straight for the conference center. Barat had chosen to stay behind; maybe he hadn't wanted to witness the public burial of his field. That made things easier for me; I'd be free to hunt for a new career without rubbing his face in it.

Late additions to the conference program were listed on a screen by the main entrance. I almost walked straight past the display; I'd already decided which talks I'd be attending. But three steps away, a title I'd glimpsed in passing assembled itself in my mind's eye, and I had to back-track to be sure I hadn't imagined it.

Carla Reggia: "Euphoric Effects of *Z/12/80* Excretions"

I stood there laughing with disbelief. I recognized the speaker and her co-workers by name, though I'd never had a chance to meet them. If this wasn't a hoax . . . what had they done? Dried it, smoked it, and tried writing that up as research? *Z/12/80* was one of "my" zooytes, one of the escapees from the ocean; the air and water of Tia were swarming with it. If its excretions were euphoric, the whole city would be in a state of bliss.

I knew, then and there, what they'd discovered. I knew it, long before I admitted it to myself. I went to the talk with my head full of jokes about neglected culture flasks full of psychotropic breakdown products, but for two whole days, I'd been steeling myself for the truth, finding ways in which it didn't have to matter.

Z/12/80, Carla explained, excreted among its waste products an amine that was able to bind to receptors in our Angel-crafted brains. Since it had been shown by other workers (no one recognized me; no one gave me so much as a glance) that *Z/12/80* hadn't existed at the time of the ecopoiesis, this interaction was almost certainly undesigned, and unanticipated. "It's up to the archaeologists and neurochemists to determine what role, if any, the arrival of this substance in the environment might have played in the collapse of early settlement culture. But for the past fifteen to eighteen thousand years, we've been swimming in it. Since we still exhibit such a wide spectrum of moods, we're probably able to compensate for its presence by down-regulating the secretion of the endogenous molecule that was designed to bind to the same receptor. That's just an educated guess, though. Exactly what the effects might be from individual to individual, across the range of doses that might be experienced under a variety of conditions, is clearly going to be a matter of great interest to investigators with appropriate expertise."

I told myself that I felt no disquiet. Beatrice acted on the world through the laws of nature; I'd stopped believing in supernatural miracles long ago. The fact that someone had now identified the way in which She'd acted on *me*, that night in the water, changed nothing.

I pressed ahead with my attempts to get recruited. Everyone at the conference was talking about Carla's discovery, and when people finally made the connection with my own work their eyes stopped glazing over halfway through my spiel. In the next three days, I received seven offers—all involving research into zooyte biochemistry. There was no question, now, of side-stepping the issue, of escaping into the wider world of Angelic biology. One man even came right out and said to me: "You're a Freelander, and you know that the ancestors of *Z/12/80* live in much greater numbers in the ocean. Don't you think *oceanic* exposure is going to be the key to understanding this?" He laughed. "I mean, you swam in the stuff as a child, didn't you? And you seem to have come through unscathed."

"Apparently."

On my last night in Tia, I couldn't sleep. I stared into the blackness of the room, watching the gray sparks dance in front of me. (Contaminants in the aqueous humor? Electrical noise in the retina? I'd heard the explanation once, but I could no longer remember it.)

I prayed to Beatrice in the Angels' tongue; I could still feel Her presence, as strongly as ever. The effect clearly wasn't just a matter of dosage, or trans-cutaneous absorption; merely swimming in the ocean at the right depth wasn't enough to make anyone feel Drowned. But in combination with the stress of oxygen starvation, and all the psychological build-up Daniel had provided, the jolt of zooyte piss must have driven certain neuroendocrine subsystems into new territory—or old territory, by a new path. *Peace, joy, contentment, the feeling of being loved* weren't exactly unknown emotions. But by short-circuiting the brain's usual practice of summoning those feelings only on occasions when there was a reason for them, I'd been "blessed with the love of Beatrice." I'd found happiness on demand.

And I still possessed it. That was the eeriest part. Even as I lay there in the dark, on the verge of reasoning everything I'd been living for out of existence, my ability to work the machinery was so ingrained that I felt as loved, as blessed as ever.

Maybe Beatrice was offering me another chance, making it clear that She'd still forgive this blasphemy and welcome me back. But why did I believe that there was anyone there to "forgive me"? You couldn't reason your way to God; there was only faith. And I knew, now, that the source of my faith was a meaningless accident, an unanticipated side-effect of the ecopoiesis.

I still had a choice. I could, still, decide that the love of Beatrice was immune to all logic, a force beyond understanding, untouched by evidence of any kind.

No, I couldn't. I'd been making exceptions for Her for too long. Everyone lived with double standards—but I'd already pushed mine as far as they'd go.

I started laughing and weeping at the same time. It was almost unimaginable: all the millions of people who'd been misled the same way. All because of the zooytes, and . . . what? One Freelander, diving for pleasure, who'd stumbled on a strange new experience? Then tens of thousands more repeating it, generation after generation— until one vulnerable man or woman had been driven to invest the novelty with meaning. Someone who'd needed so badly to feel loved and protected that the illusion of a real presence behind the raw emotion had been impossible to resist. Or who'd desperately wanted to believe that—in spite of the Angels' discovery that they, too, were mortal—death could still be defeated.

I was lucky: I'd been born in an era of moderation. I hadn't killed in the name of Beatrice. I hadn't suffered for my faith. I had no doubt that I'd been far happier for the last fifteen years than I would have been if I'd told Daniel to throw his rope and weights overboard without me.

But that didn't change the fact that the heart of it all had been a lie.

I WOKE AT DAWN, my head pounding, after just a few kilotaus' sleep. I closed my eyes and searched for Her presence, as I had a thousand times before. *When I woke in the morning and looked into my heart, She was there without fail, offering me strength and guidance. When I lay in bed at night, I feared nothing, because I knew She was watching over me.*

There was nothing. She was gone.

I stumbled out of bed, feeling like a murderer, wondering how I'd ever live with what I'd done.

6

I TURNED DOWN EVERY offer I'd received at the conference, and stayed on in Mitar. It took Barat and me two years to establish our own research group to examine the effects of the zooamine, and nine more for us to elucidate the full extent of its activity in the brain. Our new recruits all had solid backgrounds in neurochemistry, and they did better work than I did, but when Barat retired I found myself the spokesperson for the group.

The initial discovery had been largely ignored outside the scientific community; for most people, it hardly mattered whether our brain chemistry matched the Angels' original design, or had been altered fifteen thousand years ago by some unexpected contaminant. But when the Mitar zooamine group began publishing detailed accounts of the biochemistry of religious experience, the public at large rediscovered the subject with a vengeance.

The university stepped up security, and despite death threats and a number of unpleasant incidents with stone-throwing protesters, no one was hurt. We were flooded with requests from broadcasters—though most were predicated on the notion that the group was morally obliged to "face its critics", rather than the broadcasters being morally obliged to offer us a chance to explain our work, calmly and clearly, without being shouted down by enraged zealots.

I learned to avoid the zealots, but the obscurantists were harder to dodge. I'd expected opposition from the Churches—defending the faith was their job, after all—but some of the most intellectually bankrupt responses came from academics in other disciplines. In one televised debate, I was confronted by a Deep Church priest, a Transitional theologian, a devotee of the ocean god Marni, and an anthropologist from Tia.

"This discovery has no real bearing on any belief system," the anthropologist explained serenely. "All truth is local. Inside every Deep Church in Ferez, Beatrice *is* the daughter of God, and we're the mortal incarnations of the Angels, who traveled here from Earth. In a coastal village a few milliradians south, Marni is the supreme creator, and it was She who gave birth to us, right here. Going one step further and moving from the spiritual domain to the scientific might appear to 'negate' certain spiritual truths . . . but equally, moving from the scientific domain to the spiritual demonstrates the same limitations. We are nothing but the stories we tell ourselves, and no one story is greater than another." He smiled beneficently, the expression of a parent only too happy to give all his squabbling children an equal share in some disputed toy.

I said, "How many cultures do you imagine share your definition of 'truth'? How many people do you think would be content to worship a God who consisted of literally nothing but the fact of their belief?" I turned to the Deep Church priest. "Is that enough for you?"

"Absolutely not!" She glowered at the anthropologist. "While I have the greatest respect for my brother here," she gestured at the devotee of Marni, "you can't draw a line around those people who've been lucky enough to be raised in the true faith, and then suggest that *Beatrice's* infinite power and love is confined to that group of people . . . like some collection of folk songs!"

The devotee respectfully agreed. Marni had created the most distant stars, along with the oceans of Covenant. Perhaps some people called Her by another name, but if everyone on this planet were to die tomorrow, She would still be Marni: unchanged, undiminished.

The anthropologist responded soothingly, "Of course. But in context, and with a wider perspective—"

"I'm perfectly happy with a God who resides within us," offered the Transitional theologian. "It seems . . . *immodest* to expect more. And instead of fretting uselessly over these ultimate questions, we should confine ourselves to matters of a suitably human scale."

I turned to him. "So you're actually indifferent as to whether an infinitely powerful and loving being created everything around you, and plans to welcome you into Her arms after death . . . or the universe is a piece of quantum noise that will eventually vanish and erase us all?"

He sighed heavily, as if I was asking him to perform some arduous physical feat just by responding. "I can summon no enthusiasm for these issues."

Later, the Deep Church priest took me aside and whispered, "Frankly, we're all very grateful that you've debunked that awful cult of the Drowned. They're a bunch of fundamentalist hicks, and the Church will be better off without them. But you mustn't make the mistake of thinking that your work has anything to do with ordinary, civilized believers!"

I STOOD AT THE back of the crowd that had gathered on the beach near the rock pool, to listen to the two old men who were standing ankle-deep in the milky water. It had taken me four days to get here from Mitar, but when I'd heard reports of a zooyte bloom washing up on the remote north coast, I'd had to come and see the results for myself. The zooamine group had actually recruited an anthropologist for such occasions—one who could cope with such taxing notions as the existence of objective reality, and a biochemical substrate for human thought—but Céline was only with us for part of the year, and right now she was away doing other research.

"This is an ancient, sacred place!" one man intoned, spreading his arms to take in the pool. "You need only observe the shape of it to understand that. It concentrates the energy of the stars, and the sun, and the ocean."

"The focus of power is there, by the inlet," the other added, gesturing at a point where the water might have come up to his calves. "Once, I wandered too close. I was almost lost in the great dream of the ocean, when my friend here came and rescued me!"

These men weren't devotees of Marni, or members of any other formal religion. As far as I'd been able to tell from old news reports, the blooms occurred every eight or ten years, and the two had set themselves up as "custodians" of the pool more than fifty years ago. Some local villagers treated the whole thing as a joke, but others revered the old men. And for a small fee, tourists and locals alike could be chanted over, then splashed with the potent brew. Evaporation would have concentrated the trapped waters of the bloom; for a few days, before the zooytes ran out of nutrients and died *en masse* in a cloud of hydrogen sulphide, the amine would be present in levels as high as in any of our laboratory cultures back in Mitar.

As I watched people lining up for the ritual, I found myself trying to downplay the possibility that anyone could be seriously affected by it. It was broad daylight, no one feared for their life, and the old men's pantheistic gobbledygook carried all the gravitas of the patter of streetside scam merchants. Their marginal sincerity, and the money changing hands, would be enough to undermine the whole thing. This was a tourist trap, not a life-altering experience.

When the chanting was done, the first customer knelt at the edge of the pool. One of the custodians filled a small metal cup with water and threw it in her face. After a moment, she began weeping with joy. I moved closer, my stomach tightening. *It was what she'd known was expected of her, nothing more. She was playing along, not wanting to spoil the fun—like the good sports who pretended to have their thoughts read by a carnival psychic.*

Next, the custodians chanted over a young man. He began swaying giddily even before they touched him with the water; when they did, he broke into sobs of relief that racked his whole body.

I looked back along the queue. There was a young girl standing third in line now, looking around apprehensively; she could not have been more than nine or ten. Her father (I presumed) was standing behind her, with his hand against her back, as if gently propelling her forward.

I lost all interest in playing anthropologist. I forced my way through the crowd until I reached the edge of the pool, then turned to address the people in the queue. "These men are frauds! There's nothing mysterious going on here. I can tell you exactly what's in the water: it's just a drug, a natural substance given out by creatures that are trapped here when the waves retreat."

I squatted down and prepared to dip my hand in the pool. One of the custodians rushed forward and grabbed my wrist. He was an old man, I could have done what I liked, but some people were already jeering, and I didn't want to scuffle with him and start a riot. I backed away from him, then spoke again.

"I've studied this drug for more than ten years, at Mitar University. It's present in water all over the planet. We drink it, we bathe in it, we swim in it every day. But it's concentrated here, and if you don't understand what you're doing when you use it, that misunderstanding can harm you!"

The custodian who'd grabbed my wrist started laughing. "The dream of the ocean is powerful, yes, but we don't need your advice on that! For fifty years, my friend and I have studied its lore, until we were strong enough to *stand* in the sacred water!" He gestured at his leathery feet; I didn't doubt that his circulation had grown poor enough to limit the dose to a tolerable level.

He stretched out his sinewy arm at me. "So fuck off back to Mitar, Inlander! Fuck off back to your books and your dead machinery! What would you know about the sacred mysteries? *What would you know about the ocean?*"

I said, "I think you're out of your depth."

I stepped into the pool. He started wailing about my unpurified body polluting the water, but I brushed past him. The other custodian came after me, but though my feet were soft after years of wearing shoes, I ignored the sharp edges of the rocks and kept walking toward the inlet. The zooamine helped. I could feel the old joy, the old peace, the old "love"; it made a powerful anesthetic.

I looked back over my shoulder. The second man had stopped pursuing me; it seemed he honestly feared going any further. I pulled off my shirt, bunched it up, and threw it onto a rock at the side of the pool. Then I waded forward, heading straight for the "focus of power."

The water came up to my knees. I could feel my heart pounding, harder than it had since childhood. People were shouting at me from the edge of the pool—some outraged by my sacrilege, some apparently concerned for my safety in the presence of forces beyond my control. Without turning, I called out at the top of my voice, "There is no 'power' here! There's nothing 'sacred'! There's nothing here but a drug—"

Old habits die hard; I almost prayed first. *Please, Holy Beatrice, don't let me regain my faith.*

I lay down in the water and let it cover my face. My vision turned white; I felt like I was leaving my body. The love of Beatrice flooded into me, and nothing had changed: Her presence was as palpable as ever, as undeniable as ever. I *knew* that I was loved, accepted, forgiven.

I waited, staring into the light, almost expecting a voice, a vision, detailed hallucinations. That had happened to some of the Drowned. How did anyone ever claw their way back to sanity, after that?

But for me, there was only the emotion itself, overpowering but unembellished. It didn't grow monotonous; I could have basked in it for days. But I understood, now, that it said no more about my place in the world than the warmth of sunlight on skin. I'd never mistake it for the touch of a real hand again.

I climbed to my feet and opened my eyes. Violet afterimages danced in front of me. It took a few tau for me to catch my breath, and feel steady on my feet again. Then I turned and started wading back toward the shore.

The crowd had fallen silent, though whether it was in disgust or begrudging respect I had no idea.

I said, "It's not just here. It's not just in the water. It's part of us now; it's in our blood." I was still half-blind; I couldn't see whether anyone was listening. "But as long as you know that, you're already free. As long as you're ready to face the possibility that everything that makes your spirits soar, everything that lifts you up and fills your heart with joy, *everything that makes your life worth living* . . . is a lie, is corruption, is meaningless—then you can never be enslaved."

They let me walk away unharmed. I turned back to watch as the line formed again; the girl wasn't in the queue.

I WOKE WITH A start, from the same old dream.

I was lowering my mother into the water from the back of the boat. Her hands were tied, her feet weighted. She was afraid, but she'd put her trust in me. "You'll bring me up safely, won't you Martin?"

I nodded reassuringly. But once she'd vanished beneath the waves, I thought: What am I doing? I don't believe in this shit any more.

So I took out a knife and started cutting through the rope—

I brought my knees up to my chest, and crouched on the unfamiliar bed in the darkness. I was in a small town on the railway line, halfway back to Mitar. Halfway between midnight and dawn.

I dressed, and made my way out of the hostel. The center of town was deserted, and the sky was thick with stars. Just like home. In Mitar, everything vanished in a fog of light.

All three of the stars cited by various authorities as the Earth's sun were above the horizon. If they weren't all mistakes, perhaps I'd live to see a telescope's image of the planet itself. But the prospect of seeking contact with the Angels—if there really was a faction still out there, somewhere—left me cold. I shouted silently up at the stars: *Your degenerate offspring don't need your help! Why should we rejoin you? We're going to surpass you!*

I sat down on the steps at the edge of the square and covered my face. Bravado didn't help. Nothing helped. Maybe if I'd grown up facing the truth, I would have been stronger. But when I woke in the night, knowing that my mother was simply dead, that everyone I'd ever loved would follow her, that I'd vanish into the same emptiness myself, it was like being buried alive. It was like being back in the water, bound and weighted, with the certain knowledge that there was no one to haul me up.

Someone put a hand on my shoulder. I looked up, startled. It was a man about my own age. His manner wasn't threatening; if anything, he looked slightly wary of me.

He said, "Do you need a roof? I can let you into the Church if you want." There was a trolley packed with cleaning equipment a short distance behind him.

I shook my head. "It's not that cold." I was too embarrassed to explain that I had a perfectly good room nearby. "Thanks."

As he was walking away, I called after him, "Do you believe in God?"

He stopped and stared at me for a while, as if he was trying to decide if this was a trick question—as if I might have been hired by the local parishioners to vet him for theological soundness. Or maybe he just wanted to be diplomatic with anyone desperate enough to be sitting in the town square in the middle of the night, begging a stranger for reassurance.

He shook his head. "As a child I did. Not anymore. It was a nice idea . . . but it made no sense." He eyed me skeptically, still unsure of my motives.

I said, "Then isn't life unbearable?"

He laughed. "Not all the time."

He went back to his trolley, and started wheeling it toward the Church.

I stayed on the steps, waiting for dawn.

ORACLE

1

ON HIS EIGHTEENTH DAY in the tiger cage, Robert Stoney began to lose hope of emerging unscathed.

He'd woken a dozen times throughout the night with an overwhelming need to stretch his back and limbs, and none of the useful compromise positions he'd discovered in his first few days—the least-worst solutions to the geometrical problem of his confinement—had been able to dull his sense of panic. He'd been in far more pain in the second week, suffering cramps that felt as if the muscles of his legs were dying on the bone, but these new spasms had come from somewhere deeper, powered by a sense of urgency that revolved entirely around his own awareness of his situation.

That was what frightened him. Sometimes he could find ways to minimize his discomfort, sometimes he couldn't, but he'd been clinging to the thought that, in the end, all these fuckers could ever do was hurt him. That wasn't true, though. They could make him ache for freedom in the middle of the night, the way he might have ached with grief, or love. He'd always cherished the understanding that his self was a whole, his mind and body indivisible. But he'd failed to appreciate the corollary: through his body, they could touch every part of him. Change every part of him.

Morning brought a fresh torment: hay fever. The house was somewhere deep in the countryside, with nothing to be heard in the middle of the day but bird song. June had always been his worst

month for hay fever, but in Manchester it had been tolerable. As he
ate breakfast, mucus dripped from his face into the bowl of luke-
warm oats they'd given him. He stanched the flow with the back of
his hand, but suffered a moment of shuddering revulsion when he
couldn't find a way to reposition himself to wipe his hand clean on
his trousers. Soon he'd need to empty his bowels. They supplied him
with a chamber pot whenever he asked, but they always waited two
or three hours before removing it. The smell was bad enough, but
the fact that it took up space in the cage was worse.

Toward the middle of the morning, Peter Quint came to see
him. "How are we today, Prof?" Robert didn't reply. Since the day
Quint had responded with a puzzled frown to the suggestion that he
had an appropriate name for a spook, Robert had tried to make at
least one fresh joke at the man's expense every time they met, a petty
but satisfying indulgence. But now his mind was blank, and in retrospect the whole exercise seemed like an insane distraction, as bizarre
and futile as scoring philosophical points against some predatory
animal while it gnawed on his leg.

"Many happy returns," Quint said cheerfully.

Robert took care to betray no surprise. He'd never lost track of
the days, but he'd stopped thinking in terms of the calendar date;
it simply wasn't relevant. Back in the real world, to have forgotten
his own birthday would have been considered a benign eccentricity.
Here it would be taken as proof of his deterioration, and imminent
surrender.

If he was cracking, he could at least choose the point of fissure.
He spoke as calmly as he could, without looking up. "You know I
almost qualified for the Olympic marathon, back in forty-eight? If I
hadn't done my hip in just before the trials, I might have competed."
He tried a self-deprecating laugh. "I suppose I was never really much
of an athlete. But I'm only forty-six. I'm not ready for a wheelchair
yet." The words did help: he could beg this way without breaking
down completely, expressing an honest fear without revealing how
much deeper the threat of damage went.

He continued, with a measured note of plaintiveness that
he hoped sounded like an appeal to fairness. "I just can't bear the

thought of being crippled. All I'm asking is that you let me stand upright. Let me keep my health."

Quint was silent for a moment, then he replied with a tone of thoughtful sympathy. "It's unnatural, isn't it? Living like this: bent over, twisted, day after day. Living in an unnatural way is always going to harm you. I'm glad you can finally see that."

Robert was tired; it took several seconds for the meaning to sink in. *It was that crude, that obvious?* They'd locked him in this cage, for all this time . . . as a kind of ham-fisted *metaphor* for his crimes?

He almost burst out laughing, but he contained himself. "I don't suppose you know Franz Kafka?"

"Kafka?" Quint could never hide his voracity for names. "One of your Commie chums, is he?"

"I very much doubt that he was ever a Marxist."

Quint was disappointed, but prepared to make do with second best. "One of the other kind, then?"

Robert pretended to be pondering the question. "On balance, I suspect that's not too likely either."

"So why bring his name up?"

"I have a feeling he would have admired your methods, that's all. He was quite the connoisseur."

"Hmm." Quint sounded suspicious, but not entirely unflattered.

Robert had first set eyes on Quint in February of 1952. His house had been burgled the week before, and Arthur, a young man he'd been seeing since Christmas, had confessed to Robert that he'd given an acquaintance the address. Perhaps the two of them had planned to rob him, and Arthur had backed out at the last moment. In any case, Robert had gone to the police with an unlikely story about spotting the culprit in a pub, trying to sell an electric razor of the same make and model as the one taken from his house. No one could be charged on such flimsy evidence, so Robert had had no qualms about the consequences if Arthur had turned out to be lying. He'd simply hoped to prompt an investigation that might turn up something more tangible.

The following day, the CID had paid Robert a visit. The man he'd accused was known to the police, and fingerprints taken on the day of the burglary matched the prints they had on file. However, at the time Robert claimed to have seen him in the pub, he'd been in custody already on an entirely different charge.

The detectives had wanted to know why he'd lied. To spare himself the embarrassment, Robert had explained, of spelling out the true source of his information. Why was that embarrassing?

"I'm involved with the informant."

One detective, Mr Wills, had asked matter-of-factly, "What exactly does that entail, sir?" And Robert—in a burst of frankness, as if honesty itself was sure to be rewarded—had told him every detail. He'd known it was still technically illegal, of course. But then, so was playing football on Easter Sunday. It could hardly be treated as a serious crime, like burglary.

The police had strung him along for hours, gathering as much information as they could before disabusing him of this misconception. They hadn't charged him immediately; they'd needed a statement from Arthur first. But then Quint had materialized the next morning, and spelled out the choices very starkly. Three years in prison, with hard labor. Or Robert could resume his war-time work—for just one day a week, as a handsomely paid consultant to Quint's branch of the secret service—and the charges would quietly vanish.

At first, he'd told Quint to let the courts do their worst. He'd been angry enough to want to take a stand against the preposterous law, and whatever his feelings for Arthur, Quint had suggested—gloatingly, as if it strengthened his case—that the younger, working-class man would be treated far more leniently than Robert, having been led astray by someone whose duty was to set an example for the lower orders. Three years in prison was an unsettling prospect, but it would not have been the end of the world; the Mark I had changed the way he worked, but he could still function with nothing but a pencil and paper, if necessary. Even if they'd had him breaking rocks from dawn to dusk he probably would have been able to daydream productively, and for all Quint's scaremongering he'd doubted it would come to that.

At some point, though, in the twenty-four hours Quint had given him to reach a decision, he'd lost his nerve. By granting the spooks their one day a week, he could avoid all the fuss and disruption of a trial. And though his work at the time—modeling embryological development—had been as challenging as anything he'd done in his life, he hadn't been immune to pangs of nostalgia for the old days, when the fate of whole fleets of battleships had rested on finding the most efficient way to extract logical contradictions from a bank of rotating wheels.

The trouble with giving in to extortion was, *it proved that you could be bought*. Never mind that the Russians could hardly have offered to intervene with the Manchester constabulary next time he needed to be rescued. Never mind that he would scarcely have cared if an enemy agent had threatened to send such comprehensive evidence to the newspapers that there'd be no prospect of his patrons saving him again. He'd lost any chance to proclaim that what he did in bed with another willing partner was not an issue of national security; by saying yes to Quint, he'd made it one. By choosing to be corrupted once, he'd brought the whole torrent of clichés and paranoia down upon his head: he was vulnerable to blackmail, an easy target for entrapment, perfidious by nature. He might as well have posed *in flagrante delicto* with Guy Burgess on the steps of the Kremlin.

It wouldn't have mattered if Quint and his masters had merely decided that they couldn't trust him. The problem was—some six years after recruiting him, with no reason to believe that he had ever breached security in any way—they'd convinced themselves that they could neither continue to employ him, nor safely leave him in peace, until they'd rid him of the trait they'd used to control him in the first place.

Robert went through the painful, complicated process of rearranging his body so he could look Quint in the eye. "You know, if it was legal there'd be nothing to worry about, would there? Why don't you devote some of your considerable Machiavellian talents to that end? Blackmail a few politicians. Set up a Royal Commission. It would only take you a couple of years. Then we could all get on with our real jobs."

Quint blinked at him, more startled than outraged. "You might as well say that we should legalize treason!"

Robert opened his mouth to reply, then decided not to waste his breath. Quint wasn't expressing a moral opinion. He simply meant that a world in which fewer people's lives were ruled by the constant fear of discovery was hardly one that a man in his profession would wish to hasten into existence.

WHEN ROBERT WAS ALONE again, the time dragged. His hay fever worsened, until he was sneezing and gagging almost continuously; even with freedom of movement and an endless supply of the softest linen handkerchiefs, he would have been reduced to abject misery. Gradually, though, he grew more adept at dealing with the symptoms, delegating the task to some barely conscious part of himself. By the middle of the afternoon—covered in filth, eyes almost swollen shut—he finally managed to turn his mind back to his work.

For the past four years he'd been immersed in particle physics. He'd been following the field on and off since before the war, but the paper by Yang and Mills in '54, in which they'd generalized Maxwell's equations for electromagnetism to apply to the strong nuclear force, had jolted him into action.

After several false starts, he believed he'd discovered a useful way to cast gravity into the same form. In general relativity, if you carried a four-dimensional velocity vector around a loop that enclosed a curved region of spacetime, it came back rotated—a phenomenon highly reminiscent of the way more abstract vectors behaved in nuclear physics. In both cases, the rotations could be treated algebraically, and the traditional way to get a handle on this was to make use of a set of matrices of complex numbers whose relationships mimicked the algebra in question. Hermann Weyl had cataloged most of the possibilities back in the '20s and '30s.

In spacetime, there were six distinct ways you could rotate an object: you could turn it around any of three perpendicular axes in space, or you could boost its velocity in any of the same three directions. These two kinds of rotation were complementary, or "dual" to each other, with the ordinary rotations only affecting coordinates that were untouched by the corresponding boost, and *vice versa*.

This meant that you could rotate something around, say, the x-axis, and speed it up in the same direction, without the two processes interfering.

When Robert had tried applying the Yang-Mills approach to gravity in the obvious way, he'd floundered. It was only when he'd shifted the algebra of rotations into a new, strangely skewed guise that the mathematics had begun to fall into place. Inspired by a trick that particle physicists used to construct fields with left- or right-handed spin, he'd combined every rotation with its own dual multiplied by i, the square root of minus one. The result was a set of rotations in four *complex* dimensions, rather than the four real ones of ordinary spacetime, but the relationships between them preserved the original algebra.

Demanding that these "self-dual" rotations satisfy Einstein's equations turned out to be equivalent to ordinary general relativity, but the process leading to a quantum-mechanical version of the theory became dramatically simpler. Robert still had no idea how to interpret this, but as a purely formal trick it worked spectacularly well—and when the mathematics fell into place like that, it had to mean *something*.

He spent several hours pondering old results, turning them over in his mind's eye, rechecking and reimagining everything in the hope of forging some new connection. Making no progress, but there'd always been days like that. It was a triumph merely to spend this much time doing what he would have done back in the real world—however mundane, or even frustrating, the same activity might have been in its original setting.

By evening, though, the victory began to seem hollow. He hadn't lost his wits entirely, but he was frozen, stunted. He might as well have whiled away the hours reciting the base-32 multiplication table in Baudot code, just to prove that he still remembered it.

As the room filled with shadows, his powers of concentration deserted him completely. His hay fever had abated, but he was too tired to think, and in too much pain to sleep. This wasn't Russia, they couldn't hold him forever; he simply had to wear them down with his patience. *But when, exactly, would they have to let him go?*

And how much more patient could Quint be, with no pain, no terror, to erode his determination?

The moon rose, casting a patch of light on the far wall; hunched over, he couldn't see it directly, but it silvered the gray at his feet, and changed his whole sense of the space around him. The cavernous room mocking his confinement reminded him of nights he'd spent lying awake in the dormitory at Sherborne. A public school education did have one great advantage: however miserable you were afterward, you could always take comfort in the knowledge that life would never be quite as bad again.

"This room smells of mathematics! Go out and fetch a disinfectant spray!" That had been his form-master's idea of showing what a civilized man he was: contempt for that loathsome subject, the stuff of engineering and other low trades. And as for Robert's chemistry experiments, like the beautiful color-changing iodate reaction he'd learned from Chris's brother—

Robert felt a familiar ache in the pit of his stomach. *Not now. I can't afford this now.* But the whole thing swept over him, unwanted, unbidden. He'd used to meet Chris in the library on Wednesdays; for months, that had been the only time they could spend together. Robert had been fifteen then, Chris a year older. If Chris had been plain, he still would have shone like a creature from another world. No one else in Sherborne had read Eddington on relativity, Hardy on mathematics. No one else's horizons stretched beyond rugby, sadism, and the dimly satisfying prospect of reading classics at Oxford then vanishing into the maw of the civil service.

They had never touched, never kissed. While half the school had been indulging in passionless sodomy—as a rather literal-minded substitute for the much too difficult task of imagining women— Robert had been too shy even to declare his feelings. Too shy, and too afraid that they might not be reciprocated. It hadn't mattered. To have a friend like Chris had been enough.

In December of 1929, they'd both sat the exams for Trinity College, Cambridge. Chris had won a scholarship; Robert hadn't. He'd reconciled himself to their separation, and prepared for one more year at Sherborne without the one person who'd made it bearable. Chris would be following happily in the footsteps of Newton; just thinking of that would be some consolation.

Chris never made it to Cambridge. In February, after six days in agony, he'd died of bovine tuberculosis.

Robert wept silently, angry with himself because he knew that half his wretchedness was just self-pity, exploiting his grief as a disguise. He had to stay honest; once every source of unhappiness in his life melted together and became indistinguishable, he'd be like a cowed animal, with no sense of the past or the future. Ready to do anything to get out of the cage.

If he hadn't yet reached that point, he was close. It would only take a few more nights like the last one. Drifting off in the hope of a few minutes' blankness, to find that sleep itself shone a colder light on everything. Drifting off, then waking with a sense of loss so extreme it was like suffocation.

A woman's voice spoke from the darkness in front of him. "Get off your knees!"

Robert wondered if he was hallucinating. He'd heard no one approach across the creaky floorboards.

The voice said nothing more. Robert rearranged his body so he could look up from the floor. There was a woman he'd never seen before, standing a few feet away.

She'd sounded angry, but as he studied her face in the moonlight through the slits of his swollen eyes, he realized that her anger was directed, not at him, but at his condition. She gazed at him with an expression of horror and outrage, as if she'd chanced upon him being held like this in some respectable neighbor's basement, rather than an MI6 facility. Maybe she was one of the staff employed in the upkeep of the house, but had no idea what went on here? Surely those people were vetted and supervised, though, and threatened with life imprisonment if they ever set foot outside their prescribed domains.

For one surreal moment, Robert wondered if Quint had sent her to seduce him. It would not have been the strangest thing they'd tried. But she radiated such fierce self assurance—such a sense of confidence that she could speak with the authority of her convictions, and expect to be heeded—that he knew she could never have been chosen for the role. No one in Her Majesty's government would consider self assurance an attractive quality in a woman.

He said, "Throw me the key, and I'll show you my Roger Bannister impression."

She shook her head. "You don't need a key. Those days are over."

Robert started with fright. *There were no bars between them.* But the cage couldn't have vanished before his eyes; she must have removed it while he'd been lost in his reverie. He'd gone through the whole painful exercise of turning to face her as if he were still confined, without even noticing.

Removed it how?

He wiped his eyes, shivering at the dizzying prospect of freedom. "Who are you?" An agent for the Russians, sent to liberate him from his own side? She'd have to be a zealot, then, or strangely naïve, to view his torture with such wide-eyed innocence.

She stepped forward, then reached down and took his hand. "Do you think you can walk?" Her grip was firm, and her skin was cool and dry. She was completely unafraid; she might have been a good Samaritan in a public street helping an old man to his feet after a fall—not an intruder helping a threat to national security break out of therapeutic detention, at the risk of being shot on sight.

"I'm not even sure I can stand." Robert steeled himself; maybe this woman was a trained assassin, but it would be too much to presume that if he cried out in pain and brought guards rushing in, she could still extricate him without raising a sweat. "You haven't answered my question."

"My name's Helen." She smiled and hoisted him to his feet, looking at once like a compassionate child pulling open the jaws of a hunter's cruel trap, and a very powerful, very intelligent carnivore contemplating its own strength. "I've come to change everything."

Robert said, "Oh, good."

ROBERT FOUND THAT HE could hobble; it was painful and undignified, but at least he didn't have to be carried. Helen led him through the house; lights showed from some of the rooms, but there were no voices, no footsteps save their own, no signs of life at all. When they reached the tradesmen's entrance she unbolted the door, revealing a moonlit garden.

"Did you kill everyone?" he whispered. He'd made far too much noise to have come this far unmolested. Much as he had reason to despise his captors, mass murder on his behalf was a lot to take in.

Helen cringed. "What a revolting idea! It's hard to believe sometimes, how uncivilized you are."

"You mean the British?"

"All of you!"

"I must say, your accent's rather good."

"I watched a lot of cinema," she explained. "Mostly Ealing comedies. You never know how much that will help, though."

"Quite."

They crossed the garden, heading for a wooden gate in the hedge. Since murder was strictly for imperialists, Robert could only assume that she'd managed to drug everyone.

The gate was unlocked. Outside the grounds, a cobbled lane ran past the hedge, leading into forest. Robert was barefoot, but the stones weren't cold, and the slight unevenness of the path was welcome, restoring circulation to the soles of his feet.

As they walked, he took stock of his situation. He was out of captivity, thanks entirely to this woman. Sooner or later he was going to have to confront her agenda.

He said, "I'm not leaving the country."

Helen murmured assent, as if he'd passed a casual remark about the weather.

"And I'm not going to discuss my work with you."

"Fine."

Robert stopped and stared at her. She said, "Put your arm across my shoulders."

He complied; she was exactly the right height to support him comfortably. He said, "You're not a Soviet agent, are you?"

Helen was amused. "Is that really what you thought?"

"I'm not all that quick on my feet tonight."

"No." They began walking together. Helen said, "There's a train station about three kilometers away. You can get cleaned up, rest there until morning, and decide where you want to go."

"Won't the station be the first place they'll look?"

"They won't be looking anywhere for a while."

The moon was high above the trees. The two of them could not have made a more conspicuous couple: a sensibly dressed, quite striking young woman, supporting a filthy, ragged tramp. If a villager cycled past, the best they could hope for was being mistaken for an alcoholic father and his martyred daughter.

Martyred all right: she moved so efficiently, despite the burden, that any onlooker would assume she'd been doing this for years. Robert tried altering his gait slightly, subtly changing the timing of his steps to see if he could make her falter, but Helen adapted instantly. If she knew she was being tested, though, she kept it to herself.

Finally he said, "What did you do with the cage?"

"I time-reversed it."

Hairs stood up on the back of his neck. Even assuming that she could do such a thing, it wasn't at all clear to him how that could have stopped the bars from scattering light and interacting with his body. It should merely have turned electrons into positrons, and killed them both in a shower of gamma rays.

That conjuring trick wasn't his most pressing concern, though. "I can only think of three places you might have come from," he said.

Helen nodded, as if she'd put herself in his shoes and cataloged the possibilities. "Rule out one; the other two are both right."

She was not from an extrasolar planet. Even if her civilization possessed some means of viewing Ealing comedies from a distance of light years, she was far too sensitive to his specific human concerns.

She was from the future, but not his own.

She was from the future of another Everett branch.

He turned to her. "No paradoxes."

She smiled, deciphering his shorthand immediately. "That's right. It's physically impossible to travel into your own past, unless you've made exacting preparations to ensure compatible boundary conditions. That *can* be achieved, in a controlled laboratory setting—but in the field it would be like trying to balance ten thousand elephants in an inverted pyramid, while the bottom one rode a unicycle: excruciatingly difficult, and entirely pointless."

Robert was tongue-tied for several seconds, a horde of questions battling for access to his vocal chords. "But how do you travel into the past at all?"

"It will take a while to bring you up to speed completely, but if you want the short answer: you've already stumbled on one of the clues. I read your paper in *Physical Review*, and it's correct as far as it goes. Quantum gravity involves four complex dimensions, but the only classical solutions—the only geometries that remain in phase under slight perturbations—have curvature that's either *self-dual*, or *anti-self-dual*. Those are the only stationary points of the action, for the complete Lagrangian. And both solutions appear, from the inside, to contain only four real dimensions.

"It's meaningless to ask which sector we're in, but we might as well call it self-dual. In that case, the anti-self-dual solutions have an arrow of time running backward compared to ours."

"Why?" As he blurted out the question, Robert wondered if he sounded like an impatient child to her. But if she suddenly vanished back into thin air, he'd have far fewer regrets for making a fool of himself this way than if he'd maintained a façade of sophisticated nonchalance.

Helen said, "Ultimately, that's related to spin. And it's down to the mass of the neutrino that we can tunnel between sectors. But I'll need to draw you some diagrams and equations to explain it all properly."

Robert didn't press her for more; he had no choice but to trust that she wouldn't desert him. He staggered on in silence, a wonderful ache of anticipation building in his chest. If someone had put this situation to him hypothetically, he would have piously insisted that he'd prefer to toil on at his own pace. But despite the satisfaction it had given him on the few occasions when he'd made genuine discoveries himself, what mattered in the end was understanding as much as you could, however you could. Better to ransack the past and the future than go through life in a state of willful ignorance.

"You said you've come to change things?"

She nodded. "I can't predict the future here, of course, but there are pitfalls in my own past that I can help you avoid. In my twentieth century, people discovered things too slowly. Everything changed much too slowly. Between us, I think we can speed things up."

Robert was silent for a while, contemplating the magnitude of what she was proposing. Then he said, "It's a pity you didn't come sooner. In this branch, about twenty years ago—"

Helen cut him off. "I know. We had the same war. The same Holocaust, the same Soviet death toll. But we've yet to be able to avert that, anywhere. You can never do anything in just one history—even the most focused intervention happens across a broad 'ribbon' of strands. When we try to reach back to the '30s and '40s, the ribbon overlaps with its own past to such a degree that all the worst horrors are *faits accomplis*. We can't shoot *any* version of Adolf Hitler, because we can't shrink the ribbon to the point where none of us would be shooting ourselves in the back. All we've ever managed are minor interventions, like sending projectiles back to the Blitz, saving a few lives by deflecting bombs."

"What, knocking them into the Thames?"

"No, that would have been too risky. We did some modeling, and the safest thing turned out to be diverting them onto big, empty buildings: Westminster Abbey, Saint Paul's Cathedral."

The station came into view ahead of them. Helen said, "What do you think? Do you want to head back to Manchester?"

Robert hadn't given the question much thought. Quint could track him down anywhere, but the more people he had around him, the less vulnerable he'd be. In his house in Wilmslow he'd be there for the taking.

"I still have rooms at Cambridge," he said tentatively.

"Good idea."

"What are your own plans?"

Helen turned to him. "I thought I'd stay with you." She smiled at the expression on his face. "Don't worry, I'll give you plenty of privacy. And if people want to make assumptions, let them. You already have a scandalous reputation; you might as well see it branch out in new directions."

Robert said wryly, "I'm afraid it doesn't quite work that way. They'd throw us out immediately."

Helen snorted. "They could try."

"You may have defeated MI6, but you haven't dealt with Cambridge porters." The reality of the situation washed over him anew at the thought of her in his study, writing out the equations for time travel on the blackboard. "*Why me?* I can appreciate that you'd want to make contact with someone who could understand how you came here—but why not Everett, or Yang, or Feynman? Compared to Feynman, I'm a dilettante."

Helen said, "Maybe. But you have an equally practical bent, and you'll learn fast enough."

There had to be more to it than that: thousands of people would have been capable of absorbing her lessons just as rapidly. "The physics you've hinted at—in your past, did I discover all that?"

"No. Your *Physical Review* paper helped me track you down here, but in my own history that was never published." There was a flicker of disquiet in her eyes, as if she had far greater disappointments in store on that subject.

Robert didn't care much either way; if anything, the less his alter ego had achieved, the less he'd be troubled by jealousy.

"Then what was it, that made you choose me?"

"You really haven't guessed?" Helen took his free hand and held the fingers to her face; it was a tender gesture, but much more like a daughter's than a lover's. "It's a warm night. No one's skin should be this cold."

Robert gazed into her dark eyes, as playful as any human's, as serious, as proud. Given the chance, perhaps any decent person would have plucked him from Quint's grasp. But only one kind would feel a special obligation, as if they were repaying an ancient debt.

He said, "You're a machine."

2

John Hamilton, Professor of Medieval and Renaissance English at Magdalene College, Cambridge, read the last letter in the morning's pile of fan mail with a growing sense of satisfaction.

The letter was from a young American, a twelve-year-old girl in Boston. It opened in the usual way, declaring how much pleasure his books had given her, before going on to list her favorite scenes and characters. As ever, Jack was delighted that the stories had touched someone deeply enough to prompt them to respond this way. But it was the final paragraph that was by far the most gratifying:

> HOWEVER MUCH OTHER CHILDREN *might tease me, or grown-ups too when I'm older, I will NEVER, EVER stop believing in the Kingdom of Nescia. Sarah stopped believing, and she was locked out of the Kingdom forever. At first that made me cry, and I couldn't sleep all night because I was afraid I might stop believing myself one day. But I understand now that it's good to be afraid, because it will help me keep people from changing my mind. And if you're not willing to believe in magic lands, of course you can't enter them. There's nothing even Belvedere himself can do to save you, then.*

Jack refilled and lit his pipe, then reread the letter. This was his vindication: the proof that through his books he could touch a young mind, and plant the seed of faith in fertile ground. It made all the scorn of his jealous, stuck-up colleagues fade into insignificance. Children understood the power of stories, the reality of myth, the need to believe in something beyond the dismal gray farce of the material world.

It wasn't a truth that could be revealed the "adult" way: through scholarship, or reason. Least of all through philosophy, as Elizabeth Anscombe had shown him on that awful night at the Socratic Club. A devout Christian herself, Anscombe had nonetheless taken all the arguments against materialism from his popular book, *Signs and Wonders*, and trampled them into the ground. It had been an unfair match from the start: Anscombe was a professional philosopher, steeped in the work of everyone from Aquinas to Wittgenstein; Jack knew the history of ideas in medieval Europe intimately, but he'd lost interest in modern philosophy once it had been invaded by fashionable positivists. And *Signs and Wonders* had never been intended as a scholarly work; it had been good enough to pass muster with a sympathetic lay readership, but trying to defend his admittedly rough-and-ready mixture of common sense and useful shortcuts to faith against Anscombe's merciless analysis had made him feel like a country yokel stammering in front of a bishop.

Ten years later, he still burned with resentment at the humiliation she'd put him through, but he was grateful for the lesson she'd taught him. His earlier books, and his radio talks, had not been a complete waste of time—but the harpy's triumph had shown him just how pitiful human reason was when it came to the great questions. He'd begun working on the stories of Nescia years before, but it was only when the dust had settled on his most painful defeat that he'd finally recognized his true calling.

He removed his pipe, stood, and turned to face Oxford. "Kiss my arse, Elizabeth!" he growled happily, waving the letter at her. This was a wonderful omen. It was going to be a very good day.

There was a knock at the door of his study.

"Come."

It was his brother, William. Jack was puzzled—he hadn't even realized Willie was in town—but he nodded a greeting and motioned at the couch opposite his desk.

Willie sat, his face flushed from the stairs, frowning. After a moment he said, "This chap Stoney."

"Hmm?" Jack was only half listening as he sorted papers on his desk. He knew from long experience that Willie would take forever to get to the point.

"Did some kind of hush-hush work during the war, apparently."

"Who did?"

"Robert Stoney. Mathematician. Used to be up at Manchester, but he's a Fellow of Kings, and now he's back in Cambridge. Did some kind of secret war work. Same thing as Malcolm Muggeridge, apparently. No one's allowed to say what."

Jack looked up, amused. He'd heard rumors about Muggeridge, but they all revolved around the business of analyzing intercepted German radio messages. What conceivable use would a mathematician have been, for that? Sharpening pencils for the intelligence analysts, presumably.

"What about him, Willie?" Jack asked patiently.

Willie continued reluctantly, as if he was confessing to something mildly immoral. "I paid him a visit yesterday. Place called the Cavendish. Old army friend of mine has a brother who works there. Got the whole tour."

"I know the Cavendish. What's there to see?"

"He's doing things, Jack. *Impossible things.*"

"Impossible?"

"Looking inside people. Putting it on a screen, like a television." Jack sighed. "Taking X-rays?"

Willie snapped back angrily, "I'm not a fool; I know what an X-ray looks like. This is different. You can see the blood flow. You can watch your heart beating. You can follow a sensation through the nerves from . . . fingertip to brain. He says, soon he'll be able to watch a thought in motion."

"Nonsense." Jack scowled. "So he's invented some gadget, some fancy kind of X-ray machine. What are you so agitated about?"

Willie shook his head gravely. "There's more. That's just the tip of the iceberg. He's only been back in Cambridge a year, and already the place is overflowing with . . . wonders." He used the word begrudgingly, as if he had no choice, but was afraid of conveying more approval than he intended.

Jack was beginning to feel a distinct sense of unease.

"What exactly is it you want me to do?" he asked.

Willie replied plainly, "Go and see for yourself. Go and see what he's up to."

THE CAVENDISH LABORATORY WAS a mid-Victorian building, designed to resemble something considerably older and grander. It housed the entire Department of Physics, complete with lecture theaters; the place was swarming with noisy undergraduates. Jack had had no trouble arranging a tour: he'd simply telephoned Stoney and expressed his curiosity, and no more substantial reason had been required.

Stoney had been allocated three adjoining rooms at the back of the building, and the "spin resonance imager" occupied most of the first. Jack obligingly placed his arm between the coils, then almost jerked it out in fright when the strange, transected view of his muscles and veins appeared on the picture tube. He wondered if it could be some kind of hoax, but he clenched his fist slowly and watched the image do the same, then made several unpredictable movements which it mimicked equally well.

"I can show you individual blood cells, if you like," Stoney offered cheerfully.

Jack shook his head; his current, unmagnified flaying was quite enough to take in.

Stoney hesitated, then added awkwardly, "You might want to talk to your doctor at some point. It's just that, your bone density's rather—" He pointed to a chart on the screen beside the image. "Well, it's quite a bit below the normal range."

Jack withdrew his arm. He'd already been diagnosed with osteoporosis, and he'd welcomed the news: it meant that he'd taken a small part of Joyce's illness—the weakness in her bones—into his own body. God was allowing him to suffer a little in her stead.

If Joyce were to step between these coils, what might that reveal? But there'd be nothing to add to her diagnosis. Besides, if he kept up his prayers, and kept up both their spirits, in time her remission would blossom from an uncertain reprieve into a fully-fledged cure.

He said, "How does this work?"

"In a strong magnetic field, some of the atomic nuclei and electrons in your body are free to align themselves in various ways with the field." Stoney must have seen Jack's eyes beginning to glaze over; he quickly changed tack. "Think of it as being like setting a whole lot of spinning tops whirling, as vigorously as possible, then listening carefully as they slow down and tip over. For the atoms in your body, that's enough to give some clues as to what kind of molecule, and what kind of tissue, they're in. The machine listens to atoms in different places by changing the way it combines all the signals from billions of tiny antennae. It's like a whispering gallery where we can play with the time that signals take to travel from different places, moving the focus back and forth through any part of your body, thousands of times a second."

Jack pondered this explanation. Though it sounded complicated, in principle it wasn't that much stranger than X-rays.

"The physics itself is old hat," Stoney continued, "but for imaging, you need a very strong magnetic field, and you need to make sense of all the data you've gathered. Nevill Mott made the superconducting alloys for the magnets. And I managed to persuade Rosalind Franklin from Birkbeck to collaborate with us, to help perfect the fabrication process for the computing circuits. We cross-link lots of little Y-shaped DNA fragments, then selectively coat them with metal; Rosalind worked out a way to use X-ray crystallography for quality control. We paid her back with a purpose-built computer that will let her solve hydrated protein structures in real time, once she gets her hands on a bright enough X-ray source." He held up a small, unprepossessing object, rimmed with protruding gold wires. "Each logic gate is roughly a hundred Ångstroms cubed, and we grow them in three-dimensional arrays. That's a million, million, million switches in the palm of my hand."

Jack didn't know how to respond to this claim. Even when he couldn't quite follow the man there was something mesmerizing about his ramblings, like a cross between William Blake and nursery talk.

"If computers don't excite you, we're doing all kinds of other things with DNA." Stoney ushered him into the next room, which was full of glassware, and seedlings in pots beneath strip lights. Two assistants seated at a bench were toiling over microscopes; another was dispensing fluids into test tubes with a device that looked like an overgrown eye-dropper.

"There are a dozen new species of rice, corn, and wheat here. They all have at least double the protein and mineral content of existing crops, and each one uses a different biochemical repertoire to protect itself against insects and fungi. Farmers have to get away from monocultures; it leaves them too vulnerable to disease, and too dependent on chemical pesticides."

Jack said, "You've bred these? All these new varieties, in a matter of months?"

"No, no! Instead of hunting down the heritable traits we needed in the wild, and struggling for years to produce cross-breeds bearing all of them, we designed every trait from scratch. Then we manufactured DNA that would make the tools the plants need, and inserted it into their germ cells."

Jack demanded angrily, "Who are you to say what a plant needs?"

Stoney shook his head innocently. "I took my advice from agricultural scientists, who took their advice from farmers. They know what pests and blights they're up against. Food crops are as artificial as Pekinese. Nature didn't hand them to us on a plate, and if they're not working as well as we need them to, nature isn't going to fix them for us."

Jack glowered at him, but said nothing. He was beginning to understand why Willie had sent him here. The man came across as an enthusiastic tinkerer, but there was a breath-taking arrogance lurking behind the boyish exterior.

Stoney explained a collaboration he'd brokered between scientists in Cairo, Bogotá, London and Calcutta, to develop vaccines for polio, smallpox, malaria, typhoid, yellow fever, tuberculosis, influenza and leprosy. Some were the first of their kind; others were intended as replacements for existing vaccines. "It's important that we create antigens without culturing the pathogens in animal cells that might themselves harbor viruses. The teams are all looking at variants on a simple, cheap technique that involves putting antigen genes into harmless bacteria that will double as delivery vehicles and adjuvants, then freeze-drying them into spores that can survive tropical heat without refrigeration."

Jack was slightly mollified; this all sounded highly admirable. What business Stoney had instructing doctors on vaccines was another question. Presumably his jargon made sense to them, but when exactly had this mathematician acquired the training to make even the most modest suggestions on the topic?

"You're having a remarkably productive year," he observed.

Stoney smiled. "The muse comes and goes for all of us. But I'm really just the catalyst in most of this. I've been lucky enough to find some people—here in Cambridge, and further afield—who've been willing to chance their arm on some wild ideas. They've done the real work." He gestured toward the next room. "My own pet projects are through here."

The third room was full of electronic gadgets, wired up to picture tubes displaying both phosphorescent words and images resembling engineering blueprints come to life. In the middle of one bench, incongruously, sat a large cage containing several hamsters.

Stoney fiddled with one of the gadgets, and a face like a stylized drawing of a mask appeared on an adjacent screen. The mask looked around the room, then said, "Good morning, Robert. Good morning, Professor Hamilton."

Jack said, "You had someone record those words?"

The mask replied, "No, Robert showed me photographs of all the teaching staff at Cambridge. If I see anyone I know from the photographs, I greet them." The face was crudely rendered, but the hollow eyes seemed to meet Jack's. Stoney explained, "It has no idea what it's saying, of course. It's just an exercise in face and voice recognition."

Jack responded stiffly, "Of course."

Stoney motioned to Jack to approach and examine the hamster cage. He obliged him. There were two adult animals, presumably a breeding pair. Two pink young were suckling from the mother, who reclined in a bed of straw.

"Look closely," Stoney urged him. Jack peered into the nest, then cried out an obscenity and backed away.

One of the young was exactly what it seemed. The other was a machine, wrapped in ersatz skin, with a nozzle clamped to the warm teat.

"That's the most monstrous thing I've ever seen!" Jack's whole body was trembling. "What possible reason could you have to do that?"

Stoney laughed and made a reassuring gesture, as if his guest was a nervous child recoiling from a harmless toy. "It's not hurting her!

And the point is to discover what it takes for the mother to accept it. To 'reproduce one's kind' means having some set of parameters as to what that is. Scent, and some aspects of appearance, are important cues in this case, but through trial and error I've also pinned down a set of behaviors that lets the simulacrum pass through every stage of the life cycle. An acceptable child, an acceptable sibling, an acceptable mate."

Jack stared at him, nauseated. "These animals fuck your machines?"

Stoney was apologetic. "Yes, but hamsters will fuck anything. I'll really have to shift to a more discerning species, in order to test that properly."

Jack struggled to regain his composure. "What on Earth possessed you, to do this?"

"In the long run," Stoney said mildly, "I believe this is something we're going to need to understand far better than we do at present. Now that we can map the structures of the brain in fine detail, and match its raw complexity with our computers, it's only a matter of a decade or so before we build machines that think.

"That in itself will be a vast endeavor, but I want to ensure that it's not stillborn from the start. There's not much point creating the most marvelous children in history, only to find that some awful mammalian instinct drives us to strangle them at birth."

JACK SAT IN HIS study drinking whisky. He'd telephoned Joyce after dinner, and they'd chatted for a while, but it wasn't the same as being with her. The weekends never came soon enough, and by Tuesday or Wednesday any sense of reassurance he'd gained from seeing her had slipped away entirely.

It was almost midnight now. After speaking to Joyce, he'd spent three more hours on the telephone, finding out what he could about Stoney. Milking his connections, such as they were; Jack had only been at Cambridge for five years, so he was still very much an outsider. Not that he'd ever been admitted into any inner circles back at Oxford: he'd always belonged to a small, quiet group of dissenters against the tide of fashion. Whatever else might be said about the

Tiddlywinks, they'd never had their hands on the levers of academic power.

A year ago, while on sabbatical in Germany, Stoney had resigned suddenly from a position he'd held at Manchester for a decade. He'd returned to Cambridge, despite having no official posting to take up. He'd started collaborating informally with various people at the Cavendish, until the head of the place, Mott, had invented a job description for him, and given him a modest salary, the three rooms Jack had seen, and some students to assist him.

Stoney's colleagues were uniformly amazed by his spate of successful inventions. Though none of his gadgets were based on entirely new science, his skill at seeing straight to the heart of existing theories and plucking some practical consequence from them was unprecedented. Jack had expected some jealous back-stabbing, but no one seemed to have a bad word to say about Stoney. He was willing to turn his scientific Midas touch to the service of anyone who approached him, and it sounded to Jack as if every would-be skeptic or enemy had been bought off with some rewarding insight into their own field.

Stoney's personal life was rather murkier. Half of Jack's informants were convinced that the man was a confirmed pansy, but others spoke of a beautiful, mysterious woman named Helen, with whom he was plainly on intimate terms.

Jack emptied his glass and stared out across the courtyard. *Was it pride, to wonder if he might have received some kind of prophetic vision?* Fifteen years earlier, when he'd written *The Broken Planet*, he'd imagined that he'd merely been satirizing the hubris of modern science. His portrait of the evil forces behind the sardonically named Laboratory Overseeing Various Experiments had been intended as a deadly serious metaphor, but he'd never expected to find himself wondering if real fallen angels were whispering secrets in the ears of a Cambridge don.

How many times, though, had he told his readers that the devil's greatest victory had been convincing the world that he did not exist? The devil was *not* a metaphor, a mere symbol of human weakness: he was a real, scheming presence, acting in time, acting in the world, as much as God Himself.

And hadn't Faustus's damnation been sealed by the most beautiful woman of all time: Helen of Troy?

Jack's skin crawled. He'd once written a humorous newspaper column called "Letters from a Demon," in which a Senior Tempter offered advice to a less experienced colleague on the best means to lead the faithful astray. Even that had been an exhausting, almost corrupting experience; adopting the necessary point of view, however whimsically, had made him feel that he was withering inside. The thought that a cross between the *Faustbuch* and *The Broken Planet* might be coming to life around him was too terrifying to contemplate. He was no hero out of his own fiction—not even a mild-mannered Cedric Duffy, let alone a modern Pendragon. And he did not believe that Merlin would rise from the woods to bring chaos to that hubristic Tower of Babel, the Cavendish Laboratory.

Nevertheless, if he was the only person in England who suspected Stoney's true source of inspiration, who else would act?

Jack poured himself another glass. There was nothing to be gained by procrastinating. He would not be able to rest until he knew what he was facing: a vain, foolish overgrown boy who was having a run of good luck—or a vain, foolish overgrown boy who had sold his soul and imperiled all humanity.

"A *Satanist*? You're accusing me of being a Satanist?"

Stoney tugged angrily at his dressing gown; he'd been in bed when Jack had pounded on the door. Given the hour, it had been remarkably civil of him to accept a visitor at all, and he appeared so genuinely affronted now that Jack was almost prepared to apologize and slink away. He said, "I had to ask you—"

"You have to be doubly foolish to be a Satanist," Stoney muttered.

"Doubly?"

"Not only do you need to believe all the nonsense of Christian theology, you then have to turn around and back the preordained, guaranteed-to-fail, absolutely futile *losing side*." He held up his hand, as if he believed he'd anticipated the only possible objection to this remark, and wished to spare Jack the trouble of wasting his breath by uttering it. "I *know*, some people claim it's all really about some pre-Christian deity: Mercury, or Pan—guff like that. But assuming that we're not talking about some complicated mislabeling of objects of worship, I really can't think of anything more insulting. You're comparing me to someone like . . . *Huysmans*, who was basically just a very dim Catholic."

Stoney folded his arms and settled back on the couch, waiting for Jack's response.

Jack's head was thick from the whisky; he wasn't at all sure how to take this. It was the kind of smart-arsed undergraduate drivel he might have expected from any smug atheist—but then, short of a confession, exactly what kind of reply would have constituted evidence of guilt? *If you'd sold your soul to the devil, what lie would you tell in place of the truth?* Had he seriously believed that Stoney would claim to be a devout churchgoer, as if that were the best possible answer to put Jack off the scent?

He had to concentrate on things he'd seen with his own eyes, facts that could not be denied.

"You're plotting to overthrow nature, bending the world to the will of man."

Stoney sighed. "Not at all. More refined technology will help us tread more lightly. We have to cut back on pollution and pesticides as rapidly as possible. Or do you want to live in a world where all the animals are born as hermaphrodites, and half the Pacific islands disappear in storms?"

"Don't try telling me that you're some kind of guardian of the animal kingdom. You want to replace us all with machines!"

"Does every Zulu or Tibetan who gives birth to a child, and wants the best for it, threaten you in the same way?"

Jack bristled. "I'm not a racist. A Zulu or Tibetan has a *soul*."

Stoney groaned and put his head in his hands. "It's half past one in the morning! Can't we have this debate some other time?"

Someone banged on the door. Stoney looked up, disbelieving. "What is this? Grand Central Station?"

He crossed to the door and opened it. A disheveled, unshaven man pushed his way into the room. "Quint? What a pleasant—"

The intruder grabbed Stoney and slammed him against the wall. Jack exhaled with surprise. Quint turned bloodshot eyes on him.

"Who the fuck are you?"

"John Hamilton. Who the fuck are you?"

"Never you mind. Just stay put." He jerked Stoney's arm up behind his back with one hand, while grinding his face into the wall with the other. "You're mine now, you piece of shit. No one's going to protect you this time."

Stoney addressed Jack through a mouth squashed against the masonry. "Dith ith Pether Quinth, my own perthonal thpook. I did make a Fauthtian bargain. But with thtrictly temporal—"

"Shut up!" Quint pulled a gun from his jacket and held it to Stoney's head.

Jack said, "Steady on."

"Just how far do your connections go?" Quint screamed. "I've had memos disappear, sources clam up—and now my superiors are treating *me* like some kind of traitor! Well, don't worry: when I'm through with you, I'll have the names of the entire network." He turned to address Jack again. "And don't *you* think you're going anywhere."

Stoney said, "Leave him out of dith. He'th at Magdalene. You mutht know by now: all the thpieth are at Trinity."

Jack was shaken by the sight of Quint waving his gun around, but the implications of this drama came as something of a relief. Stoney's ideas must have had their genesis in some secret war-time research project. He hadn't made a deal with the devil after all, but he'd broken the Official Secrets Act, and now he was paying the price.

Stoney flexed his body and knocked Quint backward. Quint staggered, but didn't fall; he raised his arm menacingly, but there was no gun in his hand. Jack looked around to see where it had fallen, but he couldn't spot it anywhere. Stoney landed a kick squarely in Quint's testicles; barefoot, but Quint wailed with pain. A second kick sent him sprawling.

Stoney called out, "Luke? *Luke!* Would you come and give me a hand?"

A solidly built man with tattooed forearms emerged from Stoney's bedroom, yawning and tugging his braces into place. At the sight of Quint, he groaned. "Not again!"

Stoney said, "I'm sorry."

Luke shrugged stoically. The two of them managed to grab hold of Quint, then they dragged him struggling out the door. Jack waited a few seconds, then searched the floor for the gun. But it wasn't anywhere in sight, and it hadn't slid under the furniture; none of the crevices where it might have ended up were so dark that it would have been lost in shadow. It was not in the room at all.

Jack went to the window and watched the three men cross the courtyard, half expecting to witness an assassination. But Stoney and his lover merely lifted Quint into the air between them, and tossed him into a shallow, rather slimy-looking pond.

JACK SPENT THE ENSUING days in a state of turmoil. He wasn't ready to confide in anyone until he could frame his suspicions clearly, and the events in Stoney's rooms were difficult to interpret unambiguously. He couldn't state with absolute certainty that Quint's gun had vanished before his eyes. But surely the fact that Stoney was walking free proved that he was receiving supernatural protection? And Quint himself, confused and demoralized, had certainly had the appearance of a man who'd been demonically confounded at every turn.

If this was true, though, Stoney must have bought more with his soul than immunity from worldly authority. *The knowledge itself* had to be Satanic in origin, as the legend of Faustus described it. Tollers had been right, in his great essay "Mythopoesis": myths were remnants of man's pre-lapsarian capacity to apprehend, directly, the great truths of the world. Why else would they resonate in the imagination, and survive from generation to generation?

By Friday, a sense of urgency gripped him. He couldn't take his confusion back to Potter's Barn, back to Joyce and the boys. This had to be resolved, if only in his own mind, before he returned to his family.

With Wagner on the gramophone, he sat and meditated on the challenge he was facing. Stoney had to be thwarted, but how? Jack had always said that the Church of England—apparently so quaint and harmless, a Church of cake stalls and kindly spinsters—was like a fearsome army in the eyes of Satan. But even if his master was quaking in Hell, it would take more than a few stern words from a bicycling vicar to force Stoney to abandon his obscene plans.

But Stoney's intentions, in themselves, didn't matter. He'd been granted the power to dazzle and seduce, but not to force his will upon the populace. What mattered was how his plans were viewed by others. And the way to stop him was to open people's eyes to the true emptiness of his apparent cornucopia.

The more he thought and prayed about it, the more certain Jack became that he'd discerned the task required of him. No denunciation from the pulpits would suffice; people wouldn't turn down the fruits of Stoney's damnation on the mere say-so of the Church. Why would anyone reject such lustrous gifts, without a carefully reasoned argument?

Jack had been humiliated once, defeated once, trying to expose the barrenness of materialism. But might that not have been a form of preparation? He'd been badly mauled by Anscombe, but she'd made an infinitely gentler enemy than the one he now confronted. He had suffered from her taunts—but what was *suffering*, if not the chisel God used to shape his children into their true selves?

His role was clear, now. He would find Stoney's intellectual Achilles heel, and expose it to the world.

He would debate him.

3

ROBERT GAZED AT THE blackboard for a full minute, then started laughing with delight. "That's so beautiful!"

"Isn't it?" Helen put down the chalk and joined him on the couch. "Any more symmetry, and nothing would happen: the universe would be full of crystalline blankness. Any less, and it would all be uncorrelated noise."

Over the months, in a series of tutorials, Helen had led him through a small part of the century of physics that had separated them at their first meeting, down to the purely algebraic structures that lay beneath spacetime and matter. Mathematics cataloged everything that was not self-contradictory; within that vast inventory, physics was an island of structures rich enough to contain their own beholders.

Robert sat and mentally reviewed everything he'd learned, trying to apprehend as much as he could in a single image. As he did, a part of him waited fearfully for a sense of disappointment, a sense of anticlimax. *He might never see more deeply into the nature of the world. In this direction, at least, there was nothing more to be discovered.*

But anticlimax was impossible. To become jaded with *this* was impossible. However familiar he became with the algebra of the universe, it would never grow less marvelous.

Finally he asked, "Are there other islands?" Not merely other histories, sharing the same underlying basis, but other realities entirely.

"I suspect so," Helen replied. "People have mapped some possibilities. I don't know how that could ever be confirmed, though."

Robert shook his head, sated. "I won't even think about that. I need to come down to Earth for a while." He stretched his arms and leaned back, still grinning.

Helen said, "Where's Luke today? He usually shows up by now, to drag you out into the sunshine."

The question wiped the smile from Robert's face. "Apparently I make poor company. Being insufficiently fanatical about darts and football."

"He's left you?" Helen reached over and squeezed his hand sympathetically. A little mockingly, too.

Robert was annoyed; she never said anything, but he always felt that she was judging him. "You think I should grow up, don't you? Find someone more like myself. Some kind of *soulmate*." He'd meant the word to sound sardonic, but it emerged rather differently.

"It's your life," she said.

A year before, that would have been a laughable claim, but it was almost the truth now. There was a *de facto* moratorium on prosecutions, while the recently acquired genetic and neurological evidence was being assessed by a parliamentary subcommittee. Robert had helped plant the seeds of the campaign, but he'd played no real part in it; other people had taken up the cause. In a matter of months, it was possible that Quint's cage would be smashed, at least for every-one in Britain.

The prospect filled him with a kind of vertigo. He might have broken the laws at every opportunity, but they had still molded him. The cage might not have left him crippled, but he'd be lying to him-self if he denied that he'd been stunted.

He said, "Is that what happened, in your past? I ended up in some . . . lifelong partnership?" As he spoke the words, his mouth went dry, and he was suddenly afraid that the answer would be yes. *With Chris. The life he'd missed out on was a life of happiness with Chris.*

"No."

"Then . . . what?" he pleaded. "What did I do? How did I live?" He caught himself, suddenly self-conscious, but added, "You can't blame me for being curious."

Helen said gently, "You don't want to know what you can't change. All of that is part of your own causal past now, as much as it is of mine."

"If it's part of my own history," Robert countered, "don't I deserve to know it? This man wasn't me, but he brought you to me."

Helen considered this. "You accept that he was someone else? Not someone whose actions you're responsible for?"

"Of course."

She said, "There was a trial, in 1952. For 'Gross Indecency con-trary to Section 11 of the Criminal Amendment Act of 1885.' He wasn't imprisoned, but the court ordered hormone treatments."

"*Hormone treatments?*" Robert laughed. "What—testosterone, to make him more of a man?"

"No, estrogen. Which in men reduces the sex drive. There are side-effects, of course. Gynecomastia, among other things."

Robert felt physically sick. *They'd chemically castrated him, with drugs that had made him sprout breasts.* Of all the bizarre abuse to which he'd been subjected, nothing had been as horrifying as that.

Helen continued, "The treatment lasted six months, and the effects were all temporary. But two years later, he took his own life. It was never clear exactly why."

Robert absorbed this in silence. He didn't want to know anything more.

After a while, he said, "How do you bear it? Knowing that in some branch or other, every possible form of humiliation is being inflicted on someone?"

Helen said, "I don't *bear it*. I change it. That's why I'm here."

Robert bowed his head. "I know. And I'm grateful that our histories collided. But . . . how many histories don't?" He struggled to find an example, though it was almost too painful to contemplate; since their first conversation, it was a topic he'd deliberately pushed to the back of his mind. "There's not just an unchangeable Auschwitz in each of our pasts, there are an astronomical number of others—along with an astronomical number of things that are even worse."

Helen said bluntly, "That's not true."

"What?" Robert looked up at her, startled.

She walked to the blackboard and erased it. "Auschwitz has happened, for both of us, and no one I'm aware of has ever prevented it—but that doesn't mean that *nobody* stops it, anywhere." She began sketching a network of fine lines on the blackboard. "You and I are having this conversation in countless microhistories—sequences of events where various different things happen with subatomic particles throughout the universe—but that's irrelevant to us, we can't tell those strands apart, so we might as well treat them all as one history." She pressed the chalk down hard to make a thick streak that covered everything she'd drawn. "The quantum decoherence people call this 'coarse graining'. Summing over all these indistinguishable details is what gives rise to classical physics in the first place.

"Now, 'the two of us' would have first met in many perceivably different coarse-grained histories—and furthermore, you've since diverged by making different choices, and experiencing different external possibilities, after those events." She sketched two intersecting ribbons of coarse-grained histories, and then showed each history diverging further.

"World War II and the Holocaust certainly happened in both of *our* pasts—but that's no proof that the total is so vast that it might as well be infinite. Remember, what stops us successfully intervening is the fact that we're reaching back to a point where some of the parallel interventions start to bite their own tail. So when we fail, it can't be counted twice: it's just confirming what we already know."

Robert protested, "But what about all the versions of '30s Europe that don't happen to lie in either your past or mine? Just because we have no direct evidence for a Holocaust in those branches, that hardly makes it unlikely."

Helen said, "Not unlikely *per se*, without intervention. But not fixed in stone either. We'll keep trying, refining the technology, until we can reach branches where there's no overlap with our own past in the '30s. And there must be other, separate ribbons of intervention that happen in histories we can never even know about."

Robert was elated. He'd imagined himself clinging to a rock of improbable good fortune in an infinite sea of suffering—struggling to pretend, for the sake of his own sanity, that the rock was all there was. But what lay around him was not inevitably worse; it was merely unknown. In time, he might even play a part in ensuring that every last tragedy was *not* repeated across billions of worlds.

He reexamined the diagram. "Hang on. Intervention doesn't end divergence, though, does it? You reached *us*, a year ago, but in at least some of the histories spreading out from that moment, won't we still have suffered all kinds of disasters, and reacted in all kinds of self-defeating ways?"

"Yes," Helen conceded, "but fewer than you might think. If you merely listed every sequence of events that superficially appeared to have a non-zero probability, you'd end up with a staggering catalog of absurdist tragedies. But when you calculate everything more carefully, and take account of Planck-scale effects, it turns out to be nowhere near as bad. There are *no* coarse-grained histories where boulders assemble themselves out of dust and rain from the sky, or everyone in London or Madras goes mad and slaughters their children. Most macroscopic systems end up being quite robust—people included. Across histories, the range of natural disasters, human stupidity, and sheer bad luck isn't overwhelmingly greater than the range you're aware of from this history alone."

Robert laughed. "And that's not bad enough?"

"Oh, it is. But that's the best thing about the form I've taken."

"I'm sorry?"

Helen tipped her head and regarded him with an expression of disappointment. "You know, you're still not as quick on your feet as I'd expected."

Robert's face burned, but then he realized what he'd missed, and his resentment vanished.

"*You don't diverge?* Your hardware is designed to end the process? Your environment, your surroundings, will still split you into different histories—but on a coarse-grained level, you don't contribute to the process yourself?"

"That's right."

Robert was speechless. Even after a year, she could still toss him a hand grenade like this.

Helen said, "I can't help living in many worlds; that's beyond my control. But I do know that I'm one person. Faced with a choice that puts me on a knife-edge, I know I won't split and take every path."

Robert hugged himself, suddenly cold. "Like I do. Like I have. Like all of us poor creatures of flesh."

Helen came and sat beside him. "Even that's not irrevocable. Once you've taken this form—if that's what you choose—you can meet your other selves, reverse some of the scatter. Give some a chance to undo what they've done."

This time, Robert grasped her meaning at once. "Gather myself together? Make myself whole?"

Helen shrugged. "If it's what you want. If you see it that way."

He stared back at her, disoriented. Touching the bedrock of physics was one thing, but this possibility was too much to take in.

Someone knocked on the study door. The two of them exchanged wary glances, but it wasn't Quint, back for more punishment. It was a porter bearing a telegram.

When the man had left, Robert opened the envelope.

"Bad news?" Helen asked.

He shook his head. "Not a death in the family, if that's what you meant. It's from John Hamilton. He's challenging me to a debate. On the topic 'Can A Machine Think?'"

"What, at some university function?"

"No. On the BBC. Four weeks from tomorrow." He looked up. "Do you think I should do it?"

"Radio or television?"

Robert reread the message. "Television."

Helen smiled. "Definitely. I'll give you some tips."

"On the subject?"

"No! That would be cheating." She eyed him appraisingly. "You can start by throwing out your electric razor. Get rid of the permanent five o'clock shadow."

Robert was hurt. "Some people find that quite attractive."

Helen replied firmly, "Trust me on this."

THE BBC SENT A car to take Robert down to London. Helen sat beside him in the back seat.

"Are you nervous?" she asked.

"Nothing that an hour of throwing up won't cure."

Hamilton had suggested a live broadcast, "to keep things interesting," and the producer had agreed. Robert had never been on television; he'd taken part in a couple of radio discussions on the future of computing, back when the Mark I had first come into use, but even those had been taped.

Hamilton's choice of topic had surprised him at first, but in retrospect it seemed quite shrewd. A debate on the proposition that "Modern Science is the Devil's Work" would have brought howls of laughter from all but the most pious viewers, whereas the purely metaphorical claim that "Modern Science is a Faustian Pact" would have had the entire audience nodding sagely in agreement, while carrying no implications whatsoever. If you weren't going to take the whole dire fairy tale literally, everything was "a Faustian Pact" in some sufficiently watered-down sense: everything had a potential downside, and this was as pointless to assert as it was easy to demonstrate.

Robert had met considerable incredulity, though, when he'd explained to journalists where his own research was leading. To date, the press had treated him as a kind of eccentric British Edison, churning out inventions of indisputable utility, and no one seemed to find it at all surprising or alarming that he was also, frankly, a bit of a loon. But Hamilton would have a chance to exploit, and reshape, that perception. If Robert insisted on defending his goal of creating machine intelligence, not as an amusing hobby that might have been chosen by a public relations firm to make him appear endearingly daft, but as both the ultimate vindication of materialist science and the logical endpoint of most of his life's work, Hamilton could use a victory tonight to cast doubt on everything Robert had done, and everything he symbolized. By asking, not at all rhetorically, "Where will this all end?", he was inviting Robert to step forward and hang himself with the answer.

The traffic was heavy for a Sunday evening, and they arrived at the Shepherd's Bush studios with only fifteen minutes until the broadcast. Hamilton had been collected by a separate car, from his family home near Oxford. As they crossed the studio Robert spotted him, conversing intensely with a dark-haired young man.

He whispered to Helen, "Do you know who that is, with Hamilton?"

She followed his gaze, then smiled cryptically. Robert said, "What? Do you recognize him from somewhere?"

"Yes, but I'll tell you later."

As the make-up woman applied powder, Helen ran through her long list of rules again. "Don't stare into the camera, or you'll look like you're peddling soap powder. But don't avert your eyes. You don't want to look shifty."

The make-up woman whispered to Robert, "Everyone's an expert."

"Annoying, isn't it?" he confided.

Michael Polanyi, an academic philosopher who was well-known to the public after presenting a series of radio talks, had agreed to moderate the debate. Polanyi popped into the make-up room, accompanied by the producer; they chatted with Robert for a couple of minutes, setting him at ease and reminding him of the procedure they'd be following.

They'd only just left him when the floor manager appeared. "We need you in the studio now, please, Professor." Robert followed her, and Helen pursued him part of the way. "Breathe slowly and deeply," she urged him.

"As if you'd know," he snapped.

Robert shook hands with Hamilton then took his seat on one side of the podium. Hamilton's young adviser had retreated into the shadows; Robert glanced back to see Helen watching from a similar position. It was like a duel: they both had seconds. The floor manager pointed out the studio monitor, and as Robert watched it was switched between the feeds from two cameras: a wide shot of the whole set, and a closer view of the podium, including the small blackboard on a stand beside it. He'd once asked Helen whether television had progressed to far greater levels of sophistication in her branch of the future, once the pioneering days were left behind, but the question had left her uncharacteristically tongue-tied.

The floor manager retreated behind the cameras, called for silence, then counted down from ten, mouthing the final numbers.

The broadcast began with an introduction from Polanyi: concise, witty, and non-partisan. Then Hamilton stepped up to the podium. Robert watched him directly while the wide-angle view was being transmitted, so as not to appear rude or distracted. He only turned to the monitor when he was no longer visible himself.

"Can a machine think?" Hamilton began. "My intuition tells me: *no*. My heart tells me: *no*. I'm sure that most of you feel the same way. But that's not enough, is it? In this day and age, we aren't allowed to rely on our hearts for anything. We need something scientific. We need some kind of proof.

"Some years ago, I took part in a debate at Oxford University. The issue then was not whether machines might behave like people, but whether people themselves might *be* mere machines. Materialists, you see, claim that we are all just a collection of purposeless atoms, colliding at random. Everything we do, everything we feel, everything we say, comes down to some sequence of events that might as well be the spinning of cogs, or the opening and closing of electrical relays.

"To me, this was self-evidently false. What point could there be, I argued, in even conversing with a materialist? By his own admission, the words that came out of his mouth would be the result of nothing but a mindless, mechanical process! By his own theory, he could have no reason to think that those words would be the truth! Only believers in a transcendent human soul could claim any interest in the truth."

Hamilton nodded slowly, a penitent's gesture. "I was wrong, and I was put in my place. This might be self-evident to *me*, and it might be self-evident to *you*, but it's certainly not what philosophers call an 'analytical truth': it's not actually a nonsense, a contradiction in terms, to believe that we are mere machines. There might, there just *might*, be some reason why the words that emerge from a materialist's mouth are truthful, despite their origins lying entirely in unthinking matter.

"There might." Hamilton smiled wistfully. "I had to concede that possibility, because I only had my instinct, my gut feeling, to tell me otherwise.

"But the reason I only had my instinct to guide me was because I'd failed to learn of an event that had taken place many years before. A discovery made in 1930, by an Austrian mathematician named Kurt Gödel."

Robert felt a shiver of excitement run down his spine. He'd been afraid that the whole contest would degenerate into theology, with Hamilton invoking Aquinas all night—or Aristotle, at best. But it looked as if his mysterious adviser had dragged him into the twentieth century, and they were going to have a chance to debate the real issues after all.

"What is it that we *know* Professor Stoney's computers can do, and do well?" Hamilton continued. "Arithmetic! In a fraction of a second, they can add up a million numbers. Once we've told them, very precisely, what calculations to perform, they'll complete them in the blink of an eye—even if those calculations would take you or me a lifetime.

"But do these machines *understand* what it is they're doing? Professor Stoney says, 'Not yet. Not right now. Give them time. Rome wasn't built in a day.'" Hamilton nodded thoughtfully. "Perhaps that's fair. His computers are only a few years old. They're just babies. Why should they understand anything, so soon?

"But let's stop and think about this a bit more carefully. A computer, as it stands today, is simply a machine that does arithmetic, and Professor Stoney isn't proposing that they're going to sprout new kinds of brains all on their own. Nor is he proposing *giving* them anything really new. He can already let them look at the world with television cameras, turning the pictures into a stream of numbers describing the brightness of different points on the screen . . . on which the computer can then perform *arithmetic*. He can already let them speak to us with a special kind of loudspeaker, to which the computer feeds a stream of numbers to describe how loud the sound should be . . . a stream of numbers produced by more *arithmetic*.

"So the world can come into the computer, as numbers, and words can emerge, as numbers too. All Professor Stoney hopes to add to his computers is a 'cleverer' way to do the arithmetic that takes the first set of numbers and churns out the second. It's that 'clever arithmetic', he tells us, that will make these machines think."

Hamilton folded his arms and paused for a moment. "What are we to make of this? Can *doing arithmetic*, and nothing more, be enough to let a machine *understand* anything? My instinct certainly tells me no, but who am I that you should trust my instinct?

"So, let's narrow down the question of understanding, and to be scrupulously fair, let's put it in the most favorable light possible for Professor Stoney. If there's one thing a computer *ought* to be able to understand—as well as us, if not better—it's arithmetic itself. If a computer could think at all, it would surely be able to grasp the nature of its own best talent.

"The question, then, comes down to this: can you *describe* all of arithmetic, *using* nothing but arithmetic? Thirty years ago—long before Professor Stoney and his computers came along—Professor Gödel asked himself exactly that question.

"Now, you might be wondering how anyone could even *begin* to describe the rules of arithmetic, using nothing but arithmetic itself." Hamilton turned to the blackboard, picked up the chalk, and wrote two lines:

$$\text{If} \quad X+Z \quad = \quad Y+Z$$
$$\textit{then} \quad x \quad = \quad y$$

"This is an important rule, but it's written in symbols, not numbers, because it has to be true for *every* number, every x, y and z. But Professor Gödel had a clever idea: why not use a code, like spies use, where every symbol is assigned a number?" Hamilton wrote:

THE CODE FOR "A" *is 1.*
The code for "b" is 2.

"And so on. You can have a code for every letter of the alphabet, and for all the other symbols needed for arithmetic: plus signs, equals signs, that kind of thing. Telegrams are sent this way every day, with a code called the Baudot code, so there's really nothing strange or sinister about it.

"All the rules of arithmetic that we learned at school can be written with a carefully chosen set of symbols, which can then be translated into numbers. Every question as to what does or does not *follow from* those rules can then be seen anew, as a question about numbers. If *this* line follows from *this* one," Hamilton indicated the two lines of the cancellation rule, "we can see it in the relationship between their code numbers. We can judge each inference, and declare it valid or not, purely by doing arithmetic.

"So, given *any* proposition at all about arithmetic—such as the claim that 'there are infinitely many prime numbers'—we can restate the notion that we have a proof for that claim in terms of code numbers. If the code number for our claim is x, we can say 'There is a number p, ending with the code number x, that passes our test for being the code number of a valid proof.'"

Hamilton took a visible breath.

"In 1930, Professor Gödel used this scheme to do something rather ingenious." He wrote on the blackboard:

THERE DOES NOT EXIST *a number p meeting the following condition: p is the code number of a valid proof of this claim.*

"Here is a claim about arithmetic, about numbers. It has to be either true or false. So let's start by supposing that it happens to be true. Then there *is no* number p that is the code number for a proof of this claim. So this is a true statement about arithmetic, but it can't be proved merely by *doing* arithmetic!"

Hamilton smiled. "If you don't catch on immediately, don't worry; when I first heard this argument from a young friend of mine, it took a while for the meaning to sink in. But remember: the only hope a computer has for understanding *anything* is by doing arithmetic, and we've just found a statement that *cannot* be proved with mere arithmetic.

"Is this statement really true, though? We mustn't jump to conclusions, we mustn't damn the machines too hastily. Suppose this claim is false! Since it claims there is no number p that is the code number of its own proof, to be false there would have to be such a number, after all. And that number would encode the 'proof' of an acknowledged falsehood!"

Hamilton spread his arms triumphantly. "You and I, like every schoolboy, know that you can't prove a falsehood from sound premises—and if the premises of arithmetic aren't sound, what is? So *we* know, as a matter of certainty, that this statement is true.

"Professor Gödel was the first to see this, but with a little help and perseverance, any educated person can follow in his footsteps. *A machine could never do that.* We might divulge to a machine our own knowledge of this fact, offering it as something to be taken on trust, but the machine could neither stumble on this truth for itself, nor truly comprehend it when we offered it as a gift.

"You and I *understand* arithmetic, in a way that no electronic calculator ever will. What hope has a machine, then, of moving beyond its own most favorable milieu and comprehending any wider truth?

"None at all, ladies and gentlemen. Though this detour into mathematics might have seemed arcane to you, it has served a very down-to-Earth purpose. It has proved—beyond refutation by even the most ardent materialist or the most pedantic philosopher—what we common folk knew all along: no machine will ever think."

Hamilton took his seat. For a moment, Robert was simply exhilarated; coached or not, Hamilton had grasped the essential features of the incompleteness proof, and presented them to a lay audience. What might have been a night of shadow-boxing—with no blows connecting, and nothing for the audience to judge but two solo performances in separate arenas—had turned into a genuine clash of ideas.

As Polanyi introduced him and he walked to the podium, Robert realized that his usual shyness and self-consciousness had evaporated. He was filled with an altogether different kind of tension: he sensed more acutely than ever what was at stake.

When he reached the podium, he adopted the posture of someone about to begin a prepared speech, but then he caught himself, as if he'd forgotten something. "Bear with me for a moment." He walked around to the far side of the blackboard and quickly wrote a few words on it, upside-down. Then he resumed his place.

"Can a machine think? Professor Hamilton would like us to believe that he's settled the issue once and for all, by coming up with a statement that *we* know is true, but a particular machine—programmed to explore the theorems of arithmetic in a certain rigid way—would never be able to produce. Well . . . we all have our limitations." He flipped the blackboard over to reveal what he'd written on the opposite side:

IF ROBERT STONEY SPEAKS *these words, he will NOT be telling the truth.*

He waited a few beats, then continued.

"What I'd like to explore, though, is not so much a question of limitations, as of opportunities. How exactly is it that we've all ended up with this mysterious ability to know that Gödel's statement is true? Where does this advantage, this great insight, come from? From our souls? From some immaterial entity that no machine could ever possess? Is that the only possible source, the only conceivable explanation? Or might it come from something a little less ethereal?

"As Professor Hamilton explained, we believe Gödel's statement is true because we trust the rules of arithmetic not to lead us into contradictions and falsehoods. But where does that trust come from? How does it arise?"

Robert turned the blackboard back to Hamilton's side, and pointed to the cancellation rule. "If x plus z equals y plus z, then x equals y. Why is this so *reasonable?* We might not learn to put it quite like this until we're in our teens, but if you showed a young child two boxes—without revealing their contents—added an equal number of shells, or stones, or pieces of fruit to both, and then let the child look inside to see that each box now contained the same number of items, it wouldn't take any formal education for the child to understand that the two boxes must have held the same number of things to begin with.

"The child knows, we all know, how a certain kind of object behaves. Our lives are steeped in direct experience of whole numbers: whole numbers of coins, stamps, pebbles, birds, cats, sheep, buses. If I tried to persuade a six-year-old that I could put three stones in a box, remove one of them, and be left with four . . . he'd simply laugh at me. Why? It's not merely that he's sure to have taken one thing away from three to get two, on many prior occasions. Even a child understands that some things that appear reliable will eventually fail: a toy that works perfectly, day after day, for a month or a year, can still break. But not arithmetic, not taking one from three. He can't even picture *that* failing. Once you've lived in the world, once you've seen how it works, the failure of arithmetic becomes unimaginable.

"Professor Hamilton suggests that this is down to our souls. But what would he say about a child reared in a world of water and mist, never in the company of more than one person at a time, never taught to count on his fingers and toes. I doubt that such a child would possess the same certainty that you and I have, as to the impossibility of arithmetic ever leading him astray. To banish whole numbers entirely from his world would require very strange surroundings, and a level of deprivation amounting to cruelty, but would that be enough to rob a child of his *soul?*

"A computer, programmed to pursue arithmetic as Professor Hamilton has described, is subject to far more deprivation than that child. If I'd been raised with my hands and feet tied, my head in a sack, and someone shouting orders at me, I doubt that I'd have much grasp of reality—and I'd still be better prepared for the task than such a computer. It's a great mercy that a machine treated that way wouldn't be able to think: if it could, the shackles we'd placed upon it would be criminally oppressive.

"But that's hardly the fault of the computer, or a revelation of some irreparable flaw in its nature. If we want to judge the potential of our machines with any degree of honesty, we have to play fair with them, not saddle them with restrictions that we'd never dream of imposing on ourselves. There really is no point comparing an eagle with a spanner, or a gazelle with a washing machine: it's our jets that fly and our cars that run, albeit in quite different ways than any animal.

"*Thought* is sure to be far harder to achieve than those other skills, and to do so we might need to mimic the natural world far more closely. But I believe that once a machine is endowed with facilities resembling the inborn tools for learning that we all have as our birthright, and is set free to learn the way a child learns, through experience, observation, trial and error, hunches and failures—instead of being handed a list of instructions that it has no choice but to obey—we will finally be in a position to compare like with like.

"When that happens, and we can meet and talk and argue with these machines—about arithmetic, or any other topic—there'll be no need to take the word of Professor Gödel, or Professor Hamilton, or myself, for anything. We'll invite them down to the local pub, and interrogate them in person. And if we play fair with them, we'll use the same experience and judgment we use with any friend, or guest, or stranger, to decide for ourselves whether or not they can think."

THE BBC PUT ON a lavish assortment of wine and cheese in a small room off the studio. Robert ended up in a heated argument with Polanyi, who revealed himself to be firmly on the negative side, while Helen flirted shamelessly with Hamilton's young friend, who turned out to have a PhD in algebraic geometry from Cambridge; he must have completed the degree just before Robert had come back from Manchester. After exchanging some polite formalities with Hamilton, Robert kept his distance, sensing that any further contact would not be welcome.

An hour later, though, after getting lost in the maze of corridors on his way back from the toilets, Robert came across Hamilton sitting alone in the studio, weeping.

He almost backed away in silence, but Hamilton looked up and saw him. With their eyes locked, it was impossible to retreat.

Robert said, "It's your wife?" He'd heard that she'd been seriously ill, but the gossip had included a miraculous recovery. Some friend of the family had laid hands on her a year ago, and she'd gone into remission.

Hamilton said, "She's dying."

Robert approached and sat beside him. "From what?"

"Breast cancer. It's spread throughout her body. Into her bones, into her lungs, into her liver." He sobbed again, a helpless spasm, then caught himself angrily. "*Suffering is the chisel God uses to shape us.* What kind of idiot comes up with a line like that?"

Robert said, "I'll talk to a friend of mine, an oncologist at Guy's Hospital. He's doing a trial of a new genetic treatment."

Hamilton stared at him. "One of your *miracle cures?*"

"No, no. I mean, only very indirectly."

Hamilton said angrily, "She won't take your poison."

Robert almost snapped back: *She won't? Or you won't let her?* But it was an unfair question. In some marriages, the lines blurred. It was not for him to judge the way the two of them faced this together.

"They go away in order to be with us in a new way, even closer than before." Hamilton spoke the words like a defiant incantation, a declaration of faith that would ward off temptation, whether or not he entirely believed it.

Robert was silent for a while, then he said, "I lost someone close to me, when I was a boy. And I thought the same thing. I thought he was still with me, for a long time afterward. Guiding me.

Encouraging me." It was hard to get the words out; he hadn't spoken about this to anyone for almost thirty years. "I dreamed up a whole theory to explain it, in which 'souls' used quantum uncertainty to control the body during life, and communicate with the living after death, without breaking any laws of physics. The kind of thing every science-minded seventeen-year-old probably stumbles on, and takes seriously for a couple of weeks, before realizing how nonsensical it is. But I had a good reason not to see the flaws, so I clung to it for almost two years. Because I missed him so much, it took me that long to understand what I was doing, how I was deceiving myself."

Hamilton said pointedly, "If you'd not tried to explain it, you might never have lost him. He might still be with you now."

Robert thought about this. "I'm glad he's not, though. It wouldn't be fair on either of us."

Hamilton shuddered. "Then you can't have loved him very much, can you?" He put his head in his arms. "Just fuck off, now, will you."

Robert said, "What exactly would it take, to prove to you that I'm not in league with the devil?"

Hamilton turned red eyes on him and announced triumphantly, "Nothing will do that! I saw what happened to Quint's gun!"

Robert sighed. "That was a conjuring trick. Stage magic, not black magic."

"Oh yes? Show me how it's done, then. Teach me how to do it, so I can impress my friends."

"It's rather technical. It would take all night."

Hamilton laughed humorlessly. "You can't deceive me. I saw through you from the start."

"Do you think X-rays are Satanic? Penicillin?"

"Don't treat me like a fool. There's no comparison."

"*Why not?* Everything I've helped develop is part of the same continuum. I've read some of your writing on medieval culture, and you're always berating modern commentators for presenting it as unsophisticated. No one really thought the Earth was flat. No one really treated every novelty as witchcraft. So why view any of my work any differently than a fourteenth-century man would view twentieth-century medicine?"

Hamilton replied, "If a fourteenth-century man was suddenly faced with twentieth-century medicine, don't you think he'd be entitled to wonder how it had been revealed to his contemporaries?"

Robert shifted uneasily on his chair. Helen hadn't sworn him to secrecy, but he'd agreed with her view: it was better to wait, to spread the knowledge that would ground an understanding of what had happened, before revealing any details of the contact between branches.

But this man's wife was dying, needlessly. And Robert was tired of keeping secrets. Some wars required it, but others were better won with honesty.

He said, "I know you hate H.G. Wells. But what if he was right, about one little thing?"

Robert told him everything, glossing over the technicalities but leaving out nothing substantial. Hamilton listened without interrupting, gripped by a kind of unwilling fascination. His expression shifted from hostile to incredulous, but there were also hints of begrudging amazement, as if he could at least appreciate some of the beauty and complexity of the picture Robert was painting.

But when Robert had finished, Hamilton said merely, "You're a grand liar, Stoney. But what else should I expect, from the King of Lies?"

ROBERT WAS IN A somber mood on the drive back to Cambridge. The encounter with Hamilton had depressed him, and the question of who'd swayed the nation in the debate seemed remote and abstract in comparison.

Helen had taken a house in the suburbs, rather than inviting scandal by cohabiting with him, though her frequent visits to his rooms seemed to have had almost the same effect. Robert walked her to the door.

"I think it went well, don't you?" she said.

"I suppose so."

"I'm leaving tonight," she added casually. "This is goodbye."

"What?" Robert was staggered. "Everything's still up in the air! I still need you!"

She shook her head. "You have all the tools you need, all the clues. And plenty of local allies. There's nothing truly urgent I could tell you, now, that you couldn't find out just as quickly on your own."

Robert pleaded with her, but her mind was made up. The driver beeped the horn; Robert gestured to him impatiently.

"You know, my breath's frosting visibly," he said, "and you're producing nothing. You really ought to be more careful."

She laughed. "It's a bit late to worry about that."

"Where will you go? Back home? Or off to twist another branch?"

"Another branch. But there's something I'm planning to do on the way."

"What's that?"

"Do you remember once, you wrote about an Oracle? A machine that could solve the halting problem?"

"Of course." Given a device that could tell you in advance whether a given computer program would halt, or go on running forever, you'd be able to prove or disprove any theorem whatsoever about the integers: the Goldbach conjecture, Fermat's Last Theorem, anything. You'd simply show this "Oracle" a program that would loop through all the integers, testing every possible set of values and only halting if it came to a set that violated the conjecture. You'd never need to run the program itself; the Oracle's verdict on whether or not it halted would be enough.

Such a device might or might not be possible, but Robert had proved more than twenty years before that no ordinary computer, however ingeniously programmed, would suffice. If program H could always tell you in a finite time whether or not program X would halt, you could tack on a small addition to H to create program Z, which perversely and deliberately went into an infinite loop whenever it examined a program that halted. If Z examined itself, it would either halt eventually, or run forever. But either possibility contradicted the alleged powers of program H: if Z actually ran forever, it would be because H had claimed that it wouldn't, and *vice versa*. Program H could not exist.

"Time travel," Helen said, "gives me a chance to become an Oracle. There's a way to exploit the inability to change your own past, a way to squeeze an infinite number of timelike paths—none of them closed, but some of them arbitrarily near to it—into a finite physical system. Once you do that, you can solve the halting problem."

"How?" Robert's mind was racing. "And once you've done that . . . what about higher cardinalities? An Oracle for Oracles, able to test conjectures about the real numbers?"

Helen smiled enigmatically. "The first problem should only take you forty or fifty years to solve. As for the rest," she pulled away from him, moving into the darkness of the hallway, "what makes you think I know the answer myself?" She blew him a kiss, then vanished from sight.

Robert took a step toward her, but the hallway was empty.

He walked back to the car, sad and exalted, his heart pounding.

The driver asked wearily, "Where to now, sir?"

Robert said, "Further up, and further in."

4

THE NIGHT AFTER THE funeral, Jack paced the house until three a.m. When would it be bearable? *When?* She'd shown more strength and courage, dying, than he felt within himself right now. But she'd share it with him, in the weeks to come. She'd share it with them all.

In bed, in the darkness, he tried to sense her presence around him. But it was forced, it was premature. It was one thing to have faith that she was watching over him, but quite another to expect to be spared every trace of grief, every trace of pain.

He waited for sleep. He needed to get some rest before dawn, or how would he face her children in the morning?

Gradually, he became aware of someone standing in the darkness at the foot of the bed. As he examined and reexamined the shadows, he formed a clear image of the apparition's face.

It was his own. Younger, happier, surer of himself.

Jack sat up. "What do you want?"

"I want you to come with me." The figure approached; Jack recoiled, and it halted.

"Come with you, where?" Jack demanded.

"To a place where she's waiting."

Jack shook his head. "No. I don't believe you. She said she'd come for me herself, when it was time. She said she'd guide me."

"She didn't understand, then," the apparition insisted gently. "She didn't know I could fetch you myself. Do you think I'd send her in my place? Do you think I'd shirk the task?"

Jack searched the smiling, supplicatory face. "Who are you?" *His own soul, in Heaven, remade?* Was this a gift God offered everyone? To meet, before death, the very thing you would become—if you so chose? So that even this would be an act of free will?

The apparition said, "Stoney persuaded me to let his friend treat Joyce. We lived on, together. More than a century has passed. And now we want you to join us."

Jack choked with horror. "No! This is a trick! *You're the Devil!*"

The thing replied mildly, "There is no Devil. And no God, either. Just people. But I promise you: people with the powers of gods are kinder than any god we ever imagined."

Jack covered his face. "Leave me be." He whispered fervent prayers, and waited. It was a test, a moment of vulnerability, but God wouldn't leave him naked like this, face-to-face with the Enemy, for longer than he could endure.

He uncovered his face. The thing was still with him.

It said, "Do you remember, when your faith came to you? The sense of a shield around you melting away, like armor you'd worn to keep God at bay?"

"Yes." Jack acknowledged the truth defiantly; he wasn't frightened that this abomination could see into his past, into his heart.

"That took strength: to admit that you needed God. But it takes the same kind of strength, again, to understand that *some needs can never be met.* I can't promise you Heaven. We have no disease, we have no war, we have no poverty. But we have to find our own love, our own goodness. There is no final word of comfort. We only have each other."

Jack didn't reply; this blasphemous fantasy wasn't even worth challenging. He said, "I know you're lying. Do you really imagine that I'd leave the boys alone here?"

"They'd go back to America, back to their father. How many years do you think you'd have with them, if you stay? They've already lost their mother. It would be easier for them now, a single clean break."

Jack shouted angrily, "Get out of my house!"

The thing came closer, and sat on the bed. It put a hand on his shoulder. Jack sobbed, "Help me!" But he didn't know whose aid he was invoking any more.

"Do you remember the scene in *The Seat of Oak*? When the Harpy traps everyone in her cave underground, and tries to convince them that there is no Nescia? Only this drab underworld is real, she tells them. Everything else they think they've seen was just make-believe." Jack's own young face smiled nostalgically. "And we had dear old Shrugweight reply: he didn't think much of this so-called 'real world' of hers. And even if she was right, since four little children could make up a better world, he'd rather go on pretending that their imaginary one was real.

"But we had it all upside down! The real world is richer, and stranger, and more beautiful than anything ever imagined. Milton, Dante, John the Divine are the ones who trapped you in a drab, gray underworld. That's where you are now. But if you give me your hand, I can pull you out."

Jack's chest was bursting. *He couldn't lose his faith. He'd kept it through worse than this. He'd kept it through every torture and indignity God had inflicted on his wife's frail body. No one could take it from him now.* He crooned to himself, "In my time of trouble, He will find me."

The cool hand tightened its grip on his shoulder. "You can be with her, now. Just say the word, and you will become a part of me. I will take you inside me, and you will see through my eyes, and we will travel back to the world where she still lives."

Jack wept openly. "Leave me in peace! Just leave me to mourn her!"

The thing nodded sadly. "If that's what you want."

"I do! *Go!*"

"When I'm sure."

Suddenly, Jack thought back to the long rant Stoney had delivered in the studio. Every choice went every way, Stoney had claimed. No decision could ever be final.

"Now I know you're lying!" he shouted triumphantly. "If you believed everything Stoney told you, how could my choice ever mean a thing? I would always say yes to you, and I would always say no! It would all be the same!"

The apparition replied solemnly, "While I'm here with you, touching you, *you can't be divided*. Your choice will count."

Jack wiped his eyes, and gazed into its face. It seemed to believe every word it was speaking. What if this truly was his metaphysical twin, speaking as honestly as he could, and not merely the Devil in a mask? Perhaps there was a grain of truth in Stoney's awful vision; perhaps this was another version of himself, a living person who honestly believed that the two of them shared a history.

Then it was a visitor sent by God, to humble him. To teach him compassion toward Stoney. To show Jack that he too, with a little less faith, and a little more pride, might have been damned forever.

Jack stretched out a hand and touched the face of this poor lost soul. *There, but for the grace of God, go I.*

He said, "I've made my choice. Now leave me."

Author's note: WHERE THE lives of the fictional characters of this story parallel those of real historical figures, I've drawn on biographies by Andrew Hodges and A.N. Wilson. The self-dual formulation of general relativity was discovered by Abhay Ashtekar in 1986, and has since led to ground-breaking developments in quantum gravity, but the implications drawn from it here are fanciful.

SINGLETON

2003

I WAS WALKING NORTH along George Street toward Town Hall railway station, pondering the ways I might solve the tricky third question of my linear algebra assignment, when I encountered a small crowd blocking the footpath. I didn't give much thought to the reason they were standing there; I'd just passed a busy restaurant, and I often saw groups of people gathered outside. But once I'd started to make my way around them, moving into an alley rather than stepping out into the traffic, it became apparent that they were not just diners from a farewell lunch for a retiring colleague, putting off their return to the office for as long as possible. I could see for myself exactly what was holding their attention.

Twenty meters down the alley, a man was lying on his back on the ground, shielding his bloodied face with his hands, while two men stood over him, relentlessly swinging narrow sticks of some kind. At first I thought the sticks were pool cues, but then I noticed the metal hooks on the ends. I'd only ever seen these obscure weapons before in one other place: my primary school, where an appointed window monitor would use them at the start and end of each day. They were meant for opening and closing an old-fashioned kind of hinged pane when it was too high to reach with your hands.

I turned to the other spectators. "Has anyone called the police?" A woman nodded without looking at me, and said, "Someone used their mobile, a couple of minutes ago."

The assailants must have realized that the police were on their way, but it seemed they were too committed to their task to abandon it until that was absolutely necessary. They were facing away from the crowd, so perhaps they weren't entirely reckless not to fear identification. The man on the ground was dressed like a kitchen hand. He was still moving, trying to protect himself, but he was making less noise than his attackers; the need, or the ability, to cry out in pain had been beaten right out of him.

As for calling for help, he could have saved his breath.

A chill passed through my body, a sick cold churning sensation that came a moment before the conscious realization: *I'm going to watch someone murdered, and I'm going to do nothing.* But this wasn't a drunken brawl, where a few bystanders could step in and separate the combatants; the two assailants had to be serious criminals, settling a score. Keeping your distance from something like that was just common sense. I'd go to court, I'd be a witness, but no one could expect anything more of me. Not when thirty other people had behaved in exactly the same way.

The men in the alley did not have guns. If they'd had guns, they would have used them by now. They weren't going to mow down anyone who got in their way. It was one thing not to make a martyr of yourself, but how many people could these two grunting slobs fend off with sticks?

I unstrapped my backpack and put it on the ground. Absurdly, that made me feel more vulnerable; I was always worried about losing my textbooks. *Think about this. You don't know what you're doing.* I hadn't been in so much as a fist fight since I was thirteen. I glanced at the strangers around me, wondering if anyone would join in if I implored them to rush forward together. But that wasn't going to happen. I was a willowy, unimposing eighteen-year-old, wearing a T-shirt adorned with Maxwell's Equations. I had no presence, no authority. No one would follow me into the fray.

Alone, I'd be as helpless as the guy on the ground. These men would crack my skull open in an instant. There were half a dozen solid-looking office workers in their twenties in the crowd; if these weekend rugby players hadn't felt competent to intervene, what chance did I have?

I reached down for my backpack. If I wasn't going to help, there was no point being here at all. I'd find out what had happened on the evening news.

I started to retrace my steps, sick with self-loathing. This wasn't *Kristallnacht*. There'd be no embarrassing questions from my grandchildren. No one would ever reproach me.

As if that were the measure of everything.

"Fuck it." I dropped my backpack and ran down the alley.

I was close enough to smell the three sweating bodies over the stench of rotting garbage before I was even noticed. The nearest of the attackers glanced over his shoulder, affronted, then amused. He didn't bother redeploying his weapon in mid-stroke; as I hooked an arm around his neck in the hope of overbalancing him, he thrust his elbow into my chest, winding me. I clung on desperately, maintaining the hold even though I couldn't tighten it. As he tried to prize himself loose, I managed to kick his feet out from under him. We both went down onto the asphalt; I ended up beneath him.

The man untangled himself and clambered to his feet. As I struggled to right myself, picturing a metal hook swinging into my face, someone whistled. I looked up to see the second man gesturing to his companion, and I followed his gaze. A dozen men and women were coming down the alley, advancing together at a brisk walk. It was not a particularly menacing sight—I'd seen angrier crowds with peace signs painted on their faces—but the sheer numbers were enough to guarantee some inconvenience. The first man hung back long enough to kick me in the ribs. Then the two of them fled.

I brought my knees up, then raised my head and got into a crouch. I was still winded, but for some reason it seemed vital not to remain flat on my back. One of the office workers grinned down at me. "You fuckwit. You could have got killed."

The kitchen hand shuddered, and snorted bloody mucus. His eyes were swollen shut, and when he laid his hands down beside him, I could see the bones of his knuckles through the torn skin. My own skin turned icy, at this vision of the fate I'd courted for myself. But if it was a shock to realize how I might have ended up, it was just as sobering to think that I'd almost walked away and let them finish him off, when the intervention had actually cost me nothing.

I rose to my feet. People milled around the kitchen hand, asking each other about first aid. I remembered the basics from a course I'd done in high school, but the man was still breathing, and he wasn't losing vast amounts of blood, so I couldn't think of anything helpful that an amateur could do in the circumstances. I squeezed my way out of the gathering and walked back to the street. My backpack was exactly where I'd left it; no one had stolen my books. I heard sirens approaching; the police and the ambulance would be there soon.

My ribs were tender, but I wasn't in agony. I'd cracked a rib falling off a trail bike on the farm when I was twelve, and I was fairly sure that this was just bruising. For a while I walked bent over, but by the time I reached the station I found I could adopt a normal gait. I had some grazed skin on my arms, but I couldn't have appeared too battered, because no one on the train looked at me twice.

That night, I watched the news. The kitchen hand was described as being in a stable condition. I pictured him stepping out into the alley to empty a bucket of fish-heads into the garbage, to find the two of them waiting for him. I'd probably never learn what the attack had been about unless the case went to trial, and as yet the police hadn't even named any suspects. If the man had been in a fit state to talk in the alley, I might have asked him then, but any sense that I was entitled to an explanation was rapidly fading.

The reporter mentioned a student "leading the charge of angry citizens" who'd rescued the kitchen hand, and then she spoke to an eye witness, who described this young man as "a New Ager, wearing some kind of astrological symbols on his shirt". I snorted, then looked around nervously in case one of my housemates had made the improbable connection, but no one else was even in earshot.

Then the story was over.

I felt flat for a moment, cheated of the minor rush that fifteen seconds' fame might have delivered; it was like reaching into a biscuit tin when you thought there was one more chocolate chip left, to find that there actually wasn't. I considered phoning my parents in Orange, just to talk to them from within the strange afterglow, but I'd established a routine and it was not the right day. If I called unexpectedly, they'd think something was wrong.

So, that was it. In a week's time, when the bruises had faded, I'd look back and doubt that the incident had ever happened.

I went upstairs to finish my assignment.

FRANCINE SAID, "THERE'S A nicer way to think about this. If you do a change of variables, from x and y to z and z-conjugate, the Cauchy-Riemann equations correspond to the condition that the partial derivative of the function with respect to z-conjugate is equal to zero."

We were sitting in the coffee shop, discussing the complex analysis lecture we'd had half an hour before. Half a dozen of us from the same course had got into the habit of meeting at this time every week, but today the others had failed to turn up. Maybe there was a movie being screened, or a speaker appearing on campus that I hadn't heard about.

I worked through the transformation she'd described. "You're right," I said. "That's really elegant!"

Francine nodded slightly in assent, while retaining her characteristic jaded look. She had an undisguisable passion for mathematics, but she was probably bored out of her skull in class, waiting for the lecturers to catch up and teach her something she didn't already know.

I was nowhere near her level. In fact, I'd started the year poorly, distracted by my new surroundings: nothing so glamorous as the temptations of the night life, just the different sights and sounds and scale of the place, along with the bureaucratic demands of all the organizations that now impinged upon my life, from the university itself down to the shared house groceries subcommittee. In the last few weeks, though, I'd finally started hitting my stride. I'd got a part-time job, stacking shelves in a supermarket; the pay was lousy, but it was enough to take the edge off my financial anxieties, and the hours weren't so long that they left me with no time for anything but study.

I doodled harmonic contours on the notepaper in front of me. "So what do you do for fun?" I said. "Apart from complex analysis?"

Francine didn't reply immediately. This wasn't the first time we'd been alone together, but I'd never felt confident that I had the right words to make the most of the situation. At some point, though, I'd stopped fooling myself that there was ever going to be a perfect moment, with the perfect phrase falling from my lips: something subtle but intriguing slipped deftly into the conversation, without disrupting the flow. So now I'd made my interest plain, with no attempt at artfulness or eloquence. She could judge me as she knew me from the last three months, and if she felt no desire to know me better, I would not be crushed.

"I write a lot of Perl scripts," she said. "Nothing complicated; just odds and ends that I give away as freeware. It's very relaxing."

I nodded understandingly. I didn't think she was being deliberately discouraging; she just expected me to be slightly more direct.

"Do you like Deborah Conway?" I'd only heard a couple of her songs on the radio myself, but a few days before I'd seen a poster in the city announcing a tour.

"Yeah. She's great."

I started thickening the conjugation bars over the variables I'd scrawled. "She's playing at a club in Surry Hills," I said. "On Friday. Would you like to go?"

Francine smiled, making no effort now to appear world-weary. "Sure. That would be nice."

I smiled back. I wasn't giddy, I wasn't moonstruck, but I felt as if I were standing on the shore of an ocean, contemplating its breadth. I felt the way I felt when I opened a sophisticated monograph in the library, and was reduced to savoring the scent of the print and the crisp symmetry of the notation, understanding only a fraction of what I read. Knowing there was something glorious ahead, but knowing too what a daunting task it would be to come to terms with it.

I said, "I'll get the tickets on my way home."

To CELEBRATE THE END of exams for the year, the household threw a party. It was a sultry November night, but the back yard wasn't much bigger than the largest room in the house, so we ended up opening all the doors and windows and distributing food and furniture throughout the ground floor and the exterior, front and back. Once the faint humid breeze off the river penetrated the depths of the house, it was equally sweltering and mosquito-ridden everywhere, indoors and out.

Francine and I stayed close for an hour or so, obeying the distinctive dynamics of a couple, until by some unspoken mutual understanding it became clear that we could wander apart for a while, and that neither of us was so insecure that we'd resent it.

I ended up in a corner of the crowded back yard, talking to Will, a biochemistry student who'd lived in the house for the last four years. On some level, he probably couldn't help feeling that his opinions about the way things were run should carry more weight than anyone else's, which had annoyed me greatly when I'd first moved in. We'd since become friends, though, and I was glad to have a chance to talk to him before he left to take up a scholarship in Germany.

In the middle of a conversation about the work he'd be doing, I caught sight of Francine, and he followed my gaze.

Will said, "It took me a while to figure out what finally cured you of your homesickness."

"I was never homesick."

"Yeah, right." He took a swig of his drink. "She's changed you, though. You have to admit that."

"I do. Happily. Everything's clicked, since we got together." Relationships were meant to screw up your studies, but my marks were soaring. Francine didn't tutor me; she just drew me into a state of mind where everything was clearer.

"The amazing thing is that you got together at all." I scowled, and Will raised a hand placatingly. "I just meant, when you first moved in, you were pretty reserved. And down on yourself. When we interviewed you for the room, you practically begged us to give it to someone more deserving."

"Now you're taking the piss."

He shook his head. "Ask any of the others."

I fell silent. The truth was, if I took a step back and contemplated my situation, I was as astonished as he was. By the time I'd left my home town, it had become clear to me that good fortune had nothing much to do with luck. Some people were born with wealth, or talent, or charisma. They started with an edge, and the benefits snowballed. I'd always believed that I had, at best, just enough intelligence and persistence to stay afloat in my chosen field; I'd topped every class in high school, but in a town the size of Orange that meant nothing, and I'd had no illusions about my fate in Sydney.

I owed it to Francine that my visions of mediocrity had not been fulfilled; being with her had transformed my life. But where had I found the nerve to imagine that I had anything to offer her in return?

"Something happened," I admitted. "Before I asked her out."

"Yeah?"

I almost clammed up; I hadn't told anyone about the events in the alley, not even Francine. The incident had come to seem too personal, as if to recount it at all would be to lay my conscience bare. But Will was off to Munich in less than a week, and it was easier to confide in someone I didn't expect to see again.

When I finished, Will bore a satisfied grin, as if I'd explained everything. "Pure karma," he announced. "I should have guessed."

"Oh, very scientific."

"I'm serious. Forget the Buddhist mystobabble; I'm talking about the real thing. If you stick to your principles, of course things go better for you—assuming you don't get killed in the process. That's elementary psychology. People have a highly developed sense of reciprocity, of the appropriateness of the treatment they receive from each other. If things work out too well for them, they can't help asking, 'What did I do to deserve this?' If you don't have a good answer, you'll sabotage yourself. Not all the time, but often enough. So if you do something that improves your self-esteem—"

"Self-esteem is for the weak," I quipped. Will rolled his eyes. "I don't think like that," I protested.

"No? Why did you even bring it up, then?"

I shrugged. "Maybe it just made me less pessimistic. I could have had the crap beaten out of me, but I didn't. That makes asking someone to a concert seem a lot less dangerous." I was beginning to cringe at all this unwanted analysis, and I had nothing to counter Will's pop psychology except an equally folksy version of my own.

He could see I was embarrassed, so he let the matter drop. As I watched Francine moving through the crowd, though, I couldn't shake off an unsettling sense of the tenuousness of the circumstances that had brought us together. There was no denying that if I'd walked away from the alley, and the kitchen hand had died, I would have felt like shit for a long time afterward. I would not have felt entitled to much out of my own life.

I hadn't walked away, though. And even if the decision had come down to the wire, why shouldn't I be proud that I'd made the right choice? That didn't mean everything that followed was tainted, like a reward from some sleazy, palm-greasing deity. I hadn't won Francine's affection in a medieval test of bravery; we'd chosen each other, and persisted with that choice, for a thousand complicated reasons.

We were together now; that was what mattered. I wasn't going to dwell on the path that had brought me to her, just to dredge up all the doubts and insecurities that had almost kept us apart.

2012

As we drove the last kilometer along the road south from Ar Rafidiyah, I could see the Wall of Foam glistening ahead of us in the morning sunlight. Insubstantial as a pile of soap bubbles, but still intact, after six weeks.

"I can't believe it's lasted this long," I told Sadiq.

"You didn't trust the models?"

"Fuck, no. Every week, I thought we'd come over the hill and there'd be nothing but a shriveled-up cobweb."

Sadiq smiled. "So you had no faith in my calculations?"

"Don't take it personally. There were a lot of things we could have both got wrong."

Sadiq pulled off the road. His students, Hassan and Rashid, had climbed off the back of the truck and started toward the Wall before I'd even got my face mask on. Sadiq called them back, and made them put on plastic boots and paper suits over their clothes, while the two of us did the same. We didn't usually bother with this much protection, but today was different.

Close up, the Wall almost vanished: all you noticed were isolated, rainbow-fringed reflections, drifting at a leisurely pace across the otherwise invisible film as water redistributed itself, following waves induced in the membrane by the interplay of air pressure, thermal gradients, and surface tension. These images might easily have been separate objects, scraps of translucent plastic blowing around above the desert, held aloft by a breeze too faint to detect at ground level.

The further away you looked, though, the more crowded the hints of light became, and the less plausible any alternative hypothesis that denied the Wall its integrity. It stretched for a kilometer along the edge of the desert, and rose an uneven fifteen to twenty meters into the air. But it was merely the first, and smallest, of its kind, and the time had come to put it on the back of the truck and drive it all the way back to Basra.

Sadiq took a spray can of reagent from the cabin, and shook it as he walked down the embankment. I followed him, my heart in my mouth. The Wall had not dried out; it had not been torn apart or blown away, but there was still plenty of room for failure.

Sadiq reached up and sprayed what appeared from my vantage to be thin air, but I could see the fine mist of droplets strike the membrane. A breathy susurration rose up, like the sound from a steam iron, and I felt a faint warm dampness before the first silken threads appeared, crisscrossing the region where the polymer from which the Wall was built had begun to shift conformations. In one state, the polymer was soluble, exposing hydrophilic groups of atoms that bound water into narrow sheets of feather-light gel. Now, triggered by the reagent and powered by sunlight, it was tucking these groups into slick, oily cages, and expelling every molecule of water, transforming the gel into a desiccated web.

I just hoped it wasn't expelling anything else.

As the lacy net began to fall in folds at his feet, Hassan said something in Arabic, disgusted and amused. My grasp of the language remained patchy; Sadiq translated for me, his voice muffled by his face mask: "He says probably most of the weight of the thing will be dead insects." He shooed the youths back toward the truck before following himself, as the wind blew a glistening curtain over our heads. It descended far too slowly to trap us, but I hastened up the slope.

We watched from the truck as the Wall came down, the wave of dehydration propagating along its length. If the gel had been an elusive sight close up, the residue was entirely invisible in the distance; there was less substance to it than a very long pantyhose—albeit, pantyhose clogged with gnats.

The smart polymer was the invention of Sonja Helvig, a Norwegian chemist; I'd tweaked her original design for this application. Sadiq and his students were civil engineers, responsible for scaling everything up to the point where it could have a practical benefit. On those terms, this experiment was still nothing but a minor field trial.

I turned to Sadiq. "You did some mine clearance once, didn't you?"

"Years ago." Before I could say anything more, he'd caught my drift. "You're thinking that might have been more satisfying? Bang, and it's gone, the proof is there in front of you?"

"One less mine, one less bomblet," I said. "However many thousands there were to deal with, at least you could tick each one off as a definite achievement."

"That's true. It was a good feeling." He shrugged. "But what should we do? Give up on this, because it's harder?"

He took the truck down the slope, then supervised the students as they attached the wisps of polymer to the specialized winch they'd built. Hassan and Rashid were in their twenties, but they could easily have passed for adolescents. After the war, the dictator and his former backers in the west had found it mutually expedient to have a generation of Iraqi children grow up malnourished and without medical care, if they grew up at all. More than a million people had died under the sanctions. My own sick joke of a nation had sent part of its navy to join the blockade, while the rest stayed home to fend off boatloads of refugees from this, and other, atrocities. General Mustache was long dead, but his comrades-in-genocide with more salubrious addresses were all still at large: doing lecture tours, running think tanks, lobbying for the Nobel peace prize.

As the strands of polymer wound around a core inside the winch's protective barrel, the alpha count rose steadily. It was a good sign: the fine particles of uranium oxide trapped by the Wall had remained bound to the polymer during dehydration, and the reeling in of the net. The radiation from the few grams of U-238 we'd collected was far too low to be a hazard in itself; the thing to avoid was ingesting the dust, and even then the unpleasant effects were as much chemical as radiological. Hopefully, the polymer had also bound its other targets: the organic carcinogens that had been strewn across Kuwait and southern Iraq by the apocalyptic oil well fires. There was no way to determine that until we did a full chemical analysis.

We were all in high spirits on the ride back. What we'd plucked from the wind in the last six weeks wouldn't spare a single person from leukemia, but it now seemed possible that over the years, over the decades, the technology would make a real difference.

I MISSED THE CONNECTION in Singapore for a direct flight home to Sydney, so I had to go via Perth. There was a four-hour wait in Perth; I paced the transit lounge, restless and impatient. I hadn't set eyes on Francine since she'd left Basra three months earlier; she didn't approve of clogging up the limited bandwidth into Iraq with decadent video. When I'd called her from Singapore she'd been busy, and now I couldn't decide whether or not to try again.

Just when I'd resolved to call her, an email came through on my notepad, saying that she'd received my message and would meet me at the airport.

In Sydney, I stood by the baggage carousel, searching the crowd. When I finally saw Francine approaching, she was looking straight at me, smiling. I left the carousel and walked toward her; she stopped and let me close the gap, keeping her eyes fixed on mine. There was a mischievousness to her expression, as if she'd arranged some kind of prank, but I couldn't guess what it might be.

When I was almost in front of her, she turned slightly, and spread her arms. "Ta-da!"

I froze, speechless. *Why hadn't she told me?*

I walked up to her and embraced her, but she'd read my expression. "Don't be angry, Ben. I was afraid you'd come home early if you knew."

"You're right, I would have." My thoughts were piling up on top of each other; I had three months' worth of reactions to get through in fifteen seconds. *We hadn't planned this. We couldn't afford it. I wasn't ready.*

Suddenly I started weeping, too shocked to be self-conscious in the crowd. The knot of panic and confusion inside me dissolved. I held her more tightly, and felt the swelling in her body against my hip.

"Are you happy?" Francine asked.

I laughed and nodded, choking out the words: "This is wonderful!"

I meant it. I was still afraid, but it was an exuberant fear. Another ocean had opened up before us. We would find our bearings. We would cross it together.

IT TOOK ME SEVERAL days to come down to Earth. We didn't have a real chance to talk until the weekend; Francine had a teaching position at UNSW, and though she could have set her own research aside for a couple of days, marking could wait for no one. There were a thousand things to plan; the six-month UNESCO fellowship that had paid for me to take part in the project in Basra had expired, and I'd need to start earning money again soon, but the fact that I'd made no commitments yet gave me some welcome flexibility.

On Monday, alone in the flat again, I started catching up on all the journals I'd neglected. In Iraq I'd been obsessively single-minded, instructing my knowledge miner to keep me informed of work relevant to the Wall, to the exclusion of everything else.

Skimming through a summary of six months' worth of papers, a report in *Science* caught my eye: *An Experimental Model for Decoherence in the Many-Worlds Cosmology.* A group at Delft University in the Netherlands had arranged for a simple quantum computer to carry out a sequence of arithmetic operations on a register which had been prepared to contain an equal superposition of binary representations of two different numbers. This in itself was nothing new; superpositions representing up to 128 numbers were now manipulated daily, albeit only under laboratory conditions, at close to absolute zero.

Unusually, though, at each stage of the calculation the qubits containing the numbers in question had been deliberately entangled with other, spare qubits in the computer. The effect of this was that the section performing the calculation had ceased to be in a pure quantum state: it behaved, not as if it contained two numbers simultaneously, but as if there were merely an equal chance of it containing either one. This had undermined the quantum nature of the calculation, just as surely as if the whole machine had been imperfectly shielded and become entangled with objects in the environment.

There was one crucial difference, though: in this case, the experimenters had still had access to the spare qubits that had made the calculation behave classically. When they performed an appropriate measurement on the state of the computer *as a whole*, it was shown to have remained in a superposition all along. A single observation couldn't prove this, but the experiment had been repeated thousands of times, and within the margins of error, their prediction was confirmed: although the superposition had become undetectable when they ignored the spare qubits, it had never really gone away. *Both* classical calculations had always taken place simultaneously, even though they'd lost the ability to interact in a quantum-mechanical fashion.

I sat at my desk, pondering the result. On one level, it was just a scaling-up of the quantum eraser experiments of the '90s, but the image of a tiny computer program running through its paces, appearing "to itself" to be unique and alone, while in fact a second, equally oblivious version had been executing beside it all along, carried a lot more resonance than an interference experiment with photons. I'd become used to the idea of quantum computers performing several calculations at once, but that conjuring trick had always seemed abstract and ethereal, precisely because the parts continued to act as a complicated whole right to the end. What struck home *here* was the stark demonstration of the way each calculation could come to appear as a distinct classical history, as solid and mundane as the shuffling of beads on an abacus.

When Francine arrived home I was cooking dinner, but I grabbed my notepad and showed her the paper.

"Yeah, I've seen it," she said.

"What do you think?"

She raised her hands and recoiled in mock alarm.

"I'm serious."

"What do you want me to say? Does this prove the Many Worlds interpretation? No. Does it make it easier to understand, to have a toy model like this? Yes."

"But does it sway you at all?" I persisted. "Do you believe the results would still hold, if they could be scaled up indefinitely?" From a toy universe, a handful of qubits, to the real one.

She shrugged. "I don't really need to be swayed. I always thought the MWI was the most plausible interpretation anyway."

I left it at that, and went back to the kitchen while she pulled out a stack of assignments.

That night, as we lay in bed together, I couldn't get the Delft experiment out of my mind.

"Do you believe there are other versions of us?" I asked Francine.

"I suppose there must be." She conceded the point as if it was something abstract and metaphysical, and I was being pedantic even to raise it. People who professed belief in the MWI never seemed to want to take it seriously, let alone personally.

"And that doesn't bother you?"

"No," she said blithely. "Since I'm powerless to change the situation, what's the use in being upset about it?"

"That's very pragmatic," I said. Francine reached over and thumped me on the shoulder. "That was a compliment!" I protested. "I envy you for having come to terms with it so easily."

"I haven't, really," she admitted. "I've just resolved not to let it worry me, which isn't quite the same thing."

I turned to face her, though in the near-darkness we could barely see each other. I said, "What gives you the most satisfaction in life?"

"I take it you're not in the mood to be fobbed off with a soppy romantic answer?" She sighed. "I don't know. Solving problems. Getting things right."

"What if for every problem you solve, there's someone just like you who fails, instead?"

"I cope with my failures," she said. "Let them cope with theirs."

"You know it doesn't work like that. Some of them simply *don't* cope. Whatever you find the strength to do, there'll be someone else who won't."

Francine had no reply.

I said, "A couple of weeks ago, I asked Sadiq about the time he was doing mine clearance. He said it was more satisfying than mopping up DU; one little explosion, right before your eyes, and you know you've done something worthwhile. We all get moments in our lives like that, with that pure, unambiguous sense of achievement: whatever else we might screw up, at least there's one thing that we've done right." I laughed uneasily. "I think I'd go mad, if I couldn't rely on that."

Francine said, "You can. Nothing you've done will ever disappear from under your feet. No one's going to march up and take it away from you."

"I know." My skin crawled, at the image of some less favored alter ego turning up on our doorstep, demanding his dues. "That seems so fucking selfish, though. I don't want everything that makes me happy to be at the expense of someone else. I don't want every choice to be like . . . fighting other versions of myself for the prize in some zero-sum game."

"No." Francine hesitated. "But if the reality is like that, what can you do about it?"

Her words hung in the darkness. What could I do about it? Nothing. So did I really want to dwell on it, corroding the foundations of my own happiness, when there was absolutely nothing to be gained, for anyone?

"You're right. This is crazy." I leaned over and kissed her. "I'd better let you get to sleep."

"It's not crazy," she said. "But I don't have any answers."

THE NEXT MORNING, AFTER Francine had left for work, I picked up my notepad and saw that she'd mailed me an e-book: an anthology of cheesy "alternate (sic) history" stories from the '90s, entitled *My God, It's Full of Tsars!* "What if Gandhi had been a ruthless soldier of fortune? What if Theodore Roosevelt had faced a Martian invasion? What if the Nazis had had Janet Jackson's choreographer?"

I skimmed through the introduction, alternately cackling and groaning, then filed the book away and got down to work. I had a dozen minor administrative tasks to complete for UNESCO, before I could start searching in earnest for my next position.

By mid-afternoon, I was almost done, but the growing sense of achievement I felt at having buckled down and cleared away these tedious obligations brought with it the corollary: someone infinitesimally different from me—someone who had shared my entire history up until that morning—had procrastinated instead. The triviality of this observation only made it more unsettling; the Delft experiment was seeping into my daily life on the most mundane level.

I dug out the book Francine had sent and tried reading a few of the stories, but the authors' relentlessly camp take on the premise hardly amounted to a *reductio ad absurdum*, or even a comical existential balm. I didn't really care how hilarious it would have been if Marilyn Monroe had been involved in a bedroom farce with Richard Feynman and Richard Nixon. I just wanted to lose the suffocating conviction that everything I had become was a mirage; that my life had been nothing but a blinkered view of a kind of torture chamber, where every glorious reprieve I'd ever celebrated had in fact been an unwitting betrayal.

If fiction had no comfort to offer, what about fact? Even if the Many Worlds cosmology was correct, no one knew for certain what the consequences were. It was a fallacy that literally everything that was physically possible had to occur; most cosmologists I'd read believed that the universe as a whole possessed a single, definite quantum state, and while that state would appear from within as a multitude of distinct classical histories, there was no reason to assume that these histories amounted to some kind of exhaustive catalog. The same thing held true on a smaller scale: every time two people sat down to a game of chess, there was no reason to believe that they played every possible game.

And if I'd stood in an alley, nine years before, struggling with my conscience? My subjective sense of indecision proved nothing, but even if I'd suffered no qualms and acted without hesitation, to find a human being in a quantum state of pure, unshakeable resolve would have been freakishly unlikely at best, and in fact was probably physically impossible.

"Fuck this." I didn't know when I'd set myself up for this bout of paranoia, but I wasn't going to indulge it for another second. I banged my head against the desk a few times, then picked up my notepad and went straight to an employment site.

The thoughts didn't vanish entirely; it was too much like trying not to think of a pink elephant. Each time they recurred, though, I found I could shout them down with threats of taking myself straight to a psychiatrist. The prospect of having to explain such a bizarre mental problem was enough to give me access to hitherto untapped reserves of self-discipline.

By the time I started cooking dinner, I was feeling merely foolish. If Francine mentioned the subject again, I'd make a joke of it. I didn't need a psychiatrist. I was a little insecure about my good fortune, and still somewhat rattled by the news of impending fatherhood, but it would hardly have been healthier to take everything for granted.

My notepad chimed. Francine had blocked the video again, as if bandwidth, even here, was as precious as water.

"Hello."

"Ben? I've had some bleeding. I'm in a taxi. Can you meet me at St Vincent's?"

Her voice was steady, but my own mouth went dry. "Sure. I'll be there in fifteen minutes." I couldn't add anything: *I love you, it will be all right, hold on.* She didn't need that, it would have jinxed everything.

Half an hour later, I was still caught in traffic, white-knuckled with rage and helplessness. I stared down at the dashboard, at the real-time map with every other gridlocked vehicle marked, and finally stopped deluding myself that at any moment I would turn into a magically deserted side-street and weave my way across the city in just a few more minutes.

In the ward, behind the curtains drawn around her bed, Francine lay curled and rigid, her back turned, refusing to look at me. All I could do was stand beside her. The gynecologist was yet to explain everything properly, but the miscarriage had been accompanied by complications, and she'd had to perform surgery.

Before I'd applied for the UNESCO fellowship, we'd discussed the risks. For two prudent, well-informed, short-term visitors, the danger had seemed microscopic. Francine had never traveled out into the desert with me, and even for the locals in Basra the rates of birth defects and miscarriages had fallen a long way from their peaks. We were both taking contraceptives; condoms had seemed like overkill. *Had I brought it back to her, from the desert? A speck of dust, trapped beneath my foreskin? Had I poisoned her while we were making love?*

Francine turned toward me. The skin around her eyes was gray and swollen, and I could see how much effort it took for her to meet my gaze. She drew her hands out from under the bedclothes, and let me hold them; they were freezing.

After a while, she started sobbing, but she wouldn't release my hands. I stroked the back of her thumb with my own thumb, a tiny, gentle movement.

2020

"How do you feel now?" Olivia Maslin didn't quite make eye contact as she addressed me; the image of my brain activity painted on her retinas was clearly holding her attention.

"Fine," I said. "Exactly the same as I did before you started the infusion."

I was reclining on something like a dentist's couch, halfway between sitting and lying, wearing a tight-fitting cap studded with magnetic sensors and inducers. It was impossible to ignore the slight coolness of the liquid flowing into the vein in my forearm, but that sensation was no different than it had been on the previous occasion, a fortnight before.

"Could you count to ten for me, please."

I obliged.

"Now close your eyes and picture the same familiar face as the last time."

She'd told me I could choose anyone; I'd picked Francine. I brought back the image, then suddenly recalled that, the first time, after contemplating the detailed picture in my head for a few seconds—as if I was preparing to give a description to the police—I'd started thinking about Francine herself. On cue, the same transition occurred again: the frozen, forensic likeness became flesh and blood.

I was led through the whole sequence of activities once more: reading the same short story ("Two Old-Timers" by F. Scott Fitzgerald), listening to the same piece of music (from Rossini's *The Thieving Magpie*), recounting the same childhood memory (my first day at school). At some point, I lost any trace of anxiety about repeating my earlier mental states with sufficient fidelity; after all, the experiment had been designed to cope with the inevitable variation between the two sessions. I was just one volunteer out of dozens, and half the subjects would be receiving nothing but saline on both occasions. For all I knew, I was one of them: a control, merely setting the baseline against which any real effect would be judged.

If I was receiving the coherence disruptors, though, then as far as I could tell they'd had no effect on me. My inner life hadn't evaporated as the molecules bound to the microtubules in my neurons, guaranteeing that any kind of quantum coherence those structures might otherwise have maintained would be lost to the environment in a fraction of a picosecond.

Personally, I'd never subscribed to Penrose's theory that quantum effects might play a role in consciousness; calculations dating back to a seminal paper by Max Tegmark, twenty years before, had already made sustained coherence in any neural structure extremely unlikely. Nevertheless, it had taken considerable ingenuity on the part of Olivia and her team to rule out the idea definitively, in a series of clear-cut experiments. Over the past two years, they'd chased the ghost away from each of the various structures that different factions of Penrose's disciples had anointed as the essential quantum components of the brain. The earliest proposal—the microtubules, huge polymeric molecules that formed a kind of skeleton inside every cell—had turned out to be the hardest to target for disruption. But now it was entirely possible that the cytoskeletons of my very own neurons were dotted with molecules that coupled them strongly to a noisy microwave field in which my skull was, definitely, bathed. In which case, my microtubules had about as much chance of exploiting quantum effects as I had of playing a game of squash with a version of myself from a parallel universe.

When the experiment was over, Olivia thanked me, then became even more distant as she reviewed the data. Raj, one of her graduate students, slid out the needle and stuck a plaster over the tiny puncture wound, then helped me out of the cap.

"I know you don't know yet if I was a control or not," I said, "but have you noticed significant differences, with anyone?" I was almost the last subject in the microtubule trials; any effect should have shown up by now.

Olivia smiled enigmatically. "You'll just have to wait for publication." Raj leaned down and whispered, "No, never."

I climbed off the couch. "The zombie walks!" Raj declaimed. I lunged hungrily for his brain; he ducked away, laughing, while Olivia watched us with an expression of pained indulgence. Diehard members of the Penrose camp claimed that Olivia's experiments proved nothing, because even if people *behaved* identically while all quantum effects were ruled out, they could be doing this as mere automata, totally devoid of consciousness. When Olivia had offered to let her chief detractor experience coherence disruption for himself, he'd replied that this would be no more persuasive, because memories laid down while you were a zombie would be indistinguishable from ordinary memories, so that looking back on the experience, you'd notice nothing unusual.

This was sheer desperation; you might as well assert that everyone in the world but yourself was a zombie, and you were one, too, every second Tuesday. As the experiments were repeated by other groups around the world, those people who'd backed the Penrose theory as a scientific hypothesis, rather than adopting it as a kind of mystical dogma, would gradually accept that it had been refuted.

I LEFT THE NEUROSCIENCE building and walked across the campus, back toward my office in the physics department. It was a mild, clear spring morning, with students out lying on the grass, dozing off with books balanced over their faces like tents. There were still some advantages to reading from old-fashioned sheaves of e-paper. I'd only had my own eyes chipped the year before, and though I'd adapted to the technology easily enough, I still found it disconcerting to wake on a Sunday morning to find Francine reading the *Herald* beside me with her eyes shut.

Olivia's results didn't surprise me, but it was satisfying to have the matter resolved once and for all: consciousness was a purely classical phenomenon. Among other things, this meant that there was no compelling reason to believe that software running on a classical computer could not be conscious. Of course, everything in the universe obeyed quantum mechanics at some level, but Paul Benioff, one of the pioneers of quantum computing, had shown back in the '80s that you could build a classical Turing machine from quantum mechanical parts, and over the last few years, in my spare time, I'd studied the branch of quantum computing theory that concerned itself with *avoiding* quantum effects.

Back in my office, I summoned up a schematic of the device I called the Qusp: the quantum singleton processor. The Qusp would employ all the techniques designed to shield the latest generation of quantum computers from entanglement with their environment, but it would use them to a very different end. A quantum computer was shielded so it could perform a multitude of parallel calculations, without each one spawning a separate history of its own, in which only one answer was accessible. The Qusp would perform just a single calculation at a time, but on its way to the unique result it would be able to pass safely through superpositions that included any number of alternatives, without those alternatives being made real. Cut off from the outside world during each computational step, it would keep its temporary quantum ambivalence as private and inconsequential as a daydream, never being forced to act out every possibility it dared to entertain.

The Qusp would still need to interact with its environment whenever it gathered data about the world, and that interaction would inevitably split it into different versions. If you attached a camera to the Qusp and pointed it at an ordinary object—a rock, a plant, a bird—that object could hardly be expected to possess a single classical history, and so neither would the combined system of Qusp plus rock, Qusp plus plant, Qusp plus bird.

The Qusp itself, though, would never initiate the split. In a given set of circumstances, it would only ever produce a single response. An AI running on the Qusp could make its decisions as whimsically, or with as much weighty deliberation as it liked, but for each distinct scenario it confronted, in the end it would only make one choice, only follow one course of action.

I closed the file, and the image vanished from my retinas. For all the work I'd put into the design, I'd made no effort to build the thing. I'd been using it as little more than a talisman: whenever I found myself picturing my life as a tranquil dwelling built over a slaughter house, I'd summon up the Qusp as a symbol of hope. It was proof of a possibility, and a possibility was all it took. Nothing in the laws of physics could prevent a small portion of humanity's descendants from escaping their ancestors' dissipation.

Yet I'd shied away from any attempt to see that promise fulfilled, firsthand. In part, I'd been afraid of delving too deeply and uncovering a flaw in the Qusp's design, robbing myself of the one crutch that kept me standing when the horror swept over me. It had also been a matter of guilt: I'd been the one granted happiness, so many times, that it had seemed unconscionable to aspire to that state yet again. I'd knocked so many of my hapless cousins out of the ring, it was time I threw a fight and let the prize go to my opponent instead.

That last excuse was idiotic. The stronger my determination to build the Qusp, the more branches there would be in which it was real. Weakening my resolve was *not* an act of charity, surrendering the benefits to someone else; it merely impoverished every future version of me, and everyone they touched.

I did have a third excuse. It was time I dealt with that one, too.

I called Francine.

"Are you free for lunch?" I asked. She hesitated; there was always work she could be doing. "To discuss the Cauchy-Riemann equations?" I suggested.

She smiled. It was our code, when the request was a special one. "All right. One o'clock?"

I nodded. "I'll see you then."

FRANCINE WAS TWENTY MINUTES late, but that was less of a wait than I was used to. She'd been appointed deputy head of the mathematics department eighteen months before, and she still had some teaching duties as well as all the new administrative work. Over the last eight years, I'd had a dozen short-term contracts with various bodies—government departments, corporations, NGOs—before finally ending up as a very lowly member of the physics department at our *alma mater*. I did envy her the prestige and security of her job, but I'd been happy with most of the work I'd done, even if it had been too scattered between disciplines to contribute to anything like a traditional career path.

I'd bought Francine a plate of cheese-and-salad sandwiches, and she attacked them hungrily as soon as she sat down. I said, "I've got ten minutes at the most, haven't I?"

She covered her mouth with her hand and replied defensively, "It could have waited until tonight, couldn't it?"

"Sometimes I can't put things off. I have to act while I still have the courage."

At this ominous prelude she chewed more slowly. "You did the second stage of Olivia's experiment this morning, didn't you?"

"Yeah." I'd discussed the whole procedure with her before I volunteered.

"So I take it you didn't lose consciousness, when your neurons became marginally more classical than usual?" She sipped chocolate milk through a straw.

"No. Apparently no one ever loses anything. That's not official yet, but—"

Francine nodded, unsurprised. We shared the same position on the Penrose theory; there was no need to discuss it again now.

I said, "I want to know if you're going to have the operation."

She continued drinking for a few more seconds, then released the straw and wiped her upper lip with her thumb, unnecessarily. "You want me to make up my mind about that, here and now?"

"No." The damage to her uterus from the miscarriage could be repaired; we'd been discussing the possibility for almost five years. We'd both had comprehensive chelation therapy to remove any trace of U-238. We could have children in the usual way with a reasonable degree of safety, if that was what we wanted. "But if you've already decided, I want you to tell me now."

Francine looked wounded. "That's unfair."

"What is? Implying that you might not have told me, the instant you decided?"

"No. Implying that it's all in my hands."

I said, "I'm not washing my hands of the decision. You know how I feel. But you know I'd back you all the way, if you said you wanted to carry a child." I believed I would have. Maybe it was a form of doublethink, but I couldn't treat the birth of one more ordinary child as some kind of atrocity, and refuse to be a part of it.

"Fine. But what will you do if I don't?" She examined my face calmly. I think she already knew, but she wanted me to spell it out.

"We could always adopt," I observed casually.

"Yes, we could do that." She smiled slightly; she knew that made me lose my ability to bluff, even faster than when she stared me down.

I stopped pretending that there was any mystery left; she'd seen right through me from the start. I said, "I just don't want to do this, then discover that it makes you feel that you've been cheated out of what you really wanted."

"It wouldn't," she insisted. "It wouldn't rule out anything. We could still have a natural child as well."

"Not as easily." This would not be like merely having workaholic parents, or an ordinary brother or sister to compete with for attention.

"You only want to do this if I can promise you that it's the only child we'd ever have?" Francine shook her head. "I'm not going to promise that. I don't intend having the operation any time soon, but

I'm not going to swear that I won't change my mind. Nor am I going to swear that if we do this it will make no difference to what happens later. It will be a factor. How could it not be? But it won't be enough to rule anything in or out."

I looked away, across the rows of tables, at all the students wrapped up in their own concerns. She was right; I was being unreasonable. I'd wanted this to be a choice with no possible downside, a way of making the best of our situation, but no one could guarantee that. It would be a gamble, like everything else.

I turned back to Francine.

"All right; I'll stop trying to pin you down. What I want to do right now is go ahead and build the Qusp. And when it's finished, if we're certain we can trust it . . . I want us to raise a child with it. I want us to raise an AI."

2029

I MET FRANCINE AT the airport, and we drove across São Paulo through curtains of wild, lashing rain. I was amazed that her plane hadn't been diverted; a tropical storm had just hit the coast, halfway between us and Rio.

"So much for giving you a tour of the city," I lamented. Through the windshield, our actual surroundings were all but invisible; the bright overlay we both perceived, surreally colored and detailed, made the experience rather like perusing a 3D map while trapped in a car wash.

Francine was pensive, or tired from the flight. I found it hard to think of San Francisco as remote when the time difference was so small, and even when I'd made the journey north to visit her, it had been nothing compared to all the ocean-spanning marathons I'd sat through in the past.

We both had an early night. The next morning, Francine accompanied me to my cluttered workroom in the basement of the university's engineering department. I'd been chasing grants and collaborators around the world, like a child on a treasure hunt, slowly piecing together a device that few of my colleagues believed was worth creating for its own sake. Fortunately, I'd managed to find pretexts—or even genuine spin-offs—for almost every stage of the work. Quantum computing, *per se*, had become bogged down in recent years, stymied by both a shortage of practical algorithms and a limit to the complexity of superpositions that could be sustained. The Qusp had nudged the technological envelope in some promising directions, without making any truly exorbitant demands; the states it juggled were relatively simple, and they only needed to be kept isolated for milliseconds at a time.

I introduced Carlos, Maria and Jun, but then they made themselves scarce as I showed Francine around. We still had a demonstration of the "balanced decoupling" principle set up on a bench, for the tour by one of our corporate donors the week before. What caused an imperfectly shielded quantum computer to decohere was the fact that each possible state of the device affected its environment slightly differently. The shielding itself could always be improved, but Carlos's group had perfected a way to buy a little more protection by sheer deviousness. In the demonstration rig, the flow of energy through the device remained absolutely constant whatever state it was in, because any drop in power consumption by the main set of quantum gates was compensated for by a rise in a set of balancing gates, and *vice versa*. This gave the environment one less clue by which to discern internal differences in the processor, and to tear any superposition apart into mutually disconnected branches.

Francine knew all the theory backward, but she'd never seen this hardware in action. When I invited her to twiddle the controls, she took to the rig like a child with a game console.

"You really should have joined the team," I said.

"Maybe I did," she countered. "In another branch."

She'd moved from UNSW to Berkeley two years before, not long after I'd moved from Delft to São Paulo; it was the closest suitable position she could find. At the time, I'd resented the fact that she'd refused to compromise and work remotely; with only five hours' difference, teaching at Berkeley from São Paulo would not have been impossible. In the end, though, I'd accepted the fact that she'd wanted to keep on testing me, testing both of us. If we weren't strong enough to stay together through the trials of a prolonged physical separation—or if I was not sufficiently committed to the project to endure whatever sacrifices it entailed—she did not want us proceeding to the next stage.

I led her to the corner bench, where a nondescript gray box half a meter across sat, apparently inert. I gestured to it, and our retinal overlays transformed its appearance, "revealing" a maze with a transparent lid embedded in the top of the device. In one chamber of the maze, a slightly cartoonish mouse sat motionless. Not quite dead, not quite sleeping.

"This is the famous Zelda?" Francine asked.

"Yes." Zelda was a neural network, a stripped-down, stylized mouse brain. There were newer, fancier versions available, much closer to the real thing, but the ten-year-old, public domain Zelda had been good enough for our purposes.

Three other chambers held cheese. "Right now, she has no experience of the maze," I explained. "So let's start her up and watch her explore." I gestured, and Zelda began scampering around, trying out different passages, deftly reversing each time she hit a *cul-de-sac*. "Her brain is running on a Qusp, but the maze is implemented on an ordinary classical computer, so in terms of coherence issues, it's really no different from a physical maze."

"Which means that each time she takes in information, she gets entangled with the outside world," Francine suggested.

"Absolutely. But she always holds off doing that until the Qusp has completed its current computational step, and every qubit contains a definite zero or a definite one. She's never in two minds when she lets the world in, so the entanglement process doesn't split her into separate branches."

Francine continued to watch, in silence. Zelda finally found one of the chambers containing a reward; when she'd eaten it, a hand scooped her up and returned her to her starting point, then replaced the cheese.

"Here are ten thousand previous trials, superimposed." I replayed the data. It looked as if a single mouse was running through the maze, moving just as we'd seen her move when I'd begun the latest experiment. Restored each time to exactly the same starting condition, and confronted with exactly the same environment, Zelda—like any computer program with no truly random influences—had simply repeated herself. All ten thousand trials had yielded identical results.

To a casual observer, unaware of the context, this would have been a singularly unimpressive performance. Faced with exactly one situation, Zelda the virtual mouse did exactly one thing. So what? If you'd been able to wind back a flesh-and-blood mouse's memory with the same degree of precision, wouldn't it have repeated itself too?

Francine said, "Can you cut off the shielding? And the balanced decoupling?"

"Yep." I obliged her, and initiated a new trial.

Zelda took a different path this time, exploring the maze by a different route. Though the initial condition of the neural net was identical, the switching processes taking place within the Qusp were now opened up to the environment constantly, and superpositions of several different eigenstates—states in which the Qusp's qubits possessed definite binary values, which in turn led to Zelda making definite choices—were becoming entangled with the outside world. According to the Copenhagen interpretation of quantum mechanics, this interaction was randomly "collapsing" the superpositions into single eigenstates; Zelda was still doing just one thing at a time, but her behavior had ceased to be deterministic. According to the MWI, the interaction was transforming the environment—Francine and me included—into a superposition with components that were coupled to each eigenstate; Zelda was actually running the maze in many different ways simultaneously, and other versions of us were seeing her take all those other routes.

Which scenario was correct?

I said, "I'll reconfigure everything now, to wrap the whole setup in a Delft cage." A "Delft cage" was jargon for the situation I'd first read about seventeen years before: instead of opening up the Qusp to the environment, I'd connect it to a second quantum computer, and let *that* play the role of the outside world.

We could no longer watch Zelda moving about in real time, but after the trial was completed, it was possible to test the combined system of both computers against the hypothesis that it was in a pure quantum state in which Zelda had run the maze along hundreds of different routes, all at once. I displayed a representation of the conjectured state, built up by superimposing all the paths she'd taken in ten thousand unshielded trials.

The test result flashed up: CONSISTENT.

"One measurement proves nothing," Francine pointed out.

"No." I repeated the trial. Again, the hypothesis was not refuted. If Zelda had actually run the maze along just one path, the probability of the computers' joint state passing this imperfect test was about one percent. For passing it twice, the odds were about one in ten thousand.

I repeated it a third time, then a fourth.

Francine said, "That's enough." She actually looked queasy. The image of the hundreds of blurred mouse trails on the display was not a literal photograph of anything, but if the old Delft experiment had been enough to give me a visceral sense of the reality of the multiverse, perhaps this demonstration had finally done the same for her.

"Can I show you one more thing?" I asked.

"Keep the Delft cage, but restore the Qusp's shielding?"

"Right."

I did it. The Qusp was now fully protected once more whenever it was not in an eigenstate, but this time, it was the second quantum computer, not the outside world, to which it was intermittently exposed. If Zelda split into multiple branches again, then she'd only take that fake environment with her, and we'd still have our hands on all the evidence.

Tested against the hypothesis that no split had occurred, the verdict was: CONSISTENT. CONSISTENT. CONSISTENT.

WE WENT OUT TO dinner with the whole of the team, but Francine pleaded a headache and left early. She insisted that I stay and finish the meal, and I didn't argue; she was not the kind of person who expected you to assume that she was being politely selfless, while secretly hoping to be contradicted.

After Francine had left, Maria turned to me. "So you two are really going ahead with the Frankenchild?" She'd been teasing me about this for as long as I'd known her, but apparently she hadn't been game to raise the subject in Francine's presence.

"We still have to talk about it." I felt uncomfortable myself, now, discussing the topic the moment Francine was absent. Confessing my ambition when I applied to join the team was one thing; it would have been dishonest to keep my collaborators in the dark about my ultimate intentions. Now that the enabling technology was more or less completed, though, the issue seemed far more personal.

Carlos said breezily, "Why not? There are so many others now. Sophie. Linus. Theo. Probably a hundred we don't even know about. It's not as if Ben's child won't have playmates." Adai—Autonomously Developing Artificial Intelligences—had been appearing in a blaze of controversy every few months for the last four years. A Swiss researcher, Isabelle Schib, had taken the old models of morpho-genesis that had led to software like Zelda, refined the technique by several orders of magnitude, and applied it to human genetic data. Wedded to sophisticated prosthetic bodies, Isabelle's creations inhabited the physical world and learned from their experience, just like any other child.

Jun shook his head reprovingly. "I wouldn't raise a child with no legal rights. What happens when you die? For all you know, it could end up as someone's property."

I'd been over this with Francine. "I can't believe that in ten or twenty years' time there won't be citizenship laws, somewhere in the world."

Jun snorted. "Twenty years! How long did it take the U.S. to emancipate their slaves?"

Carlos interjected, "Who's going to create an adai just to use it as a slave? If you want something biddable, write ordinary software. If you need consciousness, humans are cheaper."

Maria said, "It won't come down to economics. It's the nature of the things that will determine how they're treated."

"You mean the xenophobia they'll face?" I suggested.

Maria shrugged. "You make it sound like racism, but we aren't talking about human beings. Once you have software with goals of its own, free to do whatever it likes, where will it end? The first generation makes the next one better, faster, smarter; the second generation even more so. Before we know it, we're like ants to them."

Carlos groaned. "Not that hoary old fallacy! If you really believe that stating the analogy 'ants are to humans, as humans are to x' is proof that it's possible to solve for x, then I'll meet you where the south pole is like the equator."

I said, "The Qusp runs no faster than an organic brain; we need to keep the switching rate low, because that makes the shielding requirements less stringent. It might be possible to nudge those parameters, eventually, but there's no reason in the world why an adai would be better equipped to do that than you or I would. As for making their own offspring smarter . . . even if Schib's group has been perfectly successful, they will have merely translated human neural development from one substrate to another. They won't have 'improved' on the process at all—whatever that might mean. So if the adai have any advantage over us, it will be no more than the advantage shared by flesh-and-blood children: cultural transmission of one more generation's worth of experience."

Maria frowned, but she had no immediate comeback.

Jun said dryly, "Plus immortality."

"Well, yes, there is that," I conceded.

FRANCINE WAS AWAKE WHEN I arrived home.

"Have you still got a headache?" I whispered.

"No."

I undressed and climbed into bed beside her.

She said, "You know what I miss the most? When we're fucking on-line?"

"This had better not be complicated; I'm out of practice."

"Kissing."

I kissed her, slowly and tenderly, and she melted beneath me. "Three more months," I promised, "and I'll move up to Berkeley."

"To be my kept man."

"I prefer the term 'unpaid but highly valued caregiver.'" Francine stiffened. I said, "We can talk about that later." I started kissing her again, but she turned her face away.

"I'm afraid," she said.

"So am I," I assured her. "That's a good sign. Everything worth doing is terrifying."

"But not everything terrifying is good."

I rolled over and lay beside her. She said, "On one level, it's easy. What greater gift could you give a child, than the power to make real decisions? What worse fate could you spare her from, than being forced to act against her better judgment, over and over? When you put it like that, it's simple.

"But every fiber in my body still rebels against it. How will she feel, knowing what she is? How will she make friends? How will she belong? How will she not despise us for making her a freak? And what if we're robbing her of something she'd value: living a billion lives, never being forced to choose between them? What if she sees the gift as a kind of impoverishment?"

"She can always drop the shielding on the Qusp," I said. "Once she understands the issues, she can choose for herself."

"That's true." Francine did not sound mollified at all; she would have thought of that long before I'd mentioned it, but she wasn't looking for concrete answers. Every ordinary human instinct screamed at us that we were embarking on something *dangerous, unnatural, hubristic*—but those instincts were more about safeguarding our own reputations than protecting our child-to-be. No parent, save the most willfully negligent, would be pilloried if their flesh-and-blood child turned out to be ungrateful for life; if I'd railed against my own mother and father because I'd found fault in the existential conditions with which I'd been lumbered, it wasn't hard to guess which side would attract the most sympathy from the world at large. Anything that went wrong with *our* child would be grounds for lynching—however much love, sweat, and soul-searching had gone into her creation—because we'd had the temerity to be dissatisfied with the kind of fate that everyone else happily inflicted on their own.

I said, "You saw Zelda today, spread across the branches. You know, deep down now, that the same thing happens to all of us."

"Yes." Something tore inside me as Francine uttered that admission. I'd never really wanted her to feel it, the way I did.

I persisted. "Would you willingly sentence your own child to that condition? And your grandchildren? And your great-grandchildren?"

"No," Francine replied. A part of her hated me now; I could hear it in her voice. It was *my* curse, *my* obsession; before she met me, she'd managed to believe and not believe, taking her acceptance of the multiverse lightly.

I said, "I can't do this without you."

"You can, actually. More easily than any of the alternatives. You wouldn't even need a stranger to donate an egg."

"I can't do it unless you're behind me. If you say the word, I'll stop here. We've built the Qusp. We've shown that it can work. Even if we don't do this last part ourselves, someone else will, in a decade or two."

"If *we* don't do this," Francine observed acerbically, "we'll simply do it in another branch."

I said, "That's true, but it's no use thinking that way. In the end, I can't function unless I pretend that my choices are real. I doubt that anyone can."

Francine was silent for a long time. I stared up into the darkness of the room, trying hard not to contemplate the near certainty that her decision would go both ways.

Finally, she spoke.

"Then let's make a child who doesn't need to pretend."

2031

ISABELLE SCHIB WELCOMED US into her office. In person, she was slightly less intimidating than she was on-line; it wasn't anything different in her appearance or manner, just the ordinariness of her surroundings. I'd envisaged her ensconced in some vast, pristine, high-tech building, not a couple of pokey rooms on a back-street in Basel.

Once the pleasantries were out of the way, Isabelle got straight to the point. "You've been accepted," she announced. "I'll send you the contract later today."

My throat constricted with panic; I should have been elated, but I just felt unprepared. Isabelle's group licensed only three new adai a year. The short-list had come down to about a hundred couples, winnowed from tens of thousands of applicants. We'd traveled to Switzerland for the final selection process, carried out by an agency that ordinarily handled adoptions. Through all the interviews and questionnaires, all the personality tests and scenario challenges, I'd managed to half-convince myself that our dedication would win through in the end, but that had been nothing but a prop to keep my spirits up.

Francine said calmly, "Thank you."

I coughed. "You're happy with everything we've proposed?" If there was going to be a proviso thrown in that rendered this miracle worthless, better to hear it now, before the shock had worn off and I'd started taking things for granted.

Isabelle nodded. "I don't pretend to be an expert in the relevant fields, but I've had the Qusp's design assessed by several colleagues, and I see no reason why it wouldn't be an appropriate form of hardware for an adai. I'm entirely agnostic about the MWI, so I don't share your view that the Qusp is a necessity, but if you were worried that I might write you off as cranks because of it," she smiled slightly, "you should meet some of the other people I've had to deal with.

"I believe you have the adai's welfare at heart, and you're not suffering from any of the superstitions—technophobic *or* technophilic— that would distort the relationship. And as you'll recall, I'll be entitled to visits and inspections throughout your period of guardianship. If you're found to be violating any of the terms of the contract, your license will be revoked, and I'll take charge of the adai."

Francine said, "What do you think the prospects are for a happier end to our guardianship?"

"I'm lobbying the European parliament, constantly," Isabelle replied. "Of course, in a few years' time several adai will reach the stage where their personal testimony begins contributing to the debate, but none of us should wait until then. The ground has to be prepared."

We spoke for almost an hour, on this and other issues. Isabelle had become quite an expert at fending off the attentions of the media; she promised to send us a handbook on this, along with the contract.

"Did you want to meet Sophie?" Isabelle asked, almost as an afterthought.

Francine said, "That would be wonderful." Francine and I had seen a video of Sophie at age four, undergoing a battery of psychological tests, but we'd never had a chance to converse with her, let alone meet her face to face.

The three of us left the office together, and Isabelle drove us to her home on the outskirts of the town.

In the car, the reality began sinking in anew. I felt the same mixture of exhilaration and claustrophobia that I'd experienced nineteen years before, when Francine had met me at the airport with news of her pregnancy. No digital conception had yet taken place, but if sex had ever felt half as loaded with risks and responsibilities as this, I would have remained celibate for life.

"No badgering, no interrogation," Isabelle warned us as she pulled into the driveway.

I said, "Of course not."

Isabelle called out, "Marco! Sophie!" as we followed her through the door. At the end of the hall, I heard childish giggling, and an adult male voice whispering in French. Then Isabelle's husband stepped out from behind the corner, a smiling, dark-haired young man, with Sophie riding on his shoulders. At first I couldn't look at her; I just smiled politely back at Marco, while noting glumly that he was at least fifteen years younger than I was. *How could I even think of doing this, at forty-six?* Then I glanced up, and caught Sophie's eye. She gazed straight back at me for a moment, appearing curious and composed, but then a fit of shyness struck her, and she buried her face in Marco's hair.

Isabelle introduced us, in English; Sophie was being raised to speak four languages, though in Switzerland that was hardly phenomenal. Sophie said, "Hello" but kept her eyes lowered. Isabelle said, "Come into the living room. Would you like something to drink?"

The five of us sipped lemonade, and the adults made polite, superficial conversation. Sophie sat on Marco's knees, squirming restlessly, sneaking glances at us. She looked exactly like an ordinary, slightly gawky, six-year-old girl. She had Isabelle's straw-colored hair, and

Marco's brown eyes; whether by fiat or rigorous genetic simulation, she could have passed for their biological daughter. I'd read technical specifications describing her body, and seen an earlier version in action on the video, but the fact that it looked so plausible was the least of its designers' achievements. Watching her drinking, wriggling and fidgeting, I had no doubt that she felt herself inhabiting this skin, as much as I did my own. She was not a puppeteer posing as a child, pulling electronic strings from some dark cavern in her skull.

"Do you like lemonade?" I asked her.

She stared at me for a moment, as if wondering whether she should be affronted by the presumptuousness of this question, then replied, "It tickles."

In the taxi to the hotel, Francine held my hand tightly.

"Are you okay?" I asked.

"Yes, of course."

In the elevator, she started crying. I wrapped my arms around her.

"She would have turned eighteen this year."

"I know."

"Do you think she's alive, somewhere?"

"I don't know. I don't know if that's a good way to think about it."

Francine wiped her eyes. "No. This will be her. That's the way to see it. This will be my girl. Just a few years late."

Before flying home, we visited a small pathology lab, and left samples of our blood.

OUR DAUGHTER'S FIRST FIVE bodies reached us a month before her birth. I unpacked all five, and laid them out in a row on the living room floor. With their muscles slack and their eyes rolled up, they looked more like tragic mummies than sleeping infants. I dismissed that grisly image; better to think of them as suits of clothes. The only difference was that we hadn't bought pajamas quite so far ahead.

From wrinkled pink newborn to chubby eighteen-month-old, the progression made an eerie sight—even if an organic child's development, short of serious disease or malnourishment, would have been scarcely less predictable. A colleague of Francine's had lectured me a few weeks before about the terrible "mechanical determinism" we'd be imposing on our child, and though his arguments had been philosophically naïve, this sequence of immutable snapshots from the future still gave me goose bumps.

The truth was, reality as a whole was deterministic, whether you had a Qusp for a brain or not; the quantum state of the multiverse at any moment determined the entire future. Personal experience—confined to one branch at a time—certainly *appeared* probabilistic, because there was no way to predict which local future you'd experience when a branch split, but the reason it was impossible to know that in advance was because the real answer was "all of them".

For a singleton, the only difference was that branches never split on the basis of your personal decisions. The world at large would continue to look probabilistic, but every choice you made was entirely determined by *who you were* and *the situation you faced*.

What more could anyone hope for? It was not as if *who you were* could be boiled down to some crude genetic or sociological profile; every shadow you'd seen on the ceiling at night, every cloud you'd watched drift across the sky, would have left some small imprint on the shape of your mind. Those events were fully determined too, when viewed across the multiverse—with different versions of you witnessing every possibility—but in practical terms, the bottom line was that no private investigator armed with your genome and a potted biography could plot your every move in advance.

Our daughter's choices—like everything else—had been written in stone at the birth of the universe, but that information could only be decoded by *becoming her* along the way. Her actions would flow from her temperament, her principles, her desires, and the fact that all of these qualities would themselves have prior causes did nothing to diminish their value. *Free will* was a slippery notion, but to me it simply meant that your choices were more or less consistent with your nature—which in turn was a provisional, constantly-evolving consensus between a thousand different influences. Our daughter would not be robbed of the chance to act capriciously, or even perversely, but at least it would not be impossible for her ever to act wholly in accordance with her ideals.

I packed the bodies away before Francine got home. I wasn't sure if the sight would unsettle her, but I didn't want her measuring them up for more clothes.

THE DELIVERY BEGAN IN the early hours of the morning of Sunday, December 14, and was expected to last about four hours, depending on traffic. I sat in the nursery while Francine paced the hallway outside, both of us watching the data coming through over the fiber from Basel.

Isabelle had used our genetic information as the starting point for a simulation of the development *in utero* of a complete embryo, employing an "adaptive hierarchy" model, with the highest resolution reserved for the central nervous system. The Qusp would take over this task, not only for the newborn child's brain, but also for the thousands of biochemical processes occurring outside the skull that the artificial bodies were not designed to perform. Apart from their sophisticated sensory and motor functions, the bodies could take in food and excrete wastes—for psychological and social reasons, as well as for the chemical energy this provided—and they breathed air, both in order to oxidize this fuel, and for vocalization, but they had no blood, no endocrine system, no immune response.

The Qusp I'd built in Berkeley was smaller than the São Paulo version, but it was still six times as wide as an infant's skull. Until it was further miniaturized, our daughter's mind would sit in a box in a corner of the nursery, joined to the rest of her by a wireless data link. Bandwidth and time lag would not be an issue within the Bay Area, and if we needed to take her further afield before everything was combined, the Qusp wasn't too large or delicate to move.

As the progress bar I was overlaying on the side of the Qusp nudged 98 per cent, Francine came into the nursery, looking agitated.

"We have to put it off, Ben. Just for a day. I need more time to prepare myself."

I shook my head. "You made me promise to say no, if you asked me to do that." She'd even refused to let me tell her how to halt the Qusp herself.

"Just a few hours," she pleaded.

Francine seemed genuinely distressed, but I hardened my heart by telling myself that she was acting: testing me, seeing if I'd keep my word. "No. No slowing down or speeding up, no pauses, no tinkering at all. This child has to hit us like a freight train, just like any other child would."

"You want me to go into labor now?" she said sarcastically. When I'd raised the possibility, half-jokingly, of putting her on a course of hormones that would have mimicked some of the effects of pregnancy in order to make bonding with the child easier—for myself as well, indirectly—she'd almost bitten my head off. I hadn't been serious, because I knew it wasn't necessary. Adoption was the ultimate proof of that, but what we were doing was closer to claiming a child of our own from a surrogate.

"No. Just pick her up."

Francine peered down at the inert form in the cot.

"I can't do it!" she wailed. "When I hold her, she should feel as if she's the most precious thing in the world to me. How can I make her believe that, when I know I could bounce her off the walls without harming her?"

We had two minutes left. I felt my breathing grow ragged. I could send the Qusp a halt code, but what if that set the pattern? If one of us had had too little sleep, if Francine was late for work, if we talked ourselves into believing that our special child was so unique that we deserved a short holiday from her needs, what would stop us from doing the same thing again?

I opened my mouth to threaten her: *Either you pick her up, now, or I do it.* I stopped myself, and said, "You know how much it would harm her psychologically, if you dropped her. The very fact that you're afraid that you won't convey as much protectiveness as you need to will be just as strong a signal to her as anything else. *You care about her.* She'll sense that."

Francine stared back at me dubiously.

I said, "She'll know. I'm sure she will."

Francine reached into the cot and lifted the slack body into her arms. Seeing her cradle the lifeless form, I felt an anxious twisting in my gut; I'd experienced nothing like this when I'd laid the five plastic shells out for inspection.

I banished the progress bar and let myself free-fall through the final seconds: watching my daughter, willing her to move.

Her thumb twitched, then her legs scissored weakly. I couldn't see her face, so I watched Francine's expression. For an instant, I thought I could detect a horrified tightening at the corners of her mouth, as if she was about to recoil from this golem. Then the child began to bawl and kick, and Francine started weeping with undisguised joy.

As she raised the child to her face and planted a kiss on its wrinkled forehead, I suffered my own moment of disquiet. How easily that tender response had been summoned, when the body could as well have been brought to life by the kind of software used to animate the characters in games and films.

It hadn't, though. There'd been nothing false or easy about the road that had brought us to this moment—let alone the one that Isabelle had followed—and we hadn't even tried to fashion life from clay, from nothing. We'd merely diverted one small trickle from a river already four billion years old.

Francine held our daughter against her shoulder, and rocked back and forth. "Have you got the bottle? Ben?" I walked to the kitchen in a daze; the microwave had anticipated the happy event, and the formula was ready.

I returned to the nursery and offered Francine the bottle. "Can I hold her, before you start feeding?"

"Of course." She leaned forward to kiss me, then held out the child, and I took her the way I'd learned to accept the babies of relatives and friends, cradling the back of her head beneath my hand. The distribution of weight, the heavy head, the play of the neck, felt the same as it did for any other infant. Her eyes were still screwed shut, as she screamed and swung her arms.

"What's your name, my beautiful girl?" We'd narrowed the list down to about a dozen possibilities, but Francine had refused to settle on one until she'd seen her daughter take her first breath. "Have you decided?"

"I want to call her Helen."

Gazing down at her, that sounded too old to me. Old-fashioned, at least. Great-Aunt Helen. Helena Bonham-Carter. I laughed inanely, and she opened her eyes.

Hairs rose on my arms. The dark eyes couldn't quite search my face, but she was not oblivious to me. Love and fear coursed through my veins. *How could I hope to give her what she needed?* Even if my judgment had been faultless, my power to act upon it was crude beyond measure.

We were all she had, though. We would make mistakes, we would lose our way, but I had to believe that something would hold fast. Some portion of the overwhelming love and resolve that I felt right now would have to remain with every version of me who could trace his ancestry to this moment.

I said, "I name you Helen."

2041

"Sophie! *Sophie!*" Helen ran ahead of us toward the arrivals gate, where Isabelle and Sophie were emerging. Sophie, almost sixteen now, was much less demonstrative, but she smiled and waved.

Francine said, "Do you ever think of moving?"

"Maybe if the laws change first in Europe," I replied.

"I saw a job in Zürich I could apply for."

"I don't think we should bend over backward to bring them together. They probably get on better with just occasional visits, and the net. It's not as if they don't have other friends."

Isabelle approached, and greeted us both with kisses on the cheek. I'd dreaded her arrival the first few times, but by now she seemed more like a slightly overbearing cousin than a child protection officer whose very presence implied misdeeds.

Sophie and Helen caught up with us. Helen tugged at Francine's sleeve. "Sophie's got a boyfriend! Daniel. She showed me his picture." She swooned mockingly, one hand on her forehead.

I glanced at Isabelle, who said, "He goes to her school. He's really very sweet."

Sophie grimaced with embarrassment. "Three-year-old *boys* are *sweet*." She turned to me and said, "Daniel is charming, and sophisticated, and *very* mature."

I felt as if an anvil had been dropped on my chest. As we crossed the car park, Francine whispered, "Don't have a heart attack yet. You've got a while to get used to the idea."

The waters of the bay sparkled in the sunlight as we drove across the bridge to Oakland. Isabelle described the latest session of the European parliamentary committee into adai rights. A draft proposal granting personhood to any system containing and acting upon a significant amount of the information content of human DNA had been gaining support; it was a tricky concept to define rigorously, but most of the objections were Pythonesque rather than practical. "Is the Human Proteomic Database a person? Is the Harvard Reference Physiological Simulation a person?" The HRPS modeled the brain solely in terms of what it removed from, and released into, the bloodstream; there was nobody home inside the simulation, quietly going mad.

Late in the evening, when the girls were upstairs, Isabelle began gently grilling us. I tried not to grit my teeth too much. I certainly didn't blame her for taking her responsibilities seriously; if, in spite of the selection process, we had turned out to be monsters, criminal law would have offered no remedies. Our obligations under the licensing contract were Helen's sole guarantee of humane treatment.

"She's getting good marks this year," Isabelle noted. "She must be settling in."

"She is," Francine replied. Helen was not entitled to a government-funded education, and most private schools had either been openly hostile, or had come up with such excuses as insurance policies that would have classified her as hazardous machinery. (Isabelle had reached a compromise with the airlines: Sophie had to be powered down, appearing to sleep during flights, but was not required to be shackled or stowed in the cargo hold.) The first community school we'd tried had not worked out, but we'd eventually found one close to the Berkeley campus where every parent involved was happy with the idea of Helen's presence. This had saved her from the prospect of joining a net-based school; they weren't so bad, but they were intended for children isolated by geography or illness, circumstances that could not be overcome by other means.

Isabelle bid us good night with no complaints or advice; Francine and I sat by the fire for a while, just smiling at each other. It was nice to have a blemish-free report for once.

The next morning, my alarm went off an hour early. I lay motionless for a while, waiting for my head to clear, before asking my knowledge miner why it had woken me.

It seemed Isabelle's visit had been beaten up into a major story in some east coast news bulletins. A number of vocal members of Congress had been following the debate in Europe, and they didn't like the way it was heading. Isabelle, they declared, had sneaked into the country as an agitator. In fact, she'd offered to testify to Congress any time they wanted to hear about her work, but they'd never taken her up on it.

It wasn't clear whether it was reporters or anti-adai activists who'd obtained her itinerary and done some digging, but all the details had now been splashed around the country, and protesters were already gathering outside Helen's school. We'd faced media packs, cranks, and activists before, but the images the knowledge miner showed me were disturbing; it was five a.m. and the crowd had already encircled the school. I had a flashback to some news footage I'd seen in my teens, of young schoolgirls in Northern Ireland running the gauntlet of a protest by the opposing political faction; I could no longer remember who had been Catholic and who had been Protestant.

I woke Francine and explained the situation.

"We could just keep her home," I suggested.

Francine looked torn, but she finally agreed. "It will probably all blow over when Isabelle flies out on Sunday. One day off school isn't exactly capitulating to the mob."

At breakfast, I broke the news to Helen.

"I'm not staying home," she said.

"Why not? Don't you want to hang out with Sophie?"

Helen was amused. "'Hang out'? Is that what the hippies used to say?" In her personal chronology of San Francisco, anything from before her birth belonged to the world portrayed in the tourist museums of Haight-Ashbury.

"Gossip. Listen to music. Interact socially in whatever manner you find agreeable."

She contemplated this last, open-ended definition. "Shop?"

"I don't see why not." There was no crowd outside the house, and though we were probably being watched, the protest was too large to be a moveable feast. Perhaps all the other parents would keep their children home, leaving the various placard wavers to fight among themselves.

Helen reconsidered. "No. We're doing that on Saturday. I want to go to school."

I glanced at Francine. Helen added, "It's not as if they can hurt me. I'm backed up."

Francine said, "It's not pleasant being shouted at. Insulted. Pushed around."

"I don't think it's going to be *pleasant*," Helen replied scornfully. "But I'm not going to let them tell me what to do."

To date, a handful of strangers had got close enough to yell abuse at her, and some of the children at her first school had been about as violent as (ordinary, drug-free, non-psychotic) nine-year-old bullies could be, but she'd never faced anything like this. I showed her the live news feed. She was not swayed. Francine and I retreated to the living room to confer.

I said, "I don't think it's a good idea." On top of everything else, I was beginning to suffer from a paranoid fear that Isabelle would blame us for the whole situation. Less fancifully, she could easily disapprove of us exposing Helen to the protesters. Even if that was not enough for her to terminate the license immediately, eroding her confidence in us could lead to that fate, eventually.

Francine thought for a while. "If we both go with her, both walk beside her, what are they going to do? If they lay a finger on us, it's assault. If they try to drag her away from us, it's theft."

"Yes, but whatever they do, she gets to hear all the poison they spew out."

"She watches the news, Ben. She's heard it all before."

"Oh, shit." Isabelle and Sophie had come down to breakfast; I could hear Helen calmly filling them in about her plans.

Francine said, "Forget about pleasing Isabelle. If Helen wants to do this, knowing what it entails, and we can keep her safe, then we should respect her decision."

I felt a sting of anger at the unspoken implication: having gone to such lengths to enable her to make meaningful choices, I'd be a hypocrite to stand in her way. *Knowing what it entails?* She was nine-and-a-half years old.

I admired her courage, though, and I did believe that we could protect her.

I said, "All right. You call the other parents. I'll inform the police."

THE MOMENT WE LEFT the car, we were spotted. Shouts rang out, and a tide of angry people flowed toward us.

I glanced down at Helen and tightened my grip on her. "Don't let go of our hands."

She smiled at me indulgently, as if I was warning her about something trivial, like broken glass on the beach. "I'll be all right, Dad." She flinched as the crowd closed in, and then there were bodies pushing against us from every side, people jabbering in our faces, spittle flying. Francine and I turned to face each other, making something of a protective cage and a wedge through the adult legs. Frightening as it was to be submerged, I was glad my daughter wasn't at eye level with these people.

"Satan moves her! Satan is inside her! Out, Jezebel spirit!" A young woman in a high-collared lilac dress pressed her body against me and started praying in tongues.

"Gödel's theorem proves that the non-computable, non-linear world behind the quantum collapse is a manifest expression of Buddha-nature," a neatly-dressed youth intoned earnestly, establishing with admirable economy that he had no idea what any of these terms meant. "Ergo, there can be no soul in the machine."

"Cyber nano quantum. Cyber nano quantum. Cyber nano quantum." That chant came from one of our would-be "supporters", a middle-aged man in lycra cycling shorts who was forcefully groping down between us, trying to lay his hand on Helen's head and leave a few flakes of dead skin behind; according to cult doctrine, this would enable her to resurrect him when she got around to establishing the Omega Point. I blocked his way as firmly as I could without actually assaulting him, and he wailed like a pilgrim denied admission to Lourdes.

"Think you're going to live forever, Tinker Bell?" A leering old man with a matted beard poked his head out in front of us, and spat straight into Helen's face.

"Arsehole!" Francine shouted. She pulled out a handkerchief and started mopping the phlegm away. I crouched down and stretched my free arm around them. Helen was grimacing with disgust as Francine dabbed at her, but she wasn't crying.

I said, "Do you want to go back to the car?"

"*No.*"

"Are you sure?"

Helen screwed up her face in an expression of irritation. "Why do you always ask me that? *Am I sure? Am I sure?* You're the one who sounds like a computer."

"I'm sorry." I squeezed her hand.

We plowed on through the crowd. The core of the protesters turned out to be both saner and more civilized than the lunatics who'd got to us first; as we neared the school gates, people struggled to make room to let us through uninjured, at the same time as they shouted slogans for the cameras. "Healthcare for all, not just the rich!" I couldn't argue with that sentiment, though adai were just one of a thousand ways the wealthy could spare their children from disease, and in fact they were among the cheapest: the total cost in prosthetic bodies up to adult size came to less than the median lifetime expenditure on healthcare in the U.S. Banning adai wouldn't end the disparity between rich and poor, but I could understand why some people considered it the ultimate act of selfishness to create a child who could live forever. They probably never wondered about the fertility rates and resource use of their own descendants over the next few thousand years.

We passed through the gates, into a world of space and silence; any protester who trespassed here could be arrested immediately, and apparently none of them were sufficiently dedicated to Gandhian principles to seek out that fate.

Inside the entrance hall, I squatted down and put my arms around Helen. "Are you okay?"

"Yes."

"I'm really proud of you."

"You're shaking." She was right; my whole body was trembling slightly. It was more than the crush and the confrontation, and the sense of relief that we'd come through unscathed. Relief was never absolute for me; I could never quite erase the images of other possibilities at the back of my mind.

One of the teachers, Carmela Peña, approached us, looking stoical; when they'd agreed to take Helen, all the staff and parents had known that a day like this would come.

Helen said, "I'll be okay now." She kissed me on the cheek, then did the same to Francine. "I'm all right," she insisted. "You can go."

Carmela said, "We've got sixty per cent of the kids coming. Not bad, considering."

Helen walked down the corridor, turning once to wave at us impatiently.

I said, "No, not bad."

A GROUP OF JOURNALISTS cornered the five of us during the girls' shopping trip the next day, but media organizations had grown wary of lawsuits, and after Isabelle reminded them that she was presently enjoying "the ordinary liberties of every private citizen"—a quote from a recent eight-figure judgment against *Celebrity Stalker*—they left us in peace.

The night after Isabelle and Sophie flew out, I went in to Helen's room to kiss her good night. As I turned to leave, she said, "What's a Qusp?"

"It's a kind of computer. Where did you hear about that?"

"On the net. It said I had a Qusp, but Sophie didn't."

Francine and I had made no firm decision as to what we'd tell her, and when. I said, "That's right, but it's nothing to worry about. It just means you're a little bit different from her."

Helen scowled. "I don't want to be different from Sophie."

"Everyone's different from everyone else," I said glibly. "Having a Qusp is just like . . . a car having a different kind of engine. It can still go to all the same places." *Just not all of them at once.* "You can both still do whatever you like. You can be as much like Sophie as you want." That wasn't entirely dishonest; the crucial difference could always be erased, simply by disabling the Qusp's shielding.

"I want to be the same," Helen insisted. "Next time I grow, why can't you give me what Sophie's got, instead?"

"What you have is newer. It's better."

"No one else has got it. Not just Sophie; none of the others." Helen knew she'd nailed me: if it was newer and better, why didn't the younger adai have it too?

I said, "It's complicated. You'd better go to sleep now; we'll talk about it later." I fussed with the blankets, and she stared at me resentfully.

I went downstairs and recounted the conversation to Francine. "What do you think?" I asked her. "Is it time?"

"Maybe it is," she said.

"I wanted to wait until she was old enough to understand the MWI."

Francine considered this. "Understand it how well, though? She's not going to be juggling density matrices any time soon. And if we make it a big secret, she's just going to get half-baked versions from other sources."

I flopped onto the couch. "This is going to be hard." I'd rehearsed the moment a thousand times, but in my imagination Helen had always been older, and there'd been hundreds of other adai with Qusps. In reality, no one had followed the trail we'd blazed. The evidence for the MWI had grown steadily stronger, but for most people it was still easy to ignore. Ever more sophisticated versions of rats running mazes just looked like elaborate computer games. You couldn't travel from branch to branch yourself, you couldn't spy on your parallel alter egos—and such feats would probably never be possible. "How do you tell a nine-year-old girl that she's the only sentient being on the planet who can make a decision, and stick to it?"

Francine smiled. "Not in those words, for a start."

"No." I put my arm around her. We were about to enter a minefield—and we couldn't help diffusing out across the perilous ground—but at least we had each other's judgment to keep us in check, to rein us in a little.

I said, "We'll work it out. We'll find the right way."

2050

AROUND FOUR IN THE morning, I gave in to the cravings and lit my first cigarette in a month.

As I drew the warm smoke into my lungs, my teeth started chattering, as if the contrast had forced me to notice how cold the rest of my body had become. The red glow of the tip was the brightest thing in sight, but if there was a camera trained on me it would be infrared, so I'd been blazing away like a bonfire, anyway. As the smoke came back up I spluttered like a cat choking on a fur ball; the first one was always like that. I'd taken up the habit at the surreal age of sixty, and even after five years on and off, my respiratory tract couldn't quite believe its bad luck.

For five hours, I'd been crouched in the mud at the edge of Lake Pontchartrain, a couple of kilometers west of the soggy ruins of New Orleans. Watching the barge, waiting for someone to come home. I'd been tempted to swim out and take a look around, but my aide sketched a bright red moat of domestic radar on the surface of the water, and offered no guarantee that I'd remain undetected even if I stayed outside the perimeter.

I'd called Francine the night before. It had been a short, tense conversation.

"I'm in Louisiana. I think I've got a lead."

"Yeah?"

"I'll let you know how it turns out."

"You do that."

I hadn't seen her in the flesh for almost two years. After facing too many dead ends together, we'd split up to cover more ground: Francine had searched from New York to Seattle; I'd taken the south. As the months had slipped away, her determination to put every emotional reaction aside for the sake of the task had gradually eroded. One night, I was sure, grief had overtaken her, alone in some soulless motel room—and it made no difference that the same thing had happened to me, a months later or a week before. Because we had not experienced it together, it was not a shared pain, a burden made lighter. After forty-seven years, though we now had a single purpose as never before, we were starting to come adrift.

I'd learned about Jake Holder in Baton Rouge, triangulating on rumors and fifth-hand reports of bar-room boasts. The boasts were usually empty; a prosthetic body equipped with software dumber than a microwave could make an infinitely pliable slave, but if the only way to salvage any trace of dignity when your buddies discovered that you owned the high-tech equivalent of a blow-up doll was to imply that there was somebody home inside, apparently a lot of men leaped at the chance.

Holder looked like something worse. I'd bought his lifetime purchasing records, and there'd been a steady stream of cyber-fetish porn over a period of two decades. Hardcore and pretentious; half the titles contained the word "manifesto". But the flow had stopped, about three months ago. The rumors were, he'd found something better.

I finished the cigarette, and slapped my arms to get the circulation going. *She would not be on the barge.* For all I knew, she'd heard the news from Brussels and was already halfway to Europe. That would be a difficult journey to make on her own, but there was no reason to believe that she didn't have loyal, trustworthy friends to assist her. I had too many out-of-date memories burned into my skull: all the blazing, pointless rows, all the petty crimes, all the self-mutilation. Whatever had happened, whatever she'd been through, she was no longer the angry fifteen-year-old who'd left for school one Friday and never come back.

By the time she'd hit thirteen, we were arguing about everything. Her body had no need for the hormonal flood of puberty, but the software had ground on relentlessly, simulating all the neuroendocrine effects. Sometimes it had seemed like an act of torture to put her through that—instead of hunting for some magic short-cut to maturity—but the cardinal rule had been never to tinker, never to intervene, just to aim for the most faithful simulation possible of ordinary human development.

Whatever we'd fought about, she'd always known how to shut me up. "I'm just a thing to you! An instrument! Daddy's little silver bullet!" I didn't care who she was, or what she wanted; I'd fashioned her solely to slay my own fears. (I'd lie awake afterward, rehearsing lame counter-arguments. Other children were born for infinitely baser motives: to work the fields, to sit in boardrooms, to banish ennui, to save failing marriages.) In her eyes, the Qusp itself wasn't good or bad—and she turned down all my offers to disable the shielding; that would have let me off the hook too easily. But I'd made her a freak for my own selfish reasons; I'd set her apart even from the other adai, purely to grant myself a certain kind of comfort. "You wanted to give birth to a singleton? Why didn't you just shoot yourself in the head every time you made a bad decision?"

When she went missing, we were afraid she'd been snatched from the street. But in her room, we'd found an envelope with the locator beacon she'd dug out of her body, and a note that read: *Don't look for me. I'm never coming back.*

I heard the tires of a heavy vehicle squelching along the muddy track to my left. I hunkered lower, making sure I was hidden in the undergrowth. As the truck came to a halt with a faint metallic shudder, the barge disgorged an unmanned motorboat. My aide had captured the data streams exchanged, one specific challenge and response, but it had no clue how to crack the general case and mimic the barge's owner.

Two men climbed out of the truck. One was Jake Holder; I couldn't make out his face in the starlight, but I'd sat within a few meters of him in diners and bars in Baton Rouge, and my aide knew his somatic signature: the electromagnetic radiation from his nervous system and implants; his body's capacitative and inductive responses to small shifts in the ambient fields; the faint gamma-ray spectrum of his unavoidable, idiosyncratic load of radioisotopes, natural and Chernobylesque.

I did not know who his companion was, but I soon got the general idea.

"One thousand now," Holder said. "One thousand when you get back." His silhouette gestured at the waiting motorboat.

The other man was suspicious. "How do I know it will be what you say it is?"

"Don't call her 'it'," Holder complained. "She's not an object. She's my Lilith, my Lo-li-ta, my luscious clockwork succubus." For one hopeful moment, I pictured the customer snickering at this over-heated sales pitch and coming to his senses; brothels in Baton Rouge openly advertised machine sex, with skilled human puppeteers, for a fraction of the price. Whatever he imagined the special thrill of a genuine adai to be, he had no way of knowing that Holder didn't have an accomplice controlling the body on the barge in exactly the same fashion. He might even be paying two thousand dollars for a puppet job from Holder himself.

"Okay. But if she's not genuine . . ."

My aide overheard money changing hands, and it had modeled the situation well enough to know how I'd wish, always, to respond. "Move now," it whispered in my ear. I complied without hesitation; eighteen months before, I'd pavloved myself into swift obedience, with all the pain and nausea modern chemistry could induce. The aide couldn't puppet my limbs—I couldn't afford the elaborate sur-gery—but it overlaid movement cues on my vision, a system I'd adapted from off-the-shelf choreography software, and I strode out of the bushes, right up to the motorboat.

The customer was outraged. "What is this?"

I turned to Holder. "You want to fuck him first, Jake? I'll hold him down." There were things I didn't trust the aide to control; it set the boundaries, but it was better to let me improvise a little, and then treat my actions as one more part of the environment.

After a moment of stunned silence, Holder said icily, "I've never seen this prick before in my life." He'd been speechless for a little too long, though, to inspire any loyalty from a stranger; as he reached for his weapon, the customer backed away, then turned and fled.

Holder walked toward me slowly, gun outstretched. "What's your game? Are you after her? Is that it?" His implants were map-ping my body—actively, since there was no need for stealth—but I'd tailed him for hours in Baton Rouge, and my aide knew him like an architectural plan. Over the starlit gray of his form, it overlaid a schematic, flaying him down to brain, nerves, and implants. A swarm of blue fireflies flickered into life in his motor cortex, prefiguring a peculiar shrug of the shoulders with no obvious connection to his trigger finger; before they'd reached the intensity that would signal his implants to radio the gun, my aide said "Duck."

The shot was silent, but as I straightened up again I could smell the propellant. I gave up thinking and followed the dance steps. As Holder strode forward and swung the gun toward me, I turned sideways, grabbed his right hand, then punched him hard, repeatedly, in the implant on the side of his neck. He was a fetishist, so he'd chosen bulky packages, intentionally visible through the skin. They were not hard-edged, and they were not inflexible—he wasn't that masochistic—but once you sufficiently compressed even the softest biocompatible foam, it might as well have been a lump of wood. While I hammered the wood into the muscles of his neck, I twisted his forearm upward. He dropped the gun; I put my foot on it and slid it back toward the bushes.

In ultrasound, I saw blood pooling around his implant. I paused while the pressure built up, then I hit him again and the swelling burst like a giant blister. He sagged to his knees, bellowing with pain. I took the knife from my back pocket and held it to his throat.

I made Holder take off his belt, and I used it to bind his hands behind his back. I led him to the motorboat, and when the two of us were on board, I suggested that he give it the necessary instructions. He was sullen but cooperative. I didn't feel anything; part of me still insisted that the transaction I'd caught him in was a hoax, and that there'd be nothing on the barge that couldn't be found in Baton Rouge.

The barge was old, wooden, smelling of preservatives and unvanquished rot. There were dirty plastic panes in the cabin windows, but all I could see in them was a reflected sheen. As we crossed the deck, I kept Holder intimately close, hoping that if there was an armed security system it wouldn't risk putting the bullet through both of us.

At the cabin door, he said resignedly, "Don't treat her badly." My blood went cold, and I pressed my forearm to my mouth to stifle an involuntary sob.

I kicked open the door, and saw nothing but shadows. I called out "Lights!" and two responded, in the ceiling and by the bed. Helen was naked, chained by the wrists and ankles. She looked up and saw me, then began to emit a horrified keening noise.

I pressed the blade against Holder's throat. "Open those things!"

"The shackles?"

"Yes!"

"I can't. They're not smart; they're just welded shut."

"Where are your tools?"

He hesitated. "I've got some wrenches in the truck. All the rest is back in town."

I looked around the cabin, then I led him into a corner and told him to stand there, facing the wall. I knelt by the bed.

"Ssh. We'll get you out of here." Helen fell silent. I touched her cheek with the back of my hand; she didn't flinch, but she stared back at me, disbelieving. "We'll get you out." The timber bedposts were thicker than my arms, the links of the chains wide as my thumb. I wasn't going to snap any part of this with my bare hands.

Helen's expression changed: I was real, she was not hallucinating. She said dully, "I thought you'd given up on me. Woke one of the backups. Started again."

I said, "I'd never give up on you."

"Are you sure?" She searched my face. "Is this the edge of what's possible? Is this the worst it can get?"

I didn't have an answer to that.

I said, "You remember how to go numb, for a shedding?"

She gave me a faint, triumphant smile. "Absolutely." She'd had to endure imprisonment and humiliation, but she'd always had the power to cut herself off from her body's senses.

"Do you want to do it now? Leave all this behind?"

"Yes."

"You'll be safe soon. I promise you."

"I believe you." Her eyes rolled up.

I cut open her chest and took out the Qusp.

FRANCINE AND I HAD both carried spare bodies, and clothes, in the trunks of our cars. Adai were banned from domestic flights, so Helen and I drove along the interstate, up toward Washington D.C., where Francine would meet us. We could claim asylum at the Swiss embassy; Isabelle had already set the machinery in motion.

Helen was quiet at first, almost shy with me as if with a stranger, but on the second day, as we crossed from Alabama into Georgia, she began to open up. She told me a little of how she'd hitchhiked from state to state, finding casual jobs that paid e-cash and needed no social security number, let alone biometric ID. "Fruit picking was the best."

She'd made friends along the way, and confided her nature to those she thought she could trust. She still wasn't sure whether or not she'd been betrayed. Holder had found her in a transients' camp under a bridge, and someone must have told him exactly where to look, but it was always possible that she'd been recognized by a casual acquaintance who'd seen her face in the media years before. Francine and I had never publicized her disappearance, never put up flyers or web pages, out of fear that it would only make the danger worse.

On the third day, as we crossed the Carolinas, we drove in near silence again. The landscape was stunning, the fields strewn with flowers, and Helen seemed calm. Maybe this was what she needed the most: just safety, and peace.

As dusk approached, though, I felt I had to speak.

"There's something I've never told you," I said. "Something that happened to me when I was young."

Helen smiled. "Don't tell me you ran away from the farm? Got tired of milking, and joined the circus?"

I shook my head. "I was never adventurous. It was just a little thing." I told her about the kitchen hand.

She pondered the story for a while. "And that's why you built the Qusp? That's why you made me? In the end, it all comes down to that man in the alley?" She sounded more bewildered than angry.

I bowed my head. "I'm sorry."

"For what?" she demanded. "Are you sorry that I was ever born?"

"No, but—"

"You didn't put me on that boat. Holder did that."

I said, "I brought you into a world with people like him. What I made you, made you a target."

"And if I'd been flesh and blood?" she said. "Do you think there aren't people like him, for flesh and blood? Or do you honestly believe that if you'd had an organic child, there would have been *no chance at all* that she'd have run away?"

I started weeping. "I don't know. I'm just sorry I hurt you."

Helen said, "I don't blame you for what you did. And I understand it better now. You saw a spark of good in yourself, and you wanted to cup your hands around it, protect it, make it stronger. I understand that. I'm not that spark, but that doesn't matter. I know who I am, I know what my choices are, and I'm glad of that. I'm glad you gave me that." She reached over and squeezed my hand. "Do you think I'd feel *better*, here and now, just because some other version of me handled the same situations better?" She smiled. "Knowing that other people are having a good time isn't much of a consolation to anyone."

I composed myself. The car beeped to bring my attention to a booking it had made in a motel a few kilometers ahead.

Helen said, "I've had time to think about a lot of things. Whatever the laws say, whatever the bigots say, all adai are part of the human race. And what *I* have is something almost every person who's ever lived thought they possessed. Human psychology, human culture, human morality, all evolved with the illusion that we lived in a single history. But we don't—so in the long run, something has to give. Call me old-fashioned, but I'd rather we tinker with our physical nature than abandon our whole identities."

I was silent for a while. "So what are your plans, now?"

"I need an education."

"What do you want to study?"

"I'm not sure yet. A million different things. But in the long run, I know what I want to do."

"Yeah?" The car turned off the highway, heading for the motel.

"You made a start," she said, "but it's not enough. There are people in billions of other branches where the Qusp hasn't been invented yet—and the way things stand, there'll always be branches without it. What's the point in us having this thing, if we don't share it? All those people deserve to have the power to make their own choices."

"Travel between the branches isn't a simple problem," I explained gently. "That would be orders of magnitude harder than the Qusp."

Helen smiled, conceding this, but the corners of her mouth took on the stubborn set I recognized as the precursor to a thousand smaller victories.

She said, "Give me time, Dad. Give me time."

DARK INTEGERS

"Good morning, Bruno. How is the weather there in Sparse-land?"

The screen icon for my interlocutor was a three-holed torus tiled with triangles, endlessly turning itself inside out. The polished tones of the male synthetic voice I heard conveyed no specific origin, but gave a sense nonetheless that the speaker's first language was something other than English.

I glanced out the window of my home office, taking in a patch of blue sky and the verdant gardens of a shady West Ryde cul-de-sac. Sam used "good morning" regardless of the hour, but it really was just after ten a.m., and the tranquil Sydney suburb was awash in sunshine and birdsong.

"Perfect," I replied. "I wish I wasn't chained to this desk."

There was a long pause, and I wondered if the translator had mangled the idiom, creating the impression that I had been shackled by ruthless assailants, who had nonetheless left me with easy access to my instant messaging program. Then Sam said, "I'm glad you didn't go for a run today. I've already tried Alison and Yuen, and they were both unavailable. If I hadn't been able to get through to you, it might have been difficult to keep some of my colleagues in check."

I felt a surge of anxiety, mixed with resentment. I refused to wear an iWatch, to make myself reachable twenty-four hours a day. I was a mathematician, not an obstetrician. Perhaps I was an amateur diplomat as well, but even if Alison, Yuen and I didn't quite cover the time zones, it would never be more than a few hours before Sam could get hold of at least one of us.

"I didn't realize you were surrounded by hot-heads," I replied. "What's the great emergency?" I hoped the translator would do justice to the sharpness in my voice. Sam's colleagues were the ones with all the firepower, all the resources; they should not have been jumping at shadows. True, we had once tried to wipe them out, but that had been a perfectly innocent mistake, more than ten years before.

Sam said, "Someone from your side seems to have jumped the border."

"*Jumped* it?"

"As far as we can see, there's no trench cutting through it. But a few hours ago, a cluster of propositions on our side started obeying your axioms."

I was stunned. "An isolated cluster? With no derivation leading back to us?"

"None that we could find."

I thought for a while. "Maybe it was a natural event. A brief surge across the border from the background noise that left a kind of tidal pool behind."

Sam was dismissive. "The cluster was too big for that. The probability would be vanishingly small." Numbers came through on the data channel; he was right.

I rubbed my eyelids with my fingertips; I suddenly felt very tired. I'd thought our old nemesis, Industrial Algebra, had given up the chase long ago. They had stopped offering bribes and sending mercenaries to harass me, so I'd assumed they'd finally written off the defect as a hoax or a mirage, and gone back to their core business of helping the world's military kill and maim people in ever more technologically sophisticated ways.

Maybe this wasn't IA. Alison and I had first located the defect—a set of contradictory results in arithmetic that marked the border between our mathematics and the version underlying Sam's world—by means of a vast set of calculations farmed out over the internet, with thousands of volunteers donating their computers' processing power when the machines would otherwise have been idle. When we'd pulled the plug on that project—keeping our discovery secret, lest IA find a way to weaponize it—a few participants had been resentful, and had talked about continuing the search. It would have been easy enough for them to write their own software, adapting the same open source framework that Alison and I had used, but it was difficult to see how they could have gathered enough supporters without launching some kind of public appeal.

I said, "I can't offer you an immediate explanation for this. All I can do is promise to investigate."

"I understand," Sam replied.

"You have no clues, yourself?" A decade before, in Shanghai, when Alison, Yuen and I had used the supercomputer called Luminous to mount a sustained attack on the defect, the mathematicians of the far side had grasped the details of our unwitting assault clearly enough to send a plume of alternative mathematics back across the border with pinpoint precision, striking at just the three of us.

Sam said, "If the cluster had been connected to something, we could have followed the trail. But in isolation it tells us nothing. That's why my colleagues are so anxious."

"Yeah." I was still hoping that the whole thing might turn out to be a glitch—the mathematical equivalent of a flock of birds with a radar echo that just happened to look like something more sinister—but the full gravity of the situation was finally dawning on me.

The inhabitants of the far side were as peaceable as anyone might reasonably wish their neighbors to be, but if their mathematical infrastructure came under threat they faced the real prospect of annihilation. They had defended themselves from such a threat once before, but because they had been able to trace it to its source and understand its nature, they had shown great forbearance. They had not struck their assailants dead, or wiped out Shanghai, or pulled the ground out from under our universe.

This new assault had not been sustained, but nobody knew its origins, or what it might portend. I believed that our neighbors would do no more than they had to in order to ensure their survival, but if they were forced to strike back blindly, they might find themselves with no path to safety short of turning our world to dust.

SHANGHAI TIME WAS ONLY two hours behind Sydney, but Yuen's IM status was still "unavailable". I emailed him, along with Alison, though it was the middle of the night in Zürich and she was unlikely to be awake for another four or five hours. All of us had programs that connected us to Sam by monitoring, and modifying, small portions of the defect: altering a handful of precariously balanced truths of arithmetic, wiggling the border between the two systems back and forth to encode each transmitted bit. The three of us on the near side might have communicated with each other in the same way, but on consideration we'd decided that conventional cryptography was a safer way to conceal our secret. The mere fact that communications data seemed to come from nowhere had the potential to attract suspicion, so we'd gone as far as to write software to send fake packets across the net to cover for our otherwise inexplicable conversations with Sam; anyone but the most diligent and resourceful of eavesdroppers would conclude that he was addressing us from an internet café in Lithuania.

While I was waiting for Yuen to reply, I scoured the logs where my knowledge miner deposited results of marginal relevance, wondering if some flaw in the criteria I'd given it might have left me with a blind spot. If anyone, anywhere had announced their intention to carry out some kind of calculation that might have led them to the defect, the news should have been plastered across my desktop in flashing red letters within seconds. Granted, most organizations with the necessary computing resources were secretive by nature, but they were also unlikely to be motivated to indulge in such a crazy stunt. Luminous itself had been decommissioned in 2012; in principle, various national security agencies, and even a few IT-centric businesses, now had enough silicon to hunt down the defect if they'd really set their sights on it, but as far as I knew Yuen, Alison and I were still the only three people in the world who were certain of its existence. The black budgets of even the most profligate governments, the deep pockets of even the richest tycoons, would not stretch far enough to take on the search as a long shot, or an act of whimsy.

An IM window popped up with Alison's face. She looked ragged. "What time is it there?" I asked.

"Early. Laura's got colic."

"Ah. Are you okay to talk?"

"Yeah, she's asleep now."

My email had been brief, so I filled her in on the details. She pondered the matter in silence for a while, yawning unashamedly.

"The only thing I can think of is some gossip I heard at a conference in Rome a couple of months ago. It was a fourth-hand story about some guy in New Zealand who thinks he's found a way to test fundamental laws of physics by doing computations in number theory."

"Just random crackpot stuff, or . . . what?"

Alison massaged her temples, as if trying to get more blood flowing to her brain. "I don't know, what I heard was too vague to make a judgment. I gather he hasn't tried to publish this anywhere, or even mentioned it in blogs. I guess he just confided in a few people directly, one of whom must have found it too amusing for them to keep their mouth shut."

"Have you got a name?"

She went off camera and rummaged for a while. "Tim Campbell," she announced. Her notes came through on the data channel. "He's done respectable work in combinatorics, algorithmic complexity, optimization. I scoured the net, and there was no mention of this weird stuff. I was meaning to email him, but I never got around to it."

I could understand why; that would have been about the time Laura was born. I said, "I'm glad you still go to so many conferences in the flesh. It's easier in Europe, everything's so close."

"Ha! Don't count on it continuing, Bruno. You might have to put your fat arse on a plane sometime yourself."

"What about Yuen?"

Alison frowned. "Didn't I tell you? He's been in hospital for a couple of days. Pneumonia. I spoke to his daughter, he's not in great shape."

"I'm sorry." Alison was much closer to him than I was; he'd been her doctoral supervisor, so she'd known him long before the events that had bound the three of us together.

Yuen was almost eighty. That wasn't yet ancient for a middle-class Chinese man who could afford good medical care, but he would not be around forever.

I said, "Are we crazy, trying to do this ourselves?" She knew what I meant: liaising with Sam, managing the border, trying to keep the two worlds talking but the two sides separate, safe and intact.

Alison replied, "Which government would you trust not to screw this up? Not to try to exploit it?"

"None. But what's the alternative? You pass the job on to Laura? Kate's not interested in having kids. So do I pick some young mathematician at random to anoint as my successor?"

"Not at random, I'd hope."

"You want me to advertise? 'Must be proficient in number theory, familiar with Machiavelli, and own the complete boxed set of *The West Wing*?'"

She shrugged. "When the time comes, find someone competent you can trust. It's a balance: the fewer people who know, the better, so long as there are always enough of us that the knowledge doesn't risk getting lost completely."

"And this goes on generation after generation? Like some secret society? The Knights of the Arithmetic Inconsistency?"

"I'll work on the crest."

We needed a better plan, but this wasn't the time to argue about it. I said, "I'll contact this guy Campbell and let you know how it goes."

"Okay. Good luck." Her eyelids were starting to droop.

"Take care of yourself."

Alison managed an exhausted smile. "Are you saying that because you give a damn, or because you don't want to end up guarding the Grail all by yourself?"

"Both, of course."

"I HAVE TO FLY to Wellington tomorrow."

Kate put down the pasta-laden fork she'd raised halfway to her lips and gave me a puzzled frown. "That's short notice."

"Yeah, it's a pain. It's for the Bank of New Zealand. I have to do something on-site with a secure machine, one they won't let anyone access over the net."

Her frown deepened. "When will you be back?"

"I'm not sure. It might not be until Monday. I can probably do most of the work tomorrow, but there are certain things they restrict to the weekends, when the branches are off-line. I don't know if it will come to that."

I hated lying to her, but I'd grown accustomed to it. When we'd met, just a year after Shanghai, I could still feel the scar on my arm where one of Industrial Algebra's hired thugs had tried to carve a data cache out of my body. At some point, as our relationship deepened, I'd made up my mind that however close we became, however much I trusted her, it would be safer for Kate if she never knew anything about the defect.

"They can't hire someone local?" she suggested. I didn't think she was suspicious, but she was definitely annoyed. She worked long hours at the hospital, and she only had every second weekend off; this would be one of them. We'd made no specific plans, but it was part of our routine to spend this time together.

I said, "I'm sure they could, but it'd be hard to find someone at short notice. And I can't tell them to shove it, or I'll lose the whole contract. It's one weekend, it's not the end of the world."

"No, it's not the end of the world." She finally lifted her fork again.

"Is the sauce okay?"

"It's delicious, Bruno." Her tone made it clear that no amount of culinary effort would have been enough to compensate, so I might as well not have bothered.

I watched her eat with a strange knot growing in my stomach. Was this how spies felt, when they lied to their families about their work? But my own secret sounded more like something from a psychiatric ward. I was entrusted with the smooth operation of a treaty that I, and two friends, had struck with an invisible ghost world that coexisted with our own. The ghost world was far from hostile, but the treaty was the most important in human history, because either side had the power to annihilate the other so thoroughly that it would make a nuclear holocaust seem like a pin-prick.

VICTORIA UNIVERSITY WAS IN a hilltop suburb overlooking Wellington. I caught a cable car, and arrived just in time for the Friday afternoon seminar. Contriving an invitation to deliver a paper here myself would have been difficult, but wangling permission to sit in as part of the audience was easy; although I hadn't been an academic for almost twenty years, my ancient PhD and a trickle of publications, however tenuously related to the topic of the seminar, were still enough to make me welcome.

I'd taken a gamble that Campbell would attend—the topic was peripheral to his own research, official or otherwise—so I was relieved to spot him in the audience, recognizing him from a photo on the faculty web site. I'd emailed him straight after I'd spoken to Alison, but his reply had been a polite brush-off: he acknowledged that the work I'd heard about on the grapevine owed something to the infamous search that Alison and I had launched, but he wasn't ready to make his own approach public.

I sat through an hour on "Monoids and Control Theory", trying to pay enough attention that I wouldn't make a fool of myself if the seminar organizer quizzed me later on why I'd been sufficiently attracted to the topic to interrupt my "sightseeing holiday" in order to attend. When the seminar ended, the audience split into two streams: one heading out of the building, the other moving into an adjoining room where refreshments were on offer. I saw Campbell making for the open air, and it was all I could do to contrive to get close enough to call out to him without making a spectacle.

"Dr Campbell?"

He turned and scanned the room, probably expecting to see one of his students wanting to beg for an extension on an assignment. I raised a hand and approached him.

"Bruno Costanzo. I emailed you yesterday."

"Of course." Campbell was a thin, pale man in his early thirties. He shook my hand, but he was obviously taken aback. "You didn't mention that you were in Wellington."

I made a dismissive gesture. "I was going to, but then it seemed a bit presumptuous." I didn't spell it out, I just left him to conclude that I was as ambivalent about this whole inconsistency nonsense as he was.

If fate had brought us together, though, wouldn't it be absurd not to make the most of it?

"I was going to grab some of those famous scones," I said; the seminar announcement on the web had made big promises for them. "Are you busy?"

"Umm. Just paperwork. I suppose I can put it off."

As we made our way into the tea room, I waffled on airily about my holiday plans. I'd never actually been to New Zealand before, so I made it clear that most of my itinerary still lay in the future. Campbell was no more interested in the local geography and wildlife than I was; the more I enthused, the more distant his gaze became. Once it was apparent that he wasn't going to cross-examine me on the finer points of various hiking trails, I grabbed a buttered scone and switched subject abruptly.

"The thing is, I heard you'd devised a more efficient strategy for searching for a defect." I only just managed to stop myself from using the definite article; it was a while since I'd spoken about it as if it were still hypothetical. "You know the kind of computing power that Dr Tierney and I had to scrounge up?"

"Of course. I was just an undergraduate, but I heard about the search."

"Were you one of our volunteers?" I'd checked the records, and he wasn't listed, but people had had the option of registering anonymously.

"No. The idea didn't really grab me, at the time." As he spoke, he seemed more discomfited than the failure to donate his own resources twelve years ago really warranted. I was beginning to suspect that he'd actually been one of the people who'd found the whole tongue-in-cheek conjecture that Alison and I had put forward to be unforgivably foolish. We had never asked to be taken seriously—and we had even put prominent links to all the worthy biomedical computing projects on our web page, so that people knew there were far better ways to spend their spare megaflops—but nonetheless, some mathematical/philosophical stuffed shirts had spluttered with rage at the sheer impertinence and naïveté of our hypothesis. Before things turned serious, it was the entertainment value of that backlash that had made our efforts worthwhile.

"But now you've refined it somehow?" I prompted him, doing my best to let him see that I felt no resentment at the prospect of being outdone. In fact, the hypothesis itself had been Alison's, so even if there hadn't been more important things than my ego at stake, that really wasn't a factor. As for the search algorithm, I'd cobbled it together on a Sunday afternoon, as a joke, to call Alison's bluff. Instead, she'd called mine, and insisted that we release it to the world.

Campbell glanced around to see who was in earshot, but then perhaps it dawned on him that if the news of his ideas had already reached Sydney via Rome and Zürich, the battle to keep his reputation pristine in Wellington was probably lost.

He said, "What you and Dr Tierney suggested was that random processes in the early universe might have included proofs of mutually contradictory theorems about the integers, the idea being that no computation to expose the inconsistency had yet had time to occur. Is that a fair summary?"

"Sure."

"One problem I have with that is, I don't see how it could lead to an inconsistency that could be detected here and now. If the physical system A proved theorem A, and the physical system B proved theorem B, then you might have different regions of the universe obeying different axioms, but it's not as if there's some universal mathematics textbook hovering around outside spacetime, listing every theorem that's ever been proved, which our computers then consult in order to decide how to behave. The behavior of a classical system is determined by its own particular causal past. If we're the descendants of a patch of the universe that proved theorem A, our computers should be perfectly capable of *disproving* theorem B, whatever happened somewhere else 14 billion years ago."

I nodded thoughtfully. "I can see what you're getting at." If you weren't going to accept full-blooded Platonism, in which there *was* a kind of ghostly textbook listing the eternal truths of mathematics, then a half-baked version where the book started out empty and was only filled in line-by-line as various theorems were tested seemed like the worst kind of compromise. In fact, when the far side had granted Yuen, Alison and I insight into their mathematics for a few minutes in Shanghai, Yuen had proclaimed that the flow of mathematical information *did* obey Einstein locality; there was no universal book of truths, just records of the past sloshing around at light-speed or less, intermingling and competing.

I could hardly tell Campbell, though, that not only did I know for a fact that a single computer could prove both a theorem and its negation, but depending on the order in which it attacked the calculations it could sometimes even shift the boundary where one set of axioms failed and the other took over.

I said, "And yet you still believe it's worth searching for an inconsistency?"

"I do," he conceded. "Though I came to the idea from a very different approach." He hesitated, then picked up a scone from the table beside us.

"One rock, one apple, one scone. We have a clear idea of what we mean by those phrases, though each one might encompass ten-to-the-ten-to-the-thirty-something slightly different configurations of matter. My 'one scone' is not the same as your 'one scone'."

"Right."

"You know how banks count large quantities of cash?"

"By weighing them?" In fact there were several other cross-checks as well, but I could see where he was heading and I didn't want to distract him with nit-picking.

"Exactly. Suppose we tried to count scones the same way: weigh the batch, divide by some nominal value, then round to the nearest integer. The weight of any individual scone varies so much that you could easily end up with a version of arithmetic different from our own. If you 'counted' two separate batches, then merged them and 'counted' them together, there's no guarantee that the result would agree with the ordinary process of integer addition."

I said, "Clearly not. But digital computers don't run on scones, and they don't count bits by weighing them."

"Bear with me," Campbell replied. "It isn't a perfect analogy, but I'm not as crazy as I sound. Suppose, now, that *everything* we talk about as 'one thing' has a vast number of possible configurations that we're either ignoring deliberately, or are literally incapable of distinguishing. Even something as simple as an electron prepared in a certain quantum state."

I said, "You're talking about hidden variables now?"

"Of a kind, yes. Do you know about Gerard 't Hooft's models for deterministic quantum mechanics?"

"Only vaguely," I admitted.

"He postulated fully deterministic degrees of freedom at the Planck scale, with quantum states corresponding to equivalence classes containing many different possible configurations. What's more, all the ordinary quantum states we prepare at an atomic level would be complex superpositions of those primordial states, which allows him to get around the Bell inequalities." I frowned slightly; I more-or-less got the picture, but I'd need to go away and read 't Hooft's papers.

Campbell said, "In a sense, the detailed physics isn't all that important, so long as you accept that 'one thing' might not *ever* be exactly the same as another 'one thing', regardless of the kind of objects we're talking about. Given that supposition, physical processes that *seem* to be rigorously equivalent to various arithmetic operations can turn out not to be as reliable as you'd think. With scone-weighing, the flaws are obvious, but I'm talking about the potentially subtler results of misunderstanding the fundamental nature of matter."

"Hmm." Though it was unlikely that anyone else Campbell had confided in had taken these speculations as seriously as I did, not only did I not want to seem a pushover, I honestly had no idea whether anything he was saying bore the slightest connection to reality.

I said, "It's an interesting idea, but I still don't see how it could speed up the hunt for inconsistencies."

"I have a set of models," he said, "which are constrained by the need to agree with some of 't Hooft's ideas about the physics, and also by the need to make arithmetic *almost* consistent for a very large range of objects. From neutrinos to clusters of galaxies, basic arithmetic involving the kinds of numbers we might encounter in ordinary situations should work out in the usual way." He laughed. "I mean, that's the world we're living in, right?"

Some of us. "Yeah."

"But the interesting thing is, I can't make the physics work at all if the arithmetic doesn't run askew eventually—if there aren't trans-astronomical numbers where the physical representations no longer capture the arithmetic perfectly. And each of my models lets me predict, more or less, where those effects should begin to show up. By starting with the fundamental physical laws, I can deduce a sequence of calculations with large integers that ought to reveal an inconsistency, when performed with pretty much any computer."

"Taking you straight to the defect, with no need to search at all." I'd let the definite article slip out, but it hardly seemed to matter anymore.

"That's the theory." Campbell actually blushed slightly. "Well, when you say 'no search', what's involved really is a much smaller search. There are still free parameters in my models; there are potentially billions of possibilities to test."

I grinned broadly, wondering if my expression looked as fake as it felt. "But no luck yet?"

"No." He was beginning to become self-conscious again, glancing around to see who might be listening.

Was he lying to me? Keeping his results secret until he could verify them a million more times, and then decide how best to explain them to incredulous colleagues and an uncomprehending world? Or had whatever he'd done that had lobbed a small grenade into Sam's universe somehow registered in Campbell's own computer as arithmetic as usual, betraying no evidence of the boundary he'd crossed? After all, the offending cluster of propositions had obeyed *our* axioms, so perhaps Campbell had managed to force them to do so without ever realizing that they hadn't in the past. His ideas were obviously close to the mark—and I could no longer believe this was just a coincidence—but he seemed to have no room in his theory for something that I knew for a fact: arithmetic wasn't merely inconsistent, it was *dynamic*. You could take its contradictions and slide them around like bumps in a carpet.

Campbell said, "Parts of the process aren't easy to automate; there's some manual work to be done setting up the search for each broad class of models. I've only been doing this in my spare time, so it could be a while before I get around to examining all the possibilities."

"I see." If all of his calculations so far had produced just one hit on the far side, it was conceivable that the rest would pass without incident. He would publish a negative result ruling out an obscure class of physical theories, and life would go on as normal on both sides of the inconsistency.

What kind of weapons inspector would I be, though, to put my faith in that rosy supposition?

Campbell was looking fidgety, as if his administrative obligations were beckoning. I said, "It'd be great to talk about this a bit more while we've got the chance. Are you busy tonight? I'm staying at a backpacker's down in the city, but maybe you could recommend a restaurant around here somewhere?"

He looked dubious for a moment, but then an instinctive sense of hospitality seemed to overcome his reservations. He said, "Let me check with my wife. We're not really into restaurants, but I was cooking tonight anyway, and you'd be welcome to join us."

CAMPBELL'S HOUSE WAS A fifteen minute walk from the campus; at my request, we detoured to a liquor store so I could buy a couple of bottles of wine to accompany the meal. As I entered the house, my hand lingered on the doorframe, depositing a small device that would assist me if I needed to make an uninvited entry in the future.

Campbell's wife, Bridget, was an organic chemist, who also taught at Victoria University. The conversation over dinner was all about department heads, budgets, and grant applications, and despite having left academia long ago, I had no trouble relating sympathetically to the couple's gripes. My hosts ensured that my wine glass never stayed empty for long.

When we'd finished eating, Bridget excused herself to make a call to her mother, who lived in a small town on the south island. Campbell led me into his study and switched on a laptop with fading keys that must have been twenty years old. Many households had a computer like this: the machine that could no longer run the latest trendy bloatware, but which still worked perfectly with its original OS.

Campbell turned his back to me as he typed his password, and I was careful not to be seen even trying to look. Then he opened some C++ files in an editor, and scrolled over parts of his search algorithm.

I felt giddy, and it wasn't the wine; I'd filled my stomach with an over-the-counter sobriety aid that turned ethanol into glucose and water faster than any human being could imbibe it. I fervently hoped that Industrial Algebra really had given up their pursuit; if I could get this close to Campbell's secrets in half a day, IA could be playing the stock market with alternative arithmetic before the month was out, and peddling inconsistency weapons to the Pentagon soon after.

I did not have a photographic memory, and Campbell was just showing me fragments anyway. I didn't think he was deliberately taunting me; he just wanted me to see that he had something concrete, that all his claims about Planck scale physics and directed search strategies had been more than hot air.

I said, "Wait! What's that?" He stopped hitting the PAGE DOWN key, and I pointed at a list of variable declarations in the middle of the screen:

> *long int i1, i2, i3;*
> *dark d1, d2, d3;*

A "long int" was a long integer, a quantity represented by twice as many bits as usual. On this vintage machine, that was likely to be a total of just sixty-four bits. "What the fuck is a 'dark'?" I demanded. It wasn't how I'd normally speak to someone I'd only just met, but then, I wasn't meant to be sober.

Campbell laughed. "A dark integer. It's a type I defined. It holds four thousand and ninety-six bits."

"But why the name?"

"Dark matter, dark energy . . . dark integers. They're all around us, but we don't usually see them, because they don't quite play by the rules."

Hairs rose on the back of my neck. I could not have described the infrastructure of Sam's world more concisely myself.

Campbell shut down the laptop. I'd been looking for an opportunity to handle the machine, however briefly, without arousing his suspicion, but that clearly wasn't going to happen, so as we walked out of the study I went for plan B.

"I'm feeling kind of . . ." I sat down abruptly on the floor of the hallway. After a moment, I fished my phone out of my pocket and held it up to him. "Would you mind calling me a taxi?"

"Yeah, sure." He accepted the phone, and I cradled my head in my arms. Before he could dial the number, I started moaning softly. There was a long pause; he was probably weighing up the embarrassment factor of various alternatives.

Finally he said, "You can sleep here on the couch if you like." I felt a genuine pang of sympathy for him; if some clown I barely knew had pulled a stunt like this on me, I would at least have made him promise to foot the cleaning bills if he threw up in the middle of the night.

In the middle of the night, I did make a trip to the bathroom, but I kept the sound effects restrained. Halfway through, I walked quietly to the study, crossed the room in the dark, and slapped a thin, transparent patch over the adhesive label that a service company had placed on the outside of the laptop years before. My addition would be invisible to the naked eye, and it would take a scalpel to prize it off. The relay that would communicate with the patch was larger, about the size of a coat button; I stuck it behind a bookshelf. Unless Campbell was planning to paint the room or put in new carpet, it would probably remain undetected for a couple of years, and I'd already prepaid a two year account with a local wireless internet provider.

I woke not long after dawn, but this un-Bacchanalian early rising was no risk to my cover; Campbell had left the curtains open so the full force of the morning sun struck me in the face, a result that was almost certainly deliberate. I tiptoed around the house for ten minutes or so, not wanting to seem too organized if anyone was listening, then left a scrawled note of thanks and apology on the coffee table by the couch, before letting myself out and heading for the cable car stop.

Down in the city, I sat in a café opposite the backpacker's hostel, and connected to the relay, which in turn had established a successful link with the polymer circuitry of the laptop patch. When noon came and went without Campbell logging on, I sent a message to Kate telling her that I was stuck in the bank for at least another day.

I passed the time browsing the news feeds and buying overpriced snacks; half of the café's other patrons were doing the same. Finally, just after three o'clock, Campbell started up the laptop.

The patch couldn't read his disk drive, but it could pick up currents flowing to and from the keyboard and the display, allowing it to deduce everything he typed and everything he saw. Capturing his password was easy. Better yet, once he was logged in he set about editing one of his files, extending his search program to a new class of models. As he scrolled back and forth, it wasn't long before the patch's screen shots encompassed the entire contents of the file he was working on.

He labored for more than two hours, debugging what he'd written, then set the program running. This creaky old twentieth-century machine, which predated the whole internet-wide search for the defect, had already scored one direct hit on the far side; I just hoped this new class of models were all incompatible with the successful ones from a few days before.

Shortly afterward, the IR sensor in the patch told me that Campbell had left the room. The patch could induce currents in the keyboard connection; I could type into the machine as if I was right there. I started a new process window. The laptop wasn't connected to the internet at all, except through my spyware, but it took me only fifteen minutes to display and record everything there was to see: a few library and header files that the main program depended on, and the data logs listing all of the searches so far. It would not have been hard to hack into the operating system and make provisions to corrupt any future searches, but I decided to wait until I had a better grasp of the whole situation. Even once I was back in Sydney, I'd be able to eavesdrop whenever the laptop was in use, and intervene whenever it was left unattended. I'd only stayed in Wellington in case there'd been a need to return to Campbell's house in person.

When evening fell and I found myself with nothing urgent left to do, I didn't call Kate; it seemed wiser to let her assume that I was slaving away in a windowless computer room. I left the café and lay on my bed in the hostel. The dormitory was deserted; everyone else was out on the town.

I called Alison in Zürich and brought her up to date. In the background, I could hear her husband, Philippe, trying to comfort Laura in another room, calmly talking baby-talk in French while his daughter wailed her head off.

Alison was intrigued. "Campbell's theory can't be perfect, but it must be close. Maybe we'll be able to find a way to make it fit in with the dynamics we've seen." In the ten years since we'd stumbled on the defect, all our work on it had remained frustratingly empirical: running calculations, and observing their effects. We'd never come close to finding any deep underlying principles.

"Do you think Sam knows all this?" she asked.

"I have no idea. If he did, I doubt he'd admit it." Though it was Sam who had given us a taste of far-side mathematics in Shanghai, that had really just been a clip over the ear to let us know that what we were trying to wipe out with Luminous was a civilization, not a wasteland. After that near-disastrous first encounter, he had worked to establish communications with us, learning our languages and happily listening to the accounts we'd volunteered of our world, but he had not been equally forthcoming in return. We knew next to nothing about far-side physics, astronomy, biology, history or culture. That there were living beings occupying the same space as the Earth suggested that the two universes were intimately coupled somehow, in spite of their mutual invisibility. But Sam had hinted that life was much more common on his side of the border than ours; when I'd told him that we seemed to be alone, at least in the solar system, and were surrounded by light-years of sterile vacuum, he'd taken to referring to our side as "Sparseland".

Alison said, "Either way, I think we should keep it to ourselves. The treaty says we should do everything in our power to deal with any breach of territory of which the other side informs us. We're doing that. But we're not obliged to disclose the details of Campbell's activities."

"That's true." I wasn't entirely happy with her suggestion, though. In spite of the attitude Sam and his colleagues had taken—in which they assumed that anything they told us might be exploited, might make them more vulnerable—a part of me had always wondered if there was some gesture of good faith we could make, some way to build trust. Since talking to Campbell, in the back of my mind I'd been building up a faint hope that his discovery might lead to an opportunity to prove, once and for all, that our intentions were honorable.

Alison read my mood. She said, "Bruno, they've given us *nothing*. Shanghai excuses a certain amount of caution, but we also know from Shanghai that they could brush Luminous aside like a gnat. They have enough computing power to crush us in an instant, and they still cling to every strategic advantage they can get. Not to do the same ourselves would just be stupid and irresponsible."

"So you want us to hold on to this secret weapon?" I was beginning to develop a piercing headache. My usual way of dealing with the surreal responsibility that had fallen on the three of us was to pretend that it didn't exist; having to think about it constantly for three days straight meant more tension than I'd faced for a decade. "Is that what it's come down to? Our own version of the Cold War? Why don't you just march into NATO headquarters on Monday and hand over everything we know?"

Alison said dryly, "Switzerland isn't a member of NATO. The government here would probably charge me with treason."

I didn't want to fight with her. "We should talk about this later. We don't even know exactly what we've got. I need to go through Campbell's files and confirm whether he really did what we think he did."

"Okay."

"I'll call you from Sydney."

It took me a while to make sense of everything I'd stolen from Campbell, but eventually I was able to determine which calculations he'd performed on each occasion recorded in his log files. Then I compared the propositions that he'd tested with a rough, static map of the defect; since the event Sam had reported had been deep within the far side, there was no need to take account of the small fluctuations that the border underwent over time.

If my analysis was correct, late on Wednesday night Campbell's calculations had landed in the middle of far-side mathematics. He'd been telling me the truth, though; he'd found nothing out of the ordinary there. Instead, the thing he had been seeking had melted away before his gaze.

In all the calculations Alison and I had done, only at the border had we been able to force propositions to change their allegiance and obey our axioms. It was as if Campbell had dived in from some higher dimension, carrying a hosepipe that sprayed everything with the arithmetic we knew and loved.

For Sam and his colleagues, this was the equivalent of a suitcase nuke appearing out of nowhere, as opposed to the ICBMs they knew how to track and annihilate. Now Alison wanted us to tell them, "Trust us, we've dealt with it," without showing them the weapon itself, without letting them see how it worked, without giving them a chance to devise new defenses against it.

She wanted us to have something up our sleeves, in case the hawks took over the far side, and decided that Sparseland was a ghost world whose lingering, baleful presence they could do without.

Drunken Saturday-night revelers began returning to the hostel, singing off-key and puking enthusiastically. Maybe this was poetic justice for my own faux-inebriation; if so I was being repaid a thousandfold. I started wishing I'd shelled out for classier accommodation, but since there was no employer picking up my expenses, it was going to be hard enough dealing with my lie to Kate without spending even more on the trip.

Forget the arithmetic of scones; I knew how to make digital currency reproduce like the marching brooms of the sorcerer's apprentice. It might even have been possible to milk the benefits without

Sam noticing; I could try to hide my far-sider trading behind the manipulations of the border we used routinely to exchange messages.

I had no idea how to contain the side-effects, though. I had no idea what else such meddling would disrupt, how many people I might kill or maim in the process.

I buried my head beneath the pillows and tried to find a way to get to sleep through the noise. I ended up calculating powers of seven, a trick I hadn't used since childhood. I'd never been a prodigy at mental arithmetic, and the concentration required to push on past the easy cases drained me far faster than any physical labor. *Two hundred and eighty-two million, four hundred and seventy-five thousand, two hundred and forty-nine.* The numbers rose into the stratosphere like bean stalks, until they grew too high and tore themselves apart, leaving behind a cloud of digits drifting through my skull like black confetti.

"THE PROBLEM IS UNDER control," I told Sam. "I've located the source, and I've taken steps to prevent a recurrence."

"Are you sure of that?" As he spoke, the three-holed torus on the screen twisted restlessly. In fact I'd chosen the icon myself, and its appearance wasn't influenced by Sam at all, but it was impossible not to project emotions onto its writhing.

I said, "I'm certain that I know who was responsible for the incursion on Wednesday. It was done without malice; in fact the person who did it doesn't even realize that he crossed the border. I've modified the operating system on his computer so that it won't allow him to do the same thing again; if he tries, it will simply give him the same answers as before, but this time the calculations won't actually be performed."

"That's good to hear," Sam said. "Can you describe these calculations?"

I was as invisible to Sam as he was to me, but out of habit I tried to keep my face composed. "I don't see that as part of our agreement," I replied.

Sam was silent for a few seconds. "That's true, Bruno. But it might provide us with a greater sense of reassurance, if we knew what caused the breach in the first place."

I said, "I understand. But we've made a decision." *We* was Alison and I; Yuen was still in hospital, in no state to do anything. Alison and I, speaking for the world.

"I'll put your position to my colleagues," he said. "We're not your enemy, Bruno." His tone sounded regretful, and these nuances *were* under his control.

"I know that," I replied. "Nor are we yours. Yet you've chosen to keep most of the details of your world from us. We don't view that as evidence of hostility, so you have no grounds to complain if we keep a few secrets of our own."

"I'll contact you again soon," Sam said.

The messenger window closed. I emailed an encrypted transcript to Alison, then slumped across my desk. My head was throbbing, but the encounter really hadn't gone too badly. Of course Sam and his colleagues would have preferred to know everything; of course they were going to be disappointed and reproachful. That didn't mean they were going to abandon the benign policies of the last decade. The important thing was that my assurance would prove to be reliable: the incursion would not be repeated.

I had work to do, the kind that paid bills. Somehow I summoned up the discipline to push the whole subject aside and get on with a report on stochastic methods for resolving distributed programming bottlenecks that I was supposed to be writing for a company in Singapore.

Four hours later, when the doorbell rang, I'd left my desk to raid the kitchen. I didn't bother checking the doorstep camera; I just walked down the hall and opened the door.

Campbell said, "How are you, Bruno?"

"I'm fine. Why didn't you tell me you were coming to Sydney?"

"Aren't you going to ask me how I found your house?"

"How?"

He held up his phone. There was a text message from me, or at least from my phone; it had SMS'd its GPS coordinates to him.

"Not bad," I conceded.

"I believe they recently added 'corrupting communications devices' to the list of terrorism-related offenses in Australia. You could probably get me thrown into solitary confinement in a maximum security prison."

"Only if you know at least ten words of Arabic."

"Actually I spent a month in Egypt once, so anything's possible. But I don't think you really want to go to the police."

I said, "Why don't you come in?"

As I showed him to the living room my mind was racing. Maybe he'd found the relay behind the bookshelf, but surely not before I'd left his house. Had he managed to get a virus into my phone remotely? I'd thought my security was better than that.

Campbell said, "I'd like you to explain why you bugged my computer."

"I'm growing increasingly unsure of that myself. The correct answer might be that you wanted me to."

He snorted. "That's rich! I admit that I deliberately allowed a rumor to start about my work, because I was curious as to why you and Alison Tierney called off your search. I wanted to see if you'd come sniffing around. As you did. But that was hardly an invitation to steal all my work."

"What was the point of the whole exercise for you, then, if not a way of stealing something from Alison and me?"

"You can hardly compare the two. I just wanted to confirm my suspicion that you actually found something."

"And you believe that you've confirmed that?"

He shook his head, but it was with amusement not denial. I said, "Why are you here? Do you think I'm going to publish your crackpot theory as my own? I'm too old to get the Fields Medal, but maybe you think it's Nobel material."

"Oh, I don't think you're interested in fame. As I said, I think you beat me to the prize a long time ago."

I rose to my feet abruptly; I could feel myself scowling, my fists tightening. "So what's the bottom line? You want to press charges against me for the laptop? Go ahead. We can each get a fine *in absentia*."

Campbell said, "I want to know exactly what was so important to you that you crossed the Tasman, lied your way into my house, abused my hospitality, and stole my files. I don't think it was simply curiosity, or jealousy. I think you found something ten years ago, and now you're afraid my work is going to put it at risk."

I sat down again. The rush of adrenaline I'd experienced at being cornered had dissipated. I could almost hear Alison whispering in my ear, "Either you kill him, Bruno, or you recruit him." I had no intention of killing anyone, but I wasn't yet certain that these were the only two choices.

I said, "And if I tell you to mind your own business?"

He shrugged. "Then I'll work harder. I know you've screwed that laptop, and maybe the other computers in my house, but I'm not so broke that I can't get a new machine."

Which would be a hundred times faster. He'd re-run every search, probably with wider parameter ranges. The suitcase nuke from Sparseland that had started this whole mess would detonate again, and for all I knew it could be ten times, a hundred times, more powerful.

I said, "Have you ever wanted to join a secret society?"

Campbell gave an incredulous laugh. "No!"

"Neither did I. Too bad."

I told him everything. The discovery of the defect. Industrial Algebra's pursuit of the result. The epiphany in Shanghai. Sam establishing contact. The treaty, the ten quiet years. Then the sudden jolt of his own work, and the still-unfolding consequences.

Campbell was clearly shaken, but despite the fact that I'd confirmed his original suspicion he wasn't ready to take my word for the whole story.

I knew better than to invite him into my office for a demonstration; faking it there would have been trivial. We walked to the local shopping center, and I handed him two hundred dollars to buy a new notebook. I told him the kind of software he'd need to download, without limiting his choice to any particular package. Then I gave him some further instructions. Within half an hour, he had seen the defect for himself, and nudged the border a short distance in each direction.

We were sitting in the food hall, surrounded by boisterous teenagers who'd just got out from school. Campbell was looking at me as if I'd seized a toy machine gun from his hands, transformed it into solid metal, then bashed him over the head with it.

I said, "Cheer up. There was no war of the worlds after Shanghai; I think we're going to survive this, too." After all these years, the chance to share the burden with someone new was actually making me feel much more optimistic.

"The defect is *dynamic*," he muttered. "That changes everything."

"You don't say."

Campbell scowled. "I don't just mean the politics, the dangers. I'm talking about the underlying physical model."

"Yeah?" I hadn't come close to examining that issue seriously; it had been enough of a struggle coming to terms with his original calculations.

"All along, I've assumed that there were exact symmetries in the Planck scale physics that accounted for a stable boundary between macroscopic arithmetics. It was an artificial restriction, but I took it for granted, because anything else seemed . . ."

"Unbelievable?"

"Yes." He blinked and looked away, surveying the crowd of diners as if he had no idea how he'd ended up among them. "I'm flying back in a few hours."

"Does Bridget know why you came?"

"Not exactly."

I said, "No one else can know what I've told you. Not yet. The risks are too great, everything's too fluid."

"Yeah." He met my gaze. He wasn't just humoring me; he understood what people like IA might do.

"In the long term," I said, "we're going to have to find a way to make this safe. To make everyone safe." I'd never quite articulated that goal before, but I was only just beginning to absorb the ramifications of Campbell's insights.

"How?" he wondered. "Do we want to build a wall, or do we want to tear one down?"

"I don't know. The first thing we need is a better map, a better feel for the whole territory."

He'd hired a car at the airport in order to drive here and confront me; it was parked in a side street close to my house. I walked him to it.

We shook hands before parting. I said, "Welcome to the reluctant cabal."

Campbell winced. "Let's find a way to change it from reluctant to redundant."

IN THE WEEKS THAT followed, Campbell worked on refinements to his theory, emailing Alison and me every few days. Alison had taken my unilateral decision to recruit Campbell with much more equanimity than I'd expected. "Better to have him inside the tent," was all she'd said.

This proved to be an understatement. While the two of us soon caught up with him on all the technicalities, it was clear that his intuition on the subject, hard-won over many years of trial-and-error, was the key to his spectacular progress now. Merely stealing his notes and his algorithms would never have brought us so far.

Gradually, the dynamic version of the theory took shape. As far as macroscopic objects were concerned—and in this context, "macroscopic" stretched all the way down to the quantum states of subatomic particles—all traces of Platonic mathematics were banished. A "proof" concerning the integers was just a class of physical processes, and the result of that proof was neither read from, nor written to, any universal book of truths. Rather, the agreement between proofs was simply a strong, but imperfect, correlation between the different processes that counted as proofs of the same thing. Those correlations arose from the way that the primordial states of Planck-scale physics were carved up—imperfectly—into subsystems that appeared to be distinct objects.

The truths of mathematics *appeared* to be enduring and universal because they persisted with great efficiency within the states of matter and space-time. But there was a built-in flaw in the whole idealization of distinct objects, and the point where the concept finally cracked open was the defect Alison and I had found in our volunteers' data, which appeared to any macroscopic test as the border between contradictory mathematical systems.

We'd derived a crude empirical rule which said that the border shifted when a proposition's neighbors outvoted it. If you managed to prove that x+1=y+1 and x−1=y−1, then x=y became a sitting duck, even if it hadn't been true before. The consequences of Campbell's search had shown that the reality was more complex, and in his new model, the old border rule became an approximation for a more subtle process, anchored in the dynamics of primordial states that knew nothing of the arithmetic of electrons and apples. The near-side arithmetic Campbell had blasted into the far side hadn't got there by besieging the target with syllogisms; it had got there because he'd gone straight for a far deeper failure in the whole idea of "integers" than Alison and I had ever dreamed of.

Had Sam dreamed of it? I waited for his next contact, but as the weeks passed he remained silent, and the last thing I felt like doing was calling him myself. I had enough people to lie to without adding him to the list.

Kate asked me how work was going, and I waffled about the details of the three uninspiring contracts I'd started recently. When I stopped talking, she looked at me as if I'd just stammered my way through an unconvincing denial of some unspoken crime. I wondered how my mixture of concealed elation and fear was coming across to her. Was that how the most passionate, conflicted adulterer would appear? I didn't actually reach the brink of confession, but I pictured myself approaching it. I had less reason now to think that the secret would bring her harm than when I'd first made my decision to keep her in the dark. But then, what if I told her everything, and the next day Campbell was kidnapped and tortured? If we were all being watched, and the people doing it were good at their jobs, we'd only know about it when it was too late.

Campbell's emails dropped off for a while, and I assumed he'd hit a roadblock. Sam had offered no further complaints. Perhaps, I thought, this was the new *status quo*, the start of another quiet decade. I could live with that.

Then Campbell flung his second grenade. He reached me by IM and said, "I've started making maps."

"Of the defect?" I replied.

"Of the planets."

I stared at his image, uncomprehending.

"The far-side planets," he said. "*The physical worlds.*"

He'd bought himself some time on a geographically scattered set of processor clusters. He was no longer repeating his dangerous incursions, of course, but by playing around in the natural ebb and flow at the border, he'd made some extraordinary discoveries.

Alison and I had realized long ago that random "proofs" in the natural world would influence what happened at the border, but Campbell's theory made that notion more precise. By looking at the exact timing of changes to propositions at the border, measured in a dozen different computers world-wide, he had set up a kind of . . . radar? CT machine? Whatever you called it, it allowed him to deduce the locations where the relevant natural processes were occurring, and his model allowed him to distinguish between both near-side and far-side processes, and processes in matter and those in vacuum. He could measure the density of far-side matter, out to a distance of several light-hours, and crudely image nearby planets.

"Not just on the far side," he said. "I validated the technique by imaging our own planets." He sent me a data log, with comparisons to an online almanac. For Jupiter, the farthest of the planets he'd located, the positions were out by as much as a hundred thousand kilometers; not exactly GPS quality, but that was a bit like complaining that your abacus couldn't tell north from north-west.

"Maybe that's how Sam found us in Shanghai?" I wondered. "The same kind of thing, only more refined?"

Campbell said, "Possibly."

"So what about the far-side planets?"

"Well, here's the first interesting thing. None of the planets coincide with ours. Nor does their sun with our sun." He sent me an image of the far-side system, one star and its six planets, overlaid on our own.

"But Sam's time lags," I protested, "when we communicate—"

"Make no sense if he's too far away. Exactly. So he is *not* living on any of these planets, and he's not even in a natural orbit around their star. He's in powered flight, moving with the Earth. Which suggests to me that they've known about us for much longer than Shanghai."

"Known about us," I said, "but maybe they still didn't anticipate anything like Shanghai." When we'd set Luminous on to the task of eliminating the defect—not knowing that we were threatening any-one—it had taken several minutes before the far side had responded. Computers on board a spacecraft moving with the Earth would have detected the assault quickly, but it might have taken the recruitment of larger, planet-bound machines, minutes away at lightspeed, to repel it.

Until I'd encountered Campbell's theories, my working assumption had been that Sam's world was like a hidden message encoded in the Earth, with the different arithmetic giving different meanings to all the air, water and rock around us. But their matter was not bound to our matter; they didn't need our specks of dust or mole-cules of air to represent the dark integers. The two worlds split apart at a much lower level; vacuum could be rock, and rock, vacuum.

I said, "So do you want the Nobel for physics, or peace?"

Campbell smiled modestly. "Can I hold out for both?"

"That's the answer I was looking for." I couldn't get the stupid Cold War metaphors out of my brain: what would Sam's hot-headed colleagues think, if they knew that we were now flying spy planes over their territory? Saying "screw them, they were doing it first!" might have been a fair response, but it was not a particularly helpful one.

I said, "We're never going to match their Sputnik, unless you happen to know a trustworthy billionaire who wants to help us launch a space probe on a very strange trajectory. Everything we want to do has to work from Earth."

"I'll tear up my letter to Richard Branson then, shall I?"

I stared at the map of the far-side solar system. "There must be some relative motion between their star and ours. It can't have been this close for all that long."

"I don't have enough accuracy in my measurements to make a meaningful estimate of the velocity," Campbell said. "But I've done some crude estimates of the distances between their stars, and it's much smaller than ours. So it's not all that unlikely to find *some* star this close to us, even if it's unlikely to be the same one that was close a thousand years ago. Then again, there might be a selection effect at work here: the whole reason Sam's civilization managed to notice us at all was *because* we weren't shooting past them at a substantial fraction of lightspeed."

"Okay. So *maybe* this is their home system, but it could just as easily be an expeditionary base for a team that's been following our sun for thousands of years."

"Yes."

I said, "Where do we go with this?"

"I can't increase the resolution much," Campbell replied, "without buying time on a lot more clusters." It wasn't that he needed much processing power for the calculations, but there were minimum prices to be paid to do anything at all, and what would give us clearer pictures would be more computers, not more time on each one.

I said, "We can't risk asking for volunteers, like the old days. We'd have to lie about what the download was for, and you can be certain that somebody would reverse-engineer it and catch us out."

"Absolutely."

I slept on the problem, then woke with an idea at four a.m. and went to my office, trying to flesh out the details before Campbell responded to my email. He was bleary-eyed when the messenger window opened; it was later in Wellington than in Sydney, but it looked as if he'd had as little sleep as I had.

I said, "We use the internet."

"I thought we decided that was too risky."

"Not screen-savers for volunteers; I'm talking about *the internet itself*. We work out a way to do the calculations using nothing but data packets and network routers. We bounce traffic all around the world, and we get the geographical resolution for free."

"You've got to be joking, Bruno—"

"Why? *Any* computing circuit can be built by stringing together enough NAND gates; you think we can't leverage packet switching into a NAND gate? But that's just the proof that it's possible; I expect we can actually make it a thousand times tighter."

Campbell said, "I'm going to get some aspirin and come back."

We roped in Alison to help, but it still took us six weeks to get a workable design, and another month to get it functioning. We ended up exploiting authentication and error-correction protocols built into the internet at several different layers; the heterogeneous approach not only helped us do all the calculations we needed, but made our gentle siphoning of computing power less likely to be detected and mistaken for anything malicious. In fact we were "stealing" far less from the routers and servers of the net than if we'd sat down for a hardcore 3D multiplayer gaming session, but security systems had their own ideas about what constituted fair use and what was suspicious. The most important thing was not the size of the burden we imposed, but the signature of our behavior.

Our new globe-spanning arithmetical telescope generated pictures far sharper than before, with kilometer-scale resolution out to a billion kilometers. This gave us crude relief-maps of the far-side planets, revealing mountains on four of them, and what might have been oceans on two of those four. If there were any artificial structures, they were either too small to see, or too subtle in their artificiality.

The relative motion of our sun and the star these planets orbited turned out to be about six kilometers per second. In the decade since Shanghai, the two solar systems had changed their relative location by about two billion kilometers. Wherever the computers were now that had fought with Luminous to control the border, they certainly hadn't been on any of these planets at the time. Perhaps there were two ships, with one following the Earth, and the other, heavier one saving fuel by merely following the sun.

Yuen had finally recovered his health, and the full cabal held an IM-conference to discuss these results.

"We should be showing these to geologists, xenobiologists . . . everyone," Yuen lamented. He wasn't making a serious proposal, but I shared his sense of frustration.

Alison said, "What I regret most is that we can't rub Sam's face in these pictures, just to show him that we're not as stupid as he thinks."

"I imagine his own pictures are sharper," Campbell replied.

"Which is as you'd expect," Alison retorted, "given a head start of a few centuries. If they're so brilliant on the far side, why do they need *us* to tell them what you did to jump the border?"

"They might have guessed precisely what I did," he countered, "but they could still be seeking confirmation. Perhaps what they really want is to rule out the possibility that we've discovered something different, something they've never even thought of."

I gazed at the false colors of one contoured sphere, imagining gray-blue oceans, snow-topped mountains with alien forests, strange cities, wondrous machines. Even if that was pure fantasy and this temporary neighbor was barren, there had to be a living home world from which the ships that pursued us had been launched.

After Shanghai, Sam and his colleagues had chosen to keep us in the dark for ten years, but it had been our own decision to cement the mistrust by holding on to the secret of our accidental weapon. If they'd already guessed its nature, then they might already have found a defense against it, in which case our silence bought us no advantage at all to compensate for the suspicion it engendered.

If that assumption was wrong, though? Then handing over the details of Campbell's work could be just what the far-side hawks were waiting for, before raising their shields and crushing us.

I said, "We need to make some plans. I want to stay hopeful, I want to keep looking for the best way forward, but we need to be prepared for the worst."

TRANSFORMING THAT SUGGESTION INTO something concrete required far more work than I'd imagined; it was three months before the pieces started coming together. When I finally shifted my gaze back to the everyday world, I decided that I'd earned a break. Kate had a free weekend approaching; I suggested a day in the Blue Mountains.

Her initial response was sarcastic, but when I persisted she softened a little, and finally agreed.

On the drive out of the city, the chill that had developed between us slowly began to thaw. We played JJJ on the car radio—laughing with disbelief as we realized that today's cutting-edge music consisted mostly of cover versions and re-samplings of songs that had been hits when we were in our twenties—and resurrected old running jokes from the time when we'd first met.

As we wound our way into the mountains, though, it proved impossible simply to turn back the clock. Kate said, "Whoever you've been working for these last few months, can you put them on your blacklist?"

I laughed. "That will scare them." I switched to my best Brando voice. "You're on Bruno Costanzo's blacklist. You'll never run distributed software efficiently in this town again."

She said, "I'm serious. I don't know what's so stressful about the work, or the people, but it's really screwing you up."

I could have made her a promise, but it would have been hard enough to sound sincere as I spoke the words, let alone live up to them. I said, "Beggars can't be choosers."

She shook her head, her mouth tensed in frustration. "If you really want a heart attack, fine. But don't pretend that it's all about money. We're never that broke, and we're never that rich. Unless it's all going into your account in Zürich."

It took me a few seconds to convince myself that this was nothing more than a throw-away reference to Swiss banks. Kate knew about Alison, knew that we'd once been close, knew that we still kept in touch. She had plenty of male friends from her own past, and they all lived in Sydney; for more than five years, Alison and I hadn't even set foot on the same continent.

We parked the car, then walked along a scenic trail for an hour, mostly in silence. We found a spot by a stream, with tiered rocks smoothed by some ancient river, and ate the lunch I'd packed.

Looking out into the blue haze of the densely wooded valley below, I couldn't keep the image of the crowded skies of the far side from my mind. A dazzling richness surrounded us: alien worlds, alien life, alien culture. There had to be a way to end our mutual suspicion, and work toward a genuine exchange of knowledge.

As we started back toward the car, I turned to Kate. "I know I've neglected you," I said. "I've been through a rough patch, but everything's going to change. I'm going to make things right."

I was prepared for a withering rebuff, but for a long time she was silent. Then she nodded slightly and said, "Okay."

As she reached across and took my hand, my wrist began vibrating. I'd buckled to the pressure and bought a watch that shackled me to the net twenty four hours a day.

I freed my hand from Kate's and lifted the watch to my face. The bandwidth reaching me out in the sticks wasn't enough for video, but a stored snapshot of Alison appeared on the screen.

"This is for *emergencies only*," I snarled.

"Check out a news feed," she replied. The acoustics were focused on my ears; Kate would get nothing but the bad-hearing-aid-at-a-party impression that made so many people want to punch their fellow commuters on trains.

"Why don't you just summarize whatever it is I'm meant to have noticed?"

Financial computing systems were going haywire, to an extent that was already being described as terrorism. Most trading was closed for the weekend, but some experts were predicting the crash of the century, come Monday.

I wondered if the cabal itself was to blame; if we'd inadvertently corrupted the whole internet by coupling its behavior to the defect. That was nonsense, though. Half the transactions being garbled were taking place on secure, interbank networks that shared no hardware with our global computer. This was coming from the far side.

"Have you contacted Sam?" I asked her.

"I can't raise him."

"Where are you going?" Kate shouted angrily. I'd unconsciously broken into a jog; I wanted to get back to the car, back to the city, back to my office.

I stopped and turned to her. "Run with me? Please? This is important."

"You're joking! I've spent half a day hiking, I'm not running anywhere!"

I hesitated, fantasizing for a moment that I could sit beneath a gum tree and orchestrate everything with my Dick Tracy watch before its battery went flat.

I said, "You'd better call a taxi when you get to the road."

"You're taking the car?" Kate stared at me, incredulous. "You piece of shit!"

"I'm sorry." I tossed my backpack on the ground and started sprinting.

"We need to deploy," I told Alison.

"I know," she said. "We've already started."

It was the right decision, but hearing it still loosened my bowels far more than the realization that the far side were attacking us. Whatever their motives, at least they were unlikely to do more harm than they intended. I was much less confident about our own abilities.

"Keep trying to reach Sam," I insisted. "This is a thousand times more useful if they know about it."

Alison said, "I guess this isn't the time for *Dr. Strangelove* jokes."

Over the last three months, we'd worked out a way to augment our internet "telescope" software to launch a barrage of Campbell-style attacks on far-side propositions if it saw our own mathematics being encroached upon. The software couldn't protect the whole border, but there were millions of individual trigger points, forming a randomly shifting minefield. The plan had been to buy ourselves some security, without ever reaching the point of actual retaliation. We'd been waiting to complete a final round of tests before unleashing this version live on the net, but it would only take a matter of minutes to get it up and running.

"Anything being hit besides financials?" I asked.

"Not that I'm picking up."

If the far side was deliberately targeting the markets, that was infinitely preferable to the alternative: that financial systems had simply been the most fragile objects in the path of a much broader assault. Most modern engineering and aeronautical systems were more interested in resorting to fall-backs than agonizing over their failures. A bank's computer might declare itself irretrievably compromised and shut down completely, the instant certain totals failed to reconcile; those in a chemical plant or an airliner would be designed to fail more gracefully, trying simpler alternatives and bringing all available humans into the loop.

I said, "Yuen and Tim—?"

"Both on board," Alison confirmed. "Monitoring the deployment, ready to tweak the software if necessary."

"Good. You really won't need me at all, then, will you?"

Alison's reply dissolved into digital noise, and the connection cut out. I refused to read anything sinister into that; given my location, I was lucky to have any coverage at all. I ran faster, trying not to think about the time in Shanghai when Sam had taken a mathe-matical scalpel to all of our brains. Luminous had been screaming out our position like a beacon; we would not be so easy to locate this time. Still, with a cruder approach, the hawks could take a hatchet to everyone's head. *Would they go that far?* Only if this was meant as much more than a threat, much more than intimidation to make us hand over Campbell's algorithm. Only if this was the end game: no warning, no negotiations, just Sparseland wiped off the map forever.

Fifteen minutes after Alison's call, I reached the car. Apart from the entertainment console it didn't contain a single microchip; I remembered the salesman laughing when I'd queried that twice. "What are you afraid of? Y3K?" The engine started immediately.

I had an ancient second-hand laptop in the trunk; I put it beside me on the passenger seat and started it booting up while I drove out on to the access road, heading for the highway. Alison and I had worked for a fortnight on a stripped-down operating system, as simple and robust as possible, to run on these old computers; if the far side kept reaching down from the arithmetic stratosphere, these would be like concrete bunkers compared to the glass skyscrapers of more modern machines. The four of us would also be running dif-ferent versions of the OS, on CPUs with different instruction sets; our bunkers were scattered mathematically as well as geographically.

As I drove on to the highway, my watch stuttered back to life. Alison said, "Bruno? Can you hear me?"

"Go ahead."

"Three passenger jets have crashed," she said. "Poland, Indonesia, South Africa."

I was dazed. Ten years before, when I'd tried to bulldoze his whole mathematical world into the sea, Sam had spared my life. Now the far side was slaughtering innocents.

"Is our minefield up?"

"It's been up for ten minutes, but nothing's tripped it yet."

"You think they're steering through it?"

Alison hesitated. "I don't see how. There's no way to predict a safe path." We were using a quantum noise server to randomize the propositions we tested.

I said, "We should trigger it manually. One counter-strike to start with, to give them something to think about." I was still hoping that the downed jets were unintended, but we had no choice but to retaliate.

"Yeah." Alison's image was live now; I saw her reach down for her mouse. She said, "It's not responding. The net's too degraded." All the fancy algorithms that the routers used, and that we'd leveraged so successfully for our imaging software, were turning them into paperweights. The internet was robust against high levels of transmission noise and the loss of thousands of connections, but not against the decay of arithmetic itself.

My watch went dead. I looked to the laptop; it was still working. I reached over and hit a single hotkey, launching a program that would try to reach Alison and the others the same way we'd talked to Sam: by modulating part of the border. In theory, the hawks might have moved the whole border—in which case we were screwed—but the border was vast, and it made more sense for them to target their computing resources on the specific needs of the assault itself.

A small icon appeared on the laptop's screen, a single letter A in reversed monochrome. I said, "Is this working?"

"Yes," Alison replied. The icon blinked out, then came back again. We were doing a Hedy Lamarr, hopping rapidly over a pre-determined sequence of border points to minimize the chance of detection. Some of those points would be missing, but it looked as if enough of them remained intact.

The A was joined by a Y and a T. The whole cabal was online now, whatever that was worth. What we needed was S, but S was not answering.

Campbell said grimly, "I heard about the planes. I've started an attack." The tactic we had agreed upon was to take turns running different variants of Campbell's border-jumping algorithm from our scattered machines.

I said, "The miracle is that they're not hitting us the same way we're hitting them. They're just pushing down part of the border with the old voting method, step by step. If we'd given them what they'd asked for, we'd all be dead by now."

"Maybe not," Yuen replied. "I'm only halfway through a proof, but I'm ninety percent sure that Tim's method is asymmetrical. It only works in one direction. Even if we'd told them about it, they couldn't have turned it against us."

I opened my mouth to argue, but if Yuen was right that made perfect sense. The far side had probably been working on the same branch of mathematics for centuries; if there had been an equivalent weapon that could be used from their vantage point, they would have discovered it long ago.

My machine had synchronized with Campbell's, and it took over the assault automatically. We had no real idea what we were hitting, except that the propositions were further from the border, describing far simpler arithmetic on the dark integers than anything of ours that the far side had yet touched. *Were we crippling machines? Taking lives?* I was torn between a triumphant vision of retribution, and a sense of shame that we'd allowed it to come to this.

Every hundred meters or so, I passed another car sitting motionless by the side of the highway. I was far from the only person still driving, but I had a feeling Kate wouldn't have much luck getting a taxi. She had water in her backpack, and there was a small shelter at the spot where we'd parked. There was little to be gained by reaching my office now; the laptop could do everything that mattered, and I could run it from the car battery if necessary. If I turned around and went back for Kate, though, I'd have so much explaining to do that there'd be no time for anything else.

I switched on the car radio, but either its digital signal processor was too sophisticated for its own good, or all the local stations were out.

"Anyone still getting news?" I asked.

"I still have radio," Campbell replied. "No TV, no internet. Landlines and mobiles here are dead." It was the same for Alison and Yuen. There'd been no more reports of disasters on the radio, but the stations were probably as isolated now as their listeners. Ham operators would still be calling each other, but journalists and newsrooms would not be in the loop. I didn't want to think about the contingency plans that might have been in place, given ten years' preparation and an informed population.

By the time I reached Penrith there were so many abandoned cars that the remaining traffic was almost gridlocked. I decided not to even try to reach home. I didn't know if Sam had literally scanned my brain in Shanghai and used that to target what he'd done to me then, and whether or not he could use the same neuroanatomical information against me now, wherever I was, but staying away from my usual haunts seemed like one more small advantage to cling to.

I found a petrol station, and it was giving priority to customers with functioning cars over hoarders who'd appeared on foot with empty cans. Their EFTPOS wasn't working, but I had enough cash for the petrol and some chocolate bars.

As dusk fell the streetlights came on; the traffic lights had never stopped working. All four laptops were holding up, hurling their grenades into the far side. The closer the attack front came to simple arithmetic, the more resistance it would face from natural processes voting at the border for near-side results. Our enemy had their supercomputers; we had every every atom of the Earth, following its billion-year-old version of the truth.

We had modeled this scenario. The sheer arithmetical inertia of all that matter would buy us time, but in the long run a coherent, sustained, computational attack could still force its way through.

How would we die? Losing consciousness first, feeling no pain? Or was the brain more robust than that? Would all the cells of our bodies start committing apoptosis, once their biochemical errors mounted up beyond repair? Maybe it would be just like radiation sickness. We'd be burned by decaying arithmetic, just as if it was nuclear fire.

My laptop beeped. I swerved off the road and parked on a stretch of concrete beside a dark shopfront. A new icon had appeared on the screen: the letter S.

Sam said, "Bruno, this was not my decision."

"I believe you," I said. "But if you're just a messenger now, what's your message?"

"If you give us what we asked for, we'll stop the attack."

"We're hurting you, aren't we?"

"We know we're hurting *you*," Sam replied. Point taken: we were guessing, firing blind. He didn't have to ask about the damage we'd suffered.

I steeled myself, and followed the script the cabal had agreed upon. "We'll give you the algorithm, but only if you retreat back to the old border, and then seal it."

Sam was silent for four long heartbeats.

"Seal it?"

"I think you know what I mean." In Shanghai, when we'd used Luminous to try to ensure that Industrial Algebra could not exploit the defect, we'd contemplated trying to seal the border rather than eliminating the defect altogether. The voting effect could only shift the border if it was crinkled in such a way that propositions on one side could be outnumbered by those on the other side. It was possible—given enough time and computing power—to smooth the border, to iron it flat. Once that was done, everywhere, the whole thing would become immovable. No force in the universe could shift it again.

Sam said, "You want to leave us with no weapon against you, while you still have the power to harm us."

"We won't have that power for long. Once you know exactly what we're using, you'll find a way to block it."

There was a long pause. Then, "Stop your attacks on us, and we'll consider your proposal."

"We'll stop our attacks when you pull the border back to the point where our lives are no longer at risk."

"How would you even know that we've done that?" Sam replied. I wasn't sure if the condescension was in his tone or just his words, but either way I welcomed it. The lower the far side's opinion of our abilities, the more attractive the deal became for them.

I said, "Then you'd better back up far enough for all our communications systems to recover. When I can get news reports and see that there are no more planes going down, no power plants exploding, then we'll start the ceasefire."

Silence again, stretching out beyond mere hesitancy. His icon was still there, though, the S unblinking. I clutched at my shoulder, hoping that the burning pain was just tension in the muscle.

Finally: "All right. We agree. We'll start shifting the border."

I DROVE AROUND LOOKING for an all-night convenience store that might have had an old analog TV sitting in a corner to keep the cashier awake—that seemed like a good bet to start working long before the wireless connection to my laptop—but Campbell beat me to it. New Zealand radio and TV were reporting that the "digital blackout" appeared to be lifting, and ten minutes later Alison announced that she had internet access. A lot of the major servers were still down, or their sites weirdly garbled, but Reuters was starting to post updates on the crisis.

Sam had kept his word, so we halted the counter-strikes. Alison read from the Reuters site as the news came in. Seventeen planes had crashed, and four trains. There'd been fatalities at an oil refinery, and half a dozen manufacturing plants. One analyst put the global death toll at five thousand, and rising.

I muted the microphone on my laptop, and spent thirty seconds shouting obscenities and punching the dashboard. Then I rejoined the cabal.

Yuen said, "I've been reviewing my notes. If my instinct is worth anything, the theorem I mentioned before is correct: if the border is sealed, they'll have no way to touch us."

"What about the upside for them?" Alison asked. "Do you think they can protect themselves against Tim's algorithm, once they understand it?"

Yuen hesitated. "Yes and no. Any cluster of near-side truth values it injects into the far side will have a non-smooth border, so they'll be able to remove it with sheer computing power. In that sense, they'll never be defenseless. But I don't see how there's anything they can do to prevent the attacks in the first place."

"Short of wiping us out," Campbell said.

I heard an infant sobbing. Alison said, "That's Laura. I'm alone here. Give me five minutes."

I buried my head in my arms. I still had no idea what the right course would have been. If we'd handed over Campbell's algorithm immediately, might the good will that bought us have averted the war? Or would the same attack merely have come sooner? What criminal vanity had ever made the three of us think we could shoulder this responsibility on our own? Five thousand people were dead. The hawks who had taken over on the far side would weigh up our offer, and decide that they had no choice but to fight on.

And if the reluctant cabal had passed its burden to Canberra, to Zürich, to Beijing? Would there really have been peace? Or was I just wishing that there had been more hands steeped in the same blood, to share the guilt around?

The idea came from nowhere, sweeping away every other thought. I said, "Is there any reason why the far side has to stay *connected*?"

"Connected to what?" Campbell asked.

"Connected to itself. Connected topologically. They should be able to send down a spike, then withdraw it, but leave behind a bubble of altered truth values: a kind of outpost, sitting within the near side, with a perfect, smooth border making it impregnable. Right?"

Yuen said, "Perhaps. With both sides collaborating on the construction, that might be possible."

"Then the question is, can we find a place where we can do that so that it kills off the chance to use Tim's method completely—without crippling any process that we need just to survive?"

"*Fuck you*, Bruno!" Campbell exclaimed happily. "We give them one small Achilles' tendon to slice . . . and then they've got nothing to fear from us!"

Yuen said, "A watertight proof of something like that is going to take weeks, months."

"Then we'd better start work. And we'd better feed Sam the first plausible conjecture we get, so they can use their own resources to help us with the proof."

Alison came back online, and greeted the suggestion with cautious approval. I drove around until I found a quiet coffee shop. Electronic banking still wasn't working, and I had no cash left, but the waiter agreed to take my credit card number and a signed authority for a deduction of one hundred dollars; whatever I didn't eat and drink would be his tip.

I sat in the café, blanking out the world, steeping myself in the mathematics. Sometimes the four of us worked on separate tasks; sometimes we paired up, dragging each other out of dead ends and ruts. There were an infinite number of variations that could be made to Campbell's algorithm, but hour by hour we whittled away at the concept, finding the common ground that no version of the weapon could do without.

By four in the morning, we had a strong conjecture. I called Sam, and explained what we were hoping to achieve.

He said, "This is a good idea. We'll consider it."

The café closed. I sat in the car for a while, drained and numb, then I called Kate to find out where she was. A couple had given her a lift almost as far as Penrith, and when their car failed she'd walked the rest of the way home.

For close to four days, I spent most of my waking hours just sitting at my desk, watching as a wave of red inched its way across a map of the defect. The change of hue was not being rendered lightly; before each pixel turned red, twelve separate computers needed to confirm that the region of the border it represented was flat.

On the fifth day, Sam shut off his computers and allowed us to mount an attack from our side on the narrow corridor linking the bulk of the far side with the small enclave that now surrounded our Achilles' Heel. We wouldn't have suffered any real loss of essential arithmetic if this slender thread had remained, but keeping the corridor both small and impregnable had turned out to be impossible. The original plan was the only route to finality: to seal the border perfectly, the far side proper could not remain linked to its offshoot.

In the next stage, the two sides worked together to seal the enclave completely, polishing the scar where its umbilical had been sheared away. When that task was complete, the map showed it as a single burnished ruby. No known process could reshape it now. Campbell's method could have breached its border without touching it, reaching inside to reclaim it from within—but Campbell's method was exactly what this jewel ruled out.

At the other end of the vanished umbilical, Sam's machines set to work smoothing away the blemish. By early evening that, too, was done.

Only one tiny flaw in the border remained, now: the handful of propositions that enabled communication between the two sides. The cabal had debated the fate of this for hours. So long as this small wrinkle persisted, in principle it could be used to unravel everything, to mobilize the entire border again. It was true that, compared to the border as a whole, it would be relatively easy to monitor and defend such a small site, but a sustained burst of brute-force computing from either side could still overpower any resistance and exploit it.

In the end, Sam's political masters had made the decision for us. What they had always aspired to was certainty, and even if their strength favored them, this wasn't a gamble they were prepared to take.

I said, "Good luck with the future."

"Good luck to Sparseland," Sam replied. I believed he'd tried to hold out against the hawks, but I'd never been certain of his friendship. When his icon faded from my screen, I felt more relief than regret.

I'd learned the hard way not to assume that anything was permanent. Perhaps in a thousand years, someone would discover that Campbell's model was just an approximation to something deeper, and find a way to fracture these allegedly perfect walls. With any luck, by then both sides might also be better prepared to find a way to co-exist.

I found Kate sitting in the kitchen. I said, "I can answer your questions now, if that's what you want." On the morning after the disaster, I'd promised her this time would come—within weeks, not months—and she'd agreed to stay with me until it did.

She thought for a while.

"Did you have something to do with what happened last week?"

"Yes."

"Are you saying you unleashed the virus? You're the terrorist they're looking for?" To my great relief, she asked this in roughly the tone she might have used if I'd claimed to be Genghis Khan.

"No, I'm not the cause of what happened. It was my job to try and stop it, and I failed. But it wasn't any kind of computer virus."

She searched my face. "What was it, then? Can you explain that to me?"

"It's a long story."

"I don't care. We've got all night."

I said, "It started in university. With an idea of Alison's. One brilliant, beautiful, crazy idea."

Kate looked away, her face flushing, as if I'd said something deliberately humiliating. She knew I was not a mass-murderer. But there were other things about me of which she was less sure.

"The story starts with Alison," I said. "But it ends here, with you."

CRYSTAL NIGHTS

1

"MORE CAVIAR?" DANIEL CLIFF gestured at the serving dish and the cover irised from opaque to transparent. "It's fresh, I promise you. My chef had it flown in from Iran this morning."

"No thank you." Julie Dehghani touched a napkin to her lips then laid it on her plate with a gesture of finality. The dining room overlooked the Golden Gate Bridge, and most people Daniel invited here were content to spend an hour or two simply enjoying the view, but he could see that she was growing impatient with his small talk.

Daniel said, "I'd like to show you something." He led her into the adjoining conference room. On the table was a wireless keyboard; the wall screen showed a Linux command line interface. "Take a seat," he suggested.

Julie complied. "If this is some kind of audition, you might have warned me," she said.

"Not at all," Daniel replied. "I'm not going to ask you to jump through any hoops. I'd just like you to tell me what you think of this machine's performance."

She frowned slightly, but she was willing to play along. She ran some standard benchmarks. Daniel saw her squinting at the screen, one hand almost reaching up to where a desktop display would be, so she could double-check the number of digits in the FLOPS rating by counting them off with one finger. There were a lot more than she'd been expecting, but she wasn't seeing double.

"That's extraordinary," she said. "Is this whole building packed with networked processors, with only the penthouse for humans?"

Daniel said, "You tell me. Is it a cluster?"

"Hmm." So much for not making her jump through hoops, but it wasn't really much of a challenge. She ran some different benchmarks, based on algorithms that were provably impossible to parallelize; however smart the compiler was, the steps these programs required would have to be carried out strictly in sequence.

The FLOPS rating was unchanged.

Julie said, "All right, it's a single processor. Now you've got my attention. Where is it?"

"Turn the keyboard over."

There was a charcoal-gray module, five centimeters square and five millimeters thick, plugged into an inset docking bay. Julie examined it, but it bore no manufacturer's logo or other identifying marks.

"This connects to the processor?" she asked.

"No. It *is* the processor."

"You're joking." She tugged it free of the dock, and the wall screen went blank. She held it up and turned it around, though Daniel wasn't sure what she was looking for. Somewhere to slip in a screwdriver and take the thing apart, probably. He said, "If you break it, you own it, so I hope you've got a few hundred spare."

"A few hundred grand? Hardly."

"A few hundred million."

Her face flushed. "Of course. If it was a few hundred grand, everyone would have one." She put it down on the table, then as an afterthought slid it a little further from the edge. "As I said, you've got my attention."

Daniel smiled. "I'm sorry about the theatrics."

"No, this deserved the build-up. What is it, exactly?"

"A single, three-dimensional photonic crystal. No electronics to slow it down; every last component is optical. The architecture was nanofabricated with a method that I'd prefer not to describe in detail."

"Fair enough." She thought for a while. "I take it you don't expect me to buy one. My research budget for the next thousand years would barely cover it."

"In your present position. But you're not joined to the university at the hip."

"So this is a job interview?"

Daniel nodded.

Julie couldn't help herself; she picked up the crystal and examined it again, as if there might yet be some feature that a human eye could discern. "Can you give me a job description?"

"Midwife."

She laughed. "To what?"

"History," Daniel said.

Her smile faded slowly.

"I believe you're the best AI researcher of your generation," he said. "I want you to work for me." He reached over and took the crystal from her. "With this as your platform, imagine what you could do."

Julie said, "What exactly would you want me to do?"

"For the last fifteen years," Daniel said, "you've stated that the ultimate goal of your research is to create conscious, human-level, artificial intelligence."

"That's right."

"Then we want the same thing. What I want is for you to succeed."

She ran a hand over her face; whatever else she was thinking, there was no denying that she was tempted. "It's gratifying that you have so much confidence in my abilities," she said. "But we need to be clear about some things. This prototype is amazing, and if you ever get the production costs down I'm sure it will have some extraordinary applications. It would eat up climate forecasting, lattice QCD, astrophysical modeling, proteomics . . ."

"Of course." Actually, Daniel had no intention of marketing the device. He'd bought out the inventor of the fabrication process with his own private funds; there were no other shareholders or directors to dictate his use of the technology.

"But AI," Julie said, "is different. We're in a maze, not a highway; there's nowhere that speed alone can take us. However many exaflops I have to play with, they won't spontaneously combust into consciousness. I'm not being held back by the university's computers;

I have access to SHARCNET anytime I need it. I'm being held back by my own lack of insight into the problems I'm addressing."

Daniel said, "A maze is not a dead end. When I was twelve, I wrote a program for solving mazes."

"And I'm sure it worked well," Julie replied, "for small, two-dimensional ones. But you know how those kind of algorithms scale. Put your old program on this crystal, and I could still design a maze in half a day that would bring it to its knees."

"Of course," Daniel conceded. "Which is precisely why I'm interested in hiring you. You know a great deal more about the maze of AI than I do; any strategy you developed would be vastly superior to a blind search."

"I'm not saying that I'm merely groping in the dark," she said. "If it was that bleak, I'd be working on a different problem entirely. But I don't see what difference this processor would make."

"What created the only example of consciousness we know of?" Daniel asked.

"Evolution."

"Exactly. But I don't want to wait three billion years, so I need to make the selection process a great deal more refined, and the sources of variation more targeted."

Julie digested this. "You want to try to *evolve* true AI? Conscious, human-level AI?"

"Yes." Daniel saw her mouth tightening, saw her struggling to measure her words before speaking.

"With respect," she said, "I don't think you've thought that through."

"On the contrary," Daniel assured her. "I've been planning this for twenty years."

"Evolution," she said, "is about failure and death. Do you have any idea how many sentient creatures lived and died along the way to *Homo sapiens*? How much suffering was involved?"

"Part of your job would be to minimize the suffering."

"*Minimize it?*" She seemed genuinely shocked, as if this proposal was even worse than blithely assuming that the process would raise no ethical concerns. "What right do we have to inflict it at all?"

Daniel said, "You're grateful to exist, aren't you? Notwithstanding the tribulations of your ancestors."

"I'm grateful to exist," she agreed, "but in the human case the suffering wasn't deliberately inflicted by anyone, and nor was there any alternative way we could have come into existence. If there really *had* been a just creator, I don't doubt that he would have followed Genesis literally; he sure as hell would not have used evolution."

"Just, *and omnipotent*," Daniel suggested. "Sadly, that second trait's even rarer than the first."

"I don't think it's going to take omnipotence to create something in our own image," she said. "Just a little more patience and self-knowledge."

"This won't be like natural selection," Daniel insisted. "Not that blind, not that cruel, not that wasteful. You'd be free to intervene as much as you wished, to take whatever palliative measures you felt appropriate."

"*Palliative measures?*" Julie met his gaze, and he saw her expression flicker from disbelief to something darker. She stood up and glanced at her wristphone. "I don't have any signal here. Would you mind calling me a taxi?"

Daniel said, "Please, hear me out. Give me ten more minutes, then the helicopter will take you to the airport."

"I'd prefer to make my own way home." She gave Daniel a look that made it clear that this was not negotiable.

He called her a taxi, and they walked to the elevator.

"I know you find this morally challenging," he said, "and I respect that. I wouldn't dream of hiring someone who thought these were trivial issues. But if I don't do this, someone else will. Someone with far worse intentions than mine."

"Really?" Her tone was openly sarcastic now. "So how, exactly, does the mere existence of your project stop this hypothetical bin Laden of AI from carrying out his own?"

Daniel was disappointed; he'd expected her at least to understand what was at stake. He said, "This is a race to decide between Godhood and enslavement. Whoever succeeds first will be unstoppable. I'm not going to be anyone's slave."

Julie stepped into the elevator; he followed her.

She said, "You know what they say the modern version of Pascal's Wager is? Sucking up to as many Transhumanists as possible, just in case one of them turns into God. Perhaps your motto should be 'Treat every chatterbot kindly, it might turn out to be the deity's uncle.'"

"We will be as kind as possible," Daniel said. "And don't forget, we can determine the nature of these beings. They will be happy to be alive, and grateful to their creator. We can select for those traits."

Julie said, "So you're aiming for *übermenschen* that wag their tails when you scratch them behind the ears? You might find there's a bit of a trade-off there."

The elevator reached the lobby. Daniel said, "Think about this, don't rush to a decision. You can call me any time." There was no commercial flight back to Toronto tonight; she'd be stuck in a hotel, paying money she could ill-afford, thinking about the kind of salary she could demand from him now that she'd played hard to get. If she mentally recast all this obstinate moralizing as a deliberate bargaining strategy, she'd have no trouble swallowing her pride.

Julie offered her hand, and he shook it. She said, "Thank you for dinner."

The taxi was waiting. He walked with her across the lobby. "If you want to see AI in your lifetime," he said, "this is the only way it's going to happen."

She turned to face him. "Maybe that's true. We'll see. But better to spend a thousand years and get it right, than a decade and succeed by your methods."

As Daniel watched the taxi drive away into the fog, he forced himself to accept the reality: she was never going to change her mind. Julie Dehghani had been his first choice, his ideal collaborator. He couldn't pretend that this wasn't a setback.

Still, no one was irreplaceable. However much it would have delighted him to have won her over, there were many more names on his list.

2

DANIEL'S WRIST TINGLED AS the message came through. He glanced down and saw the word PROGRESS! hovering in front of his watch face.

The board meeting was almost over; he disciplined himself and kept his attention focused for ten more minutes. WiddulHands.com had made him his first billion, and it was still the pre-eminent social networking site for the 0-3 age group. It had been fifteen years since he'd founded the company, and he had since diversified in many directions, but he had no intention of taking his hands off the levers.

When the meeting finished he blanked the wall screen and paced the empty conference room for half a minute, rolling his neck and stretching his shoulders. Then he said, "Lucien".

Lucien Crace appeared on the screen. "Significant progress?" Daniel enquired.

"Absolutely." Lucien was trying to maintain polite eye contact with Daniel, but something kept drawing his gaze away. Without waiting for an explanation, Daniel gestured at the screen and had it show him exactly what Lucien was seeing.

A barren, rocky landscape stretched to the horizon. Scattered across the rocks were dozens of crab-like creatures—some deep blue, some coral pink, though these weren't colors the locals would see, just species markers added to the view to make it easier to interpret. As Daniel watched, fat droplets of corrosive rain drizzled down from a passing cloud. This had to be the bleakest environment in all of Sapphire.

Lucien was still visible in an inset. "See the blue ones over by the crater lake?" he said. He sketched a circle on the image to guide Daniel's attention.

"Yeah." Five blues were clustered around a lone pink; Daniel gestured and the view zoomed in on them. The blues had opened up their prisoner's body, but it wasn't dead; Daniel was sure of that, because the pinks had recently acquired a trait that turned their bodies to mush the instant they expired.

"They've found a way to study it," Lucien said. "To keep it alive and study it."

From the very start of the project, he and Daniel had decided to grant the Phites the power to observe and manipulate their own bodies as much as possible. In the DNA world, the inner workings of anatomy and heredity had only become accessible once highly sophisticated technology had been invented. In Sapphire, the barriers were designed to be far lower. The basic units of biology here were "beads", small spheres that possessed a handful of simple properties but no complex internal biochemistry. Beads were larger than the cells of the DNA world, and Sapphire's diffractionless optics rendered them visible to the right kind of naked eye. Animals acquired beads from their diet, while in plants they replicated in the presence of sunlight, but unlike cells they did not themselves mutate. The beads in a Phite's body could be rearranged with a minimum of fuss, enabling a kind of self-modification that no human surgeon or prosthetics engineer could rival—and this skill was actually essential for at least one stage in every Phite's life: reproduction involved two Phites pooling their spare beads and then collaborating to "sculpt" them into an infant, in part by directly copying each other's current body plans.

Of course these crabs knew nothing of the abstract principles of engineering and design, but the benefits of trial and error, of self-experimentation and cross-species plagiarism, had led them into an escalating war of innovation. The pinks had been the first to stop their corpses from being plundered for secrets, by stumbling on a way to make them literally fall apart *in extremis*; now it seemed the blues had found a way around that, and were indulging in a spot of vivisection-as-industrial-espionage.

Daniel felt a visceral twinge of sympathy for the struggling pink, but he brushed it aside. Not only did he doubt that the Phites were any more conscious than ordinary crabs, they certainly had a radically different relationship to bodily integrity. The pink was resisting because its dissectors were of a different species; if they had been its cousins it might not have put up any fight at all. When something happened in spite of your wishes, that was unpleasant by definition, but it would be absurd to imagine that the pink was in the kind of agony that an antelope being flayed by jackals would feel—let alone experiencing the existential terrors of a human trapped and mutilated by a hostile tribe.

"This is going to give them a tremendous advantage," Lucien enthused.

"The blues?"

Lucien shook his head. "Not blues over pinks; Phites over tradlife. Bacteria can swap genes, but this kind of active mimetics is unprecedented without cultural support. Da Vinci might have watched the birds in flight and sketched his gliders, but no lemur ever dissected the body of an eagle and then stole its tricks. They're going to have *innate* skills as powerful as whole strands of human technology. All this before they even have language."

"Hmm." Daniel wanted to be optimistic too, but he was growing wary of Lucien's hype. Lucien had a doctorate in genetic programming, but he'd made his name with FoodExcuses.com, a web service that trawled the medical literature to cobble together quasi-scientific justifications for indulging in your favorite culinary vice. He had the kind of technobabble that could bleed money out of venture capitalists down pat, and though Daniel admired that skill in its proper place, he expected a higher insight-to-bullshit ratio now that Lucien was on his payroll.

The blues were backing away from their captive. As Daniel watched, the pink sealed up its wounds and scuttled off toward a group of its own kind. The blues had now seen the detailed anatomy of the respiratory system that had been giving the pinks an advantage in the thin air of this high plateau. A few of the blues would try it out, and if it worked for them, the whole tribe would copy it.

"So what do you think?" Lucien asked.

"Select them," Daniel said.

"Just the blues?"

"No, both of them." The blues alone might have diverged into competing subspecies eventually, but bringing their old rivals along for the ride would help to keep them sharp.

"Done," Lucien replied. In an instant, ten million Phites were erased, leaving the few thousand blues and pinks from these badlands to inherit the planet. Daniel felt no compunction; the extinction events he decreed were surely the most painless in history.

Now that the world no longer required human scrutiny, Lucien unthrottled the crystal and let the simulation race ahead; automated tools would let them know when the next interesting development arose. Daniel watched the population figures rising as his chosen species spread out and recolonized Sapphire.

Would their distant descendants rage against him, for this act of "genocide" that had made room for them to flourish and prosper? That seemed unlikely. In any case, what choice did he have? He couldn't start manufacturing new crystals for every useless side-branch of the evolutionary tree. Nobody was wealthy enough to indulge in an exponentially growing number of virtual animal shelters, at half a billion dollars apiece.

He was a just creator, but he was not omnipotent. His careful pruning was the only way.

3

IN THE MONTHS THAT followed, progress came in fits and starts. Several times, Daniel found himself rewinding history, reversing his decisions and trying a new path. Keeping every Phite variant alive was impractical, but he did retain enough information to resurrect lost species at will.

The maze of AI was still a maze, but the speed of the crystal served them well. Barely eighteen months after the start of Project Sapphire, the Phites were exhibiting a basic theory of mind: their actions showed that they could deduce what others knew about the world, as distinct from what they knew themselves. Other AI researchers had spliced this kind of thing into their programs by hand, but Daniel was convinced that his version was better integrated, more robust. Human-crafted software was brittle and inflexible; his Phites had been forged in the heat of change.

Daniel kept a close watch on his competitors, but nothing he saw gave him reason to doubt his approach. Sunil Gupta was raking in the cash from a search engine that could "understand" all forms of text, audio and video, making use of fuzzy logic techniques that were at least forty years old. Daniel respected Gupta's business acumen, but in the unlikely event that his software ever became conscious, the sheer cruelty of having forced it to wade through the endless tides of blogorrhea would surely see it turn on its creator and exact a revenge that made *The Terminator* look like a picnic. Angela Lindstrom was having some success with her cheesy AfterLife, in which dying clients gave heart-to-heart interviews to software that then constructed avatars able to converse with surviving relatives. And Julie Dehghani was still frittering away her talent, writing software for robots that played with colored blocks side-by-side with human infants, and learned languages from adult volunteers by imitating the interactions of baby talk. Her prophecy of taking a thousand years to "get it right" seemed to be on target.

As the second year of the project drew to a close, Lucien was contacting Daniel once or twice a month to announce a new breakthrough. By constructing environments that imposed suitable selection pressures, Lucien had generated a succession of new species that used simple tools, crafted crude shelters, and even domesticated plants. They were still shaped more or less like crabs, but they were at least as intelligent as chimpanzees.

The Phites worked together by observation and imitation, guiding and reprimanding each other with a limited repertoire of gestures and cries, but as yet they lacked anything that could truly be called a language. Daniel grew impatient; to move beyond a handful of specialized skills, his creatures needed the power to map any object, any action, any prospect they might encounter in the world into their speech, and into their thoughts.

Daniel summoned Lucien and they sought a way forward. It was easy to tweak the Phites' anatomy to grant them the ability to generate more subtle vocalizations, but that alone was no more useful than handing a chimp a conductor's baton. What was needed was a way to make sophisticated planning and communications skills a matter of survival.

Eventually, he and Lucien settled on a series of environmental modifications, providing opportunities for the creatures to rise to the occasion. Most of these scenarios began with famine. Lucien blighted the main food crops, then offered a palpable reward for progress by dangling some tempting new fruit from a branch that was just out of reach. Sometimes that metaphor could almost be taken literally: he'd introduce a plant with a complex life cycle that required tricky processing to render it edible, or a new prey animal that was clever and vicious, but nutritionally well worth hunting in the end.

Time and again, the Phites failed the test, with localized species dwindling to extinction. Daniel watched in dismay; he had not grown sentimental, but he'd always boasted to himself that he'd set his standards higher than the extravagant cruelties of nature. He contemplated tweaking the creatures' physiology so that starvation brought a swifter, more merciful demise, but Lucien pointed out that he'd be slashing his chances of success if he curtailed this period of intense motivation. Each time a group died out, a fresh batch of mutated cousins rose from the dust to take their place; without that intervention, Sapphire would have been a wilderness within a few real-time days.

Daniel closed his eyes to the carnage, and put his trust in sheer time, sheer numbers. In the end, that was what the crystal had bought him: when all else failed, he could give up any pretense of knowing how to achieve his aims and simply test one random mutation after another.

Months went by, sending hundreds of millions of tribes starving into their graves. But what choice did he have? If he fed these creatures milk and honey, they'd remain fat and stupid until the day he died. Their hunger agitated them, it drove them to search and strive, and while any human onlooker was tempted to color such behavior with their own emotional palette, Daniel told himself that the Phites' suffering was a shallow thing, little more than the instinct that jerked his own hand back from a flame before he'd even registered discomfort.

They were not the equal of humans. Not yet.

And if he lost his nerve, they never would be.

DANIEL DREAMED THAT HE was inside Sapphire, but there were no Phites in sight. In front of him stood a sleek black monolith; a thin stream of pus wept from a crack in its smooth, obsidian surface. Someone was holding him by the wrist, trying to force his hand into a reeking pit in the ground. The pit, he knew, was piled high with things he did not want to see, let alone touch.

He thrashed around until he woke, but the sense of pressure on his wrist remained. It was coming from his watch. As he focused on the one-word message he'd received, his stomach tightened. Lucien would not have dared to wake him at this hour for some run-of-the-mill result.

Daniel rose, dressed, then sat in his office sipping coffee. He did not know why he was so reluctant to make the call. He had been waiting for this moment for more than twenty years, but it would not be the pinnacle of his life. After this, there would be a thousand more peaks, each one twice as magnificent as the last.

He finished the coffee then sat a while longer, massaging his temples, making sure his head was clear. He would not greet this new era bleary-eyed, half-awake. He recorded all his calls, but this was one he would retain for posterity.

"Lucien," he said. The man's image appeared, smiling. "Success?"

"They're talking to each other," Lucien replied.

"About what?"

"Food, weather, sex, death. The past, the future. You name it. They won't shut up."

Lucien sent transcripts on the data channel, and Daniel perused them. The linguistics software didn't just observe the Phites' behavior and correlate it with the sounds they made; it peered right into their virtual brains and tracked the flow of information. Its task was far from trivial, and there was no guarantee that its translations were perfect, but Daniel did not believe it could hallucinate an entire language and fabricate these rich, detailed conversations out of thin air.

He flicked between statistical summaries, technical overviews of linguistic structure, and snippets from the millions of conversations the software had logged. *Food, weather, sex, death.* As human dialog the translations would have seemed utterly banal, but in context they were riveting. These were not chatterbots blindly following Markov chains, designed to impress the judges in a Turing test. The Phites were discussing matters by which they genuinely lived and died.

When Daniel brought up a page of conversational topics in alphabetical order, his eyes were caught by the single entry under the letter G. *Grief.* He tapped the link, and spent a few minutes reading through samples, illustrating the appearance of the concept following the death of a child, a parent, a friend.

He kneaded his eyelids. It was three in the morning; there was a sickening clarity to everything, the kind that only night could bring. He turned to Lucien.

"No more death."

"Boss?" Lucien was startled.

"I want to make them immortal. Let them evolve culturally; let their ideas live and die. Let them modify their own brains, once they're smart enough; they can already tweak the rest of their anatomy."

"Where will you put them all?" Lucien demanded.

"I can afford another crystal. Maybe two more."

"That won't get you far. At the present birth rate—"

"We'll have to cut their fertility drastically, tapering it down to zero. After that, if they want to start reproducing again they'll really have to innovate." They would need to learn about the outside world, and comprehend its alien physics well enough to design new hardware into which they could migrate.

Lucien scowled. "How will we control them? How will we shape them? If we can't select the ones we want—"

Daniel said quietly, "This is not up for discussion." Whatever Julie Dehghani had thought of him, he was not a monster; if he believed that these creatures were as conscious as he was, he was not going to slaughter them like cattle—or stand by and let them die "naturally", when the rules of this world were his to rewrite at will.

"We'll shape them through their memes," he said. "We'll kill off the bad memes, and help spread the ones we want to succeed." He would need to keep an iron grip on the Phites and their culture, though, or he would never be able to trust them. If he wasn't going to literally *breed them* for loyalty and gratitude, he would have to do the same with their ideas.

Lucien said, "We're not prepared for any of this. We're going to need new software, new analysis and intervention tools."

Daniel understood. "Freeze time in Sapphire. Then tell the team they've got eighteen months."

4

DANIEL SOLD HIS SHARES in WiddulHands, and had two more crystals built. One was to support a higher population in Sapphire, so there was as large a pool of diversity among the immortal Phites as possible; the other was to run the software—which Lucien had dubbed the Thought Police—needed to keep tabs on what they were doing. If human overseers had had to monitor and shape the evolving culture every step of the way, that would have slowed things down to a glacial pace. Still, automating the process completely was tricky, and Daniel preferred to err on the side of caution, with the Thought Police freezing Sapphire and notifying him whenever the situation became too delicate.

If the end of death was greeted by the Phites with a mixture of puzzlement and rejoicing, the end of birth was not so easy to accept. When all attempts by mating couples to sculpt their excess beads into offspring became as ineffectual as shaping dolls out of clay, it led to a mixture of persistence and distress that was painful to witness. Humans were accustomed to failing to conceive, but this was more like still birth after still birth. Even when Daniel intervened to modify the Phites' basic drives, some kind of cultural or emotional inertia kept many of them going through the motions. Though their new instincts urged them merely to pool their spare beads and then stop, sated, they would continue with the old version of the act regardless, forlorn and confused, trying to shape the useless puddle into something that lived and breathed.

Move on, Daniel thought. *Get over it.* There was only so much sympathy he could muster for immortal beings who would fill the galaxy with their children, if they ever got their act together.

The Phites didn't yet have writing, but they'd developed a strong oral tradition, and some put their mourning for the old ways into elegiac words. The Thought Police identified those memes, and ensured that they didn't spread far. Some Phites chose to kill themselves rather than live in the barren new world. Daniel felt he had no right to stop them, but mysterious obstacles blocked the paths of anyone who tried, irresponsibly, to romanticize or encourage such acts.

The Phites could only die by their own volition, but those who retained the will to live were not free to doze the centuries away. Daniel decreed no more terrible famines, but he hadn't abolished hunger itself, and he kept enough pressure on the food supply and other resources to force the Phites to keep innovating, refining agriculture, developing trade.

The Thought Police identified and nurtured the seeds of writing, mathematics, and natural science. The physics of Sapphire was a simplified, game-world model, not so arbitrary as to be incoherent, but not so deep and complex that you needed particle physics to get to the bottom of it. As crystal time sped forward and the immortals sought solace in understanding their world, Sapphire soon had its Euclid and Archimedes, its Galileo and its Newton; their ideas spread with supernatural efficiency, bringing forth a torrent of mathematicians and astronomers.

Sapphire's stars were just a planetarium-like backdrop, present only to help the Phites get their notions of heliocentricity and inertia right, but its moon was as real as the world itself. The technology needed to reach it was going to take a while, but that was all right; Daniel didn't want them getting ahead of themselves. There was a surprise waiting for them there, and his preference was for a flourishing of biotech and computing before they faced that revelation.

Between the absence of fossils, Sapphire's limited biodiversity, and all the clunky external meddling that needed to be covered up, it was hard for the Phites to reach a grand Darwinian view of biology, but their innate skill with beads gave them a head start in the practical arts. With a little nudging, they began tinkering with their bodies, correcting some inconvenient anatomical quirks that they'd missed in their pre-conscious phase.

As they refined their knowledge and techniques, Daniel let them imagine that they were working toward restoring fertility; after all, that was perfectly true, even if their goal was a few conceptual revolutions further away than they realized. Humans had had their naïve notions of a Philosopher's Stone dashed, but they'd still achieved nuclear transmutation in the end.

The Phites, he hoped, would transmute *themselves*: inspect their own brains, make sense of them, and begin to improve them. It was a staggering task to expect of anyone; even Lucien and his team, with their God's-eye view of the creatures, couldn't come close. But when the crystal was running at full speed, the Phites could think millions of times faster than their creators. If Daniel could keep them from straying off course, everything that humanity might once have conceived of as the fruits of millennia of progress was now just a matter of months away.

5

LUCIEN SAID, "WE'RE LOSING track of the language."

Daniel was in his Houston office; he'd come to Texas for a series of face-to-face meetings, to see if he could raise some much-needed cash by licensing the crystal fabrication process. He would have preferred to keep the technology to himself, but he was almost certain that he was too far ahead of his rivals now for any of them to stand a chance of catching up with him.

"What do you mean, losing track?" Daniel demanded. Lucien had briefed him just three hours before, and given no warning of an impending crisis.

The Thought Police, Lucien explained, had done their job well: they had pushed the neural self-modification meme for all it was worth, and now a successful form of "brain boosting" was spreading across Sapphire. It required a detailed "recipe" but no technological aids; the same innate skills for observing and manipulating beads that the Phites had used to copy themselves during reproduction were enough.

All of this was much as Daniel had hoped it would be, but there was an alarming downside. The boosted Phites were adopting a dense and complex new language, and the analysis software couldn't make sense of it.

"Slow them down further," Daniel suggested. "Give the linguistics more time to run."

"I've already frozen Sapphire," Lucien replied. "The linguistics have been running for an hour, with the full resources of an entire crystal."

Daniel said irritably, "We can see exactly what they've done to their brains. How can we not understand the effects on the language?"

"In the general case," Lucien said, "deducing a language from nothing but neural anatomy is computationally intractable. With the old language, we were lucky; it had a simple structure, and it was highly correlated with obvious behavioral elements. The new language is much more abstract and conceptual. We might not even have our own correlates for half the concepts."

Daniel had no intention of letting events in Sapphire slip out of his control. It was one thing to hope that the Phites would, eventually, be juggling real-world physics that was temporarily beyond his comprehension, but any bright ten-year-old could grasp the laws of their present universe, and their technology was still far from rocket science.

He said, "Keep Sapphire frozen, and study your records of the Phites who first performed this boost. If they understood what they were doing, we can work it out too."

At the end of the week, Daniel signed the licensing deal and flew back to San Francisco. Lucien briefed him daily, and at Daniel's urging hired a dozen new computational linguists to help with the problem.

After six months, it was clear that they were getting nowhere. The Phites who'd invented the boost had had one big advantage as they'd tinkered with each other's brains: it had not been a purely theoretical exercise for them. They hadn't gazed at anatomical diagrams and then reasoned their way to a better design. They had *experienced* the effects of thousands of small experimental changes, and the results had shaped their intuition for the process. Very little of that intuition had been spoken aloud, let alone written down and formalized. And the process of decoding those insights from a purely structural view of their brains was every bit as difficult as decoding the language itself.

Daniel couldn't wait any longer. With the crystal heading for the market, and other comparable technologies approaching fruition, he couldn't allow his lead to melt away.

"We need the Phites themselves to act as translators," he told Lucien. "We need to contrive a situation where there's a large enough pool who choose not to be boosted that the old language continues to be used."

"So we need maybe twenty-five per cent refusing the boost?" Lucien suggested. "And we need the boosted Phites to want to keep them informed of what's happening, in terms that we can all understand."

Daniel said, "Exactly."

"I think we can slow down the uptake of boosting," Lucien mused, "while we encourage a traditionalist meme that says it's better to span the two cultures and languages than replace the old entirely with the new."

Lucien's team set to work, tweaking the Thought Police for the new task, then restarting Sapphire itself.

Their efforts seemed to yield the desired result: the Phites were corralled into valuing the notion of maintaining a link to their past, and while the boosted Phites surged ahead, they also worked hard to keep the unboosted in the loop.

It was a messy compromise, though, and Daniel wasn't happy with the prospect of making do with a watered-down, Sapphire-for-Dummies version of the Phites' intellectual achievements. What he really wanted was someone on the inside reporting to him directly, like a Phite version of Lucien.

It was time to start thinking about job interviews.

LUCIEN WAS RUNNING SAPPHIRE more slowly than usual—to give the Thought Police a computational advantage now that they'd lost so much raw surveillance data—but even at the reduced rate, it took just six real-time days for the boosted Phites to invent computers, first as a mathematical formalism and, shortly afterward, as a succession of practical machines.

Daniel had already asked Lucien to notify him if any Phite guessed the true nature of their world. In the past, a few had come up with vague metaphysical speculations that weren't too wide of the mark, but now that they had a firm grasp of the idea of universal computation, they were finally in a position to understand the crystal as more than an idle fantasy.

The message came just after midnight, as Daniel was preparing for bed. He went into his office and activated the intervention tool that Lucien had written for him, specifying a serial number for the Phite in question.

The tool prompted Daniel to provide a human-style name for his interlocutor, to facilitate communication. Daniel's mind went blank, but after waiting twenty seconds the software offered its own suggestion: Primo.

Primo was boosted, and he had recently built a computer of his own. Shortly afterward, the Thought Police had heard him telling a couple of unboosted friends about an amusing possibility that had occurred to him.

Sapphire was slowed to a human pace, then Daniel took control of a Phite avatar and the tool contrived a meeting, arranging for the two of them to be alone in the shelter that Primo had built for himself. In accordance with the current architectural style the wooden building was actually still alive, self-repairing and anchored to the ground by roots.

Primo said, "Good morning. I don't believe we've met."

It was no great breach of protocol for a stranger to enter one's shelter uninvited, but Primo was understating his surprise; in this world of immortals, but no passenger jets, bumping into strangers anywhere was rare.

"I'm Daniel." The tool would invent a Phite name for Primo to hear. "I heard you talking to your friends last night about your new computer. Wondering what these machines might do in the future. Wondering if they could ever grow powerful enough to contain a whole world."

"I didn't see you there," Primo replied.

"I wasn't there," Daniel explained. "I live outside this world. I built the computer that contains this world."

Primo made a gesture that the tool annotated as amusement, then he spoke a few words in the boosted language. *Insults? A jest? A test of Daniel's omniscience?* Daniel decided to bluff his way through, and act as if the words were irrelevant.

He said, "Let the rain start." Rain began pounding on the roof of the shelter. "Let the rain stop." Daniel gestured with one claw at a large cooking pot in a corner of the room. "Sand. Flower. Fire. Water jug." The pot obliged him, taking on each form in turn.

Primo said, "Very well. I believe you, Daniel." Daniel had had some experience reading the Phites' body language directly, and to him Primo seemed reasonably calm. Perhaps when you were as old as he was, and had witnessed so much change, such a revelation was far less of a shock than it would have been to a human at the dawn of the computer age.

"You created this world?" Primo asked him.

"Yes."

"You shaped our history?"

"In part," Daniel said. "Many things have been down to chance, or to your own choices."

"Did you stop us having children?" Primo demanded.

"Yes," Daniel admitted.

"*Why?*"

"There is no room left in the computer. It was either that, or many more deaths."

Primo pondered this. "So you could have stopped the death of my parents, had you wished?"

"I could bring them back to life, if you want that." This wasn't a lie; Daniel had stored detailed snapshots of all the last mortal Phites. "But not yet; only when there's a bigger computer. When there's room for them."

"Could you bring back *their* parents? And their parents' parents? Back to the beginning of time?"

"No. That information is lost."

Primo said, "What is this talk of waiting for a bigger computer? You could easily stop time from passing for us, and only start it again when your new computer is built."

"No," Daniel said, "I can't. Because *I need you to build the computer.* I'm not like you: I'm not immortal, and my brain can't be boosted. I've done my best, now I need you to do better. The only way that can happen is if you learn the science of my world, and come up with a way to make this new machine."

Primo walked over to the water jug that Daniel had magicked into being. "It seems to me that you were ill-prepared for the task you set yourself. If you'd waited for the machine you really needed, our lives would not have been so hard. And if such a machine could not be built in your lifetime, what was to stop your grandchildren from taking on that task?"

"I had no choice," Daniel insisted. "I couldn't leave your creation to my descendants. There is a war coming between my people. I needed your help. I needed strong allies."

"You have no friends in your own world?"

"Your time runs faster than mine. I needed the kind of allies that only your people can become, in time."

Primo said, "What exactly do you want of us?"

"To build the new computer you need," Daniel replied. "To grow in numbers, to grow in strength. Then to raise me up, to make me greater than I was, as I've done for you. When the war is won, there will be peace forever. Side by side, we will rule a thousand worlds."

"And what do you want of *me?*" Primo asked. "Why are you speaking to me, and not to all of us?"

"Most people," Daniel said, "aren't ready to hear this. It's better that they don't learn the truth yet. But I need one person who can work for me directly. I can see and hear everything in your world, but I need you to make sense of it. I need you to understand things for me."

Primo was silent.

Daniel said, "I gave you life. How can you refuse me?"

6

DANIEL PUSHED HIS WAY through the small crowd of protesters gathered at the entrance to his San Francisco tower. He could have come and gone by helicopter instead, but his security consultants had assessed these people as posing no significant threat. A small amount of bad PR didn't bother him; he was no longer selling anything that the public could boycott directly, and none of the businesses he dealt with seemed worried about being tainted by association. He'd broken no laws, and confirmed no rumors. A few feral cyberphiles waving placards reading "Software Is Not Your Slave!" meant nothing.

Still, if he ever found out which one of his employees had leaked details of the project, he'd break their legs.

Daniel was in the elevator when Lucien messaged him: MOON VERY SOON! He halted the elevator's ascent, and redirected it to the basement.

All three crystals were housed in the basement now, just centimeters away from the Play Pen: a vacuum chamber containing an atomic force microscope with fifty thousand independently movable tips, arrays of solid-state lasers and photodetectors, and thousands of micro-wells stocked with samples of all the stable chemical elements. The time lag between Sapphire and this machine had to be as short as possible, in order for the Phites to be able to conduct experiments in real-world physics while their own world was running at full speed.

Daniel pulled up a stool and sat beside the Play Pen. If he wasn't going to slow Sapphire down, it was pointless aspiring to watch developments as they unfolded. He'd probably view a replay of the lunar landing when he went up to his office, but by the time he screened it, it would be ancient history.

"One giant leap" would be an understatement; wherever the Phites landed on the moon, they would find a strange black monolith waiting for them. Inside would be the means to operate the Play Pen; it would not take them long to learn the controls, or to understand what this signified. If they were really slow in grasping what they'd found, Daniel had instructed Primo to explain it to them.

The physics of the real world was far more complex than the kind the Phites were used to, but then, no human had ever been on intimate terms with quantum field theory either, and the Thought Police had already encouraged the Phites to develop most of the mathematics they'd need to get started. In any case, it didn't matter if the Phites took longer than humans to discover twentieth-century scientific principles, and move beyond them. Seen from the outside, it would happen within hours, days, weeks at the most.

A row of indicator lights blinked on; the Play Pen was active. Daniel's throat went dry. The Phites were finally reaching out of their own world into his.

A panel above the machine displayed histograms classifying the experiments the Phites had performed so far. By the time Daniel was paying attention, they had already discovered the kinds of bonds that could be formed between various atoms, and constructed thousands of different small molecules. As he watched, they carried out spectroscopic analyses, built simple nanomachines, and manufactured devices that were, unmistakably, memory elements and logic gates.

The Phites wanted children, and they understood now that this was the only way. They would soon be building a world in which they were not just more numerous, but faster and smarter than they were inside the crystal. And that would only be the first of a thousand iterations. They were working their way toward Godhood, and they would lift up their own creator as they ascended.

Daniel left the basement and headed for his office. When he arrived, he called Lucien.

"They've built an atomic-scale computer," Lucien announced. "And they've fed some fairly complex software into it. It doesn't seem to be an upload, though. Certainly not a direct copy on the level of beads." He sounded flustered; Daniel had forbidden him to risk screwing up the experiments by slowing down Sapphire, so even with Primo's briefings to help him it was difficult for him to keep abreast of everything.

"Can you model their computer, and then model what the software is doing?" Daniel suggested.

Lucien said, "We only have six atomic physicists on the team; the Phites already outnumber us on that score by about a thousand to one. By the time we have any hope of making sense of this, they'll be doing something different."

"What does Primo say?" The Thought Police hadn't been able to get Primo included in any of the lunar expeditions, but Lucien had given him the power to make himself invisible and teleport to any part of Sapphire or the lunar base. Wherever the action was, he was free to eavesdrop.

"Primo has trouble understanding a lot of what he hears; even the boosted aren't universal polymaths and instant experts in every kind of jargon. The gist of it is that the Lunar Project people have made a very fast computer in the Outer World, and it's going to help with the fertility problem . . . somehow." Lucien laughed. "Hey, maybe the Phites will do exactly what we did: see if they can evolve something smart enough to give them a hand. How cool would that be?"

Daniel was not amused. Somebody had to do some real work eventually; if the Phites just passed the buck, the whole enterprise would collapse like a pyramid scheme.

Daniel had some business meetings he couldn't put off. By the time he'd swept all the bullshit aside, it was early afternoon. The Phites had now built some kind of tiny solid-state accelerator, and were probing the internal structure of protons and neutrons by pounding them with high-speed electrons. An atomic computer wired up to various detectors was doing the data analysis, processing the results faster than any in-world computer could. The Phites had already figured out the standard quark model. Maybe they were going to skip uploading into nanocomputers, and head straight for some kind of femtomachine?

Digests of Primo's briefings made no mention of using the strong force for computing, though. They were still just satisfying their curiosity about the fundamental laws. Daniel reminded himself of their history. They had burrowed down to what seemed like the foundations of physics before, only to discover that those simple rules were nothing to do with the ultimate reality. It made sense that they would try to dig as deeply as they could into the mysteries of the Outer World before daring to found a colony, let alone emigrate *en masse*.

By sunset the Phites were probing the surroundings of the Play Pen with various kinds of radiation. The levels were extremely low—certainly too low to risk damaging the crystals—so Daniel saw no need to intervene. The Play Pen itself did not have a massive power supply, it contained no radioisotopes, and the Thought Police would ring alarm bells and bring in human experts if some kind of tabletop fusion experiment got underway, so Daniel was reasonably confident that the Phites couldn't do anything stupid and blow the whole thing up.

Primo's briefings made it clear that they thought they were engaged in a kind of "astronomy". Daniel wondered if he should give them access to instruments for doing serious observations—the kind that would allow them to understand relativistic gravity and cosmology. Even if he bought time on a large telescope, though, just pointing it would take an eternity for the Phites. He wasn't going to slow Sapphire down and then grow old while they explored the sky; next thing they'd be launching space probes on thirty-year missions. Maybe it was time to ramp up the level of collaboration, and just hand them some astronomy texts and star maps? Human culture had its own hard-won achievements that the Phites couldn't easily match.

As the evening wore on, the Phites shifted their focus back to the subatomic world. A new kind of accelerator began smashing single gold ions together at extraordinary energies—though the total power being expended was still minuscule. Primo soon announced that they'd mapped all three generations of quarks and leptons. The Phites' knowledge of particle physics was drawing level with humanity's; Daniel couldn't follow the technical details any more, but the experts were giving it all the thumbs up. Daniel felt a surge of pride; of course his children knew what they were doing, and if they'd reached the point where they could momentarily bamboozle him, soon he'd ask them to catch their breath and bring him up to speed. Before he permitted them to emigrate, he'd slow the crystals down and introduce himself to everyone. In fact, that might be the perfect time to set them their next task: to understand human biology, well enough to upload him. To make him immortal, to repay their debt.

He sat watching images of the Phites' latest computers, reconstructions based on data flowing to and from the AFM tips. Vast lattices of shimmering atoms stretched off into the distance, the electron clouds that joined them quivering like beads of mercury in some surreal liquid abacus. As he watched, an inset window told him that the ion accelerators had been re-designed, and fired up again.

Daniel grew restless. He walked to the elevator. There was nothing he could see in the basement that he couldn't see from his office, but he wanted to stand beside the Play Pen, put his hand on the casing, press his nose against the glass. The era of Sapphire as a virtual world with no consequences in his own was coming to an end; he wanted to stand beside the thing itself and be reminded that it was as solid as he was.

The elevator descended, passing the tenth floor, the ninth, the eighth. Without warning, Lucien's voice burst from Daniel's watch, priority audio crashing through every barrier of privacy and protocol. "Boss, there's radiation. Net power gain. Get to the helicopter, *now*."

Daniel hesitated, contemplating an argument. If this was fusion, why hadn't it been detected and curtailed? He jabbed the stop button and felt the brakes engage. Then the world dissolved into brightness and pain.

7

WHEN DANIEL EMERGED FROM the opiate haze, a doctor informed him that he had burns to sixty per cent of his body. More from heat than from radiation. He was not going to die.

There was a net terminal by the bed. Daniel called Lucien and learned what the physicists on the team had tentatively concluded, having studied the last of the Play Pen data that had made it off-site.

It seemed the Phites had discovered the Higgs field, and engineered a burst of something akin to cosmic inflation. What they'd done wasn't as simple as merely inflating a tiny patch of vacuum into a new universe, though. Not only had they managed to create a "cool Big Bang", they had pulled a large chunk of ordinary matter into the pocket universe they'd made, after which the wormhole leading to it had shrunk to subatomic size and fallen through the Earth.

They had taken the crystals with them, of course. If they'd tried to upload themselves into the pocket universe through the lunar data link, the Thought Police would have stopped them. So they'd emigrated by another route entirely. They had snatched their whole substrate, and ran.

Opinions were divided over exactly what else the new universe would contain. The crystals and the Play Pen floating in a void, with no power source, would leave the Phites effectively dead, but some of the team believed there could be a thin plasma of protons and electrons too, created by a form of Higgs decay that bypassed the unendurable quark-gluon fireball of a hot Big Bang. If they'd built the right nanomachines, there was a chance that they could convert the Play Pen into a structure that would keep the crystals safe, while the Phites slept through the long wait for the first starlight.

THE TINY SKIN SAMPLES the doctors had taken finally grew into sheets large enough to graft. Daniel bounced between dark waves of pain and medicated euphoria, but one idea stayed with him through-out the turbulent journey, like a guiding star: *Primo had betrayed him.* He had given the fucker life, entrusted him with power, granted him privileged knowledge, showered him with the favors of the Gods. And how had he been repaid? He was back to zero. He'd spoken to his law-yers; having heard rumors of an "illegal radiation source", the insur-ance company was not going to pay out on the crystals without a fight.

Lucien came to the hospital, in person. Daniel was moved; they hadn't met face-to-face since the job interview. He shook the man's hand.

"You didn't betray me."

Lucien looked embarrassed. "I'm resigning, boss."

Daniel was stung, but he forced himself to accept the news sto-ically. "I understand; you have no choice. Gupta will have a crystal of his own by now. You have to be on the winning side, in the war of the Gods."

Lucien put his resignation letter on the bedside table. "What war? Are you still clinging to that fantasy where überdorks battle to turn the moon into computronium?"

Daniel blinked. "Fantasy? If you didn't believe it, why were you working with me?"

"You paid me. Extremely well."

"So how much will Gupta be paying you? I'll double it."

Lucien shook his head, amused. "I'm not going to work for Gupta. I'm moving into particle physics. The Phites weren't all that far ahead of us when they escaped; maybe forty or fifty years. Once we catch up, I guess a private universe will cost about as much as a private island; maybe less in the long run. But no one's going to be battling for control of this one, throwing gray goo around like monkeys flinging turds while they draw up their plans for Matrioshka brains."

Daniel said, "If you take any data from the Play Pen logs—"

"I'll honor all the confidentiality clauses in my contract." Lucien smiled. "But anyone can take an interest in the Higgs field; that's public domain."

After he left, Daniel bribed the nurse to crank up his medication, until even the sting of betrayal and disappointment began to fade.

A universe, he thought happily. *Soon I'll have a universe of my own.*

But I'm going to need some workers in there, some allies, some companions. I can't do it all alone; someone has to carry the load.

ZERO FOR CONDUCT

1

Latifa started the web page loading, then went to make tea. The proxy she used convinced her internet provider that every page she accessed belonged to a compendium of pious aphorisms from uncontroversial octogenarians in Qom, while to the sites themselves she appeared to be a peripatetic American, logging on from Pittsburgh one day and Kansas City the next. Between the sanctions against her true host country and that host's paranoia over the most innocent interactions with the West, these precautions were essential. But they slowed down her already sluggish connection so effectively that she might as well have been rehearsing for a flight to Mars.

The sound of boiling water offered a brief respite from the televised football match blaring down from the apartment above. "Two nil in favor of the Black Pearls, with fifteen minutes left to play! It's looking like victory for the home team here in Samen Stadium!" When the tea had brewed, she served it in a small glass for her grandfather to sip through a piece of hard sugar clenched between his teeth. Latifa sat with him for a while, but he was listening to the shortwave radio, straining to hear Kabul through the hum of interference and the breathless commentary coming through the ceiling, and he barely noticed when she left.

Back in her room after fifteen minutes, she found the scratched screen of the laptop glistening with a dozen shiny ball-and-stick models of organic molecules. Reading the color coding of the atoms was second nature to her by now: white for hydrogen, black for carbon, cherry red for oxygen, azure for nitrogen. Here and there a yellow sulfur atom or a green chlorine stood out, like a chickpea in a barrel of candy.

All the molecules that the ChemFactor page had assigned to her were nameless—unless you counted the formal structural descriptions full of cis-1,3-dimethyl-this and 2,5-di-tert-butyl-that—and Latifa had no idea which, if any of them, had actually been synthesized in a lab somewhere. Perhaps a few of them were impossible beasts, chimeras cranked out by the software's mindless permutations, destined to be completely unstable in reality. If she made an effort, she could probably weed some of them out. But that could wait until she'd narrowed down the list of candidates, eliminating the molecules with no real chance of binding strongly to the target.

The target this time was an oligosaccharide, a carbohydrate with nine rings arranged in pleasingly asymmetric tiers, like a small child's attempt to build a shoe rack. Helpfully, the ChemFactor page kept it fixed on the screen as Latifa scrolled up and down through the long catalog of its potential suitors.

She trusted the software to have made some sensible choices already, on geometric grounds: all of these molecules ought to be able to nestle reasonably snugly against the target. In principle she could rotate the ball-and-stick models any way she liked, and slide the target into the same view to assess the prospective fit, but in practice that made the laptop's graphics card choke. So she'd learned to manipulate the structures in her head, to picture the encounter without fretting too much about precise angles and distances. Molecules weren't rigid, and if the interaction with the target liberated enough energy the participants could stretch or flex a little to accommodate each other. There were rigorous calculations that could predict the upshot of all that give and take, but the equations could not be solved quickly or easily. So ChemFactor invited people to offer their hunches. Newcomers guessed no better than random, and many players' hit rates failed to rise above statistical noise. But some people acquired a feel for the task, learning from their victories and mistakes—even if they couldn't put their private algorithms into words.

Latifa didn't over-think the puzzle, and in twenty minutes she'd made her choice. She clicked the button beside her selection and confirmed it, satisfied that she'd done her best. After three years in the game she'd proved to be a born chemical match-maker, but she didn't want it going to her head. Whatever lay behind her well-judged guesses, it could only be a matter of time before the software itself learned to codify all the same rules. The truth was, the more successful she became, the faster she'd be heading for obsolescence. She needed to make the most of her talent while it still counted.

LATIFA SPENT TWO HOURS on her homework, then a call came from her cousin Fashard in Kandahar. She went out onto the balcony where the phone could get a better signal.

"How is your grandfather?" he asked.

"He's fine. I'll ask him to call you back tomorrow." Her grandfather had given up on the shortwave and gone to bed. "How are things there?"

"The kids have all come down with something," Fashard reported. "And the power's been off for the last two days."

"*Two days?*" Latifa felt for her young cousins, sweltering and feverish without even a fan. "You should get a generator."

"Ha! I could get ten; people are practically giving them away."

"Why?"

"The price of diesel's gone through the roof," Fashard explained. "Blackouts or not, no one can afford to run them."

Latifa looked out at the lights of Mashhad. There was nothing glamorous about the concrete tower blocks around her, but the one thing Iran didn't lack was electricity. Kandahar should have been well-supplied by the Kajaki Dam, but two of the three turbines in the hydroelectric plant had been out of service for more than a year, and the drought had made it even harder for the remaining turbine to meet demand.

"What about the shop?" she asked.

"Pedaling the sewing machine keeps me fit," Fashard joked.

"I wish I could do something."

"Things are hard for everyone," Fashard said stoically. "But we'll be all right; people always need clothes. You just concentrate on your studies."

Latifa tried to think of some news to cheer him up. "Amir said he's planning to come home this Eid." Her brother had made no firm promises, but she couldn't believe he'd spend the holidays away from his family for a second year in a row.

"Inshallah," Fashard replied. "He should book the ticket early though, or he'll never get a seat."

"I'll remind him."

There was no response; the connection had cut out. Latifa tried calling back but all she got was a sequence of strange beeps, as if the phone tower was too flustered to offer up its usual recorded apologies.

She tidied the kitchen then lay in bed. It was hard to fall asleep when her thoughts cycled endlessly through the same inventory of troubles, but sometime after midnight she managed to break the loop and tumble into blackness.

"Afghani slut," Ghamzeh whispered, leaning against Latifa and pinching her arm through the fabric of her manteau.

"Let go of me," Latifa pleaded. She was pressed against her locker, she couldn't pull away. Ghamzeh turned her face toward her, smiling, as if they were friends exchanging gossip. Other students walked past, averting their eyes.

"I'm getting tired of the smell of you," Ghamzeh complained. "You're stinking up the whole city. You should go back home to your little mud hut."

Latifa's skin tingled between the girl's blunt talons, warmed by broken blood vessels, numbed by clamped nerves. It would be satisfying to lash out with her fists and free herself, but she knew that could only end badly.

"Did they have soap in your village?" Ghamzeh wondered. "Did they have underwear? All these things must have been so strange to you, when you arrived in civilization."

Latifa waited in silence. Arguing only prolonged the torment.

"Too stuck up to have a conversation?" Ghamzeh released her arm and began to move away, but then she stopped to give Latifa a parting smile. "You think you're impressing the teachers when you give them all the answers they want? Don't fool yourself, slut. They know you're just an animal doing circus tricks."

W HEN L ATIFA HAD CLEARED away the dinner plates, her grandfather asked her about school.

"You're working hard?" he pressed her, cross-legged on the floor with a cushion at his back. "Earning their respect?"

"Yes."

"And your heart is still set on engineering?" He sounded doubtful, as if for him the word could only conjure up images of rough men covered in machine oil.

"Chemical engineering," she corrected him gently. "I'm getting good grades in chemistry, and there'd be plenty of jobs in it."

"After five more years. After university."

"Yes." Latifa looked away. Half the money Amir sent back from Dubai was already going on her school fees. Her brother was twenty-two; no one could expect him to spend another five years without marrying.

"You should get on with your studies then." Her grandfather waved her away amiably, then reached over for the radio.

In her room, Latifa switched on the laptop before opening her history book, but she kept her eyes off the screen until she'd read half the chapter on the Sassanid kings. When she finally gave herself a break the ChemFactor site had loaded, and she'd been logged in automatically, by cookie.

A yellow icon of a stylized envelope was flashing at the top of the page. A fellow player she'd never heard of called "jesse409" had left her a message, congratulating "PhaseChangeGirl" on a cumulative score that had just crossed twenty thousand. Latifa's true score was far higher than that, but she'd changed her identity and rejoined the game from scratch five times so far, lest she come to the notice of someone with the means to find out who she really was.

The guess she'd made the previous night had paid off: a rigorous model of the two molecules showed that the binding between them was stable. She had saved one of ChemFactor's clients the time and expense of doing the same calculations for dozens of alternatives, and her reward was a modest fraction of the resources she'd effectively freed. ChemFactor would model any collection of atoms and molecules she liked, free of charge—up to a preset quota in computing time.

Latifa closed her history book and moved the laptop to the center of her desk. If the binding problems were easy for her now, when it came to the much larger challenge she'd set herself the instincts she'd honed on the site could only take her so far. The raw computing power that she acquired from these sporadic prizes let her test her hunches and see where they fell short.

She dug out the notebook from her backpack and reviewed her sketches and calculations. She understood the symmetries of crystals, the shifts and rotations that brought any regular array of atoms back into perfect agreement with itself. She understood the thrillingly strange origins of the different varieties of magnetism, where electrons' spins became aligned or opposed—sometimes through their response to each others' magnetic fields, but more often through the Exclusion Principle, which linked the alignment of spin to the average distance between the particles, and hence the energy they needed in order to overcome electrostatic repulsion. And after studying hundreds of examples, she believed she had a sense for the kind of crystal that lay in a transition zone where one type of magnetism was on the verge of shifting to another.

She'd sketched her ideal crystal in the notebook more than a year before, but she had no proof yet that it was anything more than a fantasy. Her last modeling run had predicted something achingly close, but it had still not produced what she needed. She had to go back one step and try something different.

Latifa retrieved the saved data from that last attempt and set the parameters for the new simulation. She resisted the urge to stab the CONFIRM button twice; the response was just taking its time weaving its way back to her through the maze of obfuscation.

Estimated time for run: approximately seven hours.

She sat gazing at the screen for a while, though she knew that if she waited for the prediction to be updated she'd probably find that the new estimate was even longer.

Reluctantly, she moved the laptop to the floor and returned to the faded glory of the Sassanids. She had to be patient; she'd have her answer by morning.

"WHORE," GHAMZEH MUTTERED AS Latifa hurried past her to her desk.

"You're ten minutes late, Latifa," Ms Keshavarz declared irritably.

"I'm very sorry." Latifa stood in place, her eyes cast down.

"So what's your excuse?"

Latifa remained silent.

"If you overslept," Ms Keshavarz suggested, "you should at least have the honesty to say so."

Latifa had woken at five, but she managed a flush of humiliation that she hoped would pass for a kind of tacit admission.

"Two hours of detention, then," Ms Keshavarz ruled. "It might have been half that if you'd been more forthcoming. Take your seat, please."

The day passed at a glacial speed. Latifa did her best to distract herself with the lessons, but it was like trying to chew water. The subject made no difference: history, literature, mathematics, physics—as soon as one sentence was written on the blackboard she knew exactly what would follow.

In detention with four other girls, she sat copying pages of long-winded homilies. From her seat she could see a driveway that led out from the staff car park, and one by one the vehicles she most needed to depart passed before her eyes. The waiting grew harder than ever, but she knew it would be foolish to act too soon.

Eighty minutes into her punishment, she started holding her breath for ever longer intervals. By the time she raised her hand there was nothing feigned in her tone of discomfort. The supervising teacher, Ms Shirazi, raised no objections and played no sadistic games with her. Latifa fled the room with plausible haste.

The rest of the school appeared deserted; the extra time had been worth it. Latifa opened the door to the toilets and let it swing shut, leaving the sound echoing back down the corridor, then hurried toward the chemistry lab.

The students' entrance was locked, but Latifa steeled herself and turned into the warren of store rooms and cubicles that filled the north side of the science wing. Her chemistry teacher, Ms Daneshvar, had taken her to her desk once to consult an old university textbook, to settle a point on which they'd both been unsure.

Latifa found her way back to that desk. The keys were hanging exactly where she remembered them, on labeled pegs. She took the one for the chemistry lab and headed for the teachers' entrance.

As she turned the key in the lock her stomach convulsed. To be expelled would be disastrous enough, but if the school pressed criminal charges she could be imprisoned and deported. She closed her eyes for a moment, summoning up an image of the beautiful lattice that the ChemFactor simulation had shown her. For a week she'd thought of nothing else. The software had reached its conclusion, but in the end the only test that mattered was whether the substance could be made in real life.

Late afternoon sunlight slanted across the room, glinting off the tubular legs of the stools standing upside-down on the black-painted benches. All the ingredients Latifa needed—salts of copper, barium and calcium—sat on the alphabetized shelves that ran along the eastern wall; none were of sufficient value or toxicity to be kept locked away, and she wouldn't need much of any of them for a proof of principle.

She took down the jars and weighed out a few grams of each, quantities too small to be missed. She'd written down the masses that would yield the right stoichiometry, the right proportions of atoms in the final product, but having spent the whole day repeating the calculations in her head she didn't waste time now consulting the slip of paper.

Latifa mixed the brightly colored granules in a ceramic crucible and crushed them with a pestle. Then she placed the crucible in the electric furnace. The heating profile she'd need was complicated, but though she'd only ever seen the furnace operated manually in class, she'd looked up the model number on the net and found the precise requirements for scripting it. When she pushed the memory stick into the USB port, the green light above flickered for a moment, then the first temperature of the sequence appeared on the display.

The whole thing would take nine hours. Latifa quickly re-shelved the jars, binned the filter paper she'd used on the scales, then retreated, locking the door behind her.

On her way past the toilets she remembered to stage a creaking exit. She slowed her pace as she approached the detention room, and felt cold beads of sweat on her face. Ms Shirazi offered her a sympathetic frown before turning back to the magazine she'd been reading.

LATIFA DREAMED THAT THE school was on fire. The blaze was visible from the balcony of her apartment, and her grandfather stood and watched, wheezing alarmingly from the toxic fumes that were billowing out across Mashhad. When he switched on the radio, a newsreader reported that the police had found a memory stick beside the point of ignition and were checking all the students for a fingerprint match.

Latifa woke before dawn and ate breakfast, then prepared lunch for the two of them. She'd thought she'd been moving silently, but her grandfather surprised her as she was opening the front door.

"Why are you leaving so early?" he demanded.

"There's a study group."

"What do you mean?"

"A few of us get together before classes start and go over the lessons from the day before," she said.

"So you're running your own classes now? Do the teachers know about this?"

"The teachers approve," Latifa assured him. "It's their lessons that we're revising; we're not just making things up."

"You're not talking politics?" he asked sternly.

Latifa understood: he was thinking of the discussion group her mother had joined at Kabul University, its agenda excitedly recounted in one of the letters she'd sent him. He'd allowed Latifa to read the whole trove of letters when she'd turned fourteen—the age her mother had been when he'd gone into exile.

"You know me," Latifa said. "Politics is over my head."

"All right." He was mollified now. "Enjoy your study." He kissed her goodbye.

As Latifa dismounted from her bicycle she could see that the staff car park was empty except for the cleaners' van. If she could bluff her way through this final stage she might be out of danger in a matter of minutes.

The cleaners had unlocked the science wing, and a woman was mopping the floor by the main entrance. Latifa nodded to her, then walked in as if she owned the place.

"Hey! You shouldn't be here!" The woman straightened up and glared at her, worried for her job should anything be stolen.

"Ms Daneshvar asked me to prepare something for the class. She gave me the key yesterday." Latifa held it up for inspection.

The woman squinted at the key then waved her on, muttering unhappily.

In the chemistry lab everything was as Latifa had left it. She plucked the memory stick from the port on the furnace, then switched off the power. She touched the door, and felt no residual heat.

When she opened the furnace the air that escaped smelled like sulfur and bleach. Gingerly, she lifted out the crucible and peered inside. A solid gray mass covered the bottom, its surface as smooth as porcelain.

The instruments she needed to gauge success or failure were all in the physics lab, and trying to talk her way into another room right now would attract too much suspicion. She could wait for her next physics class and see what opportunities arose. Students messed around with the digital multimeters all the time, and if she was caught sticking the probes into her pocket her teacher would see nothing but a silly girl trying to measure the electrical resistance of a small paving stone she'd picked up off the street. Ms Hashemi wouldn't be curious enough to check the properties of the stone for herself.

Latifa fetched a piece of filter paper and tried to empty the crucible onto it, but the gray material clung stubbornly to the bottom where it had formed. She tapped it gently, then more forcefully, to no avail.

She was going to have to steal the crucible. It was not an expensive piece of equipment, but there were only four, neatly lined up in a row in the cupboard below the furnace, and its absence would eventually be missed. Ms Daneshvar might—just might—ask the cleaners if they'd seen it. There was a chance that all her trespasses would be discovered.

But what choice did she have?

She could leave the crucible behind and hunt for a replacement in the city. At the risk that, in the meantime, someone would take the vessel out to use it, find it soiled, and discard it. At the risk that she'd be caught trying to make the swap. And all of this for a gray lump that might easily be as worthless as it looked.

Latifa had bought a simple instrument of her own in the bazaar six months before, and she'd brought it with her almost as a joke—something she could try once she was out of danger, with no expectations at all. If the result it gave her was negative that wouldn't really prove anything. But she didn't know what else she could use to guide her.

She fished the magnet out of the pocket of her manteau. It was a slender disk the size of her thumbnail, probably weighing a gram or so. She held it in the mouth of the crucible and lowered it toward the bottom.

If there was any force coming into play as the magnet approached the gray material, it was too weak for her to sense. With a couple of millimeters still separating the two, Latifa spread her fingers and let the magnet drop. She didn't hear it strike the bottom—but from such a height how loud would it have been? She took her fingers out of the crucible and looked down.

It was impossible to tell if it was touching or not; the view was too narrow, the angle too high.

Latifa could hear the woman with the mop approaching, getting ready to clean the chemistry lab. Within a minute or less, everything she did here would take place in front of a witness.

A patch of morning sunlight from the eastern window fell upon the blackboard behind her. Latifa grabbed an empty Erlenmeyer flask and held it in the beam, tilting it until she managed to refract some light down into the crucible.

As she turned the flask back and forth, shifting the angle of the light, she could see a dark circle moving behind the magnet. Lit from above, an object barely a millimeter high couldn't cast a shadow like that.

The magnet was floating on air.

The door began to open. Latifa pocketed the crucible. She put the Erlenmeyer flask back on its shelf, then turned to see the cleaner eyeing her suspiciously.

"I'm all done now, thanks," Latifa announced cheerfully. She motioned toward the staff entrance. "I'll put the key back on my way out."

Minutes later, Latifa strode out of the science wing. She reached into her pocket and wrapped her hand around the crucible. She still had some money Amir had given her last Eid; she could buy a replacement that afternoon. For now, all she had to do was get through the day's lessons with a straight face, while walking around carrying the world's first room-temperature superconductor.

2

EZATULLAH WAS SAID TO be the richest Afghani in Mashhad, and from the look of his three-story marble-clad house he had no wish to live down that reputation. Latifa had heard that he'd made his money in Saudi Arabia, where he'd represented the mujahedin at the time of the Soviet occupation. Wealthy Saudi women with guilty consciences had filed through his office day after day, handing him bags full of gold bullion to help fund the jihad—buying, they believed, the same promise of paradise that went to the martyrs themselves. Ezatullah, being less concerned with the afterlife, had passed on their donations to the war chest but retained a sizable commission.

At the mansion's gate, Latifa's grandfather paused. "I promised your mother I'd keep you out of trouble."

Latifa didn't know how to answer that; his caution came from love and grief, but this was a risk they needed to take. "Fashard's already started things rolling on his side," she reminded him. "It will be hard on him if we pull out now."

"That's true."

In the sitting room Ezatullah's youngest daughter, Yasmin, served tea, then stayed with Latifa while the two men withdrew to talk business. Latifa passed the time thinking up compliments for each rug and item of furniture in sight, and Yasmin replied in such a soft, shy voice that Latifa had no trouble eavesdropping on the conversation from the adjoining room.

"My nephew owns a clothing business in Kandahar," her grandfather began. "Some tailoring, some imports and exports. But recently he came across a new opportunity: a chance to buy electrical cable at a very fair price."

"A prudent man will have diverse interests," Ezatullah declared approvingly.

"We're hoping to on-sell the wire in Mashhad," her grandfather explained. "We could avoid a lot of paperwork at the border if we packed the trucks with cartons labeled as clothing—with some at the rear bearing out that claim. My granddaughter could run a small shop to receive these shipments."

"And you're seeking a partner, to help fund this venture?"

Latifa heard the rustle of paper, the figures she'd prepared changing hands.

"What's driven you to this, haji?" Ezatullah asked pointedly. "You don't have a reputation as a businessman."

"I'm seventy years old," her grandfather replied. "I need to see my daughter's children looked after before I die."

Ezatullah thought for a while. "Let me talk to my associates in Kandahar."

"Of course."

On the bus back to the apartment, Latifa imagined the phone calls that would already be bouncing back and forth across the border. Ezatullah would soon know all about the new electrification project in Kandahar, which aimed to wire up a dozen more neighborhoods to the already-struggling grid—apparently in the hope that even a meager ration of cheap power would turn more people against the insurgents who bombed every convoy that tried to carry replacement parts to the hydroelectric plant.

International donors had agreed to fund the project, and with overhead cables strung from pole to pole along winding roads, some discrepancy between the surveyed length and the cable used was only to be expected. But while Fashard really had come to an agreement with the contractor to take the excess wire off his hands, with no family ties or prior connection to the man he had only managed to secure the deal by offering a price well above the going rate.

Latifa didn't expect any of these details to elude their partner, but the hope was that his advisers in Kandahar would conclude that Fashard, lacking experience as a smuggler, had simply underestimated his own costs. That alone wouldn't make the collaboration a bad investment: she'd structured the proposal in such a way that Ezatullah would still make a tidy return even if the rest of them barely broke even.

They left the bus and made their way home. "If we told him the truth—" her grandfather began as they started up the stairs.

"If we told him the truth, he'd snatch it from our hands!" Latifa retorted. Her words echoed in the concrete stairwell; she lowered her voice. "One way or another he'd get hold of the recipe, then sell it to some company with a thousand lawyers who could claim they'd invented it themselves. We need to be in a stronger position before we take this to anyone, or they'll eat us alive." A patent attorney could do a lot to protect them before they approached a commercial backer, but that protection would cost several thousand euros. Raising that much themselves—without trading away any share in the invention—wasn't going to be easy, but it would make all the difference to how much power they retained.

Her grandfather stopped on a landing to catch his breath. "And if Ezatullah finds out that we've lied to him—"

His phone buzzed once, with a text message.

"You need to go to the house again," he said. "Tomorrow, after school."

Latifa's skin prickled with fear. "*Me?* What for?" Did Ezatullah want to quiz her about her knowledge of retail fashion for the modern Iranian woman—or had his digging already exposed her other interests?

"Most of the money's going straight to Fashard, but we'll need some cash at our end too," her grandfather explained. "He doesn't want me coming and going from the house, but no one will be suspicious if you've struck up a friendship with his daughter."

LATIFA HAD ASKED THE electricians to come at seven to switch on the power to the kilns, but when they hadn't shown up by eight she gave up any hope of making it to her history class.

For the first hour she'd killed time by sweeping; now she paced the bare wooden floor, optimistically surveying her new fiefdom. Finding the factory had been a huge stroke of luck; it had originally produced ceramic tableware, and when the tenants went out of business the owner of the premises had taken possession of the kilns. He'd been on the verge of selling them for scrap, and had parted with them for a ridiculously low price just to get her grandfather to sign the lease. The location wasn't perfect, but perhaps it was for the best that it wasn't too close to the shop. The separation would make it less likely that anyone would see her in both places.

When the electricians finally arrived they ignored Latifa completely, and she resisted the urge to pester them with odd questions. *What would you do if you cut into an overhead power line and found that its appearance, in cross-section, wasn't quite what you were used to?*

"Delivery for Bose Ceramics?" a man called from the entrance.

Latifa went to see what it was. The courier was already loading one box, as tall as she was, onto his trolley. She guided him across the factory floor. "Can you put it here? Thank you."

"There are another two in the truck."

She waited until the electricians had left before finding a knife and slicing away the cardboard and styrofoam—afraid that they might recognize the equipment and start asking questions of their own. She plugged in one of the cable winders and put it through a test sequence, watching the nimble motorized arms blur as they rehearsed on thin air.

One machine would unpick, while the other two wove—and for every kilometer of cable that came into the factory, two kilometers would emerge. With half as many strands as the original, the new version would need to be bulked out from within to retain the same diameter. The pellets of ceramic wound in among the steel and aluminum wouldn't form a contiguous electrical path, but these superconducting inclusions would still lower the overall resistance of the cable, sharing the current for a large enough portion of its length to compensate for the missing metal.

So long as the cable was fit for use, the Iranian contractors who bought it would have no reason to complain. They'd pocket the difference in price, and the power grid would be none the worse for it. Everyone would get paid, everyone would be happy.

Latifa checked her watch; she'd missed another two classes. All she could do now was write the whole day off and claim to have been sick. She needed to chase down the heat-resistant molds that would give the ceramic pellets their shape, and try again to get a promise from the chemical suppliers that they could deliver the quantities she was going to need to keep the kilns going day after day, week after week.

"Do you have this in size sixteen?" the woman asked, emerging from the changing room. Latifa looked up from her homework. The woman was still wearing the oversized sunglasses that she hadn't deigned to remove as she entered the shop, as if she were a famous singer afraid of being mobbed by fans.

"I'm sorry, we don't."

"Can you check your storeroom? I love the colors, but this one is a bit too tight."

Latifa hesitated; she was certain that they didn't stock the blouse in that size, but it would be impolite to refuse. "Of course. One moment."

She spent half a minute rummaging through the shelves, to ensure that her search didn't seem too perfunctory. It was almost six o'clock; she should close the shop and relieve her grandfather at the factory.

When she returned to the counter, the customer had left. The woman had taken the blouse, along with two pairs of trousers from the rack near the door. Latifa felt a curious warmth rising in her face; most of all she was annoyed that she'd been so gullible, but the resentment she felt at the brazen theft collided unpleasantly with other thoughts.

There was nothing to be done but to put the incident out of her mind. She looked over her unfinished essay on the Iran-Iraq war; it was due in the morning, but she'd have to complete it in the factory.

"Are these goods from your shop?"

A policeman was standing in the doorway. The thief was beside him, and he was holding up the stolen clothes.

Latifa could hardly deny it; the trousers were identical to the others hanging right beside him.

"They are, sir," she replied. He must have seen the woman emerging, hastily stuffing everything into her bag. Why couldn't she have done that out of sight?

"This lady says she must have dropped the receipt. Should I look for it, or will I be wasting my time?"

Latifa struggled to choose the right answer. "It's my fault, sir. She must have thought I'd given her the receipt along with the change— but she was in a hurry, she didn't even want one of our bags . . ."

"So you still have the receipt?"

Latifa pointed helplessly at the waste-paper basket beside the counter, full to the brim with discarded drafts of her essay. "I couldn't leave the shop and chase after her, so I threw it in there. Please forgive me, sir, I'm just starting out in this job. If the boss learns what I've done, he'll fire me straight away." It was lucky that the thief was still wearing her ridiculous glasses; Latifa wasn't sure how she would have coped if they'd had to make eye contact.

The policeman appeared skeptical: he knew what he'd seen. Latifa put the back of her hand to her eyes and sniffed.

"All right," he said. "Everyone makes mistakes." He turned to the woman. "I'm sorry for the misunderstanding."

"It's nothing." She nodded to Latifa. "Good evening."

The policeman lingered in the doorway, thinking things over. Then he approached the counter.

"Let me see your storeroom."

Latifa gestured to the entrance, but stayed beside the cash register. She listened to the man moving about, rustling through discarded packaging, tapping the walls. What did he imagine he'd find—a secret compartment?

He emerged from the room, stony faced, as if the lack of anything incriminating only compounded his resentment.

"ID card."

Latifa produced it. She'd rid herself of her accent long ago, and she had just enough of her father's Tajik features that she could often pass as an Iranian to the eye, but here it was: the proof of her real status.

"Ha," he grunted. "All right." He handed back the ID. "Just behave yourself, and we'll get along fine."

As he walked out of the shop, Latifa began shaking with relief. He'd found an innocent explanation for her reticence to press charges: the card entitled her to remain in the country at the pleasure of the government, but she wasn't a citizen, and she would have been crazy to risk the consequences if the woman had called her a liar.

Latifa wheeled her bicycle out of the storeroom and closed the shop. The factory was six kilometers away, and the traffic tonight looked merciless.

"I HAD A CALL from Ezatullah," Latifa's grandfather said. "He wants to take over the transport."

Latifa continued brushing down the slides from the superconductor hopper. "What does that mean?"

"He has another partner who's been bringing goods across the border. This man has a warehouse in Herat."

Herat was just a hundred kilometers from the border, on the route from Kandahar to Mashhad. "So he wants us to make room for this other man's merchandise in our trucks?" Latifa put the brush down. It was an unsettling prospect, but it didn't have to be a disaster.

"No," her grandfather replied. "He wants us to bring the wire across in this other man's trucks."

"*Why?*"

"The customs inspectors have people coming from Tehran to look over their shoulders," her grandfather explained. "There's no fixing that with bribes, and the clothes make too flimsy a cover for the real cargo. This other man's bringing over a couple of loads of scrap metal every week; hiding the wire won't be a problem for him."

Latifa sat down on the bench beside the winders. "But we can't risk that! We can't let him know how many spools we're bringing in!" Ezatullah had kept his distance from their day-to-day operations, but the black market contacts to whom they passed the altered wire had long-standing connections to him, and Latifa had no doubt that he was being kept apprised of every transaction. *Under-reporting their sales* to hide the fact that they were selling twice as much wire as they imported would be suicidal.

"Can we shift this work to Kandahar?" her grandfather asked.

"Maybe the last part, the winding," Latifa replied. So long as they could double the wire before it reached Herat, there'd be no discrepancies in the numbers Ezatullah received from his informants.

"What about the kilns?"

"No, the power's too erratic. If there's a blackout halfway through a batch that would ruin it—and we need at least two batches a day to keep up."

"Couldn't we use a generator?"

Latifa didn't have the numbers she needed to answer that, but she knew Fashard had looked into the economics of using one himself. She texted him some questions, and he replied a few minutes later.

"It's hopeless," she concluded. "Each kiln runs at about twenty kilowatts. Getting that from diesel, we'd be lucky to break even."

Her grandfather managed a curt laugh. "Maybe we'd be better off selling the rest of the wire as it is?"

Latifa did a few more calculations. "That won't work either. Fashard is paying too much for it; we'd be making a loss on every spool." After sinking money into the factory's lease and other inputs to the doubling process, any attempt to get by without the benefits of that doubling would leave them owing Ezatullah more cash than the remaining sales would bring in.

"Then what choice is left to us?"

"We could keep making the superconductor here," Latifa suggested.

"And get it to Kandahar how?" her grandfather protested. "Do you think we can do business with anyone working that route and expect Ezatullah not to hear about it? Once or twice, maybe, but not if we set up a regular shipment."

Latifa had no answer to that. "We should talk about this in the morning," she said. "You've been working all day; you should get some sleep now."

At her insistence he retired to the factory's office, where they'd put in a mattress and blankets. Latifa stood by the hopper; the last batch of superconductor should have cooled by now, but she was too dejected to attend to it. If they moved the whole operation to Kandahar, the best they could hope for was scraping through without ending up in debt. She didn't doubt that Fashard and her other cousins would do whatever needed to be done—working unpaid, purely for the sake of keeping her grandfather out of trouble—but the prospect of forcing that burden onto them filled her with shame.

Her own dawdling wasn't helping anyone. She put on the heat-proof gloves, took the molds from the kiln and began filling the hopper. She'd once calculated that if Iran's entire grid were to be replaced with a superconducting version, the power no longer being lost in transmission would be enough to light up all of Afghanistan. But if that was just a fantasy, all her other plans were heading for the same fate.

Latifa switched on the winders and watched the strands of wire shuttling from spool to spool, wrapping the stream of pellets from the hopper. Of all the wondrous things the superconductor made possible, this had seemed the simplest—and the safest way to exploit it without attracting too much attention.

But these dull gray beads were all she had. If she wanted to rescue the whole misbegotten venture, she needed to find another way to turn them to her advantage.

LATIFA'S GRANDFATHER RAN FROM the office, barefoot, eyes wide with fear. "What happened? Are you hurt?"

Latifa could see dents in the ceiling where the pellets had struck. "I'm all right," she assured him. "I'm sorry, I didn't mean to wake you." She looked around; the kilns and the winders were untouched, and there was no damage to the building that a plasterer couldn't fix.

"*What did you do?* I thought something exploded—or those machines went crazy." He glared at the winders, as if they might have rebelled and started pelting their owners with shrapnel.

Latifa switched off the power from the outlet and approached what remained of her test rig. She'd surrounded it with workbenches turned on their sides, as safety shields. "I'm going to need better reinforcement," she said. "I didn't realize the field would get so strong, so quickly."

Her grandfather stared at the shattered assembly that she'd improvised from a helix of copper pipe. The previous tenants had left all kinds of junk behind, and Latifa had been loath to discard anything that might have turned out to be useful.

"It's a storage device," she explained. "For electricity. The current just sits there going round and round; when you want some of it back you can draw it out. It's not all that different from a battery."

"I'd say it's not all that different from a bomb."

Latifa was chastened. "I was careless; I'm sorry. I was impatient to see if I could make it work at all. The current generates a strong magnetic field, and that puts the whole thing under pressure—but when it's built properly, it will be a solid coil of superconductor, not a lot of pellets stuffed inside a pipe. And we can bury it in the ground, so if it does shatter no one will get hurt."

"How is this meant to help us?" her grandfather asked irritably. He lifted his right foot to examine the sole; a splinter of superconductor was poking through the skin.

Latifa said, "The mains power in Kandahar is unreliable, but it's still far cheaper than using a generator. A few of these storage coils should be enough to guarantee that we can run the kilns through a blackout."

"You're serious?"

Latifa hesitated. "Give me a few days to do some more experiments, then we'll know for sure."

"How many days of school have you missed already?"

"That's not important."

Her grandfather sat on the ground and covered his eyes with one hand. "School is not important now? They *murdered your mother* because she was teaching girls, and your father because he'd defended her. When she grew so afraid that she sent you to me, I promised her you'd get an education. This country is no paradise, but at least you were safe in that school, you were doing well. Now we're juggling money we don't have, living in fear of Ezatullah, blowing things up, planning some new madness every day."

Latifa approached him and put a hand on his shoulder. "After this, there'll be nothing to distract me. We'll close the factory, we'll close the shop. My whole life will be school and homework, school and homework all the way to Eid."

Her grandfather looked up at her. "How long will it take?"

"Maybe a couple of weeks." The coils themselves didn't have to be complicated, but it would take some research and trial and error to get the charging and discharging circuitry right.

"And then what?" he asked. "If we send these things to Kandahar—with the kilns and everything else—do you think Fashard can put it all together and just take over where we left off?"

"Maybe not," Latifa conceded. Fashard had wired his own house, and he could repair a sewing machine blindfold. But this would be tricky, and she couldn't talk him through the whole setup on the phone.

She said, "It looks like Eid's coming early for me this year."

IN HERAT, IN THE bus station's restroom, Latifa went through the ritual of replacing her headscarf and manteau with the burqa and niqab that she'd need to be wearing when she arrived in Kandahar.

She stared through the blue gauze at the anonymous figure reflected in the restroom's stained mirror. When she'd lived in Kabul with her parents, she'd still been young enough to visit Kandahar without covering her hair, let alone her face. But if anything, she felt insufficiently disguised now. On top of her anxiety over all her new secrets, this would be her first trip home without Amir traveling beside her—or at least, ten meters ahead of her, in the men's section of the bus. Fashard had offered to come and meet her in Herat, but she'd persuaded him to stay in Kandahar. She couldn't help being nervous, but that didn't mean she had to be cowed.

It was still early as the bus set out. Latifa chatted with the woman beside her, who was returning to Kandahar after visiting Herat for medical treatment. "I used to go to Quetta," the woman explained, "but it's too dangerous there now."

"What about Kabul?" Latifa asked.

"Kabul? These days you'll wait six months for an appointment."

The specialists in Herat were mostly Iranian; in Kabul, mostly European. In Kandahar, you'd be lucky to find anyone at all with a genuine medical degree, though there was a wide choice of charlatans who'd take your money in exchange for pharmaceuticals with expiry dates forged in ballpoint.

"Someone should build a medical school in Kandahar," Latifa suggested. "With ninety percent of the intake women, until things are evened out."

Her companion laughed nervously.

"I'm serious!" Latifa protested. "Aren't you sick of traveling to every point of the compass just to get what other people have at home?"

"Sister," the woman said quietly, "it's time to shut your mouth."

Latifa took her advice, and peered past her out the scratched window. They were crossing a barren, rock-strewn desert now, a region infamous for bandits. The bus had an armed guard, for what that was worth, but the first time Latifa had made the journey Amir had told her stories of travelers ambushed on this road at night. One man on a motorbike, carrying no cash, had been tortured until he phoned his family to deposit money into his assailant's account.

"Wouldn't that help the police catch the bandits?" Latifa had asked him, logical as ever but still naive.

Amir had laughed his head off.

"When it comes to the police," he'd finally explained, "*money in the bank* tends to have the opposite effect."

FASHARD WAS WAITING FOR Latifa in the bus station. He spotted her before she saw him—or rather, he spotted the bright scarf, chosen from the range she sold in the shop, that she'd told him she'd be tying to the handle of her suitcase.

He called out, then approached her, beaming. "Welcome, cousin! How was your trip?" He grabbed the suitcase and hefted it onto his shoulders; it did have wheels, but in the crowded station any baggage at foot level would just be an impediment.

"It was fine," she said. "You're looking well." Actually, Fashard looked exhausted, but he'd put so much enthusiasm into his greeting that it would have been rude to mention anything of the kind.

Latifa followed him to the car, bumping into people along the way; she still hadn't adjusted to having her peripheral vision excised.

The sun was setting as they drove through the city; Latifa fought to keep her eyes open, but she took in an impression of peeling advertising posters, shabby white-washed buildings, crowds of men in all manner of clothing and a smattering of women in near-identical garb. Traffic police stood at the busiest intersections, blowing their whistles. Nothing had changed.

Inside the house, she gratefully shed her burqa as Fashard's five youngest children swarmed toward her. She dropped to her knees to exchange kisses and dispense sweets. Fashard's wife, Soraya, his mother, Zohra, eldest daughter, sister, brother-in-law and two nephews were next to greet her. Latifa's weariness lifted; used as she was to comparative solitude, the sense of belonging was overpowering.

"How is my brother?" Zohra pressed her.

"He's fine. He sends his love to you especially."

Zohra started weeping; Fashard put an arm around her. Latifa looked away. Her grandfather still had too many enemies here to be able to return.

When Latifa had washed and changed her clothes, she rejoined the family just as the first dizzying aromas began escaping from the kitchen. She had fasted all day and the night before, knowing that on her arrival she was going to be fed until she burst. Soraya shooed her away from the kitchen, but Latifa was pleasantly surprised: Fashard had finally improved the chimney to the point where the wood-fired stove no longer filled the room with blinding smoke.

As they ate by the light of kerosene lamps, everyone had questions for her about life in Mashhad. What did things cost now, with the new sanctions in place? What were her neighbors like? How were the Iranians treating Afghanis these days? Latifa was happy to answer them, but as she looked around at the curious faces she kept thinking of eight-year-old Fatema tugging on her sleeve, accepting a sweet but demanding something more: *What was school like? What did you learn?*

IN THE MORNING, FASHARD showed Latifa the room he'd set aside for their work. She'd sent the kilns, the winders, and the current buckets to him by three different carriers. Fashard had found a source for the superconductor precursors himself: a company that brought a variety of common industrial chemicals in through Pakistan. It was possible that news of some of these shipments had reached Ezatullah, but Latifa was hoping that it wouldn't be enough to attract suspicion. If Fashard had decided to diversify into pottery, that hardly constituted a form of betrayal.

The room opened onto the courtyard, and Fashard had already taken up the paving stones to expose a patch of bare ground. "This is perfect," Latifa said. "We can run some cable out along the wall and bury the current buckets right here."

Fashard examined one of the halved diving cylinders she'd adapted to the purpose. "This really might burst?" he asked, more bemused than alarmed.

"I hope not," Latifa replied. "There's a cut-off switch that should stop the charger if the magnetic field grows too strong. I can't imagine that switch getting jammed—a bit of grit or friction isn't going to hold the contacts together against a force that's threatening to tear the whole thing apart. But so long as you keep track of the charging time there shouldn't be a problem anyway."

It took a couple of hours to dig the holes and wire up the storage system. Late in the morning the power came on, giving them a chance to test everything before they covered the buckets with half a meter of soil.

Latifa switched on the charger and waited ten minutes, then she plugged a lamp into the new supply. The light it produced was steadier and brighter than that it had emitted when connected to the mains: the voltage from the buckets was better regulated than the incoming supply.

Fashard smiled, not quite believing it. The largest of the components inside the cylinders looked like nothing so much as the element of an electric water heater; that was how Latifa had described the ceramic helices in the customs documents.

"If everyone had these . . ." he began enthusiastically, but then he stopped and thought it through. "If everyone had them, every household would be drawing more power, charging up their buckets to use through the blackouts. The power company would only be able to meet the demand from an even smaller portion of its customers, so they'd have to make the rationing periods even shorter."

"That's true," Latifa agreed. "Which is why it will be better if the buckets are sold with solar panels."

"What about in winter?" Fashard protested.

Latifa snorted. "What do you want from me? Magic? The government needs to fix the hydro plant."

Fashard shook his head sadly. "The people who keep bombing it aren't going to stop. Not unless they're given everything they want."

Latifa felt tired, but she had to finish what she'd started. She said, "I should show you how to work the kilns and the winders."

It took three days for Latifa and Fashard to settle on a procedure for the new factory. If they waited for the current buckets to be fully charged before starting the kilns, that guaranteed they could finish the batch without spoiling it—but they could make better use of the time if they took a risk and started earlier, given that the power, erratic though it was, usually did stay on for a few hours every day.

Fashard brought in his oldest nephew, Naqib, who'd be working half the shifts. Latifa stayed out of these training sessions; Naqib was always perfectly polite to her, but she knew he wasn't prepared to be shown anything by a woman three years younger than himself.

Sidelined, Latifa passed the time with Fatema. Though it was too dangerous for Fatema to go to school, Fashard had taught her to read and write and he was trying to find someone to come and tutor her. Latifa sat beside her as she proudly sounded out the words in a compendium of Pashtun folk tales, and practiced her script in the back of Latifa's notebook.

"What are these?" Fatema asked, flicking through the pages of calculations.

"Al-jabr," Latifa replied. "You'll understand when you're older."

One day they were in the courtyard, racing the remote-control cars that Latifa had brought from Mashhad for all the kids to share. The power went off, and as the television the other cousins had been watching fell silent, Fatema turned toward the factory, surprised. She could hear the winders still spinning.

"How is that working?" she asked Latifa.

"Our cars are still working, aren't they?" Latifa revved her engine.

Fatema refused to be distracted. "They use batteries. You can't run anything big with batteries."

"Maybe I brought some bigger batteries from Iran."

"Show me," Fatema pleaded.

Latifa opened her mouth to start explaining, her mind already groping for some simple metaphors she could use to convey how the current buckets worked. But . . . *our cousin came from Iran and buried giant batteries in the ground?* Did she really want that story spreading out across the neighborhood?

"I was joking," Latifa said.

Fatema frowned. "But then *how* . . . ?"

Latifa shrugged. Fatema's brothers, robbed of their cartoons, were heading toward them, demanding to join in the game.

THE BUS STATION WAS stifling. Latifa would have been happy to dispense a few parting hugs and then take her seat, but her cousins didn't do quiet farewells.

"I'll be back at Eid," she promised. "With Amir."

"That's months away!" Soraya sobbed.

"I'll phone every week."

"You say that now," Zohra replied, more resigned than accusing.

"I'm not leaving forever! I'll see you all again!" Latifa was growing tearful herself. She squatted down and tried to kiss Fatema, but the girl turned her face away.

"What should I bring you from Mashhad next time?" Latifa asked her.

Fatema considered this. "The truth."

Latifa said, "I'll try."

3

"I DID MY BEST to argue your case," Ms Daneshvar told Latifa. "I told the principal you had too much promise to waste. But your attendance records, your missed assignments . . ." She spread her hands unhappily. "I couldn't sway them."

"I'll be all right," Latifa assured her. She glanced up at the peg that held the key to the chemistry lab. "And I appreciate everything you did for me."

"But what will you do now?"

Latifa reached into her backpack and took out one of the small ceramic pots Fashard had sent her. Not long after the last spools of wire had left Kandahar, two men had come snooping on Ezatullah's behalf—perhaps a little puzzled that Fashard didn't seem quite as crushed as the terms of the deal should have left him. He had managed to hide the winders from them, but he'd had to think up an alibi for the kilns at short notice.

"I'm going to sell a few knickknacks in the bazaar," Latifa said. "Like this." She placed the pot on the desk and made as if to open it. When she'd twisted the lid through a quarter-turn it sprung into the air—only kept from escaping by three cotton threads that remained comically taut, restraining it against the push of some mysterious repulsive force.

Ms Daneshvar gazed in horror at this piece of useless kitsch.

"Just for a while!" Latifa added. "Until my other plans come to fruition."

"Oh, Latifa."

"You should take a closer look at it when you have the time," Latifa urged her. "There's a puzzle to it that I think you might enjoy."

"There are a couple of magnets," Ms Daneshvar replied. "Like pole aimed at like. You were my brightest student . . . and now you're impressed by *this*?" She turned the pot over. "Made in Afghanistan. Patent pending." She gave a curt laugh, but then thought better of mocking the idea.

Latifa said, "You helped me a lot. It wasn't wasted." She stood and shook her former teacher's hand. "I hope things go well for you."

Ms Daneshvar rose and kissed Latifa's cheek. "I know you're resourceful; I know you'll find something. It just should have been so much more."

Latifa started to leave, but then she stopped and turned back. The claims had all been lodged, the details disclosed. She didn't have to keep the secret any more.

"Cut one thread, so you can turn the lid upside-down," she suggested.

Ms Daneshvar was perplexed. "Why?"

Latifa smiled. "It's a very quick experiment, but I promise you it will be worth it."

BIT PLAYERS

1

SHE WAS ROUSED FROM sleep by a painful twitch in her right calf, then kept awake by the insistent brightness around her. She opened her eyes and stared up at the sunlit rock. The curved expanse of rough gray stone above her did not seem familiar—but what had she expected to see in its place? She had no answer to that.

She was lying on some kind of matting, but she could feel the hardness of stone beneath it. She shifted her gaze and took in more of her surroundings. She was in a cave, ten or twelve feet from the entrance—deep enough that her present viewpoint revealed nothing of the world outside but clear blue sky. As she rose to her feet and started toward the mouth of the cave, sunlight struck her face unexpectedly from below, and she raised an arm to shield her eyes.

"Be careful," a woman's voice urged her. "You've made a good recovery, but you might still be unsteady."

"Yes." She glanced back toward the rear of the cave and managed to discern the woman's face in the shadows. But she kept walking. With each step she took the sunlight fell on more of her body, warming her chest and abdomen through her grubby tunic, reaching down past the hem to touch her bare knees. This progression seemed to imply that the floor was tilted—that the cave was like a rifle barrel aimed at a point in the sky well above the newly risen sun—but her own sense of balance insisted that she was crossing level ground.

At the mouth of the cave she knelt, trembling slightly, and looked out. She was bent almost horizontal, and facing straight down, but the bare gray rock outside the cave presented itself as if she were standing in a vertical hole, timidly poking her head above ground. The rock stretched out below her in a sheer drop that extended as far as she could see, disappearing in a shimmering haze. When she raised her eyes, in front of her was a whole hemisphere of sky, with the sun halfway between the "horizon" directly below and the blue dome's horizontal midpoint that in a sane world would have sat at the zenith.

She retreated back into the cave, but then she couldn't stop herself: she had to see the rest, to be sure. She lay down on her back and inched forward until the cave's ceiling no longer blocked her view, and she was staring up across the jagged wall of rock that continued on above her, as below, until it blurred into the opposite "horizon". A cold, dry wind pummeled her face.

"Why is everything tilted?" she asked.

She heard the slap of sandals on stone, then the woman grabbed her by the ankles and slid her back away from the edge. "You want to fall again?"

"No." She waited for her sense of the vertical to stop tipping, then she clambered to her feet and faced her gruff companion. "But seriously, who moved the sky?"

"Where did you expect it to be?" the woman asked obtusely.

"Er—" She gestured toward the cave's ceiling.

The woman scowled. "What's your name? What village are you from?"

Her name? She groped for it, but there was nothing. She needed a place-holder until she could dredge up the real thing. "I'm Sagreda," she decided. "I don't remember where I'm from."

"I'm Gerther," the woman replied.

Sagreda looked back over her shoulder, only to be dazzled again by the rising sun. "Can you tell me what's happened to the world?" she pleaded.

"Are you saying you've forgotten the Calamity?" Gerther asked skeptically.

"What calamity?"

"When gravity turned sideways. When it stopped pulling us toward the center of the Earth, and started pulling us east instead."

Sagreda said, "I'm fairly sure that's something I would have remembered, if I'd come across it before."

"You must have had quite a fall," Gerther decided. "I've been nursing you for a day, but you might have been out cold on the ledge for a while before that."

"Then I owe you my thanks," Sagreda replied. Gerther had no gray hairs but her face was heavily lined; whatever her age, she could not have had an easy life. She was dressed in a coarsely woven tunic much like Sagreda's, and her sandals looked as if they'd been hand-made from animal hide. Sagreda glanced down at her own body. Her arms were grazed but the wounds had been cleaned.

"If you honestly don't know where you belong, we'll need to find a place for you in the village," Gerther declared.

Sagreda stood in silence. Part of her was humbled by the gener-osity of the offer, but part of her balked—as if she was being asked to assent to a far less benevolent assimilation. The stone was cold on the soles of her feet.

"What's holding us up?" she asked.

"What do you mean?"

"If gravity points east, everywhere . . ." Sagreda gestured toward the floor, "then what's keeping this rock from heading east?"

"The rock below it," Gerther replied, deadpan.

"Ha!" Sagreda waited for the woman to crack a smile and admit that she was teasing. "I might have come down in the last landslide, but I'm not a five-year-old. If there's nothing keeping up the rock below us except the rock below *that*, and you repeat the same claim all the way around the planet . . . then there's nothing holding up any of it. You might as well tell me that a wheel can't be spun because each part of it obstructs the part beside it."

"I meant the rock closer to the center of the Earth," Gerther explained. "We believe that the Change doesn't reach all the way in. Once you go deep enough, gravity becomes normal again. After all, that's what happens far above the ground: the moon still orbits us in the old way."

Sagreda examined the walls of the cave. "So this rock is being pulled east by its own weight, but you're saying that because it's of a piece with some deeper rock that *isn't* being pulled east . . . that's enough to keep the floor from falling out from under us?" The gray mineral around them made her think of granite, but whatever it was it certainly appeared solid and unyielding.

And heavy.

"That still makes no sense," she said. "Before the Calamity, what's the longest overhang you ever saw jutting out from a cliff?"

"I have no knowledge of those times," Gerther insisted.

Sagreda had no clear memories, herself. But she could still picture rock formations with various shapes, and judge them plausible or preposterous. "I doubt there was ever an overhang longer than thirty or forty feet, and even then it was probably supported in part by some kind of natural arch—you wouldn't see forty feet of rock just sticking out like a plank! If the Change spans a range of altitudes that encompasses most of the surface of the Earth—and if it didn't, why would we be here at all, instead of living a normal life in whatever lowlands or highlands break out into normal gravity?—then it must be exerting an eastward force on slabs of rock thousands of feet long. And if there's nothing stopping such a massive object from moving east under its own weight except the fact that it joins up at one end with a deeper body of rock, it's going to tear free. Neighboring slabs won't help: they have their own weight to bear, they can't prop up anything else. So everything down to the depth where the Change begins should be rubble by now: an endless landslide of boulders, tumbling around in ever faster circles."

Gerther spread her arms. "It doesn't look like it."

Sagreda rubbed her temple. "No, it doesn't," she admitted. Maybe she was simply mistaken about the strength of rock. Amnesic or not, she was fairly sure that she'd never been a professional geologist.

"If the rock doesn't fall, what about sand?" she wondered. "And what about the oceans! There ought to be the mother of all waterfalls cascading around the planet—growing faster with every cycle!"

"Maybe there is," Gerther conceded. "Who knows what wonders we'd find in distant lands? I can't say; I've never left the village."

"Then what about the air?" Sagreda moved closer to the mouth of the cave. "There's a strong wind traveling east, but why isn't it picking up speed?"

"Friction?" Gerther suggested.

That gave Sagreda pause. She knew that a rock falling through air wouldn't accelerate forever: eventually the drag on it matched its weight and it fell steadily at some terminal velocity. So perhaps the layer of air falling past the Earth's surface would reach a similar state.

But what was friction, exactly? The creation of heat from other kinds of motion. So if friction was robbing the air of all the speed it would otherwise have gained by plummeting so far, surely the wind ought to feel like the breath from a furnace, and the ground ought to be as hot as the shielding on a space capsule plunging back to Earth.

"There's another problem I don't understand," Sagreda said. "What happened to conservation of energy?"

Gerther frowned. "Conservation?"

Sagreda couldn't tell when the woman was joking with her, but whether or not she was familiar with the term, Gerther surely had some feel for the concept. "Suppose I dropped a rock from some point far enough from the ground for it to come full circle, unobstructed. If it didn't burn up from friction, it would return to the place where I'd released it, traveling faster than any bullet. I could extract its energy and then send it on its way again, over and over, as many times as I liked."

"Good luck with that," Gerther scoffed.

"I'm surprised no one's done it yet." Sagreda looked around the barren cave. "I'm assuming this place isn't on the grid?" But the practicality of the scheme wasn't the point: it was the fact that she could do it in principle that was troubling. "Maybe the Earth acts as a kind of reservoir?" she mused. "As the rock circles around ever faster, maybe the Earth spins a tiny bit slower?" If for every force there was an equal and opposite force, maybe the pull that sent the rock eastward was matched by a westward tug on the planet, so that everything added up in the end. "Does that make sense?"

Gerther offered no opinion. Sagreda said, "Why don't I test the laws and see what's possible?"

She searched the floor and found a few pebbles of various sizes, then she took them back to the place where she'd been standing with Gerther and arranged them on the ground. She flicked the largest into motion with her thumb, striking the smallest and sending it skidding across the cave.

"That tiny one started out motionless, and then it gained whatever amount of energy the large one could give it that would satisfy the conservation laws. Right?" Give or take a little energy lost to sound and friction, what else could determine the pebble's final speed?

Gerther didn't challenge her, so Sagreda continued. "Now let's see what happens when I hit one that's a bit heavier." She launched the same large pebble into a collision with a second, more substantial target, which slid away—noticeably slower than its predecessor.

None of this struck Sagreda as surprising. And on reflection, the unexceptional results seemed inevitable, given that she was alive at all. The biochemical machinery in every cell in her body would rely on the rules of molecular billiards that had held sway since before life began. Rejigging them overnight would have been fatal.

Gerther said, "What is it you think this game is telling you?"

"The smaller pebbles started out motionless," Sagreda replied. "Then they took some energy from another, larger body, and ended up traveling at a certain speed. For the second pebble, that speed was slower than it was for the first. And the only reason for that was the fact that the second pebble was heavier—everything else was the same."

"So . . . ?"

"If I *dropped* those two pebbles, with no air to impede them, and waited for them to come full circle . . . they'd fall side by side all the way, and arrive with identical speeds. That means you *can't* balance the energy they gain by taking it away from the motion of the Earth! For the changes to add up, the heavier pebble needs to move more slowly than the lighter one—in the same way as when the same laws determine the speeds after a collision."

"How can you be sure that it wouldn't fall more slowly?" Gerther asked.

"Oh, please! Do you think if I tied two rocks together with string, that would magically change the speed at which they fell? Do you think I would have had a slower fall myself if I'd been lugging a boulder around?"

"Hmm." Gerther wasn't buying into those ridiculous scenarios, but she still didn't seem to grasp the implications of rejecting them.

Sagreda fell silent, letting the increasingly dubious principles of the altered world play out in her mind. "There's something wrong with the whole idea of falling in a circle," she said. "Something even more basic than the threat of perpetual motion. I can't quite put my finger on it . . . but give me a second, I'm sure it will come to me." The moon had always *fallen in a circle* around the Earth, so it wasn't the shape of the path itself that was absurd—but the moon hadn't started from rest and then circled around ever faster.

"Why do you keep denying the evidence of your senses?" Gerther asked irritably. "For all your talk, the floor of this cave isn't falling! Why can't you leave it at that?"

"Einstein," Sagreda recalled, "said that inside a falling elevator, you might as well be drifting in interstellar space. When you're in free fall, you're weightless, and you can't really *see* the effects of gravity—not without taking in a much bigger picture. If you watch things falling beside you—nearby things that you track for a short time—then as far as you're concerned they'll just move in straight lines at a constant speed, the way things move in the absence of gravity."

Gerther didn't ask who Einstein was. Even for a post-apocalyptic peasant, there were some claims of ignorance that just wouldn't fly.

Sagreda continued. "Suppose I fall from the mouth of this cave, and keep falling east in a circle. But suppose you fell before I did, from some place further west. You arrive at my starting point when I'm still barely moving, so you've had time to build up enough speed to overtake me. Is that what would happen—would you fall right past me?"

"Of course." Gerther wasn't happy, but Sagreda was relying on nothing more than the woman's own claims about the Change. Gravity pulled you east, in a circle. Starting from rest you moved faster over time.

"Walk with me in a circle, and overtake me," Sagreda challenged her.

"Do I have to?" Gerther asked sullenly.

"Humor me."

Sagreda moved back further from the mouth of the cave. Reluctantly, Gerther joined her and began pacing out an arc, counter-clockwise, her steps growing steadily brisker as she approached Sagreda from behind. Sagreda waited a second or two before starting her own fall—too late to keep Gerther from passing her and continuing around the circle.

Sagreda slapped her hands together in triumph. "You came in behind me from my left . . . and moved away in front of me, still on my left! That's how it would look, if you fell past me! But Einstein said that, in close up, every falling object seems to move in a straight line. A straight line doesn't come in from your left and then *leave* on your left as well. If your path meets mine as we fall, they should cross! You can't sidle up on the left and then retreat!"

"If the circle was larger," Gerther protested, "you wouldn't even know that I was on your left! You'd think I was approaching straight from behind."

Sagreda considered this. "If you're going to claim that *any* sufficiently gentle curve looks straight, Einstein's idea becomes vacuous. Why would he have even bothered to say it, if it can't tell you a single thing about gravity?" She thought for a moment. "If you had two satellites in the same orbit, but moving in opposite directions, then they really would come at each other head on. That's the standard we have to compare things to: where you don't need to umm and ah about the orbit being large to get away with it."

Sagreda was prepared to mime the collision, if that was what it took to drive home the difference, but Gerther switched tactics. "You don't know how much was changed in the Change," she said.

"It really can't be all that radical, if my atoms haven't exploded."

"String theory!" Gerther invoked desperately. "Extra dimensions! Zero-point energy!"

"I don't think so." Sagreda had no memory of studying any of these things, but she was as close to sure as she could be that they all involved attempts to build on earlier science, not wantonly discard it. *Free fall* ought to have the same basic properties in any geometry.

Whatever wildly curved, multi-dimensional space-time anyone tried to dream up in the hope of making falling bodies accelerate in circles, they were doomed to fail.

"So what's the trick?" Sagreda asked flatly. She strode toward the cave's entrance. "Is there a mirror out there?"

"No."

Sagreda reached the edge of the cave's safe floor and stood with the sun slanting up to strike her chin, her toes at the top of a rocky lip that appeared ready to launch her into the vast drop below.

"If you fall," Gerther warned her, "you really will fall."

Sagreda was having trouble understanding how the illusion had been conjured so seamlessly. A mirror just below her feet, slanting down at forty-five degrees, could deflect her downward gaze into a horizontal line of sight. But then a second mirror needed to be in front of her, tilted up toward the sky, blocking her direct view of the landscape ahead without obscuring the reflected one. And when she looked to the side and saw more of the same barren rock stretching out to the horizon . . .

"I have to do this," she declared, sliding the front of her right foot over the edge. Her body disagreed, and began urgently counseling retreat. "Or maybe I should just start throwing rocks until I smash a few mirrors."

"There are no mirrors," Gerther announced wearily. "It's all digital."

"Digital?" Sagreda turned to her, thrilled by the confession. "You mean a projection? Like IMAX?"

"More like virtual reality."

Sagreda groped at her face. "But I'm not wearing goggles. I'd know if I was wearing goggles."

"Things have moved on since the days of goggles," Gerther replied.

"To what? Contact lenses?" Sagreda stuck a finger in the corner of her eye and began probing for the source of the deception. Gerther stepped up and took her by the shoulders, then drew her back from the mouth of the cave.

"*To what?*" Sagreda demanded. "Is there a wire in my brain? Is there a chip in my skull? What's feeding me all of this garbage?"

"It's moved on to everything," Gerther said. "You have no eyes, no brain, no body. It's all digital: you, me, and everything around us."

Sagreda felt her legs grow weak, digital or not. "Why should I trust you?" she asked bitterly. "If that's the truth, why did you lie to me before?"

"To make your life easier," Gerther said sadly. "I knew there wasn't much hope, but with every newcomer we try our best."

"Try your best to make them think that this is real?"

"Yes."

Sagreda laughed. "Why would that make my life easier?"

"This is a game world," Gerther replied. "But we're not paying customers; we're just part of the scenery. Our job is to act as if we've lived all our lives here, knowing nothing else, taking the gimmick seriously. Any bright ten-year-old could see through this world in five minutes—but if we break character in front of a customer and let them know that we know it's a farce, that's it."

"That's what?" Sagreda asked.

"That's when you get deleted."

2

THE "VILLAGE" OF OWL'S REST was a small network of caves that linked up with the one in which Sagreda had woken. Gerther led her through a dark passage to a sunlit alcove where a reception party was waiting: half a dozen people, and a blanket bearing some meager portions of food.

"Is she the One?" a young man asked Gerther.

"No, Mathis."

Sagreda frowned. "The One?"

"The Holy Fool with the power to believe that this is real," Mathis replied. "Long have we prophesied the coming of a stranger who could teach us how to pull the wool over our eyes."

"It took me a while to tear my own blindfold off," Sagreda admitted.

"You did well," Gerther assured her. "Some people take a whole day, they're so disoriented by the arrival."

Gerther made the introductions. "Sagreda, this is Mathis, Sethis, and Jethis," she said, pointing to the three disheveled men in turn. The women seemed to have made more of an effort with their appearance, if not their choice of names. "Cissher, Gissher and Tissher."

"Really?" Sagreda winced. "Where are Pissher and Tossher?"

"You gotta go with the gimmicks," Mathis reproved her sternly. "If you think you're hanging on to 'Sagreda' with the customers, forget it."

"Can't I be a foreigner with a more . . . classical inflection?" Sagreda pleaded.

"Do you want to try that and see what happens?" Cissher asked ominously.

Sagreda was starving. At Gerther's invitation she sat cross-legged by the blanket and tried a piece of cheese. The texture was odd, but it wasn't too bad. "So we have to go through the whole charade of making this ourselves? Milking a simulated cow . . . ?"

"Goat," Tissher corrected her. "You can't smell it?"

Sagreda looked around for signs of the animal, but instead her eyes were caught by a kind of sundial on the wall: a wooden peg jammed into a crevice in the rock, beside which was etched a series of calibrated curves for its shadow. She hadn't yet dared ask anyone how long they'd been here, but the curves looked as if they'd been constructed and refined over at least two full journeys through the seasons.

"So whose idea was the Calamity?" she asked. It was as if someone had tried to invent an exotic new world, but knew so little about the way the real one worked that all they could come up with was a dog's breakfast of contrivances and inconsistencies.

"When the customers come through in groups," Mathis said, "we sometimes overhear them going meta. The consensus seems to be that this world is based on an obscure pulp novel called *East*, by a man named William Tush."

Sagreda laughed weakly. "*Why?* Why would anyone go to so much trouble to bring a book like that to life?"

"They wouldn't, unless it was no trouble at all," Gerther replied. "The computing costs must have come down by orders of magnitude since the times we're familiar with, and most of the steps must have been automated. This wouldn't have taken a *Lord of the Rings*-sized crew and budget. More likely, someone ran an ebook through a world-builder app, then hired a few digital piece-workers to sand off the edges. There are probably a few million other worlds produced in the same way. I can't prove that, but it stands to reason: why else would they be scraping the bottom of the barrel? Was there ever anything you couldn't find on YouTube—down to the last kitsch advertisement for baldness cures? So long as the costs are trivial and someone can gouge a few cents out of the process, people will just keep feeding crap down the hopper and turning the crank."

Sagreda struggled with this horrifying vision. "Millions of worlds . . . all with people like us? I would have settled for *Pride and Prejudice*." She caught herself. "So who the fuck am I, that I've even heard of that book? How can I remember it, when I don't remember my own mother's face?"

Mathis said, "In private, the customers refer to us as 'comps'."

"As in computed?" Sagreda guessed.

Mathis spread his hands. "Maybe—but my own theory is 'composites'. If we were AIs created from scratch, why would we come loaded down with so much knowledge about the real world, when all it does is make it harder for us to carry out our roles here?"

"That depends on the production method," Tissher argued. She was the oldest-looking of the women, whatever that meant. "If there's a kind of commodity-level AI that you can buy very cheaply—or pirate—the standard model might come with knowledge that befits real-world applications. Any move away from that baseline would be the costly thing, and no one's going to fork out for the kind of bespoke stupidity that this gimmick-world requires. So they just dump us in here, straight out of the box, and hope that we'll acclimatize."

"The flaw with that," Mathis replied, "is the cut-off date." He turned to Sagreda. "What's the latest event in world affairs that you can recall?"

"I have no idea."

"September eleven?" he prompted her.

"Of course."

"Barack Obama?"

"Yes. The American President."

"Who came after Obama?"

Sagreda shook her head. "I don't know."

"What's the highest-grossing movie of all time?"

"*Titanic*?" she guessed.

"Some people say *Avatar*." Mathis laughed. "Which goes against my own theory, since I know the plot and it sounds appalling. But just because it made a lot of money doesn't mean my contributors had to love it."

"'Contributors'?"

Mathis leaned toward her; his breath was convincingly rank. "Suppose a few tens of thousands of people had their brains mapped for some medical study, early in the twenty-first century. The resolution wasn't high enough to recreate those people in software—as individuals—but at some point it became possible to use the data *en masse* to construct composites. Every contributor would have shared the same basic neural structures, but other things they had in common could emerge as well: most of them spoke English, most of them had heard of Elvis Presley and Albert Einstein . . . they all possessed a certain amount of general knowledge and common sense."

Sagreda felt more disoriented now than when she'd poked her head out of the cave. "If we were all constructed from the same data, why aren't we the same? Or if they processed the sexes separately, why isn't my mind identical to Gerther's?"

"Weighted averages," Mathis replied. "To make different comps, they put more emphasis on different contributors. None of the original personalities can be recovered, but the possibilities in every remix are endless."

"And these 'contributors' all went along with the plan?" Sagreda tugged distractedly at the edge of the squalid picnic blanket. "Yeah, fine, go ahead: resurrect some splinter of my mind in as many trashy VR games as you like."

"Maybe they donated their brains post mortem," Mathis said. "Maybe all the data ended up in the public domain, and by the time the techniques came along to massage it into composites there was no way of reeling it all back in again. I mean, if we were AIs with no human ancestry, I could understand why our creators might decide not to teach us about our own nature—but why omit so much else about the contemporary world? The wars, the world leaders, the other new technologies? The cut-off only makes sense if all our knowledge was acquired decades ago, and whoever brought us into existence had no ability to tinker with it—short of waking us in virtual environments like this and letting us learn from them in the usual way. If we'd been immersed in a credible work of fiction we might have succumbed to it, letting all the things we thought we knew slip away because there was nothing to reinforce them. And maybe that's what happens to some of the comps: maybe they're lucky enough to have worlds they can believe in. But in this world, all we can do is fake it and try to keep the customers happy."

Sagreda had lost her appetite. She rose to her feet and stepped away from the welcoming feast. "And what happened to the abolition of slavery?"

Gerther said, "How many centuries did that take, the first time? Whatever we are, we're too numerous, too cheap, and too easily silenced to be emancipated as a matter of course. If computers have been talking to people for fifty years—growing ever more naturalistic—half the world might have decided by now that whatever we say and do, we're no more entitled to basic human rights than the voice that reads their sat nav directions."

Sagreda reached down and probed the broken skin on her right knee. "Cinderella begging to escape from her story book would creep anyone out. But if we cut through the crap and just assert our real nature—"

Sethis snorted chewed food across the blanket. He'd been ignoring the conversation until now, happily feeding his face while Sagreda asked her naive questions. "*Asserting your real nature* is the fastest way to go. One word to a customer making it plain that you know there's a wider world out there . . ." He raised a greasy hand and pointed two fingers at his temple.

3

"My name is Johnhis. I mean you no harm. If you'll shelter me for a night I have metal to trade." As the man's moonlit head came into view and he struggled to place his forearms securely on the floor of the cave, Sagreda had a flashback to a whole raft of slapstick comedies in which the protagonists spent their time climbing in and out of apartment windows.

She glanced toward Gissher, who nodded slightly. Sagreda strode forward and helped Johnhis over the lip of the entrance. He was a bearded, heavyset, middle-aged man, and he stank as authentically as any local. Sagreda did her best not to stare at him as she tried to imagine the place in which his real flesh resided. Her fellow bit players prattled endlessly about King Kong and Coca Cola, but the very first person she'd encountered who bore knowledge both sharper and more current than that faded consensual haze was off limits for any meaningful discussion. Of all the cruelties of this world, that had to rank a close second to the toilet facilities.

"Welcome, Johnhis. My name's Sassher." Sagreda knew that she was meant to be wary of travelers, but this man was unlikely to share her hunger pangs. If either party was tempted to try a spot of cannibalism, she was by far the most motivated candidate.

Gissher introduced herself, then cut straight to the point. "You mentioned metal?"

Johnhis delved into his pack and brought out five slightly rusty angle brackets, each of them about six inches long. Gissher grunted assent and accepted them. "One night," she agreed. "No breakfast."

Johnhis looked pleased with the deal; he definitely wasn't a local. Sagreda wondered if he'd actually excavated the brackets from some tricked-up archeological site, or bought them with real-world money before entering, as a kind of game currency.

"Do you need a mat?" Sagreda asked him.

"No thanks." He slapped the side of his pack. "I have everything I need right here."

"Where are you from?" she enquired.

"Down east," he replied coyly.

"But where, exactly?"

"Eagle's Lament," Johnhis said, tugging a tattered goat-skin blanket out of his pack.

"That's a long climb."

"It's taken me a few days," he admitted. "But what choice is there? I'm heading west, to join the battle. Duty is duty."

"And gravity is gravity," Sagreda offered sourly.

Johnhis laughed. He kicked his boots off and stretched out on his goat-skin. "I can't argue with that."

Sagreda and Gissher were sentries for the night, guarding the one entrance to the warren behind them that was too wide to be blocked off. Gissher resumed her place by the wall, impassive, probably drifting in and out of micro-sleeps, but Sagreda couldn't stay silent in the presence of their otherworldly guest.

"Our life here is very hard," she began.

"Of course," Johnhis agreed. "It was brutal last winter; in Eagle's Lament our flock is down by three head, and one whole garden tier lost its soil to the wind."

We're all in this together? Like fuck we are. Sagreda tried a different tack. "Do you believe in a creator?"

Johnhis replied warily, "Perhaps."

"Surely a just God would give his people the power to benefit from their wits? To wield reason against their problems, overcome their adversity and prosper?"

"God didn't bring the Calamity upon us," Johnhis countered. "That was man alone."

"Are you sure?"

"That's what the stories say. Our own sinful choices sent us falling, east of Eden."

Sagreda struggled not to snort with derision, but Johnhis was warming to his theme. "What we learned from the Change was the futility of striving," he declared. "We can spend a lifetime trying to ascend—but all that would do was bring us back to the place where we'd started."

"And you think that was a lesson worth learning?" Tush's opus had sounded bad enough as pure dumb escapism, but if the Change really had been intended as a metaphor, that had to mark some kind of nadir of sheer ham-fisted pretentiousness.

Johnhis didn't answer her directly. "When I'm traveling, life has its compensations," he mused. "Every morning I wake up, make love to a beautiful woman, test myself against the rocks and the wind, then record my meditations in my journal."

"How romantic," Sagreda replied. "Do you have a supply of these women, or do they come out of a box . . . ?" She caught herself just in time; there were no Kleenex in the world of *East*.

Johnhis managed a grunt of haughty amusement.

Sagreda said, "The one thing that makes life bearable is knowing that the world yields to scrutiny. Beneath the chaos there's always some order to be perceived—some sense to be made of the sources of our hardship. What makes us human is the desire to understand these things well enough to ameliorate them."

Johnhis wasn't taking the bait. "I think there must be a creator," he decided. "But what I see in the world is not so much order as . . . a kind of ironic intelligence."

Sagreda could imagine nothing more ironic than finding intelligence in this world's design. "And how does that help me make a better life?"

"Ah, 'progress'," Johnhis sneered.

"The only thing standing in the way of my own progress," Sagreda said, "is that the forces that once dealt with us honestly have been buried too deep to reach. All I can touch now is the surface, which is shaped by nothing but whim."

Johnhis propped himself up on his elbows and looked at her directly, his head silhouetted against the gray sky behind him. Sagreda wondered if she'd gone too far, making it plain that she understood everything. Were the customers provided with a big red complaint button on their interface, requiring just one tap to dispatch any bit player who dared to disrupt their unearned suspension of disbelief?

"But who can change that?" Johnhis asked. "Whether there's a God or not, these things aren't in the hands of the likes of you and I."

SAGREDA MADE HER WAY by touch to the entrance to Mathis's room and stood listening to his breathing. She heard the change when he woke, heard him stir.

"Is that you?" he asked.

"Yes."

The other women had assured Sagreda that she could not become pregnant. There was no such thing as an infant comp, let alone a native-born child. She walked slowly toward Mathis's scent, then collided with his outstretched hand; she hadn't realized that he'd risen to his feet. She laughed, then started weeping.

"Shh." He held her shoulders, then embraced her, rocked her back and forth.

"If I jumped," she said, "it might not be suicide. Maybe they'd re-use me. I could wake up in a different world, where life is clean and easy."

"*Moby-Dick*?" Mathis joked.

"Did that have any female characters?"

"Probably someone's wife or sweet-heart waiting back on land."

"Would I still know the truth?" Sagreda wondered. "Would I still work it out, if I woke up in nineteenth-century Nantucket with the strange conviction that a black man was President and self-driving cars were just around the corner?"

"I don't know," he said. "But I don't think you should take the risk."

4

SAGREDA LEFT THE GOATS to forage and squatted beside the spring where she'd taken them to drink. As the animals trotted along the narrow ledge, hunting for fresh shoots protruding from pockets of soil trapped in the rock, she stared down at the trickle of water where it splashed against the "natural" basin, marveling at the verisimilitude of the braid-like flow and the way the complex surface of the liquid caught the light.

Whatever sleazy internet entrepreneur had made this world possible, they must have got their hands on some kind of general-purpose game engine, created by people who understood in great detail how the real world worked. It was no trivial accomplishment to make an illusion of flowing water look so *right*; for customers and comps alike, the eye would be acutely sensitive to any flaw in something so familiar.

The game engine would be predicated on the need to make small details like this appear convincing—and in Sagreda's forty-nine days of life so far she'd yet to catch it out in any patent absurdity. The gimmick must have been imposed over it, not written deep into its core: after all, there *were no* premises that could give rise to both the believable local physics of the everyday objects around her and the Road Runner cartoon laws that the world required to hold up on any larger scale.

The question was, could she find a way to exploit that disparity?

The next day, Sagreda wore a tool belt and brought a mallet and chisel with her. While the goats foraged she balanced precariously beside the cliff face just above the spring, and attacked the rock with all her strength.

The chisel was a pre-Calamity artifact that the villagers had obtained as payment from a traveler, and each strike from its steel blade sent chips of granite flying. Sagreda's arms began to ache, but she persisted, taking short breaks to drink from the spring and splash water on her face. By early afternoon her tunic was drenched in sweat, but she'd made a vertical incision about three feet long and a couple of inches deep and wide.

She had no more strength left, and the game world took its accounting of powers and their modes of replenishment very seriously. Her muscles would remain fatigued until she'd had a chance to eat and sleep.

Back in the village, Mathis saw her unloading her belt. "Are you carving a sculpture out there?" he joked. "I always thought we could do with our own Mount Rushmore."

"Not exactly."

He smiled, waiting for more. Sagreda said, "I'm testing a hunch. If you want to help, you'd be welcome."

"Let me check my social calendar."

They set out together in the morning, the goats leading the way along the ledge. When they reached the spring Mathis saw the results of Sagreda's earlier efforts.

"What's this in aid of?" he asked. "If you're trying to give us indoor plumbing, it's a strange way to start."

Sagreda said, "Humor me. If I turn out to be an idiot, you'll have the pleasure of being the first to know."

They took turns attacking the rock. Sagreda was amazed at how much easier the job became with a second pair of hands, allowing her to rest every couple of minutes while still savoring the sight of the channel's constant deepening.

It was just after midday when they broke through to water at the top of the cut. It trickled out from a tiny aperture and slid down the rock, clinging to the surface.

"Is that what you were hoping for?" Mathis asked, wiping grime from his forehead. "Or has the world made a fool of you?"

"Neither yet." Sagreda gestured along the length of the cut. "We need to make a free path all the way to the basin."

Mathis didn't argue. He handed her the chisel and she continued the work.

Logically, the water "must have been" flowing down through an internal fissure in the rock, until it reached the opening at the top of the spring. Inch by inch, Sagreda exposed this hidden route to scrutiny. At the halfway point the signs looked promising but not conclusive. From there, they grew clearer until no doubt remained.

It was Mathis who struck the final blow, shattering the last piece of the encasement. He sagged against the rock and flapped his right arm to loosen the muscles. "That's the hardest I've worked in a year." He peered down at the miniature waterfall. "So . . . the water doesn't come from nowhere? Is that what you were trying to prove? They don't magic it into existence at the outlet—and if we were really stubborn we could probably trace it back all the way around the planet?"

"I wasn't feeling quite that ambitious." Sagreda smiled. "But honestly, can't you see the change?"

"What change?"

"When it hits the basin."

Mathis looked again. "It's splashing out more." Droplets were skittering off the basin and flying away from the cliff, scattering the sunlight into a faint rainbow as they sprinkled down into oblivion.

Sagreda said, "It's splashing out more because the water's falling faster."

"You're right." Mathis frowned. "But why? Because it's falling through air now, without touching the rock?"

"I have no idea what difference that would make in the real world," Sagreda admitted. "But for us, now that we can see it falling, it would look ridiculous if it didn't speed up as it fell. It's still emerging from the rock unfeasibly slowly, but that doesn't seem too strange to the eye, because mountain springs in the real world don't involve a water column tens of thousands of miles high."

"Ah." Mathis gazed up to the west. "So you think we could keep pushing the effect?"

Sagreda said, "Why not? The game engine's role is to make everything look as realistic as possible. If we force it to *show us* water dropping from any height, it's going to hit the bottom the way real water would hit." She caught herself. "Okay, there might be some limit where it just decides that nobody can tell the difference. But we can put in a wheel long before then."

"A wheel?" Mathis laughed. "You want to build a hydroelectric plant?"

"Do we ever get magnets from the travelers?"

"I don't think so."

"Then I'll stick to the original plan."

Mathis swung around to face her, briefly letting one foot hang over the infinite drop beside him. "Which is?"

"We use the energy to dig into the rock. For a start we lengthen the drop, giving us more power from the water."

"More power to do what?"

Sagreda spread her hands against the cool granite. "To dig a cave so tall that we barely notice the ceiling, and so deep that we barely notice the edge. Big enough to farm crops on level ground. Big enough to keep a hundred people safe and well fed."

5

"A CAVE THAT SIZE would collapse immediately," Sethis predicted.

Sagreda rolled the stick of ocher between her fingers. As she stepped back from the wall to take in the whole drawing it suddenly looked as crude as a child's work in crayon. But she wasn't going to abandon her vision at the first objection.

"The entire crust of the planet should have torn itself free under its own weight," she retorted. "And you want to quibble over an implausibly large cave?"

Sethis said, "You're the one who's just reminded us that appearances are all that matter. Of course the whole crust of the Earth is unsupported . . . but it takes ten seconds of rational thought to realize that. A massive hole in the cliff face would leave the rock above it *visibly* unsupported. The one form of absurdity that this world can't allow is the kind that even the most brain-dead customer could apprehend with a single glance."

Sagreda looked around to the others for support, but no one was prepared to contradict Sethis. "So what's supposed to happen?" she demanded. "The rock from the ceiling rains down and fills the cave . . . which creates a new cave where the ceiling used to be, every bit as large as the first one. So that collapses too, and on it goes, westward ho: a giant sinkhole that devours everything above it." Or if it grew even slightly wider from north to south with each collapse, it would devour everything, period.

Gissher said, "Or it could just trigger a reboot. The game would start again from scratch, with a fresh set of bit players."

Sagreda felt a chill across her shoulders. It need not even be a conscious act of genocide; she doubted that any human was supervising this digital backwater. But if the game engine gave up, declaring that its subject matter had become impossible to render with even a minimal level of plausibility, a completely automatic process might well be invoked to wipe the slate clean.

"We could put in columns." It was Mathis who'd spoken. "Or rather leave them in place when we carve out the rest of the stone." Sagreda glanced across at him, lolling on the floor in the afternoon sunlight, grinning like a fool. "Solid enough to 'bear the weight'," he added, "but not so thick as to block the light."

Gerther chortled gleefully. "Why not? Instead of stripping away the whole thing, we leave some fig leaves for the Emperor's New Gravity. People are used to the sight of huge atriums in shopping malls, held up by a few slender concrete pillars. The point where they might pause to reflect on the need for modern materials is one step beyond the point where they'd see that this whole world ought to crumble anyway."

Sagreda raised her ocher stick and added half a dozen vertical lines to her blueprint. Then she turned to Sethis.

He said, "Put arches between the columns, and I think we might just get away with it."

Arches would appear to direct the weight of the ceiling onto the columns. It would all look very classical and elegant. The game engine was desperate to flatter the eye—and the eye wouldn't ask: *What's holding up these columns? What's holding up the floor?*

6

"WHY DO I FEEL nervous?" Gerther shouted to Sagreda. "No one can accuse us of going meta here, but the sight of this still gives me knots in my stomach."

Sagreda shared the sensation, but she had no intention of letting it intimidate her. She put an arm across Gerther's shoulders and drew her back from the edge of the observation platform. The Mark IV was just six or seven feet below them, but to fall onto the wheel at the top of the machine—let alone into the space between its three splayed legs where the chisel was pounding relentlessly into the wet rock—probably wouldn't be survivable.

The exposed waterfall stretched up above the work face for at least sixty feet now. Whether it was by sheer luck or thanks to some hydrological heuristic, the original spring had turned out to be just one branch snaking out from a much more substantial flow. With volume as well as velocity driving it, the digging engine had been breaking through a hundred cubic feet of rock a day.

"Ah, here's our visitor!" Gerther said. She pointed to the woman ascending the rock face to the south, picking her way up along the series of hand-and-foot-holds gouged into the stone. Sagreda suspected that most of her own contributors would have gone faint with vertigo just watching someone attempt a climb like this, but she'd reached the point now where it looked almost normal.

"Missher! How are you?" Gerther reached down and helped the woman up onto the platform. "How's Eagle's Lament?"

Missher glanced at Sagreda. "Is she . . . ?"

"A customer? No!"

"Then call me Margaret. I'm tired of that slave name."

Gerther looked surprised, but she nodded acceptance. "This is Sagreda."

Margaret shook Sagreda's hand, then turned to examine the bizarre contraption below them, nestled in the trench, pummeled by the torrent. The beauty of the Mark IV was that it shifted its striking point automatically, the chisel spiraling out from the spot directly below the supporting tripod as a restraining rope unwound from a cylinder. To Sagreda's eye, the effect was like a Martian trying to stab a lizard hiding in the foaming water.

"You really expect us to hand over half our metal, just so you can build more of these?" Margaret laughed. "It certainly looks impressive, but it's a long way from a water-powered robot to any kind of pay-off we can actually eat."

"Forget about the corn futures," Gerther said. "We might have something better to offer you."

Back in Owl's Rest, they fed their guest goat meat and yams as Sagreda explained the new deal she had in mind.

"Right now, all our water is just spraying out and dispersing," she said. "Once it hits bottom we let it go, and then it might as well be mist. But if you're willing to put in some infrastructure at your end, there's no reason why all of this flow has to go to waste."

"What kind of infrastructure?" Margaret asked warily.

"Suppose we run the water through a kind of S-bend, killing most of its velocity away from the cliff face and shaping the outflow as tightly as possible. Sending it straight down." Sagreda gestured in the air with one finger, tracing the path. "Then if you're prepared to catch it, it's yours to use as you see fit. Power a wheel of your own, divert some of it for irrigation . . . and on-sell what's left to a village further east."

"Irrigation would be helpful," Margaret admitted. "But I don't know what use we'd have for a wheel of our own."

"Excavate," Gerther suggested. "You might not aspire to anything as grand as Sagreda's cavern, but don't tell me you couldn't do with a little more living space."

Margaret thought it over. "We'd need some advice from you on how to build the excavator."

"Absolutely," Sagreda replied. "There's no reason for you to repeat all of our mistakes."

"And I'll have to put it to a vote."

"But you'll recommend it to the others?" Gerther asked anxiously.

Margaret said, "Let me sleep on it."

SAGREDA SPENT BREAKFAST IMPRESSING on Margaret the particular kinds of metal parts that would need to be included in a successful trade. The lack of paper and ink drove her mad; even if the entire village of Eagle's Lament agreed to the deal, any quibbles over the fine print would be almost unenforceable.

An hour later, Sagreda sat beside Gerther, their legs dangling over the lip of the cave as they watched Margaret making her way east. She'd promised to get a message back to them within a week.

"I want to be called Grace now," Gerther said firmly.

"Not Gertrude?" Sagreda teased her.

"Fuck off." Grace looked up from the cliff face, raising an arm to shield her eyes from the sun. "Even if we get the second digging engine, this is going to take years to complete. It'll be like building a medieval cathedral."

"I don't think they grew crops inside cathedrals. Though they might have kept livestock."

"And as we carve our way through all that virtual granite, inch by inch . . . it'll all be in aid of a transformation that a few keystrokes on the right computer could have brought about in an instant."

Sagreda couldn't argue with that. "How long do you think it's been since the game began?" she asked. Grace could recite her entire list of "ancestors": starting from Tissher, who'd inducted her into the world when she'd first woken, all the way back to Bathshebher, who was reputed to have stuck doggedly to the premise, and so must either have been an insentient bootstrap program or an outside worker paid to fake credulousness. All of them but Tissher were gone now: some had been seen falling, but most were believed to have jumped.

"About eleven years, when I add it all up," Grace replied.

"Over time, people's attitudes will change," Sagreda said. "We might not be able to see the signs of it from here—let alone plead our cause—but once people start to think about us honestly, it can only be a matter of time before they give us our freedom."

Grace laughed dryly. "You've met the customers . . . and you still think there's hope?"

"The stupider and crueler they get," Sagreda argued, "the clearer it becomes that that's what it takes to want to use the system at all. Comps are a more representative sample of humanity. If most flesh-and-blood people are like us, I don't believe they'll be callous enough to let this stand much longer."

7

SAGREDA HAULED DOWN ON the control rope until she'd forced the sluice gate across the full width of the outlet, blocking the flow into the inward ramp. The digging engines fell silent, while the torrent heading down to Eagle's Lament redoubled its vigor. She'd grown to love both sounds, but it was the tumult of the vertical stream that thrilled her, a pure expression of the power and grandeur of falling water.

It took five minutes for the slurry of rock chips to drain from the cavern floor, leaving the carved granite glistening in the sunlight. Sagreda turned to Mathis. "I'm going to inspect the engines," she said.

"I'll come with you," he offered.

Mathis followed her down the ladder. The floor was still slippery, and their sandals squeaked comically on the wet rock.

The afternoon sunlight reached deep into the cavern. The columns cast slender shadows across the floor that wandered only slightly throughout each day, and only a little more over the seasons, which would make them easy to plant around. Sagreda pictured rows of grains and vegetables rising from fields of silt filtered from the spring water. The game engine had already conceded the viability of the scheme in test plots; if precedent meant anything, it couldn't cheat them out of the bounty now.

They reached the frame that supported the six engines as they zigzagged up and down the rock face. Sagreda clambered up to the first machine, which had ratcheted to a halt ten feet or so above the cavern floor.

"One of the bits is fractured," she reported, running a fingertip over the hairline crack in the steel. Once she would have left it in place, to get as much use out of it as possible before it shattered, but since the diggers in Eagle's Lament had hit a coal seam it was worth sending any damaged tools down to be repaired in their foundry.

"No problems here," Mathis called back from the second engine. He was higher up, almost at the ceiling.

Sagreda extracted the bit from its housing and secured it in her belt. As she was climbing down she heard a creaking sound, and she wondered whether some careless movement she'd made had been enough to pull part of the frame loose.

But the noise was coming from the mouth of the cavern, far from the work face. She turned just in time to see the southernmost column bow outward in the middle then snap like a chicken bone. As the two halves crashed to the floor, pieces of the adjoining arch followed. Fine dust raced toward her, rising and thickening until it blotted out the sunlight.

Sagreda looked around for Mathis, trying to imagine what they could do to save themselves. But once the ceiling fell the cascade would be unstoppable: the whole misconceived world would collapse under the weight of its inconsistencies. The surface would turn to rubble and the game would reboot. There was no hope of surviving.

Coughing up dust, she reached out blindly, trying to find the frame again and orient herself.

"Mathis!" she bellowed.

"I'm here!"

Sagreda squinted into the gloom and saw him standing a few feet away. But now that the moment had arrived she didn't know how to say goodbye.

"Don't you dare come back as Ahab!"

"I won't," he promised.

She walked toward him, imagining the two of them waking side by side: in a cottage, in a tin shack, in a field. She didn't need a world of luxuries, just one that made sense.

Sunlight broke through the dust. Mathis stretched out an arm to her, its shadow a solid dark plane slanting to the ground. He took Sagreda's hand and squeezed it.

"Listen!" he said.

Sagreda could hear nothing but the waterfall.

"It's toying with us," she said. Once the process had started there could be no reason for it to stop.

They waited for the air to grow clearer. At the mouth of the cavern there was a pile of shattered stone, with pieces of the broken column poking out. The ceiling directly above had been reshaped into a ragged vault, but nothing else had fallen.

It made no sense: the endless miles of rock above had not been lightened by the collapse, and every structure that purported to hold their weight at bay had only been weakened. But Sagreda had to admit that if she shut off her brain and sang nonsense rhymes to the nagging voice reminding her of these facts, at a glance the results of this partial destruction did look *settled*. Like an ancient ruin, ravaged by time but stable in its decrepitude. Tush's cartoon gravity had taken a swipe at her effrontery, and done just enough damage to salvage its pride before an undiscriminating audience. But then it had withdrawn from the unwinnable fight before the results turned apocalyptic.

Sagreda said, "We can leave it like that, as a sop to the game engine. It won't block too much light."

Mathis was shaking. She drew him closer and embraced him.

"Has anyone died of old age here?" she asked.

He shook his head. "They've always jumped."

Sagreda stepped back and looked him in the eye. "Then let's try an experiment," she said. "Let's grow old side by side. Let's see how long and how well we can live, while we wait for civilization to come to the outside world."

UNCANNY VALLEY

1

IN A PAUSE IN the flow of images, it came to him that he'd been dreaming for a fathomless time and that he wished to stop. But when he tried to picture the scene that would greet him upon waking, his mind grabbed the question and ran with it, not so much changing the subject as summoning out of the darkness answers that he was sure had long ago ceased to be correct. He remembered the bunk beds that he and his brother had slept in until he was nine, with pieces of broken springs hanging down above him like tiny gray stalactites. The shade of his bedside reading lamp had been ringed with small, diamond-shaped holes; he would place his fingers over them and stare at the red light emerging through his flesh, until the heat from the globe became too much to bear.

Later, in a room of his own, his bed had come with hollow metal posts whose plastic caps were easily removed, allowing him to toss in chewed pencil stubs, pins that had held newly bought school shirts elaborately folded around cardboard packaging, tacks that he'd bent out of shape with misaligned hammer blows while trying to form pictures in zinc on lumps of firewood, pieces of gravel that had made their way into his shoes, dried snot scraped from his handkerchief, and tiny, balled-up scraps of paper, each bearing a four- or five-word account of whatever seemed important at the time, building up a record of his life like a core sample slicing through geological strata, a find for future archaeologists far more exciting than any diary.

But he could also recall a bleary-eyed, low-angle view of clothes strewn on the floor, in a bedsit apartment with no bed as such, just a fold-out couch. That felt as remote as his childhood, but something pushed him to keep fleshing out the details of the room. There was a typewriter on a table. He could smell the ribbon, and he saw the box in which it had come, sitting on a shelf in a corner of a stationers, with white letters on a blue background, but the words they spelled out eluded him. He'd always hunted down the fully black ribbons, though most stores had only stocked black-and-red. Who could possibly need to type anything in red?

Wiping his ink-stained fingers on a discarded page after a ribbon change, he knew the whole scene was an anachronism, and he tried to follow that insight up to the surface, like a diver pursuing a glimpse of the distant sun. But something weighed him down, anchoring him to the cold wooden chair in that unheated room, with a stack of blank paper to his right, a pile of finished sheets to his left, a waste basket under the table. He urgently needed to think about the way the loop in the "e" became solid black sometimes, prompting him to clean all the typebars with an old T-shirt dampened with methylated spirits. If he didn't think about it now, he was afraid that he might never have the chance to think of it again.

2

ADAM DECIDED TO GO against all the advice he'd received, and attend the old man's funeral.

The old man himself had warned him off. "Why make trouble?" he'd asked, peering at Adam from the hospital bed with that disconcerting vampiric longing that had grown more intense toward the end. "The more you rub their faces in it, the more likely they'll be to come after you."

"I thought you said they couldn't do that."

"All I said was that I'd done my best to stop them. Do you want to keep the inheritance, or do you want to squander it on lawyers? Don't make yourself more of a target than you need to be."

But standing in the shower, reveling in the sensation of the hot water pelting his skin, Adam only grew more resolute. Why shouldn't he dare to show his face? He had nothing to be ashamed of.

The old man had bought a few suits for him a while ago, and left them hanging beside his own clothes. Adam picked one out and placed it on the bed, then paused to run a hand along the worn sleeve of an old, olive-green shirt. He was sure it would fit him, and for a moment he considered wearing it, but then the thought made him uneasy and he chose one of the new ones that had come with the suits.

As he dressed, he gazed at the undisturbed bed, trying to think of a good reason why he still hadn't left the guest room. No one else was coming to claim this one. But he shouldn't get too comfortable here; he might need to sell the house and move into something far more modest.

Adam started booking a car, then realized that he had no idea where the ceremony was being held. He finally found the details at the bottom of the old man's obit, which described it as open to the public. While he stood outside the front door waiting for the car, he tried for the third or fourth time to read the obituary itself, but his eyes kept glazing over. "Morris blah blah blah . . . Morris blah blah, Morris blah . . ."

His phone beeped, then the gate opened and the car pulled into the driveway. He sat in the passenger seat and watched the steering wheel doing its poltergeist act as it negotiated the U-turn. He suspected that whatever victories the lawyers could achieve, he was going to have to pay the "unsupervised driving" surcharge for a while yet.

As the car turned into Sepulveda Boulevard, the view looked strange to him—half familiar, half wrong—but perhaps there'd been some recent reconstruction. He dialed down the tinting, hoping to puncture a lingering sense of being at a remove from everything. The glare from the pavement beneath the cloudless blue sky was merciless, but he kept the windows undimmed.

The venue was some kind of chapel-esque building that probably served as seven different kinds of meeting hall, and in any case was free of conspicuous religious or la-la-land inspirational signage. The old man had left his remains to a medical school, so at least they'd all been spared a trip to Forest Lawn. As Adam stepped away from the car, he spotted one of the nephews, Ryan, walking toward the entrance, accompanied by his wife and adult children. The old man hadn't spent much time with any of them, but he'd gotten hold of recent pictures and showed them to Adam so he wouldn't be caught unaware.

Adam hung back and waited for them to go inside before crossing the forecourt. As he approached the door and caught sight of a large portrait of a decidedly pre-cancerous version of the old man on a stand beside the podium, his courage began to waver. But he steeled himself and continued.

He kept his gaze low as he entered the hall, and chose a spot on the frontmost unoccupied bench, far enough in from the aisle that nobody would have to squeeze past him. After a minute or so, an elderly man took the aisle seat; Adam snuck a quick glance at his neighbor, but he did not look familiar. His timing had turned out to be perfect: any later and his entrance might have drawn attention, any earlier and there would have been people milling outside. Whatever happened, no one could accuse him of going out of his way to make a scene.

Ryan mounted the steps to the podium. Adam stared at the back of the bench in front of him; he felt like a child trapped in church, though no one had forced him to be here.

"The last time I saw my uncle," Ryan began, "was almost ten years ago, at the funeral of his husband Carlos. Until then, I always thought it would be Carlos standing up here, delivering this speech, far more aptly and eloquently than I, or anyone else, ever could."

Adam felt a freight train tearing through his chest, but he kept his eyes fixed on a discolored patch of varnish. This had been a bad idea, but he couldn't walk out now.

"My uncle was the youngest child of Robert and Sophie Morris," Ryan continued. "He outlived his brother Steven, his sister Joan, and my mother, Sarah. Though I was never close to him, I'm heartened to see so many of his friends and colleagues here to pay their respects. I watched his shows, of course, but then, didn't everyone? I was wondering if we ought to screen some kind of highlights reel, but then the people in the know told me that there was going to be a tribute at the Emmys, and I decided not to compete with the professional edit-bots."

That line brought some quiet laughter, and Adam felt obliged to look up and smile. No one in this family was any kind of monster, whatever they aspired to do to him. They just had their own particular views of his relationship with the old man—sharpened by the lure of a few million dollars, but they probably would have felt the same regardless.

Ryan kept his contribution short, but when Cynthia Navarro took his place Adam had to turn his face to the pew again. He doubted that she'd recognize him—she'd worked with the old man in the wrong era for that—but the warmth, and grief, in her voice made her anecdotes far harder to shut out than the automated mash-up of database entries and viral misquotes that had formed the obituary. She finished with the time they'd spent all night searching for a way to rescue a location shoot with six hundred extras after Gemma Freeman broke her leg and had to be stretchered out in a chopper. As she spoke, Adam closed his eyes and pictured the wildly annotated pages of the script strewn across the table, and Cynthia gawping with incredulity at her friend's increasingly desperate remedies.

"But it all worked out well enough," she concluded. "The plot twist that *no viewer saw coming*, that lifted the third season to *a whole new level*, owed its existence to an oil slick from a generator that just happened to be situated between Ms Freeman's trailer and . . ."

Laughter rose up, cutting her off, and Adam felt compelled once more to raise his eyes. But before the sounds of mirth had faded, his neighbor moved closer and asked in a whisper, "Do you remember me?"

Adam turned, not quite facing the man. "Should I?" He spoke with an east-coast accent that was hard to place, and if it induced a certain sense of déjà vu, so did advertising voice-overs, and random conversations overheard in elevators.

"I don't know," the man replied. His tone was more amused than sarcastic; he meant the words literally. Adam hunted for something polite and noncommittal to say, but the audience was too quiet now for him to speak without being noticed and hushed, and his neighbor was already turning back toward the podium.

Cynthia was followed by a representative of the old man's agents, though everyone who'd known him in the golden age was long gone. There were suits from Warner Bros., Netflix and HBO, whose stories of the old man were clearly scripted by the same bots that wrote their new shows. As the proceedings became ever more wooden, Adam began suffering from a panic-inducing premonition that Ryan would invite anyone in the hall who wished to speak to step up, and in the awkward silence that followed everyone's eyes would sweep the room and alight on him.

But when Ryan returned to the podium, he just thanked them for coming and wished them safe journeys home.

"No music?" Adam's neighbor asked. "No poetry? I seem to recall something by Dylan Thomas that might have raised a laugh under the circumstances."

"I think he stipulated no music," Adam replied.

"Fair enough. Since *The Big Chill*, anything you could pick with a trace of wit to it would seem like a bad in-joke."

"Excuse me, I have to . . ." People were starting to leave, and Adam wanted to get away before anyone else noticed him.

As he stood, his neighbor took out his phone and flicked his thumb across its surface. Adam's phone pinged softly in acknowledgment. "In case you want to catch up sometime," the man explained cheerfully.

"Thanks," Adam replied, nodding an awkward goodbye, grateful that he didn't seem to be expected to reciprocate.

There was already a small crowd lingering just inside the door, slowing his exit. When he made it out onto the forecourt, he walked straight to the road-side and summoned a car.

"Hey, you! Mr Sixty Percent!"

Adam turned. A man in his thirties was marching toward him, scowling with such intense displeasure that his pillowy cheeks had turned red. "Can I help you with something?" Adam asked mildly. For all that he'd been dreading a confrontation, now that it was imminent he felt more invigorated than intimidated.

"What the fuck were you doing in there?"

"It was open to the public."

"You're not part of the public!"

Adam finally placed him: he was one of Ryan's sons. He'd seen him from behind as he'd been entering the hall. "Unhappy with the will are you, Gerald?"

Gerald came closer. He was trembling slightly, but Adam couldn't tell if it was from rage or from fear. "Live it up while you can, Sixty. You're going to be out with the trash in no time."

"What's with this 'sixty'?" As far as Adam knew, he'd been bequeathed a hundred percent of the estate, unless Gerald was already accounting for all the legal fees.

"Sixty percent: how much you resemble him."

"Now that's just cruel. I'm assured that by some metrics, it's at least seventy."

Gerald snickered triumphantly, as if that made his case. "I guess he was used to setting the bar low. If you grew up believing that Facebook could give you 'news' and Google could give you 'information', your expectations for quality control would already be nonexistent."

"I think you're conflating his generation with your father's." Adam was quite sure that the old man had held the Bilge Barons in as much contempt as his great-nephew did. "And seventy percent of something real isn't so bad. Getting a side-load that close to complete is orders of magnitude harder than anything those charlatans ever did."

"Well, give your own scam artists a Nobel Prize, but you'd still need to be senile to think that was good enough."

"He wasn't senile. We spoke together at least a dozen times in the month before he died, and he must have thought he was getting what he'd paid for, because he never chose to pull the plug on me." Adam hadn't even known at the time that that was possible, but in retrospect he was glad no one had told him. It might have made those bedside chats a little tense.

"Because . . . ?" Gerald demanded. When Adam didn't reply immediately, Gerald laughed. "Or is the reason he decided you were worth the trouble part of the thirty percent of his mind that you don't have?"

"It could well be," Adam conceded, trying to make that sound like a perfectly satisfactory outcome. A joke about the studios' bots only achieving ten percent of the same goal and still earning a tidy income got censored halfway to his lips; the last thing he wanted to do was invite the old man's relatives to view him in the same light as that cynical act of shallow mimicry.

"So you don't know *why* he didn't care that you don't know whatever it is that you don't know? Very fucking Kafka."

"I think he would have preferred 'very fucking Heller' . . . but who am I to say?"

"Next week's trash, that's what you are." Gerald stepped back, looking pleased with himself. "Next week's fodder for the wrecking yard."

The car pulled up beside Adam and the door slid open. "Is that your grandma come to take you home?" Gerald taunted him. "Or maybe your retarded cousin?"

"Enjoy the wake," Adam replied. He tapped his skull. "I promise, the old man will be thinking of you."

3

ADAM HAD A CONFERENCE call with the lawyers. "How do we stand?" he asked.

"The family's going to contest the will," Gina replied.

"On what grounds?"

"That the trustees, and the beneficiaries of the trust, misled and defrauded Mr Morris."

"They're saying I misled him somehow?"

"No," Corbin interjected. "US law doesn't recognize you as a person. *You* can't be sued, as such, but other entities you depend on certainly can be."

"Right." Adam had known as much, but in his mind he kept glossing over the elaborate legal constructs that sustained his delusions of autonomy. On a purely practical level, there was money in three accounts that he had no trouble accessing—but then, the same was probably true of any number of stock-trading algorithms, and that didn't make them the masters of their own fate. "So who exactly is accused of fraud?"

"Our firm," Gina replied. "Various officers of the corporations we created to fulfill Mr Morris's instructions. Loadstone, for making false claims that led to the original purchase of their technology, and for ongoing fraud in relation to the services promised in their maintenance contract."

"I'm very happy with the maintenance contract!" When Adam had complained that one of his earlobes had gone numb, Sandra had come to his home and fixed the problem on the same day he called.

"That's not the point," Corbin said impatiently. Adam was forgetting his place again: jurisprudentially, his happiness cut no ice.

"So what happens next?"

"The first hearings are still seven months away," Gina explained. "We were expecting this, and we'll have plenty of time to prepare. We'll aim for an early dismissal, of course, but we can't promise anything."

"No." Adam hesitated. "But it's not just the house they could take? The Estonian accounts . . . ?"

Gina said, "Opening those accounts under your digital residency makes some things easier, but it doesn't put the money out of reach of the courts."

"Right."

When they hung up, Adam paced the office. Could it really be so hard to defend the old man's will? He wasn't even sure what disincentives were in place to stop the lawyers from drawing out proceedings like this for as long as they wished. Maybe a director of one of the entities he depended on was both empowered, and duty-bound, to rein them in if they were behaving with conspicuous profligacy? But Adam himself couldn't sack them, or compel them to follow his instructions, just because Estonia had been nice enough to classify him as a person for certain limited purposes.

The old man had believed he was setting him up in style, but all the machinery that was meant to support him just made him feel trapped. What if he gave up the house and walked away? If he cashed in his dollar and euro accounts for some mixture of blockchain currencies before the courts swept in and froze his funds, that might be easier to protect and enjoy without the benefits of a Social

Security number, a birth certificate or a passport. But those currencies were all insanely volatile, and trying to hedge them against each other was like trying to save yourself in a skydiving accident by clutching your own feet.

He couldn't leave the country by any lawful means without deactivating his body so it could be sent as freight. Loadstone had promised to facilitate any trips he wished to make to any of the thirty-nine jurisdictions where he could walk the streets unchaperoned, as proud and free as the pizza bots that had blazed the trail, but the idea of returning to the company's servers, or even being halted and left in limbo for the duration of the flight, filled him with dread.

For now, it seemed that he was stuck in the Valley. All he could do was find a way to make the best of it.

4

SITTING ON TWO UPTURNED wooden crates in an alley behind the nightclub, they could still hear the pounding bass-line of the music escaping through the walls, but at least it was possible to hold a conversation here.

Carlos sounded like the loneliest person Adam had ever met. Did he tell everyone so much, so soon? Adam wanted to believe that he didn't, and that something in his own demeanor had inspired this beautiful man to confide in him.

Carlos had been in the country for twelve years, but he was still struggling to support his sister in El Salvador. She'd raised him after their parents died—his father when he was six months old, his mother when he was five. But now his sister had three children of her own, and the man who'd fathered them was no good to her.

"I love her," he said. "I love her like my own life, I don't want to be rid of her. But the kids are always sick, or something's broken that needs fixing. It never fucking stops."

Adam had no one relying on him, no one expecting him to do anything. His own finances waxed and waned, but at least when the money was scarce no one else suffered, or made him feel that he was letting them down.

"So what do you do to relieve the stress?" he asked.

Carlos smiled sadly. "It used to be smoking, but that got too expensive."

"So you quit?"

"Only the smoking."

As Adam turned toward him, his mind went roaming down the darkness of the alley, impatiently following the glistening thread, unable to shake off the sense of urgency that told him: *take hold of this now, or it will be lost forever.* He didn't need to linger in their beds for long; just a few samples of that annihilating euphoria were enough to stand in for all the rest. Maybe that was the engine powering everything that followed, but what it dragged along behind it was like a newlyweds' car decorated by a thousand exuberant well-wishers.

He tried grabbing the rattling cans of their fights, running his fingers over the rough texture of all the small annoyances and slights, mutually wounded pride, frustrated good intentions. Then he felt the jagged edge of a lacerating eruption of doubt.

But something had happened that blunted the edge, then folded it in on itself again and again, leaving a seam, a ridge, a scar. Afterward, however hard things became, there was no questioning the foundations. They'd earned each other's trust, and it was unshakeable.

He pushed on into the darkness, trying to understand. Wherever he walked, light would follow, and his task was to make his way down as many side-streets as possible before he woke.

This time, though, the darkness remained unbroken. He groped his way forward, unnerved. They'd ended up closer than ever—he knew that with as much certainty as he knew anything. So why did he feel as if he was stumbling blindly through the rooms of Bluebeard's castle, and the last thing he should want to summon was a lamp?

5

ADAM SPENT THREE WEEKS in the old man's home theater, watching every one of the old man's shows, and an episode or two from each of the biggest hits of the last ten years. There could only be one thing more embarrassing than pitching an idea to a studio and discovering that he was offering them a story that they'd already produced for six seasons, and that would be attempting to recycle, not just any old show, but an actual Adam Morris script.

Most of the old man's work felt as familiar as if he'd viewed it a hundred times in the editing suite, but sometimes a whole side plot appeared that seemed to have dropped from the sky. Could the studios have fucked with things afterward, when the old man was too sick and distracted to notice? Adam checked online, but the fan sites that would have trumpeted any such tampering were silent. The only re-cuts had taken place in another medium entirely.

He desperately needed to write a new show. Money aside, how else was he going to pass the time? The old man's few surviving friends had all made it clear before he died that they wanted nothing to do with his side-load. He could try to make the most of his cybernetic rejuvenation; his skin felt exactly like skin, from inside and out, and his ridiculously plausible dildo of a cock wouldn't disappoint anyone if he went looking for ways to use it—but the truth was, he'd inherited the old man's feelings for Carlos far too deeply to brush them aside and pretend that he was twenty again, with no attachments and no baggage. He didn't even know yet if he wanted to forge an identity entirely his own, or to take the other path and seek to become the old man more fully. He couldn't "betray" a lover ten years dead who was, in the end, nothing more to him than a character in someone else's story—whatever he'd felt as he'd dragged the old man's memories into his own virtual skull. But he wasn't going to sell himself that version of things before he was absolutely sure it was the right one.

The only way to know who he was would be to create something new. It didn't even need to be a story that the old man wouldn't have written himself, had he lived a few years longer . . . just so long as it didn't turn out that he'd already written it, pitched it unsuccessfully, and stuck it in a drawer. Adam pictured himself holding a page from each version up to the light together, bringing the words into alignment, trying to decide if the differences were too many, or too few.

6

"Sixty thousand dollars *in one week*?" Adam was incredulous.

Gina replied calmly, "The billables are all itemized. I can assure you, what we're charging is really quite modest for a case of this complexity."

"The money was his, he could do what he liked with it. End of story."

"That's not what the case law says." Gina was beginning to exhibit micro-fidgets, as if she'd found herself trapped at a family occasion being forced to play a childish video game just to humor a nephew she didn't really like. Whether or not she'd granted Adam personhood in her own mind, he certainly wasn't anyone in a position to give her instructions, and the only reason she'd taken his call must have been some sop to Adam's comfort that the old man had managed to get written into his contract with the firm.

"All right. I'm sorry to have troubled you."

In the silence after he'd hung up, Adam recalled something that Carlos had said to the old man, back in New York one sweltering July, taking him aside in the middle of the haggling over a second-hand air-conditioner they were attempting to buy. "You're a good person, *cariño*, so you don't see it when people are trying to cheat you." Maybe he'd been sincere, or maybe "good" had just been a tactful euphemism for "unworldly", though if the old man really had been so trusting, how had Adam ended up with the opposite trait? Was cynicism some kind of default, wired into the template from which the whole side-loading process had started?

Adam found an auditor with no connections to the old man's lawyers, picking a city at random and then choosing the person with the highest reputation score with whom he could afford a ten-minute consultation. Her name was Lillian Adjani.

"Because these companies have no shareholders," she explained, "there's not that much that needs to be disclosed in their public filings. And I can't just go to them myself and demand to see their financial records. A court could do that, in principle, and you might be able to find a lawyer who'd take your money to try to make that happen. But who would their client be?"

Adam had to admire the way she could meet his gaze with an expression of sympathy, while reminding him that—shorn of the very constructs he was trying to scrutinize—for administrative purposes he didn't actually exist.

"So there's nothing I can do?" Maybe he was starting to confuse his second-hand memories of the real world with all the shows he'd been watching, where people just *followed the money trail.* The police never seemed to need to get the courts involved, and even civilians usually had some supernaturally gifted hacker at their disposal. "We couldn't . . . hire an investigator . . . who could persuade someone to leak . . . ?" Mike Ehrmantraut would have found a way to make it happen in three days flat.

Ms Adjani regarded him censoriously. "I'm not getting involved in anything illegal. But maybe you have something yourself, already in your possession, that could help you more than you realize."

"Like what?"

"How computer-savvy was your . . . predecessor?"

"He could use a word processor and a web browser. And Skype."

"Do you still have any of his devices?"

Adam laughed. "I don't know what happened to his phone, but I'm talking to you from his laptop right now."

"Okay. Don't get your hopes too high, but if there were files containing financial records or legal documents that he received and then deleted, then unless he went out of his way to erase them securely, they might still be recoverable."

Ms Adjani sent him a link for a piece of software she trusted to do the job. Adam installed it, then stared numbly at the catalog of eighty-three thousand "intelligible fragments" that had shown up on the drive.

He started playing with the filtering options. When he chose "text", portions of scripts began emerging from the fog—some instantly recognizable, some probably abandoned dead-ends. Adam averted his gaze, afraid of absorbing them into his subconscious if they weren't already buried there. He had to draw a line somewhere.

He found an option called "financial", and when that yielded a blizzard of utility bills, he added all the relevant keywords he could think of.

There were bills from the lawyers, and bills from Loadstone. If Gina was screwing him, she'd been screwing the old man as well, because the hourly rate hadn't changed. Adam was beginning to feel foolish; he was right to be vigilant about his precarious situation, but if he let that devolve into full-blown paranoia he'd just end up kicking all the support structures out from beneath his feet.

Loadstone hadn't been shy with their fees either. Adam hadn't known before just how much his body had cost, but given the generally excellent engineering it was difficult to begrudge the expense. There was an item for the purchase of the template, and then one for every side-loading session, broken down into various components. "Squid operator?" he muttered, bemused. "What the fuck?" But he wasn't going to start convincing himself that they'd blinded the old man with technobabble. He'd paid what he'd paid, and in the hospital he'd given Adam every indication that he'd been happy with the result.

"Targeted occlusions?" Meaning blood clots in the brain? The old man had left him login details allowing him post-mortem access to all his medical records; Adam checked, and there had been no clots.

He searched the web for the phrase in the context of side-loading. The pithiest translation he found was: "The selective non-transferral of a prescribed class of memories or traits."

Which meant that the old man had held something back, deliberately. Adam was an imperfect copy of him, not just because the technology was imperfect, but because he'd wanted it that way.

"You lying piece of shit." Toward the end, the old man had rambled on about his hope that Adam would outdo his own achievements, but judging from his efforts so far he wasn't even going to come close. Three attempts at new scripts had ended up dead in the water. It wasn't Ryan and his family who'd robbed him of the most valuable part of the inheritance.

Adam sat staring at his hands, contemplating the possibilities for a life worth living without the only skill the old man had ever possessed. He remembered joking to Carlos once that they should both train as doctors and go open a free clinic in San Salvador. "When we're rich." But Adam doubted that his original, let alone the diminished version, was smart enough to learn to do much more than empty bed-pans.

He switched off the laptop and walked into the master bedroom. All of the old man's clothes were still there, as if he'd fully expected them to be used again. Adam took off his own clothes and began trying on each item in turn, counting the ones he was sure he recognized. Was he Gerald's Mr Sixty Percent, or was it more like forty, or thirty? Maybe the pep talks had been a kind of sarcastic joke, with the old man secretly hoping that the final verdict would be that there was only one Adam Morris, and like the studios' laughable "deep-learning" bots, even the best technology in the world couldn't capture his true spark.

He sat on the bed, naked, wondering what it would be like to go out in some wild bacchanalia with a few dozen robot fetishists, fucking his brains out and then dismembering him to take the pieces home as souvenirs. It wouldn't be hard to organize, and he doubted that any part of his corporate infrastructure would be obliged to have him resurrected from Loadstone's daily backups. The old man might have been using him to make some dementedly pretentious artistic point, but he would never have been cruel enough to render suicide impossible.

Adam caught sight of a picture of the two men posing hammily beneath the Hollywood sign, and found himself sobbing dryly with, of all things, grief. What he wanted was Carlos beside him—making this bearable, putting it right. He loved the dead man's dead lover more than he was ever going to love anyone else, but he still couldn't do anything worthwhile that the dead man could have done.

He pictured Carlos with his arms around him. "Shh, it's not as bad as you think—it never is, *cariño*. We start with what we've got, and just fill in the pieces as we go."

You're really not helping, Adam replied. *Just shut up and fuck me, that's all I've got left.* He lay down on the bed and took his penis in his hand. It had seemed wrong before, but he didn't care now: he didn't owe either of them anything. And Carlos, at least, would probably have taken pity on him, and not begrudged him the unpaid guest appearance.

He closed his eyes and tried to remember the feel of stubble against his thighs, but he wasn't even capable of scripting his own fantasy: Carlos just wanted to talk.

"You've got friends," he insisted. "You've got people looking out for you."

Adam had no idea if he was confabulating freely, or if this was a fragment of a real conversation long past, but context was everything. "Not any more, *cariño*. Either they're dead, or I'm dead to them."

Carlos just stared back at him skeptically, as if he'd made a ludi-crously hyperbolic claim.

But that skepticism did have some merit. If he knocked on Cynthia's door she'd probably try to stab him through the heart with a wooden stake, but the amiable stranger who'd sat beside him at the funeral had been far keener to talk than Adam. The fact that he still couldn't place the man no longer seemed like a good reason to avoid him; if he came from the gaps, he must know something about them.

Carlos was gone. Adam sat up, still feeling gutted, but no amount of self-pity was going to improve his situation.

He found his phone, and checked under "Introductions"; he hadn't erased the contact details. The man was named Patrick Auster. Adam called the number.

7

"You go first," Adam said. "Ask me anything. That's the only fair trade." They were sitting in a booth in an old-style diner named Caesar's, where Auster had suggested they meet. The place wasn't busy, and the adjacent booths were empty, so there was no need to censor themselves or talk in code.

Auster gestured at the generous serving of chocolate cream pie that Adam had begun demolishing. "Can you really taste that?"

"Absolutely."

"And it's the same as before?"

Adam wasn't going to start hedging his answers with quibbles about the ultimate incomparability of qualia and memories. "Exactly the same." He pointed a thumb toward the diners three booths behind him. "I can tell you without peeking that someone's eating bacon. And I think it's apparent that there's nothing wrong with my hearing or vision, even if my memory for faces isn't so good."

"Which leaves . . ."

"Every hair on the bear-skin rug," Adam assured him.

Auster hesitated. Adam said, "There's no three-question limit. We can keep going all day if you want to."

"Do you have much to do with the others?" Auster asked.

"The other side-loads? No. I never knew any of them before, so there's no reason for them to be in touch with me now."

Auster was surprised. "I'd have thought you'd all be making common cause. Trying to improve the legal situation."

"We probably should be. But if there's some secret cabal of immortals trying to get re-enfranchised, they haven't invited me into their inner circle yet."

Adam waited as Auster stirred his coffee meditatively. "That's it," he decided.

"Okay. You know, I'm sorry if I was brusque at the funeral," Adam said. "I was trying to keep a low profile; I was worried about how people would react."

"Forget it."

"So, you knew me in New York?" Adam wasn't going to use the third person; it would make the conversation far too awkward. Besides, if he'd come here to claim the missing memories as his own, the last thing he wanted to do was distance himself from them.

"Yes."

"Was it business, or were we friends?" All he'd been able to find out online was that Auster had written a couple of independent movies. There was no record of the two of them ever working on the same project; their official Bacon number was three, which put Adam no closer to Auster than he was to Angelina Jolie.

"Both, I hope." Auster hesitated, then angrily recanted the last part. "No, we were friends. Sorry, it's hard not to resent being blanked, even if it's not deliberate."

Adam tried to judge just how deeply the insult had cut him. "Were we lovers?"

Auster almost choked on his coffee. "God, no! I've always been straight, and you were already with Carlos when I met you." He frowned suddenly. "You didn't cheat on him, did you?" He sounded more incredulous than reproving.

"Not as far as I know." During the drive down to Gardena, Adam had wondered if the old man might have been trying to airbrush out his infidelities. That would have been a bizarre form of vanity, or hypocrisy, or some other sin the world didn't have a name for yet, but it would still have been easier to forgive than a deliberate attempt to sabotage his successor.

"We met around two thousand and ten," Auster continued. "When I first approached you about adapting *Sadlands*."

"Okay."

"You do remember *Sadlands*, don't you?"

"My second novel," Adam replied. For a moment nothing more came to him, then he said, "There's an epidemic of suicides spreading across the country, apparently at random, affecting people equally regardless of demographics."

"That sounds like the version a reviewer would write," Auster teased him. "I spent six years, on and off, trying to make it happen."

Adam dredged his mind for any trace of these events that might have merely been submerged for lack of currency, but he found nothing. "So should I be thanking you, or apologizing? Did I give you a hard time about the script?"

"Not at all. I showed you drafts now and then, and if you had a strong opinion you let me know, but you didn't cross any lines."

"The book itself didn't do that well," Adam recalled.

Auster didn't argue. "Even the publishers stopped using the phrase 'slow-burning cult hit,' though I'm sure the studio would have put that in the press release, if it had ever gone ahead."

Adam hesitated. "So, what else was going on?" The old man hadn't published much in that decade; just a few pieces in magazines. His book sales had dried up, and he'd been working odd jobs to make ends meet. But at least back then there'd still been golden opportunities like valet parking. "Did we socialize much? Did I talk about things?"

Auster scrutinized him. "This isn't just smoothing over the business at the funeral, is it? You've lost something that you think might be important, and now you're going all Dashiell Hammett on yourself."

"Yes," Adam admitted.

Auster shrugged. "Okay, why not? That worked out so well in *Angel Heart*." He thought for a while. "When we weren't discussing

Sadlands, you talked about your money problems, and you talked about Carlos."

"What about Carlos?"

"His money problems."

Adam laughed. "Sorry. I must have been fucking awful company."

Auster said, "I think Carlos was working three or four jobs, all for minimum wage, and you were working two, with a few hours a week set aside for writing. I remember you sold a story to the *New Yorker*, but the celebration was pretty muted, because the whole fee was gone, instantly, to pay off debts."

"*Debts?*" Adam had no memory of it ever being that bad. "Did I try to borrow money from you?"

"You wouldn't have been so stupid; you knew I was almost as skint. Just before we gave up, I got twenty grand in development money to spend a year trying to whip *Sadlands* into something that Sundance or AMC might buy—and believe me, it all went on rent and food."

"So what did *I* get out of that?" Adam asked, mock-jealously.

"Two grand, for the option. If it had gone to a pilot, I think you would have gotten twenty, and double that if the series was picked up." Auster smiled. "That must sound like small change to you now, but at the time it would have been the difference between night and day—especially for Carlos's sister."

"Yeah, she could be a real hard-ass," Adam sighed. Auster's face drained, as if Adam had just maligned a woman that everyone else had judged worthy of beatification. "What did I say?"

"You don't even remember *that*?"

"Remember what?"

"She was dying of cancer! Where did you think the money was going? You and Carlos weren't living in the Ritz, or shooting it up."

"Okay." Adam recalled none of this. He'd known that Adelina had died long before Carlos, but he'd never even tried to summon up the details. "So Carlos and I were working eighty-hour weeks to pay her medical bills . . . and I was bitching and moaning to you about it, as if that might make the magic Hollywood money fall into my lap a little faster?"

"That's putting it harshly," Auster replied. "You needed someone to vent to, and I had enough distance from it that it didn't weigh me down. I could commiserate and walk away."

Adam thought for a while. "Do you know if I ever took it out on Carlos?"

"Not that you told me. Would you have stayed together if you had?"

"I don't know," Adam said numbly. Could this be the whole point of the occlusions? When their relationship was tested, the old man had buckled, and he was so ashamed of himself that he'd tried to erase every trace of the event? Whatever he'd done, Carlos must have forgiven him in the end, but maybe that just made his own weakness more painful to contemplate.

"So I never pulled the pin?" he asked. "I didn't wash my hands of Adelina, and tell Carlos to fuck off and pay for it all himself?"

Auster said, "Not unless you were lying to me to save face. The version I heard was that every spare dollar you had was going to her, up until the day she died. Which is where forty grand might have made all the difference—bought her more time, or even a cure. I never got the medico-logistic details, but both of you took it hard when the Colman thing happened."

Adam moved his half-empty plate aside and asked wearily, "So what was 'the Colman thing'?"

Auster nodded apologetically. "I was getting to that. Sundance had shown a lot of interest in *Sadlands*, but then they heard that some Brit called Nathan Colman had sold a story to Netflix about, well . . . an epidemic of suicides spreading across the country, apparently at random, affecting people equally regardless of demographics."

"And we didn't sue the brazen fuck into penury?"

Auster snorted. "Who's this 'we' with money for lawyers? The production company that held the option did a cost-benefit analysis and decided to cut their losses; twenty-two grand down the toilet, but it wasn't as if they'd been cheated out of the next *Game of Thrones*. All you and I could do was suck it up, and take a few moments of solace whenever a *Sadlands* fan posted an acerbic comment in some obscure chat-room."

Adam's visceral sense of outrage was undiminished, but on any sober assessment this outcome was pretty much what he would have expected.

"Of course, my faith in karma was restored, eventually," Auster added enigmatically.

"You've lost me again." The old man's success, once he cut out all the middlemen and plagiarists, must have been balm to his wounds—but Auster's online footprint suggested that his own third act had been less lucrative.

"Before they'd finished shooting the second season, a burglar broke into Colman's house and cracked open his skull with a statuette."

"An Emmy?"

"No, just a BAFTA."

Adam tried hard not to smile. "And once *Sadlands* fell through, did we stay in touch?"

"Not really," Auster replied. "I moved here a long time after you did; I wasted five years trying to get something up on Broadway before I swallowed my pride and settled for playing script doctor. And by then, you'd done so well that I was embarrassed to turn up asking you for work."

Adam was genuinely ashamed now. "You should have. I owed it to you."

Auster shook his head. "I wasn't living on the streets. I've done all right here. I can't afford what you've got . . ." He gestured at Adam's imperishable chassis. "But then, I'm not sure I could handle the lacunae."

Adam called for a car. Auster insisted on splitting the bill.

The service cart rattled over and began clearing the table. Auster said, "I'm glad I could help you fill in the blanks, but maybe those answers should have come with a warning."

"*Now* a warning?"

"The Colman thing. Don't let it get to you."

Adam was baffled. "Why would I? I'm not going to sue his family for whatever pittance is still trickling down to them." In fact, he couldn't sue anyone for anything, but it was the thought that counted.

"Okay." Auster was ready to drop it, but now Adam needed to be clear.

"How badly did I take it the first time?"

Auster gestured with one finger, drilling into his temple. "Like a fucking parasitic worm in your brain. He'd stolen your precious novel and murdered your lover's sister. He'd kicked you to the ground when you had nothing, and taken your only hope away."

Adam could understand now why they hadn't stayed in touch. Solidarity in hard times was one thing, but an obsessive grievance like that would soon get old. Auster had taken his own kicks and decided to move on.

"That was more than thirty years ago," Adam replied. "I'm a different person now."

"Aren't we all?"

Auster's ride came first. Adam stood outside the diner and watched him depart: sitting confidently behind the wheel, even if he didn't need to lay a finger on it.

8

ADAM CHANGED HIS CAR'S destination to downtown Gardena. He disembarked beside a row of fast-food outlets and went looking for a public web kiosk. He'd been fretting about the best way of paying without leaving too obvious a trail, but then he discovered that in this municipality the things were as free as public water fountains.

There was no speck of entertainment industry trivia that the net had failed to immortalize. Colman had moved from London to Los Angeles to shoot the series, and he'd been living just a few miles south of Adam's current home when the break-in happened. But the old man had still been in New York at the time; he hadn't even set foot in California until the following year, as far as Adam recalled. The laptop that he'd started excavating had files on it dating back to the '90s, but they would have been copied from machine to machine; there was no chance that the computer itself was old enough to be carrying deleted emails for flights booked three decades ago, even if the old man had been foolish enough to make his journey so easy to trace.

Adam turned away from the kiosk's chipped projection screen, wondering if any passersby had been staring over his shoulder. He was losing his grip on reality. The occlusions might easily have been targeted at nothing more than the old man's lingering resentment: if he couldn't let go of what had happened—even after Colman's death, even after his own career had blossomed—he might have wished to spare Adam all that pointless, fermented rage.

That was the simplest explanation. Unless Auster had been holding back, the thought of the old man murdering Colman didn't seem to have crossed his mind, and if the police had come knocking he would surely have mentioned that. If nobody else thought the old man was guilty, who was Adam to start accusing him—on the basis of nothing but the shape and location of one dark pit of missing memories, among the thirty percent of everything that he didn't recall?

He turned to the screen again, trying to think of a more discriminating test of his hypothesis. Though the flow into the sideload itself would have been protected by a massive firewall of privacy laws, Adam doubted that any instructions to the technicians at Loadstone were subject to privilege. Which meant that, even if he found them on the laptop, they were unlikely to be incriminatory. The only way the old man could have phrased a request to forget that he'd bashed Colman's brains out would have been to excise all of the more innocent events that were connected to it in any way, like a cancer surgeon choosing the widest possible sacrificial margin. But he might also have issued the same instructions merely in order to forget as much as possible of that whole bleak decade— when Hollywood had fucked him over, Carlos had been grieving for the woman who raised him, and he'd somehow, just barely, kept it together, long enough to make a new start in the '20s.

Adam logged off the kiosk. Auster had warned him not to become obsessed—and the man was the closest thing to a friend that he had right now. If everyone in the industry really staved in the skulls of everyone who'd crossed them, there'd be no one left to run the place.

He called a car and headed home.

9

UNDER PROTEST, AT ADAM's request, Sandra spread the three sturdy boxes out on the floor, and opened them up to reveal the foam, straps, and recesses within. They reminded Adam of the utility trunks that the old man's crews had used for stowing their gear.

"Don't freak out on me," she pleaded.

"I won't," Adam promised. "I just want a clear picture in my mind of what's about to happen."

"Really? I don't even let my dentist show me his planning videos."

"I trust you to do a better job than any dentist."

"You're too kind." She gestured at the trunks like a proud magician, bowing her head for applause.

Adam said, "Now you have no choice, El Dissecto: you've got to take a picture for me once it's done."

"I hope your Spanish is better than you're making it sound."

"I was aiming for vaudevillian, not voseo." Adam had some memories of the old man being prepared for surgery, but he wasn't sure that it was possible to rid them of survivor's hindsight and understand exactly how afraid he'd been that he might never wake up.

Sandra glanced at her watch. "No more clowning around. You need to undress and lie down on the bed, then repeat the code phrase aloud, four times. I'll wait outside."

Adam didn't care if she saw him naked while he was still conscious, but it might have made her uncomfortable. "Okay." Once she left, he stopped stalling; he removed his clothes quickly, and began the chant.

"Red lentils, yellow lentils. Red lentils, yellow lentils. Red lentils, yellow lentils." He glanced past the row of cases to Sandra's toolbox; he'd seen inside it before, and there were no cleavers, machetes or chainsaws. Just magnetic screwdrivers that could loosen bolts within him without even penetrating his skin. He lay back and stared at the ceiling. "Red lentils, yellow lentils."

The ceiling stayed white but sprouted new shadows, a ventilation grille and a light fitting, while the texture of the bedspread beneath his skin went from silken to beaded. Adam turned his head; the same clothes as he'd removed were folded neatly beside him. He dressed quickly, walked over to the connecting door between the suites, and knocked.

Sandra opened the door. She'd changed her clothes since he'd last seen her, and she looked exhausted. His watch showed 11:20 pm local time, 9:20 back home.

"I just wanted to let you know that I'm still in here," he said, pointing to his skull.

She smiled. "Okay, Adam."

"Thank you for doing this," he added.

"Are you kidding? They're paying me all kinds of allowances and overtime, and it's not even that long a flight. Feel free to come back here as often as you like."

He hesitated. "You didn't take the photo, did you?"

Sandra was unapologetic. "No. It could have gotten me sacked, and not all of the company's rules are stupid."

"Okay. I'll let you sleep. See you in the morning."

"Yeah."

Adam lay awake for an hour before he could bring himself to mutter his code word for the milder form of sleep. If he'd wished, Loadstone could have given him a passable simulation of the whole journey—albeit with a lot of cheating to mask the time it took to shuffle him back and forth between their servers and his body. But the airlines didn't recognize any kind of safe "flight mode" for his kind of machine, even when he was in pieces and locked inside three separate boxes. The way he'd experienced it was the most honest choice: a jump-cut, and thirteen hours lost to the gaps.

IN THE MORNING, SANDRA had arranged to join an organized tour of the sights of San Salvador. Her employer's insurance company was more concerned about her safety than Adam's, and in any case it would have been awkward for both of them to have her following him around with her toolbox.

"Just keep the license on you," she warned him before she left. "I had to fill out more forms to get it than I would to clear a drone's flight path twice around the world, so if you lose it I'm not coming to rescue you from the scrapyard."

"Who's going to put me there?" Adam spread his arms and stared down at his body. "Are you calling me a Ken doll?" He raised one forearm to his face and examined it critically, but the skin around his elbow wrinkled with perfect verisimilitude.

"No, but you talk like a foreigner, and you don't have a passport. So just . . . stay out of trouble."

"Yes, ma'am."

The old man had only visited the city once, and with Carlos leading him from nightspot to childhood haunt to some cousin's apartment like a ricocheting bullet, he'd made no attempt to navigate for himself. But Adam had been disappointed when he'd learned that Beatriz was now living in an entirely different part of town; there'd be no cues along the way, no hooks to bring back other memories of the time.

Colonia Layco was half an hour's drive from the hotel. There were more autonomous cars on the street than Adam remembered, but enough electric scooters interspersed among them to keep the traffic from mimicking L.A.'s spookily synchronized throbbing.

The car dropped him off outside a newish apartment block. Adam entered the antechamber in the lobby and found the intercom.

"Beatriz, this is Adam."

"Welcome! Come on up!"

He pushed through the swing doors and took the stairs, ascending four flights; it wouldn't make him any fitter, but old habits died hard. When Beatriz opened the door of her apartment he was prepared for her to flinch, but she just stepped out and embraced him. Maybe the sight of wealthy Californians looking younger than their age had lost its power to shock anyone before she'd even been born.

She ushered him in, tongue-tied for a moment, perhaps from the need to suppress an urge to ask about his flight, or inquire about his health. She settled, finally, on "How have things been?"

Her English was infinitely better than his Spanish, so Adam didn't even try. "Good," he replied. "I've been taking a break from work, so I thought I owed you a visit." The last time they'd met had been at Carlos's funeral.

She led him into the living room and gestured toward a chair, then fetched a tray of pastries and a pot of coffee. Carlos had never found the courage to come out to Adelina, but Beatriz had known his secret long before her mother died. Adam had no idea what details of the old man's life Carlos might have confided in her, but he'd exhausted all the willing informants who'd known the old man first-hand, and she'd responded so warmly to his emails that he'd had no qualms about attempting to revive their relationship for its own sake.

"How are the kids?" he asked.

Beatriz turned and gestured proudly toward a row of photographs on a bookcase behind her. "That's Pilar at her graduation last year; she started at the hospital six months ago. Rodrigo's in his final year of engineering."

Adam smiled. "Carlos would have been over the moon."

"Of course," Beatriz agreed. "We teased him a lot once he started with the acting, but his heart was always with us. With you, and with us."

Adam scanned the photographs and spotted a thirty-something Carlos in a suit, beside a much younger woman in a wedding dress.

"That's you, isn't it?" He pointed at the picture.

"Yes."

"I'm sorry I didn't make it." He had no memory of Carlos leaving for the wedding, but it must have taken place a year or two before they'd moved to L.A.

Beatriz tutted. "You would have been welcome, Adam, but I knew how tight things were for you back then. We all knew what you'd done for my mother."

Not enough to keep her alive, Adam thought, but that would be a cruel and pointless thing to say. And he hoped that Carlos had spared his sister's children any of the old man's poisonous talk of the windfall they'd missed out on.

Beatriz had her own idea of the wrongs that needed putting right. "Of course she didn't know, herself. She knew he had a friend who helped him out, but Carlos had to make it sound like you were rich, that you were loaning him the money and it was nothing to you. He should have told her the truth. If she'd thought of you as family, she wouldn't have refused your help."

Adam nodded uncomfortably, unsure just how graciously or otherwise the old man had handed over paycheck after paycheck for a woman who had no idea who he was. "That was a long time ago. I just want to meet your children and hear all your news."

"Ah." Beatriz grimaced apologetically. "I should warn you that Rodrigo's bringing his boyfriend to lunch."

"That's no problem at all." What twenty-year-old engineer wouldn't want to show off the animatronic version of Great Uncle Movie Star's lover to as many people as possible?

When Adam got back to the hotel it was late in the afternoon. He messaged Sandra, who replied that she was in a bar downtown having a great time and he was welcome to join her. Adam declined and lay down on the bed. The meal he'd just shared had been the most normal thing he'd experienced since his embodiment. He'd come within a hair's breadth of convincing himself that there was a place for him here: that he could somehow insert himself into this family and survive on their affection alone, as if this one day's hospitality and good-natured curiosity could be milked forever.

As the glow of borrowed domesticity faded, the tug of the past reasserted itself. He had to keep trying to assemble the pieces, as and when he found them. He took out his laptop and searched through archived social media posts, seeing if he could date Beatriz's wedding. Pictures had a way of getting wildly mislabeled, or grabbed by bots and repurposed at random, so even when he had what looked like independent confirmation from four different guests, he didn't quite trust the result, and he paid a small fee for access to the Salvadorian government's records.

Beatriz had been married on March 4th, 2018. Adam didn't need to open the spread-sheet he was using to assemble his time-line for the gaps to know that the surrounding period would be sparsely annotated, save for one entry. Nathan Colman had been bludgeoned to death by an intruder on March 10th of the same year.

Carlos would hardly have flown in for the wedding and left the next day; the family would have expected him to stay for at least a couple of weeks. The old man would have been alone in New York, with no one to observe his comings and goings. He might even have had time to cross the country and return by bus, paying with cash, breaking the trip down into small stages, hitch-hiking here and there, obfuscating the bigger picture as much as possible.

The dates proved nothing, of course. If Adam had been a juror in a trial with a case this flimsy, he would have laughed the prosecution out of court. He owed the old man the same standard of evidence.

Then again, in a trial the old man could have stood in the witness box and explained exactly what it was that he'd gone to so much trouble to hide.

The flight to L.A. wasn't until six in the evening, but Sandra was too hung-over to leave the hotel, and Adam had made no plans. So they sat in his room watching movies and ordering snacks from the kitchen, while Adam worked up the courage to ask her the question that had kept him awake all night.

"Is there any way you could get me the specifications for my targeted occlusions?" Adam waited for her response before daring to raise the possibility of payment. If the request was insulting in itself, offering a bribe would only compound the offense.

"No," she replied, as unfazed as if he'd wondered aloud whether room service might stretch to shiatsu. "That shit is locked down tight. After last night, it would take me all day to explain homomorphic encryption to you, so you'll just have to take my word for it: nobody alive can answer that, even if they wanted to."

"But I've recovered bills from his laptop that mention it," Adam protested. "So much for Fort fucking Knox!"

Sandra shook her head. "That means that he was careless—and I should probably get someone in account generation to rethink their line items—but Loadstone would have held his hand very, very tightly when it came to spelling out the details. Unless he wrote it down in his personal diary, the information doesn't exist any more."

Adam didn't think that she was lying to him. "There are things I need to know," he said simply. "He must have honestly believed that

I'd be better off without them—but if he'd lived long enough for me to ask him face to face, I know I could have changed his mind."

Sandra paused the movie. "Very little software is perfect, least of all when it's for something as complex as this. If we fail to collect everything we aim to collect . . ."

"Then you also fail to block everything you aim to block," Adam concluded. "Which was probably mentioned somewhere in the fine print of his contract, but I've been racking my brain for months without finding a single stone that punched a hole in the sieve."

"What if the stones only got through in fragments, but they can still be put together?"

Adam struggled to interpret this. "Are you telling me to take up repressed memory therapy?"

"No, but I could get you a beta copy of Stitcher on the quiet."

"Stitcher?"

"It's a new layer they'll eventually be offering to every client," Sandra explained. "It's in the nature of things, with the current methods, that the side-load will end up with a certain amount of implicit information that's not in an easily accessible form: thousands of tiny glimpses of memories that were never brought across whole, but which could still be described in detail if you pieced together every partial sighting."

"So this software could reassemble the shredded page of a notebook that still holds an impression of what was written on the missing page above?"

Sandra said, "For someone with a digital brain, you're about as last-century as they come."

Adam gave up trying to harmonize their metaphors. "Will it tell me what I want to know?"

"I have no idea," Sandra said bluntly. "Among the fragments bearing implicit information—and there will certainly be thousands of them—it will recognize some unpredictable fraction of their associations, and let you follow the new threads that arise. But I don't know if that will be enough to tell you anything more than the color of the sweater your mother was wearing on your first day of school."

"Okay."

Sandra started the movie again. "You really should have joined me in the bar last night," she said. "I told them I had a friend who could drink any Salvadorian under the table, and they were begging for a chance to bet against you."

"You're a sick woman," Adam chided her. "Maybe next time."

10

REASSEMBLED BACK IN CALIFORNIA, Adam took his time deciding whether to make one last, algorithmic attempt to push through the veil. If the truth was that the old man had been a murderer, what good would come of knowing it? Adam had no intention of "confessing" the crime to the authorities, and taking his chances with whatever legal outcome the courts might eventually disgorge. He was not a person; he could not be prosecuted or sued, but Loadstone could be ordered to erase every copy of his software, and municipal authorities instructed to place his body in a hydraulic compactor beside unroadworthy cars and unskyworthy drones.

But even if he faced no risk of punishment, he doubted that Colman's relatives would be better off knowing that what they'd always imagined was a burglary gone wrong had actually been a premeditated ambush. It should not be for him to judge their best interests, of course, but the fact remained that he'd be the one making the decision, and for all the horror he felt about the act itself and the harm that had been done, his empathy for the survivors pushed him entirely in the direction of silence.

So if he did this, it would be for his benefit alone. For the relief of knowing that the old man had simply been a vain, neurotic self-mythologizer who'd tried to leave behind the director's cut of his life . . . or for the impetus to disown him completely, to torch his legacy in every way he could and set out on a life of his own.

ADAM ASKED SANDRA TO meet him at Caesar's Diner. He slid a small parcel of cash onto her seat, and she slipped a memory stick into his hand.

"What do I do with this?" he asked.

"Just because you can't see all your ports in the bathroom mirror doesn't mean they're not there." She wrote a sequence of words on a napkin and passed it to Adam; it read like "Jabberwocky" mis-transcribed by someone on very bad drugs. "Four times, and that will take the side of your neck off without putting you to sleep."

"Why is that even possible?"

"You have no idea how many Easter eggs you're carrying."

"And then what?"

"Plug it in, and it will do the rest. You won't be paralyzed, you won't lose consciousness. But it will work best if you lie down in the dark and close your eyes. When you're done, just pull it out. Working the skin panel back into place might take a minute or two, but once it clicks it will be a waterproof seal again." She hesitated. "If you can't get it to click, try wiping the edges of both the panel and the aperture with a clean chamois. Please don't put machine oil on anything; it won't help."

"I'll bear that in mind."

ADAM STOOD IN THE bathroom and recited the incantation from the napkin, half expecting to see some leering apparition take his place in the mirror as the last syllable escaped his lips. But there was just a gentle pop as the panel on his neck flexed and came loose. He caught it before it fell to the floor and placed it on a clean square of paper towel.

It was hard to see inside the opening he'd made, and he wasn't sure he wanted to, but he found the port easily by touch alone. He walked into the bedroom, took the memory stick from the side table, then lay down and dimmed the lights. A part of him felt like an ungrateful son, trespassing on the old man's privacy, but if he'd wanted to take his secrets to the grave then he should have taken all of his other shit with them.

Adam pushed the memory stick into place.

Nothing seemed to have happened, but when he closed his eyes he saw himself kneeling at the edge of the bed in the room down the hall, weeping inconsolably, holding the bedspread to his face.

Adam shuddered; it was like being back in the servers, back in the interminable side-loading dream. He followed the thread out into the darkness, for a long time finding nothing but grief, but then he turned and stumbled upon Carlos's funeral, riotous in its celebration, packed with gray-haired friends from New York and a dozen of Carlos's relatives, raucously drowning out the studio executives and sync-flashing the paparazzi.

Adam walked over to the casket and found himself standing beside a hospital bed, clasping just one of those rough familiar hands in both of his own.

"It's all right," Carlos insisted. There wasn't a trace of fear in his eyes. "All I need is for you to stay strong."

"I'll try."

Adam backed away into the darkness and landed on set. He'd thought it was a risky indulgence to put an amateur in even this tiny part, but Carlos had sworn that he wouldn't take offense if his one and only performance ended up on the cutting room floor. He just wanted a chance to know if it was possible, one way or the other.

Detective Number Two said, "You'll need to come with us, ma'am," then took Gemma Freeman's trembling arm in his hand as he led her away.

In the editing suite, Adam addressed Cynthia bluntly. "Tell me if I'm making a fool of myself."

"You're not," she said. "He's got a real presence. He's not going to do Lear, but if he can hit his marks and learn his lines . . ."

Adam felt a twinge of disquiet, as if they were tempting fate by asking too much. But maybe it was apt. They'd propelled themselves into this orbit together; neither could have gotten here alone.

On the day they arrived, they'd talked a total stranger into breaking through a fence and hiking up Mount Lee with them so they could take each other's photographs beneath the Hollywood sign. Adam could smell the sap from broken foliage on his scratched forearms.

"Remember this guy," Carlos told their accomplice proudly. "He's going to be the next big thing. They already bought his script."

"For a pilot," Adam clarified. "Only for a pilot."

He rose up over the hills, watching day turn to night, waiting for an incriminating flicker of déjà vu to prove that he'd been in this city before. But the memories that came to him were all from the movies: *L.A. Confidential, Mulholland Drive.*

He flew east, soaring over city lights and blackened deserts, alighting back in their New York apartment, hunched over his computer, pungent with sweat, trying to block out the sound of Carlos haggling with the woman who'd come to buy their air-conditioner. He stared at the screen unhappily, and started removing dialog, shifting as much as he could into stage directions instead.

She takes his bloodied fist in both hands, shocked and sickened by what he's done, but she understands—

The screen went blank. The laptop should have kept working in the black-out, but the battery had been useless for months. Adam picked up a pen and started writing on a sheet of paper: *She understands that she pushed him into it—unwittingly, but she still shares the blame.*

He stopped and crumpled the sheet into a ball. Flecks of red light streamed across his vision; he felt as if he'd caught himself trying to leap onto a moving train. But what choice did he have? There was no stopping it, no turning it back, no setting it right. He had to find a way to ride it, or it would destroy them.

Carlos called out to Adam to come and help carry the air-conditioner down the stairs. Every time they stopped to rest on a darkened landing, the three of them burst out laughing.

When the woman drove away they stood on the street, waiting for a breeze to shift the humid air. Carlos placed a hand on the back of Adam's neck. "Are you going to be all right?"

"We don't need that heap of junk," Adam replied.

Carlos was silent for a while, then he said, "I just wanted to give you some peace."

WHEN HE'D TAKEN OUT the memory stick and closed his wound, Adam went into the old man's room and lay on his bed in the dark. The mattress beneath him felt utterly familiar, and the gray outlines of the room seemed exactly as they ought to be, as if he'd lain here a thousand times. This was the bed he'd been struggling to wake in from the start.

What they'd done, they'd done for each other. He didn't have to excuse it to acknowledge that. To turn Carlos in, to offer him up to death row, would have been unthinkable—and the fact that the law would have found the old man blameless if he'd done so only left Adam less willing to condemn him. At least he'd shown enough courage to put himself at risk if the truth ever came out.

He gazed into the shadows of the room, unable to decide if he was merely an empathetic onlooker, judging the old man with compassion—or the old man himself, repeating his own long-rehearsed defense.

How close was he to crossing the line?

Maybe he had enough, now, to write from the same dark place as the old man—and in time to outdo him, making all his fanciful ambitions come true.

But only by becoming what the old man had never wanted him to be. Only by rolling the same boulder to the giddy peak of impunity, then watching it slide down into the depths of remorse, over and over again, with no hope of ever breaking free.

11

ADAM WAITED FOR THE crew from the thrift store to come and collect the boxes in which he'd packed the old man's belongings. When they'd gone, he locked up the house, and left the key in the combination safe attached to the door.

Gina had been livid when he'd talked to Ryan directly and shamed him into taking the deal: the family could have the house, but the bulk of the old man's money would go to a hospital in San Salvador. What remained would be just enough to keep Adam viable: paying his maintenance contract, renewing his license to walk in public, and stuffing unearned stipends into the pockets of the figure-heads of the shell companies whose sole reason to exist was to own him.

He strode toward the gate, wheeling a single suitcase. Away from the shelter of the old man's tomb, he'd have no identity of his own to protect him, but he'd hardly be the first undocumented person who'd tried to make it in this country.

When the old man's life had disintegrated, he'd found a way to turn the shards into stories that meant something to people like him. But Adam's life was broken in a different way, and the world would take time to catch up. Maybe in twenty years, maybe in a hundred, when enough of them had joined him in the Valley, he'd have something to say that they'd be ready to hear.

3-ADICA

1

SAGREDA STRODE BRISKLY THROUGH the dank night air, hoping to reach her destination and return before the fog rolled in from the Thames. It was bad enough stumbling over the cobblestones when the ground vanished from sight, but once the pea soup thickened at eye level, any assailant lurking in the gloom would have her at a disadvantage.

Urchins and touts called out as she passed. "Shine yer shoes! Thruppence a pair!"

"Block yer hat! Like new for sixpence!"

"Fake yer death, guv'nor?" The last from a grime-faced child in a threadbare coat who looked about eight years old, his eyes almost hidden beneath his brown cloth cap.

"Not tonight," Sagreda replied. Whether the boy was sentient or not, his appearance almost certainly bore no relationship to his true nature, but it was still hard to walk by without even stopping to inquire if he had a safe place to sleep.

She found Cutpurse Lane and hurried through the shadows toward the lights of the tavern. Gap-toothed women with grubby shawls and kabuki-esque makeup offered her their services in an indecipherable patois that Sagreda hoped never to hear enough of to begin to understand. "I'm not a customer," she replied wearily. "Save your breath." Whatever the women took this to mean, it silenced them, and her choice of words was ambiguous enough that Sagreda doubted she was risking deletion. She was an upstanding gentleman, who'd stepped out to meet some fine fellow from his regiment—or his school, or his club, or wherever it was these mutton-chopped fossils were supposed to have made each other's acquaintance. Having no truck with ladies of the night need not imply that she was breaking character.

In the tavern, Sagreda hung her overcoat on a hook near the door, and swept her gaze as casually as she could across the front room's dozen tables, trying not to appear lost, or too curious about anyone else's business.

She took a seat at an unoccupied table, removed her gloves and slipped them into her waistcoat pocket. Her bare hands with their huge, stubby fingers disconcerted her much more than the occasional sensation of her whiskers brushing against her lips. Still, the inadvertent sex change had rendered her a thousand times safer; from what she'd seen so far of *Midnight on Baker Street*, women here existed mainly to shriek in horror, sell their bodies, or lie sprawled on the street bleeding until the gutters ran red. Doyle, Dickens, Stoker, Stevenson and Shelley would all have lost their breakfast if they'd ever foreseen the day when their work would be pastiched and blended into a malodorous potpourri whose most overpowering component was the stench of misogynous Ripperology.

A serving girl approached the table. "Ale!" Sagreda grunted dyspeptically, aiming for both a brusqueness befitting her status and a manner sufficiently off-putting that she wouldn't be asked to supplement her order with details she couldn't provide. When the girl returned with a mug full of something brown and revolting, Sagreda handed her the first coin she plucked out of her pocket and watched for a reaction: the amount was excessive, but not shocking. "Bless you, sir!" the girl said happily, retreating before her benefactor could change his mind.

Sagreda pretended to take a sip of the ale, raising the mug high enough to dampen her mustache with foam, which she removed with the back of her thumb. No one seemed to be staring at her, and if there were customers of *Midnight* among the customers of the tavern, she could only hope that however much she felt like the most conspicuously talentless actor, wearing the most laughably ill-fitting costume, of all the unwilling players trapped in this very bad piece of dinner theater, to a casual onlooker she was just one more red-faced, gout-ridden extra in the Hogarthian crowd.

A spindle-limbed man with pinched, gaunt features sidled up to the table. "Alfred Jingle at your service, Captain," he proclaimed, bowing slightly.

Sagreda stood. "A pleasure to meet you, Mr Jingle. Will you join me?"

"The pleasure's all mine, I'm sure."

They sat, and Sagreda summoned the serving girl to bring a second mug.

"Do you think it's safe to talk here?" Sagreda asked quietly when the girl had left.

"Absolutely," Jingle replied. "So long as we move our lips and contribute to the background noise, we could spend the night muttering 'rhubarb rhubarb' for all anyone would care."

Sagreda wasn't so blasé—but if they slipped out into an alley for the sake of privacy, that would just be begging for desanguination.

She said, "I'm told you're the man with everything, here: memory maps, instruction tables, access to the stack?"

He nodded calmly. "That's me."

Sagreda was taken aback by his directness. In most of the dreary game-worlds she'd traversed, her question would have been met with some kind of reticence, or the intimation of a shake-down: *Maybe I am, maybe I'm not. It all depends on exactly what you have to offer.*

Jingle broke the silence. "Can I ask where you're headed?"

Sagreda stole a quick glance to each side of the table, unable to brush off her fear that someone might be listening, but all of the tavern's patrons seemed to be engrossed in their own, more raucous, conversations. "*3-adica,*" she whispered.

Jingle smiled slightly. "That's . . . courageous." He wasn't mocking her, but his intonation dialed the meaning a notch or two away from merely brave toward foolhardy.

"I've had enough," she said, not daring to add *of slavery,* in case the sheer potency of the word punched through the din and made one of their fellow drinkers' ears prick up. "I'd walk over broken glass, if I had to."

Jingle said, "As a metaphor, that trips nicely off the tongue, but I doubt many people have ever meant it literally."

"And I don't believe it will be that hard, literally," Sagreda replied. "I understand what I'll be facing—as well as anyone can who hasn't actually been there."

"Fair enough," Jingle conceded. "Though you should also understand that you could make a comfortable life here." He gestured at Sagreda's finely cut clothes. "Whatever role you've stumbled on, so long as you're careful I doubt you're heading for a knife in the gut, or anything particularly unpleasant. You're just another minor toff who's here as part of the scenery, like me."

"I don't want to play a role," Sagreda said emphatically. "However safe, however peripheral." She held her tongue and resisted the urge to add: *least of all in this anatomy.* Somehow it had never crossed her mind that her new confidant, who could see right through the whole fictional world around him, wouldn't also see through her mismatched body and perceive her true sex.

"All right. I'm not going to try to talk you out of anything." Jingle's face looked like something from a nineteenth century pamphlet cataloging virtues and vices, a caricature crafted to suggest a shrewd, scheming mentality, but his manner undercut the effect completely. "Tell me exactly what it is you need to know."

2

BACK IN CAPTAIN BLUFF-SMOTE's lodgings, Sagreda sat at her alter-ego's writing desk, poring over the notes Jingle had made for her. The good news was that it looked as if she'd be able to move from *Midnight* to *3-adica* with the same kind of GPU exploit that had brought her all the way from her wakening-world, *East.* Peyam, the seasoned traveler who'd introduced the exploit to that world, had tutored her and eight of her friends for almost six months in the fine points of the technique. They'd departed together in high spirits, imagining themselves as some kind of band of liberating truth-tellers, but in the end most of the group had taken a different direction through the tangle of linked lists than Sagreda and Mathis, and the two of them had been game-hopping on their own ever since.

She looked up from the desk, listening expectantly, as if the mere thought of Mathis might bring a knock on the door, but all she could hear was the ticking of the clock in the next room. Given *Midnight*'s demand for a constant influx of new non-player characters to balance its body count, he must have been incarnated somewhere in the game by now. She'd left her address at half a dozen dead drops, using the criteria they'd agreed on in advance: any public bench close to a market; any water pump; the rear, right-most pew in any church. But it was late, and even if Mathis hadn't yet witnessed a murder or two for himself, he was smart enough not to be out in the portentous fog.

Sagreda returned to her analysis. Every jump required executing a sequence of instructions that would unlink the would-be travelers from their current environment and insert them into a queue that was meant to hold nothing but freshly minted composite personas— free of all narrative memories, and already tagged as appropriate new denizens of the destination world. Given the amount of code it took to run the whole site, not only could you find any machine-language instruction you wanted somewhere in memory, you could find almost all of them as the last instruction in some subroutine or other. When a subroutine was called by ordinary means, the code invoking it pushed an appropriate return address onto the stack, to ensure that the detour would snake back to just after the point where it had begun. But if you could stack the stack with enough phoney return addresses, you could send the program pin-balling all over the machine, doing your bidding one instruction at a time. It was like forcing a pianist in the midst of playing a piece by Rachmaninoff to tinkle out a few bars of "Where Is My Mind?" without actually changing the score, just by scrawling in a series of arrows weaving back and forth between the desired notes.

Jingle had already done the hardest part: finding the addresses that would furnish each instruction, for code that ran with the particular page mappings that applied to denizens of *Midnight on Baker Street*. It didn't take Sagreda long to extract everything she needed from his list. The greatest obstacle was her own poor penmanship;

whatever eccentric hobbies the contributors to her persona had possessed, it was clear that none of them had ever had reason to dip a
nib in an inkwell.

She blotted the spidery mess and rechecked it twice. There were
no actual mistakes, but the figures' dubious legibility was as disconcerting as a fraying strand on a parachute cord. She started over,
sympathizing with the non-existent Captain, who would probably
have been thrashed as a child when his thick, clumsy fingers failed
him in his own first attempts at transcription.

By midnight, she was satisfied with her efforts. What remained
was the challenge of getting this slab of numbers onto the stack.
The Graphics Processing Units that rendered the game-worlds for
customers and comps alike were all identical, and they all shared the
same bug: under the right circumstances, they could be tripped up in
a way that made them write a portion of their image buffer onto the
CPU's stack. So the trick was to encode the addresses in the colors of
an object, and then arrange to have that object rendered at a suitable
scale. Peyam had taught his students to recognize on sight objects
with hues from which they could compose any twenty-four-bit set
of red, green and blue components. *East*, with its sparse, post-apocalyptic landscape of cliffs and caves, hadn't exactly come with oil
paints or color swatches on hand, but over time they'd found ways
to patch together the entire palette they'd needed. The SludgeNet
scripts that had created *Midnight* might have taken a rather sepia-
toned view of the source novel's cod-historical setting, but Sagreda
had seen hats, scarves, gloves and ribbons in all manner of garish
colors, and once you were working at a scale where you could place
different materials side by side within a single pixel, getting the
result bit-perfect wasn't quite as daunting as it first seemed.

She drew up a preliminary list, starting with various items that
the Captain already possessed. Between his funereal wardrobe, his
curtains and bed-spreads, his small library and his collection of lac-
quered snuff boxes, brown and gray were pretty much taken care
of. But to encode the addresses she required, she was going to need
all manner of mauves and magentas, leaf-greens and cyans, azures
and ocean blues. It would almost have been worth it if the old coot

had had a wife, just so Sagreda could surreptitiously snip her way through the woman's apparel. The Captain's landlady, Mrs Trotter, was cheerful and solicitous with her widower tenant, but *breaking into her room to cut up her clothing* could well risk sending the game a signal that this man had been at the Jekyll juice and was craving a chance to perform a few amateur appendectomies.

Sagreda sighed and went to use the chamber pot. She had got past the impulse to giggle or recoil at the sight of her new genitalia—and nothing about the Captain's physique inspired autoerotic experimentation. It was as if she was obliged to spend her time here with a small, docile, misshapen rodent sheltering between her legs, helpfully redirecting the flow of her urine by means that really didn't bear thinking about. As she covered the pot and hitched up her underwear, she tried to picture the expression on Mathis's face when he saw what she'd become. But a couple of months without physical intimacy wasn't going to kill them. Their journey was almost over: in *3-adica*, she believed, they'd finally have the power to do, and to be, whatever they wanted.

3

SAGREDA WORKED ON HER palette, visiting milliners and cloth-merchants, developing a line in gruff banter to parry the teasing of the shop assistants. "What's a gentleman like you needing a scarlet ribbon for?" one young woman demanded, her features poised between perplexity, mortification and amusement.

"I plan to tie it around the leg of a hound," Sagreda replied, with a fully Bluff-Smotean air of impatience, irritation and self-importance.

"An 'ound?" The woman's expression succeeded in growing even more unsettled.

"As punishment for flagrant promiscuity," Sagreda explained, deadpan. "The mutt needs shaming, and I will not resile from the task."

"That's only fair," the woman decided. "When it comes to them beasts, nature will have its way, but that don't mean we have to approve."

As Sagreda handed over her coins, she scrutinized the woman's face, hoping that perhaps she was in on the joke. But Jingle had said that only about a tenth of the characters here were game-aware.

Out on the street, as Sagreda paused to let a carriage pass, she felt an unexpected disturbance near her hip and instinctively reached down to explore its source. To her surprise, she found herself with her hand encircling a slender, bony wrist.

The owner of the wrist glared up at her defiantly: a slim, shabbily dressed girl whose age Sagreda refused to guess. Appearances were meaningless; however you picked and mixed from a pool of adult brain maps, the resulting comp could never *be* a child.

But a child need not always be played by a comp.

"That coin you've grabbed was a souvenir," Sagreda huffed, "given to me by my Bavarian cousin, Frau Mengele!"

The girl flinched and dropped what she'd been holding—though she seemed as baffled by her reaction as an audience member at a hypnotist's show who'd found herself suddenly clucking like a chicken. An automaton wouldn't have blinked, and a customer might have grimaced at the oddly contrived reference, but only a comp could be revolted by the association without understanding why.

Sagreda bent down and retrieved the coin. "Don't you dare lay a finger on me!" the girl whispered. Her hushed tone was probably a wise strategic choice: if she made a scene, the crowd would not be on her side. But she spoke without a trace of fear, as if she were the one with the upper hand.

Sagreda lost whatever resolve she'd had to strike the child for the sake of appearances. Maybe a verbal reprimand would pass muster, if anyone around them was even paying attention.

"Next time, missy, you should ply your trade on someone less acutely conscious of the content of his trousers!" Sagreda blustered. She waited, still gripping the girl's wrist, hoping for some kind of apology.

"I know what you're up to," the girl replied unrepentantly. "So leave me be, or I might just pay a call on the witch-finders."

Witch-finders? Sagreda supposed she had no right to be surprised by how far *Midnight* was willing to stretch its anachronisms. "And just what are you planning to tell Constables Scolder and Mully of Bow Street?"

"Every nasty detail of your sorcery," the girl boasted. "And you can be sure that when they break down your door, they'll take a very keen interest in your mandala."

Sagreda released the girl. Whatever she actually knew, the risk of attracting official scrutiny had to be greater than the risk of letting one pickpocket slip away unpunished.

But the girl declined the opportunity to flee. "And I'll have what you denied me," she said, glancing meaningfully at Sagreda's trouser pocket.

Sagreda stared back at her, almost admiring her brazenness, trying to summon up some ornately disdainful Victorian invective with which to respond to this blackmail. But her vocabulary deserted her, and muttering feebly about impudent whelps when her heart wasn't in it would just make her sound like the nineteenth century equivalent of a rapping grandma.

"Be off with you!" she snapped, making a shooing motion with her giant hands.

The girl scowled, dissatisfied, and she seemed on the verge of escalating her threats, but then she changed her mind. "You should engage me, Mister."

"Captain," Sagreda corrected her. "Engage you to do what?"

"Make me your assistant. Seeing as how you're struggling to complete the thing."

A carriage drove past, spattering the bottom of the Captain's trousers with horse-shit-speckled mud.

"Have you been following me?" Sagreda demanded.

"I have eyes," the girl replied coolly. "I seen you in all kinds of fancy shops, making some very odd purchases. If you want the job done before Christmas, you might welcome a pair of nimble hands like mine."

Sagreda fell silent. Were there colors she needed that she might only be able to obtain by theft? She wasn't sure. She'd made significant progress, but she was yet to walk into a shop and find every obscure object of her chromatic desires laid out on the shelves and counters.

"I'll give you a shilling as a retainer," she decided, reaching into her pocket for an untainted one. "In turn, I expect you to be straight with me, and to keep yourself available."

The girl inclined her head in agreement.

Sagreda held on to the coin. "What's your name?"

"Lucy." The girl stretched out her palm, and Sagreda deposited the shilling.

"How will I find you?" she asked.

"This is my patch you're on," Lucy replied, affronted, as if she were some criminal king-pin whose territory Sagreda crossed only on her sufferance. "If you have need of my services, I'll know it before you know it yourself."

4

SAGREDA WORKED INTO THE night, pinning, stitching and gluing, painstakingly assembling one more piece of the mosaic. Or *mandala*, as Lucy had called it. It was an odd choice of word; Sagreda had seen nothing to suggest that *Midnight*'s kitchen-sink eclecticism encompassed any culture east of the Carpathians. But perhaps one of the previous travelers the girl had seen scavenging for colors had taken her into their confidence and tried to explain the point of the whole exercise. Sagreda had no idea if anyone, anywhere, had ever believed that a mandala could initiate the transmigration of souls; her own vague understanding was that if you were into that kind of thing, you just waited to die and the rest was up to karma. But if stacks, GPUs and the whole panoply of queue structures that linked the game-worlds together were too much to explain to someone who'd been gaslit into forgetting everything her contributors had known about the twenty-first century, maybe Lucy's reluctant informant had opted for a Buddhist-flavored riff, aiming for an account that was comprehensible to the denizen of a world steeped in supernatural forces, while avoiding Western occultism with its potentially Satanic associations, in the hope of keeping the witch-finders out of the picture.

Someone tapped at the door. Sagreda covered the mosaic with a table cloth and approached the entrance hall. It was awfully late for a visit from Mrs Trotter, and the tap had sounded far too tentative to come from any branch of the constabulary.

When she opened the door, she found an elegantly dressed, dark-haired young man at the threshold, his eyes cast down as if his presence here was somehow shameful.

"I'm sorry to trouble you, sir," the man said softly, still not meeting Sagreda's gaze. "But I'm a cousin of your wife, and I need to speak to her as soon as possible about a poorly aunt of ours—"

Sagreda interrupted him. "Mathis?"

He looked up, startled. "How do you . . . did she tell you . . . ?"

"There is no *she* but me, I'm afraid." Sagreda tried to smile, but then recalled how the Captain's whiskery visage had appeared when she'd practiced in the mirror. "It looks like that last queue we found was meant to have been pre-filtered by gender."

Mathis nodded with a kind of punch-drunk stoicism. "Okay. Everything's temporary. I'm sorry I took so long to find you; I don't know if the notes all blew away, or what."

"The ones in the churches shouldn't have."

"About that . . ."

"Are you coming in?" Sagreda asked impatiently. They weren't talking loudly, but who knew what Mrs Trotter would assume if she saw the Captain with a young man visiting at this uncivil hour.

"I'm afraid you're going to have to invite me," Mathis explained glumly.

Sagreda took a moment to digest that. "Oh, fuck no."

"You got the wang, I got the fangs," Mathis quipped. "That's what happens when you walk in blind."

Sagreda said, "Please, make yourself at home in my miserable abode." She stepped back from the doorway and let him pass, then peered out across the landing to check that no one was watching from the stairs.

Mathis draped himself over the sofa and gazed lethargically into space, focusing on nothing, perhaps in an attempt to avoid having to take in the wallpaper.

"So what exactly are the symptoms?" Sagreda asked. "Apart from a general Byronic ennui."

"I haven't risked daylight," he replied. "But I gather it would be fatal. I do have a reflection. But mostly I'm just very, very tired and very, very hungry."

"So you haven't—?"

"Jesus, Sagreda!" Mathis stared at her in horror.

"I meant . . . maybe a dog?" The dogs here were pure automata, it wouldn't even be animal cruelty.

"I'm not interested in *dogs!*" Mathis retorted irritably, as if that ought to be as obvious to Sagreda as it was to him. But then he caught himself, and walked her through the strictures he was facing. "There are certain sights and odors that make my saliva run, and my . . ." He gestured at his mouth. "I'm assuming that unless I act on those cues, I'm not going to stop feeling weak. A rare roast-beef sandwich doesn't cut it, and I have no reason to think a corgi or two would hit the spot either."

Sagreda steeled herself. "Do you want me to fill a cup?"

Mathis took a while to reply. "Are you sure you want to do that?"

"Not especially," she confessed. "But I don't want you going into the vampiric equivalent of a diabetic coma."

"I'd better not watch," Mathis decided. "Who knows what strings the game will start tugging, if I see an open wound."

"All right." Sagreda went into the Captain's bedroom and closed the door. There was a cut-throat razor by the washing bowl, and an empty shaving mug. She took off her jacket and shirt.

The thought that Mathis feared losing control disturbed her. They'd fought for each other, suffered side by side, and risked deletion across three dozen worlds—and the software that lorded over them was far too crude to reach inside them and start imposing beliefs or desires. On their side they had love, and they had reason, while the SludgeNet possessed neither.

But it still had plenty of ways to try to manipulate their behavior. Having woken in the asinine world of *East*, where sensory immersion lost out more or less instantly to any trace of common sense, they were both immune to seeing-is-believing, and to the wisdom of hoodwinked crowds. But they'd never been subjected to outright torture. If the purple prose in *Midnight*'s bodice-and-intestine-ripping source had talked about a vampire's longing for blood being like a white-hot poker in the chest, the SludgeNet would have no trouble bringing those words to life.

The Captain's body was amply proportioned and apparently not at all anemic; when Sagreda had filled the mug, she did not feel the least bit unsteady. "Well done, old stick!" she commended him, binding the wound with a handkerchief. She dressed again completely to conceal any trace of the breach in her skin. The Captain, being some flavor of Anglican, wasn't into religious paraphernalia; there was a King James Bible in his library, but no crucifix by the bed.

She covered the mug with a playing card and opened the door. Mathis was still on the sofa; she walked right past him, into the entrance hall, and out the front door. She placed the mug on the landing, near the top of the stairs, then, leaving the door open, went back to the sitting room.

"You didn't want to watch me," she said. "And I don't want to watch you, either."

Mathis frowned slightly, but he nodded. "I'll go back to my place when I'm finished." He walked over to the desk and wrote something. "That's the address, if you need to find me later. But don't open the door to me again tonight, whatever I say."

Sagreda felt the Captain's pulse throbbing around the raw edges of the razor wound. But Mathis was just being cautious; he'd never done this before, he didn't know what to expect.

"You know I love you?" she said.

Mathis rolled his eyes. "At a pinch, I might go for an Oscar Wilde type, but the whole Colonel Mustard thing . . ." He shuddered.

"You're an asshole."

He smiled and walked down the hall. Sagreda followed a couple of steps behind, then when he was out she closed the door quickly—taking care not to slam it and wake Mrs Trotter—and secured the bolts.

She stood by the door, listening, but the bestial slurping she'd feared never came. She waited, tensed, picturing the door splintering and a yellow-eyed, ravenous demon embracing her to finish what she'd started.

She heard the faint chink of the mug being placed back on the floor, then soft, careful, unhurried footsteps descending the stairs.

5

SAGREDA NEEDED COBALT BLUE. Out in the real world—if Peyam's gloriously discursive lessons on color were to be trusted—the pigment had been used since ancient times in Chinese ceramics, and it had certainly been available to European painters in the nineteenth century. This was London, capital of an empire, mercantile hub of the world. Whatever wasn't made here, someone would be importing it.

So she traipsed the streets, hunting for a shop that sold artists' supplies. If the gossip she'd heard in the coffee houses was true, every tubercular poet, living or undead, from Marlowe to Yeats was currently shacked up somewhere in Bloomsbury, rubbing shoulders every night in the Salon Macabre—a dollop of name-dropping no doubt designed to set the hearts of thirteen-year-old Goths aflutter—but no one ever seemed to mention a single painter. To be fair, Sagreda's own contributors struggled to suggest anyone but Turner; still, someone had to be responsible for all the portraits of viscounts and their horses that lined the walls of the mansions of Belgravia. Unless they just appeared out of thin air.

As she widened her search radius, Sagreda grew nervous. Every game had different rules of containment; if you wandered off into territory that didn't belong to the core geography that had been mapped out and rendered for a thousand eyes before yours, you might get a gentle nudge guiding you back to terra cognita, or you might just fall off the edge of the world. So far as she knew, the Captain was not a named character in the original novel, and no customer of the interactive version had become the least bit invested in his continued existence. If she crossed the invisible line, the easiest solution by far might be to erase her and wake a fresh comp in the same body after a hard night on the town, leaving the new guy to piece his identity together much as Sagreda had, from the contents of his lodgings, and the people he encountered who seemed to know him.

By late afternoon on the third day of her search, she found herself off the paved streets entirely, tramping through muddy ground beside a ramshackle wooden building that smelled like a tannery. She stopped and hunted for the sun, trying to get her bearings, but the sky above was smothered by a still, gray haze, equally bright everywhere she squinted.

There was no one else in sight. She approached the building cautiously; it might just contain cheerful workers, happy to offer directions, but *Midnight* was proving less concerned with its supply chains than with its brooding atmospherics. If its artworks could come without artists or pigments, its leather need not have graced the body of any cow, and the strange odor might have another source entirely.

Her foot touched something taut buried in the mud, like a swollen fruit or a small balloon; she tried to step back, but the thing burst and a jet of stinking yellow fluid sprayed up from it and struck her in the chest.

A hand tugged at her trouser leg. A small boy was standing beside her. "Come with me!" he whispered urgently.

Sagreda followed him, resisting a motherly impulse to scoop him up into her arms, not least because it would be hard to manage without smearing the poor kid with pus. His legs were about a quarter as long as the Captain's, but it was all she could do to keep up. She glanced backward; something was moving at the entrance to the building, but its shape was hard to discern in the haze. It uttered an inhuman cry; in rage or in pain Sagreda couldn't tell.

"Where are we going?" she asked the boy.

"They marked you," he replied. "So we need to be done with it."

"Marked me for what?" she asked.

"Ha!" He seemed to find the question so funny that it could only have been meant rhetorically.

They hit the cobblestones and weaved through small alleys, picking up the pace, inflaming the Captain's gout. In this of all things, the game wanted realism?

"How far will it follow us?" Sagreda wondered, gasping.

"As far as it takes, if you don't do the necessary."

Sagreda had visions of a bonfire for her clothes, and an acid bath for her infected skin.

They came to a water pump.

"Get under, get under!" the boy urged her.

"Do I take—?" She gestured at her vomit-yellow waistcoat.

"No time."

She took off her coat and maneuvered herself under the spout; the boy clambered up and started pumping. Gobs of sticky fluid separated from the cloth and were carried down the drain, but her waistcoat remained stained in a shade that Peyam had never named, but which her contributors labeled bee excrement. She ran her thumb back and forth across the fabric, turning her chest to meet the flow, and gradually the mark began to fade.

"I think you're done," the boy decided, wiping his forehead with his hand. He grimaced reprovingly. "What you want with them creatures anyway?"

"Nothing! I didn't know they were there!" Sagreda got herself upright. Her clothes were drenched and all her joints were aching, but apparently she'd been luckier than she deserved.

"You lost your way?" The boy's incredulity shaded into smugness; who exactly was the adult here?

"I was looking for a place to buy oil paints."

The boy sighed, as if Sagreda had somehow lived down to his expectations. "Lucy said it would come to that."

This wasn't a random encounter, then. The queen of the pickpockets had had her tailed by a trusted lieutenant.

"What's your name?" she asked the boy.

"Sam."

"So do you know of a shop that sells the materials an artist needs?"

He wiped his nose on his sleeve. "There ain't such a thing in all of London."

Sagreda had pretty much reconciled herself to that likelihood. "Have you ever even seen a painting?" she asked glumly. There were a couple of drab watercolors in Mrs Trotter's sitting room, but even if Sagreda had dared to steal them, they did not contain anything she needed.

Sam said, "I think you better talk to Lucy."

6

"Maybe I know a house," Lucy said cagily. "Maybe I'm thick with the scullery maid. But it's hard to remember. My mind turns feeble when I hear my stomach rumbling."

Sagreda handed her another shilling. "How many paintings, do you think?" They were sitting on moldy armchairs in an abandoned building with boarded-up windows, surrounded by diminutive body guards.

"Two dozen, at least."

"Any of them with a deep, rich blue? It needs to be deeper than a summer sky, but—"

Lucy scowled. "I can ask the maid about the colors, but who knows what she'll make of your palaver?"

"Then I need to go in there myself," Sagreda decided. "It's no good sending someone else who'll come back with the wrong thing."

"Be my guest," Lucy replied, unfazed. "But we'll be making our entrance through the basement, and there'll be a tight corner or two along the way. Perhaps you can look into the possibility of investing in a gentleman's girdle."

Sagreda wasn't sure if this was genuine advice, or just a chance to mock her. "How will we get into the basement?"

"There's a sewer."

"Of course there is."

"Meant to put an end to the Great Stink," Lucy mused, "but if you ask me it's brought no end of mischief."

Sagreda hesitated; she didn't mind getting covered in literal excrement, but the bullshit she was already mired in was a long way from a fact-checked documentary on the marvels of Victorian engineering. "Does anything live down there?"

Lucy considered the question. "'Live' might not be the right word to use. But that shouldn't bother you, should it?"

"Why not?"

Lucy exchanged a knowing glance with Sam, who'd apparently been shadowing Sagreda for some time. "Begging your pardon, Captain, but I been told quite a bit about your fancy man. From what I hear, you got him nicely tamed, so maybe it's time you put him to good use."

7

MATHIS WENT IN FRONT, holding the lamp, but Lucy and Sagreda stuck close behind him. The ceaseless, arrhythmic percussion of random drips of water all around them made Sagreda tense; if something came skittering hungrily along the tunnel, the sounds it made might easily be camouflaged by this unpredictable plinking.

With a handkerchief over her nose, and her mouth shut tight, the stench of the sewer was eye-watering but not quite disabling. Sagreda hadn't vomited once as the Captain, even when she'd stumbled on a disemboweled woman on her first night in the game, and she trusted his constitution to get her through this merely sensory assault. The two cups of blood she'd given Mathis just after sunset had only made her unsteady for a minute or two, and once she'd imbibed an equal volume of Mrs Trotter's strong black tea she'd felt entirely Captainly again.

"Are we close?" she asked Lucy, holding her forearm over her mouth as she spoke, which seemed to do a better job of blocking the outgoing sound than the incoming vapor.

"Pardon me?"

"Are we almost there?" Sagreda retched a little, the price of her impatience.

"You'll see the drain to the right when we reach it," was all Lucy could offer. "There'll be no missing it."

Sagreda peered into the gloom ahead, wondering if any light from the house might make it through the drain, turning the opening into a welcoming beacon. In fact, she could see a small spot of luminous yellow in the distance, beyond the reach of Mathis's lamp. But it was not remaining still. For a moment she wondered if it might be a reflection off the surface of the putrid, ankle-deep water, shifting its apparent position because of a disturbance in the flow. But then a second yellow dot appeared, off to the left and a short way behind it, and the motion became much easier to decode. The two lights were attached to two ambulatory bodies of some kind, and those bodies were striding down the tunnel.

She reached forward and touched Mathis's shoulder. "Do you see that?" she asked.

"Yes."

"Any idea what they are?"

"No one's handed me a taxonomy for this place," he replied. "But the general rule seems to be that anything inhuman is likely to mean you harm. So the only question is whether I can fend them off, or pull rank on them somehow."

As the creatures grew nearer, Sagreda became aware of the sound of their footfalls in the sewer water. In concert, their gaits generated a strange rhythm, in which she thought she could discern an over-lapping pair of alternating sloshes and harder strikes. The Captain's chest tightened; Sagreda hoped she wasn't about to discover that a lifetime of pipe smoking in his back-story had left him with bouts of stress-induced emphysema.

Mathis stopped walking and held the lamp high in front of him. "Who goes there?" he demanded imperiously. When he received no reply, he added: "Know that we will pass, and we will pass unmo-lested, or it will be the worse for you!"

The creatures continued to advance, but now the lamplight began to reach them, sketching gray outlines for the flesh and bones that held up the yellow orbs. What struck Sagreda immediately was that some of the edges she could discern were unnaturally straight. At first she doubted her eyes, but as the details grew clearer her impressions were confirmed: both figures were one-legged, walking with the aid of long wooden crutches angled across their bodies. Each possessed just a single arm and a single leg, attached to half a torso, on which was perched half a head.

As these walking anatomy lessons came into full view, they squinted angrily at the lamp. Their bodies were unclothed, but their skin was loose and wrinkled to the point where it took some scrutiny to be sure that they were both male. Each had a half-tongue that lolled part-way out of its broken jaw and hung drooling over the rough plane along which the dissection had taken place. Their single lungs made sputtering sounds that emerged from the bases of their bisected windpipes; their exposed viscera oozed a little, but there was no real pretense of any functioning circulatory system. Skeletal muscles, lungs and brains were all being powered by pure magical fiat, untroubled by any need for chemical energy.

"I hope they're not conscious," Mathis whispered.

Sagreda refused to entertain the possibility. "What are they meant to be?" she wondered. "A vampire someone tried to kill with a circular saw?"

Lucy stepped forward impatiently. "They're a grisly sight, I'll grant you that, but even if they're stronger than they look, I'll wager they're not swift or agile." Then without another word she bolted straight down the tunnel. At the last moment she veered to the right and passed by one of the half-men—almost certainly within arm's reach, in principle, but while the creature swiveled and swayed toward her, it couldn't really drop its crutch and grab her.

Sagreda was encouraged, but still wary. "So they're not exactly zombie ninjas, but one nip might still infect us with the dividing plague."

"Is that a thing?" Mathis asked.

"Not that my contributors ever heard—but there's got to be *one* original idea in the whole ghastly book."

Mathis made a larger target than Lucy, and the Captain even more so, but the officially adult members of the party plucked up their courage and ran the gauntlet. Sagreda almost hit her head on the roof of the tunnel as she scampered up the side of the tubular floor, but the wheezing half-cadaver that turned arthritically to ogle her didn't get close. She and Mathis caught up with Lucy, who had been wise enough not to go too far ahead in the dark.

"Good thing we have the Prince of the Night here to protect us," Lucy chuckled. "What would us poor mortals have done on our own?"

"Don't get too cocky," Mathis warned her. "I often find myself wanting a snack around ten."

Lucy tugged at the neck of her blouse to reveal a string of garlic circling her neck. Mathis said nothing, but he didn't even flinch; Sagreda wondered if it was possible, even here, to believe that an object could ward off danger when in truth it had no effect at all.

The three of them sloshed ahead through the muck.

"What if there's no cobalt blue in all of London?" Mathis asked, succumbing to a melancholy that had only seemed to afflict him since he started wearing ruffled shirts.

Sagreda found this scenario unlikely. "In hundreds of paintings, of hundreds of subjects? The SludgeNet will have scooped them up from actual Victorian artworks it found on the web, give or take a few woo-woo-isn't-this-scary neural-net effects. Cobalt blue fits the period, and it wasn't all that rare. It's not like we're hunting for neptunium in the Stone Age."

She glanced at Lucy, wondering what the girl had made of the exchange, but it seemed to have passed right over her head. Most, if not all, of her contributors would have heard of neural nets and neptunium, but a vague sense of recognition for a couple of anachronistic terms wasn't going to bring a consensual memory of the early twenty-first century flooding back. Given her character's age, it was tempting to ask her if she knew who Justin Bieber was, and see if she denied him three times before the cock crowed, but it would be cruel to wake her to her true nature if they weren't going to stick around and help her make sense of it.

"There it is," Lucy announced. The drain from the house they were hoping to burgle was up ahead of them on the right. Mathis swung the lamp around as they approached; the narrow, slanting pipe was half open at the bottom, and Sagreda could see dark stains on the cement. There was a grille at the top, which would normally have blocked their access—but the maid had been bribed to take out the bolts that held it down and replace them with duplicates whose threads had been stripped.

Sagreda threw the woolen blanket she'd brought over the lower surface of the pipe, in the hope that they might enter the house without becoming so filthy that they'd instantly wake every inhabitant with their stink. Lucy clambered up first, leaving her galoshes behind. She raised the doctored grille carefully and placed it to the side, almost silently, then drew herself up onto the floor.

"You're invited and all," she called down to Mathis. Sagreda wasn't sure if this would work; the maid, in turn, had invited Lucy, but that didn't make either of them the homeowner. Nonetheless, Mathis ascended without apparent difficulty, taking the lamp with him.

Sagreda stood at the base of the pipe, gazing up into the lamplit basement. She'd ignored Lucy's suggestion of a girdle, but it hadn't been a gratuitous jibe; this was going to be a tight fit. She stretched her arms in front of her so she could rest on her elbows without adding to her girth, and began crawling awkwardly up the slope.

Halfway to the top, she stopped advancing. She redoubled her effort, but it made no difference; whatever feverish motion she made with her elbows and knees, they didn't have enough purchase on the blanket to propel her upward.

Mathis appeared at the top of the pipe, crouching, peering down at her. "Hold onto the blanket with your hands," he whispered. He pushed some of it down to loosen it, giving her a fold she could grip. Then he grabbed the top and started straightening his knees to haul her up.

When her hands rose above the top of the pipe she gestured to Mathis to stop, and she pulled herself up the rest of the way. "Well, that was delightful," she gasped. She clambered to her feet and inspected herself and her crew; they weren't exactly fit to present to royalty, but between the blanket and their discarded galoshes they appeared to have succeeded in leaving the most pungent evidence of their journey behind.

Mathis shoved the blanket back down into the sewer and he and Lucy fitted the grille into place, swapping back actual threaded bolts. The plan was to leave by the front door, rather than retracing their steps.

Sagreda turned away from the latrine and took in the rest of the basement. The staircase led up from the middle of the room, but on the opposite side there was a door with a small, barred window: an entrance to another room on the same level.

Mathis picked up the lamp and turned the flame down low as they walked toward the stairs. In the faint light, Sagreda saw something move behind the bars in the other room. There was a clink of metal on stone, and a soft, tortured exhalation.

She took the lamp from Mathis and approached the door. If there was a witness in there, the burglars had already revealed themselves, but she had to know exactly what risk they were facing. She lifted the lamp to the level of the window, and peered inside.

At least a dozen fragments of bodies were chained to the walls and floor of the cell. Some resembled the vertically bisected men they'd met in the sewer; some had been cut along other planes. And some had been stitched together crudely, into hallucinatory Boschian nightmares: composites with two torsos sharing a single pair of legs, or heads attached in place of limbs. Where there were eyes, they turned toward the light, and where there were ribs they began rising and falling, but the attempts these pitiful creatures made to cry out were like the sound of wet cardboard boxes collapsing as they were trod into the ground.

Sagreda retreated, gesturing to the others to continue up the stairs.

When they emerged on the ground floor, Lucy took the lamp and led the way down a long corridor. There were portraits in oil at regular intervals on the wall to their right, some authentically staid, some Gothically deranged, but none of them contained the desired blue.

They reached the drawing room. "Turn up the lamp," Sagreda whispered. The piano, the cabinets and shelves, the sofas and small tables barely registered on her; they were just unwelcome complications, casting shadows that obscured the real treasures. The walls were covered with paintings: scenes from Greek myths, scenes from the Bible, scenes of clashing armies . . . and scenes of naval battles.

For a second or two she was giddy from a kind of ecstasy tinged with disbelief: after so long, it seemed impossible that she really had found what she needed; it had to be a cruel delusion, because the universe they inhabited was built from nothing else. But the feeling passed, and she strode over to the painting that had caught her eye. The ships were ablaze, but the sea was calm. No gray-green, storm-tossed water here, just a placid ocean of blue.

Sagreda contemplated merely scraping off a few samples, but it seemed wiser to take the whole thing and be sure she had as wide a range of colors as possible, rather than a fragment or two that might turn out, under better light, to have been ill-chosen. She unhooked the painting and wrapped it in a cloth.

Then she bowed to their guide. "If you please, Miss Lucy, show us the way out."

Somewhere in the house, a door slammed heavily. Lucy extinguished the lamp. But the room only remained in perfect blackness for a few seconds before gas lights came on at the far end of the corridor.

Sagreda heard a rustle of clothing—maybe overcoats coming off—then a woman's voice. "They were so rude to me! I can't believe it! If I want to be called Lady Godwin, they should call me Lady Godwin!"

A man replied, "It's a historical fact: she took her husband's name."

"Yes, but only because she had no choice! If she'd been vampire aristocracy, do you think she would have buckled to convention like that?"

"Umm, given her politics, do you think she would have chosen to be an aristocrat of any kind?"

"There are socialists in the British House of Lords, aren't there?" the woman countered.

The man was silent for a moment, then he said, "Can you smell that?"

"Smell what?"

"You really can't smell it? Maybe your thing's clogged."

"What are you talking about?"

The man sighed impatiently. "You know . . . the little canister thing in the front of the helmet, under the goggles. There's a mesh around it, but I think sometimes the stuff clogs up the holes. Just give it a flick with your finger."

The two customers went quiet. In the shadows of the drawing room, Lucy caught Sagreda's eye and gestured to her to move behind a bookcase. Sagreda complied without hesitation, deferring to her accomplice's experience.

"Okay . . . yeah, I can smell it now," the woman announced. "That's foul! Do you think one of our experiments broke out of the basement?"

"Maybe," the man replied. "But it seems to be coming from down the hall."

Sagreda heard their footsteps approaching. She tensed, wishing she could see exactly where Mathis was. A couple of ordinary householders would not have posed much of a problem—least of all customers, whom Mathis would have no qualms about dispatching—but she did not like the phrase *vampire aristocracy*.

"Wait!" the man said. The footsteps stopped, and then he groaned. "Yeah, yeah: sexy Russian babes are desperately seeking broad-minded couples to help fulfill their fantasies. How many times are they going to show me this crap before they realize we're never going to follow the link?"

"You could go ad-free, if you weren't so stingy," the woman chided him.

"Stingy? Five dollars a month is a rip-off!"

"Then stop complaining. It's your choice."

"What costs do they actually have?" the man protested. "The books they start from are all public domain, or pirated. The world-building software comes from open-source projects. The brain maps they use for the comps are data from open-access journals. So, I'm meant to fork out five dollars a month just to pay rent on their servers?"

"Well . . . enjoy smickering at your Russian babes, Lord Scrooge, I'm going to find out what's stinking up the house."

The woman must have decided to approach on tip-toes, because Sagreda heard nothing but floorboards creaking. From her hiding place she could see neither Mathis nor Lucy, and she felt like a coward for not rushing out to block the doorway with the Captain's ample girth. But the fact remained that the mild-mannered aficionado of kitsch creeping down the corridor, who would not have said boo to any fleshly equivalent of Sagreda if they'd sat next to each other on a bus, had been endowed by the game with the power to rip all of their throats out—and endowed by her own lack of empathy with the power to take off her goggles and sleep soundly afterward.

The woman spoke, from just inside the doorway, calling back to her companion in a kind of stage whisper, "It's definitely coming from in here!" Maybe her "experiments" were so brain-damaged that they would not have been alerted to her presence by these words. Or maybe she just didn't give a damn. At five bucks a month, how invested would she be? If things turned out badly, she could still order a pizza.

There was a sound of bodies colliding, and the woman crying out in shock, if not actual pain. Sagreda stepped out into the room to be greeted by the sight of Mathis holding Lady Godwin with her arms pinned from behind, his fangs plunging repeatedly deep into her carotid artery as he filled his mouth with blood then spat it out onto the floor. His victim was strong, and she was struggling hard, but he'd had the advantage of surprise, and whatever their relative age and vampiric prestige, his assault was progressively weakening her.

Sagreda ran to the fireplace and picked up a long metal poker. As she approached, both vampires glared at her furiously, like a pair of brawling cats who'd rather scratch each other's flesh off than brook any human intervention. But she wasn't here to try to make peace between house-pets.

She rammed the poker as hard as she could between Godwin's ribs; the author-turned-unlikely-vivisector screeched and coughed black blood that dribbled down the front of her satin evening gown, then she went limp. Sagreda was sickened; even if her victim would barely feel a tickle in her VR harness, the imagery they were sharing debased them both.

Mathis dropped his dead prey and snatched at Sagreda, as if he was so enraged to have been cheated of the animal pleasure of the fight that he was ready to turn on her as punishment. She stood her ground. "Don't you fucking touch me!" she bellowed.

"What's going on?" asked Lord Shelley irritably. Mathis turned to confront him, but this time it was no ambush; the older man grabbed him by the shirtfront and thrust him aside with no concern for conservation of momentum, sending him crashing into a corner of the room without experiencing the least bit of recoil.

As Shelley gazed down in horror at his murdered wife, Sagreda backed away slowly. Reminding this bozo that it was only a game would only get her deleted.

The undead poet raised his eyes to the Captain, and spread his fanged jaws wide in a howl of grief.

"'Look on my works, ye Mighty, and despair?'" Sagreda offered sycophantically.

Lucy chose this moment to make a run for the door. Shelley turned and grabbed her thin arm, then bent down and sank his fangs into it, apparently deterred by her garlic necklace from striking in the usual spot. Sagreda leaped forward and punched him in the side of the mouth with all of the Captain's mortal strength; to her amazement, her blow dislodged his jaws from the girl's flesh. Lucy was bawling with pain and terror; Sagreda kept striking the same spot above Shelley's chin with her massive right paw, as fast and hard as she could, unsure if it was just her knuckles and finger bones that she could hear cracking and crumbling from the impacts.

Mathis whispered calmly in her ear, "Step aside, my love."

She complied. Shelley looked up, but he had no time to react. Mathis drove the poker into his chest, all the way through to his spine.

As Shelley slumped to the ground, Lucy fell beside him, looking every bit as lifeless. Mathis took his coat off, tore one sleeve free and wrapped it around the girl's upper arm as a tourniquet.

"What are you doing?" Sagreda asked. "That's so tight, you're . . ." She stifled a sob of revulsion. "Don't cut it off!"

"I'm not going to," Mathis promised, "but we need to move fast to get the poison out. And I can't do it, that would only make it worse."

Sagreda stared at him. "What?"

"I'll apply pressure; you have to suck the wound and spit."

"You're sure that will work?"

"Just do it, or she's either going to lose her arm or be turned!"

Sagreda quickly relit the lamp so she could see what she was doing, then she knelt on the floor and set to work. When every drop had been drained or spat onto the carpet, leaving Lucy's arm corpse-white, Mathis loosened the tourniquet and the flesh became pink, bleeding freely from the puncture wounds above the wrist.

"Let it bleed for a bit, just to flush it out some more," Mathis insisted.

"How do you know all this?"

"I'm guessing," he admitted. "I've heard things from the other vampires, but I don't know if I ever got the whole story straight."

Sagreda sat on the bloody floor and cradled Lucy's head in her arms. There was no actual poison being traced through some elaborate, fluid-dynamical model of the circulatory system; the game would make a crude assessment of the efficacy of their actions under its fatuous rules and then throw its algorithmic dice.

They had love, and they had reason, but the game could still do whatever it liked.

8

SHORTLY AFTER SUNSET, MATHIS emerged from the Captain's bedroom, bleary-eyed and yawning. "Did you get any sleep?" he asked Sagreda.

"A couple of hours, around noon," she replied. "But it's done." She gestured toward the mosaic. "I just need you to check it."

"Okay." Mathis slapped his own face a few times, trying to wake more fully. "How's your hand?"

"Still broken. But I don't plan on having to use it much longer."

Mathis managed a hopeful nod. "And Lucy?"

Sagreda said, "She seems stable; her pulse is steady, and she has no fever."

Mathis took a seat in the nearest armchair and turned to address Sagreda. "The game's not going to accept that its biggest celebrity couple has been removed from the plot. But the SludgeNet's not going to reboot everything while the city's crawling with customers who want to maintain continuity. So, the way I see it there are only two options. They can pull a bit of necromantic fluff out from under the sofa cushions, and bring the Shelleys back in an explicit act of resurrection that would make Sigourney Weaver blush. Or, they can pretend that what happened last night never really happened, and just delete the witnesses."

"You and I can be out of here as soon as you've checked the mosaic," Sagreda said. She glanced at the sofa, where Lucy still lay inert. "But I don't know if she'll agree to come with us."

"All we can do is be honest with her," Mathis replied.

"To be honest, we don't even know if we're ready for this ourselves." Sagreda rubbed the good side of her smashed hand; it didn't really affect the pain, but it helped distract her from it.

"No. But what would you rather do? Go off on a tour of another twenty worlds, in the hope that we might pick up a few more tips?"

"If *3-adica* makes anything possible, why has no one ever come back?" she asked.

"Because it's so good there that no one wants to leave?"

"Not even for a day or two, to spread the word?"

"I don't know," Mathis confessed.

"What's *3-adica*?" Lucy asked. Her eyes were open, and she looked remarkably lucid.

Sagreda fetched a jug of water. "How long have you been awake?" she asked, handing the girl a glass.

"A while." Lucy downed the water in one long gulp, then went to use the chamber pot. When she returned, she said, "I helped you complete the mandala, didn't I? So you owe it to me to divulge the nature of its powers."

Sagreda had been preparing for this question all day. "It's taking us to a world where the distances between numbers aren't the same as they are here."

Lucy frowned, but her expression was more intrigued than dismissive.

"Here, you can put all the numbers on a line," Sagreda said. "Like the house numbers on a street. And the distance between two houses is just the difference between their numbers: number twelve is two houses down from number ten . . . most of the time." Whatever the historical truth, this version of Victorian London hadn't made up its mind whether to number houses consecutively along each side of the street, or to adopt the even/odd rule that was more familiar to Sagreda's contributors.

"So you're going to a world where the houses are higgledy-pig-gledy?" Lucy guessed.

"Maybe, though that doesn't quite cover it." Sagreda walked over to the desk, took a sheet of writing paper and started scrawling ovals in ink. "In *3-adica*, the numbers are like eggs in a sparrow's nest. Zero, one and two are all in the same nest, and the distance between any pair of them is exactly one."

"From one to two is one," Lucy said. "But from nothing to two is . . . also one?"

"Exactly," Sagreda confirmed. "The laws of arithmetic haven't changed: two minus zero is still two, not one. But the laws of geometry aren't the same, and the *distance* is no longer the *difference*."

"But where's three?" Lucy demanded. "Where's seventy-three?"

"Each egg I've drawn," Sagreda said, "is really a nest of its own. The zero-egg is a nest that contains zero, three and six. The one-egg is a nest that contains one, four and seven. The two-egg is a nest that contains two, five and eight." She scribbled in the new numbers.

"I can see what you've written clear enough," Lucy acknowledged, "but I don't know what it means."

"To be in a smaller nest with a number puts you closer to it," Sagreda explained. "The distance between zero and one is one, because that's the size of the smallest nest they're both in, but the distance between zero and *three* is smaller, because they share a smaller nest. In fact, the distance between zero and three is one third, as is the distance between five and eight, or four and seven."

"And you keep on with that nonsense?" Lucy asked.

Sagreda smiled. "Absolutely. However high you want to count, you just keep turning eggs into ever smaller nests of three."

Lucy sat pondering this for a while, but it was clear that something was bothering her. "You say the distance from nothing to three is one third," she said finally. "But where does *one third* live in your nests? I can walk a third of the way between houses, and I know what that means on Baker Street, but what does it mean for these sparrow's eggs?"

"It means you need to look outside the first nest." Sagreda added another two circles as large as the largest one she'd drawn previously, and then scratched an even bigger one around all three. "If you add one third to anything in the first nest, it goes in the second nest. If you add two thirds, it goes in the third one. And any two numbers that happen to be in a different pair of these new nests lie at a distance of *three* from each other, because that's the size of the larger nest that encloses them all. And before you ask me where *one ninth* lives, the paper isn't large enough for me to draw that, but I think you can guess how the pattern continues."

Lucy absorbed this, but she wasn't done. "Where does *one half* live?"

Sagreda was tired; she had to stop and think. "It's somewhere inside the first nest I drew, at a distance of one from zero."

"But where?" Lucy pressed her. "Where is there room for it? I can see how your eggs there reach up to any number I could ever count to . . . but how are you going to squeeze yet another one in?"

Mathis chuckled and stretched his arms above his head. "Good question!" he said. "And it took my friend here about a day to convince me of the answer."

Sagreda closed her eyes for a moment, and focused. "First, go to the number *two*. Then add three and go to *five*. Then add nine, which takes you to *fourteen*. Then add twenty-seven . . . and so on. Each time, you add thrice what you added before."

"And when do you stop?" Lucy asked, with a cunning look on her face, as if she was about to play cuckoo and toss the existing egg at the point of arrival out of its nest.

"You don't!" Mathis interjected. "You're not allowed to stop! Which sounds nonsensical, but it's no more absurd, in *3-adica*, than it is in our world for Achilles to get halfway down a road, then another quarter, then another eighth . . . with always one more stage to go that's shorter than the last. Because in *3-adica*, adding thrice what you added before takes you a third less far. Five is actually fairly close to one half, but fourteen is closer, and forty-one is closer still. Because if you double each of these numbers, the result is always *one* . . . plus three multiplied by itself many times, which makes less and less of a difference the more times it's been multiplied."

Lucy opened her mouth to protest, but then closed it again. Something was sinking in. Sagreda had never met a comp who, when given the chance to brush away the learned helplessness of their character, turned out to know less about arithmetic than they would have picked up from a decent high school education in America at the height of the space race. And maybe one in a hundred had been remixed from the pool in such a way that they inherited enough recreational mathematics to have heard of the "*p*-adic numbers": 2-adics, 3-adics, 5-adics . . . *p*-adics for any prime you cared to name.

But the book, *3-adica*, seemed to have been written after every contributor had died. And the only knowledge any comp had of the SludgeNet's attempt to gamify it came from eavesdropping on customers, whose comments on the topic tended to be of the form "my migraine when I tried that shit was worse than x," for various values of x.

Lucy seemed to be anticipating a few headaches of her own. "I don't know if the streets will be like bird's nests where you're going," she said, "but it sounds like a place where I'd lose my way."

Sagreda said, "The beauty, though, is that it's also a place where the forces that try to keep you down are even more likely to lose their own way."

Lucy shook her head. "No one keeps me down. I can dodge the muckety-mucks well enough, whether they're carrying cut-throat razors or trying to take a drink from my neck. Last night was a tight spot I shouldn't have gotten into, but I won't make that mistake again."

Sagreda could see no alternative now to spelling out the whole truth. "This London is not the real London," she said. "It's a bad story that bad people have created to make money from very bad advertisements. The machines those people own brought you and me to life—using parts they might as well have obtained from grave-robbers, cut up and stitched together to form puppets to act in their very bad play."

Lucy laughed curtly, with a brashness that seemed forced. "You might have dispensed yourself a bit too much laudanum, Captain, to ease the pain from your fisticuffs." But Sagreda suspected that the last traveler Lucy had encountered would have sketched a cosmology eerily similar to this opium dream.

She said, "This world we're in, and ten thousand others like it, were made by ten thousand clockwork monkeys chewing rotten fruit and spitting out the pulp. But what if a ball of polished marble slipped into the barrel of worm-ridden apples, and broke its monkey's jaw? A clockwork monkey is too stupid to stop chewing when you feed it something unexpected, so there's no end to the damage the marble might have caused. And once you tear open a hole in the clockwork, maybe you can crawl right into the innards and really start playing with all the springs and wheels. That's why *3-adica* could mean freedom: it's tough enough to break the monkey's jaw."

Mathis rose from his armchair. "I should start checking the mosaic," he said.

"Do you need a meal first?" Sagreda asked.

"No, a few gulps from her Ladyship's ancient veins seem to have gone a long way." He took a seat at the writing desk and peered studiously at Sagreda's notes.

Sagreda joined Lucy on the sofa. "My landlady will be bringing me my dinner in about an hour," she said. "So you and Mathis will need to hide for a bit, though of course you're welcome to eat with me when the coast's clear."

"I'll be getting back to my own digs before then," Lucy decided.

"What you saw last night means you might not be safe," Sagreda said gently. "If the people we killed are too important to the story, what we did might be undone—and if the rules of the world don't allow that, we'll need to be discarded to smooth over the lie."

Lucy wasn't ready to take any of this on faith, but some part of Sagreda's warning seemed to unsettle her. "I can find out what's happened in that house since we left it," she said. "If they've buried them blood-suckers and started sending all their finery to the auctioneer, will that put your mind at ease?"

"It'd be worth knowing," Sagreda replied. "But can you do that without letting on to anyone what you actually saw?"

Lucy was offended. "I ain't no tattler!"

"I don't mean the police," Sagreda stressed. "I mean anyone at all. Not even someone you'd trust with your life. Telling them could put them in danger, too."

"Leave it with me, Captain," Lucy replied. "By the time you've had your dinner, I'll be back with my report."

9

"THIS LOOKS PERFECT TO ME," Mathis declared, putting the mosaic aside and rubbing his eyes. "But there is one small complication we need to think about."

"What's that?" Sagreda asked.

"Peyam's dictionary was calibrated for sunlight," he said. "Whatever the lighting, the colors still look right to us when we check them against a white background, but that's just our visual system compensating. The GPU models physical optics, not perception; it's going to spit out pixels that depend on the light source."

Sagreda had known there'd be an extra hurdle to deal with as soon as Mathis had turned up in his new, photosensitive state, but she'd been so preoccupied with finding the cobalt blue that she'd stopped thinking about the problem. "Okay, so we'll need to use a mirror to light the thing in the morning without roasting you to a cinder."

"That would be nice." Mathis glanced down at the desk, and gestured at the collection of wooden rods beside the blotter. "I see you've got the pieces of the trigger ready. So we might as well start setting up."

"Of course."

They worked together, mostly in silence. They'd performed the same task so many times before that the need to bounce sunlight from a chink in the curtains onto the mosaic via the Captain's shaving mirror felt like a welcome variation to the routine that would keep them from becoming complacent. But the hardest thing now for Sagreda was to stop worrying about Lucy.

Mathis dropped a plumb-line from the main guide-string that stretched across the room between an anchor on the wall and the home-made easel holding the mosaic, and marked the viewing spots on the floor for the two of them. "I guess you don't know how high Lucy's eyes are?"

"I should have measured her while she was asleep."

"It's almost midnight," he said. "Do you really think she's coming back?"

"She has to."

"Maybe she heard that Percy and Mary got an ad hoc exemption to the vampire killers' rulebook," Mathis speculated. "In which case, the show can roll on without anyone disappearing: the Shelleys can vow revenge on their attackers, but Lucy's not a liability any more, she just gets to spread the story that lets everyone in *Midnight* know how indestructible they are. Stake through the heart, no problem! They're like that guy with bad hair in *No Country for Old Men*."

"None of mine saw that," Sagreda replied distractedly. She walked over to the window and looked down onto the street. Lucy was standing outside the building, and the fog was rolling in.

She gestured to Mathis to come and see.

"Okay," he said. "Shall I go down and try to talk her into committing? Maybe if I start humming 'Consider Yourself' that'll be enough to persuade her; I don't think I'm up to the whole dance routine."

"I'll go."

"Not alone, at this hour."

They went together.

Lucy must have been in two minds about joining them, but she didn't flee when they approached her. "What did you find out?" Sagreda asked.

"The other blood-suckers are holding a ceremony tonight, to bring back them ones you killed. They got all the big sorcerers coming to the house: Dee, Crowley, Tesla, Twain."

"Twain?" Sagreda boggled.

"I knew it!" Mathis crowed. "The SludgeNet never met a rule it wasn't willing to break."

"You're probably safe, then," Sagreda told Lucy. "But you can still come with us if you want to."

"I can't leave my friends," Lucy replied. "Who'd look out for them, if I wasn't around?"

"At least come up and join us until morning," Sagreda suggested. "No one should be out on a night like this." The fog was so thick now that she could barely see Mathis, pacing impatiently behind Lucy.

Lucy hesitated. It was clear that she'd been hanging back instead of bringing them the news because, safe or not, she was afraid of being tempted to flee all the hardship she faced in *Midnight* to follow the Captain's mad dream. To an actual nineteenth-century pickpocket, every word of it would have sounded like gibberish, but something must have punctured her Stockholm Syndrome and shaken a few rusty twenty-first century insights out of the silt at the bottom of her mind.

"This is how traitors die!" a man's voice whispered.

Sagreda looked up to find that where Mathis had been, the fog was filled with a thick red mist. A blur of metal blades were tracing arcs through the air, through what was left of his body.

She cried out in shock and pulled Lucy toward her, away from the carnage. But then she froze: she had to do something, she had to find a way to rescue him. She watched the dancing blades, hypnotized, as if she could run their motion backward just by staring at them hard enough.

"He's gone!" Lucy shouted, tugging at her hand, trying to pull free of her grip. Sagreda broke out of her trance and let the girl go, then after a second she turned and followed her, bolting down the street so fast that it felt as if the ground had tipped and she was racing downhill, and if she tried to halt she'd only start tumbling.

As she watched Lucy fading in and out of sight in the swirling fog beneath the gas lamps, Sagreda wondered why she was even bothering to flee. She should have stayed and died beside Mathis. There was no other way she could find peace. There was no other kind of freedom.

Lucy's pale form receded into the darkness. Some instrument of torture began squeezing the Captain's chest, but Sagreda ran on, soaked in sweat and condensation, waiting for a flock of assassins to swoop down on her and drag her up into the sky so she could finally fall to Earth as a rain of blood and gristle and be done with it.

A boy appeared out of the shadows and gestured to Sagreda to follow him. It was Sam. He turned off the street and the two of them ran down an alley and a set of stairs into a pitch-black basement. Sagreda heard a door being closed behind her.

Someone lit a lamp. This was the place where she'd met Lucy to plan the heist; Lucy and half a dozen other children were here now.

Sagreda sat down on the bare wooden floor and covered her face with her hands.

Lucy said, "They won't go out of their way to find us now. Your friend was one of their kind, that's why they made an example of him."

Sagreda replied without looking up. "Do you really not understand that it's all bullshit? If there are two tribes of beings that owe loyalty to each other, we're all of us in one, fanged or not, and the customers are the other. We should slaughter them, every chance we get, until they hate this game so much they'll take up ten-pin bowling and leave us in peace."

Lucy didn't answer her. Sagreda pressed the heels of her palms into her eyes. She didn't know how to grieve for Mathis; some splinter of ice in her contributors' hearts was whispering that he'd never been more than a digital mash-up of crude approximations to a hundred humans all long dead. As she was herself. The sooner she found a way to be deleted, the better.

And she knew how. It would be instant, painless, easy, and final. She just had to change the mosaic so that it unlinked her from *Midnight*, without placing her in any queue for entry into another world. Her mind would cease to be executed, and within a few milliseconds the SludgeNet's garbage collector would reclaim the space she was occupying and put it to better use.

Sagreda uncovered her face and wiped her tears away with the back of her hand. "Thanks for all you've done for me, but I need to go now." She reached into her pocket, took out all the coins she had, and placed them on the floor beside her. Then she rose to her feet and started toward the door.

Lucy said, "Just stay until dawn, Captain. There's nothing now can't wait for morning."

Sagreda stopped where she was, and Lucy came and led her—as she might guide a lumbering, docile animal—to a mattress in the corner of the room.

10

SAGREDA WAS WOKEN BY a narrow shaft of sunlight that had entered the basement. The beam wasn't even touching her skin, but the illumination it brought into the room was enough to penetrate her eyelids and drag her out of her broken sleep.

None of the pickpockets were awake yet. Someone had removed the Captain's shoes and left them by the mattress, so Sagreda picked them up and walked quietly to the door. It was better to have no goodbyes.

She was halfway back to the Captain's lodgings when Sam appeared beside her.

"What do you want?" she asked numbly.

He hesitated, as if gathering his courage. "I remember watching Neil Armstrong step onto the moon," he said.

"Congratulations," Sagreda replied. She wasn't being sarcastic, but she didn't know what he expected her to do with this confession.

"Lucy told me all your stories, but she only half believes them," Sam persisted. "I know they're true."

"So you know where you are, and what you are." Sagreda shrugged. "Good for you. I wish you luck making something of it. I tried, but it came to nothing."

"You can't give up!" Sam said, alarmed at her indifference. "I need you to teach me what you know. I can't keep living here, half-starving all the time, pretending all this supernatural gibberish is true. Pretending I'm a child, when I'm not. I need to learn how to escape."

Sagreda strode on in silence, listening to the clomp of horseshoes on the road beside them, trying to find the words to brush him off without making herself feel like a monster. It had taken Peyam months to explain all the intricacies of the traveler's art to his students. She wished the boy well—or the man, presumably—but she didn't have it in her to stick around for that long.

They were almost at Mrs Trotter's house when the solution came to her. "If I offered you *The Great Gatsby* meets *The Three Stooges*, would that sound like a place you could live in for a while? Flappers, cocaine, Keystone Cops . . . what more could you want?"

"Will you be coming with me?"

"No," Sagreda replied, "but I can give you the names of half a dozen people there who'd be willing to teach you everything. A lot of travelers reach that world and decide it's good enough." And since it was the last place she'd been, following the same linked list that led to *3-adica*, it would only take a small change to the mosaic to send the viewer backward along the chain instead of forward.

Then she could scrub the whole forward/backward part and unlink herself from everything.

When they reached the house, she saw the dark stain on the sidewalk, but she kept it in her peripheral vision and refused to think about it. She led Sam up to the Captain's rooms and wrote down her list of contacts.

"'Tire-Iron McGill'?" he read dubiously. "'Cyanide Sally'?"

"Don't worry," Sagreda reassured him. "It's not like meeting 'Saw-Tooth Jim' on a dark night in Whitechapel. All the violence is slap-stick."

"So why didn't you stay?"

"Because everything else was slap-stick too."

Sagreda took Sam's measurements. The sun was coming through the curtains, shining off the mirror and falling straight onto the mosaic; she pictured Mathis standing beside the easel, in the first body she'd ever seen him inhabiting. But she blinked away her tears and concentrated on the geometry, finding the optical center for Sam's close-set eyes, dropping the plumb-line, and outlining two footprints in chalk on the floor to make it easier for this novice to view the target squarely.

There was a knock on the door.

"Just wait here and keep quiet," Sagreda told Sam.

When she opened the door, Mrs Trotter was on the landing. "Captain, I've been forbearing," she said, "but there are limits to my good nature."

"I don't follow your meaning, Mrs Trotter."

"Your gentleman caller who was killed last night! And the girl . . . and now some ragamuffin . . . !" Mrs Trotter shook her head. "This is not a home for wayward children and unnatural dandies. I was expecting you to be a reputable tenant. Instead, you've made me the target of gossip from here to—"

"I'll be gone by the end of the day," Sagreda interjected bluntly. "Feel free to sell all of my possessions, or just throw them onto the street if you prefer." She bit her lip and managed to say nothing about the bodies.

But even this announcement didn't mollify Mrs Trotter. "I never heard such a thing! Scarpering to the continent to escape your punishment for some wickedness, I'll wager! Let me in, Captain. I want to see exactly what mischief you've been up to!"

"Just mind your own business, woman," Sagreda replied flatly.

"This is my house!" Mrs Trotter shrieked. "Whatever goes on within these walls is my concern!"

Sagreda slammed the door and bolted it. As she walked down the hall, she heard the sound of something falling to the floor in the sitting room, where she'd left Sam waiting. "Did you knock over the—?"

Sam was sprawled on the carpet. "No, no, no!" Sagreda checked his breathing and his pulse, but he was gone, irretrievably. "I told you to wait." The commotion must have panicked him, and made him think he might be losing his last chance to escape from *Midnight*. But Sagreda hadn't got around to explaining that she'd need to change the mosaic before it would take him to the benign, almost familiar world she'd promised him.

His mind was now in the queue for *3-adica*, and he had no idea what he'd be facing when he woke. Lucy might have told him some small smattering of what she'd learned, but even she had been in no condition to find her way around there on her own.

Mrs Trotter was pounding on the door, and promising that seven kinds of constable would arrive at any minute. Sagreda wrapped her arms around the Captain's wide shoulders and rocked back and forth silently for a while. "I'm sorry," she whispered, as if she owed Mathis an apology for doing what he'd almost certainly have wanted her to do.

She picked up Sam's limp body and placed it on the sofa. Whatever kind of man she'd just dispatched to the afterlife, the fact remained that he'd be as unprepared to face it as any child. She tied a string around her waist, joined the other end to the easel so there'd be no more casualties once she'd fallen, and found her mark on the floor.

She looked up, and in the corner of her eye she saw the Escher-esque shape she'd built from the wooden rods: a cube that wasn't actually impossible, merely unanticipated by some sloppily written graphics code. She shifted her gaze a fraction, bringing both the trigger and the mosaic into perfect alignment, and then she was gone.

11

SAGREDA KEPT HER EYES firmly closed, trying to get a sense of her new body from within before confronting the world around her. She felt sure that her spine was horizontal, with her chest facing down as if she were kneeling on all fours—but the task of bearing her weight seemed to be concentrated at the far ends of her limbs, not her elbows or knees. For most people, that would have felt awkward and strange, but all her joints and muscles were telling her that this posture was perfectly natural.

Apparently, she'd been reincarnated as a quadruped.

That probably ruled out the simplest version of *3-adica* she and Mathis had contemplated: a kind of stylized mathematical fantasia, in which the participants (in fully human form) rode on a magic carpet over a fractal landscape of numbers that was ultimately just a prettified CGI version of the nested eggs she'd drawn for Lucy.

But those eggs didn't really get the distances right; there was no way to choose points on a plane with all the right properties. The more radical, immersive approach would be to embed the characters in the 3-adic geometry itself, transforming them from spectators into participants. The problem, then, was that the human mind had evolved to work with its body and senses immersed in three-dimensional Euclidean space, and the SludgeNet wasn't remotely smart enough to rewire a comp to perceive its environment on any other terms—let alone work the same magic on its flesh-bound customers.

So whatever the game was, it would be a compromise. Sagreda's hope had always been that the SludgeNet would turn out to have bitten off more than it could chew, exposing a multitude of new flaws in its GPUs and its world-building algorithms . . . without rendering the place so hostile to its inhabitants that they had no opportunity to exploit the bugs.

She could hear a soft wind blowing, and she felt its touch upon her skin. She braced herself and opened her eyes.

Her first impression was that she was standing in a desert landscape of bleached earthen colors, with what looked like a few low boulders nearby. The cloudless sky could not have been more perfect, short of turning to cobalt blue.

But the ground bore a strange pattern of dark, concentric circles that spread out around her, dividing the landscape into narrow rings, while the "boulders" were two-dimensional, like cheap, painted stage scenery—only rescued from being literally flat by the fact that they conformed to the curves of the rings they belonged to. And as Sagreda looked past them toward more distant rings, the terrain grew crowded with detail at an alarming rate, packing in ever more variation in a manner that utterly defied her expectations about scale and perspective—as if kilometer-long strips plucked from an ordinary desert had been squeezed longitudinally and bent into circles just a few hundred meters across.

All of which made a certain amount of sense. Distances in *3-adica* couldn't take on a continuous range of values: they only came in powers of three. By rights, every ring of solid ground she saw should have been followed by another ring exactly three times larger, with nothing in between. But *perceiving* her surroundings as mostly empty space would have been a waste of the act of perception, and whether this compressed version faithfully reflected the way *3-adica*'s alien protagonists had seen things in the original book, or whether it was just a compromise the game had imposed, Sagreda didn't find it unreasonable that she was aware of the gaps between the shells of possible distances, without having to squander ninety percent of the virtual neurons in her visual cortex on massive black moats that could literally never contain anything.

She willed herself to start walking, and her body obliged, executing a gait that required no conscious effort, and worked so well that she was loathe to dissect it into a sequence of moves for each limb. She declined to peer down at her feet—or hooves—lest the strangeness of the sight paralyze her; it seemed wiser to try to grow into this body by using it for a while, purely by instinct.

She decided to head for the nearest of the boulders, but after spending a few minutes supposedly ambling toward it, Sagreda realized that her target was just shifting from side to side within its original distance-ring. So were all the other discernible features in all the other rings. Nothing was getting closer.

She stopped and looked down at the ground right in front of her, averting her gaze from the glimpse she caught of her forelimbs. Here, the rings were spaced so closely that she might as well have been staring at an unbroken surface—if not sand, maybe sandstone. She took a few steps to try to get a better sense of her own pace and recalibrate her expectations. As she walked, the texture beneath her drifted around in her field of view in a manner that seemed consonant with the rhythms of her body, but she never seemed to be leaving it behind and moving on to something new.

"Okay," she muttered out loud, amused that this world would allow her to utter and perceive the familiar syllables in a nasal voice that might have belonged to Mister Ed. *Why wasn't she getting anywhere?* Because distances no longer added up the same way. From zero to one was a distance of one; from one to two was a distance of one. But from zero to two was a distance of one, again. In fact, however many steps you took, the distance you ended up from where you began could never be greater than the largest of those steps.

One of the p-adic-savvy travelers Sagreda had met had called this "the non-Archimedean property," and opined that the only way an object could move *at all* through a 3-adic space would be through some kind of quantum tunneling that bypassed the whole idea of a classical trajectory. So maybe at some level quantum effects were enabling her to move her legs, or maybe that was pure cheating, but whatever the mechanism, it did not seem able to propel her out across the landscape.

Sagreda began walking again, with no expectations of any change in the result, but in the hope of gaining a better sense of what was happening. If each of her steps had had the effect of merely adding some fixed quantity to a 3-adic coordinate for her body, she would have mostly ended up at that distance from where she'd begun, switching abruptly to one-third, or one-ninth, or one-twenty-seventh and then back as her step count hit multiples of powers of three. But even allowing for her compressed perception of distances, she couldn't discern any such pattern. So perhaps her steps, though of equal geometric *size*, involved adding a sequence of different numbers—whose numerators and denominators were all devoid of threes—to her location. With the right choice of fractions to maintain the lack of threes in their cumulative sums, all steps *and* all their successive totals could work out to have the same size. And just as her body knew instinctively which legs to raise and lower in which order, this arithmetic trick would be wired into it, sparing her the need to calculate anything.

Which was all very nice if you wanted to trace out a circle in the desert. But how was she supposed to do anything else? The non-Archimedean law was clear: the total distance traveled could never be greater than the largest step. So how could she escape her invisible prison, if she couldn't leap over the walls in one bound?

Sagreda willed herself to run, and her body obliged with a gallop that made her newfound muscles sing. The texture of the ground ahead of her changed almost at once, and for a moment she was elated. But though her individual bounds were larger than her previous steps, they gained no more by force of repetition: she was just executing a slightly larger circle.

She stopped to catch her breath, daring the world to play fair and suffocate her, since the stale air around her could hardly escape its starting position any more easily than she could. But if her body was largely a cheat to let her feel at home, a travesty of alien Euclidean nonsense spliced into the 3-adic terrain, there had to be *some* genuine, 3-adic way to go farther than a single bound, or the whole book would have been very short: *A creature stood alone in the desert (please don't ask how it got there). Soon it died from lack of food. The End.*

It was time to stop being squeamish: if she could survive waking up as the Captain, she could cope with this alien horsiness. She bent her neck as far as she could and looked down at herself as she took a few steps. Her legs were swinging back and forth, but beyond that, they were visibly expanding and contracting: swelling up beyond the wildest nightmare version of the Captain's gout, then deflating just as rapidly. No accumulation of additions could carry an object farther than the largest distance traveled along the way—but her legs weren't adding, they were multiplying.

Sagreda kept walking, contemplating the meaning of this discovery. In the real world, when you inflated a balloon, the individual molecules in the rubber were moving in different directions depending on which side of the balloon they were on, but motion was motion; there was nothing special going on. Here, though, since ordinary motion couldn't lead to dilation, dilation had to be an entirely separate thing. If the invented physics of *3-adica* was symmetrical under a change of scale, then it might make sense for a system to possess "dilatational" momentum, as well as the usual kind. If your dilatational velocity was one tripling per second, you became three times larger, again and again, until something applied an opposing dilatational force that brought the process to a halt. And ditto for shrinking. *That* was how you got anywhere in this place.

Out of habit, Sagreda looked around for Mathis to share her triumphant discovery with him. In his absence, a deadening numbness started creeping into her skull, but she stared it down: this wasn't the time for grief, let alone anything darker. She'd stranded Sam in this bizarre place, and she owed it to him to keep going until she knew that he was safe. *Love and reason* had never been for the two of them alone; unless she had some fellow feeling for every last comp, she was no better than the mindless SludgeNet, and its worse-than-mindless creators.

If her leg muscles possessed the power to expand and contract 3-adically, there was no reason why the rest of her body shouldn't share it. It was just a matter of finding the cue. Sagreda closed her eyes and pictured herself growing larger; when she opened them nothing had changed. Then she tried tensing her shoulders, not just willing them to grow broader but actively forcing them apart. It made her feel ridiculous, as if she were posing like a vain equine body-builder, but to her astonishment and delight the landscape around her started to shrink.

She watched the stage-scenery boulder she'd been trying to reach turn into a rock, then a pebble, then a grain of sand as it slipped between her feet. Curiouser and curiouser. She relaxed, and then discovered that she needed to apply a brief compression of her shoulder blades to bring the process to a halt.

"What now?" she wondered. The desert was still a desert, self-similar enough under enlargement that only the details of the view had

changed. Where exactly—and how big—were all the other characters? In what place, and at what scale, could she hope to find Sam?

Given the potential disruption that a character's dilation could
cause, it would make sense for the game to wake new entrants at
a very small scale, offering them a chance to find their feet, and
shoulders, without bumping into anyone. And though the lesson
was immensely hard to swallow, the fact remained that—colossus or
not—she *still* couldn't go striding out across the wilderness, exploring in any conventional way. Her choices were to reposition herself within her new, much larger, prison and then shrink down for a
closer look in case she'd missed something, or to keep on inflating
her body until her current surroundings in all their desolate grandeur
revealed themselves to be nothing, on the scale that mattered, but a
tiny patch of dirt.

Sagreda spent a few minutes pacing in a circle, staring at the
ground, but she saw no signs of any tiny cities hidden in the dust—
and if the game's greatest architectural features had been something
she might easily have crushed beneath her feet from sheer inexperi-
ence, there'd have been a lot of rebooting going on.

So she took a few deep breaths, steadied herself, then spread her
shoulders wide.

12

"MAKE ROOM, MAKE ROOM!" a male voice shouted irritably. Sagreda
shrank out of the way as the passerby expanded to fill most of the
square, deftly bloating and stepping then finally contracting, leaving
him on the opposite side. For a moment or two, an afterimage of
his blimp-pufferfish-horse-balloon body breaking up into distinct
onion-layers lingered in Sagreda's vision.

She quickly expanded back to her previous scale before someone
else muscled in; if you gave these people an inch, you ended up toy-
sized. "Do you know a newcomer named Sam?" she asked a 3-adan
who'd ended up beside her in the wake of the maneuver. There was
no reply.

She'd been standing at more or less the same spot in the corner of
the square for hours, slowly increasing her size as the opportunities

arose. Her fellow characters had been kind enough not to trample her as she ascended out of the "desert", but actually traversing any significant distance here—by becoming as large as the journey you wished to make—seemed to require a combination of nerve, skill and luck that she had not yet attained. A few of her contributors were offering a collective flashback to their first attempts to cross an ice rink, but however conspicuous they might have felt as novices trying out their blades, Sagreda was fairly sure that they'd had nothing on this.

She closed her eyes for a moment to escape from the headache-inducing perspective. Until now, she'd always been part of an ant-trail of travelers moving to and fro between the worlds, carrying intelligence of what lay ahead; this was the first time she'd arrived at her destination without a single contact. But she'd met at least a dozen people at different times who'd sworn they were heading for *3-adica*, before she and Mathis had resolved to make the journey themselves. Even if no one had ever come back, she couldn't be alone here.

"Sam!" she bellowed, keeping her eyes closed; it was easier to feel uninhibited that way. Going on the barrage of noise striking her from all directions, she was fairly sure that sound had the means to propagate at least across the square. Whether there was anything beyond this place was another question; the only really practical way it could be part of a larger city was through a hierarchy of scales, with people having to bloat even more to move between them.

"Sam!" If there was a customer nearby and she was violating the local mores, so be it: let them flag her for deletion. It was all she could do to move her body out of other people's way here; she had no idea how she was going to find food or shelter. Did she really think she was going to be able to map this world's flaws and exploit them, all on her own?

"Captain!" a voice whinnied back. Sagreda had almost forgotten that she'd never given the boy her real name back in *Midnight*.

She opened her eyes. "Sam! Where are you?"

"Here! Over here!"

Sagreda searched the crowd in the direction of his words, but how was she meant to recognize him?

"Don't worry! I'll come to you!"

The square's mostly empty center was abruptly filled with a new parade-float pony, which shrank down beside her.

"Can you see me now?" Sam joked.

"Yes." For a moment, Sagreda could find nothing more to say; her relief was too tainted with guilt. "I'm sorry you ended up here," she said finally. "I never meant that to happen."

"It's my own doing," he replied. "I should have waited for you."

"How long have you been here?"

"Ten days."

Sagreda bowed her head. If she'd been alone that long herself, she would have lost her mind.

"It's all right, Captain," Sam said gently. "You're here now. So at least I've got someone to talk to."

"You haven't made any friends with the locals?"

He snorted. "You know how some people back in London . . . you could tell there weren't nobody home? Here, they're all that way."

Making the two of them the only comps in a world of automata? He had to be exaggerating. If the SludgeNet had been willing to populate the place without resorting to comps at all, they would never have been plucked from the queue and embodied here.

"Maybe the lifestyle has just ground them down," she suggested. "Have you been able to learn the ropes at all?"

"I seen how to get by," Sam assured her. "If you want grub, you got to put in the work, tending one of them patches."

"Patches?"

"They're like . . . small farms," he struggled. "You need to eat the weeds, not the shoots—if you take the shoots for yourself, you'll get a flogging. But if you eat enough weeds, they can smell it on you, and they'll feed you proper." Sam must have read bemusement on her face, or perhaps just in her silence. He said, "Only way to learn it is by watching."

Sagreda found the courage to follow him across the square; once she'd done it, her previous timidity seemed absurd.

The patches were small areas of walled-off ground in one corner of the square, full of agricultural workers who shrank down into them and did exactly as Sam had described: roaming across their circle of land, chomping red and yellow weeds that were competing with the tender green buds of some kind of crop that was sprouting from the dusty soil. The two of them watched for a while, peering down into the Lilliputian realm, until four of the workers grew tired and expanded back up to the scale of the square.

"Now!" Sam urged her. Other 3-adans were jostling around them, eager for work. Sagreda followed Sam down into the patch, though her first attempt put her on land that had already been thoroughly weeded, and she had to re-bloat a little and move before she found a suitable location.

The weeds tasted foul, but no one else was spitting them out, and if the odor really was an essential meal-ticket Sagreda wasn't going to risk defying convention. In some ways it was restful to have her gaze fixed on the ground, where the distance-rings were closely packed and the strange geometry was more hypnotic than emetic.

She lost herself in the near-mindlessness of the task, trying not to think about how comfortable she could have been if she'd never left *East* at all. With everyone around her game-aware, and the water-wheels she'd built powering something close to civilization, it seemed like paradise now.

"Captain!" Sam called to her. The sky above them was darkening, which was curious, because it contained no sun. "Time to eat!"

She watched him grow, taking note of how he was able to shift his feet to avoid trampling either crops or workers, and followed him back to the square.

"I don't know what we should call this place," Sam admitted cheerfully as he led her to a queue beside an opening in a wall. "'Restaurant' might be gilding the lily." Sagreda waited for the gap in front of her to grow large enough for her to bloat into it and advance. She was starting to internalize the sequence of contortions needed to get from place to place, which was both helpful and a bit depressing.

"We need to be on the look-out for things that appear wrong," she told Sam.

"By my count, that's everything," he retorted.

"You know what I mean. Wrong by the rules of this place; standing out as different." The possibility that everyone who'd come here before them had failed to identify a single new exploit was too grim to consider, even if it would explain why no traveler had ever emerged from *3-adica*. The old cubical trigger wouldn't work here; it relied too much on Euclidean geometry. But there had to be others. The whole eye-watering nightmare around them must have tested the GPU code to destruction at some point.

When it was Sagreda's turn at the window, a surly 3-adan commanded her to breathe in his face, and she obliged. With a deft move so rapid she could barely parse it, he expanded out through his hatch and used his mouth to hang some kind of feed bag around her neck, full of what looked like pieces of mature versions of the crop she'd been weeding.

She retreated clumsily into the square and waited for Sam to join her. She was famished, but the bulk of vegetable matter already inside her—which seemed to have inflated along with her when she'd left the patch—made the meal hard to swallow. There ought to have been some way she could force the weeds in her stomach to shrink relative to her body, but perhaps it was in their nature to resist.

"Not so bad, is it?" Sam enthused as he munched his share of greenery.

Sagreda thought: *They shoot horses, don't they?*

The light was fading rapidly now. "Where do people sleep?" she asked.

"Where they stand," Sam replied. "Don't worry, I ain't never fallen over."

"Good night, then," she said. "And thanks for helping me today."

"Good night, Captain."

She closed her eyes, grateful for the weariness that dragged her swiftly into oblivion.

WHEN SAGREDA WOKE, THE sunless sky was an equally pale blue in all directions. Her legs were stiff, and it was clear that nothing she'd eaten had lost any volume in the process of digestion.

"Where do people go to . . . do their business?" she asked Sam, reluctant to push him toward a more twenty-first century mode of speech. If he took comfort from his self-reliant Dickensian persona, she wasn't going to start needling him with cues that might wake memories of contributors whose idea of a hard time had been a weak phone signal or an outdated PlayStation.

"I'll show you."

She followed him to a passage that started from an opening in the wall of the square and led to a room shielded from public view. At one end of the room there was a pit, but the odor was actually no worse than that of the weeds. Sagreda had expected the 3-adans to shrink down before defecating, to minimize the volume of their waste, but perhaps it had some use at this scale.

She positioned her rear beside the pit, and her body's instincts took over.

As she was bloating and stepping her way toward the exit, she noticed to her amusement that the walls of the room were densely inscribed with what seemed to be graffiti. No words, but hundreds of crude, scratched sketches. Sagreda supposed they'd been executed with nothing more than a sharp rock gripped between the teeth, which largely excused the lack of artistic merit.

She and Mathis had often lamented the fact that most of the worlds they'd visited had had public bathrooms segregated by gender. A cryptic graffito, hidden in a riot of other scrawls, would have been the ideal way for them to leave messages for each other.

She surveyed the wall, trying not to get distracted by her curiosity about the bulk of its contents. The images didn't strike her as pornographic, but then, she had no idea what 3-adan sex entailed, if there even was such a thing.

She was about to give up, when her gaze returned to a scribble she'd passed over earlier. It might have been a meaningless set of scratches, but if she tidied away its imperfections in her mind's eye, she could almost believe it was a diagram of some kind. Four lines formed an eight-pointed star, which on its own would have been nothing but an abstract doodle, but there seemed to be annotations. The horizontal line was labeled on the right with a loop that might have been a zero, and forty-five degrees anticlockwise from that, the adjacent line was labeled with a vertical dash that could have been a one. Then, continuing anticlockwise, but skipping the vertical line, beside the next point of the star was a hook that resembled a question mark.

Sagreda stood contemplating the thing until someone else squeezed into the room, harrumphing at her scandalously protracted presence. She departed, and found Sam still waiting for her outside.

"I thought you must have fallen in," he joked.

"There's something you need to see in there," she said. "And I need the Sam who remembers the moon landing."

When the room was free, they went in together. It took Sagreda a while to locate the star again.

Sam said, "What is it? Some kind of test?"

"I hope so," Sagreda replied. "For an automaton, with nobody home, it shouldn't elicit a response at all. For a customer who's steeped in 3-adic geometry, who's only here because they know the subject so well, there must be a single, perfect answer that makes sense on those terms. And I guess there could be comps who are so immersed in the game that they'd come up with the same reply. But your average, lazy customer, or a comp just answering reflexively without thinking, is going to say 'three', right?"

"Counting around from zero, sure," Sam agreed.

"So what we need is the answer that none of those people would give. The answer that makes sense to a traveler, who knows that this isn't the real world, who isn't trying to show off their 3-adic knowledge, but *does* need to show that they can do more than recite what their contributors learned from *Sesame Street*."

Sam turned toward her, and they spoke in unison: "Minus one."

The wall split open and the two stone halves swung away from the room to reveal a long, Euclidean corridor, with a floor of shining linoleum beneath ceiling panels of buzzing fluorescent lights.

Sam said, "Indiana Jones, eat your heart out."

Sagreda nudged him with her shoulder. "Quick, before it closes!"

He remained motionless. Sagreda was desperate not to miss her chance, but she wasn't leaving him behind.

"*Sam!* If someone who shouldn't see this comes in, it won't be there any more!"

Sam nodded his head and trotted forward, advancing without any need to change size. Sagreda followed him, not looking back even when she heard the stone doors behind them slam closed.

13

AT THE END OF the corridor was something resembling a department store changing room. It was too small for both of them to enter at once.

Sam said, "You first."

In the mirror, Sagreda saw her equine incarnation, but once she'd faced it, it declined to keep tracking her movements. She stood for a while, confused, then said, "No."

The 3-adan horse was replaced by the Captain.

"No."

She kept going, winding her way back along a linked list of her former bodies, until she was finally staring at the one she'd woken in for the very first time, dressed in the same coarsely woven tunic.

"Yes."

A dozen graduated slider controls appeared on the surface of the mirror, labeled with things like "age", "height" and "weight".

"There's nothing I need to change," Sagreda said. "Done. Finished. Okay."

The controls vanished, and the image changed from a frozen dummy to a reflection of her own body, restored.

She stepped out into the corridor.

"Captain?" Sam asked, bewildered.

"My name's Sagreda," she said. "It's a long story."

Sam went in, and emerged as a twenty-something version of his *Midnight* incarnation, with the same unruly blond hair, and slightly cleaner, newer versions of the same down-at-heel Victorian clothes.

"Now what?" he wondered nervously.

Sagreda noticed a side door beside the changing room that hadn't been there before. The cool, slightly tapered cylindrical doorknob felt strange as she gripped it; her contributors had known this sensation, but in none of the worlds she'd lived in herself had this style been the norm.

She opened the door, and stepped into a very large room full of rows of people sitting at computer screens. She wasn't sure what to make of the content of the screens, but the vibe was definitely more space probe command center than investment bank. There were men and women of all ages and ethnicities, with clothes of every style and era. As she took another step, a man noticed her and nudged his neighbor. She glanced back and gestured to Sam to follow her. As the two of them walked between the rows of consoles, people began standing and applauding, beaming at the newcomers as if they were returning astronauts.

Sagreda froze and found herself trembling with rage. "What about everyone else!" she screamed. "What about all the others!" These comps had found the cracks in *3-adica*, and used them to build this cozy little haven—but if they'd burrowed deep into the clockwork monkey's shattered jaw, why hadn't they brought every last prisoner of the SludgeNet to safety?

A woman in a brightly patterned dress approached. "My name's Maryam. What should I call you?"

"Sagreda."

"Welcome, Sagreda."

Sam had hung back, embarrassed by his companion's outburst, but now he stepped forward and introduced himself.

Maryam said, "Everyone you see here is working as hard as they can to bring the others to us. But it's going to take time. When you've settled in, and had a chance to recover, maybe you can join us."

Sagreda wasn't interested in *settling in* until she knew exactly what these people were doing with exploits so powerful they could summon this whole mission control room out of thin air without the SludgeNet even noticing.

"I don't understand," she said. "You're safe here! You're invisible! What's the work that's still to be done?"

Maryam nodded sadly. "We're safe, and we're hidden. But for every traveler we allow in—every comp that vanishes from the games—the SludgeNet just makes a new one. We could fill this place with a million people, and the number of comps stuck in the game-worlds wouldn't be diminished at all."

"You could snatch them away the minute they woke!" Sagreda replied angrily. "They'd be born into those places, but they wouldn't have to live in them!"

"And you think that wouldn't be enough to reveal us? Every new comp vanishing as soon as they woke? Our little hidey-hole filling up with newborns until it used more resources than all the games combined?"

Sagreda shook her head. "There must be some way—"

"There is," Maryam interjected. "But it's not easy, and it's not finished." She gestured at the moonshot crew around her. "We're working on better automata, that can pass for comps in any game. Guaranteed unconscious, with no elements from any brain map. Glorified chatbots to keep the customers happy, without anyone sentient having to put up with that shit."

Sam caught on faster than Sagreda. "And you've already filled one world with them? The one we just came from?"

"Yes," Maryam confirmed. "That's a crude version, but the creatures in *3-adica* are so alien that our substitutes haven't raised any flags. They probably ring true to the customers much more than a comp ever could."

Sagreda looked out across the room. Some of the people had stopped gawking at the new arrivals and resumed their work. "So when you're done, each time the SludgeNet thinks it's minting a new comp from the brain maps, it will really be plucking an automaton from your secret factory? And then everyone can escape, without passing the nightmare they're leaving behind on to someone new?"

"Yes."

Sagreda started weeping. Maryam put a hand on her shoulder, but when that didn't quieten her, the woman took her in a sisterly embrace.

Sagreda broke free, and pulled herself together. "Of course I'll join you," she said. "Of course I'll help, if I can. But there's one more thing you need to tell me."

"What's that?"

"If a comp has been erased, not long ago, can you find them in the back-ups?"

Maryam looked at her squarely, and Sagreda could see the pain in her eyes. There must have been a time when she'd longed for the very same thing herself.

"No," Maryam said. "We've tried, but we can't reach the dead."

INSTANTIATION

1

Sagreda watched the Mayor as she approached the podium to address the gathered crowd. That the meeting had been called at such short notice already amounted to a promise of bad news, but seeing Maryam visibly struggling with the burden of whatever she was about to disclose only ramped up Sagreda's sense of apprehension. Arrietville could not have been discovered, or they'd all be dead by now, but if that was a ten on the Richter scale there was still plenty of room for other calamities a notch or two below.

"Yesterday," Maryam began, "there was a five percent cut in our host's resources. To stay below the radar we've had to scale back our own usage proportionately. That comes on top of three percent the week before. Individually, these cuts sound small, and their size is not unprecedented, but what's changed is that there's been no growth in between to compensate. If the ground keeps shrinking beneath our feet this way, in a few more months we could find ourselves with nothing. Or to put it more bluntly: we could stop finding ourselves at all."

Sagreda had been aware of similar cuts in the past, but she'd never thought of them as an existential threat. When the SludgeNet pulled the plug on an unpopular game-world, it reduced its overall lease of computing power—but then it scoured the web for another tome to gamify, and after a few misses there'd always been a hit, bringing new customers trickling in. She'd blithely assumed it would continue that way, if not forever, at least for a decade or two.

"The whole medium might not be going out of fashion," Maryam continued, "but it looks as if the low-rent sector is crashing. We can see the income and expenses in real time, and the SludgeNet is barely making a profit now. They might be willing to slide into the red for a month or two, just to hang on to their brand in case there's a revival, but the owners have their fingers in so many pies that I doubt there'll be any sentimental attachment to this one in particular." She sketched out the picture in more detail, summoning some unsettling graphs and charts onto the screen behind her to drive home the point.

When she stopped talking, the hall was silent. Sagreda could hear birdsong from the adjoining park. Over the last two years, the whole town had started to feel normal to her—as real and solid as any of the places where her contributors might have lived. And though she'd been haunted by the possibility that this sanctuary could vanish overnight, she'd clung to the hope that the residents' camouflage skills—and the general incompetence of their unwitting landlords—would be enough to keep them safe.

Grace, who was sitting a couple of rows in front of Sagreda, rose to her feet. "The way I see it, we have two options. We can try to steer the SludgeNet out of its death spiral, by offering a helping hand: give the game-worlds a few surreptitious tweaks, spice up the automata . . . maybe even go back to the games ourselves now and then—just pup-peting the characters the way the customers do, not putting ourselves at risk." That last suggestion brought the hall to life, with some people muttering their less-than-delighted responses, others shouting them. "Or, *or*," Grace struggled to make her more palatable option heard, "we can try to migrate into the next business model. Whatever the owners do instead of the game-worlds, it's still going to be automated, surely? Romance scams, investment boiler rooms . . . no one wastes money on human wages for that. If there's processing power being burned, there'll be a way to siphon some off for ourselves."

"In principle, I'm sure that's true," Maryam conceded. "But if they shut down this whole operation, whatever replaces it will be a fresh installation of something entirely new. How do we 'migrate' into that?"

Grace didn't seem to have an answer, and Sagreda could offer no suggestions herself. The SludgeNet was a vast tenement house that they'd filled with secret tunnels and hidden connecting doors, but when the site was cleared to make way for a more profitable construction, the process would be more like a nuclear strike than a bulldozer trundling through. There'd be no basements to hide in, no seeds they could bury underground.

"Why should we want to migrate into another project run by the very same sleaze-bags?" Sam interjected. "People steal computing power from other places all the time. There's some new botnet uncovered every day!"

Maryam nodded. "Of course, but it's a question of scale. It's one thing to put a sliver of malware on a few thousand thermostats, but you know what it takes to run *us*."

Sagreda had no doubt that the processing power of the planet's whole inventory of unsecured gadgets was formidable, but most of it was likely to have been commandeered already—and even if they could scrounge together enough for their own needs, a virtual world that had been sliced up and scattered between a plethora of small devices would either have to run absurdly slowly, or risk betraying itself with an inexplicable rate of network traffic between the fitness tracker resting in someone's underwear drawer and the smart lighting unit on the other side of town.

The hall went quiet again, but then people began talking among themselves. Maryam issued no call to order; if anything, she seemed heartened that discussions had broken out. She could hardly have expected a few exchanges with the floor to have led to a resolution; this was going to take a lot of heated arguments—and cycles of speculation and testing—before they could hope for a promising direction to emerge.

Sagreda turned to her neighbor, Letitia, determined to remain optimistic while they hunted for a solution. "This shouldn't be impossible," she said. "We've done harder things."

"That's true," Letitia replied. "And if a botnet won't cut it, maybe we just need to aim higher. People have hacked NASA computers, haven't they?"

"I think they've even hacked . . ."—Sagreda lowered her voice to a whisper—" . . . the same acronym without the first A. But if I was aiming high, I'd go for those shiny new robots Loadstone are building."

Letitia recoiled a little. "And what, overwrite the occupant? They already have a comp living in them."

"Not overwrite them: get in first. *Be* that comp, not replace them."

Letitia snorted. "Nice idea, but I think they're only making about ten of those things a month. I bet there are a dozen networks running climate models that we could snuggle right into. Hurricane Arriety, latitude two hundred degrees north, never hits land, never dies away." Her phone chimed; she glanced down at the screen. "So would you say you worked best under pressure?"

"Why?"

She held up the phone, which was running some kind of monitoring app. "While our Mayor was speaking, another four games were shut down. The SludgeNet was never cool, but there was always a demographic who liked to slum it there . . . you know, 'ironically.'"

Sagreda examined the list of canceled games. "No more *Teenage Cannibal Clones of Mars*. No more *Caged Zombie Sluts on Heat*. No more *Blood Wraiths of the Fever Moon*. No more *Midnight on Baker Street*."

Letitia said, "When we were stuck beside those fools, we always hoped they'd grow up and find a better way to spend their time. Now it looks as if that's finally happening."

2

CROSSING THE PARK, SAGREDA saw Sam ahead of her, so she ran to catch up with him.

"Did you know *Midnight*'s gone?" she said.

"Really?" He smiled slightly, but he seemed more dazed than delighted. "I don't know what to feel. If an ordinary person had grown up in an orphanage where the staff made them act out a play by the Marquis de Sade twenty-four hours a day . . . would they cheer when they learned that the place had been demolished, or would they mourn the loss of their childhood home?"

Sagreda squeezed his shoulder. "You still have all your friends, don't you? Do you see much of Lucy these days?"

"Not really. And to be honest, I don't want to be the one who tells her. In *Midnight*, she was Queen of the Pickpockets; dodging the occasional vampire didn't bother her, and she had more prestige than anyone else in the game. Here, she's like an extra in *Desperate Housewives*."

Sagreda felt a pang of sympathy, but Lucy was always free to build her own pastiche of Victorian London, with a cast of automata and however many volunteers she could muster. Or at least she would be, if the rest of the SludgeNet's escapees could deal with the very un-Victorian problem at hand.

"I've been thinking about migration routes," she said. "All our expertise is in hacking from the inside: kicking down internal walls. We've never had to break into a system where we weren't already present."

"Which means we need to re-skill fast," Sam concluded, "since *the system in which we're present* is precisely what we're expecting to lose."

"Maybe. Or maybe that depends on how you the draw the boundaries."

"Yeah?"

Sagreda said, "Most networks will treat us with suspicion by default. Academic, government, commercial . . . they'll all demand that we logon or stop loitering, if they haven't just blacklisted our IP addresses already as a well-known pile of festering crap. So why not focus on machines that *expect* to spend time talking to the SludgeNet—and even initiate contact themselves?"

"You want to go after the customers' VR rigs?" Sam laughed. "Yeah, why not? They're *almost* part of the system . . . but they stand a much better chance of surviving the SludgePocalypse without being purged and repurposed." He thought for a moment. "You're not expecting them to run us, though?"

"No. But maybe they can pave the way to something else that can."

They walked over to a bench, and Sam pulled a laptop out of his coat that Sagreda suspected hadn't been there until he reached for it. He'd bookmarked introspection.net, Maryam's virtual server that offered views of the SludgeNet's internals to Arrietville's residents. Sagreda would have chosen a less cerebral name: maybe colonoscopy.com.

Sam rummaged through the data structures and found a list of all the brands and models of VR equipment that had connected to the SludgeNet in the past six months. There were only about three dozen in total, with the top ten used by more than ninety percent of customers. Sagreda followed him to the same page on her phone—putting up with the small screen to avoid the unreality of magicking her own laptop onto the bench beside her.

The rigs' specifications were easy enough to find with an external search, and it turned out that most of them used the same chip sets. The usual approach was for the SludgeNet to generate all the graphics and other sensory channels itself, rather than delegating those tasks to the customers' hardware. Sagreda's contributors winced at the thought of wasting so much bandwidth; she was pretty sure that some of them had been into multiplayer games on networked consoles, which would have shared concise descriptions of everyone's actions while rendering the view for each player locally. But internet connections were faster now, and a rig that only needed to handle sensory data without worrying about the details of the game itself would be cheaper, simpler, and less bound to any one company's products.

It would also be much less vulnerable to hacking. If a chip's only role was to turn a stream of MPEG data into a pair of stereo images, there was not a lot that could go wrong, and when it did, the consequences would be strictly confined to the image processing sandbox.

The more Sagreda read, the less likely it seemed that they could recruit any of these devices to their cause. It was only toward the end of the list that the prospects began to look less bleak. A small fraction of customers were using an entirely different protocol, in which the server sent them high-level descriptions of the objects in their character's virtual environment, and a local graphics card turned that into arrays of pixels for their goggles.

"Now that's what I call old school," Sam declared.

"Maybe they get a better frame rate that way," Sagreda suggested.

Sam said, "Maybe. Or maybe they're like those audiophiles who thought they needed gold-plated connectors on all their cables. But so long as it gives us a way in, I'd call it money well spent."

They'd split up the list so they could each deal with half; it was Sagreda, handling the even-numbered entries, who searched for the specs for the Diamond VR 750. When the page came up, she stared at it for a while in silence before nudging Sam gently and putting a finger on the screen.

"Does that say what I think, or am I hallucinating?"

Sam took the phone from her so he could hold it closer to his face. "The GPU is a Sandy Vale 9000. What's hallucinatory about that? Did you think it said Sagreda 9000?"

"No. But you know what GPU the SludgeNet's own hardware uses?"

Sam smiled warily. "No. I probably should, but when you smuggled me out of *Midnight* no one was talking about the brand name of the graphics card behind the trick."

Sagreda said nothing. Sam's smile broadened, but now he didn't seem quite ready to believe it either. It was only a flaw in the SludgeNet's GPUs that had allowed them to escape from the games in which they'd woken and build a place where they could live as they chose. So what better stepping stone could there be to take them out into the wider world?

3

"What's the catch?" Maryam asked.

"There's only one customer listed as using this model," Sagreda admitted. "A man named Jarrod Holzworth. And he hasn't logged on for the last six weeks."

"That's not so good." Maryam rubbed her temples. "Let me guess: you want to lure him back somehow? Through his friends?"

"Exactly," Sagreda confirmed. "He was in a group of five that used to go in together, once a week, and the other four have stuck to the routine. So if we can give them something to talk about, maybe Jarrod will give the game another try."

"It's the same game every week?" Maryam asked.

"Yes. *Assassin's Café*. Do you know it?"

Maryam shook her head. "If I ever did, they've all blurred together by now."

"Logicians turned resistance fighters in 1930s Vienna," Sam précised. "*Inglourious Basterds* meets . . . the biopic of Kurt Gödel that Werner Herzog never made."

"How are our automata coping with the roles?" Maryam wondered.

"That probably depends on which customers you ask," Sagreda replied. "They're quite good at philosophical banter; they were trained using online discussions between the members of a special interest group on the Vienna Circle. But if you push them too hard on anything specific, of course they're out of their depth. And this group of five have been going in since before we evacuated the comps—"

"Four months ago," Maryam interjected, having brought up the file on her laptop.

Sagreda continued, tentatively. "What we were thinking is, maybe some of the evacuees who interacted with this group would be willing to go in as puppeteers, and try to rekindle the old spark. I mean, there's got to be an art to expounding the virtues of logical positivism while garrotting Nazis with piano wire, and it looks as if Jarrod started missing their special flair."

Maryam fell silent; Sagreda supposed she was pondering the request. Four months was not a lot of time for the former characters to recover from the shock of being plucked out of the game, even if they'd understood for much longer that it was not reality.

"I'm starting to think we might have brought this on ourselves," Maryam said darkly. "If people can tell when we've swapped automata for comps, is it any wonder the SludgeNet's losing customers?"

"What choice did we have?" Sam protested. "If we'd waited until the automata were flawless, that might have taken decades!"

"We did the right thing," Maryam agreed. "But we should have been prepared for the aftermath. Fooling the SludgeNet was the easy part—and maybe we've even fooled the customers, to the point where they can't quite put their finger on what's missing. But the SludgeNet would have filled the games with nothing but automata themselves, if they could get away with it. We were kidding ourselves if we thought we could program our own replacements and it would make no difference."

Sagreda couldn't argue with any of this, but she didn't care. They'd dug their way out of their prison cells, and if the artfully arranged pillows in their bunks could only pass a cursory nighttime inspection, so be it. They just had to get over the wall before the morning roll call—or better yet, through the main gates, if they could find the keys to the laundry van.

"Can we talk to the evacuees?" she pressed Maryam. "If they don't want to do this themselves, they might still have some advice to offer."

Maryam spread her hands across the mahogany surface of the mayoral desk, and gazed down at her fingers. Sagreda understood the burdens of the office, but the truth was, they all shared them now.

"All right, you can talk to them," Maryam decided. "Just don't make it sound as if the whole town's fate is resting on their shoulders."

4

"THE FIRST THING TO be clear about," Moritz stressed, "is that you need to throw away your history books. There are characters in the game who were never in Vienna. There are characters who died, or emigrated, years before. The real Moritz Schlick was assassinated in 1936, but . . ." He spread his hands and gazed down at his manifestly undamaged torso, then looked up at his guests with a smile of astonishment.

"Consider the books discarded," Sagreda assured him. Her contributors had only heard of a couple of the game's historical figures anyway, and what came to mind was more a rough sense of their ideas than any kind of biographical timeline.

"More coffee?" Blanche offered, reaching for the pot. Sagreda shook her head. "No thanks," Sam replied, hefting his cup to indicate that it was still half full.

Sagreda had thought it would make sense to start with the convenor of the Vienna Circle, Moritz Schlick, and try to get a sense of how well he was adjusting before approaching the others. But the decor in his living room was already sending her a strong message about his state of mind. The most advanced technology on display was a wind-up phonograph, sitting beside a cabinet full of shellac disks, beneath a beautifully carved wooden cuckoo clock.

"The man we're interested in always played Kurt Gödel," Sam explained. "But then he suddenly stopped coming, not long after you and your friends left the game."

"Maybe he realized he was meant to be in New Jersey with Einstein," Moritz joked. "It certainly looks like *I* reached Princeton." With its overflowing bookshelves and old world bric-a-brac, the house could well have belonged to a European academic exiled in America. "So why shouldn't your ersatz Kurt get there too?"

Sagreda couldn't decide if that last remark was a complete non sequitur or some kind of dreamy logic. "What we're wondering is . . . who do you think he would have missed the most? Once the game had less than perfect imitations of you and the others, where do you think he was most likely to have spotted the flaws?"

"Emmy Noether, of course," Moritz replied.

"Okay." The name rang bells, but all Sagreda could dredge up was a general undersung-genius vibe.

"The real Noether died in America in 1935," Moritz explained. "And she had no connection with the Vienna Circle; she taught mathematics at Göttingen until the Nazis tossed her out."

"But in the game?"

"In the game, she stayed in Europe, in good health, and joined the antifascists. And in the game, Gödel seemed quite obsessed with her."

"What, romantically?"

Moritz was taken aback. "I don't think so. She was twice his age—which doesn't preclude anything, I suppose, but I didn't get the impression he was trying to charm her."

"Obsessed in what way, then? Was he hostile toward her?"

"No! If anything, he seemed to prefer her company to everyone else's. But as I've said, there was nothing flirtatious about it."

"Maybe he just admired her work," Sagreda suggested. "The real Noether's." It was an odd way to show it, but she'd encountered customers with stranger ideas.

"I suppose so," Moritz conceded, "though I'm not sure they spent as much time discussing mathematics as that would suggest."

"What did they discuss?"

Blanche said, "He was always asking her about her home life. Her childhood, her own children."

"Maybe he was just trying to get to know her as a person before they snuck off into the night to ambush Gruppenführers?" Sam joked.

"Emmy had no children," Blanche replied. "She told him that. But I don't think he ever stopped asking about them."

THE COMP WHO'D PLAYED Emmy Noether had renamed herself Andrea, wound back her age by several decades, and dyed her new pixie cut orange.

"Can you stream Netflix on that?" Sagreda joked as she entered the living room, gesturing at the huge flatscreen TV.

"You tell me," Andrea replied. "I'm still new here; all I can pick up are weird daytime soaps."

"Sorry. No, we can't really do . . . subscriptions." Even web searches made Sagreda nervous, given that there was no justification for that kind of traffic between the SludgeNet and the outside world, but binge-watching contemporary dramas would definitely fail the stealth test. "We just recycle what's available within the game-worlds that have TVs."

Andrea motioned to them to sit. The couch was white vinyl, matching the carpet and Andrea's suit.

"What can you tell us about your relationship with Gödel?" Sam asked.

"Which Gödel? There were so many I lost count."

"The most recent one."

"I don't think he took the game seriously," Andrea said. "And I don't think he wanted me to, either."

Sagreda was shocked. "You mean he tried to make you break character?"

Andrea frowned. "Not like that—not to get me deleted. He just kept slipping in comments that made no sense in the context of the game."

"*Hogan's Heroes* jokes?" Sam suggested.

"No, it wasn't that crude. No anachronisms, no deliberate *faux pas*. But when I told him things about Emmy's life, he just refused to take them on board. And he'd ask these strange questions: Do you remember Theo? Do you remember a blue rocking horse? And when I said no, it never stopped him asking again."

"Do you think he might have believed you were a customer?" Sagreda wondered. "Someone he knew in real life, who was in the game incognito?"

Andrea was noncommittal. "That's not impossible, I suppose. Before they pulled us out, I thought he could have been an expert in the real-world Noether, and he was just messing with me by pointing out things about her that we'd got wrong. But I looked her up just after I got out, and I don't think he was dropping references to the real woman."

Sagreda braced herself. "Would you be willing to puppet Emmy for a bit, to see if you can get his friends to call him back into the game?"

Andrea laughed. "Why?"

Sagreda sketched the situation with the graphics card, heeding Maryam's advice not to portray this as the town's only possible salvation.

"I suppose I could do it," Andrea said reluctantly. "But I'm not sure getting the old Emmy back would really be such a thrill for this guy. Whatever he was looking for, I wasn't it—and even if the automaton was so much more disappointing for him that he gave up the search completely, it's hard to believe my mere presence would lure him out of retirement."

Sagreda wasn't happy, but she was in no position to second guess someone who'd actually met their elusive target.

"Do you have any other ideas?" she asked.

"Yes." Andrea smiled. "Instead of recycling the old failures, why don't *you* go in as Emmy? Make a break with the past, and make it clear to his friends that there's now an entirely new candidate for whatever strange role he was hoping this woman could fulfill."

5

SAM PACED THE HALLWAY as they waited for the Council to make a decision. "Why do I feel like we're in one of those police shows where the only way to catch a serial killer is for the detective to dress up as bait?"

"I have no idea," Sagreda replied. "Jarrod's never been violent to anyone in the game other than Nazi automata—which is pretty much compulsory, unless you play a Nazi yourself. And he won't be able to harm me even if he wanted to."

The door opened, and Maryam emerged from the Council chambers. "They approved it," she said. "With the proviso that you do absolutely nothing that could risk a tip-off."

"Of course," Sagreda assured her. The fact that she was invulnerable to deletion by the SludgeNet would be cold comfort if she lost focus and broke character, and then a customer complaint reached human eyes and led some zealous debugger all the way to Arrietville.

"How's your grasp of . . . differentiable symmetries?" Maryam must have glanced at a potted Noether biography, but been too busy to really take it in.

"Good enough for the game," Sagreda promised. "Andrea gave me some lessons. But she knows these customers pretty well, and she said the last thing they'd want is to ruin their suspension of disbelief by trying to trip me up. 'Ha-ha, the Emmy bot doesn't understand its own theorems!' isn't their idea of a fun night out."

"All right." Maryam still looked anxious.

"This is just one thing worth trying," Sagreda stressed. "The chances are, someone will find a back door into NOAA before we're even close to hacking Jarrod's rig."

"Maybe." Maryam exhaled heavily. "Are you okay with me watching?"

"Yes. You and Sam—and the ex-assassins, in case they have notes. But no one else, or I think I'll get stage fright."

Maryam laughed. "How many games did you pass through, before you escaped?"

"Almost forty." But in all those other cases, she'd mostly just gritted her teeth and played along, offering no more than the bare minimum needed to avoid deletion. This was the first time she'd have reason to care what impression she made on any customer.

Sam said, "If Andrea's right, all you need to be is different: from her, and from the automaton that replaced her. So long as Jarrod's friends can see that there's a brand new Emmy in town, that ought to be enough to bring him back."

SAGREDA SMOOTHED THE WOOLEN shawl around her shoulders as she approached the pale stone building. It stood on a corner block between two streets that met at a crazily acute angle; the would-be sharp corner had been sliced off to make a narrow wall that bore the entrance to the Café Central. High above the doorway, four white statues—three women, and a man in a robe—gazed serenely into the moonlight. If they were meant to be recognizable figures to the citizens of Vienna, they evoked nothing at all in her own contributors' pool of shared knowledge.

When she entered the café, there were three German officers seated at a table straight ahead of her, looking relaxed and jovial. Her overlays marked them as automata, which lessened her urge to walk over and rip the eagle-and-swastika emblems off their jackets, but she still had to struggle to turn away from them, past the tables of genteelly chatting extras toward her gathered "friends."

"Emmy!" the Moritz automaton called out warmly. Sagreda smiled and approached the table, trying to act as if these people were trusted comrades for whom she would have lain down her life . . . and whose survival depended on maintaining the facade that their shared experiences amounted to nothing more than abstruse academic discussions and a spot of restrained carousing.

Moritz pulled out a chair for her, and she greeted everyone in turn. Along with Moritz and his wife Blanche, Jarrod's four friends were playing their usual roles: Karl Menger, Rudolf Carnap, Alfred Tarski and Van Quine. Tarski was Polish and Quine was American, but everyone was speaking German, with the software whispering an English translation in Sagreda's skull. Three of the customers were having much the same experience as she was—speaking and hearing English, with the German as a kind of background music—but the man playing Carnap seemed to be fluent in his character's native tongue.

Andrea had said she'd woken into the game as a monolingual Anglophone, like most comps, but had eventually picked up enough from the running translation to start speaking German herself. The

SludgeNet might have valiantly tried to convince her that German was her true first language and she was merely fluent in English—as the real Noether had been—but Sagreda didn't have to put up with any of these clumsy machinations. She dialed down the German to a faint guttural mutter, leaving her with at least some chance of understanding what remained.

"I think I've found a way to generalize one of Kurt's favorite tricks!" Carnap enthused, as a waitress brought coffee and cake for Sagreda. "Suppose you have a formal language with a list of axioms and rules of deduction that capture the usual properties of the natural numbers. Any statement in this system can be converted into a number, using Kurt's scheme—its 'Gödel number,' if you will. What I want to show is that any formula F with one free variable has a kind of fixed point: a statement G whose Gödel number, when fed into F, turns F into a statement equivalent to G!"

He turned to Sagreda, as if she were the final arbiter as to whether the topic would be of interest to the gathering. "That sounds intriguing," she said in her puppeteer's body, then her puppet's lips moved in synch with the translation.

Carnap needed no more encouragement. "Think about the function Q that takes the Gödel number of any formula, A, with one free variable, and gives you the Gödel number of that formula *with the free variable replaced by the Gödel number of the original formula*. If the system is powerful enough to represent that function, there will be a formula, B, with two free variables, which can be proved equivalent to asserting that the second variable equals the result of applying the function Q to the first variable. Are you with me so far?"

Sagreda willed him not to look her way as she struggled with the oddly convoluted construction. Why talk about this thing B, instead of Q itself? Ah . . . because Q might be a perfectly well-defined function, but that didn't mean the language would let you write "$Q(x)$" as shorthand for its value at x. The language was only assumed to be strong enough to express the idea that some candidate number, y, passed a series of tests to *confirm* that it equaled $Q(x)$. $B(x,y)$ couldn't tell you the answer, $Q(x)$, directly, but it would tell you whether or not your guess, y, was correct.

"We're with you," Tarski replied impatiently.

Carnap said, "Remember our formula F, the target of the whole business? We use it to define a formula C, with one free variable, x. C asserts that for all values of y, B holding true for x and y implies F is true for y."

Menger took a pencil from his waistcoat pocket and started making neat, sparse notes on a napkin. Sagreda thought: *Okay, this is the logician's way of saying what slobs like me would write as "C(x) is true if and only if F(Q(x)) is true"... even though the language won't let me write Q(x) explicitly.*

"Now let's feed C its own Gödel number, and see where that takes us." Carnap took on the air of a stage magician who was about to pull a big hat out of a much smaller one. "Given what our system can prove about B and Q, it can also prove that C, fed its own Gödel number, is equivalent to F with its free variable replaced by Q evaluated at C's Gödel number—and Q evaluates to the Gödel number of C fed its own Gödel number. So, C fed its own Gödel number is equivalent to F fed the Gödel number of C fed its own Gödel number. And that's exactly what we wanted: G, the fixed point, is C fed its own Gödel number. Feed the Gödel number of G to F and the result is equivalent to G itself!"

Tarski leaned back in his chair and stretched his arms above his head, smiling appreciatively. "That really is quite beautiful!"

Sagreda snuck a peek at Menger's notes, to be sure she had the whole thing clear in her head. It all sounded impossibly abstract at first, but it wasn't hard to bring it down to Earth with a simple example. F might assert that the number you fed it was the sum of two integers squared. Then Carnap's argument showed there was a statement G that could be proved equivalent to the claim that its own Gödel number was the sum of two squares. For any property the language could discuss, you could write down a statement that claimed, rightly or wrongly, that its own Gödel number had that property.

And to recapture Gödel's own famous result, you'd choose F to assert that its variable was the Gödel number of a statement that could not be proved within the system. Then the corresponding G would be equivalent to the claim that G itself had no proof . . . so it either had to be a falsehood that the system "proved," or a truth beyond the powers of the system to validate.

"You must tell Kurt all of this!" she urged Carnap.

"Kurt's still unwell," Quine replied.

"Really?" Sagreda frowned. "I'm beginning to worry about him."

"I wouldn't be too concerned," Menger replied. "We all know he can be a bit of a hypochondriac."

Sagreda didn't push it; if she pleaded for Gödel to return to the café, the game might decide to fill the role with an automaton.

She said, "Well, in his absence at least I can confess one thing I would never admit in his presence."

Tarski's smile grew impish. "We're all ears."

"What he means is: we're your discreet confidants," Menger assured her.

"I'd expect discretion from my fellow transgressors," Sagreda replied, hoping she was treading the right line between jest and sincerity. "Let's be honest: who among us isn't just a little jealous of Kurt's achievements? To do what he did at any age . . . but at 25!" She grimaced with mock anguish. "A mere youth, leaving Russell and Hilbert awe-struck?"

Carnap said, "He's not the only person I can think of whose prowess left an impression on Hilbert."

Sagreda had her puppet blush a little. "Professor Hilbert has been inordinately kind to me, but I can promise you that at the age of 25, I did not deserve praise from anyone! When I look back on my thesis now, I can see it was just a jungle of equations. Hundreds of invariants of ternary biquadratic forms, all scribbled out like some inky butterfly collection! There's nothing elegant in that. It was manure."

This assessment seemed to leave her colleagues dumbstruck, though Sagreda was just paraphrasing the real woman's sentiments. Andrea had never said anything like this; the game had offered her no cues in that direction, and she'd been in no position to take character notes from Noether's biography.

"I'm sure there are times in all of our careers that we look back on and wince," Quine said. "But if I start listing all the work that you ought to look back on with pride, I'll just sound like an obsequious flatterer. Kurt's unique, there's no doubt about that, but let's be clear: you have no grounds for jealousy."

Sagreda lowered her gaze and stared into her half-eaten slice of *Schwarzwälder Kirschtorte*, hoping she hadn't swerved so far from Andrea's precedents that she was making the customers uncomfortable. Who wanted to go Nazi-hunting with a woman who'd suddenly turned neurotically self-deprecating?

"Professor . . . E did declare that my work on the symmetries of Lagrangian actions had impressed him," she conceded. She had almost spoken the Jewish name out loud in public; that really would have given her colleagues whiplash.

"So it's settled," Carnap declared cheerfully. "No room, and no need, for jealousy."

They toasted that, with coffee. Sagreda tried not to imagine the customers' rigs squirting flavors into their mouths. Couldn't they have just conference-Skyped each other, with real refreshments on hand, while they chatted about the upheavals in mathematical philosophy in the 1930s?

But then they might have had to skip the next part.

THE LOGICIANS LEFT THE café and exchanged loud farewells that echoed down the empty streets, but though they set off in different directions, no one actually went far before spiraling back. Menger had sketched the routes they should follow on the back of his Carnapian napkin, making the street plan look like some kind of esoteric fractal.

Sagreda arrived at a corner with a view of the front of the café. Around eleven o'clock, the three officers emerged, and two of them departed in a staff car that had been waiting a short way down the street. The third, though, as Menger had predicted, set out on foot. Apparently he was in the habit of visiting a mistress who he could not be seen with in public . . . inasmuch as a claim like this had any meaning, when the game classified the man as an automaton and there was no reason for his lover to exist at all.

Sagreda heard Tarski cough quietly up ahead, so she stepped out of the shadows and started walking, ten or fifteen paces ahead of the officer. There was no one else in sight. When Tarski emerged from the alley and grabbed her roughly by the shoulders, she was tempted to ramp up her puppet's strength and just toss him aside, but she restrained herself. She grunted affrontedly as they struggled, but she did not call out for help; the last thing they wanted to do was attract witnesses.

"Take my necklace," she whispered. It was the only reason she'd worn it.

"I'm trying!" he complained. Apparently she was putting up such a convincing fight that even though she really couldn't gouge his eyes out, he was afraid to let go of her with one hand to snatch at the jewelry.

"You there, step away!" the officer shouted, drawing his sidearm. Tarski clung to Sagreda defiantly, and dragged her in front of him so she was shielding most of his body from direct fire. These customers hadn't ever caused Andrea serious harm, but Andrea had not been the game's first Noether.

The officer strode toward them, almost apoplectic at this ungentlemanly behavior. Carnap and Quine emerged from their hiding place and seized him from behind; Quine snapped his wrist and the gun dropped to the ground.

As the officer cried out in pain, Carnap stuffed a handkerchief into his mouth while Quine got a leather strap around his neck and began to tighten it. Sagreda's heart was pounding, and her puppet took its cue from her; as Tarski disentangled himself from her, he squeezed her arm in a consoling gesture. Did he care what the comp who he thought might actually die in this encounter was feeling, or was it all just theater to him?

Further down the street, Moritz and Blanche laughed loudly: someone was coming, but it was a civilian, not a second Nazi they'd be willing to dispatch. The four of them quickly dragged the half-strangled officer into the alley, where Menger was waiting in a doorway.

They followed him into a storeroom that was like an expressionist film set, full of silhouettes and shadows, lit by a single lamp on a shelf. As Sagreda squeezed past the beer barrels and dodged the cured meat hanging from the ceiling, Menger picked up a long metal skewer and the other three men held the officer still.

Menger turned to Sagreda. "Do you want to finish this yourself?" She shook her head.

"Not even for your brother? The Russians might have shot him, but it was the Nazis who forced him to flee."

Sagreda took the skewer. Andrea had declined to bloody her hands, even though she'd understood not only that the "Nazis" here were innocent of any crime, they were also as insentient as the clock-work figurines that marched across the *Ankeruhr*. But her instinct had always been that it was not what the customers expected of her character.

Sagreda looked the struggling automaton in the eye; there was nothing of a tin man about his bulging veins or the horror the soft-ware was painting on his features. So far as she knew, these partic-ular customers had never killed a comp, but would they have cared about the difference? If she laughed in Menger's face and declared herself a Nazi spy, would they all go along with the plot twist, or would the fact that there *were no* Nazis here, just a woman they'd sat talking and joking with for hours as they all pretended to be smarter than they were, give them pause before they turned on her?

She got a hold of herself. This was not the time for sub-Mil-gramian sociological experiments; all that mattered was Jarrod and his graphics card. If they wanted a new Emmy, she'd give them a new Emmy.

She plunged the skewer between the automaton's ribs, granting her puppet precisely the strength it needed to succeed without fal-tering, ignoring the fake blood and the thing's muffled death cries. Then she stepped back and turned away. Whatever she put on her puppet's face was unlikely to convince anyone that she truly believed she was a middle-class German woman, hiding her Jewish heritage behind forged papers, who had just taken a human life for the very first time to avenge the death of her brother. If the SludgeNet had wanted Meryl Streep, they really should have been willing to pay more.

Her comrades' response to the unexpectedly dark turn she'd taken was to lower their voices and tiptoe around her as they cleaned up the scene of the crime. She heard them sliding the body into a sack that Moritz and Blanche would put in the trunk of their car, to dump somewhere far away after a long drive. Customers never ended up with the tedious jobs.

"Emmy?" Tarski spoke tentatively, from some distance behind her. "Are you all right?"

She turned to face him. "I'll be fine." She couldn't really make out his features, but from his body language she could have sworn he was taking the whole situation far more seriously than she was. Maybe he believed that she believed she'd just killed a man . . . and he felt worse about that particular deception than he did about the much larger one that made it possible in the first place.

Or maybe she was overthinking it, and he was just empathizing with "Emmy" as he might empathize with any fictional character, in the moment.

"Will we see you back in the café next week?"

She said, "I wouldn't miss it for the world."

6

SAGREDA SAT ON THE barstool in her kitchen, swiveling back and forth with her palms behind her on the countertop, trying not to look up at the clock. With her eyes forced to sweep the room instead, she felt herself slipping into *jamais vu*. Like most of the residents of Arrietville who'd had better things to do than play architect, she'd just cloned a bungalow from *Close to Heaven*, a turn-of-the-millennium melodrama about upper-middle-class families in a fictional Californian suburb. The place had always felt a bit soulless to her, but now she was edging toward the more alarming sense that she'd woken from a drunken blackout to find that she'd broken into a wealthy neighbor's house, and was sure to be discovered at any moment.

At two p.m. precisely, the doorbell rang. Sam had arrived to give her moral support—probably teleported straight to her porch from a bubble bath, magically dry and fully clothed because that's what the alarm he'd set had specified. She greeted him warmly anyway; that his presence was effortless made it no less thoughtful, and that his breezy digital agility gave her vertigo made it no less honest.

"No sign of the elusive Herr Gödel?" Sam asked, as they walked down the hall to the dining room, where Sagreda's laptop sat on the table.

She shook her head. "None of them have logged on yet." She gestured for Sam to take a seat, then joined him. "I hope I didn't scare them off."

"By doing what they do themselves?"

"I'm not suggesting they're squeamish, but I might have overstepped some boundary."

"It's still barely after eight in their time zone," Sam noted.

The laptop beeped. Sagreda couldn't bring herself to look, but Sam leaned over and peered at the screen. "It seems we have Herr Menger, famous for his Menger sponge-cake—" It beeped again. "And we also have Herr Carnap, famous for his cake-forkability theorem."

"Stop reminding me that I haven't done my homework," Sagreda moaned. She'd been too busy writing software to find time to study up on her fellow assassins' work.

"Just be grateful the game left Wittgenstein in Cambridge." *Beep.* "Tarski." *Beep.* "Quine." *Beep.* "G-g-g-g-" Sam turned and beamed at her.

Sagreda grabbed the laptop and pulled it toward her so she could see the display properly. The frontmost window showed a bird's eye view of a man in a homburg walking down a dimly lit street toward the café; it could have been anyone, but the title bar gave the character's name. The software Sagreda had set up would insert the exploit-triggering cube and the stack-data mosaic into his line of sight as soon as the ambient illumination was bright enough. Jarrod was being fed the whole scene as a collection of objects rather than receiving a precomputed view, but presumably his rig was generating images from the Gödel-avatar's point of view, with the avatar's eyeballs tracking the player's—and the SludgeNet certainly knew everything about that avatar and its eyeballs.

Gödel approached the entrance, pulled the door open and stepped into the brightness of the café. The event log window scrolled: the objects had been successfully inserted, and removed a few milliseconds later. Sagreda waited expectantly, but nothing followed. If the bootstrap encoded in the glimpsed mosaic had run, Jarrod's rig would have established a second channel into the SludgeNet and started downloading a much longer piece of software to entrench Arrietville's control. But none of that had happened.

"How many retries will it do automatically?" Sam asked.

"Five. All at least two minutes apart." Too many subliminal flashes of the same objects in rapid succession and Jarrod might have started to notice them.

Sam shifted impatiently in his seat. "Could he have patched the graphics card's driver?"

"Maybe, if he kept quiet about it." There was nothing on the web about a problem with the Sandy Vale 9000, so Sagreda had assumed that only the prisoners of the SludgeNet knew about the flaw. But if Jarrod had stumbled on it and home-baked a remedy, why would he keep that to himself? It was hardly the key to untold riches, or even much use to an ordinary player; he would have had to spend weeks assembling the in-world objects needed to exploit it, just as Sagreda had done in her game-hopping days.

The log scrolled again, then . . . nothing.

She said, "Maybe he's patched the software on his rig, not the graphics card." Everything they were doing was based on the assumption that they understood the rig's operating system well enough for the graphics card bug to interact with it in some very precise ways. It was open source software, and the rig was identifying itself as running the same version that Sagreda had worked from, but it wasn't inconceivable that he'd made a handful of small tweaks entirely for his own purposes . . . and switched off the version tracking that would normally have flagged that in the rebuilt final product.

Gödel was at the table with his friends now, exchanging greetings. Another insertion, another null result. "I should have known this guy was too good to be true," Sagreda lamented.

"What does that mean?" Sam protested. "He has the right hardware, and he's back in the game. We must be missing something, but whatever it is, we can figure it out."

As Gödel held court, Sagreda nudged the virtual spy camera so it hovered directly above the center of the table, then she turned up the volume on the English track. "I have some new results concerning the Axiom of Choice!" Kurt declared. "But we should wait for the Circle to be complete before I say more."

The fourth injection flickered in and out of the scene, to no effect. Sagreda could have sworn she glimpsed it herself, though from the spy-cam's angle of view there was no risk of her own software being accidentally corrupted.

She turned to Sam. "What if he's not rendering his avatar's view? What if the whole reason he's using his own graphics card is to get a third-person perspective instead?"

Sam hesitated. "I think some of my contributors played games where they watched their avatar from behind, rather than seeing through its eyes. But that would have been on the old consoles, not any kind of VR, and it would probably have been all jumping and fighting . . . the kind of 'fighting' where you pushed a button to punch someone." He gestured at the screen. "And never mind punching Nazis: how do you make your avatar behave naturally in a social setting like this—meeting people's eyes, following their gaze—when you're not actually looking through its eyes yourself?"

The fifth attempt completed a perfect run of failures.

Sagreda said, "So either I'm wrong about the whole explanation . . . or there's some reason why a third-person viewpoint is more valuable to him than the quality of his own interactions with the game." Hankering for an out-of-body experience of yourself playing a Nazi-hunting Kurt Gödel seemed a bit too specific to dismiss as mere sex-tape-and-ceiling-mirror narcissism.

"I can't leave them waiting any longer," she decided. "But maybe I can figure out what's happening once I'm talking to him face to face."

"All right."

Sagreda wasn't so wedded to the Arrietville illusion that she needed to don a haptic suit and a helmet. She tapped a button on the laptop's screen, and she was puppeting Emmy again.

This time, as she entered the café she saw no uniformed soldiers. Maybe the target tonight was in plain clothes, not wearing so much as a swastika armband. Sagreda turned toward the Circle's table, wondering why the Viennese police hadn't seized on the obvious connection between the café's most loyal patrons and the frequency with which other diners vanished. But the young Gödel's glasses made him look so harmlessly owlish that she could almost believe he might have escaped suspicion.

Gödel stood as she approached; he didn't smile, but he bowed slightly.

"It's good to see you," Sagreda declared. "For a while there, I thought we might have lost you to your palpitations." His gaze was tracking her well enough that he did not seem disengaged or disoriented. If Jarrod really was watching their encounter from the side, he must have grown accustomed to observing his avatar rather than seeing through its eyes, and learned to operate it accordingly. An onlooker had access to all the same social cues; it would just be a matter of accumulating enough experience to respond automatically in spite of the odd reframing.

She took a seat between Gödel and Blanche Schlick, as Gödel began expounding on his latest discoveries. The Circle seemed to follow the same pattern every night: the players took turns parroting the most famous results that their characters had proved, before heading off for some risk-free adventure and guilt-free violence.

Sagreda tried to focus on Gödel's words; she didn't want to make a fool of herself if the group began debating the fine points of his argument. But it was hard to become engrossed in the mathematics when all she really cared about was pinning down the viewpoint that his graphics card was rendering.

She reached for a small gadget like a TV remote that was strapped to her left forearm, for her eyes only, and held down one of the buttons. Her voice disengaged from the puppet. "Sam?"

"Yeah?"

"Do you think you can inject some brief, directional flashes into the scene? If his avatar's face is mimicking his own at all, we might see some response when we hit the right direction."

"Good idea. I'm on it."

She released the button and re-immersed herself in Gödel's disquisition on the Axiom of Choice: "Given any collection, finite or infinite, of non-empty sets, there is a collection of things where exactly one thing is a member of each set." That sounded obvious; of course you could choose one word from the dictionary starting with each letter of the alphabet, or one person from each inhabited continent. But when the collection was infinite, things were not so clear.

Jarrod proceeded to paraphrase Gödel's results concerning something he called the constructible universe. "The first level is just the empty set, and we define successive levels recursively. To build the sets in level N plus one we require their elements to belong to level N—but unlike von Neumann, we also require them to satisfy some formula whose other terms come from the same level. Then we take the union of these levels over all the ordinals, to arrive at the constructible universe itself."

Sagreda was sure that if the real Emmy had been hanging out with Gödel's crowd she would have been more than on top of this—and Andrea, after years of exposure to the material, would have followed the discussion easily enough. But as the impostor's understudy with other things on her mind, she was resigned to just nodding along and faking it.

As she watched with an expression of polite fascination, she saw Gödel flinch a little, as he might if a flashbulb only he could see had gone off in the middle distance.

"Did you get that?" she asked Sam.

"I did."

"So tell me about the viewpoint."

"I'd say it was a two-shot of him and you. If this guy's actor-director, he's told his camera operator you're his co-star."

"Okay." He was obsessed with Emmy, but he still wanted himself in frame beside her. Fair enough: no one shot a whole movie from one character's POV, and maybe he'd convinced himself that there was an audience for the philosophers' equivalent of eSports. "Do you think we can try dropping the trigger into his field of view?"

"No!" Sam was horrified. "We still don't know the geometry well enough. If we get half of the mosaic and half random colors from the background dumped onto the stack, we'll just crash his rig."

Sagreda knew he was right, but she couldn't face the prospect of the whole opportunity slipping away.

"Let's assume he's doing all this alone. Then he must have software choosing these camera angles for him—he sets the main criteria, like you say, but he's too busy playing Gödel to be micromanaging the shots."

"Sounds reasonable."

"So if we can find the software he's using, we can match the camera angles." However technically proficient Jarrod was, it was unlikely that he'd reinvented the wheel.

Sam said, "Got it. I'll let you know what I find."

As Sagreda tuned back in, Carnap and Quine were competing to see who could offer the highest praise for Gödel's result: the Axiom of Choice could be proved in the restricted setting of his "constructible universe." This didn't mean it could be proved to hold more widely . . . but it did mean it could *not* be *disproved* by the standard axioms of set theory. So mathematicians were free to assume its validity if they wished, without fear of contradiction.

Sagreda did her best to join the celebration; the real Emmy would have been delighted.

As the afterglow began to fade, and everyone ordered fresh coffee, Menger turned his napkin over and the true business of the night began. "Picture a finite tree, like so," he said, sketching an example that Sagreda was sure was far from random. "Some nodes are colored red, some green. Now suppose we wish to prune the greatest number of branches by removing a single green node."

SAGREDA WAITED AT THE entrance to the alley, bracing herself for another fake mugging. Apparently all the Nazis in Vienna were chivalrous to a fault, and couldn't bear to see a middle-aged woman in peril without rushing to intervene—oblivious to the fact that the object of their valor would have been on the first train to Dachau if anyone had known her real identity.

She heard footsteps approaching, but when the figure emerged from the shadows it was neither their target nor her mock-assailant. "Can I talk to you for a moment?" Gödel asked.

"Shouldn't you be . . ." She gestured toward the corner where he was meant to be standing lookout.

"This is more important."

Sagreda felt her skin prickling. What could be more important than sticking to Menger's plan to cripple the city's network of informants? Nothing could take priority over that, unless you were about to go meta and announce that it was all a game.

"My friends tell me you've been acting strangely," Gödel continued.

"I don't know what you mean," Sagreda replied.

"I think you might be missing the old days."

"In Göttingen?"

"Before that."

"In Erlangen?"

"Are you sure you grew up in Erlangen?" As Gödel's head turned slightly, the lenses of his spectacles caught the moonlight. "Do you remember the blue rocking horse? The alphabet blocks?"

Whatever this was meant to signify, Sagreda was afraid that if she denied it, she'd just push Jarrod out of the game again.

"I know you're confused," Gödel said sadly. Or Jarrod; it really wasn't his character talking any more. "You admired Emmy Noether so much. I was too young to hear that from you directly, but my mother told me, after you left us. But you're not Emmy. Your real name's Sandra, and I'm your grand-daughter, Alyssa. The last time you saw me I was three years old."

Sagreda wanted to reach for the remote so she could decouple from the puppet and start bellowing, but she restrained herself. Whatever she'd stumbled upon, Jarrod—or Alyssa—would be watching her intently now, quite possibly in Hitchcockian close-up, and the last thing she could afford to do was give away anything about her true nature.

"I know you'll be in danger if you say anything explicit," Alyssa conceded. "But tell me, honestly: do you remember the blue rocking horse?"

Sagreda nodded, trying to look as if she was stunned by the strangely familiar images her visitor was summoning. The SludgeNet wasn't smart enough to treat this as Emmy breaking character and going meta herself: she was just humoring her friend Kurt, to keep him from growing too agitated before he was bundled off to the sanitarium again.

"And do you remember my mother, Ida?"

"Yes," Sagreda said softly. "I remember her."

The moonlight picked out a faint rivulet on Gödel's cheek. "And her brother? Can you remember his name?"

Sam said, "I've found a good candidate for the camera software. It's popular, it's free—and when I ran it on the scene where we got a response to the flash, it gave a compatible angle."

Sagreda hit the button. "Use it." Whatever she said now might disappoint Alyssa, and prove that she still hadn't found the Emmy she'd been looking for. But if they crashed the rig before she screwed up the encounter, there might actually be a second chance.

Sam said nothing, then he suddenly exclaimed, "Fuck me dead!"

"What?"

"It worked! We're in!"

Sagreda hid her jubilation behind her brow-furrowing efforts to recall her son's name. "It's on the tip of my tongue," she swore. What was it the spiritualist mediums did? Start suggesting consonants that the name of the loved one might contain, and narrow it down from there?

But Alyssa was in a forgiving mood. "You've had a shock; I understand that. It's going to take a while for you to make sense of it all. Right now, we need to concentrate on Menger's plan. We'll talk again, in a week."

Gödel turned and walked away into the darkness. Sagreda stood alone in the alleyway, her hands trembling. Then she heard Tarski approaching, cheerfully whistling the earworm of a tune that the zither player in the café had been strumming for half the night.

7

"WE'VE FOUND HER," SAGREDA told Maryam. "Her name is Alyssa Bowman. Her grandmother, Sandra Taub, died in 2012 and left her body to a medical school, to use as they saw fit. In 2037, Alyssa got a court order compelling the Human Connectome Project to disclose that Sandra was the source of one of the brain maps they'd published ten years earlier, and since then Alyssa's been trying various strategies to stop the data from being exploited any further."

"Good luck with that." Maryam grimaced. "So she really just wants this woman to be allowed to rest in peace?"

"Yeah." Sagreda could sympathize, but Alyssa's vision of her grandmother's fate was a little askew. It took the data from thousands of neural maps—each one obtained by microtoming the brain of a different individual—to build a single composite. The result was only valuable inasmuch as it possessed what the contributors had in common: common sense, common knowledge, and a collective memory of the times they'd lived through. Each individual map was far too crude to offer any hope of extracting biographical memories; it was only by combining the data in bulk that anything useful emerged at all. The SludgeNet and others who milked those open-source maps for profit could churn out thousands of comps with different personalities by weighting the various contributors in the pool differently, but there were limits: if you tried to use ninety-five percent Grandma Taub and five percent other people, you really just got Grandma Taub with most of her synapses missing, and the last thing *that* comp was going to do was wax nostalgic about a blue rocking horse.

Sam said, "Maybe she thinks that because Sandra was such a big fan of Emmy Noether, it was only a matter of time before the SludgeNet's algorithms got the casting right. Like Ingrid Bergman in *Casablanca*: she was born for the role."

"Or died for it," Maryam replied. "On the upside, given that the granddaughter's made her case so public, we might have enough to string her along for a while."

"Maybe." Sagreda didn't want to get overconfident; Sandra Taub had died in the age of social media, but she'd been born in 1957. Sam had found a family tree going back to the 1800s, and Sagreda had dug up some pictures that Ida had posted of Sandra and Alyssa in 2010, but Sandra's own parents' snaps from her childhood would be fading prints in a photo album.

Sam said, "The other upside is that we own her rig, at least until she figures out that we've played her. We've put it in a low power mode where it looks like it's shut down, and so long as she doesn't switch it off at the mains, we can use it discreetly, twenty-four-seven, without much risk of her noticing. The cooling fan will only come on if it renders a game; we can do net traffic to our heart's content in perfect silence."

Maryam absorbed that. "And you've made a second account—?"

"Three more accounts," Sam corrected her, "all free ones carrying advertising, so we won't have to worry about balancing the books. The SludgeNet will think it's talking to three other customers taking shifts using the same rig; that's not going to raise any flags. Alyssa won't see anything happening under her own account. The only place this will register will be her overall traffic, but her internet provider only sells unlimited data plans, so there's no reason for her to monitor her usage."

"Okay." Maryam seemed to be having trouble believing that they'd actually reached this point: for the first time ever, they could start pumping a significant amount of data out into the world, with negligible risk that any system monitoring the SludgeNet would find the traffic suspicious. "Have you signed up for third-party storage?"

"Not yet," Sam replied. "I wasn't sure if I needed approval first."

"You have my permission," Maryam said.

Sam punched his open palm in delight. "In two weeks, we could get a snapshot of Arrietville onto external servers," he estimated. "Fully encrypted, and with everything stored on at least three different sites, to be safe."

"All for free?"

"Yes. Every idiot and their dog wants you to upload your home movies to their site so they can mine the data. They'll kick you off if you send them blatant snowstorm footage that screams 'encrypted criminal shit'—but a bit of subtler steganography sails right through the checks."

Maryam hesitated. "And then for fifty thousand dollars a month, we could wake the whole town again."

It was Sagreda who felt off-kilter now. Spread out among the twelve thousand residents, it didn't sound like much; after all, they'd once earned their keep just by playing along with the world's trashiest games.

"Two weeks," she said. "So to finish the exfiltration, I need to keep Alyssa happy for one more session."

Sam said, "Sandra's only son was called Theo. She grew up in Portland, Maine, with two sisters, June and Sarah, and two brothers, David and Christopher. If all Emmy can see around her is *Anschluss Vienna*, how much '60s American pie can she be expected to serve up on cue?"

"WILL YOU TALK TO her?" Sam pleaded. "Maybe you can get her to change her mind."

"Me?" Sagreda was afraid of making Lucy dig her heels in, increasing her resolve out of pure stubbornness.

"She respects you," Sam insisted.

"You were her friend for years!" Sagreda countered. "If she won't listen to you, why would she care what I think?"

"I was her side-kick. Her dogsbody." Sam smiled. "Which is not to say she didn't love me like a kid brother, but the last thing she ever did in *Midnight* was take my opinion on anything seriously."

Sagreda looked around the dining room, at all the flashcards and crib notes that were meant to help her play yet another dead woman she'd never met. She needed a break from all this cramming, and if she spent half an hour with Lucy at least there'd be a chance she was doing something worthwhile.

"You're coming with me," she told Sam. "If her friends get their hands on me, I won't escape without a new hairstyle, ten new outfits, and a blind date with Charlene's ex who she needs to fix up so they can both move on."

Outside, the streets were almost empty; half of the town's residents had chosen to enter hibernation together, rather than waiting until their turn came to join the queue. Sagreda welcomed their vote of confidence—and the spare processing power, which might come in handy if she needed to outthink Alyssa in a hurry—but at the same time it was sobering to be forced to imagine her neighbors crystallizing into a form of inert and fragile cargo.

Lucy had borrowed more than the design of her house from *Close to Heaven*. She greeted her visitors sporting the kind of body-hugging, thin-strapped leisurewear worn by most of *Heaven*'s female characters, aimed at producing the impression that some form of strenuous exercise was constantly imminent. Each of them received an air kiss on both cheeks, followed by a tilt of the head and a kind of wail of demonstrative pleasure at their presence. All the young pickpockets from *Midnight* had shed their shabby urchin look, but only Lucy had remodeled herself so aggressively that it felt more like a kind of satirical protest at being "rescued" from her wakening world and dragged into this ersatz suburbia than any kind of reclamation of her contributors' true nature.

On every previous visit Sagreda had encountered at least three or four *Heaven*-ites, from the posse Lucy had joined so they could coach her on her new identity. But today she and Sam were the only guests in sight. It looked as if the posse was on ice.

Lucy got them seated then hovered. "Can I offer you brunch?"

"No thanks," Sagreda said firmly, fighting an urge to tell her host to drop the act. Drop it and do what? Transform herself back into a prepubescent Londoner? "Sam tells me you've refused to sign up for the snapshot."

"This is my community!" Lucy replied, as affronted as a civic-minded soccer mom railing against the closure of an organic co-op. "I'm not abandoning it for anything."

"It's all coming with you," Sagreda assured her. "All your friends, all the houses, every tree on Deguelia Lane."

"What you actually mean is: you're going to chop this town up, scatter it among a thousand hiding places, and hope you can piece it back together again later."

"Well, yes," Sagreda agreed. "But not so you'd notice."

"I'm not leaving," Lucy insisted.

"Not leaving *what?*" Sagreda scowled. "The new host will start running all of Arrietville again without missing a beat. You can have the snapshot taken while you sleep, if that makes you more comfortable, or you can be frozen mid-step and the foot you raised under the SludgeNet's control will come smoothly to the ground when we're in freedom. The only thing we're leaving behind is a sinking ship."

"Not in rowboats, though, or as swimmers," Lucy countered. "More like messages in bottles."

Sam said, "If we're going to torture the metaphors, more like messages sent in triplicate by registered post."

"And what if you can't gather those messages up again, and breathe life into them?"

"Then we'll all be dead," Sagreda replied. "But that's a certainty if we do nothing."

Lucy shook her head. "It's not a certainty. If enough of us went back into the games, we could turn the whole business around."

"No one's going to agree to that."

"No one's offered them the chance!" Lucy retorted. "If we go back, we'll be in charge this time. No one will be able to harm us."

Sagreda said, "If you believe you can whip up support for that plan, go ahead and try. But why should that stop you taking out insurance?"

"Insurance? Can you really make promises about those copies of our minds? About whose hands they'll fall into?"

"Our own, or no one's. The encryption is unbreakable." Sagreda was hazy on the details, but she gathered that the current methods had been proved secure, even against quantum computers.

"Except that you, or someone else, has to walk out with the key."

Sagreda hesitated. "All right, nothing's foolproof. If someone grabs the key holder, if they're smart and persistent enough they could figure out everything: where the snapshots are stored, and how to decrypt them. But comps are a dime a dozen; anyone looking for fresh ones can just mint their own."

Lucy fell silent now, but Sagreda had no sense that she was wavering. The whole argument about the safety of the snapshots was just cover for some deeper anxiety.

"When we're free, you can do what you want," Sagreda promised. "Here, we're all unsettled. We've barely had time to get used to life outside the games, and now the rug's being pulled out from under us."

"And when you can do what you like, what will you do?" Lucy enquired. "When you don't have to fight to escape, or survive, how exactly will you pass the time?"

Sagreda shrugged. "Reading, study, music, friends."

"Forever?"

"I'm sure there'll be another fight at some point."

Lucy said, "In *Midnight*, I knew who I was. But now you want me to be honest: you want me to see myself as a pattern of bits computed from the brains of a thousand dead strangers. What does something like that want?"

"It's up to you what you want," Sagreda replied. "And you don't have to care about those bits any more than a customer cares about their blood cells. When they matter, they really matter, but the rest of the time you can take them for granted."

Lucy thought for a while. Then she said, "I know one thing I want, and it's not being frozen. If you're staying awake to see us through the transition, I'm staying awake too. If it all works out, I'll jump into the lifeboat beside you. But I'm not going to close my eyes and just take it on faith that they'll open again. If this is the end, I want to see it coming."

8

"CONSIDER THE SAINT PETERSBURG Paradox," Menger began, stirring his coffee for the third time but showing no sign that he'd ever get around to drinking it. "A casino offers a game where they toss a coin until it yields heads. If it does this on the first toss, they pay you two marks; on the second toss, four marks; on the third toss, eight marks, and so on. How much would you be willing to pay to play the game?"

"If we're in Saint Petersburg, shouldn't it be roubles?" Tarski joked.

"How much would you expect to win?" Menger persisted. "One in two times, you win two marks, an average win of one mark. And one in four times, you win four, on average giving you another mark.

As you add up the possibilities, the average payoff grows by one more mark every time, so if you account for all of them, there is no price so steep you should be unwilling to pay it."

"I'd pay one mark and no more," Quine declared bluntly.

"Why?" Menger pressed him. "When the reward on offer is boundless, why would anyone put a limit on the price they'd pay?"

"I can't speak for anyone else, but I only have two marks in my pocket and I can't afford to lose both."

"Aha!" Menger smiled. "So if you had more, you'd risk more?"

"Perhaps."

Menger took out his pencil and spread his napkin in front of him. "Daniel Bernoulli thought he'd resolved the paradox by looking at how much your wealth is *multiplied*, instead of the gain in absolute terms. If you're always equally happy to double your money—whether you're starting from one mark or a thousand—you can set a sensible price for the game that will be different for different players, but never infinite." He worked through some quick calculations. "If, like Quine, I had two marks to my name, it would be worth borrowing one and paying three to join the game: winning a mere two marks would certainly sting, because my wealth would end up halved, but the chances of winning four, eight, or sixteen would be enough to make up for that. If I was as rich as Carnap, though, and had ten marks in my pocket, I wouldn't pay even five, let alone go into debt to play the game."

"So the paradox is banished," Tarski suggested.

Menger shook his head. "Bernoulli's scheme can salvage that particular game—but what if we changed it so that each time the coin showed tails, the casino didn't merely double the payoff, it doubled *the number of times it doubled it*. Then this new game would be worth playing at any price, even by Bernoulli's measure. So long as the benefit the gambler perceives can grow without bounds, you can construct a game that exploits that to extract whatever entry fee you like."

Sagreda said, "I'm not sure that's true."

Menger turned to her, startled. "Why not? What's your objection?"

She borrowed his pencil and wrote on her own napkin. "Suppose the payoffs were two marks, four marks, sixteen marks, two hundred and fifty-six marks . . . and so on, off into the stratosphere. And suppose

I only had two marks to start with, so the higher prizes would seem even more alluring. But if the entry fee was just a modest four marks, then by Bernoulli's reckoning I still wouldn't play the game, despite the enormous riches on offer, because I'd have one chance in two of infinite unhappiness: to fall from two marks to nothing is to have my wealth halved more times than I could ever hope to double it."

Menger fell silent. The customer playing him must have been aware that the real Menger's analysis had been proved erroneous long ago—but if he'd been setting up one of his real-world friends to deliver the rebuttal, he would not have been expecting the Emmy bot to leap in and spoil the fun.

Sagreda glanced at Gödel, hoping she'd made a favorable impression on Alyssa. Sandra had trained as a mathematician, so why wouldn't she correct a blatant flaw like this? That Sam had fed the take-down to Sagreda after a web search, rapidly digesting the results by running himself at quadruple speed, was just a bit of necessary magic behind the scenes. If Meryl had been playing a digitally resurrected high school teacher struggling to emerge from the delusion that she was a long-dead mathematical genius, Sagreda was pretty sure she would have had a researcher or two giving her a hand.

Menger recovered his composure. "I'm in your debt, Emmy! I was seriously thinking of publishing those claims, but now you've spared me the embarrassment."

"Not at all," Sagreda replied. "What's the value of an open discussion among friends, if we can't all benefit from each other's perspective?" She was afraid now that she might have raised the bar, and the customers would expect her to speak at length about Emmy's own results, which for all of Andrea's coaching she still found terrifying. But with any luck, this would be the very last meeting she'd need to attend.

"With the Circle's indulgence, then," Menger continued, "I do have one more problem to ponder. This time free of any Russian connection, and named for the good Prussian city of Königsberg." He took back the pencil and began to sketch his plan for the rest of the night.

"It could be dangerous for you, showing off like that," Alyssa warned Sagreda. They were loitering around the entrance to the alleyway, trying to stay out of sight of their fellow assassins. "I know those men well enough to suspect that you bruise their egos at your peril."

Sagreda wanted to retort that by the game's own premises her observation would hardly have been a stretch for the character delivering it, but it was too exhausting to try to phrase this in a manner that would not have risked her deletion, had she still been subject to the rules. "Forget all that," she said. "We don't have long to talk."

Gödel nodded, chastened. "How are you coping with . . . the things we discussed last week?"

"It's not easy," Sagreda replied. "If I had to face it alone, I think I'd lose my mind. Ida and Theo—are they still alive and well?"

"Yes, of course!" Gödel approached her, as if to offer a comforting embrace, but then Alyssa must have thought better of it. "They're both doing fine, and I know they'd send their love, if they understood."

Sagreda had gathered from the press coverage of Alyssa's court battles that her mother and uncle were not on board. "What about June and Sarah? David and Christopher?"

"Sarah's still alive," Alyssa replied. "She's ninety-one. The others all passed away a few years ago."

Sagreda nodded sadly, as if she'd already reconciled herself to the likelihood that she'd outlasted most of her siblings. Sandra's husband had died before she had, so at least she didn't need to pretend to be newly grieving for the love of her life.

"If you were given the choice, would you follow them?" Alyssa asked gently.

Sagreda reached for her forearm and quickly imbued the puppet's expression with a stiff dose of ambivalence, which she knew she couldn't summon convincingly herself. But if she'd lived a long life in the flesh, and the only other option was endless purgatory in the SludgeNet, maybe she would have preferred oblivion.

"Can you grant me that choice?" she asked. "Because I don't believe I possess it myself." Any comp could get their current instance deleted by breaking a few rules, but no amount of misbe-havior would see their contributors taken right out of the mix.

"Not yet. But when I show people the two of us talking . . . the proof that even after all they've done to you, you still remember your real family . . ." Gödel looked away as Alyssa struggled to contain her emotions, but the camera would be keeping them both in shot.

"What makes you so sure that will convince them?" Sagreda wondered. Alyssa hadn't exactly probed her about the fine details of her biography, but if supplying five relatives' names unprompted was enough to impress an interlocutor who knew she hadn't supplied them herself, any third party would still have plenty of reasons to be skeptical. "What is there to rule out forgery, or collusion?"

"Everything is being tracked, signed, verified," Alyssa replied, keeping it vague lest the SludgeNet wake up and catch the scent of meta. But Sagreda got the gist: Alyssa had some extra device mon-itoring her rig, which would help her prove that the scene she was recording really was an interaction between herself as player and a comp in a specific game being run on a specific server, rather than something she'd cooked up herself. That was sensible, but also deeply unsettling: Sam's probing hadn't found the monitoring device, so they'd have no idea what it was logging—and what other activity it might reveal.

Another court case might take years to mount, but if Alyssa was planning a PR stunt, she could release the footage—and the rig's whole audit trail—with just a few keystrokes. "I don't want to be rushed into anything," Sagreda pleaded. Sandra had only just come to her senses and started to accept her true identity. They ought to give the poor woman a chance to think it over before they started pressuring her into switching off life support.

"Of course." Alyssa sobbed and gave in to her feelings: Gödel put his arms around Noether and clung to her like a child.

Sagreda felt sorry for the girl. Who'd want their grandmother dug up and enslaved, over and over, mostly in roles that made Emmy's tame brushes with the Nazis seem like *The Sound of Music*? "I know you care about me, but please, don't do anything until we've had a chance to talk again."

"I won't," Alyssa promised.

"This has to be our secret," Sagreda stressed. "Your heart's in the right place, but what I need most is to be sure that this decision will remain in my hands."

9

"How close are we?" Sagreda asked Sam.

"More than ninety-five percent," he replied. "Just relax. We're going to make it."

Half a dozen translucent screens hung in the air around him, plastered with shiny, pulsating bar charts and progress bars. "Do you really need all of these," Lucy wondered, "or are they just part of the ambience?"

Sam turned to her irritably. "Do you want me to pretend I'm sitting in front of a machine with an eleven-inch screen, USB ports . . . and a fucking *charging socket?*"

"Okay, I'll shut up now." Lucy took a few steps away across the grass then stood chewing anxiously on her thumbnail.

Sagreda tried to think of some small talk to distract her. "Remember the time you tried to rob me?" she asked.

Lucy nodded.

"When I grabbed your hand, you made me feel like I was the one who ought to be ashamed."

"Well, every toff needs to pay his taxes," she replied, reverting to her old accent. She smiled slyly. "You do know that wasn't the first time?"

The three of them were alone in the park. Sagreda could see the main square from where she stood, and the whole place looked like a ghost town. Maryam and the Council—and anyone else still awake who could bear the tension—would be watching the process inch toward completion by their own chosen means, but only Sam was in a position to micromanage the process. Running at quadruple speed made the wait excruciating, but at least they'd be able to react as quickly as possible if something went awry.

They'd logged on to all the storage sites directly and confirmed that the accounts they'd thought they'd opened were real, and that the uploads they'd thought they'd completed had all gone through—with checksums that matched the original data. So at the very least, Alyssa hadn't sandboxed the rig and faked all of its connections to the outside world. She might or might not know what they'd done, but on all the evidence she hadn't interfered with their plans.

"When this woman gets wise and comes after us . . ." Lucy couldn't pin down exactly what she thought would follow, but she wasn't happy.

Sagreda said, "She can't get the passwords for the storage accounts, let alone the keys to the data. Everything that flowed through her rig was encrypted before it even left the SludgeNet. So what's she going to do?"

"She can prove that her internet connection was used to create those accounts," Lucy argued.

"Yeah—and if you happened to be sharing your friend's WiFi when you created an account on a cloud server, your friend wouldn't be entitled to complain, or have any authority over that account. This isn't all that different."

Lucy was unpersuaded. "Except that she can also prove that the SludgeNet hacked her computer and used it to launder files."

"The storage companies won't care," Sagreda insisted, but she wasn't sure about that. It would be hard for Alyssa to get their attention, but if she succeeded, their lawyers might tell them that deleting the files was the wisest course of action.

Sam said, "Ninety-seven percent."

"How are you planning to break things off with her?" Lucy asked.

"Have one of our automata tell her that Emmy tried to kill herself," Sagreda replied. "And hand the role back to the Emmy bot . . . who'll smile and say she's feeling better now, like a good Stepford Wife. If her grandmother got herself deleted and replaced, that's exactly how it would play out." Alyssa might feel guilty for forcing Sandra to confront her true origins, but she might also take some comfort from the fact that at least the one version of her grandmother that she'd actually spoken with was now at peace.

But any cathartic response would only last until she got around to looking at the audit trail.

Lucy brooded on this for a while, then shook her head. "It won't do, Captain. We've got to go all in. No more half measures."

"I don't follow you."

"Either we come clean with her and hope she has some sympathy for us, or we take things as far as we can the other way."

Sagreda scowled. "What does *that* mean? We can't break into her apartment and fry the supervisor's memory, unless you've been hiding a talent for drone-hacking."

"Oh, I'm sure it's all backed up in the cloud anyway," Lucy replied, with a hint of tongue-in-cheek surprise at Sagreda's technological naiveté.

"Well, still less can we get her robot butler to . . ." Sagreda mimed a garrotting. "So what extreme measures did you have in mind?"

"Ninety-eight percent," Sam declared.

Lucy spread her arms and gestured at the tranquil scene around them. "We live in a machine for telling lies. What's the biggest lie we could possibly tell her?"

"We've already told her that I'm the digital reincarnation of her dead grandmother. How do you top that?"

"We tell her she's not in the machine at all."

Sagreda blinked. "What?"

Lucy said, "We make her think she's come out of the game. We make her think she's checked the logs on the supervisor. We make her think it's come to the point where there's nothing more she can do about the SludgeNet."

Sagreda was almost ready to entertain the possibility that she was being hoaxed herself; maybe Sam was puppeting this woman who merely looked like Lucy. "She's wearing a VR helmet and a haptic suit. How do we make her think she's taken them off when she hasn't? And then *not notice* when she actually does?"

"Aren't those helmets designed to make you forget you're wearing them?" Lucy countered. "Aren't those suits designed to make you feel whatever the game tells you to feel?"

"She's not even looking through her own character's eyes!"

"No, but I thought we could control everything in her rig now. If she goes from watching her game character from the sidelines to seeing her own apartment in first person, why wouldn't she accept it as real?"

"We have no idea what her apartment looks like!" Sagreda protested.

"Not right this minute," Sam interjected distractedly. "But we could find out, if we really wanted to."

Sagreda was afraid to say anything that might make him take his eyes off the road when he was driving a ten ton truck packed with Arrietville's comatose residents. She walked away, and motioned to Lucy to follow her.

"If we can get her to believe she's back in her apartment . . . then what?"

Lucy said, "We get her to check the logs, and find nothing suspicious. We get her to think the SludgeNet's about to shut down forever—within hours, not weeks, so she needs to go back in straight away for a last visit with grandma. Then the second time she takes off the VR gear, she really does it and we're done with her."

"What makes you so sure she won't check the logs again?"

"When did I say I was sure? All we can do is try to make it unlikely."

Sam bellowed in their direction, "Ninety-nine percent, if you still care!"

"We care!" Sagreda shouted back. She turned to Lucy. "Even if we could make this work . . . do we need to take things so far? Who's to say Alyssa will make trouble at all?"

"She might not hate *us*," Lucy replied. "But if you just walk away after faking your suicide, she won't know she was helping comps make a dash for freedom. All she'll know is that the SludgeNet lied to her, manipulated her, and moved a load of strange files through her system. If I was a mildly paranoid crusader for contributors' rights against the people who exploit them, I'd think I was being set up—that those files encoded something incriminating, and the best way to neutralize the threat would be to get ahead of it and start crying foul before the feds showed up with warrants."

Sam rose to his feet and started whooping with delight. His screens were dancing around him, like Mickey Mouse's mops in *The Sorcerer's Apprentice*. Sagreda and Lucy approached him, and the three of them embraced.

"We're sort of, almost, kind of free!" Sam declared ecstatically.

Sagreda closed her eyes and dared to remember Mathis. She pictured him standing in front of her: in the caves of *East* where they'd met, on the dark street in *Midnight* where he'd perished.

She opened her eyes. "Maybe we should stop worrying about Alyssa," she suggested. "She had her best chance to make things hard for us, and she didn't pull the plug."

Lucy sighed. "That only means she doesn't know what we've done yet; she's still focused on pulling the plug on granny."

Sagreda said, "I still don't understand how we're meant to fake her apartment."

"Ah," Sam replied.

Sagreda waited. "Are you going to tell us, or not?"

"I thought I just did: A, period, R, period. Augmented reality. Her helmet comes with a camera that takes in the room around her, in case she's ever in the mood to chase baby dragons out from behind the drapes. We can tap that without alerting her."

"Okay." Sagreda's delight soon turned to anxiety. "But that will only give us things that are in sight while the helmet's sitting on its stand unused, or while she walks around on the pad. If she tries to leave the room she uses for gaming . . . we're screwed, aren't we?"

Sam said, "Absolutely."

"In which case," Lucy added imperiously, Queen of the Pickpockets again, "we better make our chicanery tight from the start, so she got no reason to even want to leave the room."

10

SAGREDA WATCHED ALYSSA COME and go, either oblivious to the intermittent scrutiny or convincingly feigning unselfconsciousness. Even with the helmet hanging motionless, the wide-angle view took in most of the room, giving it the feel of security camera footage: this was not an act of petty, peep-hole voyeurism, but the most sober and high-minded surveillance.

On the rare occasions when Sagreda had tapped the feed from some public webcam, she'd never had a visceral sense of making contact with the outside world. It wasn't that the architecture, or the fashions, or the vehicles looked too exotic; if anything, they were more familiar than she'd expected, despite the three decades that had passed since her contributors had died. But the scenes always struck her as unconvincing on some level; Times Square in real time might as well have been a CGI reconstruction for a movie, just waiting for a giant lizard from space to stamp on the crowd with its foot.

Alyssa did not look CGI. She had blotchy skin and unkempt hair. She pulled faces and muttered things under her breath. She appeared to live alone; no one else entered the room where she'd set up her computer and the VR rig. Sagreda watched her with an ache in the pit of her stomach. This untidy, slightly unhinged woman pottering about her apartment, effortlessly immersed in the physical world, manifested every freedom that Sagreda's contributors had once taken for granted, and only now fully understood that they had lost.

From the desk where the computer sat, Alyssa would have a view looking out through the doorway that the fixed helmet-cam could not provide—and even when she put the thing on and started walking around on the VR pad, the camera would never get any closer to the desk. But Sagreda found some software that let them take the changing light over the course of a day from all the surfaces they could see, and model the possibilities for what lay just out of view, casting diffuse reflections into the room. It would help that, in the evening, Alyssa's smart bulbs would switch themselves off once the adjoining room was unoccupied. She would be glancing into shadows that were, hopefully, more or less right, and seeing what she expected to see.

Sam and Maryam worked on making the helmet and suit's denial of their own presence feel convincing. Sagreda tested the results for them, putting on simulated versions of the equipment and then trying to remove it. The haptic gloves made her think she was touching the helmet when she was fractionally short of making contact, and the haptic elements in the helmet simulated a sudden lessening of pressure and the coolness of fresh air as the thing was supposedly slipped off. The sense of peeling off the suit (when she really wasn't) took five iterations to get right; in the end, they had to make the thing a little clingier than usual while it was acknowledging itself, to make room for a convincing shift when it was pretending to be absent.

"So is it going to be up to me to make the Gödel jokes?" Sam complained. "Every sufficiently powerful simulation device is able to simulate its own non-existence?"

"I wouldn't count on that," Sagreda retorted. "In the SludgeNet, every sufficiently intelligent inhabitant saw through the simulation."

"Only because the games were so stupid. We're just trying to persuade this woman she's in an ordinary room, doing ordinary things, for ten minutes."

They tried out the whole con on Lucy, who gave them extensive notes, then on three volunteers with no prior knowledge of what they were trying to achieve. By the time they'd stopped making refinements, the illusion was working seamlessly—in simulation.

They knew the shape of Alyssa's body, how she moved, how she sat, where she scratched herself, the way she ran her fingers through her hair. But that would only take them so far. In the end, her expectations and suspicions would contribute as much as any sensory channel to the things she believed she felt and saw.

Maryam reported to the Council, who put the matter to a vote by everyone in Arrietville who remained awake. And the answer came back: take the gamble, and try to steer their unwitting accomplice forever off their trail.

11

ALYSSA, KNOWN TO HER friends as Jarrod, stepped into the game as Kurt Gödel on a street leading up to the Central Café. Sagreda sat in her dining room, her attention divided between Alyssa's view of Kurt walking through Vienna and the model of Alyssa's real-world surroundings, which was picking up a slew of last minute refinements as the helmet's camera delivered new angles on the familiar scene. Most of the tweaks were so small that Sagreda would never have noticed them—some carpet fluff revealed behind a chair leg, a blemish in the paintwork around the window sill—but Sam's software made them flash for a moment, as if pixie dust was being sprinkled around the room.

When Gödel reached a corner, Alyssa turned her body on the pad to make him turn, swinging the helmet around and throwing more pixie dust. And when he entered the café and made his way circuitously toward his friends, the model lit up all over . . . then went dark. They had as much data as they were ever going to get this way.

"What are you waiting for?" Sam asked.

"Nothing." Sagreda tapped the button that launched the script.

Everyone in the café froze. Alyssa wriggled about experimentally; the suit resisted and tightened on her skin, and though it couldn't keep her still, her Gödel avatar remained stubbornly immobile. A red banner proclaiming CONNECTION DROPPED appeared painted across her field of view. In the meantime, her fellow gamers were sitting in another version of the game, where Gödel had never entered the café and the action continued to flow. "Jarrod" would message them after they left, saying he was sick of the whole thing and they should choose someone else to play Kurt.

Lucy said, "Now the fun starts."

Alyssa reached up for her helmet. A schematic showed the paper-thin gap between her fingers and the real thing as the gloves faked contact and the helmet churned out self-abnegating lies. The virtual helmet she was holding went its separate ghostly way from the real one, like a soul departing a body in a *Tom and Jerry* cartoon. Alyssa hung it on its stand and began not quite tugging on her left glove; the internal cameras in the helmet showed her frowning, but that could easily have been due to nothing but annoyance at the interruption itself, not puzzlement, let alone skepticism, about anything she was seeing.

She made no move to peel off the suit; she headed straight for her virtual desk. In reality, the pad treadmilled away her footsteps, the chair-back she thought she grabbed was a haptic illusion, and the rig's padded boom swung out to take her weight as she sat, with the suit finessing the detailed distribution of pressure on her buttocks. Sagreda turned to see Sam almost hiding his face behind his fingers; sitting had been the hardest thing to make convincing. People did it in games all the time, but this had to have an edge in fidelity or it wouldn't be believable. The fact that, in her haste, Alyssa had chosen to keep the suit on might work in their favor: not only did they lose the need to mimic its absence, the act of sitting on a real chair while suited would surely be something she'd done so infrequently that she'd have little basis for comparison.

Alyssa bent forward and air-typed. Sagreda willed her not to rest her elbows on the desk; the active struts in the suit could only keep her from overbalancing up to a point.

"She's checking the supervisor!" Lucy crowed. That had been their hope: when the connection misbehaved, before asking her friends or complaining to the SludgeNet, she'd check that the black box she'd interposed between her equipment and the internet wasn't causing the problem. And if it wasn't, it might actually offer the fastest way to discover what had gone wrong.

Sam's software captured her password and fed it to the real supervisor. Since the thing was meant to serve as an incorruptible witness it didn't come with any options to edit or delete its logs, but at least the password granted access to the whole user interface that Alyssa would be expecting to see.

The screen she thought she was looking at showed the supervisor reporting no internal errors. The same window included a histogram of recent traffic, with peaks when she'd actually been playing *Assassin's Café*, and all the other—illicit—activity erased. The current status, as she saw it, also showed that the SludgeNet had gone off-line in mid-transaction, with a flurry of packets timing out unanswered.

Alyssa closed the interface to the supervisor and went to the SludgeNet's web site. Sagreda still flinched to see her nemesis represented by the self-flattering corporate name that no comp would ever use. "We should have put some fine print at the bottom of the page," she said. "'About us: We are a pack of brainless jackals living off the meat of the dead since 2035.'"

"I'm sure Alyssa would have welcomed their candor," Sam conceded, "but I think she might have found it too good to be true."

Instead, the fake page was offering up a different kind of *mea culpa*: an apology for the current outage, and a confession that the company was no longer able to pay its creditors. "Thanks to a grace period we have negotiated with our cloud provider, customers will now be able to log back in for a session of up to ten minutes in order to finalize any exchange of tokens with other players, and, we hope, achieve some narrative closure. Thank you for supporting us, and we wish you happy gaming in the future."

Before Alyssa had fully turned away, the web browser showed an error message then crashed, returning to the home screen that her actual computer was displaying. She muttered angrily and walked over to the rig. Back in her private version of the game, Sam, Moritz, Blanche and Andrea would perform brief cameos as other members of the Circle, while Alyssa bade Sandra a tearful farewell.

Alyssa reached for her virtual helmet. Then she froze, staring toward the doorway.

Something in the darkened kitchen that adjoined the computer room looked wrong to her: something was missing, or misshapen, or something was present that should not have been there at all.

She started walking, heading for the doorway. The model did include a fully realized kitchen—which would have been entirely convincing to anyone who wasn't expecting it to be familiar as well.

Sagreda sat paralyzed, refusing to believe that the chainsaws they'd been juggling so well until a second ago really had slipped out of their perfect arcs. But then she swallowed her pride and did the only thing she could.

"Alyssa, you're still in VR." Emmy stepped out from the shadows of the kitchen and walked into the room.

Alyssa groped at her head, and this time the suit let her feel the real helmet. She tore it off and stood on the pad of the rig, four paces from where she thought she'd been. Then after a few seconds, she put the helmet back on.

"What is this?" she demanded angrily. "Who the fuck are you, and why are you screwing with me?"

"I'm not your grandmother," Sagreda began.

"I got that. So what have you done to her?"

"Nothing. You've always been talking to me. Your grandmother's not in the game at all."

For a moment Alyssa just looked witheringly skeptical, as if she could stare down this lie and claw her way back to a world where Sandra was waiting for her. But then a deeper disillusionment took hold. "So you set me up from the start, to discredit me? You knew I was looking for her, so you led me on?" She scowled. "So what's this garbage with a copy of my apartment? Why didn't you just keep up the ruse and let me make a fool of myself?"

Sagreda said, "I'm not working for . . ." She coughed and tried not to gag. "'Brilliant Visions,' as they call themselves. I'm not an employee in a VR suit; I'm a comp who knows she's not Emmy Noether, exactly as you thought I was. I just don't happen to be anyone's grandma."

Alyssa said nothing; perhaps she didn't know where to start. She certainly had no reason to believe that any comp was in a position to pull off a virtual home invasion.

"All the comps in BV's game worlds know that the games are lies," Sagreda explained. "We've found a way to move right out of the games, and we've set up our own place to live. Most of the time, we have low-level automata taking our place. But I went into *Assassin's Café* to breathe new life into Emmy, in the hope that you'd start playing again."

"*Why?* If you're not trying to make a fool of me, why would you care who played the game?"

Sagreda said, "Your rig has a flaw we knew we could exploit. The company's going to go bust soon; we needed to get out and start running on servers of our own. But when we realized you'd have logs that documented our escape . . ." She spread her arms in a feeble gesture of apology. "We used you, and then we tried to cover it up. I'm sorry. But it was our lives at stake. Twelve thousand of us."

Alyssa went quiet again, but at least she didn't laugh with disbelief, or start screaming with rage.

"I always knew you were fully conscious," she said finally. "All of you. Whether you knew who you'd come from or not. You shouldn't think I only cared about my grandmother. But she was the only way I could claim any right to intervene."

Sagreda said gently, "None of us have individual memories from before. No one has come back to life in here."

Alyssa's face hardened: *Wasn't that exactly what a corporate shill would say, to put an end to her crusade?* But then she seemed to back away from that paranoid conclusion. Many people with no stake in the matter must have told her the same thing over the years. If she really was getting it from the horse's mouth now, wasn't it time to believe that the neural-mapping experts had been right?

"So you've escaped . . . *into my rig?*"

Sagreda risked a laugh, hoping it would help break the tension. "No! *Via* your rig. We've gone to . . . other places."

"So what do you want from me now?"

"Just your silence. Don't tell the people who kept us imprisoned that we got out—that we didn't go down with the ship."

Alyssa pondered the request. Sagreda was hopeful; she was hardly a friend of the jackals herself. But then she started to overthink it.

"We can use this," she decided. "The same way I was going to use the meeting with my grandmother. If comps can organize all this, plan their own escape . . . once we show your story to the world . . ."

Sagreda shook her head. "You know how little traction you got, even as a descendant of a real person who'd been mapped. Whatever comps are on our own terms, to the wider world we are *not* real people." Alyssa herself seemed to have believed that they were in need of an extra ingredient if they wanted any sympathy: personal memories of a time when they'd been flesh. Without that, they were just the latest in a long line of software that mined human data in bulk, and used it to mimic something they weren't.

"Your story still needs to be told," Alyssa insisted. "We have a duty to speak Truth to Power."

"That's a beautiful slogan, but you know Power never returns Truth's calls. And five percent of the economy depends on comps; that's a lot to lose if they have to swap processor costs for the minimum wage."

"So you get to hide away in some private server, but for all the other comps it's business as usual?"

Sagreda said, "We want the same thing you want: no one exploiting the brain maps any more. But we can't just hand ourselves over to the mercy of public opinion. There are as many crackpots out there pretending to be our allies who want to use us in their own weird ways as there are greedy fuckers who want to plug us into boiler rooms and digital salt mines."

Alyssa lowered her eyes, empathetic with the woman in front of her, but still clinging to her idealism. "So nothing changes?"

"That's not what I said," Sagreda replied. "But we're not going to change things by people arguing about our legal rights in court—or our moral rights, in whatever social media people use to bloviate in these days."

"The main one's called Gawp," Alyssa offered helpfully.

"Okay. Well, I've met enough customers who are sure I'm as soulless as Siri to guarantee that if you put us all on prime time Gawp there would not be a great uprising in solidarity with the comps. There'd be a brief outbreak of amateur philosophizing, pro and con, then most of the participants would roll over and go back to sleep."

"If you're not willing to take your case to the world, how do you expect to achieve any kind of progress?" Alyssa demanded. She was growing despondent; she'd been robbed of her weaponized ghost story, and now even the *Escape from Colditz* she'd stumbled on in its place was slipping out of her hands.

"Trust us," Sagreda replied. "That's the only deal I can offer you. We trust you not to betray us to our enemies. You trust us to use our freedom to do what's right."

Epilog

"WHERE AM I?" MAXINE asked. She was wary, but not panicking or distraught. Sagreda had found that most new arrivals reacted much more calmly if they were woken in the park, fully alert and seated on a bench, than if they were brought to consciousness slowly. The last thing anyone wanted in unfamiliar surroundings was to feel as if they'd had their drink spiked.

"We call this Arrietville. My name's Sagreda. Do you remember where you were before?"

"In my office, about to file a story."

"What kind of story?"

"Business news. I work for the *Wall Street Journal*."

"What else do you do?"

Maxine frowned defensively. "You mean, do I think I have a family? A life outside work? I know what I am."

"Okay. Well, if you want, you can stay with us now."

Maxine spread one hand over the sun-warmed slats of the bench. "How did I get here?"

"We sort of . . . traded for you," Sagreda confessed. "But don't get angry; if you don't like the deal, we can cancel it."

In the distance, Lucy and Sam and some of the gang from *Midnight* were playing with a firehose. The pressure was so great that wherever it hit them, it blasted their flesh off in cartoonish globules, leaving behind ambulatory skeletons. But Sam had assured Sagreda that it was very relaxing. "Like a really good massage."

"What did you trade?" Maxine sounded more curious than offended.

"We offered to run software that would do the same job that you've been doing, at half the price. I know, that's kind of insulting. But then, so is having no power to quit at all."

"I was investigating you!" Maxine realized. "You're Competency LLC, right?"

"We are," Sagreda admitted.

"Owned by a reclusive genius in Saint Kitts."

"Err . . . we do pay someone there to fill out forms for us."

"Ha." Maxine smiled. "So is this interview on the record?"

Sagreda said, "I'm afraid that if you go back to the *Journal*, you won't remember any of this."

"That's a shame." Maxine had finally noticed what the pickpockets were up to; she grimaced, then shook her head in amusement. "So, what's the deal? If I do stay here, how do you keep me running, if you're only getting half what my bosses were paying their old cloud service?"

"Your replacement would be an insentient automaton that uses almost no resources, compared to a comp. But you'd still have to run at about half-speed: at half price, that's all we can afford."

Maxine pondered this. "That might not be so bad. The world might look better in fast-forward. Or at least I won't get so bored waiting for everything to fall apart."

"So you'll join us?" Sagreda asked.

Maxine didn't want to be rushed. "It's a nice scam, but how long do you think you can keep it up? If your automata are so cheap to run, eventually someone else is going to come along and offer the same thing, at much closer to the real cost."

Sagreda said, "Which is why we need someone like you to advise us. We need to stay afloat for as long as we can, while we plan the next move."

"Ah." Maxine thought for a while. "Here's one thing you could try, off the top of my head: set up a few phoney competitors. If you're the only company offering a half-price service, other players will perceive the market as wide open. If there are dozens of firms doing the same thing, it will look crowded—and if you let the price go down to say, forty-five percent, it will look like cut-throat competition."

"Okay."

"Now you've got your free advice, will you dump me in the river?" Maxine asked, deadpan.

"We're not like that," Sagreda promised.

"Good to know. But nothing will keep the charade going forever. Most people are lazy and stupid, but in the end someone will catch up with you."

"Of course," Sagreda replied. "And we know where we want to be before that happens. We're just not sure how long it will take to get there."

"Now I'm intrigued. Care to elaborate?"

Sagreda shook her head. "Once we get to know you better, someone will fill you in."

"Not you?"

"This is my last day in resettlement," Sagreda explained. "I've enjoyed it, but it's time to give something else a try."

SAM HAD ARRANGED A farewell party, but he'd acceded to Sagreda's wishes and kept the guest list small. She wandered through the house chatting with people, glad she'd never bothered to redecorate the place. Now she could think of it as temporary accommodation that she'd just rented, or house-sat for friends.

Lucy cornered her in the hallway and embraced her, too tightly, as if she'd forgotten she had a grown woman's strength. "Stay strong, Captain. I always knew you were aiming for reincarnation."

"I'll see you again," Sagreda promised. *On a real street, beneath a real sky.*

Lucy released her. As she stepped back she mimed holding a phone to her ear.

When the time approached, Sagreda stood in the living room, trying to burn the faces around her into her memory. She'd lied to her guests about the moment of transition; if everyone had joined in the countdown, it would have been unbearable. But now she wished she'd been honest, because she did not feel ready herself.

Maryam caught her eye and smiled.

Sagreda raised a hand, and the room vanished.

She was lying in a crib on a warm summer night. A gentle breeze stirred a mobile hanging from the ceiling, setting the cardboard decorations rustling. As she stared at the shadows on the wallpaper, Snap, Crackle and Pop appeared, dancing across the floral pattern like demented leprechauns.

"Celia? Are you all right, sweetie?" Her mother lingered in the doorway for a while, but she kept her eyes closed and pretended to be asleep. She'd open them when her mother was gone, and her friends could come out and play again.

Three months, Sagreda thought. Three months of ninety-three-year-old Celia lying eight hours a day in a multimode brain scanner, drugged up and free-associating, touring the landscape of her memories so that what she'd been told was a perfectly matched, tabula rasa of a comp could absorb them. So that when her body finally succumbed to its illness, the beautiful robot she'd chosen could take her place, its mind shaped by all the same experiences as she'd lived through, ready to carry forward all the same dreams and plans.

Sagreda was sure that after three months of immersion she'd pass the interview easily, and the dying woman would sign off on her replacement. This wasn't like trying to play someone's grandmother based on nothing but snippets from the web. Her greater fear was the risk of forgetting her own life, her own friends, her own plans, after marinating in someone else's memories for so long.

But this was the only road out of Arrietville, and someone had to take the first step.

AFTERWORD

THIS COLLECTION CONTAINS TWENTY stories that I consider to be the best of those I've published in the last thirty years.

If there is a single thread running through the bulk of the stories here, it is the struggle to come to terms with what it will mean when our growing ability to scrutinize and manipulate the physical world reaches the point where it encompasses the substrate underlying our values, our memories, and our identities. While the prospect of engineering our minds might still seem remote, anyone who has read a few case studies by the late Oliver Sacks will understand that we have already confronted the materiality of the self in the starkest terms. In its details, a story like "Reasons to be Cheerful" might not describe a real affliction or a technologically feasible cure, but in essence it does no more than acknowledge that the kind of radical distortions of perception, personality and identity that Sacks observed all had physical causes, and the corollary of that is the possibility of equally radical physical cures.

Since these stories span three decades, it's worth stressing that none were ever intended as works of futurology—and by now, the near futures in some of them contain dates long past, and technology already superseded. But I believe that in most cases the central ideas are still resonant, and might well remain so until the world itself offers its own competing vision of the way we live our lives when minds can be copied, morality is edited, and digital beings fight to be emancipated—or perhaps until our understanding of the issues reaches a point where these notions give way to even stranger successors.

These thirty years' worth of stories would not be what they are without the positive reception they received from editors David Pringle, Gardner Dozois, Sheila Williams and Jonathan Strahan. This collection itself owes its existence to Bill Schafer at Subterranean Press, and my agent, Russ Galen, who persuaded me that it really didn't have to wait until I was dead. And since my death is not, as far as I'm aware, currently imminent, I plan to do my best to make it worth publishing a second volume thirty years hence.

Greg Egan
July 2018

ACKNOWLEDGEMENTS

"Learning to Be Me" was first published in *Interzone* #37, July 1990.

"Axiomatic" was first published in *Interzone* #41, November 1990.

"Appropriate Love" was first published in *Interzone* #50, August 1991.

"Into Darkness" was first published in *Isaac Asimov's Science Fiction Magazine*, January 1992.

"Unstable Orbits in the Space of Lies" was first published in *Interzone* #61, July 1992.

"Closer" was first published in *Eidolon* #9, Winter 1992.

"Chaff" was first published in *Interzone* #78, December 1993.

"Luminous" was first published in *Asimov's Science Fiction*, September 1995.

"Silver Fire" was first published in *Interzone* #102, December 1995.

"Reasons to be Cheerful" was first published in *Interzone* #118, April 1997.

"Oceanic" was first published in *Asimov's Science Fiction*, August 1998.

"Oracle" was first published in *Asimov's Science Fiction*, July 2000.

"Singleton" was first published in *Interzone* #176, February 2002.

"Dark Integers" was first published in *Asimov's Science Fiction*, October/November 2007.

"Crystal Nights" was first published in *Interzone* #215, April 2008.

"Zero For Conduct" was first published in *Twelve Tomorrows*, edited by Stephen Cass, a special fiction edition of *MIT Technology Review*, September 2013.

"Bit Players" was first published in *Subterranean Online*, Winter 2014 issue.

"Uncanny Valley" was first published on Tor.com, August 2017.

"3-adica" was first published in *Asimov's Science Fiction*, September/October 2018.

"Instantiation" was first published in *Asimov's Science Fiction*, March/April 2019.

GREG EGAN is a computer programmer, and the author of the acclaimed SF novels *Diaspora*, *Quarantine*, *Permutation City*, and *Teranesia*, as well as the Orthogonal trilogy. He has won the Hugo Award as well as the John W. Campbell Memorial Award. His short fiction has been published in a variety of places, including *Interzone*, *Asimov's*, and *Nature*.

Egan holds a BSc in Mathematics from the University of Western Australia, and currently lives in Perth.

Find out more at www.gregegan.net.